I0650797

FOR SEVENTY-FIVE YEARS: THE UNIQUE MAGAZINE

Fall 1999

ISSN 0898-5073

Cover by Rick Berry

Weird Tales® is published 4 times a year by DNA Publications, Inc., in association with Terminus Publishing Co., Inc. Postmaster and others: send all changes of address and other subscription matters to DNA Publications, Inc., PO Box 2988, Radford VA 24143–2988. Editorial matters should be addressed to Terminus Publishing Co., Inc., 123 Crooked Lane, King of Prussia PA 19406–2570. Single copies, $4.95 in U.S.A. & possessions; $6.00 by mail to Canada, $9.00 by first class mail elsewhere. Subscriptions: 4 issues (one year) $16.00 in U.S.A. & possessions; $22.00 in Canada, $35.00 elsewhere, in U.S. funds. Publisher is not responsible for loss of manuscripts in publisher's hands or in transit; please see page 5 for more details. Copyright © 1999 by Terminus Publishing Co., Inc.; all rights reserved; reproduction prohibited without prior permission. Typeset, printed, & bound in the United States of America. *Weird Tales*® is a registered trademark owned by Weird Tales, Limited.

THE EYRIE

NOBODY WROTE!

That was the plaintive cry when Mad ran an empty letter column once, as a joke, complete with a cartoon of cobwebs growing from the editorial mailbox. Alas, we're not kidding.

This may be a fluke caused by the timing of distribution and when we have to compose this editorial, but the fact remains. It is not that we have any concerns for the future of *Weird Tales®*, which continues to sell better than ever, both in stores and through subscriptions.

But this letter column is going to lose something without your participation, folks. Could it be that we're just living in a post-epistolatory age? Could it be that the advent of the Internet has just caused people to forget how to put pen (or typewriter, or printer) to paper? There was a time when a magazine like this got *sacks* of mail. That time has apparently passed. But we press bravely on.

Now, let us move on to a Topic. Editorials can go just so far talking about the management of the magazine. One then proceeds to an Essay, rather the way Horace Gold did so brilliantly in *Galaxy* for so many years. Therefore, essaying forth:

Scary Places.

We were back in Niagara Falls again this Spring, for the first EerieCon, a pleasant if not entirely eerie event, featuring, among others, such *Weird Tales®* contributors as Brian Lumley and Allen Koszowski, and the eminent local publisher W. Paul Ganley, who has published many books by, among others, Lumley and someone called Darrell Schweitzer.

We wandered yet again among the monuments to tackiness on the Canadian side of the Falls, a region which, but for the interesting and more than a century old Niagara Falls Museum (which

was there for Abraham Lincoln to visit), might be described as a place next to which the Atlantic City boardwalk looks tasteful, elegant, and up-scale.

Which is not to knock Niagara Falls. There is a place in life for pleasant tackiness. Within a very small area the Canadians have crammed an impressive number of funhouses, wax museums, and other oddities, including a miniature golf course with life-sized dinosaurs in it. Not everything is as feeble as the Castle Dracula which we described a few editorials back — a place where the special effects really *do* consist of somebody popping a paper bag behind your back at one point. Much more imaginative (and impressive within the limited budget of this sort of thing) was a place called, if we remember the name correctly, Alien Encounters wherein, after wandering through a collection of science-fiction movie costumes as paraphernalia, the visitor is taken by a white-coated "scientist" to view an extraterrestrial "corpse" supposedly just shipped in from Area 51.

An alarm goes off. One of the aliens isn't dead, but has escaped! You're hurried out of the room and down a dark, winding corridor, where the alien scratches and thumps behind doors and in the ceiling, appears in silhouette behind a page of glass, and so on. At one point it is a little too obvious that one of the "effects" is a vacuum-cleaner being switched on, but otherwise we'd give this one E for Effort, and suggest it may be a better way to spend your Canadian dollars than pouring them down a slot machine in the local casino.

But what this place wasn't, of course, was *scary*, any more than the Castle Dracula down the street was scary. More fun, but not scary.

What makes a scary place? Horror fiction is replete with any number of haunted houses, and the Gothic field from which modern horror is descended (from the Castle of Otranto by way of the House of Usher) very much centered on frightening *places;* so it behooves us to actually consider what makes a place, in fiction or in real life, disturbing to be in.

Joyce Kilmer wrote in a poem we had to memorize in grade school:

> I've never seen a haunted house,
> but I hear there are such things.
> They hold the talk of spirits,
> their mirth and sorrowings.

That's some of it. Assuming you're not a devoutly believing psychic who can pick up "vibrations" anywhere, can we even analyze what makes a place seem "haunted," in the absence of actual ghosts appearing?

Think about it.

While we were thinking about it, we saw a fanzine in which the editor described a visit to the site of the notorious Andersonville prison camp in Georgia, where numerous atrocities were committed during the Civil War, enough so that the commander there was the only Confederate to be hanged after the Late Unpleasantness ceased. The article included several photographs, showing what looked like nothing more than an empty field and a fence. Nothing at all.

But no doubt if one were *there*, the impression might be very different. Andersonville, as the author of that article made clear, was a haunted place.

It's all a matter of memories and associations. The "haunting" is in the mind of the beholder.

If we put aside the category of obviously dangerous places such as ravines filled with rattlesnakes and cliffs where boulders constantly come tumbling down on one's head, or other situations of imminent physical menace, then a "scary" place is one with a horrible story attached to it, and nothing more.

We'll admit that most "haunted" place we ever visited was the Anne Frank house in Amsterdam, where, if you don't know the story, there isn't that much to see: an old, cramped Dutch house within which a cabinet swings away to reveal a stairway into the secret "annex" where the Frank family hid from the Nazis for about four years before they were finally betrayed. (And if you look out the window, you can understand how they almost got away with it. The multi-gabled, almost medieval houses completely fill

STAFF:

Publisher: Warren Lapine
Editors: George H. Scithers
& Darrell Schweitzer
Managing Editor: Carol Adams
Art Editor: Diane Weinstein
Assistant Editors: Kyle Phillips, Pat Buard,
& Robert Waters,
Computer Consultant: David J. Williams III
Typesetter: Owlswick Press
Printer: Morgan Publishing Co., Inc.

MANUSCRIPT SUBMISSIONS:

Before sending us your material, please send us a business-sized envelope, with postage affixed, addressed to you, for our guidelines.

The address for this and all other editorial matters: **Weird Tales®, 123 Crooked Lane, King of Prussia PA 19406-2570.**

The address for all new subscriptions, subscribers' changes of address, advertising, and all other money matters is: **DNA Publications, Inc., PO Box 2988, Radford VA 24143–2988.**

Yes; we read unsolicited submissions — but *only* if they are in standard manuscript format. To survive, all editors insist on a few Rules: each submission must be in proper format and must include a return envelope, addressed to you, with enough postage affixed to bring the manuscript back to you. If you want us to discard the manuscript if we don't buy it, tell us so, but include a business-letter-sized envelope, addressed to you, with proper postage affixed, so we can send you our comments. No loose stamps, please!

We recommend either or both of two books on writing (after all, we wrote one of them!): *On Writing Science Fiction: the Editors Strike Back!* by Scithers, Schweitzer, & John M. Ford; $19.50 in hardcover; and Barry B. Longyear's *Science-Fiction Writer's Workshop,* $9.50 in trade paperback, available from Owlswick Press, 123 Crooked Lane, King of Prussia PA 19406-2570. These prices include shipping & handling. If you live in Pennsylvania, please include 6% sales tax.

We are not responsible for manuscripts in our hands or in transit. You *must* keep a copy of every manuscript you send out. You *must* put your name and address on the first page of every manuscript. And please: *no* binders, folders, or padded envelopes; and especially: *no* registered or certified mail for which we would have to stand in line at the post office!

the block, so that the "annex" juts out into an open space not accessible or visible from the street; it would have taken a careful survey by helicopter to spot it.) Of course we know the story of what happened there, and there are pathetic traces of evidence left, such as the yellowing pictures of 1930s matinee stars Anne seems to have tacked up on the walls. Then you look out from the front of the house, you can gaze down at the cobblestone street by the canal and realize that it looked just like that — that it could have been yesterday — when German military vehicles came screeching to a halt and the Gestapo came storming into the house.

You have to know the *story*. To a visitor from Mars, it would be just another house, but once the associations are in place, one feels a certain chill. It is not an *imaginative* resonance such as you'd feel from a really good ghost story, but the emotion is similar. That was a haunted place. Andersonville is haunted, because of its story. After all, the idea behind most ghost tales is that Lady So-and-So was hideously beheaded/walled-up/strangled/etcetera back in the 15th century (they had some really nasty etceteras back then!) and has restlessly roamed the halls of Ghastly-Gloom Manor ever since because her story is not finished. But you have to *know* the story, and inevitably in the classical ghostly fiction, you do.

It's easy to see, then, how the belief in hauntings arose. A real place (such as the Anne Frank house, Andersonville, or, we can well presume to a far greater degree, Auschwitz) where something terrible actually happened *feels* different to the sensitive person. It is easy to imagine that the scene of a crime is haunted by the memory of the victims. Before long there may well be "sightings." Are there ever apparitions reported at the sites of Jack the Ripper's butcheries? We've been there, at night, and but for the preponderance of tourists, those would be scary places. Haunted places remind us of our mortality, and not merely because the East End is not exactly the safest part of London to go wandering about after dark.

When the story fades, so does the feeling. We've seen any number of medieval dungeons, including an awful black hole in Stirling Castle in Scotland where you can't even see the bottom . . . but these are just curiosities. Perhaps they have been cleansed by the passage of time.

We've also been to a couple of "haunted" houses. The one that's in the guidebooks is the Winchester Mystery House in San Jose, California, a vast and labyrinthine structure which looks quite cheerful on the outside, but which might be described as a Rococco Gormenghast. It was the home of a lady who inherited the Winchester Rifle fortune in the 19th century. She was a spiritualist who became obsessed with guilt over all the people killed by Winchester rifles. Her medium (who, if she didn't have connections to the building trade, should have) said that as long as Mrs. Winchester kept building onto the house, as long as it was never finished, the spirits of the dead rifle victims couldn't get her.

She was awesomely rich. She indulged herself, adding room after room, in an increasingly complex maze, with such oddities as doors that open onto blank walls, stairways that don't go anywhere; a crescent-shaped window with spiders worked into the glass, looking down on a garden, the bushes of which are arranged in some secret, mystical pattern; and lots more. As the lady grew older, she put in stairways with two-inch stairs because she couldn't raise her feet. There are nine or ten showers, all at precisely Mrs. Winchster's height (just under five feet), and a shaft where she could look down and see what the servants were doing in several rooms on several floors, all at once. The seance room is particularly peculiar. There is one door going in. It was locked from the outside when a seance was in progress. There are several doors which may be opened from the inside, but not from the outside — so if you got scared, you could run out, but not get back in again. Before the San Francisco earthquake of 1906, there were several towers.

The Winchester Mystery House is one of the most bizarre architectural accumulations anywhere on Earth. It isn't quite "scary," because nothing particularly awful happened there. There were no gruesome murders. People didn't just vanish, for all it's possible to see how you could get *lost* in such a place. But the *story* is there, written in the very house itself, of this grim, sorrowful woman's utter obsession with herself. If such a place didn't exist in real life, it would be quite an imaginative feat to make it up — and make it convincing — in fiction. It's an *eerie* place, to say the least, even in broad daylight.

The other "haunted" house we've visited was a private dwelling in Bucks County, north of Philadelphia. You can find a very imaginative (i.e., fast-and-loose with the details) description in Schweitzer and Van Hollander's story "The Throwing Suit" (in *Transients and Other Disquieting Stories*): another mismatched architectural

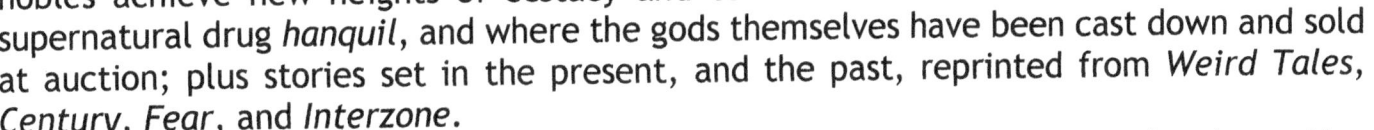

pile, a centuries-old farmhouse onto which additions have been made, followed by additions to the additions, in entirely different styles, until there are countless gables, creaking doors, and, yes, stairways that go nowhere. We clowned around, even at one point (at night, after we had supposedly left) supplying a "ghostly" hand scratching at the window — but the shivery feeling *was* there. At the very heart of the house was the oldest part, a dirt-floored cellar built in the last years of the 17th century (our British readers may laugh, but 1690 is *old* by American standards!). Massive, worm-riddled, rough-hewn beams still held up the ceiling. The cellar was dark and damp. In this house, the story goes, a little girl died long ago, in the middle of the winter, when the ground was frozen solid so that no grave could be dug outside until spring. So her family buried her in the cellar . . . and she's been heard crying in the night ever since . . .

People who actually believe in ghosts might be *really* scared by that one, for all there are no reports of the dead child actually harming anyone. But it was *so* suggestive, that it's not exactly surprising that Schweitzer and Van Hollander used it in a story, albeit minus the child ghost who didn't fit into the plot. (Which is the difference between what the *believer* does and what the artist does, the latter being far freer to shape the material — but that's another essay, and we digress.)

These then are the elements of a "haunted" place: a place that's unusual, either physically or by association; and a story of something painful or terrible, which *isn't over yet*, and which therefore resonates.

(Of course you may argue that the terrible stories of the Anne Frank House or Andersonville are over and done with; but the potential for evil revealed is never over and done with — which, you could also argue, is likewise true of those medieval dungeons. As maybe it was only the *immediacy* which was washed away by time.)

The most famous — and best — haunted house in literature is probably Shirley Jackson's Hill House, which she describes so memorably:

Hill House, not sane, stood by itself against its hills, holding darkness within; it had stood so for eighty years and might stand for eighty more. Within, walls continued upright, bricks met neatly, floors were firm, and doors were sensibly shut; silence lay steadily against the wood and stone of Hill House, and whatever walked there, walked alone.

It is a *genuinely* scary place, but the source of the fear proves to be not so much the architecture but the mind of the protagonist, who could well be projecting herself onto the house. *The Haunting of Hill House*, like that other great masterpiece of ambiguous supernaturalism, Henry James's "The Turn of the Screw," never quite resolves matters, even with the famous ending, which repeats exactly the same description quoted above.

One possible way to read it is that the house hasn't been haunted by an actual ghost anywhere in the book, but that Eleanor, the doomed protagonist, is so obsessed with her own fears and longings that *she* is haunting it at the end. *She* is the one who walks alone, either literally, or because her terrible story is now indelibly associated with the place.

This is how a "scary place" is created in literature. It is the secret of Hill House, the Overlook Hotel, and Castle Dracula. In real life, such a place makes us uneasy because of what we know happened there. In fiction, it's because of what the author *made* happen there.

Hark! A letter at last!

As we were composing this editorial, *one*, count 'em, *one* letter of comment on #316 arrived in the post. Mr. **George Smith** writes:

I could not agree more with your editorial in #316 if I had written it myself. The proliferation of non-objective art — in every field — is sickening. From the flimflam man who paints steel drums and hangs them from a ceiling for a thousand bucks a pop, to the slacker writer who can't be bothered with spelling, punctuation, or grammar, incompetency has been elevated to the pedestal of genius. The only worse thing than the idiots who buy this dreck (who should not be allowed to handle money) are the so-called art critics who hail these incomprehensible botches as art. . . . Clarity and comprehension are the cornerstones of all art. If people cannot understand what you are trying to say, you have failed as an artist. Regardless of how many art critics and college professors herald you as a daring leader in the art field.

To which we can only respond that the editorial was about poetry, not the visual arts, and, in any case, be careful. Many brilliant innovators were first greeted with cries of incomprehension — Beethoven, Dali, Walt Whitman — when all

they needed was a little getting used to. As for some of the "incomprehensible" painters of this century, we think the jury is still out on both Jackson Pollock and his contemporary and rival, J.T. Orang (an orangutan from the Topeka Zoo whose paintings won prizes as abstract art in the '50s). The visual arts are a lot tricker, and come down to the entirely subjective criterion of whether or not it is pleasing to the eye. But with poetry, or any sort of writing, the standard has to be, "Does this make any sense?" We have no patience with word-salad passed off as literature.

Rudyard Kipling, no mean poet himself, in his 1904 story, "Wireless," wrote of ". . . the high-water mark that but two of the sons of Adam have reached. Remember that in all the millions permitted there are no more than five — five little lines — of which one can say: 'These are the pure Magic. These are the clear Vision. The rest is only poetry.' "

Here are two of those lines:

Charm'd magic casements, opening on the foam
Of perilous seas, in faery lands forlorn.
                                    — *John Keats*

and the other three:

A savage place! as holy and enchanted
As e'er beneath a waning moon was haunted
By woman wailing for her demon-lover!
                    — *Samuel Taylor Coleridge*

But we still aren't getting letters. Let us assume then that American society has completely forgotten the concept of the paper letter. Our e-mail address: **owlswick@netaxs.com**

Use this for queries and letters *only*. Give letters of comment to the magazine the topic header "Weird Letter." Do *not*, under any circumstances, send us an electronic submission unless we have specifically asked you to. It will be deleted unread. (Use common sense. We get 500 manuscripts a month. If we got all that as e-mail it would crash our server. Besides, we are not about either to print out all those stories in order to read them or to squint at them on screen.)

We still want to hear from you!

A few recent books we recommend:

Beecher Smith, an active force in the Horror Writers Association, used to have as his claim to fame that he once was Elvis Presley's lawyer, but lately he has turned out to be a fine anthologist of horror stories, and has lately published **More**

Monsters from Memphis, from Zapizdat Publications, one of those many small imprints which are the life of the Horror field these days. There are twenty-two stories, all centered more or less on Memphis (Tennessee, not Egypt, which could be the subject of another, very different spooky anthology . . .), many of them by relative newcomers, but with a few better-known names among them: Brent Monahan, Steve Rasnic Tem, Janet Berliner, Tom Picarilli, etc. It is a sequel to the earlier (and still available) **Monsters from Memphis** (1997), which featured Monahan, Picarilli, Don Webb, etc. These are of interest to people who've never been to Tennessee, as any good regional writing is. That's $12.95 for the original *Monsters* and $14.95 for *More Monsters,* from Zapizdat Publications, P.O. Box 326, Palo Alto CA 94302.

Subterranean Press is well-named. As horror continues to retreat from the mass-market, the *real* action is increasingly in "underground" books like this story colection: **Crypt Orchards** by David J. Schow, a 500-copy, beautifully designed edition, which will *not* be in paperback any time soon but hopefully will be reprinted in facsimilie in some more enlightened future as part of a retrospective of '90s classics. Schow, who should be familiar to long-time *Weird Tales*® readers, is a polished, clever, witty, *unflinching* writer who combines horror and dark humor as well as anyone since the late, great Robert Bloch. Indeed, Bloch's shade hovers over this book, with an introduction *by* Bloch, Schow's playscript version of Bloch's "Final Performance," and much more in the Blochian spirit. Schow is one of the few writers of his generation who can actually make psychos interesting. He also writes nasty-funny stories about Hollywood, such as "Gills," which also appeared in *Weird Tales*® 315. Signed, lettered edition, $100. Signed, numbered edition, $35.00. Order from: P.O. Box 190106, Burton MI 48519.

The Most Popular Story for issue #316 obviously can't be determined yet. As of this writing we've got one first-place vote for Keith Taylor's "Daggers and a Serpent." We like that story quite a lot, but the results are hardly definitive. We are happy to announce that we've since purchased a sequel from Mr. Taylor's agent. But the results of reader voting for #316 will have to be announced next time, if at all. We need *you* to clear away some of the cobwebs from our editorial mailbox!   Ω

SHADOWINGS

by Douglas E. Winter

"She had somehow gotten out of bounds, wandered off the playing field and into a place where the rules she was used to no longer applied."

— Stephen King, *The Girl Who Loved Tom Gordon*

Elizabeth Hand is at the forefront of a new generation of fabulists: Writers whose fiction, although insistently unreal, sweeps aside traditional demarcations of genre — fairy tale, fantasy, science fiction, horror — in pursuit of transcendent investigations of myth and metaphor. Hand's novels include her debut, *Winterlong* (1990), and the acclaimed *Waking the Moon* (1995); more recently, the dystopian Glimmering (1997) offered a bleak yet moving alternate history of the 1990s. With *Black Light* (HarperPrism, hc, 276 pp., $25.00), she revisits familiar settings and themes, crafting an unexpected sequel to *Waking The Moon* that will delight her devoted readers.

The novel begins in Jonathan Carroll country — a pseudoreality jazzed on pop mythology that coexists, and occasionally collides, with a dark wonderland inhabited by more primal forces. But its story is pure Elizabeth Hand, a journey of reawakening (and, indeed, rebirth) that twines past and future into a present whose meaning is tenuous and terrifying.

It is 1974, and Charlotte "Lit" Moylan, the daughter of television troupers, dances out of high school and into adulthood in a remote corner of upstate New York: Kamensic Village, a recurrent locale of Hand's fiction that is haven to creatures of celebrity and the celestial. Her narrative recounts that violent ceremony known as the coming of age, in which innocence succumbs to a seemingly eternal corruptor.

Lit's nemesis is her godfather, Axel Kern, a legendary underground film auteur and blend of Andy Warhol, Kenneth Anger, Aleister Crowley and Viking Berserker gone Hollywood — and beyond. At age twelve, Lit had viewed a grotesque cave painting of a man merged into animal, its hideous head crowned by antlers. It is Kern's self-portrait, and it is not a work of impression-

ism. When Kern and his many secrets return to Kamensic Village, Lit is seventeen and ripe, physically and spiritually, for revelation.

The credo of *Black Light* is the essential tenet of twentieth-century fantasy, from Arthur Machen to Clive Barker: "We no longer perceive the sacred in our world . . ." Lit's reminiscence is a fierce scratching at the surface of things, the search for the story inside the story — or, indeed, beyond the story. In Kamensic Village, as in other waystations on the journey to Elfland, Middle Earth or Oz, the machinations of women and men are puny distractions. The real story — the true story — is told far beyond the fields we know: "In a way, it is the only thing on earth that really does happen: gods living and dying, their avatars struggling to be born and reborn."

Lit is destined — indeed, chosen — for initiation into an ancient mystery whose essence exposes the myth of Dionysus as reality. Like an artist (or, indeed, a writer of the fantastic), she views our world with a peculiar doubling of vision, one that glimpses an immaculate something that waits beyond the veil of the ordinary:

"I recognized that color: it was the blue that shades the sky sometimes in your dreams, the blue you see when a kingfisher dives and for an instant everything before you coheres into one thing, bird lake sky self: and then is gone. That is the color I saw then, and somehow I knew that this was the sky, a truer sky than I had ever seen, and that I was gazing up into it from the bottom of the deep and troubled mere that was our world."

As the use of "mere" suggests, Hand's style, although striving to cast a feverish spell, occasionally insists too strongly that we are reading a tale of fantasy. Colors are recounted with neo-psychedelic abandon, and uncomfortable similes leap from the page. In odd moments, Hand's prose summons too much attention to itself, and *Black Light* careens dangerously toward the precious.

Black Light is a fine work from a fine writer. Yet it seems curiously inbred, focused so intently on invoking Hand's prior fiction and, in turn, its literary and mythological precedents that it cannot (or perhaps refuses to) engage a readership beyond that traditionally devoted to novels of fantasy and science fiction. Devotees will love this book, but it is difficult to believe that *Black Light* will win over many new readers — and that is truly unfortunate.

The introverted aesthetics of *Black Light* are replicated, with more disastrous results, in *The Plato Papers,* a slender epistolary novel by Peter Ackroyd (Chatto & Windus, hc, 139 pp., £12.99), which proceeds from a time-honored premise: In the distant future — A.D. 3700 — when the stars have dimmed, the machines have been destroyed, and humanity itself may have evolved into ethereal beings of mind and spirit, a visionary known as Plato offers discourses on the mysteries of our troubled past. And, of course, he has it all wrong. Plato explicates *The Origin of Species* as a novel by Charles Dickens and lectures on the comedic pantomimes of Sigmund Freud, which makes for charming humor, but the joke soon wears thin — on the reader as well as Plato's peers. The orator is placed on trial for proposing that another reality resides in the darkness below, a truth that would challenge the convenient mythologies of this heavenly plane. Ackroyd, whose remarkable novels include *Hawksmoor* and *Chatterton,* indulges a penchant for the abstruse; but this is no *Riddley Walker,* simply a minor post-apocalyptic fable that might have worked at story length but cannot quite make itself into a novel.

The distant and insistently northern fantasies of *Black Light* and *The Plato Papers* find a stark counterpoint in *Locoland,* a first novel by Chris Morris (Creative Arts, tpb, 146 pp., $12.00). Its inspiration is that infamous seventies con on feminists and polite society, the movie *Snuff,* whose posters promised that it was filmed South of the Border — "where life is cheap!" *Locoland* is a full-throttle mingling of Hunter Thompson, Harry Crews and the increasingly tired mythology of the snuff film, but it can't quite find its stride — is it grim noir, black comedy, or acid picaresque? Morris travels the long and winding

"I've been waiting for you!"

(and drug-addled) road down Mexico way, as seen by a quartet of mugging and ultimately annoying California kids. Sex and violence follow and inevitably entwine; but the narrative is a victim of its own casualness and stoner chic — it is difficult to feel much of anything for anyone, save as these sort of hapless characters in search of a way out of their hollow lives. One is almost tempted, in a *Friday the 13th* way, to cheer for them all to become intimate with power tools. Morris's prose has poise, and a lean momentum that puts bricksized novels to shame; *Locoland* is a flawed but promising debut.

A far more satisfying — and bleak and nasty — first novel, also set in the American Southwest and Mexico, is the astonishingly violent *God Is a Bullet* by Boston Teran (Alfred A. Knopf, hc, 309 pp., $24.00). This blood-soaked narrative is an apt refutation of that gaggle of glib doomsayers who keep mouthing the words "horror is dead" without having the first clue about its pervasiveness on the bookshelves of America. In these pages, Teran delivers more sincere deviance and terror than a whole year of vampire novels, with a style that is sometimes breathtaking. *God Is a Bullet* warps the Manson murders into a nightmare that does not end: Twenty-five years after another famous atrocity, the Left-Handed Path, a cult of twisted and drugged-up glee killers, commits their latest home invasion, kidnapping a fourteen-year-old girl after butchering her mother and stepfather. The authorities are insistently (and intentionally) clueless, and the lost girl's only hope is her father, a police desk jockey — who, in turn, embraces a tenuous lead: a junkie and ex-cult member who plans her own ritual of vengeance. Their uneasy partnership makes for an adventure that reads a little bit like *The Searchers* meets *Cannibal Holocaust*; and although the novel falters in its endgame, *God Is a Bullet* is a relentless read, the kind of book that assures us that horror is alive and well and ready to rake the eyes of any reader with the courage to look for it.

Certainly the literature of horror remains prominent on the bestseller lists, in the names and texts of its more obvious writers — including, of course, Stephen King. His latest, *The Girl Who Loved Tom Gordon* (Scribner, hc, 224 pp., $16.95), is a finely-tuned, engaging, and effective novel that confronts the issue of faith in our secular and ominous times. Nine-year-old Trisha McFarland becomes lost on the Appala-

chian Trail during an outing with her brother and newly-divorced mom: "She was suddenly drowning in isolation, choking on a bright and yet oppressive sense of herself as a living being cast out from her fellows." Her journey through those deep, dark woods — a modern Grimm fairy tale — becomes a metaphor for society's confused slouch toward the millennium, as we stagger with an increasing sense of aloneness into a future that is uncertain and fraught with peril: "She had somehow gotten out of bounds, wandered off the playing field and into a place where the rules she was used to no longer applied." Faith, King reminds us, is something more than an element of religion — it isa way of finding belief in ourselves.

A similar theme is at the heart of *Others*, the new novel by Britain's bestselling writer of horror fiction, James Herbert (Macmillan, hc, 504 pp., £16.99). This is Herbert's most autobiographical book, based loosely on a story told to him by his mother about a shadowy hospital ward filled with misshaped and malformed children. *Others* opens, quite literally, in Hell, as a rakish and decadent Hollywood film star is offered redemption through reincarnation, but for an unknown purpose. Fast-forward to the present and the twisted body and psyche of Nicholas Dismas, a private detective whose investigation of a missing child leads him inexorably into the mysteries of a secret society of outcasts — and, in turn, into the mysteries of his own existence.

The Devil with You! The Lost Bloch: Volume One (Subterranean, hc, 330 pp., $40.00), champions the "missing" short novels of another of horror's brand names, the late Robert Bloch. Edited and introduced by David J. Schow, *The Devil with You!* presents the title piece and three other sizable texts written by Bloch for *Amazing Stories, Imaginative Tales,* and other pulp magazines of the forties and fifties. Each resounds with Bloch's characteristic style, the sometimes deadpan, sometimes punny mingling of humor and horror — what might be called stand-up tragedy — that informed his more famous work. As a result, this is a literary treasure trove, an opportunity to experience one of the true masters in works of fiction that are, for this generation, effectively new — and quite revelatory. Clearly this is a labor of love for Schow and Stefan R. Dziemianowicz (who acted as research associate and provides a foreword), but *The Devil with You!* is not a labor — indeed, it is a love — to read.   Ω

TOM O'BEDLAM AND THE KING OF DREAMS
by Darrell Schweitzer

illustrated by Stephen E. Fabian

From the hag and the hungry goblin
That into rags would rend ye,
And the spirit that stands
By the naked man
In the Book of Moons defend ye.
                                    — Traditional

If that doesn't work, alack, alas,
and something nasty comes to pass,
the sole advice that I can tell
is you should surely run like hell.
                        — Somewhat less traditional

Tom O'Bedlam awoke:

His days were always like that, beginning with a flash, a crash, like a sunburst, in the discontinuity of his muddled mind, his diseased wit, having lost track of his five senses before he ever learned to count to four.

It was getting a bit tiresome.

For Tom O'Bedlam had been mad for many and many a year, and madness was the glory of it, yet still he had begun to feel the weight of those years, the number of them, and he heard the chattering voices of all the memories they contained.

But only just a little. Ask a madman and he will explain that mad folk do not age as do the rest of us. They are almost deaf to the stealthy footsteps of Time.

It's not enough. For stealthy Time is not entirely deaf to *them.*

And in that year when King Harry of England was resting from the arduous task of beheading wives; though he might do it again and he might not; and the ghosts of headless ladies howling through Hampton Court were becoming tedious — *ahem!* — in *that* year, King Henry rested, England rested, the headsman got a day off, but Tom O'Bedlam awoke.

He saw things clearly. That was the terror of it.

The scales fell from his eyes, and when he groped around to find them in the dazzling sunlight, he could not.

Thomas of Bedlam and his friend Nick the Gaoler, who had been Tom's keeper in Bethlehem Mercy Hospital for the Knocked-a-Brained some years before (and there was no mercy there!) until madness had liberated them both — this Tom and this Nicholas still danced in the streets of London midday and midnight. They stood upon their hands and ran around in circles, their toes sticking through their soleless shoes to catch the money people tossed to them.

They stood like posts against gales, their colored tatters trailing like so many pennons. Their bells jangled. They spoke portentous prophecies to which, of course, no one listened.

Thus things were as they had long been, for he was *the* Tom O'Bedlam, the genuine archetype, the standard, the legend, against whom all other lunatics were measured.

But Tom's joints ached. He sprang to his step less springingly than before.

And, in one tiny corner of his mind, like a pebble dropping from the ceiling in a vast cavern, its faint sound growing and growing as it echoed, Tom O' Bedlam began to doubt.

The magnificent edifice of his lunacy cracked, just a little bit.

And One came to him, bearing an hourglass. This was in the springtime, amid the songs and festivals of May. The crowds tossed pennies. Madmen leapt through their accustomed contortions, and no one but Tom seemed to notice the terribly, terribly thin fellow with the hourglass, like a bundle of sticks come alive, his cloak so gauzy you could see right through it, though in his passage all the color seemed bleached out of the day.

This One came, in a cloud of greyness.

Tom and Nick stopped gambolling. The onlookers shrugged and went off after other amusements.

Now the houses all around seemed to nod like giants in their sleep, and shadows seemed to rise, like the bedclothes of those nodding giants, in time with their gigantic snores.

Tom and Nick were alone, in the gathering darkness at noon, and bony hands held up an hourglass, and a voice like a creaking coffin-lid cried out, "Look, look, and look well. I'm afraid you're running out of sand, as any sensible person can see."

The eyes of the speaker gaped at them, like open graves.

Tom laughed, a little nervously, and replied, "But we are *not* sensible!"

He reached out and spun the hourglass, so it tumbled end over end in its frame.

The bearer, snarling, whirled his cloak around himself and vanished in stages, like smoke from a cannon shot slowly dissipating.

The shadows retreated. Colors returned, but grudgingly.

And people came back into that narrow street. Tom and Nick rattled their bells, but no one gave them anything.

"Just common beggars," someone said.

And Tom sat down in the mud and dreamed while he was awake, or awoke, from waking, into a higher state which cannot quite be described. A vision came to him, of the two of them struggling up a slope of pouring sand, inside an hourglass, which tumbled end over end.

He told Nick what he saw.

"I can't see it, Tom, but I believe you. I'm so afraid."

And Tom looked into Nick's eyes and beheld, not the grey-haired, wrinkle-faced person who was there now, but a child who suddenly awakened because a nightmare came galloping through his dreams.

Tom said, "Be comforted."

But Nick was not comforted.

Tom sent forth his dream, like a tide across flat sand, to touch on brighter, stranger things.

Meanwhile, a common beggar nudged him out of his reverie with an outstretched hand and said, "Give me some money."

Tom saw at once that the beggar was not mad at all, but merely wretched, one who went hungry more often than not, who slept in the gutter when he'd been chased off doorsteps, who shivered in winter's cold and would likely die there.

He took a stick from the ground and a little mud, and drew a map on the beggar's palm, where X marked the spot beneath which an old Saxon king reclined in a ship inside a mound.

"Here is gold more than you can count or carry," said Tom. "Only beware of the what sleeps with the one who sleeps," for he knew that the dragon of the king's avarice lay coiled on his dead breast like a serpent.

The beggar went away, scratching his head and staring at his palm.

Tom realized that the man was to no degree less sane than he had been before their meeting, and so was unlikely to understand the gift Tom had given him.

"Do you suppose I'm losing my touch?"

Nick looked at him, again afraid, like that child staring up out of the deep well of passing years.

"Oh Tom! Don't say such things!"

And silently, then, the seasons turned, Spring into Summer and Summer into Autumn like the shadows of turning pages of a book; and Time's footsteps were left a little ways behind; and silently Tom got up out of the mud, for all the pain in his joints or shortness in his breath; silently Tom stood, and Nick went with him, and they walked away from London until they came to a place of ancient stones.

The leaves of autumn lay all about, covering the stones and the ground. Tom and Nick stood still, their toes crunching down through the leaves into the soft earth.

The leaves stirred. A whirling wind shaped them. The Autumn King revealed himself, like a whale rising out of the sea; all red and yellow and golden were his beard and cloak in the masses of leaves.

"Haven't we met before?" said Tom.

"Aye, and this is possibly our last meeting."

The Autumn King's soldiery rose out of the leaves, their burnished armor gleaming. They moved, rustling and creaking like scarecrows made out of the husks left behind when the harvest is long since taken away. Beneath their visors were only leaves.

They lurched toward Tom and Nick in the chilling of the air.

Tom took off his hat and bowed low before the King, making a sweeping, grand gesture with his hat, and he said, "Majesty, yes, we have met before, and this may indeed be our last meeting. I cannot be sure, for, true I've felt an autumnal humour of late within me, but there is no time for us to continue this audience, alas, for it's time for Winter."

And Tom blew hard and Tom blew cold, and in the blast of his breath the Autumn King and all his minions were blown clean away.

Tom felt smug for an instant. He held his chin in his hand and nodded sagely, muttering, "I'll miss the old bugger, you know, but he always was such a bother. Maybe this is the last time, and maybe it isn't, but I am more a windbag than he even yet."

He laughed. Nick afforded a cautious smile.

by Darrell Schweitzer

Only a madman would have believed in such things. Tom looked at Nick. Nick looked at Tom. They tried very hard to believe.

(And somewhere in the vast and haunted cavern of Mad Tom's mind, another pebble fell, rattling.)

Barefoot and wretched, shivering in the winter's snow, they made their way back to London, where no one knew them, no one turned to the sound of their jangling bells, and all the doors were shut, the windows shuttered, bolts bolted firmly in place.

"O Tom," wailed Nick at last. "What has all this got us?"

"It's got us where we are, not where we are not."

"And what might *that* mean?"

"Nick, I fear for you, for your madness is flaking away like ill-kept plaster, like pebbles rattling down from the ceiling in a cave, if you pause to ask what something *means*, for *mean* is for *mean*-spirited folk who take little accounts in huge ledgers and waste their souls away trying to make the numbers add up. We madmen do not *mean*. We utter cryptically and let someone else figure it out. Thus do we escape the ledgers, the figures, and hear not Time's wingèd chariot when one of the horses throws a shoe."

Nick hopped up and down in the cold.

"Just now all I hear is my teeth chattering."

Somewhere, in the darkness of London, a dog barked; a maiden sang; a pikeman tramped through the icy streets in iron-shod boots, thinking only of warm beer; a villain died with his throat cut and his face drowned in his soup; a poet heard the chimes at midnight and thought that'd make a good line; but where Tom and Nick were, in the empty street, beneath the shuttered windows and leaning rooftops, nothing happened at all.

And Tom began to doubt. A flash of sanity came to him, like a knife to the heart.

It came to him that the insane are merely in pain and not amusing at all, that the two of them were just dirty old frauds who would soon die in the winter's cold, that there was no transcendence in their songs, their babblings, their antics; that in all the world *things made sense* when written down in careful ledgers, in neat columns; and all dreams and fancies were like snowflakes in the dark, which may blow up against a lighted window for an instant, then drift away and are gone.

And One bearing a scythe approached them,

like a smudge spreading across the snow.

Tom tipped his hat. "We have met before, Lord."

The other, all in black, his scythe gleaming, whispered. "We have, but never before have you deigned to tarry and chat. I'm flattered."

"Nor can we now, Dread Alas."

"I think you can. I pause. We converse like sensible gentlemen."

"But you have a schedule to keep. You've written it all down in neat columns, in your ledger. I only seek to remind you, Your Deathfulness, of the vast importance of your work, which cannot be stayed or delayed or frayed."

Snow whirled in the air, though the sky was clear and uncaring stars gleamed far above. Dread Alas drew back his scythe for a swing and said, "Just hold still, the two of you. This won't take a moment."

Tom, at this critical juncture, didn't know what to do. Inspiration failed him. He could only grasp at the thinnest of straws.

"But wait, Sir."

"That I cannot."

"Already speaking, you have —"

"So?"

"Now that the moment has passed, *you're behind schedule!*"

This sort of thing had worked before, for Tom knew that all the Dreads and Alases and Deaths were exacting creatures, obsessed with neatness and with schedules. There had been Cousin Snip, whom he and Nick had left in hopeless confusion by asking him how he could possibly tread too and fro in the world and up and down it if he didn't know in what order to put down his feet.

That worked, once. Tom, his invention failing, sanity pressing in on him from all sides, pebbles rattling like rain within the cavern of his mind, could only hope it would work again.

But Dread Alas merely planted his scythe in the snow, took out a notebook, flipped through the clacking pages (for they were made of bone or stone, certainly not paper), and said, "Well, there's a plague I'm supposed to be doing soon, and the numbers are plus-or-minus a few thousand, so I could work both of you in."

He snapped the book shut.

"Then again," he said, hefting his scythe, "I have an *extra* moment just now, because someone else took care of a villain I was supposed to deal with —"

It was Nick who saved them, Nick who suddenly somersaulted onto his hands and wobbled in the snow. He shouted. He gobbled like a turkey. He garbled bits of old songs. He intoned hideous prophecies, backwards so they wouldn't come true.

Dread Alas paused, puzzled.

"No time!" said Nick. "No time at all, Dreadfully, Alasfully! We cannot linger. We cannot chat or stand still for even a moment, for a *geas* is upon us, which is like a *wyrd* only weirder; and we are the two of us the bold and trusty servants, the messengers and paladins of the King of Dreams, who outranks you and your whole family — Great Auntie Death and Cousin Snip and Uncle Slice, not to mention Clotho, Lachesis, and Atropos — for do not dreams soar beyond the reach of mere fate and time and death and meaning?"

Dread Alas, who was actually just the third cousin twice removed of the youngest nephew of Lord Pluto, King of Hades, and who was only allowed to collect souls because, with all the wars and plagues going around, the family was shorthanded — Dread Alas wasn't entirely sure who outranked whom. There was nothing in his notebook to clarify the matter.

He clacked through the pages forlornly.

"Well, I, uh —"

"And while you're figuring that out," said Nick, "my friend and I must be on our way, for we are on a special quest for our master the King of Dreams —"

He somersaulted backwards onto his feet, not as gracefully as he once had; in fact landing with a splash in a half-frozen puddle, but he caught hold of a post and hauled himself up and grabbed Tom by the arm. He drew him near and whispered, "Run!"

"That sounds entirely too sensible," said Tom.

"Just *run!*"

They ran as they had not run in years, through the streets and squares and courtyards of London, vaulting over fences and walls, past the tramping pikeman, who merely turned to watch as they passed; leaping over the throat-cut, soup-soaked villain who had been tossed out a window into a lane; all the while glancing back to see if they were pursued.

When they could run no further, both of them fell to the ground panting. Tom clung to Nick's shoulder and gasped, "Bless Momus and Bacchus and Gooble-Gobble-One-of-Us and all the ridiculous gods, Nick. *My* madness may have faltered, but, that was *pretty good.* You raved magnificently. I am impressed. Take cheer, Nick. Take cheer!"

But Nick took no cheer.

"What do you mean, 'faltered?' "

"I have been plagued by tremors of mundanity of late. I'm not as mad as I used to be, I fear."

"Then I fear indeed, for we are lost."

"Lost, how?"

"Found."

"What?"

"Oh, Tom, I did not rave at all. I *lied.*"

"What difference?"

"Any sane person can *lie.*"

"And they do, every day."

"Tom, all I did was stitch together a tatter of your old routines, speaking words you've spoken in the past. 'Twas but an imitation, a lifeless, strutting phantom —"

"I thought it strutted nicely —"

"Upon this stage of life, a poor player, soon to get the hook —"

So the conversation went on some while, as they shivered disconsolately, and Time's Wingèd Chariot completed its repairs and drew ever nearer. Once they spied a black, hooded figure with a scythe slipping in and out of the crack around the door of a house; but this was some other Death or Dread who followed a different schedule, and it did not pause to note them or to converse.

Near to dawn, as Nick was weeping for the futility of chasing after a madness which recedes like a tide over flat sand, Tom tried again to comfort him, and put his arm around him and shook him, saying, "Well, what about the King of Dreams?"

"*Is* there a king of dreams?"

"There seems to be a king of everything else."

"It's a crazy idea, Tom."

"Exactly."

It was, in fact, the thinnest of straws, but all they had to grasp at.

II

Forth from my sad and darksome cell,
Or from the deepe abyss of hell,
Mad Tom is come into the worlde againe
To see if he can cure his distempered braine.
— Traditional

Or maybe not.
— Definitely a later interpolation

These were the dreams of the Saxon king,

by Darrell Schweitzer

asleep beneath his mound, with the dragon of avarice curled on his breast.

These were the dreams of giants, hurled from England's shores by Brutus the Trojan long before London was born, giants who now lay grimacing in the depths of the sea, their golden teeth gleaming.

These were dreams of beggars, maidens, madmen, villains dead in their soup; of soldiers, sailors, candlestick-makers, old men in their beds and babies in their cradles, of corpses in coffins. These were the dreams of fallen leaves. Of stones.

And the King of Dreams opened his eyes, in the dark depths of that secret sea on which the world of waking men, of sane men, floats like a thin scum.

He gazed upward, intently.

He caused Tom O'Bedlam to dream once again, and he caused Tom and Nick to rise up, whether waking or dreaming they knew not; walking, waking, dreaming, they ascended, as if climbing stairs, and only a madman could have explained it, but no madman would ever try.

A miracle then.

Tom and Nick walked through the fading darkness, in the first light of dawn; and they thought they saw a King rise up beyond the edge of the world and put on a silver mask, which was the Moon, and then change it for a golden mask which was the Sun. London stirred, awakening. A wagon creaked. A dog barked yet again. The maiden, who had been singing now poured slops out a window.

Tom and Nick leapt aside nimbly enough.

They nearly tripped over the throat-cut villain yet again.

Stumbling backwards they came into street which was still dark, which was Day of Doom Street, and retreating further into the darkness, they came to a courtyard, or a Close, which was Day of Doom Close, and Tom and Nick did not doubt it.

They came to a door, whereon was painted a grinning, bone-faced harlequin.

"I think we belong here," said Tom.

He pressed the door open. It creaked like a coffin-lid. The two of them made their way down cold, stone steps onto a rough wooden floor. The room around them was dim, shadowy. Dust motes danced in flickering candlelight. Boards creaked. Nick jumped back, startled at some sound or some movement. He bumped into an array of glass bottles, which crashed to the floor.

"And now look what you've done!" someone shouted. "Look! Don't just stand there! Help me clean up the mess!"

The speaker was an old man with a long, tangled beard. He wore a robe like a wizard's, with moons and stars embroidered in it, but stained and in worse repair than any wizard would tolerate. In his hand he held a thin, clay flask. Something steamed in there. It might have just been tea.

Tom looked around for a broom or a mop. Nick started to gather fragments of glass in his hand.

"Oh, never mind! The work of centuries ruined! Elixer vitae, the universal solvent — which dissolves itself and so transcends matter — the fluids of transmutation and transfiguration and transmigration, all wasted, spilled down through the floor to make the mice drunken. What does it matter? I was hoping for maybe a couple of Salamanders of Eternity to come traipsing through that door."

"Sorry," said Nick.

"You two don't happen to be Salamanders?"

Tom touched himself here and there, as if to make sure he was still who he had been the last time he checked. "No. Sorry."

"We thought, because of the sign on the door, that this was a haven for the mad," said Nick.

"Oh, *that*. That's just to scare off obnoxious tradesmen and peddlers. I can't stand such tiresome, mundane folk."

"Oh."

"But sometimes I think I *am* mad."

"There's a great future in it," said Tom. "Very promising." (And as he spoke he thought he was lying, as Nick had lied, just repeating snatches of old routines. But somehow he couldn't quite *dis*believe everything he said, and he clung to that single straw.)

"But you're not exactly, quite, *mad*, are you?" said Nick.

"No, I am the next best thing. I am an alchemist. Fred the Alchemist, at your service. Afeared Frederick, my detractors call me. As long as you're here, you might as well have some breakfast."

Though madmen such as Tom and Nick were widely reputed to live on air, the bread and broth and beer the alchemist offered them was most welcome. (Though Tom had a vision of a tiny version of himself floating face-down in the soup, a thin stream of a darker fluid leaking off to one side.) They sat around a wooden table. Fred pushed aside books and bottles and assorted clutter to make room for them. A homunculus wriggled out of a flimsy box and flopped off the edge of the table, onto the floor. A stuffed crocodile suddenly came to life and followed after.

Tom noticed that the floorboards where the bottles had spilled earlier were now gleaming gold.

"That's an old trick," said Fred. "It fails to impress after a while."

"I know some who'd be impressed," said Nick.

"A vulgar thing for vulgar minds."

"Not to mention vulgar purses," said Tom.

"Exactly," said the alchemist. He put his hands on Tom and Nick's shoulders, and drew the three of them together into a huddle. "I see, gentlemen, that we are all of like minds, not the same, but similar enough. I think you are sent to me for a purpose, there being a destiny that shapes our ends, transplant them, water them, put white picket fences around them as we may —"

"Uh, Tom —" said Nick.

"We are sent by the King of Dreams," said Tom, not entirely lying, as a certain inspiration came to him again. "It is our quest."

"For what?" said Afeared Fred.

"We're not sure. We're getting to that."

"Uh, Tom —" said Nick, with rising urgency.

"No matter," said Fred. "We three are brothers, like knights on an adventure. We will share this quest. Oh! How wonderful!"

"I'm wondering," said Tom.

And Fred the alchemist told them, at great length, with much explication and consulting of arcane volumes, pointing to illustrations and strange woodcuts, how he was on a quest of his own, through his alchemy, for the Ideal, that perfect beauty which exists beyond all mortal things, beyond time and eternity. He had seen her once, from afar, in his youth, but glimpsed her in the form of an ineffably beautiful maiden, and now, many years later, after much hardship and poverty and sorrow, he was no closer than ever to regaining that vision. ("What a crazy thing to do," said Tom, and he too saw the alchemist as a brother.) But the alchemist hadn't given up. Even if the Salamanders of Eternity he had been attempting to conjure hadn't shown up on schedule, there was always tomorrow, always the night after that, always a page to be turned, a concoction to be concocted, a casting to be cast —

"We shall swear our souls to this end!" cried Fred. "Yes, yes, like one of those knights at Camelot when the Holy Grail came floating into the room during the Pentecost feast and everybody got second helpings. Yes! Yes!"

by Darrell Schweitzer

"Yes!" said Tom, and he was much heartened, and hopeful again, for this was genuine madness.

"Uh, *Tom!*" Nick yanked at Tom's arm and turned him around and pointed.

There at the bottom of the stairs, standing in the middle of the golden floorboards like an enormous copybook blot, was One in the familiar black, hooded robe, with regulation scythe, hourglass and notebook. Only this One was taller than the rest, more massive (though you could see through him, like a wisp of dark cloud), and Tom somehow knew that this wasn't any junior cousin three times removed, or elderly auntie or doddering Great-Great-Grandfather Rigor Mortis, but the King of Reapers ("I'm always meeting royalty," Tom said to himself), Catastrophicus Maximus, the boss, the one in charge, to whom even the Four Horsemen of the Apocalypse referred their more difficult cases.

"I have come for you all," spoke a voice like an earthquake. Plaster and small stones rattled down from the ceiling as the room shook.

"He's been around before," said Fred. "Such a bother." He got up and struck at the newcomer with a broom. "Shoo! Scat!" The broom passed right through, as through a shadow.

"I don't think that's going to help," said Nick.

The alchemist sat down slowly, despairing.

"I guess not. It's not fair. I was *that* close —"

Catastrophicus Maximus put his hourglass down on the table. Within, Tom could make out tiny figures of himself, Nick, and Fred the Afeared swimming desperately against the sand, which had almost completely drained from the upper chamber of the hourglass. Holding his scythe under one arm, Catastrophicus Maximus paged through his notebook. The pages crashed together, like muted thunder, each of them a gravestone with a name and date already written on it.

Tom had seen such a thing before. He suspected it was standard issue. The pages turned, one by one. He looked for the one with his name on it.

"Ah, here we go." More plaster fell. A large piece fell directly through the specter's head and hit the floor with a crash. Catastrophicus Maximus glanced up, irritated, then resumed. "Yes, here. A blank page. I can write the three of you in immediately. No delays, no excuses, no frills. *Now!*"

And the creature's skeletal forefinger began to glow, and he started writing.

"But our quest," said Tom.

"We have dreams to dream yet," said Nick.

"I'm still waiting for those damned Salamanders," said Afeared Fred. "They were supposed to help. I had hoped to attain the Ideal."

"I'll add a footnote to that effect," said Catastrophicus Maximus, who continued writing.

Tom looked at Nick. Nick looked at Tom. Tom shrugged. There was nothing left for it, nothing he could do, but one reflex, little more than a spasm.

He flipped over the hourglass and set the double-chamber tumbling. Sand poured up, and down, and up. The tiny figures within vanished.

"STOP THAT!!!" The whole house trembled and swayed like a thing alive. A heavy timber snapped and came crashing down through the table. It was all Catastrophicus Maximus could do to snatch his hourglass out of harm's way. He dropped his notebook. His scythe went clattering through a shelf of bottles and jars. Wriggly, glowing things with half-human faces, misplaced eyes, and voices entirely innocent of key or harmony flopped onto the floor, singing an insipidly cheerful anthem, which enraged Maximus all the more. He stomped ineffectually, his footsteps too light to be heard or have much effect under the circumstances.

Tom looked at Nick. Nick looked at Tom. They both looked at Fred, who grabbed them both by the arms and hauled them out of there. "Run!" he said.

They ran, Tom and Nick following Fred. Catastrophicus Maximus had recovered his scythe. One long swing cut through the walls of the room. The rest of the ceiling caved in. An enormous bed with a fat lady in it dropped into the room. "Ooh! I'll raise your rent for this!" she squealed, but by then Fred and the others were out the opposite end of the room and struggling up a narrow, twisting passage to a cramped landing which afforded no refuge, then up another stair, and another, until at last they burst out onto the roof, from which there was no place to go.

A wooden tub with a mast and sail set in it rocked on swaying sawhorses at the edge of the roof.

They could hear the footsteps of Catastrophicus Maximus drawing nearer now, stamping furiously up the narrow stair.

The wooden tub had a name written on it: *H.M.S. Folly.*

Tom and Nick looked at Fred, who said quickly, "We *are* all fools, aren't we?"

Without further ado, the three of them clambered aboard.

A familiar, hooded figure emerged onto the roof. The great scythe swung back.

Fred unfurled the sail, which filled with wind. "Heave to, boys! Heave to! At times like this I think I'm losing my mind."

"That's good!" said Tom. "Very good!"

And he dared to hope even more.

They heaved, all three of them throwing their weight to one side. The H.M.S. Folly tottered, then fell over the side of the roof.

And only a madman could have expected what came next. They didn't crash into the street below. Instead, a burning golden cloud seemed to fill the whole world. The H.M.S. Folly rose, slowly, through the cloud until the light above them was almost too much to look upon. Tom shaded his eyes, and could barely make out the huge mask of the Sun which was worn by the King of Dreams, and he more imagined than saw the vast eyes behind that mask gazing down on him, with benevolence, even with fondness.

He knew then that he was healed, that his madness was once again complete.

He sang for the King of Dreams in the special language of lunatics.

Nick joined in.

Fred remarked, "I think I can make some of that out."

"Good!" said Tom. "Very good!"

The King of Dreams set aside his mask of the Sun and put on the tarnished and spotted silver mask of the Moon. The H.M.S. Folly sailed on a sea of swirling stars, beneath a moonlit sky.

There was a faint thunder, far behind. Tom turned once, and saw a black-robed figure swimming in the stars, considerably encumbered by his scythe and his hourglass. A wave of stars washed over him, and he was gone.

The wooden tub came to rest on a glowing shore. There, as heroes of old, Tom and Nick fought and slew a dragon, whose name was Doubt or Dread or Reason, or perhaps all three. They came to a cottage where an old lady was scrubbing all the color out of people's lives, making them dull, drab, and melancholy, storing the colors thus pilfered in clay jars, carefully sealed and numbered. Tom, Nick, and an increasingly less fearful Fred rushed in, shouting, and spilled a shelf of jars. They left bright smears and handprints everywhere, while Mother Sereda shrieked and chased after them with a broom, which passed right through them as if she were

trying to beat away the light that streams in through suddenly opened shutters.

There, in the Land of Dreams, which is beyond the reach of Time, the place of the marvelous, the impossible, the mad, they met an honest politician, a generous rich man, and a merciful judge, who led them up a hillside, as a young girl fell from the Moon.

As they neared, they saw her descending, like a shooting star at first, then more gently, like a luminous leaf settling to earth. They came upon her as she lay amid the grasses, her face like a perfect pearl, her long hair trailing in the wind like finest silk.

And Fred the Alchemist knew her, for she was the Ideal, some village girl he had known long ago when he was a boy and had loved from afar. But of course this was not the girl herself, only the perfect image of her he had formed in mind and memory and dream.

The alchemist became that boy again, his youth regained. He and the girl sailed away over the star-sea in the wooden-tub ship, and vanished from sight as the King of Dreams in his lunar mask began to set below the horizon, until only his eyes and forehead were still showing.

Now the others were gone. Tom and Nick stood alone on the shore.

The Moon continued to set.

Nick suddenly shouted, "Hey! What about us?" but Tom hushed him.

A wind blew between the stars, over the rippling sea, and on the wind came the voice of the King of Dreams, who said, "I am a lie, but you have dreamed me, and so I am also true. Therefore, be rewarded."

He reached up with his golden hands and broke an hourglass as if it were an egg, and golden sand came raining down.

Tom and Nick fell, down through the stars, the golden sand swirling around them. It seemed they viewed a thousand years at once, and saw many things even a madman could not put into words. There was an impossible version of London where gleaming towers seemed to float above a layer of soiled clouds, and great metal birds roared overhead. Though this was the sort of vision madmen might properly have, they turned away, and swam back through the centuries toward the London they knew. Once they passed Catastrophicus Maximus, who was completely helpless without his hourglass. He fluttered his arms uselessly.

They paused once to save England from a

by Darrell Schweitzer

great, lumbering fleet of ships, like dark castles under sail, sent forth by a monarch who knew not dreams or fancies or joy, only misery and fear, which he wanted to share; but Tom and Nick borrowed lanterns from the Man in the Moon and walked upon the waters of the North Sea, and they directed the ships as one directs traffic, pointing to say, *You, that way!* and *You! Over there!* and so the ships of Philip of Spain were scattered.

They saw an England which became great, ruled by one called the Fairie Queen.

But this was not the place for them.

Not quite.

The King of Dreams spoke to them one last time, saying, "Be not aged. Fear not death. For you are impossible yourselves. You are dreams. Therefore exist as dreams."

And they regained their youth and found themselves back in the London they had known when they were young, before King Harry had whacked off even one queen's head.

They landed with a thump in the middle of a crowded street.

Some sort of procession was passing by. There were richly-clad nobles, guards, bishops. Then, in a fine carriage, the King, with his first queen, who, at that time, he still loved.

"You!" someone shouted. "This is no place for beggars. Be off."

But Tom bowed low, with a grand, graceful sweep, and then explained himself, blurting out all at once of his adventures and how he had, incidentally, saved an England not yet born. Not that he expected any reward for that. It was all in a day's work.

"Oh, I see! You're *mad!* Here's a penny for you!"

Tom stood on his hands. He caught the penny between his toes. Ω

TOM O'BEDLAM AND THE KING OF DREAMS

INSIDE THE EARTH, UNDER THE SEA
by Hugh B. Cave

illustrated by Allen Koszowski

"The statuette, idol, fetish, or whatever it was, had been captured some months before in the wooded swamps south of New Orleans during a raid on a supposed voodoo meeting; and so singular and hideous were the rites connected with it, that the police could not but realize that they had stumbled on a dark cult totally unknown to them, and infinitely more diabolic than even the blackest of the African voodoo circles."

— H.P. Lovecraft, *The Call of Cthulhu.*"

As the shadows deepened over the mountains, the drummers came from the *honfour* to take their places in the peristyle, and Rick Colson felt himself snap to attention on his bench under the hanging lanterns. It was not his first time in Haiti. He had visited this Caribbean land of sorcery and poverty half a dozen times before. He even spoke the peasants' Creole well enough to be understood.

Nor was this his first voodoo service. He had attended half a dozen, from simple *mangé loas* to the week-long Dahomeyan rites at La Souvenance, and had written about them for assorted magazines and newspapers.

On this September, 1990, evening he was in Haiti to write about the boat people for a newspaper in Miami. And he was here at a voodoo service in the Southern Peninsula town of Léogane because of interesting rumors about the *houngan* in charge. Marcel Antoine was said to possess powers that were little short of awesome.

The service was a *brulé zin,* in which two young women were to be made *kanzo* by, among other things, dipping their hands in the seven pots of boiling oil. Not having witnessed such a ceremony before, Colson spent most of the night taking notes. Then at dawn, when the night-long affair was over and the drums at last fell silent, he approached Antoine to thank the *houngan* for his hospitality.

The two shook hands. "Please be kind enough to give me your name and address," said Antoine, a small, dark man with hypnotic eyes and a white-toothed smile. "I expect to be in Miami in a few days and would like to call on you."

"You're going to Miami?"

"Indeed."

Colson wrote his name, home address and phone number on a notebook page and tore out the page. As he handed it over, he frowned. This was Léogane. One of the things he wished to write about was the continuing flight of desperate Haitians to the United States, and one of the seacoast towns from which those people set sail in rickety homemade boats was said to be Léogane. "You'll be traveling by boat, friend?" Colson asked.

The *houngan* shrugged.

"I wonder if I might make the journey with you," said Colson.

"What, *m'sié?*"

"I'm here in your country to write about your problems. As a friend, not a critic. If I could make such a trip with you, and see for myself what it's like to be one of the so-called boat people, I might be able to write something helpful. What do you say?"

Marcel Antoine pondered the question for a moment, then sadly shook his head. "The two men who operate the boat on which I have booked passage would never permit you to write about them."

"How will they know?"

"You mean you would travel as one of *us?* A boat person?"

"Why not?"

"It will cost you."

"How much?"

"For this boat, which is owned by two Haitians who live in the Bahamas, the fee is fifteen hundred American dollars."

Colson had heard of a boat owned by two Haitian brothers, Emile and Jules Sastine, who lived in the Bahamas. Some of what he had heard about the Sastine brothers was ugly and frightening. It would make a terrific story, he told himself. "When do you sail?" he asked.

The *houngan* leaned forward to peer at the watch on Colson's wrist. "In less than two hours, *m'sié.*"

"And the brothers have room for me?"

"They asked me yesterday, in fact, if I knew of one more person they could sign up. They dislike sailing without a full load."

"I'm your man, then," Colson said.

"And what about the car you came in?"

"It's a rental. I know a shop-keeper in Léogane who will drive it back to Port-au-Prince for me."

"And you have as much as fifteen hundred American dollars in your pocket?" Antoine asked with a frown.

"As it happens, yes. In my job one has to be prepared for opportunities like this."

"Then come, *ami.*" With a smile, the little *houngan* extended his hand. "It is time for us to make ready."

Colson would never have been accepted as a passenger had he been white, of course. As an African-American with money enough for his fare, he became just one of the eighteen passengers who boarded the sailing vessel *Vagabond* at eight o'clock that morning. The first thing he noticed was that the motorized sailboat was barely large enough to hold that many.

There were no cabin accommodations. For his fifteen hundred American dollars he was expected to find a place on deck for himself and whatever possessions he had brought with him.

Actually, he was better off than most. His luggage was at a *pension* in Port-au-Prince, and on arriving in the States he could phone for it to be sent to him. These others knew they would not be returning to Haiti and had their worldly goods with them, in rope-tied boxes, cheap cardboard suitcases, or burlap bags. Those at the bottom of the economic scale had nothing at all, having sold everything they possessed to pay for their passage.

With Emile Sastine at the wheel and her ancient engine wheezing like a crone with a bad cold, the *Vagabond* crawled out of Léogane to begin her journey. Jules, the younger brother, hoisted the craft's ragged sails and the engine was silent. So began that eventful voyage about which Rick Colson wrote in the Miami paper for which he worked. But if you happened to read the story and think you know what really happened, think again. No one would have believed the real story, Colson decided. Only with reluctance did he tell it even to me.

Under a blazing Caribbean sun, Rick Colson shed his jacket, stopped talking to Marcel Antoine, the *houngan,* and struck up a conversation with a middle-aged woman seated on the other side of him. After all, he was a reporter and had come on this journey to write about these sad people and their problems.

"Why are you leaving your beloved homeland, *commère?*"

She turned to peer at him — a woman who on close inspection had to be about forty but who, because of fatigue and despair, looked nearly twice that age. "What?" she mumbled through broken yellow teeth.

"Why are you going to America? What will you do there?"

"I go because I am hungry. And because my man was foolish enough to speak out for Aristide."

"Foolish, *commère?*"

"Well, brave, then. Whatever. My Theaud spoke up for the only good leader we have had in years, and men came to drag him away to prison. Or so they said. I now know that Theaud never got there. They killed him on the way, and left his body in a ditch beside the road."

Colson talked to her awhile, then wormed his way through the press of bodies and found another he could talk to. This one was a girl of eighteen or so, half naked in a ragged, feed-bag dress, but dark-eyed and almost regally handsome. He told her his name and asked hers.

She shook her head.

"You don't want to tell me your name?"

She shook her head again.

"Why?"

"Because I am running away from a father I hate. He is a Tonton Macoute. He kills people for money. And if he ever finds out I am in America, he will turn the world upside down to find me and silence me."

"Very well." Colson nodded. "Your name does not matter. But tell me more about these Tontons."

"Don't you know? Where have you been living in Haiti? In the Dondon caves? On top of Morne Macaya?"

"I know a little about them, of course. How Papa Doc created them to be his private army. But I need to know more."

She shook her head at him, as if to say, "What a shame you are so ignorant." Then she fell silent for a moment, perhaps wondering whether she should continue talking to him. Finally she said with a shrug, "Very well. Let me tell you how my father used to come home at night, after working all day in Port-au-Prince. We lived in Carrefour, and of course, had he been like other people, he would have taken a *tap-tap*. But no. Oh, no! He would stop a car — any car — and point his gun at the driver and open the door and get in. He would say to the driver, "Take me to Carrefour!" The driver might be a doctor on his way to the hospital, you understand. He might be anyone doing anything, and what he had to do might be of the greatest importance to himself or others. But my father would say, "Take me to Carrefour!" and jab his gun into the driver's ribs, and, of course, the driver would obey. Unless, of course, he was too terrified. Once, my father boasted of having dragged a driver out of his car and taken the car himself, leaving the poor man in the gutter. So that is why I am going to America. And, if you must know, I stole the money for my passage from my father. But if he didn't steal it himself, he earned it by doing things that are wholly evil."

So it went. All that day Colson crawled about the deck talking to people. Some, of course, would not talk to him. They were afraid. Others, before responding to his overtures, looked about them carefully to see who might be listening — to see, especially, whether the owners of the sailing craft, Emile and Jules Sastine, might be listening or watching. But enough of them talked for him to be sure of one thing:

These people were not fleeing from their homeland. They loved their homeland. They were fleeing from political oppression, from fear of being murdered for their beliefs, from despair, or from hunger. And all they hoped for in the country to which they were fleeing was a chance — even a slim chance — to be free of fear again, to work, to earn a little money, and not to be always hungry.

The night fell like a great black weight over the sea, and all movement ceased except for a few scattered sounds of moaning as the huddled passengers sought to keep warm.

His work done for the time being, Colson slept, too — alongside his new friend, little Marcel Antoine, the *houngan* who was rumored to have such awesome powers.

A sudden harsh rasping sound jarred Colson awake.

There was commotion then. The passengers on deck scrambled to their feet, some clinging to their neighbors for support. Questions filled the

night, drowning out the sea-sounds. Up on deck, from the Sastines' cabin, rushed the older brother, Emile, seeming to demand an explanation from Jules, who struggled with the wheel. For a few minutes Rick Colson found it impossible to think, and could not even answer the frantic questions of his friend, the *houngan*, who clung to him as the boat lurched and swayed.

Then, having had some experience in such things, Colson said quietly, "We're aground, Marcel. God knows where, but that fool at the wheel has run us into shallow water. Probably some reef on the edge of the Bahamas."

The older Sastine rushed about as best he could under such crowded conditions, admonishing all to relax and keep calm. "There is nothing to fear!" he shouted in Creole. "Everything will be all right!"

When there was light enough to see by, half an hour later, it proved Colson to be more correct, though what the vessel had run aground on was not a submerged reef but a tiny island only five or six times as big as the boat itself.

"All right!" Emil Sastine shouted. "You have to go ashore, all of you, so my brother and I can float her again. We can't get her off with all you people on board. Go!"

Dim in the pale glow of dawn, the speck of land was some twenty yards distant. No doubt the water between the boat and the beach was shallow, but the passengers — most of them hill people who did not know the sea that well — could not be sure of that, and cried out in fear.

"We could drown!"

"I can't swim!"

"There could be crocodiles!"

"Get off the boat," said Emil Sastine. "Now! Get off the boat so we can float her, or you'll be here forever, all of you!" And suddenly, seemingly from nowhere, a weapon appeared in his hands.

It was not a simple handgun, but a military rifle of a kind that could spew a whole torrent of bullets. Most of the passengers probably did not know what kind of gun it was. Rick Colson did. "Wait a minute, Sastine," Colson said, lifting a hand. "No need to get violent." And turning to the passengers, he said even more quietly, "Let me see how deep it is."

Silence gripped the boat as he stepped to the side. The Sastine brothers were both armed now — they must have had their weapons at hand all the time, just out of sight. Fear kept the passengers quiet. All watched as Colson slid over the side, hung by his hands for a few seconds, then let go.

The water was shoulder deep. "Wait a minute," he said, and took a few steps toward shore to make sure the bottom was what it seemed to be. Then, "All right," he said, waving. "No problem. We go ashore and wait. The boats floats, and they fix any damage. We wade back out and get aboard again." In Creole it did not sound quite that casual — the language of the Haitian peasant has its limitations — but his meaning was clear enough.

If, he thought, *remembering some of the stories he had heard, they let us aboard again. The Sastine brothers are from the Bahamas and probably know these waters well. They certainly have charts. Running aground here might not be the accident it seems to be.*

He led the passengers ashore, most of them scared half to death, some even crying in their despair. But they were not really following *him,* Colson knew. They were following the man at his side, Marcel Antoine, the *houngan,* who while trudging ashore through the ever more shallow water, kept looking back over his shoulder at the boat.

Colson looked back, too. Lighter by the weight of its passengers, the craft floated free again. Emil Sastine stood motionless by the wheel, watching. His brother had disappeared below, perhaps to assess the damage.

Perhaps.

But, anyway, there was a little more room on the island. Once ashore, those who for hour after hour had huddled body to body on the *Vagabond*'s deck were able to spread out, stretch their aching arms, breathe a bit more freely. But with the brothers' guns menacing them and the brothers snarling at them, they had not dared to gather up their meager possessions before leaving the boat. They had no food, no water, and the island itself had nothing to offer — not even a blade of grass. Standing there on that oversized pancake of sand, dripping seawater, they stared at the boat in silence, waiting for what might happen next.

All but little Marcel Antoine, the *houngan.* He looked at Rick Colson and his bony fingers tugged at Colson's sleeve. "Come," he muttered, and led the way to a part of the island where the two might talk without being overheard.

"*M'sié,*" said the voodoo priest, hunkering down on the sand, "what do you know about those two?"

Colson hesitated. Should he confide in the fellow? Tell him of the phone call he had made from his friend's shop in Léogane before boarding the *Vagabond?* He was silent while making up his mind. Then he shrugged.

"I've heard rumors, Marcel. They may have done this before."

"So I believe."

"More than once, in fact. It may be the way they operate. Line up a boatload of desperate people, take their money — for which most of them have sold everything they own — then leave them stranded on some God-forsaken flyspeck like this one. That way they avoid the risk of being caught trying to smuggle them into the States."

Marcel Antoine nodded. "So we are to perish here."

"Well, maybe n—"

But Antoine had turned away. Without looking back, he walked to an empty patch of sand and stood there with his hands at his sides, his back toward Colson and the others. Perhaps, Colson thought, he was praying to his voodoo gods. Who could say?

Colson turned to glance at the *Vagabond.* On deck, Emile Sastine still stood by the wheel. The smaller brother had just emerged from below and was striding toward him.

On the flyspeck island the huddled passengers had been reluctant to move any farther from the boat than they had to. Now they stopped whispering among themselves and watched in silence, as though sensing they were about to be betrayed.

The brothers exchanged words and looked toward the island. Jules then stepped to the wheel and Emile went below. In a moment the craft's wheezy old engine sputtered to life, and suddenly the *Vagabond* was in motion.

Heading out, away from shore!

Leaving her eighteen passengers stranded on a barren flyspeck of land without food or water!

Leaving them there to die!

The eighteen — all but *houngan* Marcel Antoine, who was otherwise busy, and reporter Rick Colson, who was watching Antoine — screamed and wept and frantically waved their arms. Some of them ran clumsily into the sea a short distance as if they would swim after the boat, but quickly realized the hopelessness of pursuit and stumbled, gasping, back to shore.

Marcel Antoine scooped up some sand and, bending forward from the waist, let it dribble slowly through his fingers while he intoned a voodoo chant.

Colson walked over to him and said, "Which *loa* are you hoping to talk to, Marcel?"

The *houngan* looked up. "The old ones, *m'sié*. The very old ones. And may *Le Bon Dieu* be with us, for what I do here is almost too dangerous to think about!"

Colson nodded, and was silent. The man from the hills continued his chanting.

"*Papa Legba, ouvri bayé! Papa Legba, Attibon Legba, ouvri bayé pou nou passé!*" Over and over, the same words, rising in volume as they were repeated. And then the chanting became *langage,* the old African tongue that no one could translate anymore, not even the *houngans* and *mambos* who used it. But the gods knew its meaning. Especially the old, old ones.

They would respond.

Antoine stood up, visibly exhausted and trembling. Reaching out, he grabbed at Colson's hand and looked toward the retreating Vagabond. Colson, not knowing what to expect — knowing only that certain voodoo *houngans* and mambos possessed incredible powers — looked in the same direction and waited, cold as ice, for what might happen.

Alongside the fleeing boat the sea suddenly began to boil. The sun was above the horizon now; the water was liquid gold. All at once it was molten gold, fiery gold, and burst apart like a monstrous display of fireworks. Into view first came the head of the huge creature causing the disturbance: a bulbous thing like the head of an octopus, whose face was a froth of giant feelers.

Then came the creature's body. Scaly. Rubbery. A gigantic sea-serpent kind of thing with enormous forefeet. Claws on the forefeet like the claws of a huge lobster.

Out of the sea it reared, bending over the boat. On deck the Sastine brothers were pygmies, dwarfs, terrified human bugs racing about waving their arms, screaming their heads off.

The monstrous serpent, dragon, snake — whatever it was — curled above the deck, seemingly powered by long, narrow wings protruding from its scaly body. Its octopus head swooped down, breathing fire. The giant feelers swept the boat's deck in search of prey. The fleeing Sastines, their screams plainly heard on the island, were swept up into the monster's maw.

Slowly then, apparently satisfied, the thing sank back into the sea. Slowly the sea stopped churning and became calm.

by **Hugh B. Cave**

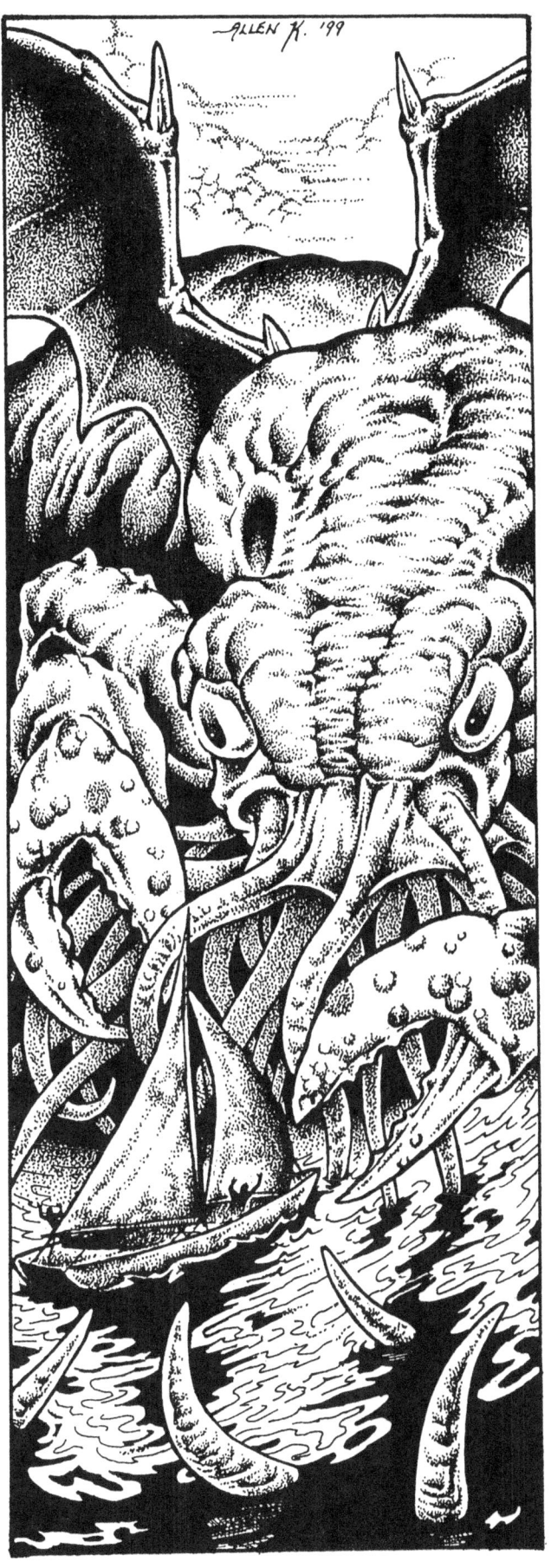

"What in God's name — ?" Rick Colson gasped.

"One of the Old Ones," whispered Marcel Antoine in awe. "One of the Great Old Ones from under the sea or inside the earth. I have never dared to call on them before. And now — God help me — I must use all the power at my command. *I must make that one obey me....*"

"*Obey* you? Colson gasped.

"Why not? I have heard that some sorcerers are able to compel even *demons* to obey. Here —"

The little *houngan* fell to his knees and scooped up a handful of sand. Letting the sand dribble through his fingers to form a star-shaped pattern on the ground in front of him, he raised his eyes to the sky and began a kind of throaty chant.

Colson could not translate the words. They were again langage, sounding like Creole but not really the peasant tongue. Over and over he voiced the same phrase. Was the word "Cthulhu" a part of it?

Suddenly Colson looked at the boat again.

Strange. Before boarding the *Vagabond* he had telephoned the U.S. Embassy and told them of the voyage. Asked them to have the U.S. Coast Guard track the Sastines' boat in case something like this might happen. And no doubt a Coast Guard plane or vessel was somewhere in the vicinity. But that would not explain the boat's present behavior.

Because the ship was not continuing on its course, as might be expected with her only human occupants now in the maw of that monstrous thing that had risen from the sea to stop her flight.

Inexplicably, with her noisy engine now silent, she was drifting — if drifting was the word — *back toward the island!*

The breeze — what there was of it — should have been propelling her away from the island. But she was coming back!

In a few minutes she would be close enough again for those on the island to wade out to her and climb aboard. And continue her voyage, even without the help of the Coast Guard.

Colson stopped staring at the craft and turned to look at Marcel Antoine. The little Haitian *houngan* was rising from his knees. His countrymen, shouting for joy, rushed into the sea.

"Come, my friend," the *houngan* said to Rick Colson. "We can leave this place now. Perhaps the old ones will even escort us to our destination."

Ω

THE MANNIKIN'S CHILD

Miners, climbers, quarriers —
Sometimes they meet her underground.
They try to catch her,
But she won't go.
She says they have it wrong.

No, says the girl,
My mother didn't guess the mannikin's name.
She didn't try, not really.
She didn't want me brought up by my father,
The king who loved only gold.
Better to live underground
Where the gold grows
Deep in the elemental earth.

The mannikin took me.
He brews, he bakes, he spins gold.
He teaches the arts of the earth.

She doesn't give her name.
She turns in their hands,
Stamps her foot,
And the earth opens under her.
She vanishes beneath the stone.

— **Ruth Berman**

FROM ALFANO'S RELIQUARY
by Andy Duncan

illustrated by Rodger Gerberding

In your time the Church is unimportant, and popes die of old age, but I am speaking of my time. In the years after Charlemagne, I served no fewer than nineteen of Christ's apostles on Earth, all scrofulous old Romans who perched on the edge of the throne of St. Peter for a season or two, pissing their vestments whenever the tapestries rustled. Such men attracted the clumsiest of assassins. Emetics were used as poisons. Frayed garrotes, unable to withstand the throes, snapped. Feebly struggling pontiffs were dropped repeatedly from low balconies. Cheaply made bread knives, shoved gracelessly into breastbones, splintered. One subtle fellow hacked away at the side of the chest opposite the victim's heart, causing needless delay and unpleasantness. It was not an age of efficiency. Yet because these murderers were seldom rushed, and tended to bring, as secondary instruments, rocks and hammers, the night's work eventually would be accomplished, and yet another prelate would be sent mewling to hell.

Of all the popes I served, only Stephen VII moved boldly against his enemy, but, of course, only Stephen VII was mad. Always awake, always anxious, he scampered along the corridors throughout the night, causing restless sleepers to dream of rats. Some nights, unobserved, I stood at intersections, a shadowed column among other columns, and watched him pass. He was a fat man with spindly legs and tiny feet. Even by day he never quite stood still, but teetered, like a balancing turnip. During mundane audiences, for no discernible reason, his sagging, ruined face would bubble with rage, and he would scuttle about the room until the mood was past, kicking dogs, bishops, furniture, with his absurd feet. He never kicked me.

These fits were not serious. Stephen feared no one in the chamber. He perceived no real enemies in his covetous entourage, in the fearful and filthy peasantry of Rome, in the restive occupation army of recently godless Franks. Certainly he perceived no threat in me, his mute counselor, at least not initially. No, the sloping garret of his skull had room for only one enemy, and that single enemy was already dead.

Many men derive comfort from their enemies — I have relished mine through the centuries — but Stephen chewed his like bitter cud. His hated predecessor, Pope Formosus, lay at rest within the Aurelian Walls, his head soothed by cool marble, yet as far beyond Stephen's grasp as the harem-couch of the Moslem caliph. Between the two popes yawned the unspanned gulf of the grave.

For months after buying the Papacy, Stephen brooded about his thousand imagined injuries. He and Arnulf, the fitfully holy, never Roman emperor, carried on an interminable secret conversation, employing a corps of exhausted messengers who struggled back and forth across the mountains. Some of Stephen's most telling points went over precipices and had to be repeated.

Then, after a night of unusually resolute galloping about the palace, Stephen summoned me.

When the guard announced my arrival in his sleeping chamber, Stephen was creeping about beneath the tapestries, an obscene bulge among the unicorns. His attempts to plug the ratholes were unceasing. I knelt as he thrashed free of the decorations, then, blessed, rose to loom over him, as I loomed over everyone in the papal court. I gazed coolly down on the pope.

"My bastard predecessor has fouled his plot of sanctified earth long enough," Stephen said. "Bring me Formosus. Rouse him from his undeserved rest, that he may stand accused before God and His Holy Church." He chuckled and added, "You are accustomed to such damp work, eh, Alfano?"

I inclined my head modestly. Stephen knew I first served the Church by stocking reliquaries — transmuting unused bits of rotting paupers into the toes and teeth of saints. I had, in fact, procured one of the heads of John the Baptist so popular among pilgrims in those days. Stephen knew I was uniquely suited to this work: A childhood of labor in the steaming dye-works of Amalfi robbed me of my sense of smell. Stephen also knew that in my years of papal service, I had not so much as touched a shovel. But I merely nodded in answer to his baiting. I was mute and wise; I had outlived six popes.

Stephen's bloated fingers toyed with the wattles beneath his chin. "It will be another Resurrection," Stephen said, "but one not born of love."

I took care to kiss his ring with my usual fervor — no more, no less — on my way out, as I hurried to put into motion the abomination.

Within the hour, I was striding along a narrow corridor that spiraled downward beneath the floor of Formosus's favorite Roman church. Somewhere above was a noisy, crowded altar; somewhere below were the peaceful, crowded vaults. I kept my head bowed in reverence to the low, uneven ceiling. A half-dozen guards and workmen shuffled behind me, clanking and panting in the clammy dark.

Beside me was my invaluable servant Torriti, whose mumblings offered an unobstructed view into the thoughts of the ignorant. With his left hand he held aloft a guttering torch; with his right he crossed himself repeatedly.

"To judge the dead!" Torriti whispered. "Is this not God's task and God's alone? What will the townspeople think? And the pilgrims? And the Franks? And the many friends of Formosus? What of them? Ah! It is an ill omen."

At a sign from me, Torriti lapsed into silence, but his right hand continued to sketch the outlines of his fear and doubt. His shaven head gleamed in the play of the torchlight upon the walls of the crypt.

At the end of the corridor, as the workmen wrestled the bundle from its tomb, I gathered my cloak about me for warmth. I recalled that Formosus blessed me one day, not long before his death, with unusual gravity, saying: "God our Father has blessed me, and with this right hand I bless you in turn. Now you, in turn, will bless another, and he, in turn, another, and at each step something of the power of God's blessing is lost. Each downward rung has less of God and more of man." Then this chamber is the holiest in Christendom, I thought, for it contains the two men who are closest to God. I would have laughed, but my yawping bark grated my ears, and I seldom indulged. Safer, too, to keep laughter inside, with the uncounted other blasphemies.

Do not be misled. Formosus did not count me among his intimates. Yet I was valuable to him, as I was valuable for decades to the Lord and His Apostle of the moment. Because I could not speak, I was in great demand as an audience. When pontiffs tired of confiding and confessing to an unresponsive God, they confided and confessed to me. I shone with the outward and visible signs they craved. Oh, the litany of gestures, subtle facial expressions, head movements! I was summoned at all hours of the day and night, and I always earned my blessing.

I served the popes in another way as well. Many ambitious men unfamiliar with my unique position foolishly thought me a trained ape, a gangling half-wit, deaf or stupid as well as mute. They indiscreetly confessed their sins in my presence — and so they received their reward on Earth and not in Heaven.

For these offices I enjoyed dank and verminous accommodations that were among the finest in Rome; a modest treasury sufficient to buy most of the citizens, as needed; many ornate titles, garments and privileges; and a place in all processionals — though cheers, I noted, tended to falter as I passed. I retired each night to my lumpy couch with a guiltless soul and, better still, a full belly. I was most proud of that, for I survived my youth only by huddling with other miserable beggars each day in the portico of the Lateran for a portion of meat, bread and wine, the fruits of the *domas cultae*. Ah, those sanctified fields and vineyards, always heard of but never seen! Surely there, we thought, the starving could pluck and eat in peace, free of the pious prattle that we choked down with our meals in Rome.

In this we were correct. As I rose higher in the Church, the meals grew more substantial and the piety less burdensome. I saw the lame and the dying leaping like frogs around a finger bone that had been fondling a milkmaid not two weeks before.

I saw some of them healed.

Torriti cleared his throat. Before me yawned the open tomb. Behind me, at the bend in the corridor, waited Torriti, the guards, and the workmen bearing Formosus on a litter. The torchlight surrounding them was distant and feeble. I stood alone in the flow of darkness from the tomb.

"Is there more?" Torriti asked.

I brusquely shook my head, my reverie over, and hastened up the slope toward the light.

As a witness to Pope Stephen's infamous

cadaver synod, I recall most vividly that the decaying corpse of Pope Formosus made a stubborn and unruly defendant. Perhaps it merely sagged beneath the weight of the charges: perjury, coveting the Papacy, arcane violations of bureaucratic procedure; new items were added daily. At any rate, attendants had to be watchful, for whenever propped upright on the papal throne, the corpse began slowly, almost imperceptibly, to lean forward, like an arthritic reaching for his shoes.

I thought it imprudent for Sergius, a toadying bishop who was one of Stephen's chief spokesmen, to stand close enough to the defendant for his spittle to fleck Formosus's face as he railed. This dramatic effect was for Stephen's benefit, no doubt, but a more dramatic effect ensued when Formosus lurched over onto Sergius, and accuser and defendant fell together to the floor. The corpse seemed to clutch at Sergius's robes and hiss the breath of the grave into his face. Sergius, gibbering blasphemies, scuttled backward to be rid of Formosus's lolling head, of his unwholesome purple vestments spilling across the flagstones like a dark and seductive pool.

Stephen began to howl. "Villain! Wretched, scraping, puking villain!" He charged across the chamber, and the hapless Sergius quailed beneath his fouled robes, not realizing the pope was addressing Formosus until Stephen kicked the dead man in the stomach. As the pope wrenched his foot free, Sergius choked and turned away — displaying a squeamishness he would not display years later, after he himself acquired the Papacy.

Thereafter, stout ropes bound the defendant to the throne during trial. Even then, welling bubbles of noxious gases kept Formosus's robes astir. Their gentle, flirtatious undulations seemed to mock the sweat and labor of the many strutting accusers.

Each night I sat with the prisoner in his cell to hear and transcribe any statements or confessions he might wish to make, and also to frustrate his escape. This was a redundant precaution given the thickness of the door, the stoutness of the lock, the presence, in the corridor outside, of a turnkey. That worthy man cared not for his duty, and gagged on his rations, but I was comfortable enough with my cheese and my biscuit, my seared nostrils, and my rich and varied thoughts. I asked Formosus how his trial was proceeding thus far.

Less and less of God, and more and more of man.

by Andy Duncan

It is of God, as well, I replied. It is mad, and pointless, and inefficient. It is godlike.

As are you.

One night Stephen demanded that the prisoner and I dine with him in his apartments. Course after course was set before the moldering guest, then cleared away untouched. Stephen gobbled his fowl and fruits as always. Only I, who knew starvation, truly appreciated the textures of the meal. Stephen downed much wine and spouted opinions in unusually high spirits. Alone with his deceased predecessor and his mute factotum, his conversational brilliance was unrivaled. He spoke at length about Regino's generally excellent *De harmonica institutione,* in which he nevertheless spied some errors of interest to the trained musician. He spoke about the well-chewed topic of the millennium — did the worthy Formosus and the good Alfano believe, as did some in the Church, that the tenth century would be the final act of history? Some histories will end even sooner, I thought, and I fancied a responsive twinkle in the sockets to my left.

On the darkest night of the year, as Formosus and I traded silences, I heard the clanking of the lock and the screeching of the hinges. The door swung open to admit Stephen, who cast me from the cell with the briefest glance and a backward wave of his hand. As I bowed low in passing, he crossed to Formosus's bunk on the far wall; he was as brisk and placid as a man striding into a corner to piss. Through the grille in the door I saw him stoop over Formosus, muttering inaudibly, and lift the corpse's right hand, the hand with which Formosus blessed. Stephen pawed at the hand's middle three fingers, clutched them and violently tugged them, stripping the bones. With an oath, he cast aside a wad of flesh. Do you squirm at this? Your day has seen worse.

Stephen lifted one of his dainty feet, his bulk swaying precariously, and stomped once, twice, upon Formosus's hand. Then he produced a knife and sawed into the fingers until they broke loose with a crack. I watched Stephen pocket the fingers, then murmur into the better of Formosus's crumpled ears, then press his own ear against the corpse's lips, then murmur again. Twice he straightened, with poisonous glances toward the door.

When he emerged, after an hour of these whispered confidences, he glared coldly at me and stated, evenly, "He has much to say of *you,* Alfano." Without speaking further, he trotted away, his heels resounding off the stone like tiny hooves.

I entered the cell.

He thinks I am his enemy, I said. What have you told him?

He has heard nothing but the chittering in his mind.

He thinks I am his enemy, I repeated. He has made me his enemy.

You have made yourself what you are.

Why not? I asked. I have touched the shrouds of harlots and turned them into martyrs. I have touched the bones of plowmen and made them into saints.

I stood over Formosus's corpse, held my hand just above his body, not quite touching it, and laughed until I winced.

When closeted with a corpse, one has little to do but plot, so I soon had various plans at my disposal. I pridefully chose the most complex.

Days passed. Formosus was found guilty, as this was the only possible verdict, and was deemed unfit for Christian burial, as this was the only possible punishment. A hired mob paraded his corpse through the streets and flung it into the Tiber. Several of the most vocal and physically imposing members of the mob were doubly salaried, in the employ both of Stephen and of my good assistant Torriti. Torriti's minions managed to exert considerable influence over the mob's route and its final riverbank destination, so that the body was flung into the water past sunset and at a spot directly upstream from where Torriti and I waited.

Dressed in the coarse robes of fishermen, we crouched in darkness on the slimy planks of a floating mill. Its grist wheel ground mindlessly, helpless to stop the current, as we raked our barge poles through the scum.

"We have become fishers of men," Torriti whispered. I watched him carefully for other signs of wit, and was relieved to see none.

Recovering Formosus's body was not strictly necessary — rumors and visions already were darting through the crowds, thanks to the calculated loose talk of my emissaries and to native Roman credulity — but I was nevertheless relieved when, after several minutes, Torriti yelped at the sight of Formosus's gaping jaw at the end of his hook.

When we spread the sack of bones across the planks, we saw that the Tiber had claimed parts of the late pontiff, but that the mauled right hand

FROM ALFANO'S RELIQUARY

was still joined at the wrist. "Thank you, my Lord, for your divine assistance," Torriti whispered, as I swung down the cleaver.

We stripped the corpse of its tattered surplice, dumped it into a wagon, pitched over it a concealing layer of hay, and trundled it for safekeeping to an ambitious hermit who lived in the shadows of the Colosseum. I considered merely returning Formosus to the fishes, but as a former procurer of relics, I knew the value of thrift.

Those members of the mob with the most spiritual fervor had smeared the surplice with excrement, presumably their own, but we dared not risk laundering lest the ruined cloth shred altogether. Also, the pitifully soiled garment would add a note of pathos.

With the distinctive surplice over my shoulders, and the mauled right hand protruding from my right sleeve, I made a convincing vision indeed in my three brief appearances. Each time I was illuminated in a window, gazing in upon a member of a pro-Formosus faction noted for zealous and sometimes violent piety: first, a Frankish lieutenant; second, the elder son of a city aristocrat; third, a leading conniver of the papal court. All saw precisely what the roiling streets without and the prayerful anguish within had prepared them to see, a sight a good deal more convincing and terrifying than I actually could have been.

The lieutenant leaped from his supper table, drew his sword, slammed it blade-first into the floorboards, and began to weep in astonishing Frankish profusion, beads of tears and soup alternating in his beard.

The elder son thrashed and twisted and cocooned himself in fabrics — sheets, cushions, even the canopy of his bed — leaving only his twitching face naked and suggestive of the sensuous inheritances he had dreamt of moments before.

The papal functionary merely fainted, a pile of robes on a marble floor. But as with the Frank and the noble, I made sure to move the clawlike right hand in a way that aped the spastic movements of a blessing.

The effect was immediate and gratifying. Within hours, the members of Stephen's guard were being eviscerated in the streets, and every altar was thronged with keening flagellants begging forgiveness for the city's sin. Several people claimed to have been healed of lameness, blindness and, I believe, suppurating wounds by the triumphant shade of the desecrated Formosus — people who, Torriti assured me, were not on our payroll. Similarly, the earthquake that collapsed the Lateran basilica, widely viewed at the time as divine judgment, was, if not divine, certainly beyond my powers to engineer. Suffice to say that after weeks of chaos, Stephen was dragged shrieking from his chambers and cast into jail, where he was found strangled soon afterward, apparently by an unusually resilient garrote.

My own death, many years later, proved uninteresting, even commonplace. Among the broken columns of the *disabitato*, that pagan city of ruins, were swamps and stagnant pools that bred black toads. In summers a dark mist sprawled from these evil bogs and breathed fever into the town. One year I inhaled unwisely and, weakened by advanced age, died.

No portion of my carcass ever was enshrined and offered to the pilgrim trade. Neither venerated nor desecrated, I was allowed to decay at my leisure. Many in torment long for less. Yet I ask you: What altarpiece saint with upturned face and outspread hands and the painted eyes of a cow could take a cadaver's claw and a shit-stained surplice and endow them with even a taint of the miraculous? Ω

BELLE DAME

She is beautiful,
Dancing, beckoning for me,
With hands of bare bone.

— Catherine Mintz

Shark Attack: A Love Story
by James Van Pelt

illustrated by Denis Tiani

Willard was day-dreaming about Elsa when the shark caught Benford, the new mail boy, directly in front of Willard's desk. Lost in his dream, Willard didn't look up from the stack of forms he was filling out mechanically. Bustle and commotion were standard fare at The First North American Trust Title Company, and the boy's silent waving of arms wasn't enough to distract Willard. Then the boy screeched.

Willard dropped his pen and pulled his feet off the aquamarine blue shag carpet. The shark, a small one if its head were an indication, probably five or six feet long, had Benford by the calf. He screeched again, then started slapping at the fish with a thick manila folder. Papers squirted from it into the air, spiraling about like sea gulls. The boy twisted in an effort to get loose and his pants tore along the seam. Willard saw a long stretch of white leg that ended at green boxer shorts.

"Help!" Benford said, his face an etching of pain and fear. He reached for Willard. Using his chair as a step, Willard climbed to the top of his desk, knelt on the desk pad and extended his hand to the boy.

"Grab on!" cried Willard, and their hands locked. For a second, he thought the shark had lost. Benford moved toward the desk, and his face beamed with hope. Then the shark regripped, shook back and forth angrily, sending ripples in the carpet that lapped against the other desks, and drug Benford under.

Benford's hand disappeared last, fingers still bent as if Willard had never let go. The carpet closed over him and the last papers drifted down to float on its now placid, blue nap. Then a dark swirl of red eddied at the spot, bloodying some of the pages. Within a few eye blinks, the color faded away and only the stained papers remained.

The attack lasted less than fifteen seconds.

Willard dropped his forehead to his hands.

When he had first seen a dorsal fin cutting through the carpet days earlier, he'd glanced around to see if anyone else noticed. Elsa, the prim title clerk he dreamed of in the desk beside his, didn't raise her head. A drooping of tight blond curls covered her eyes. Her cool looking, pale fingers moved efficiently to the next form and she began writing. The fin continued down the long rows of desks, avoiding a secretary carrying a stack of papers.

Later, he saw three fins circling the water cooler. They moved hypnotically around and around, and when Humphrey, the chief accountant, walked to the cooler for a drink, Willard bit down an urge to yell a warning. The fins widened their circle while the fat man filled and drank four tiny cupfuls of water. A bubble hiccupped in the large glass bottle each time.

No one else seemed to see them. He had attempted several times to tell Elsa. Once, he leaned toward her and almost spoke — the words were on his lips — but she glanced at him, her eyes bright, brown and shy, and he said nothing. He loved her eyes and the tiny wrinkles that radiated from their corners like she had spent time squinting at sun light. Lifeguard eyes, he thought. Protective eyes.

In the year since she had joined the firm, he'd never had enough nerve to talk to her, and she had not spoken to him, even when he left funny little sticky notes on her computer screen like, "HELP! I'M DROWNING IN DOS!" She'd smile faintly in his direction, then pull the note free and tuck it into a desk drawer. He wanted desperately to talk to her now, to alert her.

A heavy slap next to his ear startled a scream out of him.

"What the hell are you doing, Willard?" bellowed Mr. Trusty, the office manager. He was wearing his favorite grey, pin striped suit and an orange tie with the words, *Get your butt in gear*, printed over and over in black. "God damn it, Willard. You look like a seal crouched like that. Get off there right now." Mr. Trusty slapped the desk again.

"Yes, sir," said Willard, and he slid off the top into his chair. He braced his feet on a ledge in the desk so he wouldn't be touching the carpet.

"The deeds on the Hinson deal and the Arlington Estate have to be finished and at the bank tomorrow morning. I can't have you flipping out when there's work to be done. You'll stay late tonight."

The other workers began to clean their desks, putting folders into file cabinets and packing brief cases. It was quitting time. Mr. Trusty saw the papers strewn at his feet. His cold, grey eyes scanned the office. "Where is that little squid, Benford?" He kicked one of the pages. "Pick up this mess."

When Mr. Trusty turned and headed toward his office, Willard sucked in a sharp breath. The back of Mr. Trusty's jacket bulged slightly. Something between his shoulder blades pushed the jacket out, giving him a mild hunch back. Mr. Trusty grinned at another title agent a couple of desks away and said good night. His smile was full of teeth. Willard hadn't paid much attention to this before, but Mr. Trusty's face, when he smiled, was mostly shiny, white bone.

Other employees walked by Willard's desk. A couple nodded as they passed, but most didn't seem to see him. Their eyes were blank and, Willard realized with a rush, fish like. Several of them had oddly bulging backs, and Willard wondered if this had always been the case and he'd never thought about it, or if the bulges were new. He watched one man, one he didn't know well — Quinton or Quigley — as he walked away. Before he reached the door, Quinton or Quigley placed his briefcase on a desk, bent down behind it, as if he were picking something off the carpet, and didn't reappear. A fin sliced between the desk legs and sank out of sight near the photocopy machine. Although the office was almost empty, briefcases rested on many desks.

Willard didn't know what to do, but he did know that nothing was going to get him onto the carpet now, not after what he'd seen.

He wished he was back in his bachelor's apartment with its comfortable chairs and neatly swept, beach brown, hardwood floors, where he'd sit at his kitchen table and work for hours constructing ships in bottles. Not ones from kits, but ones he made on his own from balsa stock that would go into antique wine bottles he'd buy at flea markets and garage sales. Using special glues and long tweezers, he'd place each pre-painted piece in its place, plank by plank, until finally he'd attach the tiny spools and pulleys and raise the toy sails. Willard imagined standing on their decks, the wind at his back, the solid thud of waves passing beneath the hull, the smell of birds and islands and exotic flowers in his nose, and beside him, Elsa, tanned and laughing and

by James Van Pelt

37

loving. Willard never sailed his ships alone in his dreams.

A fleet lined the living room on shelves he'd built specially for them, and track lighting illuminated his best ones like art work in museums. Only his landlord had seen the collection.

Now that it was after five, the office was mostly empty. The steady patter of computer keys, the ringing of phones and the shuffling of papers was replaced by the buzz from the florescent lights.

A soft sobbing attracted his attention. He turned. Elsa's hands hid her face and her shoulders trembled. She sobbed again.

"Elsa?" he said.

Her crying continued. "That poor boy," she said, finally. Her voice was low, and even though it was caught in a sob, melodious. "That poor, poor boy."

Willard almost leapt to his feet; then he remembered the carpet. "You saw!" he whispered in exultation.

She said, "It ate him right there." She dabbed a napkin under her eyes.

"How long have you seen?"

"Since the first, I guess." She pulled a book from a drawer in her desk. "I've been reading about them. They're just big eating machines, you know."

A tall, grey fin glided smoothly past Willard's desk. It slid through the carpet for twenty feet, then circled back. Another fin joined it, then a third and fourth. A glimpse of tail fin broached the carpet and a wide expanse of solid, dark back. By the size of the fin, Willard guessed the largest might be fifteen feet long.

"There are so many," said Elsa.

A weighty thud almost knocked Willard out of his chair. He braced his hand on the seat, and a fin scraped it. The knuckles shown white, then beads of blood welled through the skin. He scrambled to the desk top again. Elsa climbed to the top of her desk too.

"Why are they going after us?" asked Willard. "They never bothered us before."

Fins crossed back and forth in front of him. His chair rumbled away, snagged on the back of one of the larger fish. The shark turned in its path, shaking the chair off; then its broad head broke the surface, mouth agape, teeth glistening and it ate the chair, dragging it under in one bite.

"Feeding frenzy," said Elsa. "They're stirred up."

The carpet undulated from their passage.

Strong, fishy smells filled the air, like seaweed baking in the sun.

"It must be the blood," said Willard. He pointed to the late Benford's papers on the floor, many darkly stained. A fin cruised through the middle of them, pushing some aside. "Maybe I can draw them off." He yanked some tissues out of a box and blotted blood off his knuckles. Squeezing, he coaxed a few more drops from each one, then wadded the tissues and threw them as far as he could. They fluttered down ten feet away.

He waited hopefully, but after two or three minutes, it was obvious that the sharks weren't interested.

"It's not enough," said Elsa. "We'll have to out-wait them."

They watched the sharks' activity. It seemed they'd settled into a waiting mode of their own. Generally their circles were counterclockwise, although one would break the pattern and dash through the blood-stained papers once in a while, and several times the flurry of fins and splashing showed they were still agitated.

After a long time, Willard said, "Why didn't you tell me you saw the sharks days ago?"

She scrunched her knees around to make herself more comfortable. "Until you tried to help . . ." She gestured at the papers on the floor. "I thought I was the only one. Why doesn't anyone else see them?"

Through the western facing windows, the sun neared the horizon. Desks and computers cast long shadows across the blue carpet. Willard shrugged. "Denial, I guess, or they're with them."

She said, "Why didn't you tell me?"

He blushed, then turned his head away to hide it. He was about to say, "Because I was shy," but a movement in the back of the office stopped him. He stood on his desk to see better. Coming toward them, a fin five feet tall wended its way between the desks. "I don't think we'll be able to out-wait them after all," he said. "We're really in trouble."

The wave from its passage tumbled telephones to the floor. Desks rose and fell in its wake.

"Uh oh," said Elsa as she dug through the top drawer of her desk. She sat up holding a nail file.

"That won't stop it," said Willard. He imagined the shark that could have a fin that size. It'd swallow him and the desk and still want more.

Elsa stabbed her hand. She winced and stabbed it again.

Shark Attack: A Love Story

"What are you doing!" shouted Willard.

"We'll have to divert them." She looked around the top of her desk, her hand dripping freely. The fin moved ponderously by. "Dang," she said. "Don't look." She unbuttoned her blouse, took it off and smeared the blood into it. "It needs to be fresh and there has to be a lot."

"Better hurry," said Willard.

The fin started back. Elsa wadded the blood-soaked garment into a ball, thought for a second, dropped a paper weight into it, and tossed it fifty feet away.

"It'll take a minute for them to notice," she said, "if they do."

Their reaction, though, was almost immediate. Three fins broke from the pack and headed for the blouse. With majestic grandeur, the massive shark ignored their desks in favor of the fresh scent. At least for the moment, no sharks were near them.

Willard's desk was twelve feet from Elsa's. He studied the carpet between them for sign of a ripple or any hint of a shark waiting below.

"Better do it," said Elsa.

He took a deep breath, jumped on the floor and onto her desk. She grabbed his arm to steady him. The fins closed in on the blouse.

"That won't hold them long," Willard said. "Should we go desk to desk, or sprint for the door."

She looked panicked, and he could see the memory of Benford surfacing in her eyes. She steadied herself and said evenly, "Desk to desk."

Fifteen desks later, they stood in the tiled hallway that led to the elevator. Willard propped his hands on his knees and breathed in loud gasps. Elsa said, "I've never seen one out here. Have you?"

He willed his breathing to slow down. "No, but I'll feel better when I get home."

He straightened himself. She clasped her bleeding hand next to her chest in a fist. A streak of blood marred one side of her pink camisole, and she was shivering.

"Maybe you could come with me," he said, "and I could bandage that." He could hear his heart in his ears. It was only the adrenaline from the rush to the door that gave him the nerve to be so bold.

She looked at him sternly. "Turn around," she said.

"Excuse me?"

"Turn around."

Confused, he did. She pressed her hand against his neck, then felt his backbone to his belt. He remembered the bulges under some of the employee's clothes, and he understood.

"You're a nice man," she said. "What kind of floors do you have?"

He laughed. "Hardwood."

"I'd be happy to go home with you."

As they walked away, they heard the crashing of office furniture. Frustrated, the sharks had begun to feed on each other. Ω

CURSE OF THE SATYR'S WIFE

His hooves scar the hardwood
and leave slashes on the sofa.
His pointed horns and ears
have several points to make.
He is the first and the last
of the great lovers, a priapic
battering ram, a premier party
animal no woman can deny.

When she returns from work
she finds the signs of his
debauchery everywhere:
paté and crackers underfoot,
empty bottles of wine
littering the coffee table
like a spent phallic regiment,
the tv on a cable channel
where xxx-action never dies.

The sweet pungent smoke
that fills the air conceals
other fragrances left behind.
Yet the dishes in the sink,
the foil packets in the trash,
confirm her suspicions
that others have been by.

Whether the moon is new or full
he is always ready for a ride.
Whether the room is dark or light,
whether she screams or fights
or lies motionless in her plight,
his shaggy thighs part her own:
he rapes her each and every night.

— Bruce Boston

WEBMAGE
by Kelly David McCullough

ilustrated by Russell Morgan

"Mtp/mweb.DecLocus//GorePres2000.umn. edu ~ comstockhall301," I said. It was my current home site on the mweb. "Execute."

"I hear and obey, Ravirn," replied Melchior.

My webgoblin familiar scratched a hexagram into the wood with his right index claw and then spat out a netspider. The tiny magical creature scuttled across the stained table to the diagram. There it set an anchor line, crossed into the etched design, and vanished. A few minutes later it returned, at which point Melchior grabbed it and returned it to his mouth.

"Mm mm. Delicious and nutritious, tastes just like chicken."

"Can the editorials, Mel. I know they taste terrible. That's one of the reasons I created you in the first place. I just want to know if my room at the dorm is empty."

The webgoblin stuck its spider-occupied tongue out at me. I snapped my fingers in exasperation, calling a wisp-light into being. I sent it to dance a few inches in front of Melchior's eyes. The goblin hopped back and growled a little. When the wisp showed no signs of departing, he sighed and swallowed the spider.

"Processing," said the goblin, in a mechanical voice. Then after a few minutes, "Reporting. Your room in Comstock at the U of M in the President Gore Decision Locus is currently vacant."

"Thank you, Mel. That wasn't so bad, now was it?" I dispelled the wisp. No sense in aggravating him.

"Ick, ack, ptooie." The goblin spat, his voice returning to its normal whiny growl. "When your grandmother wrote the code for those things, why did she make them so bitter?"

"I'm tempted to say it's just another manifestation of her sparkling temperament. But that's not actually the case. Uncle Varian asked her once while I was around. She said that it's to remind us that the spiders are serious and potentially dangerous magical constructs, not toys."

"Hmph. Why don't you fix them?"

"There are several reasons." I ticked them off on my fingers. "First, I'm not the one who has to

eat them. Second, their programming is much more involved and nasty than it's worth. Third, they're virtually bug free, if you'll pardon the pun. Fourth, and finally, it would seriously irritate grandmother and I'm not stupid enough to do that. Now, before you come up with any more distracting questions, I have orders. Establish a Locus Transfer Protocol link with the Comstock hub. Then, as soon as that's done, initiate transfer. Execute."

The little goblin glared at me, but went to work. I watched him pull a piece of chalk, a string, and a stick out of his belly pouch. Then he moved the rug away from the center of the small room. Using the stick and string to measure he drew a large hexagram on the floor. Into the center of this he spat another netspider. It blinked out the second it landed in the diagram, leaving a little glowing blob of gold silk pulsing on the spot where it hit.

"Connecting to GorePres2000," intoned the goblin.

There was a long pause in which the pulsing became ragged. A few moments later it abruptly changed from gold to green. "Connect," said Melchior. "Initiating Gate procedure."

He dropped to his knees and grabbed the node. As he pulled at it the green glow spread outward filling the whole hexagram. Once the diagram was all green, the light rose to form a hexagonal column about six feet in height and two feet across.

"Gate established. There you go, boss. We can leave whenever you're ready."

"Thank you, Mel. That was nicely done." I stood and stretched, flexing my shoulders. Just then there was a loud crashing noise from elsewhere in the building. That would be the cousins coming to see who had invaded their demesne. And, as much as I might love to stay and chat with my dear dear relatives, Atropos' brood is notorious for killing first and trading pleasantries later.

"Perfect timing," I said to Melchior. "Shall we be going?"

"Yes, yes," said Melchior. "She scares me even

more than your grandmother." The goblin was hopping from one clawed foot to the other in obvious agitation. He was also tugging at the corner of my cloak. I twitched it out of his hand.

"We go now!" he shrilled. The doorknob turned, as someone tried to open it.

"I do believe you're right, Mel." He was. I really didn't want to be there when they got through.

I turned and stepped into the column of light. As I did so there was a tremendous thud and the door shuddered and groaned. A half second later the sound was repeated. Long cracks appeared in the thick wooden timbers.

"Melchior, Locus Transfer now," I said. "Execute."

Melchior, joining me on the hexagram, hissed out a string of spaghetti logic. The light began to shift from green to blue. As Melchior finished, a third impact buckled the door completely. I drew my rapier. A half second later a broad bladed hunting spear hurtled though a gap at the top of the ruined door, coming straight for me. It would be touchy, but I thought we would be gone before it got to me. Still, it never hurts to be careful. I brought my sword up to parry the missile just as the light finished its transition. As the head of the spear entered the lighted area, the room wavered around us and vanished.

There was a shower of sparks as the iron spearpoint grated along the edge of the rapier. The contact deflected the missile so that it went past my left shoulder and buried itself solidly in my roommate's Hootie and the Blowfish poster. It also left my hand stinging and numb by turns.

"That," I said to Melchior, "was entirely too close." I dropped the sword and stepped to my dorm room door where I hooked the chain.

"Has anyone ever told you that you have a gift for stating the obvious?" asked my goblin. He was livid, literally. His face and neck, normally indigo, had faded almost to periwinkle. "Were you trying to get us killed, or are you just stupid?" That was too much.

"Melchior! That's enough. When I wrote you I included a certain amount of self determination, and a wicked streak of sarcasm. But I will not tolerate insolence or insubordination. Go to your desk."

"Your least whim is my veriest desire, O prince. I dance to your bidding." The webgoblin leaped up onto the small desk on my side of the room.

"Melchior, Laptop," said I, tired of hearing his whining. "Execute."

"No sooner commanded than performed."

by Kelly David McCullough

The goblin's flesh began to flow like soft wax. Five minutes later the transformation was complete. What had once been a nasty tempered little manling was now a shiny WebRunner 2,000cs PPCP cell laptop. A small blue logo that bore a suspicious resemblance to Melchior was positioned just below the screen on the left.

While the goblin was altering his appearance to better fit in with his surroundings, so was I. The black cloak and the rapier went into a trunk at the foot of the bed. The tights, likewise black, and the emerald tunic were stuffed into a laundry bag. The high leather boots were retained to go over a pair of black jeans. I topped that off with a green "Nobody Wins" T-shirt and a TechSec leather jacket before checking myself in the mirror to see if I had forgotten anything.

Boy, had I ever. "Shit," I mumbled. The face that stared back at me was not one I could wear around here. I invoked the spell that rounded my slightly pointed ears and reshaped the vertical slit in my green eyes to a more human circle. My long black hair, fine bone structure and dead white skin I left intact. On a campus with as large a Goth population as the U of M, they were normal enough to make the concealing of them a waste of magical resources; a cardinal sin in the Lachesis clan. That done, the transformation was complete. Prince Ravirn of the house of Lachesis, forty third in line for the throne, was gone. In his place was Ravi Latcher, a double major in Classics and Computer Science. A junior with mid-terms to study for. I ducked back into the main room and started stuffing books into my shoulder bag. That was when I remembered the spear. Ran into it is more like the truth, but that's neither here nor there.

"Damn! If Rod comes back and finds that thing there I'm never going to hear the end of it." I pulled the weapon loose and tossed it under the bed. That left the rip in the poster and the hole in the wall to be dealt with. Sighing, I flipped the cover of the laptop up and began typing.

```
Space bar.
Enter password.
• • • • • • •
Correct.
Run Melchior. Execute.
I hear and obey!
```

The laptop shifted back to its webgoblin form. "What is it now? I didn't even have all my inits in the right places. You know how I hate that."

He can get in a real snit when that happens and I didn't feel like picking a fight with my laptop three days before term papers were due. He had a nasty habit of crashing at the most inconvenient times when he was angry. I decided to be placating.

"I know, I know. I'm really sorry about that. You've been doing good work lately and I haven't been praising you enough. But I really don't have time for this right now." I waved vaguely at the wall. "I was supposed to meet my study group in Walter Library ten minutes ago. I want you to fix Rod's poster and then catch up to me there."

"I don't see why you can't just do it yourself."

"Because I don't have time to code a real spell, and if I just paste an illusion over it I'll forget about it. Then the illusion will wear off at the most inconvenient possible time and I'll end up having a huge argument with Rod."

"True, pathetic, but true." I let that slide by and he continued. "Get moving, I'll be along in fifteen minutes or so."

"Great." I opened the door then looked over my shoulder. "Oh, and Melchior."

"Yes?"

"I don't want you terrorizing the sorority girls on your way over."

"But —!"

"No, Mel. Stay away from the football team too, OK?"

"Yeah, sure. If I have to leave the Greeks alone I might as well not have any fun."

"Thanks, Mel. You're a prince."

"No, you're the prince. I'm just a lowly goblin flunky, doomed to a life of menial labor." Melchior wrenched a razor sharp tooth from his mouth and spat a netspider into his hand. He squeezed it until silk came out and then threaded that onto the tooth. "No one appreciates my simple graces."

"Good-bye, Mel."

As Melchior began to sew up the rip in the poster I ducked out and closed the door. Then I took the back stairs three at a time. When I hit the mall I sprinted. It was October, one of the good ones, and the air was crisp but not icy. In the clear fall air the full moon seemed close enough to touch and the smells of dry leaves and dying grass were enough to paint a grin on my lips. There was nothing like fall in Minnesota. I gloried in it as I raced across the lawn.

Melchior caught me as I was dashing up the library steps. Somehow, he had gotten there ahead of me.

"Boss!" he whispered loudly, from behind a pillar. "Hey, Boss."

I turned, startled. He had gotten there too fast. "How did you manage to fix the poster and get here before I did?"

"I didn't fix the poster." He raised a closed hand to forestall my complaint. "We have much bigger problems than an annoyed roommate. This popped through into the room right after you left."

He opened the hand. In it was a small broken thing, a netspider, and it wasn't one of mine. I took it and popped it into my mouth. The flavor was even worse than the ones my grandmother had coded. It was also familiar.

"Atropos," I said. "This came from my cousins, or worse, my Aunt. Are you jamming?"

"As much as possible, but they're using some pretty heavy code breaking algorithms. Their webhounds will have us locked down within ten minutes."

That wasn't much time, and it didn't leave me with a lot of options.

"I guess I'm going to have to take a pass on my study night," I said. "Melchior, bugout. Execute."

"Executing," said the goblin. "Waiting for connection." There was a long pause. "Lachesis.web system connect denied."

"What!?"

"Melchior is unable to create an Mweb socket connection at this time," he said. "The system may be down or there may be insufficient system resources at this time. Try again later."

We were being counter jammed. That was very bad. It meant they had me at least partially localized. It also meant that Atropos was directly involved. It would take her direct authority to seal access to a whole node or band of nodes.

"Right. Melchior, Sidedoor. Execute." The goblin's eyes glazed over and a low hum emerged from his mouth. After a moment he spoke again. "Unable to open carrier wave connection. Access denied." In a more normal voice he continued. "Sorry, Boss. It doesn't look good. I can't get in anywhere and we only have about five more minutes before we're locked down."

"All right. If she wants to take this to extremes we'll take it to extremes. Melchior, Scorched Earth. Execute." His eyes got very wide and he looked like he wanted to object, but I had phrased it as a direct order and he had no choice.

"Loading," said the goblin.

There was a long pause as Melchior prepped the spell. It was too big to keep in active memory.

I had time to wonder if I was overreacting. Melchior's voice came again.

"Executing."

Then it was too late for second thoughts. Scorched Earth is not a spell that can be aborted halfway. Ultimately all spells draw power from the same source, the primal chaos that churns between the worlds. Most use the predigested forces that my grandmother and her sisters channel into the net via their mainframe webservers. Scorched Earth isn't like that. It taps directly into the interworld chaos. That means it is both very dangerous and very powerful. It also means that I don't have to have web access to run it. Melchior's voice interrupted my train of thought.

"Scorched Earth successfully implemented," he said.

And, with those simple words, the nastiest virus I could code was released into the mweb. If it worked right, it would scramble the routers for my whole node band and put my Aunt's webhounds smack in the middle of a data storm. There was no way they would be able to track me through that. There was even a chance they might be completely fragged. I chuckled at the thought.

"Uh, Boss," said Melchior.

"Yes. What is it, Mel."

"I just lost contact with the carrier wave."

"I thought you couldn't get in."

"I couldn't, but that's not what I mean. I mean it just cut out completely."

"It can't do that, unless . . ." I trailed off as a really ugly thought occurred to me. I looked at Melchior and he nodded his head in agreement.

"There's no carrier wave and no Mweb line," he said. "I can't even get a ping off the backbone. I think we just took the entire net down, Boss."

Sitting at the desk in my dorm room I cradled my head in my hands. Melchior sat on the floor nearby. For four hours we had been trying to get some kind of link going to the net. Nothing had worked. There was very little doubt now that we had crashed the whole damn thing.

"Well, Mel, I think it's time we admitted the —" He held a hand up, cutting me off.

He cocked his long pointed ears this way and that for a few moments and then got up and walked to the ethernet jack in the wall. Looking confused, he wetted a fingertip and stuck it into the socket. A moment later he let out a prolonged modulated whistle.

by Kelly David McCullough

"Uh, Boss. I don't know if you're going to believe this, but you've got new mail."

"Coming over the local net?"

"Yes, indeedy."

"What is it?"

"It's from your cousin Cerice, she wants a visual ASAP."

"Over the local line? That's going to lock a lot of folks out of their online services. Where is she mailing from?"

"Cerice@shara.gob via aol.com."

"Well, so much for AOL for the next twenty minutes or so. I wonder what she's doing in this DecLocus. I thought she was home in Clotho's domain. I suppose that I'll just have to ask. Vlink Ravirn@melchior.gob via umn.edu. Execute."

"Aye, aye. Searching for Shara.gob." I used the brief pause that followed to drop the spell that altered my appearance. "Contact, waiting for a response from Shara.gob. Lock. Annexing extra bandwidth. Vltp linking initiated."

Melchior opened his eyes and mouth wide. Three beams of light, one green, one blue, one red shot forth from these orifices and intersected at a point about four feet in front of his head. A translucent golden globe appeared at this juncture. After a moment it fogged and then filled with the three dimensional image of a strikingly beautiful young woman. Her hair was so pale as to be almost white, but aside from that her features bore a strong resemblance to my own.

"Cerice, my darling," I said. "You're as ravishing as ever. It's an absolute pleasure to rest my weary eyes on your delightful features once again."

"Charming as always, Ravirn. Your absence must be sorely felt at your grandmother's court."

"Alas, I think not. Lachesis is not overfond of me. I believe my nature pains her more than my manner charms."

"Speaking of which," said Cerice, her attitude shifting from courtly circumlocution to business-like directness, "you have a major problem."

"Huh?" I replied. The change in gears was jarring.

"Look, I know that family politics call for a lot of polite nonsense and frills before finally broaching the real subject for conversation. But, I just don't have the time."

"All right, I'm willing to dispense with formality. I was dying to ask you how you happened to be in this particular DecLocus at this exact moment anyway. I thought you were home."

"I was until two hours ago

"But —" She cut me off smoothly.

"Yes, I know. The net's down. I hacked into Clotho's mainframe and used it to open a single use one way gate."

"That must have been a cast iron bitch to do."

She smiled. "It wasn't that bad. You're not the only competent coder in this generation. And, no, I'm not going to tell you how I did it, so don't even ask."

"Hey, I wouldn't even dr——" She cut me off again.

"I don't want to hear it, Ravirn. I didn't call to exchange hacking tricks. I called to let you know that you're in hot water all the way up to your eyeballs."

"How so?"

"Atropos wants your head."

"That's not news. My grandmother merely mislikes me, her sister on the other hand has always held a special black little place in her heart for me. It's because of my hacking. Atropos writes lousy security algorithms and then blames me when I happen to point that out to her."

"Ravirn, don't be more of an idiot than usual. We both know that she's security mad, and that her firewalls and program killers are better than either Clotho's or Lachesis'. We also both know that's why you bother to crack them. You're an egotistical bastard where it comes to your hacking skills, and Atropos is the only opponent you think is worth your effort. So, time and again you hack into the command line at Atropos.Web just to prove that you can. Unfortunately you haven't the wit to do it without leaving a calling card of some kind so that you can gloat about it later."

"Well, yeah, but . . ."

"But me no buts. As I said, I haven't the time. Neither have you. Not after you crashed the whole net. That was not real smart."

"It wasn't actually my intention."

"Intention or not, that was the result, and it's given Atropos the opportunity she's been waiting for. The net hadn't been down for five minutes when she showed up at Clotho's demesne. They called council and when Lachesis arrived Atropos demanded your head. Your grandmother apparently has a higher opinion of you than you think, because she absolutely refused to hear of it. Unfortunately for you, Clotho sided with Atropos."

I felt a sort of rushing sensation in my head. I had always known, in the abstract at least, that something like this could happen, but I had never really believed it.

"I'm screwed," I whispered.

"Yes, you are. Atropos couldn't just cut your thread without unanimous agreement of course, but with the net crashed and Clotho backing her she was able to get Lachesis to agree not to interfere with a proxy assassination attempt."

"Who?"

"Moric, Dairn, and Hwyl."

"All three!? Just for poor little old me?"

"Lachesis agreed to only one attempt. Atropos didn't want it to fail."

"When was the conference?"

"About an hour ago."

"Powers and Incarnations, I've got to get moving." I started to tell Melchior to close the connection, then paused. "Cerice, thank you. If I survive, I'll owe you my life. If not . . . Well, if not, I'll still owe you a great deal, but you'll likely have a hard time collecting. I have to know, why did you warn me?"

"Because you're my favorite cross cousin. Despite your pigheadedness, arrogance, and willful idiocy, you are quite charming in an impish sort of way. The world and I would be the poorer for your passing. Now go." Her hand waved briefly and then the picture faded away.

"Melchior, log us off and shut down all incoming modem traffic."

"Yes sir, right away, sir. Logging off and shutting down modem, sir. Then will we be running away, sir?"

"Damn straight we'll be running away."

"Very good, sir. Brightest thing you've done all day, sir."

"Don't push your luck, blue boy. I might leave you as a distraction for the assassins. Now, Mel, I want you to — Powers and Incarnations." It hit me like a ton of bricks.

"Ah I'm not sure I'm familiar with that one, boss."

"Mel, the net is down. The hit team will be coming the same way Cerice did. That means we have no way of knowing when they'll arrive. For that matter they could be here already."

The impulse to run out the door right then was almost overwhelming. I choked it down. I had to run, but I had to run smart. Moving as quickly as possible I grabbed my rapier and a left handed shoulder holster out of the trunk. When those were strapped in place I leaned down and tapped the combination into the speed-draw gun-safe bolted to the underside of the bed. The drawer popped open and I pulled out my beat-on but much loved Colt 45. Before holstering

the old model 1911 I worked the slide to chamber a round, flipped the secondary safety on and popped the clip. Then I loaded another bullet and returned it to the pistol. Also in the little drawer were two more clips, a box of slugs, and a dozen Krugerands. I tucked them into my jacket. As no one had yet broken my door in I took the time to kick off my boots and jeans and swap them for TechSec racing leathers. Finally I grabbed the shoulder bag I keep packed for emergencies.

"Come on, Melchior." I opened the flap on the bag. "Let's go."

"It's about time," replied the goblin, as he climbed into the bag. "You were going so slow I thought you were going to put down roots."

"Listen," I began. But then I thought better of it. "Later, if I'm still alive, I think I'm going to rework your OS." I grabbed my motorcycle helmet and gauntlets, and opened the door.

On the other side was a huge figure dressed in lamalar armor. From the demon-face helm a voice said, "Say goodnight, Gracie." Then a massive fist holding an Afghani punch-dagger slammed into my chest, right over the heart. The blow knocked me halfway across the room. It also cracked a rib, but thanks to the multi-layer Kevlar lining that TechSec built into all its racing gear, it failed to kill me.

I didn't think I would get that lucky twice. Hand to hand in a small room with my cousin Moric was a recipe for a quick death. His abilities as a sorcerer were not fantastic, but for the past couple of hundred years he had focused them on physical enhancement and on that score there weren't many in the family who could match him.

No, in this case discretion was the only part of valor. Unfortunately he was between me and the door. That left me only one possible exit and I took it. Holding my helmet in front of me I crashed through the window. That solved the immediate problem, but it also left me outside of the window of my twentieth floor dorm room.

"Melchior, Fear Of Falling. Execute now, now, now!"

The goblin stuck his head out of the bag. "I-aiee! Executing."

We had dropped nine floors. A prerecorded version of a spell spewed from the tiny blue lips, at 56,800 kilobaud, it sounded like a whippoor-will on speed, but it did the trick. Three floors above the ground our headlong plunge became a leisurely drift. I pulled on my helmet and gloves. It looked like I was going to need them before I ever got to my motorcycle.

My feet had barely touched ground when something struck me above the collar bone and then burned its way across my neck. More by reflex than conscious thought I tucked my chin into my chest. That caused the second arrow to strike the chin piece of my helmet instead of my throat. The arrow shattered, my helmet cracked, and my head just about came off my neck. Groggily I turned and headed for River Road and the cover of the cars parked there. Two more arrows hit me in the back as I went, but didn't pierce the Kevlar. I was going to need a new jacket and pile of pain killers, but at least I wasn't leaking any precious bodily fluids.

Once I reached the road I ducked behind an old Dodge Ram pickup and opened my jacket far enough to grab my pistol. Then I carefully zipped it again. I needed all the protection I could get. I also needed a plan.

If this conflict stayed a purely physical one I was going to die. There was no way around that. Sure I'm a lot stronger, tougher and faster than a normal human. But then so is everyone in my extended family. And when you put me on a scale filled only with my relatives the picture changes completely. I weigh in firmly in the featherweight division. Moric and his brothers on the other hand are all ultra-heavyweights with attitude.

Unfortunately I don't do my best thinking under pressure, and nothing came to mind immediately. The arrows smashing into the truck I was leaned against didn't help either. So a plan would have to wait until I put a little more distance between me and my homicidal cousins. The only problem was how to do that. The archer, probably Dairn who pulls a 225-pound bow, was shooting at me from the ramp where my cycle was parked, effectively cutting me off from it.

Well, I couldn't stay where I was. Moric would be out of the dorm and back in the game shortly. And Hwyl was out there somewhere as well. To my left River Road wound lazily past the parking ramp and Dairn. To the right it curved sharply north and went under the Washington Avenue bridge. Directly across from me was a thin strip of trees followed by a steep plunge into the Mississippi. I considered the choices and then, keeping the cars between me and the ramp as much as possible, I headed for the bridge. I was almost there when I heard a low gurgling growl. I winced. Intellectually I had known that Hwyl must be around someplace. Emotionally I had been pretending he didn't exist. So much for that. I tapped my shoulder bag.

"Mel?" I whispered. "Are you still alive in there?"

A muffled voice replied, "Battered, but serviceable, boss. What do you want?"

"Melchior, Redeye. Execute."

"Executing," said the webgoblin, and whistled the spell.

My visual range expanded to include the infrared and I peered at the gap under the bridge. On the left side, near one the abutments, a broad hulking inhuman shape lurked. Eyes, lamp bright in the IR range, glared out at me. It was Hwyl all right. Great. Being careful not to make any sudden movements I thumbed the 45's secondary safety off. The beavertail primary, was of course deactivated by the grip of my hand on the pistol butt.

Hwyl took a step towards me. My intestines did a backflip with a half twist. I wanted nothing more than to run blindly away. The things Hwyl has used his magic to do to himself give me the screaming creepies. Forcing myself to move with precision I snapped the pistol up into line and fired four quick rounds at his knees. The booming sound of the shots covered the noise, but I could see bone and tissue shatter and pulp under the impact of the heavy copper jacketed slugs. I turned to my right and ran up the slope to the bridge.

While I ran I cursed under my breath. It might take as long as two minutes for Hwyl's injuries to mend, but mend they would, especially with a full moon. Lacking silver weapons there was nothing I could do to him that would keep him down. That was why I aimed for the knees. Almost any other wound he could have taken and kept coming, but nobody, not even a were like Hwyl, can walk with broken knees.

My options were rapidly narrowing. By forcing me away from the passage under the bridge Hwyl had pushed me onto a killing ground. The space I entered now was narrow and enclosed on both sides. If Moric or Dairn could close off the other end it would be all over.

On my left was the long barren expanse of concrete that made up the car deck of the Washington Avenue bridge. On my right the alien, stainless steel angles of the Weisman Art Museum gleamed in the moonlight. The twisted mirrors of its construction threw my distorted reflection back at me. Something about it spoke to me, and I paused in my headlong flight to look at it. I held out my hands to touch the cold metal and the warped picture in its depths seemed to offer me refuge. It was exactly the message I needed to hear.

Turning around, I grabbed hold of one of the I-beams that supported the upper deck of the bridge. A quick layback ascent brought me to the pedestrian surface above. It also placed me only a few yards from the doors to the Weisman. I turned towards them and ran. They were locked. They were also glass. A small concrete and steel ash tray stood beside the doors. I bent, picked it up, and heaved it through the glass into the lobby.

A brutal clanging began thrashing the air as the alarm went off. As a sort of counterpoint I could hear the approaching wail of police sirens. Those were probably in response to the gun shots. In a few minutes the whole area was going to be flooded with cops. I winced at the thought. Unless those police officers were very lucky they were going to end up going toe to toe with my cousins. That was likely to get a lot of people killed. The only thing I could do about that was to remove myself from the equation as quickly as possible.

With that as an additional spur — like I needed another one — I raced down the main stairs and into the Red Gallery, where the current traveling show was housed. It was called *A Distorted Mirror: Our World Through the Eyes of the New Surrealists*. I turned right, past a sculpture of a giant melting Chihuahua, and started looking for the right sort of painting. Before there was an electronic web tying the worlds together there was an artistic one. Almost from humanity's beginning there have been artists interested in representing and interpreting the world around them. A small but significant number of those artists could see past their own world and into the others beyond. In the early years my grandmother and her sisters had used those gateways as their only means to travel between the spheres.

Of course, as the centuries went by and technology advanced they developed better and better means of travel and control, eventually settling on the mweb as the ideal solution. It was quick, it was powerful and it was easy to integrate with the growing electronic nets of the outer worlds. But the old ways still existed, they had just fallen into disuse.

There were drawbacks of course. Each of the artistic gateways goes to only one other world and there is no way to reset them. They are also slow to make and difficult to use, to say nothing

of the interface. On the other hand, anything that stood a chance of getting me out of this DecLocus alive was worth trying.

That thought was abruptly punctuated by a sharp yell from outside followed by a couple of shots. I looked back towards the entrance to the gallery and found my eye caught by a splotch of bright jewel tones on a panel near the door. Even from where I was standing I could tell it was what I needed.

I dashed over and was pleased to see that not only was it a gate, but it even looked like it might be to someplace nice. That was a big plus in my book. I didn't want to cross over into some raving, psychotic, artist's personal vision of hell. I grabbed Melchior out of the bag and dropped him on the floor.

"Mel, I need you to set up a DecLocus transfer to wherever this picture goes. But first we're going to need to make sure that no one follows us through."

The webgoblin looked at me suspiciously. "How do you propose to do that?" he asked.

"You're not going to like this, Mel. But it's the only way. Melchior, Burnt Offerings. Exe——" The little bastard cut me off.

"I really don't think that's such a good idea, boss. Not only is it excruciatingly painful, but if anything goes wrong we could be —" I held up a hand and he ran down.

"I don't want to hear it, Mel. Melchior, Burnt Offerings. Execute."

"Executing," came the resigned response. Then, he waited for me to do my part.

It was my turn to try and think of an excuse to avoid what came next. He was right, this was going to hurt. But I couldn't think of anything else. I stuck the tip of my left pinkie finger into my mouth and bit down hard on the first joint. The pain was incredible, and I thought I was going to black out, but it was this or die. I bit down harder. The blood started to flow and I gagged but kept biting. Abruptly, with a sickening pop, I felt the cartilage go and the tip of my finger came off in my mouth. I spat it onto the floor and then turned away and threw up.

When I turned back Melchior had paired the fingertip with one of his own and, using the blood from his maimed hand, was inscribing a diagram around them. From his bloodied lips came a steady stream of spell data. Now, we would see if it worked. It was a good theory, and I had run it through my spell-checker looking for bugs at least a dozen times, but for obvious reasons this was not an enchantment that I had been willing to beta-test.

I pulled a sterile wound dressing from my bag and quickly wrapped my finger. As I did this Melchior finished the diagram. A moment later the paired fingertips began to swell and metamorphose. Within a minute they had become miniature versions of the goblin and I. Within two they were approaching us in size. Within three they had grown to exact duplicates and my consciousness expanded to fill the body of my doppelgänger. I opened my second set of eyes and instantly developed a skull splitting headache. The effort of managing two bodies was bad enough, but the quadroscopic vision provided by four eyes was the real killer.

At least it wasn't going to last long. One way or another the situation was going to be resolved in the next few minutes. Not-I reached down and grabbed the fake Melchior. I handed not-me the bag. Not-I took it, put not-Melchior into it and went out the door of the gallery. I closed my eyes and concentrated on managing not-I. Melchior reversed those priorities as he worked on creating a pre-web DecLocus gateway, while letting not-him sit vacantly in not-my bag.

Not-I staggered a couple of times on the stairs, but made it to the main floor without falling. Not-I turned towards the front doors where Moric had just arrived. As not-I watched, there were a couple more shots and sparks danced across the back of his armor. He didn't even seem to notice. That wasn't exactly a big surprise. The armor was modeled on a suit my aunt Electra had designed and nothing short of an anti-tank missile was going to breach it. He turned then and saw not-me. Smiling he advanced.

"Ah, dear little Ravirn. How nice of you to come out and meet me. Did you simply run out of places to hide? Or did you finally remember the nobility of your blood and decide to look your death in the face?"

"Neither," not-I replied. "I decided that if I was going to go I should at least take one of you with me."

Not-I raised not-my hands and pointed them at Moric. Internally I braced myself. Then I opened a line into the interworld chaos and let it pour down the channel that led from my body to my doppelgänger's. It was like opening up my veins and pouring liquid fire into them. Both of my bodies crashed to their knee and I felt my own right kneecap fracture. Compared to the pain of the linkage it was barely worth noting.

I was intentionally violating every rule I had ever been taught about the proper management of magical power. Normally we only tap the raw chaos in a very carefully channeled way and all sorts of precautions are taken to contain it. That is why it can be very dangerous to tamper with even something as simple as a netspider. Muck up the tap and instant charcoal.

I felt the skin of my doppelgänger crisping as though it were my own as its underdeveloped nervous and magical channels struggled to handle the overload. There was no chance. My uncle Mordechi had died this way when a particularly involved enchantment melted down on him, and he had been a better pure sorcerer than I was ever likely to be. It was in fact that death, which I had had the misfortune to witness from close at hand, which had given me the original idea for Burnt Offerings.

Not-I watched as the power I had summoned shot from not-my hands and wreathed my cousin in flames. His armor protected him from some of the fury that was smashing at him, but it couldn't keep out all of it and after only a second or two he was swept from his feet. I didn't see what happened after that because not-my eyeballs chose that moment to melt down.

The pain was my entire universe and I fought like mad to free myself from it and the linkage which connected my two bodies. It was hard, and I wasn't sure that I would be able to do it especially with the agony that washed across me. But if I didn't manage to sever that pathway, when the chaos tap finished consuming that body it would backlash into my own and that would be it for me.

Mentally I cut at the link with everything I had, but it was very strong. It had to be, forged as it was from the sympathetic resonance between me and the fingertip which I had used as a seed for the doppelgänger. Symbolically we were still part of the same whole, and breaking your own internal self image apart is not a task I recommend. In point of fact, it's just about impossible, a circumstance that I was discovering to my great dismay. It didn't look like I was going to be able to do it. I was going to die.

"Boss!" Melchior's scream impacted on my ear from a distance of millimeters. "Boss! The gateway is open. Let's get the hell out of here!" There was pain in his tone. No surprise there, not-Melchior must have been getting pretty badly charred in not-my shoulder bag.

Fighting through the pain I forced my eyes

open. My vision was blurry from the tears of agony that streamed down my face, but I could still see the depth and life which had come to suffuse the picture. It was too bad that I wasn't going to live to see the world on the other side. It looked like a nice place.

"Thanks, Mel. You've done me proud. Why don't you step through and find someplace nice to settle down. I don't think my great aunt is going to want to leave you in one piece if she finds you, even if I'm gone. Take care of yourself." I closed my eyes again. It was emotionally too hard to keep them focused on that escape I had almost made.

"Boss, come on. You've got to move. If you don't they're going to find you and kill you."

"Don't worry about it, Mel. By the time they get here I'll already be gone. The doppelgänger's just about burned out and the backlash should be along to get me in a few seconds. But, thanks for caring."

"Don't be an idiot, Ravirn. The net's backbone is down. Once we're through with the gate closed behind us the doppelgänger link will be severed."

"What?" I thought about that for a moment and realized he might be right, but only if I hurried. I had at best five more seconds before not-I finished flaming out. After that . . .

I reached up with one hand and grabbed the edge of the picture frame. I started to stand and rediscovered my broken knee. My leg folded under me and I almost lost my grip on the picture frame. I had three seconds left. Placing my other hand next to my first I pulled myself up and into the picture.

The pain as my broken knee hit the panel below the painting was enough — when added to the feedback coming from the doppelgänger — to knock me out.

I don't remember what happened next, but I must have gotten lucky and fallen in the right direction, because when I woke up ten minutes later I was still among the living. I was also in another world. I was on a rounded green hill in the middle of a fairy circle made from crushed beer cans. Melchior was beside me. I looked at his maimed left hand and a wave of guilt washed over me.

"Sorry, about the hand, Mel."

"It's okay, boss. I understand. If that scrawny carcass of yours turned up without mine alongside it, your cousins would never believe they had the real thing. Even with your actual flesh, in the form of your fingertip, providing the signature they'd know that something was up. It is after all common knowledge that you couldn't find your ass with both hands and a map if you didn't have my help."

"You know what, Mel. I'm going to ignore that comment because of your recent service above and beyond the call of duty. And I'm not going to erase your hard drive and start from scratch like I should."

"Gosh, boss, you're all heart."

"Thank you, Mel. But now, putting all that aside for a moment, what do you think, trash her files, a virus, change all of her passwords?"

"What are you talking about?" asked Melchior, his tone one of deep concern.

"Getting even with Atropos."

"Are you out of your teeny tiny little mind . . ." He trailed off into a sigh and then began again, "Do we have to? Can't we just stay dead for a while and let things cool off?"

I shook my head. "Of course not. If I quit hacking, Atropos wins. Besides, if you can't tempt a fate once in while, where's the fun in life. Come on, let's get to work." Ω

DRAWBACK

When I look up at the moon
My form begins to change
I start to feel strange
My cells — then re-arrange
It's cool to be a werewolf
Unless you have the mange!

—Daniel Paul Medici

THE SECRET EXHIBITION

The Secret Exhibition

by Brian Stableford

illustrated by George Barr

Claudius Jaseph came to the island in the fourteenth year of our beloved Emperor's reign. He came in early June with the summer migrants — borne by one of those freak tides of fashion which afflict the idle rich. Given that more than half the island's standing population — at least since it was purged of honest fishermen — consists of writers, composers, players, painters, necromancers, mystics, and similar recipients of unsteady aristocratic patronage, the last thing it requires its seasonal visitors to bring is *more* writers, composers, players, painters, necromancers, and mystics, but wealth inevitably nurtures an addiction to novelty. Were the rich ever to become content with what they have they would no longer be able to spend the dividends of their capital and the entire Imperial economy would lurch towards collapse — or so the Physiocrats assure us.

I was not particularly put out by news of Jaseph's impending arrival, although I had every right to be. My friends will probably tell you that I was positively incandescent with envy, but artists always tend to conceive of one another as uncontrollable knots of child-like emotion, each one thinking that he or she is the only one clever enough to play the role without actually fitting it. I made the acidic remarks expected of me, because appearances must be kept up, but I had seen other portraitists sail in on the wayward tide and sail on soon enough. I had no reason to think, as June began, that Claudius Jaseph would be any different.

"This one will offer you real competition," Hecate Rain assured me, as we lounged on the terrace of the Sprite, looking out over the harbour. She was drinking absinthe; there was iced water in my own glass. "They say that his brushwork is superb, his accuracy uncanny. More to the point, dear Axel, he makes a fetish of painting women, just as you have always done. They say that he plays them off against one another with consummate cruelty: the wives whose beauty is beginning to fade, desperate to be captured on canvas one last time, while they are still desirable; the daughters just coming into their inheritance of pulchritude, intoxicated and deranged by a magnetism they cannot yet control. Those have always been your favourite victims, have they not?"

"Victims?" I echoed, with ostentatious alarm. "Have I victims? Am I reckoned a murderer, and not a humble painter after all? Are you labouring under the delusion that I put away my palette when night falls, to don my black domino and take up my gleaming dagger?"

"In poetic terms, that is exactly what you do," said Hecate. She is, of course, a poet, although she has a necromancer's given name. "By day you regard your sitters with a cool and clinical eye, impassively noting their flaws and gently erasing them from the images that appear by degrees upon your canvas. After dark, your face changes completely; your gaze becomes avid and your lips are reddened with lust. You think of yourself as a mere seducer, a plunderer of trivia, but in your heart of hearts you hate your subjects with a fervour you could never admit to yourself. You may call what you do to them *making love,* and they may even believe it — were the rich not appallingly gullible none of us would be here — but you are driving a metaphorical dagger deep into their bodies, ripping their very souls to shreds."

"The rich have no souls to be ripped," I told her. "Nor, my sweet, have we — not even in *poetic terms.* You really ought to leave such nonsense to Vashti and her fellow dabblers in distress."

"You prove my point," she riposted. "You are, at heart, a vulgar materialist. Lust, to you, is no more than a weapon."

"Your *original* point, I believe, was that this upstart veteran of a single exhibition at Myrica Mavor's metropolitan gallery is equipped to lay waste to my best-laid schemes. Have your rumour-mongers told you that he is as adept with the dagger as the brush?"

"Given that he is fifteen years your junior," said Hecate, revelling in the hurtful nature of the datum, "his dagger might be expected to be a good deal brighter and sharper — but they say that he is one of those rare men who really does *love* women. He never flatters them, by day or by night. He is honest, and he knows how precious they truly are. Myrica told me herself — so mournfully I had to believe her — that he would not lend her his very best work to show in the gallery. There are those among his creations, it seems, which he adores so absolutely that he consigns them to a secret exhibition which none but he and a favoured few may ever view. He refuses to accept his fee in such cases, for he believes that the portraits have souls of their own, which ought never to be sold."

I had to admit, on hearing this, that Jaseph seemed to have discovered an entirely new way of breaking hearts. What woman, hearing the rumour which Hecate had just quoted — even knowing that it came from the artist's agent — could resist the temptation to commission a portrait, quietly hoping that it might acquire a soul of its own and thus prove worthy to be retained in the secret exhibition? What woman, in pursuit of that aim, would not offer herself to the artist with *exceptional* abandon, hoping to prove her

worthiness by the luxury of her surrender? And what woman, told in the end that her portrait was, after all, to be returned to her husband or father in exchange for the contracted price, would not suffer a disappointment far greater than any that I had ever contrived to inflict?

But I was *not* jealous. Hecate had misjudged me, as poets are so often wont to misjudge their one-time lovers. I do not hate my sitters, and there is nothing cynical about the manner in which I flatter them with my art. I *do* make love to those who are willing — and how many women sit for a portrait who are *not* willing, once they have seen what artistry can accomplish? — but I take nothing from them but trivial affection. No woman has ever killed herself for me.

That, alas, was the next rumour to reach Hecate's avid ears, and she spared no time in spreading it. By the time Claudius Jaseph actually arrived, with Lady Hintermann and the Marquis of Caissot on Ramon Rabirio's yacht, even the Sisters of Shalimar knew the record of his power, and certainly had not divined it in their skrying-glasses. No less than three of the sitters whose portraits had made their appearance on Myrica Mavor's hallowed walls were dead. Naomi Lynhurst, daughter of the Marquis of Castelle, had thrown herself into the city's least-known river, not even from a bridge but through an iron-capped manhole in the steel-sprung pavement that had reduced it to the status of a sewer. Sarah, Lady Generoix had hanged herself with a bell-rope in the Church of St Syncletica. Worst of all, Roxane, the elder daughter of the Duke of Alectryon, had opened a vein in her arm with a barber's surgical razor, cutting all the way from the shoulder to the wrist with a single imperious sweep.

I had painted Roxane myself, and might have made love to her had I not feared the intelligence and wrath of her father. Given time, I would certainly have painted Naomi and Sarah had they lived to be a little older. Not one of them was twenty when she died; Naomi was barely seventeen.

One such death might have been regarded as tragic happenstance, even two might have been dismissed as macabre coincidence, but three looked uncommonly like the devil's work to everyone who believed in the devil. And what effect did this seeming devil's-work have on Claudius Jaseph and his reputation? According to what Myrica had told Hecate, the man was devastated by grief, but relied upon the feverish

THE SECRET EXHIBITION

expertise of his art to pull him through — and he had so many commissions impending that he was receiving bribes for preferential treatment higher than the price I usually asked for my paintings.

I knew, even before Rabirio's yacht set down its anchor, that the summer would be an unprecedentedly profitable season for the island's magicians.

As chance would have it, it was at a séance rather than a party that I first met the man that my friends had appointed my arch-rival. I am not a necrophile by habit or inclination, but when Vashti Savage told me that Alectryon's distraught wife had demanded that she summon the spirit of her dear departed daughter, and that she could not do it without a full coven of thirteen persons who had some sound connection with the dead girl, I immediately agreed to lend my hands to the circle. How could I possibly have refused?

Perhaps it was disingenuous of me not to ask who else would be there, and stupid of me not to realise that Jaseph was still regarded as a *friend* by the bereaved matron rather than the agent of the family's misery. Suffice it to say that he *was* there, with Myrica Mavor in attendance, and that the only man who cast a hateful glance in his direction was the duke — and even he was forced to be discreet, because the duke, for all that he had served as a general and won at least three battles, was always circumspect in the face of his wife's determination.

Myrica was the only woman not fluttering for Jaseph's attention. Even Hecate — who must have known that she had several too may wrinkles to catch the eye of an *accurate* artist — was reduced to using her elbows on the opposition, to no avail whatever. I was amazed by the brazen manner in which the opposition in question was led and effortlessly outclassed by Alectryon's surviving daughter Dian, but sibling rivalry can be a terrible thing.

Jaseph was everything that had been said of him: not merely handsome but *boldly* handsome. His hair was raven-black but not in the least shiny; it seemed to soak up all the light that fell upon it. His eyes were so darkly violet as to be hardly less than black themselves, but his skin was remarkably pale. The island's summer sun had not yet made the slightest impression upon his complexion, although I judged that the wide-brimmed hat he wore — also black, of course — would not protect him as fully as he expected,

given the whiteness of our pavements and the tendency of light to reflect. His black silk shirt had all the gloss that his hair lacked, and seemed to have leaked more than a little to his leather trews, which were worn tight enough to exaggerate his leanness and display the sinuous movement of his hips as he swayed on the spot or crossed a room.

I was very glad that I had dressed myself in burgundy and twilight grey — mercifully, I never wear black to séances — and could not possibly be thought by anyone there to have entered into a sartorial competition. I was not nearly so glad that Jaseph made unreasonable haste to brush off his admiring coterie — his brushwork *was* good — in order that he might introduce himself to me. He seemed, as he crossed the room, to be deeply relieved to have shaken off his lovely admirers. Indeed, he seemed every inch the haunted man, too distracted by sorrow to pay attention to female wiles — but I assumed that it was an act, contrived to suit the occasion.

"I see your work everywhere I go," he said, after telling me what a privilege it was to meet me.

"I fear that I've been too long becalmed on the island," I lamented, trying hard to make my insincerity glaring. "I simply can't abide the bitter winters in the city, nor the awful stink that summer liberates from the culverts and alleys. Fortunately, the island's summer visitors are kind enough to keep me busy, and generous enough to display my work on their walls. I fear that I have not seen *any* of your work — Myrica must have sold it to the kind of people who prefer to keep their portraits in their town houses."

"I'm barely starting out," he told me. "I hardly dare to hope that my work will be as generously distributed as yours when I reach your age." In retrospect, I suppose he must have meant it as a mere observation, with no insult intended, but I had lived too long as an artist among artists. I construed the phrase "gener-

by **Brian Stableford**

ously distributed" as a calculated euphemism for "commonplace," or even "cheap."

"Generosity has always been a fault of mine," I assured him. "It allows me to paint older women extraordinarily well, favouring the cherished memory over the vulgar fact. I fear that I am incapable of the brutality which accuracy demands."

I was implying — cruelly, I admit — that he was not. A shadow of anguish passed over his face as I said it, but I was unrepentant.

"I have never been brutal in my art," he said, in a low tone. "Nor in my life, no matter what anyone may think."

"Existence itself is brutal to blossoms which emerge in the spring," I said, with a softness that could easily have been taken for consolation. "Those which are too tender to bear the glare of maturity shrivel before their time. Parents always hold themselves responsible, but they should not seek solace in necromancy; forgiveness from beyond the grave is always hollow."

"You are not a believer, then?" Jaseph said, raising an eyebrow in faint surprise. "Does Madame Vashti know that you doubt her honesty?"

"She knows that I do not," I told him. "She forgives me my conviction that she is mistaken in her interpretation of what she sees with her mind's eye and hears with her inner ear."

"I firmly believe," he said — and if his sincerity was feigned he was a consummate actor — "that the souls of the dead outlive the wasting of the flesh. I am convinced, too, that the survival of intelligence is not the whole of it. Either the ancient Egyptians were right to say that we have several souls, or...." He was interrupted then by the ever-efficient Vashti, calling us to order and demanding that we take our seats.

Like any unbeliever, I have little patience with the extravagance of folly, and I forgot what Claudius Jaseph had been saying as soon as I took my allotted place between Hecate Rain and the Lady Dian. Had I remembered it, and taken the trouble to pursue it when I had the chance, I might have gained access to the secret exhibition earlier than I did. For all his manifest contempt, Jaseph reckoned me an artist, and he must have seen the merit in my own portrait of the Lady Roxane. He would surely have talked to me as one artist to another had I only given him the chance — but my arrogance and carelessness prevented me from realising that.

As I took Dian's little hand in mine I felt her shiver, but I am sure it was excitement rather than fear. Even at seventeen, she had no fear. She was not one of the tender ones, destined to shrivel early in the oppressive heat of maturity; she was one of those who would turn the brutality of the world back upon itself, hurting others as much as she herself was hurt.

I thought that a good thing while I held the lady Dian's hand at Vashti's table, and I think so still, in spite of the fact that a little of her returned brutality was to exact its pain from me.

Vashti never dressed her séances with overmuch trumpery — which is one of the reasons I consider her honest, an authentic artist rather than a shallow cheat — and there was no shrieking and groaning about her performance. She did not wail, nor did she command; she simply slipped into her trance and waited for inspiration to come.

It came, in the beginning, in the form of a whole sequence of persons who impressed their own dubious individuality upon hers. They claimed, as they always did, to have lived in the time of Odysseus, Alexander or Attila the Conqueror, to have been captains, courtesans or the catamites of cardinals. Every voice was eager to sell its secrets for an ounce of attention — which is. alas, exactly what the whole sum of their so-called secrets was worth.

The task of calling Lady Roxane had been delegated to Hecate, who executed the duty with all due dignity, although I do not know to this day whether she really believes in the power of magic or not.

And in the end, it seemed, the Lady Roxane deigned to present herself.

Whether Alectryon's wife had come in search of reassurance as to the Lady Roxane's fate in the world beyond the world — as she was bound to pretend — or in search of some signal that she need not hold herself at all responsible for her daughter's suicide, she was to be disappointed.

"Do not mourn for me," said the girl's voice, emitted from the versatile throat of Vashti Savage. "I did what needed to be done, carefully and without impairment of my reason. I desired to be dead, and I am."

"Have you found Paradise?" Hecate asked, as she had doubtless been instructed to do.

"I have not looked for it," replied the voice from beyond. "I did not die in the hope of finding bliss, any more than I feared to die for dread of eternal torment. In truth, I have not the capacity for either state. All warmth is in the flesh, be it love or pain; there is none in the soul. Do not grieve for me; I have left suffering far behind."

Had Hecate not been occupied I would have whispered in her ear, saying that this was not the news Vashti's spirits usually brought, and seemed to contradict the testimony of her other voices. As things were, however, I felt compelled to remain silent. Hecate's hand was quite steady within my own, but the Lady Dian's was still tremulous, and she had to clasp my fingers a little too hard in order to suppress the tremor.

"Why did you choose to depart when your life was hardly begun?" asked Hecate, with frank curiosity.

"I did not," said the other. "My *life* was finished. I had business elsewhere."

"Business! What business?" The interruption, inevitably, came from the duke; I imagined the duchess's painted and pointed fingernails digging into his hand by way of complaint.

"Something finer than commerce, father," the voice replied, as freely as any daughter might who was beyond the reach of parental displeasure. "Finer by far, and richer too — but not in any currency you would understand. There is metal more precious than gold, and light far brighter than the glow of Heaven."

I was interested by that, not as a revelation of what might await me beyond death, but as a revelation of hitherto unsuspected subtleties in Vashti Savage. Who, I wondered, could have put such heretical notions in her head?

I guessed the answer, of course: Claudius Jaseph. Vashti had been using her elbows too, in that undignified scrimmage for the man's attention, but she had already seen him privately, by way of preparation for her séance. Had she, I wondered, nursed the ludicrous hope that he might express the desire to paint her, even though she could not pay a twentieth of the kind of fee that the Duke of Alectryon could lay out, let alone the kind of bribe that would claim the artist's *immediate* attention? Was this strange performance for *his* sake?

The candlelight was far from bright, but my eyes were well enough adjusted to pick out the lines of Jaseph's pallid face. I could no longer believe that his haunted look was feigned; his eyes were wide with anguish, and he was listening as if with avid terror, fearful to miss a single word and yet fearful of what each and every word might declare.

I expected the next question to be raised by the impatient duchess, but it came instead from her impertinent daughter. "What can you tell me of my future, Roxane? What lies in store for us all?" I assumed that the second element was added by way of apology for the selfishness of the first.

"Your future is your own to make, little sister," said the voice. "You might make it with courage, or with love — but not, I think, with both."

Dian's hand tightened again when she heard that, but I judged the force as petulance rather than gratitude or anxiety.

"Why?" asked the duchess, at last. "For the love of Heaven, Roxane, *why did you do it?*"

I wondered how many of the thirteen people joined in Vashti's circle had already taken it for granted that the answer to the question was: *Not for love of Heaven but for love of Claudius Jaseph, who would not place my image in his secret exhibition, discarding all others.*

What the supposed spirit actually said was: "Because it was necessary, under the tyranny of reason."

My unbelief remained unshaken, but I thought it brave of Vashti Savage as well as cunning to place the word *tyranny* in the mouth of a lost soul. In an world like ours, where we must always speak of our *beloved* emperor and the *nobility* of his myriad dukes and barons, tyranny is not a word that trips lightly from the tongues of the unentranced.

The duchess felt that she had not had a proper answer to her question, but the spirit disagreed. The Lady Roxane, if she had indeed come to give account of herself, had no more to tell us.

When the circle had broken, the nine females present soon gravitated to their momentary sun, leaving the remainder of the males a trifle bereft. Jaseph seemed even less grateful for their attentions now than he had before, but that only made them press in upon him all the harder, competing to soothe his evident distress with their kindness and sympathy.

In such circumstances as that, fate may make

strange bedfellows. I am certain that the Duke of Alectryon acted on the spur of the moment, driven towards me by the sight of his wife and daughter dancing attendance on a man whom he thought he had reason enough to hate.

"Master Rathenius," he said, as he set himself abruptly before me. They were the first words he had addressed to me since his steward had paid me for the portrait of Roxane I had completed twenty months before.

"Lord Alectryon," I replied, with a sober bow. "I am deeply sorry for your loss."

He was not interested in my condolences. "I want you to paint my daughter," he said, unceremoniously. "Whatever you have on your easel, put it away. You must start tomorrow. Take as long as you like."

If the first of these sentences was surprising, the last was astounding. The words were innocuous enough in themselves, but the implication of the poor man's eyes was positively tortured. I wondered if he knew what he was saying, and whether I dared to take the inference that impressed itself upon my startled mind.

Most of the men who have commissioned me to paint portraits of their wives, sisters, and daughters have thought my reputation as a lecher exaggerated, as artists' reputations usually are. Even those who have taken it seriously have always considered it irrelevant to themselves; the well-born have an inbred tendency to believe that they are utterly immune to the misfortunes that descend upon the less fortunate, and this often gives them an unbreakable faith in the exceptional virtue of their own womenfolk. Alectryon was not so stupid. He knew what I was, and I knew that he knew — which was why I had made no effort to press myself on the Lady Roxane while she sat for me. I had known that I was under threat because of the duke's insistence on keeping very careful account of the *time* his daughter spent in my studio, negotiating minutes and hours with as much attention to detail as his steward lavished upon the calculation of my expenses. He had used that means to inform me, subtly, that any *extra* time I might lavish upon his daughter would be just as minutely assessed.

Now, by contrast, he was inviting me to spend *as long as I liked* with his younger — and recently his only — daughter.

I looked hard at Alectryon before I lowered my head again to acknowledge my acceptance of the commission. Then I looked hard at Dian and her mother, fawning upon the unhappy Claudius Jaseph in the far corner of the room, and understood that *her* time was already half-pledged to another. I realised that Alectryon was making a desperate attempt to head off trouble, and that he could not have been certain himself how far he was prepared to go in that cause.

Had the commissioning of Dian's portrait been a military matter, the duke would undoubtedly have brought his manuvre to a successful conclusion — but this was peace-time, and summer, and the island is even further from the empire's heart than Alectryon's estates. Dian wanted Claudius Jaseph to paint her, and her mother wanted Claudius Jaseph to paint her, and in the end the only way that the luckless duke could preserve his will was to let them have theirs.

Absurdly, but perhaps inevitably, the agreement was made that Dian was to sit for *two* portraits. In the mornings, she would go to Claudius Jaseph; in the afternoons, to me.

It was not, of course, a formal contest. In the undeclared thoughts of everyone on the island, however, it would be a duel whose like had not been seen since Thorold of Lamry cast a gauntlet before the self-styled black magician Herod Ojas and cut him to ribbons with his sabre, only to die three days afterwards from a trivial self-inflicted cut that became septic and turned his blood to bile.

I did not need to consult Hecate Rain's inbuilt barometer to know that the island's opinion-makers would put the odds against my making the better painting at three to one, and the odds against my making the better seduction at thirty to one. It would have done me no good to protest that the contest was not of my making. The fact was that it had been made — and that I, alas, had been appointed Alectryon's champion.

The only consolation I could find, at the time, was that I was certain to collect my fee, whereas Jaseph — if his reputation was deserved — might choose to forgo his if the margin of his victory was as great as popular opinion believed. That, I knew, was what the Lady Dian must crave, as her sister must have craved it before her, however absurd the ambition might be.

"What kind of a world do we live in," I lamented to an absinthe-befuddled Hecate, as I kindly put her to bed before taking myself off to my own home, "when those who believe in souls have no desire more ardent than to have them stolen by a painting?"

"Axel," she said, severely, "you have no romance in your own soul, and will never understand it in others."

I slept well, unintimidated by the thought of the odds stacked against me, and spent the first two hours of the following morning making my studio fit to receive a sitter of the highest rank. This required a deal of tidying up but not, alas, the unceremonious removal from my easel of some half-accomplished masterpiece.

When everything had been made ready, I went to see Myrica Mavor in the quayside cottage that served as her summer residence.

"You're wasting your time, Axel," she told me, immediately. "I have none of his paintings here to show you. Those which were on loan were returned, those which were for sale were sold. If you are afraid to go to Alectryon's house to compare the two portraits of Roxane you must go to Caissot, or the Hintermanns — they brought their trophies with them, to bear witness to the excellence of their lucky find."

"I am not here to measure Jaseph's abilities as a draughtsman," I told her, suppressing my resentment of her accusation of cowardice. "If you have judged him an artist, he is an artist; I do not need to see for myself how expert his brushwork is. But why, given that he *is* an artist, have you taken the trouble to boost his reputation with such silly rumours?"

"Axel! Can you possibly think....?"

"Of course I can think," I told her, with calculated rudeness. "Now, what is all this nonsense about a secret exhibition? What on earth made you think of it? Could you not imagine the effect it might have on his sitters?"

"Of course I could imagine," she retorted, coldly. "That is why I would never have invented such a silly story, or encouraged its dissemination. It simply is not true, dear Axel, that every rumour which advertises an artist's exceptional giftedness is invented by his agent. In my opinion, this particular rumour was not the cause of the suicides but their result. It was perhaps inevitable that jealous and ignorant people — whose numbers are by no means few in the city — should begin to whisper suspicion that the deaths were connected by more than coincidence. I do not know what foul-minded person made up this tale of a collection of portraits never placed on public exhibition, kept locked away in a windowless vault, but I know that it is pure malice. If Claudius *has* kept some portraits from public view, it is for his own reasons, not because

the portraits contain the captive souls of the women who had posed for them. In any case, all three of the portraits of the women who died have been displayed. Roxane's is on the island now."

"The rumour I heard said that the three had died of disappointment, because they were not thought worthy of the secret exhibition," I informed her.

"There you are," said Myrica, bitterly. "The malicious fools cannot make up their minds. Does he steal souls from his victims, or disappoint them by refusing to steal their souls? They seek to damn him either way, and they do so by piling new infamies upon the old. I have said it a thousand times and I will say it a thousand more: *he has committed no crime; he is guilty of no sin.* His work is sublime, and the devil hates sublimity; that is the sole cause of his bad luck."

Her indignation seemed real enough. I judged that if she *had* made up the tale of the secret exhibition to promote her protegé she had long since repented of it. Alas, it is in the nature of rumours that those which do not wither and die in infancy are amplified and embellished with the passage of time; further decoration is the nourishment which sustains them. The rumour of Jaseph's secret legacy had taken root, and its monstrousness had grown beyond its inventor's original intention.

"What further infamy has been added to the first?" I asked her, as gently as I could.

She hesitated, but she knew my reputation as an unbeliever. "In the city," she said, "it is now being whispered that the souls trapped within the portraits were perverted by their unnatural imprisonment and turned to evil. Denied whatever sustenance souls require from flesh, they are reputed to have become exceedingly hungry, acquiring a kind of will which permits them to leech the soul-stuff from anyone who saw them. Not only have their losers been driven to despair and suicide, it is now said, but any unsuspecting art-lover who might be allowed access to the

secret vault where Jaseph kept the paintings will be in dire danger of a similar fate. Preposterous, is it not?"

"Preposterous," I agreed.

Myrica sighed. "The air is far cleaner here on the island," she said, "and even rumours cannot reek so offensively as they do in narrow metropolitan streets — but the boat which brought the new tale to my ears will leak it nevertheless to the entire harbour."

"I fear that it will not be sufficient to dissuade the Lady Dian and her mother," I told her, soberly. "What effect do you think this silly competition will have on the girl?"

Myrica shrugged her shoulders. "If you fear that," she said, skeptical as to the honesty of my concern for the girl's welfare, "you have only to withdraw."

"And deny Alectryon? He might forgive me for failing, but he would never forgive me for not trying, since he has commanded me to do so. Unfortunately, I do not think he knows himself what licence he has given me — and whatever I decide, I shall probably be blamed for the outcome."

Myrica raised an eyebrow at that. "If I were you," she said, skeptically, "I'd content myself with painting. I shall do everything in my power to make sure that Claudius does the same. It would be best for everyone if the lady's emotions remained uninvolved. If you came here for reassurance, you have all that I can give."

I wished that she had sounded more confident that she had any power at all over Claudius Jaseph's ambitions, but I had indeed come for reassurance and I did indeed have all that she could give.

I went back to my own house, to keep my appointment and begin my work.

The uglier rumours that had now crossed the calm summer sea were soon common knowledge from St Aidan's Head to the Devil's Rocks. The account of Claudius Jaseph's secret exhibition had grown even further while the infection spread.

Those who were not true aesthetes, it was now said, were immune to the vampiric predation of the ensouled portraits — but anyone capable of perceiving the genius which had gone into their creation would be lost as soon as he beheld them. The souls of the sensitive would be sucked out of them, shredded and parcelled out among the avid images while the baleful ringmaster of the sinister circus, Claudius Jaseph, looked on and laughed.

No artist or aristocrat could ever *believe* such wild tales, of course, but that did not prevent their being passed on. Nor, alas, could it prevent their adding to the dark glamour of their subject. Although Claudius Jaseph certainly did not seem to enjoy his notoriety, he made no constructive attempt to refute the charges laid against him. Instead, he hid himself away in the cottage that Myrica Mavor had procured for him, which was set alone on the topmost height of the promontory which extended to the broken rocks of St Aidan's Point.

The Lady Dian proved to be a good sitter, far less impatient than her sister had been, even though she came to me having already posed for Jaseph for three hours and more. She came to me in clean clothes, with her auburn hair very neatly groomed. It was only to be expected that she would change between sessions, given that she would not want to appear identically clad in two different portraits, but I could not help wondering what she wore for Jaseph. What she wore for me was a gown of white silk trimmed with crimson, pinned with enamelled brooches; the sleeves were ruffled and the neckline very moderate. It seemed to me that she was trying to appear younger than she was — which immediately suggested that when she sat for Jaseph she tried to appear older.

Roxane had been the more beautiful of the two sisters — there had been an admirable *hauteur* about her, and she was longer in the limbs — but Dian was the more robust. At first sight, she gave the impression that she might bruise easily enough, but I had already begun to penetrate that illusion at Vashti's séance. When I brought my artist's sight to bear, it was perfectly obvious that her porcelain surface hid a curious combination of her father's cynicism and her mother's determination. She had no imperious *hauteur* because she had no vanity; she was less inclined than her long-limbed sister to overestimate her reach, and thus better able to make her grasp secure.

I realised, too, that the thought of sitting for two portraits at the same time had begun to amuse her tremendously once she had given it due consideration. It had occurred to her that the implicit competition would drive both artists to excel themselves, and that the extra effort Jaseph and I were required to invest would work to her advantage, her *glory*. She must have calculated, too, that if Jaseph were foolish enough to sustain his myth by refusing to deliver his portrait, she would have the best of both worlds. She would be part of the notorious secret exhibition *and* in pride of place in Alectryon's manse.

I was kind to her during her first few sittings, but I made not the slightest attempt to make love to her. I had decided that Myrica Mavor's advice was sound, and that it was dangerous to take advantage of an implication which the duke might easily refuse to admit that he had ever made.

It had long been my habit to begin my amorous advances as soon as a painting had begun, with a little scolding counterbalanced by more than a little flattery. I would use my hands to tilt the face of the sitter one way and another, to smooth the cloth upon her bosom, to caress her wrists as if by way of encouragement or thanks. Slowly but surely, as the portrait took shape, my words would grow more affectionate, my hands more adventurous, building a crescendo of emotional response that could only have one conclusion. With Dian, however, I was careful to strike an exact balance between instruction and apology, and I kept my hands strictly to myself.

The inevitable result of this unaccustomed self-restraint was, of course, that the desire I sought to set aside was amplified by restraint. My determination to make sure that the girl did not fall in love with me was translated by perversity into a process by which I found myself falling headlong in love with her.

By the time the Lady Dian had spent four afternoons with me I could not get her out of my head; every time I closed my eyes her face confronted me, strangely compounded out of flesh and paint, half-person and half-portrait — and as the face on the canvas gradually took shape and became clearer, so did the haunting image.

I knew and understood what was happening. I never lost my sense of perspective — but my understanding could not diminish the intensity of my feelings. I berated myself mercilessly, but scolding only served to inflame the unrepentant emotion. Everything I did, everything I thought, added to my confusion.

Then, for the first time, I *did* become jealous of Claudius Jaseph — and my jealousy added further fuel to the fire. Then, and only then, was the competition between us joined in deadly earnest — and despite that I was still an unbeliever, I began to feel that it might indeed be a competition for the lady's very soul.

By the fifth day, I could see that Dian was changing before my expert eyes. Her skin grew gradually paler, her hair gradually wilder, her eyes more hollow and more feverish. The white silk which lay upon her bosom seemed shadowed, if not actually tarnished. She was haunted — and not by the ghost of her unlucky sister. I knew that Jaseph was the cause, but I was uncertain as to the precise nature of the leverage. Had Myrica prevailed upon him to be as cold and businesslike as I had determined to be, and was his coldness distressing her? Was she pining for him as I was for her? Or had he rudely rejected Myrica's advice and set out upon a course of seduction that was confusing and draining her? Was she wilting beneath the assault of his flatteries and demands?

On the morning of the sixth day, while Dian was with Jaseph, Alectryon came to see me. "You pose as a reasonable man," he said to me, without preamble. "You deny the very existence of the soul — but you always do so in your accursed artist's fashion, all sarcasm and theatricality. I want to know the truth of your beliefs, Rathenius. Do you believe that souls can be stolen, or made captive?"

"Not in any literal sense," I told him, sincerely. "But with all due respect to the military precision of your thinking, my lord, there *is* such a thing as poetic truth. Matter is obedient to the laws of nature; your artillerists can calculate the flight of a cannonball, the range of a musket-shot, the blast of a petard. Mind is different; it is compounded out of our hopes, fears, and beliefs. We are what we pretend to be, and if we care to insist that we have souls, we can and do ensoul ourselves. The hope that our souls survive our death is insufficient to establish the fact, but it *is* sufficient to establish the appearance — and beyond the mere appearances of mind, there is insufficient substance to repair the error. If a believer in the soul were to be convinced that her

soul had been stolen, the loss would be tangible enough.''

"Damn you!" he said, radiating wrath. "I wanted a straight and simple answer, not one of your fancy speeches."

"The world would be a far less confusing place," I told him, as temperately as I could, "if the straight and simple answers were also the true ones. Alas, they are not."

He did not want to believe me, but he could not deny that the world was sorely confused. "Can you stop Jaseph?" he said, shortly. "Can you prevent him destroying Dian as he destroyed Roxane?"

The straight and simple answer was that whatever Jaseph might have done he had *not* destroyed Roxane. The straight and simple truth was that Roxane had destroyed herself, with Jaseph a catalyst at most — but I could not tell him that. Seen straightly and simply, the truth was Dian had more backbone than her sister, and would likely survive no matter what, even if she were slightly bruised in body and mind — but I could not tell him that, either.

"I will try," was what I actually said. "I do not know whether I can succeed, but you have my solemn word that I will try."

"Do what you have to," he said, his eyes dark and his cheek bones outstanding. "If you can't, I might have to — and I don't want that."

Whatever cynics may think about the dubious nobility of our aristocracy, the myth is not without its force — or perhaps even the straight-thinking Alectryon understood that if Claudius Jaseph were struck down by a masked assassin, he would lose his daughter just as surely as he would if Jaseph had his wicked way with her.

I spent the afternoon making plans while I painted, but I do not remember what they were. They were driven from my mind as soon as events took a turn that I had not anticipated — a turn that I had not even considered possible. When I laid down my brush, a little earlier than usual, and signalled to Dian that she could relax her pose, she stood up and came directly to me.

I thought that she had come to measure my progress, and I stood aside — I am not one of those artists who will not let unfinished work be seen — but she did not even glance at the canvas.

"Master Rathenius," she said, "will you make love to me?"

I was speechless.

"You have a reputation as a lover," she added, as if by way of explanation, and only paused for a moment before adding: "but you did not make love to my sister. She thought that society had misjudged you — but I told her even then that you were simply afraid of my father. Was that true?"

"Yes," I said, simply and straightly. "And I still am."

She smiled rather than say out loud that she did not believe me. "You have never seen the portrait which Claudius made of Roxane, have you?" she said. "It hangs side by side with your own, in one of the drawing-rooms, still beribboned in black."

"I have never seen any of his paintings," I told her. "They say that his version is far the better of the two — more neatly done, more accurate, and more revealing."

"It is," she said, brutally. "But his present work is not as good. Something is holding him back. Whereas you...." At last she condescended to glance at the canvas, approvingly.

She honestly thought that she was paying me a compliment. What she was actually saying was that Claudius needed more encouragement to do his best work — the work that would outshine *my* best. She wanted to excite his jealousy!

Perhaps, if the world were a simpler place, I would have begun to love her less when she displayed her true colours. Perhaps, if I were a better man, my stomach would have revolted against the notion of being *used*. In the event, the world is not and I am not — and what good would it have done, in any case, to harden my heart and my face and say: *I cannot make love to you*?

I took her face in my hands and kissed it. I kissed her hands. I abandoned myself to my wonderful, wayward feelings.

I remembered what Hecate Rain had said about the quality of my lust, but I *knew* that it was an empty slander. I loved Dian with all my heart, and everything I did with her I did for love. All the fear in the world could not have prevented me, nor all the principle.

It was, in any case, a mere extension into a different kind of action of all the care and genius I had already lavished upon her painting. Art is a form of lust, and portraiture a kind of possession. There is no violation more intimate than that committed by an artist's eye; the engagement of the flesh is no more than confirmation. That is why artists cannot marry, cannot be faithful, cannot even linger long over their affairs. It is in the nature of art that the artist must move on, from one portrait to another and one love to another.

If only Claudius Jaseph had understood that, he might have made a great artist. He had the eye, and he had the hand, but he believed in the soul and *more than the soul*, and that was his damnation. *Fidelity* destroyed him, whatever the world may think and whatever rumour may say.

I am, of course, true after my own particular fashion. While I made love to the lady Dian, I was as utterly committed to her flesh as I was to her appearance. While I stroked her warm skin *she* was the universe which contained my sense of touch; space and time had lost their empire. While I looked into her eyes, into the darkest depths of her pupils, she was the shell of my imagination, the only host of my desire. I was hers, and she knew it. Whatever she had expected, and however meanly she had sought to dispose of herself, for as long as the moment lasted she was everything to me.

I think she realised, although she could not yet bring herself to admit the fact, that no matter how clever his hands might be Claudius Jaseph had not the means to match me in the art of making love. I think she realised that for all his delicacy and all his accuracy there was something lacking in him.

Although I did not know it yet, the truth was that he could never have lost himself in her as I could lose myself, because something of him was already lost, and irredeemably committed.

When we had finished, and dressed ourselves, languidly revelling in our calmness and satisfaction, she said: "Will you let him know, or shall I?" She did not mean, of course, that either of us would ever be so vulgar as to *tell* him.

"Leave it to me," I said, as I was bound to do. "That way, if anyone else is hurt, it will be me."

Jaseph was, of course, astonished to see me. He was a young man and he was new to the island. He did not know me, and he did not know my world. He probably felt that I had snubbed him when I had made no effort to pick up the threads of the conversation he had initiated at Vashti Savage's séance. He probably took the gossip about our competition more seriously than it needed to be taken — or perhaps less seriously.

"What do you want, Master Rathenius?" he said, without even offering to pour me a glass of the wine that he was drinking.

"It happened that I was passing," I lied — transparently, for I could not possibly have been bound for the rocks at the point — "and I remembered that I had not yet bid you a proper welcome. We met for the first time in such awkward circumstances — necromancy inevitably casts a pall over professional courtesy. We are artists, after all, and rivals. We ought to be friends, even though we should never admit to the world that we are anything but deadly enemies."

"I never thought you were my enemy!" he protested.

"Of course not," I said, serenely. "Even the world knows, deep down, that we are not. But we must put on a bold show, for both our sakes. Rivalry is good for business. While we are deadly enemies, who would dare to insult either one of us by offering a lower fee than the other commands? I am deeply indebted to you for the masterly way in which you handled Alectryon and his wife. It will make both our fortunes!"

"The contest was none of my making," he assured me.

"You are far too modest," I assured him in return. "If you paint half as well as you manufacture rumours, you will be summoned to the capital in no time, installed in a tower in the Imperial Palace. You will paint the greatest ladies in the world, and Alectryon will bathe in the glory of having found you."

"I do not manufacture rumours," he said, coldly. "If my words are twisted by others, exaggerated to ludicrous effect, and soiled by the filth of common gossip, that is the malice of the world at work — and my misfortune." I noticed his admission that the seed of the rumours had been sown by his own words.

"Misfortune!" I echoed, sardonically. "Do you mean the misfortune that forced Alectryon to pay the highest price ever paid for a painting made on the island? Do you mean the misfortune that delivers the loveliest girl in the land to your door every morning, so that you might have the privilege of her inspiration? I can assure you that I count none of that *misfortune,* even though I have by far the lesser share."

"Are you drunk, Master Rathenius?" Jaseph asked, looking at me as if he believed that it might be true.

"Not a drop of wine has passed my lips," I informed him, merrily, "and I never touch absinthe. Dear Hecate loves the disorder it brings to her mind, but that is the kind of poet she is; I hate the disorder it brings to my hand, because that is the kind of artist I am." I looked pointedly at the glass in his own hand, but he was not about to be offended by such an empty slight.

"Well, I am glad to have brought you such good fortune," he said, with a bitterness that seemed rather premature, "and sorry that you seem to be anticipating a reversal in that fortune when I leave. In truth, though, I have no plans to visit the Empire's heart. I am quite at home here — in the city, at least. I am not sure that I shall learn to love the island as much as you do."

"No doubt you'll return to the city in the Autumn," I said. "Alectryon always does — and he'll be doubly determined to make sure that his daughter goes with him."

"I would rather have avoided this commission," he said, bluntly. "If anything were to happen to Dian, in the wake of what happened to her sister...."

"But you did not love her sister?" I said — implying, of course, that he *might* love Dian.

He stared at me as if I were a snake that had formerly kept its fangs concealed.

"I see her every day," I reminded him. "I see the light in her eye, the shadow on her cheek. *She* is in love with you, if only because her sister was. She is *very* enthusiastic to outshine her sister. It must be terribly difficult, don't you think, for a girl to grow to womanhood knowing that her sister is just a little more beautiful as well as just a little older? And young women are so ruthless, are they not? They take their rivalries so much more seriously than you and I."

"I am not in love with her," Jaseph said, pronouncing each word with the utmost care — partly because he wanted to be believed and partly because he did not know what I was trying to accomplish.

"I fear that she will not rest until you are," I said, with a sigh. "She longs to be part of your legendary secret exhibition, in order that she might prove once and for all which was the better of Alectryon's daughters. She is old enough to know that it will be her last chance, for her rival has placed herself beyond the reach of age and misfortune. Roxane will be as young and lovely

forever as she is in the portraits that hang side by side in Alectryon's house."

Jaseph's expression was ugly now. It is astonishing how ugly a handsome face can become, if one can only irritate it cleverly enough. "I am not in love with the lady Dian," he repeated, with the air of one trying to convince himself.

"She has made up her mind that you shall be," I reminded him, "and she is her father's daughter. She will stop at nothing. It is a pity the rumours of your secret exhibition have been so wildly magnified. This time next year, hardly anyone will remember them — but for the moment....will you take some advice, Claudius, from a fellow artist?"

The straight and simple answer would have been *no*, but he had curiosity enough to ask: "What advice?"

"If you really do have paintings which you will not show to the world, at least show them to Dian. If they really are locked in a vault on the mainland, fetch them here. De-mystify them."

He laughed. I do not think he intended the laughter as an insult, but it certainly hurt me, although there was a raw note in it which suggested that it hurt him too. "*De-mystify them!*" he repeated, as if it were the most ludicrous suggestion he had ever heard. "If only I could! For the love of Heaven, man, you have not *begun* to understand — and you call yourself an artist! You stupid, sordid *flatterer.*"

The flagrant insult hurt less than the subtler one, as flagrant insults usually do. "Bravo!" I said, stoutly. "You seem to be getting the hang of the politics of rivalry."

He stood up abruptly, and hurled his wine-glass at the wall, the way petty lordlings sometimes do when they want to put on a show of camaraderie, or emotion, or any similar affectation.

It shattered, of course. Wine-glasses obey the laws of matter, not the perversities of mind.

"Do you want to look at my secret exhibition?" he demanded, implying by his tone that I had been angling for exactly such an invitation. "Do you dare, having heard what they say of it?"

"Is it here?" I asked, mildly.

"Do you think I could go anywhere without it? Could I leave my shadow in a mainland vault, or my soul? The lock which secures it is the prison of my heart. In the city, to be sure, I keep it in a cellar; but on the island, I make do with a little room. You know what they have begun to say, do you not? That if you are a tasteless fool, you have nothing to fear — but that if you are a true artist, they will steal your soul through your rapt gaze."

"I thought you were not responsible for the rumours," I said, still speaking with conscientious gentleness. "Are they not the malice of the world, and your misfortune?"

He beckoned me, as imperiously as Alectryon might have. I followed as meekly as I would have had he been our beloved emperor himself. I was curious. How could I have done otherwise, even if I had thought that there really was a risk?

I stepped into Claudius Jaseph's little room without the least hint of trepidation, not doubting for a moment that I would remain in a fit state to come out again, and not fearing for an instant that my capability might demonstrate my aesthetic imbecility.

I had underestimated the risk-but I was right not to be afraid. I was equal to the challenge, and more than equal.

There were three paintings in the room, each one covered by a linen cloth deeply stained by generations of paint and turpentine. Jaseph whipped the protective coverings away, one by one, to reveal the faces beneath.

I recognised each face the instant it was displayed. The first was Naomi Lynhurst, daughter of the Marquis of Castelle. The second was Sarah, Lady Generoix. The third was Roxane, the elder daughter of the Duke of Alectryon,

The criminal stupidity of rumour is that it always seems to omit the most telling detail of all. Even Myrica Mavor had observed the crucial uncertainty in the silly stories that were being bruited about. Had the sitters killed themselves because their souls had been stolen, or because their souls had been deemed unworthy of theft? In truth, the hidden treasure trove whose existence had sparked so much speculation did not consist of paintings that Claudius Jaseph had refused to deliver to their commissioners, but paintings which he had made alongside the ones that he *had* delivered. Whatever had compelled the young women to commit suicide, it was certainly not his refusal to admit them to his secret exhibition.

I now understood why Jaseph had laughed at my suggestion that he show the lady Dian the secret exhibition. Roxane was a part of it, and Jaseph was determined that her sister would *not* be added to it. In fact, he was determined that no one else should ever be added to it, *if he could possibly help it.*

by **Brian Stableford**

You will recall that I had not seen any of Jaseph's paintings before I stepped into that room. I have seen a dozen since, of course, but I did not need any such standard of comparison to know that the paintings which comprised the secret exhibition were unlike any that had ever been painted before, even by Claudius Jaseph. The works that Myrica Mavor had exhibited had been complimented for their brushwork and their accuracy, but no one would have noticed such mere matters of detail had Myrica's paintings had the quality that *these* works had.

I had told the Duke of Alectryon the truth, although he could not find the intelligence to understand what I had said. I am a materialist. I do not believe in the soul as an objective entity obedient to natural law — but I do believe that we provide the light in which we see our inner selves, and that if we decide to see our inner selves as souls, our decision is not without real effect.

Claudius Jaseph believed in the soul, and he was an artist. When he painted, he painted what he saw, what he felt, and what he *believed in*. I saw, now, that I had been utterly wrong. He *had* loved the lady Roxane, with a fervour that had defied his intention to be faithful to Sarah, lady Generoix, just as the love he had discovered for Sarah had defied his intention to be faithful to Naomi Lynhurst. There is, alas, only so much destruction of that kind that a man can take.

Each of the three paintings was infected by a lust so powerful as to be tangible in the warm and sullen air. *No one* could have looked at them without response, a true artist least of all.

I looked them, one by one, and was *possessed* — not by any demon, even in *poetic* truth, but by a passion so raw that it cut into me like a dagger. Perhaps a lesser man would have felt less, but no man ever lived who was so devoid of aesthetic sensibility as to be incapable of feeling the frank and flamboyant eroticism of those images. Perhaps it was an illusion, a mere fantasy — but it

was real enough to rake my heart and leave me more breathless than any passion I had ever spent on my own account....even the passion I had spent that very afternoon, with the lovely lady Dian.

Anyone will tell you that the eyes of a good portrait have life enough to allow the portrait's gaze to follow you around a room, and any artist will tell you how simple it is to work that trick — but the eyes of Naomi Lynhurst looked into mine with so much life that I might have drowned in he tide of her hunger. She looked at me with love: commanding, undeniable, irresistible love.

We pretend that when we say "I love you" we are describing an emotion, and we are not *entirely* dishonest in saying so — but what the lover also means, above and beyond that, is that he or she is determined to place the other under a moral obligation to submit to the lover's will. Naomi Lynhurst had no voice, but her eyes spoke of a love much fiercer than any ever signified by mere spoken words.

Alas, she was not alone. Beside her was Sarah, lady Generoix, who had come after her, and had been forced to break down a barrier of love already pledged, emotion already exhausted. Her lust was less coloured by illusion, the force of her gaze more brutal and more cynical, but not one whit less powerful. Her image might have been a masterpiece, were it not set next to the portrait of Roxane, daughter of Alectryon. Roxane had a kind of *hauteur* that neither of the others had ever possessed; it magnified and purified her lust into something that would have been literally demonic, if there really were literal demons to tempt and plague us. Because there are not, I knew that what the portrait embodied was purely human, even child-like — a prospect which I found more frightening by far.

While I stared at Roxane, who had been forced to displace Sarah even as Sarah had displaced Naomi, she seduced me with her painted eyes — and the force of her seduction was implacable as well as intoxicating, adamantine as well as irresistible.

Claudius Jaseph whispered in my ear: "*Now* do you understand, you petty flatterer? Can you see what a man who *loves* women sees when he is honestly beguiled? Do you see now why the spirit of the lady Roxane cares neither for Heaven nor for Hell? Can you see what has been stolen from her soul, to leave her the mere shell that she is, even beyond the grave? Can you see what art really is, what power it really has, when it is the province of a *true* artist? *Have you ever before seen love, or felt lust, isolated from all confusion?*"

He meant to imply that the answer was no. He meant to imply that whatever I had called love before, and lust too, was something merely superficial — and that I was not and never would be a *true* artist. He was wrong, of course.

"They are good," I said, but not because I hoped to damn them with faint praise. The word *good* has as many meanings as it has inflections. "Your skill is growing by leaps and bounds. A lesser man would have reached his limit before this sequence was even started, as lesser men always have before, but I can see that you are not done yet."

Whatever he had expected, it was not that. That is the beauty of competition — one always has that last slim chance to surprise the adversary, to leave him wrong-footed.

"*Not done yet?*" he whispered. "What in Heaven's name do you mean by that, Rathenius?"

He was mad, of course. Had he been only mad, he might have made better use of his talent, but he was moral too. The combination is deadly.

I was still held captive by Roxane's stare, but I had a voice and she had not — and I had no soul to be stolen. "I can hardly wait to see the square completed," I said. "Your portrait of Dian will be even better than these, of course. She loves you so intensely, and yet so *cleverly*. You must have captured that cleverness in your canvas, and it will give your work the one quality it still lacks: maturity. That is the curse of the young, is it not? However fierce the passion naïve and immature sitters might inspire, one always feels slightly *silly* taking advantage of them. Dian will help you overcome that. She is quite unique, is she not?"

I was improvising, of course. Had I had time to prepare, I might have made the lie less transparent, the nonsense less confused — but my audience was exceptionally uncritical. The paintings had no intelligence of their own, of course, even by his own account — the one thing seemingly left to the insipid spectre summoned by Vashti Savage was intelligence — but in Claudius Jaseph's eyes the love and lust that they made captive were no mere artifice of the artist's brush. To him, they were literal, and they had the power to move matter as well as mind — and because he believed that, it was so, at least in the effect they were able to have on *him*. The claws they used to rake *my* heart were metaphorical;

THE SECRET EXHIBITION

they drew no blood. The claws with which the furies from the heart of Hell reached out for *him* sent him cowering, fearful for his flesh.

Anyone will tell you that a good portrait can appear to be looking at every one of its observers simultaneously, and that the only way to escape their gaze is to cover them up or leave the room. Claudius Jaseph did neither. Instead, he sank to his knees and begged for mercy, while the fever of Roxane's jealousy scoured his inner being, supported and amplified by the wrath of those he had already betrayed.

He bled, from his nose and his mouth-and finally, from his eyes. He bled, but he did not die. They did not intend to let him escape as easily as that; they knew too much about the world beyond the world to think it punishment enough for him.

I would like to think, of course, that there was a little jealousy of his own in the brainstorm which wrecked his mind, but I shall never be sure. I had tried to let him know that Dian had offered herself to me, and that I had accepted her offer gladly and triumphantly, but he might have been too distracted to take the hint. He had wrapped himself so tightly in his own fantasies of love and duty that he had almost ceased to care about the precise facts of life.

I covered the paintings one by one, leaving Roxane till last. Then I carried Claudius Jaseph from the room, and laid him tenderly upon his bed. I wiped the blood and tears from his face, and gave him wine to drink. He drank it gluttonously.

By the time I left him alone, he was as well as could be expected.

Claudius Jaseph fled the island that night. He did not return to the city. Rumour has it that he was seen in one of the northern provinces a year later, but nothing has been heard of him since then. No one knows what happened to that extraordinary product of his erotic obsessions which gossips called the secret exhibition. I sometimes drop dark hints to the effect that I was not only the last person to see it but am also privy to the secret of its fate, but in truth I can do no more than guess.

Perhaps my guess is correct — but I make so many, and I can never decide which one is most likely. My favourite account is that he took a bright dagger to the portraits, ripping them to shreds one by one — saving Roxane for last, of course — in the hope that he might liberate the dream-stuff he had stolen from their souls. On the other hand, he might equally well have burned them, or thrown them over the side of whatever boat it was that carried him away from the island. It is even possible he has them still: his three demonic brides, who love him as angrily and as faithfully as he loves them.

He might, of course, have destroyed two before he even left the island, taking one and one alone away with him, in the hope that the one might forgive him everything, in exchange for a devotion so utter and absolute that he would never touch a brush again, nor look at anyone or anything with an artist's appraising eye. That, I believe, is what many poets would call a happy ending — but I would not agree. Nor, of course, would my dear Hecate Rain.

As Hecate and I sat on the terrace outside the Sprite in late July, shielding ourselves from the harsh rays of the sun with huge white hats, while she drank absinthe and I drank iced water, she said: "I always knew that you would win, of course. Claudius had the greater talent, but he was temperamentally unsound. If you were not so ridiculously lazy, you might turn out work of that quality far more often, but given that you are what you are, I fear that you will never again produce anything half as good as your portrait of the lady Dian."

"You misjudge me," I said. "Everyone does. Alectryon has quite forgotten that he asked me for my help, and lets it be known to anyone who cares to listen that I am a dirty scoundrel. Even Dian believes that I took unfair advantage of her when she was exceptionally vulnerable — but I love her still, just as I love you. I always will."

"Those who murder in the name of art always pretend to love their victims," she informed me — or perhaps it was the absinthe speaking, in its usual disordered fashion.

"No one I have painted has ever felt the need to kill herself," I reminded her, "or even to kill anyone else. If that makes me less of an artist, or less of a lover, I am content to be diminished." Ω

THE WHARTELEY BROTHERS

ALLEN K. 9

"It grew fast and big for the same reason that Wilbur grew fast and big — but it beat him because it had a greater share of the outsidedness in it. You needn't ask how Wilbur called it out of the air. He didn't call it out. *It was his twin brother, but it looked more like the father than he did.*"   "The Dunwich Horror" by H.P. Lovecraft

by Allen Koszowski

FOR SEVENTY-SIX YEARS: THE UNIQUE MAGAZINE   ISSN 0898-5073
Winter 1999/2000   Cover by Bob Eggleton

Weird Tales® is published 4 times a year by DNA Publications, Inc., in association with Terminus Publishing
Co., Inc. Postmaster and others: send all changes of address and other subscription matters to DNA
Publications, Inc., PO Box 2988, Radford VA 24143–2988. Editorial matters should be addressed to Terminus
Publishing Co., Inc., 123 Crooked Lane, King of Prussia PA 19406–2570. Single copies, $4.95 in U.S.A. &
possessions; $6.00 by mail to Canada, $9.00 by first class mail elsewhere. Subscriptions: 4 issues (one year)
$16.00 in U.S.A. & possessions; $22.00 in Canada, $35.00 elsewhere, in U.S. funds. Publisher is not responsible
for loss of manuscripts in publisher's hands or in transit; please see page 5 for more details. Copyright ©
1999 by Terminus Publishing Co., Inc.; all rights reserved; reproduction prohibited without prior permission.
Typeset, printed, & bound in the United States of America.
Weird Tales® is a registered trademark owned by Weird Tales, Limited.

THE EYRIE

The Eyrie needs letters! We mention again that we really do want to hear from you. You can send e-mail to us at **owlswick@netaxs.com**. Make "weird letter" the topic line of your e-mail.

However, *do not* send story submissions this way. They will not be read. Be sensible: if we got 200+ submissions a week, around 5000 words each, via e-mail, our server would crash. But we do want your letters.

Is Horror Coming Back? Everyone, ourselves included, has been so gloomy about the state of the horror field for so many years now, that it's something of a surprise to be able to notice some signs of resurgence. A bookstore clerk we were talking to recently told us that horror is starting to sell again. She had twice within recent weeks expanded the horror section in her store. Sales were that much better. She guessed that the kids who grew up on such authors as R.L. Stine are now college age and ready for adult fiction.

This is more than an interesting point of demographics. It represents, we think, a crucial moment. Now is our chance to re-establish Horror with an audience which has, basically, no memory of the great Horror Boom of the '80s and the subsequent bust. We may reasonably ask: are we going to repeat the mistakes of the past, or has somebody learned something?

The answers aren't in yet. One further encouraging sign is the presence of a large horror anthology from Avon books with the title *999*. It's edited by Al Sarrantonio (hardcover, 665 pp. $27.50), and is a deliberate attempt to recreate the impact of Kirby McCauley's monumental *Dark Forces* (1980) which ushered in the *previous* horror boom in precisely the same way, by serving as a sampler of what's available in the field. The lady from the bookstore reported that *999* is doing very well for her. Readers who know only two or three Horror names — King, Koontz,

Barker, perhaps — can be told, "Look, here's a way to find out about a whole lot of other writers you might like."

It's a good book, and it will doubtless clean up all the awards. It does such a service to the field that we are even willing to congratulate Mr. Sarrantonio in advance on his awards, and forgive him for somehow implying that there has been no professional horror magazine around since *Night Cry* folded back about 1988.

We hasten to point out that since then *Weird Tales*® has published stories by eight of his contributors and devoted special issues to five of them.

As of this writing, we haven't read it all, but so far our favorite is the Joyce Carol Oates novella. There are also very serviceable stories by Ramsey Campbell, Stephen King, Thomas Ligotti, Kim Newman, Gene Wolfe, F. Paul Wilson, T.E.D. Klein, Thomas Disch, and several others, stories which any editor might look upon with envy.

We confess we couldn't make any sense out of the Tim Powers story, and the Edward Lee, once one gets past one real howler of a line ("Paone squinted through grit teeth; without his glasses he couldn't see three feet past his face," which seems to imply that his eyes are in his mouth . . .) proves to be a fast-moving, decently written, quite gory crime story of the hardboiled type, but not weird or supernatural at all.

So here we are at the crossroads once again, as we were a decade ago when some folks tried to turn Horror into something they called Dark Suspense: are we going for the Ominous and Magical, the *imaginative* side of Darkness, or are we going to (in Stephen King's words) "go for the grossout" *all over again?*

We think you can guess where *Weird Tales*® stands on this. We prefer Thomas Ligotti's (or Joyce Carol Oates's) suggestive shadows to Mr. Lee's explicitly popping viscera.

It's a matter of aesthetic choices, which are then borne out by economics. The marketplace will ultimately decide what kind of horror is to continue. We're convinced that we've made the right choice with *Weird Tales®*, which is one reason why we're one of the few survivors from the previous period of Horror ascendancy. We've been at it for twelve years now, which in this field is a very long time.

At the same time we can't deny that readers of the popping-viscera school propelled the career of, say, Rex Miller of *Slob* on to some success, though readers today might well ask, "Rex *who?*" These thing run in cycles. The *Friday the 13th* movies ran their course, and movie and TV horror then evolved into a form of specialized, knowing parody, as exemplified by such films as *Scream* and the phenomenally popular *Buffy the Vampire-Slayer* TV series (which we admit being fans of).

But it isn't *all* cycles, inevitable and impersonal as the tides, which no one may command. Artists, writers, and directors *can* choose.

So, which shall it be, a chill up the spine or a swift upchuck?

We even notice that Hollywood is, in its own faltering way, rediscovering the horror film. This, too, says something interesting about demographics, but otherwise the results are mixed. If you haven't seen the recent remake of *The Haunting*, avoid it at all costs. It is worse than a travesty; it's a two-in-one desecration of a great book (*The Haunting of Hill House* by Shirley Jackson) and a great film (*The Haunting*, directed by Robert Wise) perpetrated by a director whose previous credits include *Speed 2* and who, demonstrably, has no understanding whatsoever of how to make a supernatural horror film.

The new *Haunting* is a virtual textbook case of how not to do it, aimed, apparently, at those people who were too coarse in their sensibilities or just plain too dim-witted to appreciate the real (Robert Wise) version, arguably the finest ghost film ever made.

It's very much like saying, "Duh . . . what *The Turn of the Screw* needs is some raw sex, lots of explosions and chases, and a big rubbery monster." Well, *Hill House* has now acquired most of the forgoing. It's become a special-effects movie, full of attempted thrills-and-chills. Shirley Jackson fans may leave the rest to their horrified imagination when we mention that there's a very contrived, very stupid, *on-screen decapitation.* We may be glad that Jackson didn't live to see this, even as she mercifully escaped the awful TV movie-of-the-week version of "The Lottery" a

STAFF:

Publisher: Warren Lapine
Editors: George H. Scithers
& Darrell Schweitzer
Managing Editor: Carol Adams
Art Editor: Diane Weinstein
Assistant Editors: Kyle Phillips, Pat Buard,
& Robert Waters,
Computer Consultant: David J. Williams III
Typesetter: Owlswick Press
Printer: Morgan Publishing Co., Inc.

MANUSCRIPT SUBMISSIONS:

Before sending us your material, please send us a business-sized envelope, with postage affixed, addressed to you, for our guidelines.

The address for this and all other editorial matters: **Weird Tales®, 123 Crooked Lane, King of Prussia PA 19406-2570.**

The address for all new subscriptions, subscribers' changes of address, advertising, and all other money matters is: **DNA Publications, Inc., PO Box 2988, Radford VA 24143–2988.**

Yes; we read unsolicited submissions — but *only* if they are in standard manuscript format. To survive, all editors insist on a few Rules: each submission must be in proper format and must include a return envelope, addressed to you, with enough postage affixed to bring the manuscript back to you. If you want us to discard the manuscript if we don't buy it, tell us so, but include a business-letter-sized envelope, addressed to you, with proper postage affixed, so we can send you our comments. No loose stamps, please!

We recommend either or both of two books on writing (after all, we wrote one of them!): *On Writing Science Fiction: the Editors Strike Back!* by Scithers, Schweitzer, & John M. Ford; $19.50 in hardcover; and Barry B. Longyear's *Science-Fiction Writer's Workshop,* $9.50 in trade paperback, available from Owlswick Press, 123 Crooked Lane, King of Prussia PA 19406-2570. These prices include shipping & handling. If you live in Pennsylvania, please include 6% sales tax.

We are not responsible for manuscripts in our hands or in transit. You *must* keep a copy of every manuscript you send out. You *must* put your name and address on the first page of every manuscript. And please: *no* binders, folders, or padded envelopes; and especially: *no* registered or certified mail for which we would have to stand in line at the post office!

couple years ago. Like *that* awful botch, the new *Haunting* manages a total gutting of the story's logic and psychology. Details which had been profoundly and suggestively meaningful in the original (both novel and film) are turned into absurd coincidences. Brilliant writing has become fluent cliché. If the new version were only, as with the new *Psycho*, a reverential copy of a past masterpiece, it would be, at least, harmless, useless, and swiftly forgotten. But we're not so lucky.

In this case, for all Horror may be making more of a comeback, it would seem that Hollywood has learned nothing.

But next on the agenda comes *The Blair Witch Project*, an astonishingly successful low-budget film which may well be the *Night of the Living Dead* of the '90s. This is an interesting amateur film, a pseudo-documentary shot with hand-held cameras with a cast of unknowns, about three film students who go out to make a documentary about the legendary (i.e. made-up) Blair Witch and come to an awful end.

The film is allegedly the footage they shot, found after their mysterious disappearance. The minuscule budget (about $35,000), the total absence of special effects, and lack of professional actors are all turned into assets. *The Blair Witch Project* really looks like an inadvertently compelling, student effort, a Zapruder film of the supernatural. It is quite convincing as a *hoax*, to the point that there are apparently now whole web sites devoted to the proposition that the documentary is real. But the success of the hoax undermines the *story*. There is no conclusion, no revelation. The film just stops as the character holding the camera, presumably, dies.

The best compromise, in the hands of a more professional crew, would have been to condense the "documentary" part down to about forty minutes, have the lost film be found and viewed by other characters, and then *tell the rest of the story*. But never mind. What is intriguing about *The Blair Witch Project* is not so much the film itself, but the way audiences are responding to it. Of necessity, this is a movie which must work by suggestion. Audiences love it. It excites the imagination, which is what such movies are all about. After a generation of slasher films, *horror* is actually being reinvented.

The strongest sign of this re-invention is M. Night Shyamalan's *The Sixth Sense*, which is simply splendid. Bruce Willis proves that when he's not running around and shooting people, he can give quite a sensitive performance. He plays a child-psychologist alongside an absolutely phe-

nomenal little boy (Haley Joel Osment), whose character's problem is that he sees dead people. It's a ghost story, of course, which could be taken as "realistic" if you believe in the psychic, but in any case it is absolutely convincing emotionally, both genuinely frightening and quite moving.

There's precisely the right balance of explicitness and restraint, and a whopper of a surprise ending (which we refuse to give away), fulfilling Lord Dunsany's requirement that such endings should make us react, "What? . . . Why, *of course.*"

So there it is, the best supernatural film in thirty years, by our reckoning (since *Rosemary's Baby*, 1969), and it is successful. The horror aesthetic which we've been promoting all along in *Weird Tales*®, and which goes back a whole lot farther — to Le Fanu and M.R. James and Arthur Machen and Lovecraft — has not merely survived, but has, in at least a limited way, triumphed.

That we think to be a good thing. Now all we have to do is figure out how to get that new and ravenously hungry Horror audience to read *Weird Tales*® . . .

We actually got some letters at last, which will enable us to have a more lively and interesting letter column. The editorial last time, about Weird Poetry, drew a lot of response, much of which was like that of **Mike Barnhill** of Orlando, Florida, who writes: *Yeahhh! Finally, a magazine that treasures weird poetry. Like many baby-boomers I was bored and bred on poetry in high school English class. Dissecting the classics for hidden meanings left me dazed and confused. My reaction to too many 'great' poems was "Huh?" . . . What a pleasure, then, to find a clear and present dangerous poem like Steve McComas's "anybody home?" where my reaction was a more appropriate "Aghhh!"*

While we're unsure of the precise definitions of some of the critical terms Mr. Barnhill uses, we tend to agree, and recall Archibald MacLeish's comment that a poem "should not mean, but *be*," which we understand as saying that its impact should be emotional first and foremost, rather than as a dry intellectual puzzle to be deciphered.

Nicholas Ozment of Lanesboro, MN, follows this up with praise for The Den in the same issue: *I read S.T. Joshi's column with growing enthusiasm. Joshi perceptively addressed poetry's decline over the past eighty years.*

It can hardly be put more bluntly than Joshi puts it:

"The 1920s are currently remembered as the era of Modernism; one would like to think that in the distant future it will be judged as the period when literature and perhaps other arts took a wrong turn that has condemned entire branches of aesthetics to irrelevance. Poetry is one of these."

Why wait for the distant future?

Modernist and Post-Modernist writers have tried to work their spoiling on prose fiction as well, but the reading public would not surrender all its literature to the exclusive domain of the literati.

Weird Tales is indeed a bastion that has held up the standard of well-written poetry. Perhaps one reason why weird poetry has continued to build on traditional roots is this: since the subject matter of a weird poem is necessarily unfamiliar, bizarre, or strange, it must be couched in the familiar and concrete. If both form and subject matter are bizarre, you have not a weird poem, but one that is surreal. And there is a marked difference, as different as the "story" off a Bob Dylan record sleeve is from a story by Thomas Ligotti.

Thus weird poets have carried on poetic traditions which Post-Modernist and contemporary poets have rejected — if they studied them at all.

We suppose that the main tradition is *content*, as opposed to "word salad," which is the equivalent of throwing a bunch of metal spoons into the air in hopes that the resultant clatter will turn into a musical composition.

But the legendary fanzine writer **Richard E. Geis** recently took us to task in a review of that same issue (*WT* #317) for "lazy" poetry, which seems to imply that he wants everything to be rhymed and metered, with no exceptions. That's a position we are *not* willing to take or defend. We will admit even to admiring some of the work of T.S. Eliot and Allen Ginsberg, and while we like some clear *content* in a poem, we refuse to restrict the form. There is indeed some use for unrhymed, unmetered verse, for all that Mr. Geis would doubtless agree with the sentiment that:

Anybody, just ANYBODY,
can chop up language
into tidy, bite-sized bits,
and string it out,
and call the result
a poem.

But then, what *is* the above? It's surely not prose. There is some poetry where the "music" is reduced to the single device of the *line*, that chopping up into tidy bits being a very powerful

"I've been waiting for you!

You have this fantasy, I know. You'd like to escape the mundane world of regimented work weeks, pre packaged vacations, overbearing in-laws and government restrictions. You dream of distant worlds of high adventure where naked women satisfy your every desire. Come to my world. I'll make your fantasy real!"

form of punctuation, used for emphasis, or even irony.

One further note on this subject comes via e-mail from **Sholder Greye**, who writes: *I am moved to write to you by your recent obnoxious editorials concerning what is "correct" in literature. You are promulgating the same old snobbery and self-righteous provincial bullshit that for some reason plagues so many practitioners of genre-writing, and I'm just tired of it....*

And who, please tell me, bestowed on YOU the blazing white torch of empyrean judgment with which to set aflame anything that doesn't pass the muster against your infallible aesthetic? ... it is sheerest nonsense and Victorianism and arrogance to assert an absolute "definition" of literature against which all that makes claim to it must be measured....

The whole idea of Modernism at the beginning of this century (and, to an even greater degree, Post-Modernism in the mid-to-late portion) was that literature is a PERSONAL experience, a psychological one; a book speaks to each reader in a different way because that reader brings his own experiences and views to it....

Your dismissal of anything you don't personally understand as "word salad" is an insult to our entire culture and it certainly illuminates a source of ... the inbred mediocrity that calls itself "horror" or even "weird" in your pages season after season....

Reading fiction is a simultaneous personal and social activity; it is something done in private, a kind of masturbation, but it is also something shared with others, a kind of sexual union; and like sex, everyone's got his or her own fantasies, and everyone's looking for a unique someone to fulfill them: and we've each and every one of us got our own ideas of what that someone looks like. So don't presume to tell ME what "makes sense."

All colorful metaphors aside, we can only say it's a dirty job, but someone's got to do it. Someone's got to *begin* to do it.

We do not claim that the Revolution achieves fulfillment here. But we do hope to start something, by, quite explicitly, rejecting Modernism and Post-Modernism and Post-Post Modernism, and Deconstruction ("You know what the Mafia does when they discover Deconstructionism? Why, they make you an offer you can't understand."), and if we have to clear away the rubble (and rubbish) all the way down to the Victorian level before it is possible to rebuild, well, it's got to be done.

In the Victorian Age, poetry was widely read.

Kipling, Swinburne, Hardy, Tennyson, and many more had real cultural impact. Poetry was a public medium, within the reach of any literate person. Today it is an esoteric pursuit of a few specialists, dead in the general culture for generations, except maybe in song lyrics.

You have defined the problem of Post-Modernism very neatly: a total absence of standards. If any piece of writing has its own unique, subjective value, depending on what the reader brings to it, then the scrawlings of an illiterate schoolboy are just as valid as Yeats (our favorite poet), so why bother to learn to write like Yeats? On what basis, then, can we reject a manuscript, since according to Post-Modernism all stories are equally (subjectively) valid?

We do not think that a magazine edited that way would last very long, and we think that poetry published that way is precisely why, as Joshi put it, the entire form has been by and large condemned to irrelevance.

We respect your view and thank you for expressing it so vividly, but we still think that Post-Modernism is the problem, not the solution. The solution, we are still trying to work out.

But, lest someone coming in on the conversation late think they've wandered into *The Journal of Poetic Theory*, here's a letter about something else. **Anne McCombs** of Cheverly MD comments about our "Scary Places" editorial, and specifically about the Winchester Mystery House: *It was the haunted house of my youth, as I grew up in neighboring Santa Clara. Back in those days, 30–40 years ago, the proprietors emphasized the "haunted" nature of the house much more than they do now — their billboards showed the house in black silhouette, with a skull formed from the central windows and doors. The impression was reinforced by the fact that at the time, little restoration or refurbishing had been done, so the place was dusty, cobwebbed, and (aside from the daily tours) seemed abandoned.*

The tour guides told the story you summarized in your essay, adding that the medium had claimed that as long as construction continued twenty-four hours a day, Mrs. Winchester would never die, and that when the hammers finally fell silent, so did her heart.

I could not tour the place without being wracked by nightmares for weeks afterwards, even in my late teens. I remember the vivid terror of one room in particular. In the Winchester House, as you may recall, there is a ballroom with two stained-glass windows, each bearing a quotation from Shakespeare. One reads (if I recall correctly), "These same thoughts people this little world," and the other says, "Wide unclasp the tables of their thoughts." The windows were placed so that sunlight can never shine through them, and nobody knows what their significance to Mrs. Winchester might have been. All I can recall of my nightmare was that the meaning of the windows was revealed, and the horror of the revelation — a classic Lovecraftian "Things Man Was Not Meant to Know Moment" — brought me to consciousness paralyzed with terror. Of course, once I was awake, I don't remember what the meaning itself was!!!

But, coexisting with the house's prototypical tale of eeriness, is the other story I heard in my youth. When I was 8 or 10, my parents happened to volunteer to chauffeur the widow of Mrs. Winchester's personal physician, the night the old woman gave a talk to the local PTA. According to her, the stories of Mrs. Winchester were sadly distorted.

True, Sarah Winchester held seances and believed in spiritualism, but such beliefs were very common in her day. (Arthur Conan Doyle, for instance, was a well-known spiritualist.) And she was, without question, reclusive in the extreme. But the real reason for the unending building project was not to appease restless spirits, but to offer aid and comfort to the living.

There was a severe economic depression in California at the time. Victorians believed strongly in Good Works (probably more so than contemporary society), but they preferred to assist the needy by helping them to make themselves useful, rather than simply putting them on the dole. Sarah Winchester, who had essentially unlimited wealth, was able to give honest work to a great number of people in the building trades . . . and (again following Victorian mores, as well as her aversion to the public eye) she did not want any sort of credit for her philanthropy, so she made no effort to squelch the bizarre rumors that arose from her strange project.

So there you have two stories, one of a "grim, sorrowful woman's utter obsession with herself," and the other, somehow equally sad, of a recluse, unconcerned for her own reputation, who nevertheless reached out to help others less fortunate than herself. Perhaps both tales are true.

But we want to know what awful secret was revealed when you understood the mystery of the windows, in your dream . . . what a story that would make!

Author **Andy Duncan** has suggested another "Scary Place" which is much closer at hand, which somehow we've never visited: . . . the ruins of Eastern State Penitentiary in Philadelphia. I cannot recommend too highly a self-guided tour of this monument to folly and inhumanity, which is open to anyone willing to don a hard-hat and sign her life away. It was built in the early 19th century as a grand reformers' experiment, the embodiment of Bentham's spoked-wheel "Panopticon" plan for the modern prison.

De Tocqueville and Dickens visited it, as it was the most expensive public building in the United States to that date . . . crammed full of unfortunates as recently as the Nixon administration. Amazingly the thing has been neither maintained nor demolished since. It has been allowed, like Hill House, to go its pestilential ways undisturbed.

There it squats, a short walk from the Museum of Art and the cheery, sunny green acres along the Schuykill, its massive gray walls a rebuke to all that. Chattering tourists stop talking and avert their eyes as they hurry through its shadow, and locals give it wide berth. Locked inside are acres of crumbling corridors, dank cells, rusted bars, flaking red paint, rickety stairs, all permeated by a nearly visible Usher-like miasma of gloom and sourness and walled-up despair.

But most disturbing of all is the exercise yard, which is technically off-limits to visitors, but, like all other off-limits areas, is easily reached by walking around a saw horse, or clambering over a sodden pile of detritus, or ducking low. Here, in the psychological center of the labyrinth, the eye of the swirling stone, is a nightmare garden of waist-thick Lovecraftian weeds, thirty feet high, their great greasy leaves the size of hammocks, standing preternaturally still even in violent weather, obviously fed not by rain or the soil beneath the pulverized tarmac but by damned souls and tears.

Wandering Eastern State Penitentiary for a few hours is an unforgettable experience, especially if you lose track of time, as I did, and have to hurry to retrace your steps to get out of the maze by lock-up.

This is one tourist attraction you do not want to be trapped in overnight.

Almost back to poetry for a moment, here's a odd, belated comment we just got from **Lisa Becker** who actually lives in a Dunwich Township in Ontario: "A Dunwich School Primer" just freaked me out. (This is a good thing.) I bought a copy of the Necronomicon when I was twelve, not knowing what it was. It just looked cool, like something that would give my mother a stroke and me some late-night willies.

When I finally began reading Lovecraft at fourteen, I was hooked. I have the dog-eared books that I read over and over, and the "good copies" that are kept on the top shelf in the library and dusted with the reference afforded the Bible.

Two nights ago, while my husband was at work, I was sitting here in the trailer with my laptop when a severe storm hit. The power went out and my battery went dead. So I lit a candle and grabbed the first thing I could find which coincidentally (Ha!) happened to be Weird Tales #315. The poem is bad enough on a sunny day, but in the middle of a storm, by candlelight . . . well, it may have been the wrong thing to be reading. . . . Just thought you'd like to know you scared the crap out of me. Many thanks!

Which is very odd, because we thought "A Dunwich School Primer" was *funny* . . .

And yet another letter on matters poetical, from **Mark Francis** of Medford MA, who writes: *The causes for poetry's general diminishment suggested in "The Eyrie" and in S.T. Joshi's essay . . . are perhaps a wee bit pat and narrow. Not all contemporary mainstream poetry is enigmatic, prosaic, or lacking in fire and imagination. That poetry is not much bought, or read or quoted in this country — not necessarily the state of things abroad — may have more to do with the nature and biases of contemporary American education and the media; the decline of traditional arts, and of literacy . . . and the consequences of ever more mindless consumerism ("a nation of shoppers"). Poet-critics themselves have declared poetry's co-option by the academic establishment — as social and economic phenomenon — has had a large and telling impact on the form's confinement.*

Yes, indeed. We are interested in arranging the form's jailbreak. We know there *are* good poets out there. But finding them is the difficulty. We'd like to use *Weird Tales*® as a platform for bringing some of them together.

A moment of silence as word has come (though it will be old news by the time you read this) that **Marion Zimmer Bradley** has just died. She will be sorely missed. She was not only a noteworthy and enormously popular novelist, but a genuine patroness of the arts, who did her best to contribute to the field which made her so famous, by editing her various anthologies and by editing and publishing *Marion Zimmer Bradley's Fantasy Magazine*, which provided encouragement and support for many new — and many established — writers, and which will, we hope, continue her legacy.

Yes, we really got a lot of letters about the **Stories** in the last couple of issues, and these are very much appreciated. The "I liked this/I didn't like that . . ." letters are street lamps for editors, lighting the way by which we can steer the magazine. They may not always get printed in the letter column, but they do enable us to compile the **Most Popular Story** listings.

There were enough votes this time to give us a winner, and the winner is . . . (Unearth the casket, please . . .) "Webmage" by Kelly David McCullough, which is a very impressive showing for a first-time author and what we hope will one day be seen as the launch of an illustrious career. Many readers compared the story to the work of the late Roger Zelazny, which is high praise indeed in these parts.

Runners up (close behind) were (tied) Andy Duncan's "From Alfano's Reliquary" and Brian Stableford's "The Secret Exhibition." And one reader insisted that the Stableford is the best story we have ever published, and hopes it will be nominated for a Nebula.

Not a bad idea, we think.   Ω

THE DEN

by S. T. Joshi

Several recent works by some of our best-known writers bring to the forefront the vexing question of whether a work that eschews the supernatural can properly be classified as belonging to the horror genre. It was not so long ago that some of our pundits were looking forward, either with glee or with dismay, to the demise of supernaturalism: "horror" would no longer exist, but in its place would come some new amalgams — psychological suspense, "dark suspense," or merely suspense. In spite of the perennial (and, to my mind, inexplicable) popularity of the vampire tale, the terrors of the real world — serial killers, child pornographers, terrorists, and such like — would now be the focus of our little realm, and those authors who refused or were unwilling to follow along would simply be left behind.

It hasn't turned out that way. To be sure, "horror" has lately been shrinking as a marketing category, but the shrinkage has affected both the supernatural and the non-supernatural tale. The serial killer subgenre seems utterly played out (as early as 1991 Ramsey Campbell played a pungent riff on it by writing his *comic* serial killer novel, *The Count of Eleven*), and the former cutting-edge category of "dark suspense" has gone the way of dark fantasy and splatterpunk. But non-supernatural terror is not about to yield without a fight, and two best-selling writers have recently tried their hand at it.

First on the docket is Thomas Harris's *Hannibal* (Delacorte Press, 1999). Harris, of course, has never written supernatural fiction: after abandoning journalism, he began his literary career with a dreadful potboiler, *Black Sunday* (1975), followed by the admirable *Red Dragon* (1981)

and *The Silence of the Lambs* (1988), to which *Hannibal* is a much-awaited sequel. In refreshing contrast to the dreary prolificity of some of our other best-selling authors, Harris has habitually taken years to write his novels, and on the whole they are rather good. They will by no means enshrine him in the higher echelons of the literary pantheon, but they are among the more engaging works of popular fiction in recent years.

To my mind, however, none of his works falls into the realm of the horror tale, chiefly because Harris deliberately chooses to emphasize detection rather than the psychological aberration of his villains. The serial killers in both *Red Dragon* and *The Silence of the Lambs* are, to be sure, quite perverse; but because Harris is determined to keep their identities (and, largely, their motivations) a mystery until the end, he only infrequently allows himself the opportunity to depict their twisted psyches — as, say, Robert Bloch does in *Psycho*, making that work an authentic tale of horror. It need hardly be pointed out that this decision by Harris has no bearing on the qualitative evaluation of his novels; it merely affects the works' genre classification.

Hannibal is an avowed sequel to *The Silence of the Lambs*, and it features many characters familiar from its predecessor. Dr. Hannibal Lecter, the psychiatrist-turned-serial-killer (and occasional cannibal), was a shadowy figure in Harris's two previous novels, but is very much at center stage in this one; so is Clarice Starling, the FBI operative who hunted down the serial killer in *Silence*. *Hannibal* opens superbly, with a gripping confrontation between Starling and some drug dealers in Washington, D.C.; the resulting loss of life, fueled by biased press reports, causes Starling to be vilified, even though she acted in self-defense. After years of silence, Lecter writes to her, urging her to resist her superiors, who are seeking to make her a scapegoat. We ultimately learn that Lecter is living well in Florence, Italy, disguised as a museum curator.

About a quarter of the way through the novel, however, things start to go downhill. We learn that the wealthy Mason Verger — one of Lecter's first victims (he survived, although much of his face was eaten away by the hungry villain) — has offered a $3 million reward for the capture of Lecter alive; Verger naturally wishes to exact some particularly loathsome revenge on his nemesis. Accordingly, an unscrupulous Italian police officer strives to catch Lecter, whose disguise he has seen through; but he ends up being Hannibal's next victim. This entire Florence segment reads rather like an overenthusiastic travelogue: Harris cannot resist including every possible bit of information he has soaked up about Italy, going well beyond the bounds of verisimilitude and sounding on occasion like an encyclopedia.

But if the first half of *Hannibal* is somewhat of a disappointment to those who admired Harris's two previous works, the second half plummets into realms of dreadfulness not seen since the heyday of Harold Robbins and Irving Wallace. Several flashbacks portray Lecter's childhood in Lithuania; and we are asked to believe that he became a serial-killer-cum-cannibal because he saw his sister caught, killed, and eaten by starving soldiers in World War II. This may be bathetic enough, but the ending of the novel is worse still. It was only to be expected that Verger's cohorts would suffer the very fate — being eaten by a herd of man-eating wild pigs — they had outlined for Lecter; but Harris goes on and destroys the uneasy relationship between Lecter and Starling that lent such vivid tension to *The Silence of the Lambs*. Lecter, it appears, sees in Starling a kind of replacement for his devoured sister, and so he rescues both himself and her from Verger, drugs her, and hypnotizes her so that she becomes his companion (and presumable lover). At the conclusion of the novel we see them enjoying an opera in Buenos Aires.

All this is really too preposterous. Would Starling be so amenable to hypnotic control? And could Harris really have thought that this conclusion would prove satisfying to the readers of his previous novels? It has become obvious that Harris himself has, after a fashion, fallen in love with Lecter: he takes care to portray Hannibal's enemies as even more repulsive, hypocritical, and avaricious than Hannibal himself; and of course they lack his elegance, refinement (the first thing Lecter does after he settles in Virginia is to purchase a clavichord), courage, and psychological fortitude. And then there is an absurd and irrelevant subplot involving Mason Verger's sister, a lesbian bodybuilder who is so determined to bear a child that she secures some of her brother's sperm and promptly kills him.

There has been much speculation as to why Harris wrote *Hannibal* — or, rather, wrote it as he did. Some think it is a self-parody; others think that Harris has simply lost the ability to write well. I am skeptical of both these theories, especially the latter: the first 100 pages of *Hannibal* are scintillating, not only in their brisk action but in occasional flashes of tart wit ("There is a common emotion we all recognize and have not yet named — the happy anticipation of being able to feel contempt"). Another theory — that Harris wrote this book merely to fulfill a contractual obligation to write a sequel to *The Silence of the Lambs* — is more plausible. I have no evidence of its truth, but it seems likely to me. One can only hope that, within the next decade, Harris produces another novel that eliminates the bad taste this one has left in our mouths.

The plot of Harris's *Hannibal* is so involved as almost to defy description. By contrast, the plot of Stephen King's *The Girl Who Loved Tom Gordon* (Scribners, 1999) can be summed up in one short sentence: A girl gets lost in the woods but eventually finds her way out. This doesn't sound like a prepossessing theme for a novel, and it is not: this little book begs comparison with *Cujo* as perhaps the very nadir of King's work. It is not surprising that *Cujo* is also non-supernatural: King seems to have much difficulty with this form. (He has troubles with the supernatural as well, but that's another matter.) While there is some merit in *Misery* (1987) and considerable merit in *Gerald's Game* (1992) and *Dolores Claiborne* (1993), *The Girl Who Loved Tom Gordon* is a work we would be much better off without.

Nine-year-old Patricia (Trisha) McFarland gets lost with remarkable ease in the Maine woods when she deliberately falls behind her quarreling mother and brother (the novel provides much opportunity for King to wring his hands about divorce, the breakup of the family, and such), and suffers a variety of other indignities — continual mosquito and wasp bites, shortage of food (she lives for more than a week on nuts and berries), exhaustion that leads to hallucinations, and on and on. What carries her through her ordeal, apparently, is her devotion to Tom Gordon, a (real) pitcher for the Boston Red Sox, whose performances she hears on her handy Walkman.

The first problem with this novel is that King takes too many literary short-cuts. Early on, Trisha falls head over heels down a precipitous incline, and much of the contents of her backpack — food, a video game, etc. — are seriously damaged; but of course her Walkman survives intact. King knows that the advancement of the plot — at least the plot he has in mind — depends on the operation of the Walkman as a radio, so he defies plausibility and simply decrees that the Walkman will work. King immediately compounds this error by another one: the moment Trisha turns the Walkman on to check its condition, she hears a news report of her disappearance! This is simply laziness on King's part: the coincidence here strains credulity to such an extent that the entire novel from this point onward seems unreal. We know we are only reading a book, not an account of something that might actually have happened.

Trisha gains the feeling that if Tom Gordon (a "closer") gains a save at the end of a game she is listening to, then she will herself be saved. Sure enough, he does, and so is she — although not for another week or so. King is straining hard to make a variety of baseball elements stand as metaphors for real life; and the most egregious one occurs toward the end. The religiously devout Gordon has evidently stated (and King presents his utterance in pompous italics): *It's God's nature to come on in the bottom of the ninth.* This kind of TV-commercial philosophy may be entirely appropriate for a writer who has himself become a brand name; but to any serious reader it will seem shallow and implausible to the point of grotesquerie. And yet, King intends us to see this as the guiding metaphor of the entire book. In a fatuous letter that accompanies the novel as a press release, King states: *The Girl Who Loved Tom Gordon* isn't about Tom Gordon or baseball, and not really about love, either. It's about survival, and God . . ." How so? How, exactly, has God "come on in the bottom of the ninth"? A bear threatens Trisha just as she is about to be rescued; are we to think that the hunter who clips an ear off the animal, and so

drives him away, is a manifestation of God? The very notion that God has somehow intervened to assist Trisha is an unintentional insult, for it is abundantly clear that Trisha has survived entirely through her own determination and willpower. It would be a good idea if King were to refrain in the future from ludicrous theologizing and stick to telling a good story. And it would be even better if he actually came up with a good story to tell.

Ramsey Campbell has long felt comfortable working without the help of the supernatural, as such grim but masterful works as *The Face That Must Die* (1979) and *The Count of Eleven* testify. His two most recent works — *The Last Voice They Hear* (Tor, 1998) and *Silent Children* (Tor, forthcoming in early 2000) — continue the tradition ably. They may perhaps not rank among the very best of Campbell's works, but even middling Campbell is better than the best that nearly anyone else has to offer. Campbell has told me that the two novels comprise "a pair . . . in terms of shared themes" — specifically, the theme of the peril that can so easily befall children.

The Last Voice They Hear weaves several seemingly unrelated narrative strands together into a unified and gripping climax. The bulk of the novel focuses upon Geoff Davenport, the host of a TV news show whose half-brother disappeared when he was eighteen. Throughout the novel we are provided with glimpses of the shoddy, abusive treatment Ben received from his parents, who clearly preferred Geoff. Ben begins to make enigmatic phone calls to Geoff and also to leave him a succession of envelopes at various locations, usually containing photographs of sites associated with their childhood. Things take a sudden turn for the worse when Ben causes Gail's parents' car to crash in Scotland. He then performs the sadistic ploy that he has used on the eight elderly couples he has previously killed: he uses glue to bind their arms around each other and to seal their lips in an everlasting kiss — a grotesque parody of the affection he himself failed to receive from his own parents and grandparents.

Ben then contrives a still more heinous act: pretending to be Gail's father, he kidnaps Geoff's three-year-old son, Paul, from the television station's day care center in London and takes him back to his home town, Liverpool. Geoff eventually tracks Ben and Paul to an amusement park in Blackpool; Geoff manages to save Paul, but Ben jumps off a tower to his death.

The Last Voice They Hear manages, without overstating the matter, to convey a variety of social messages at once, but its central point is clear: the abuse of children can have lasting and catastrophic effects, and can engender psychopathic behavior years later. Some readers might perhaps wish a more exhaustive dwelling on Ben's ill-treatment during his youth, but in a few deft strokes Campbell portrays the humiliation a boy must feel when his own parents or grandparents — figures whose authority he has been brought up not to question — display contempt or loathing for him.

Silent Children is a still finer work than its predecessor and ranks close to the summit of Campbell's non-supernatural work. The novel deals largely with Hector Woollie, a handyman who has murdered several children; one of them Woollie had buried under the floor of a house in the suburb of Wembley, which he was renovating. The house was owned by Roger and Leslie Ames, a married couple who subsequently divorced. After months of trying to sell the house, Leslie and her thirteen-year-old son Ian decide to move back into it, despite the unsavory reputation it has now gained throughout the placid middle-class neighborhood.

She takes in Jack Lamb, an American horror writer, as a roomer. At this point we are led to expect a hackneyed romance between Jack and Leslie, and sure enough they become attracted to each other and engage in sex not long after Jack moves in. Leslie envisions marrying Jack, who might also provide an adult male authority figure for her wayward son.

But Campbell has lulled us into a false sense of security. Jack, it turns out, is none other than the son of Hector Woollie. Although by no means afflicted with Hector's psychosis, he is haunted by the possibility that, as a teenager, he may on occasion have unwittingly helped Woollie dispose of children while assisting in his father's renovation work. Much of the tension in the novel arises from repeated attempts by Hector — who is believed dead, having staged his own apparent death so as to escape the police — to contact Jack. At one point Hector voices Jack's most deep-seated fear: "I wonder how much like your dad you really are deep down." Later Woollie kidnaps seven-year-old Charlotte, daughter of the woman Roger Ames has now married, as well as Leslie's son Ian; the rest of the novel is devoted to efforts to rescue the children.

The one overriding feature of *Silent Children* — above its smooth-flowing prose, its tense moments of suspense, and its revelations of a diseased mind — is the vividness of its character portrayal. Even minor characters are rendered so crisply and vividly that they immediately come to life. Major figures such as Leslie and Jack are fully formed, complex personalities who are etched with increasing subtlety with each passing chapter. Campbell has depicted the teenager Ian Ames with especial felicity, capturing in all its paradoxical confusion the burgeoning character of a boy on the verge of young manhood. A distinctly satirical edge enlivens many descriptions of character and incident: Campbell is relentless in exposing the pettiness, hypocrisy, and selfishness that can typify middle-class suburban life. Few characters in the novel emerge as wholly admirable. Although the reader's sympathy resides chiefly with Leslie, and secondarily with Jack and Ian, even they are flawed individuals struggling as best they can to live up to their own ideals.

Oddly, Hector Woollie seems somewhat cloudy, specifically in regard to the psychological aberrations that led him to his multiple murders of children. There is, by design, no such intense and relentless focus on his psychotic mentality as there is on Horridge in *The Face That Must Die* or even on Jack Orchard in *The Count of Eleven:* Woollie is merely one of a network of characters whose accidental intermingling has produced the chilling scenario.

I have not left myself much room to study the question of whether any of the works under discussion actually qualify as tales of horror. To my mind none of them really do. H.P. Lovecraft's well-known remark — that genuine weird fiction "must not be confounded with a type externally similar but psychologically widely different; the literature of mere physical fear and the mundanely gruesome" — seems to me to hit the nail exactly on the head as far as the current batch of books is concerned. *Hannibal* is merely a novel of the "mundanely gruesome," while the others are novels of adventure, suspense, or crime. Genre distinctions can occasionally be excessively rigid, and some of our finest works — from Lovecraft's *At the Mountains of Madness* to Thomas Tryon's *Harvest Home* — are those that defy convenient categorization; but distinctions are still important, lest anything that contains a little blood or a madman or a serial killer be deemed a tale of horror.

Harris has worked entirely in the realm of psychological suspense; both King and Campbell have alternated from supernaturalism to non-supernaturalism, but both show signs of inclining toward the latter. In Campbell's case a definitive shift over to the non-supernatural camp would be particularly regrettable, if the scintillating brilliance of some of his recent work — notably *The House on Nazareth Hill* (1996), the finest haunted house novel ever written — is any sign. It may perhaps be easier to create a sense of unease in the reader by depicting children in peril — whether in the woods or in the hands of a maniac — but the particular type of skill that can create a convincing supernatural scenario is not widely distributed among literary figures, and its successful manipulation brings great rewards. Let us hope that there are enough writers out there, whether veterans or novices, who can carry on that tradition. Ω

by S. T. Joshi   15

EMISSARIES OF DOOM
by Keith Taylor

illustrated by Stephen E. Fabian

I

The land of Egypt was overthrown. Every man was his own guide; they had no superiors. The land was in chiefships and princedoms, each killed the other among noble and mean.

— Papyrus of the late Nineteenth Dynasty

"The noble Tayo, emissary of the King of Kush, brings submission and tribute to the Living Horus!"

The Kushite retinue hardly did honour to the Living Horus, Setekh-Nekht, Pharaoh of Egypt. Among the many courtiers, officials, scribes and priests who watched it approach, none was impressed.

The southern ruler had sent an offering so scant it amounted to a direct insult.

Among the greater priests, but a little aside, stood a tall man with narrow Syrian eyes and a pointed chin-beard. His pleated, folded robe of snowy linen was the conventional vestment. Above it and across his chest, he wore a black garment which imitated the pelt of a jackal, the beast sacred to Anubis.

For two hours he had been using considerable discipline not to yawn. Now it appeared the tedious routine might be broken a little by a display of Pharaoh's anger.

He was right.

Setekh-Nekht's eyes flashed beneath the Double Crown. He said wrathfully, "Take this trash away!" said the Pharaoh. "Let the savage return alive by my grace to his master. Tell him Pharaoh bids him send gold from the mines between the Second and Third Cataracts. Egypt's ministers will inform him of the amount. Egypt's Viceroy in Kush will see to its collection."

Tayo stood upright, his eyes burning with a malevolent, prideful glare.

The bearded priest sighed very slightly.

Seven feet tall and muscled like a lion, he had many times the physical presence of Setekh-Nekht, but those watching reckoned him foolish to display it. His voice boomed like a conch. "O mighty Pharaoh! The Viceroy appointed by you died on the day I left Mi'amh. Another, it seems, must be set in authority over Kush. My master and I will revere him —" Tayo paused, and went on with an open sneer, "— as we do the Living Horus."

The bearded priest of Anubis released a tiny sigh. This savage was foolish indeed. His chances of living out the day grew smaller with each word he uttered — with each haughty look.

Setekh-Nekht sat like a carven image for a moment. The real carven images on the back-rest of his throne, the goddesses Nekhebet and Wazt, vulture and cobra, protectors of the king, seemed to wait on his sacred words.

He soon uttered them. "Take this Kushite and beat him with rods! That he may bear Egypt's commands to the King of Kush, let him live, yet beat him most soundly. Pharaoh has spoken."

Six soldiers converged on the barbarian giant. Roaring like the beast he resembled, he broke the arm of the first with his ebony sceptre of office. Seizing another by the throat, he lifted him into the air and hurled him at two more, while courtiers darted back and additional soldiers rushed forward.

The bearded priest remained where he was, amused at this latest show of men's madness. Then a flash of concern crossed his lean face. Rameses, the Crown Prince, had taken a sword as though to subdue the lunatic in person. The Queen stretched out her hand and called him back.

The priest, being closer, closed his own hand on the prince's strong arm. "Be guided, Great One. Egypt needs you, and see, there is no reason for you to dirty your hands."

Young, soldierly, and deeply aware that he carried a great name, Rameses would not have listened, but the priest's touch rooted him to the floor somehow. Tribute fell from the hands of the Kushite retinue, and its bearers wailed on their bellies. An elephant tusk crashed to the floor, logs of black wood bounced and rolled, and a curious red-haired ape scuttled for safety. The keepers of

by Keith Taylor

two fine leopards alone held to their wits — and the leashes of the snarling animals, since letting them loose in the throne room would mean dying in quick lime.

Three soldiers dove for the envoy's legs and pulled him down. Two more gripped his arms. Another two levelled spears at his sweating chest. It required the whole seven to hold him quiescent.

Setekh-Nekht said harshly, "Impale him! When he is dead, send his head back to Kush in a sack of salt."

Taking advantage of the uproar, the bearded priest spoke softly to his attendant, a young lesser priest. "Go. Observe the execution and describe it to me later."

"Yes, holy one."

Frowning, the man in vestments of Anubis watched the envoy hustled from Pharaoh's presence. His somewhat oblique eyes widened in speculation. Prince Rameses was looking at him in much the same way, as he noticed in a moment.

"Pardon my meddling, O heir to Pharaoh."

Rameses said dryly, "You did not merely meddle. You presumed to use sorcery on me, Kamose, for I could not stir in spite of wishing it. I shall ask you to explain that later. For now, tell me why you are so interested in how that man will die."

"I think he is more than he seems, Great One." The priest named Kamose tugged pensively at his chin-beard. "And I should like to know if it is true that the Viceroy of Kush died on the very day this Tayo set forth. Also, *how* it happened."

Prince Rameses shrugged. "This is the first I have heard of it."

"And I."

A quarter-hour later, the one Kamose had sent to observe the Kushite's death came back. His forehead and cheeks dripped sweat. Soldiers came closely behind him. Eddies of gossip and surprise whirled through the packed courtiers, to be quelled at once by the ancient habit of gravity in Pharaoh's presence. The news, whatever it was, travelled as far as the feline-faced Royal Secretary and Butler before he stopped it. Kamose's ears and brain extracted three significant words from the murmurs.

Kushite . . . magician . . . escaped.

The second word touched him most sharply. Kamose himself was widely known as Egypt's greatest magician. Some of those who said it were even fit to judge. Certainly, if there were other contenders, their names escaped him. To their jealous fury, even the priests of Thoth could supply none.

"Is that true?"

"Yes, holy one."

"Tell me everything later."

"Tell me with him," Prince Rameses added grimly.

He mounted the throne-dais again, to stand beside his parents. Protocol swallowed embarrassment. Although Kamose behaved with the rest as though nothing had happened, his thoughts were seething — and they reached deeper than sensation or outrage. These events had significance.

The affront from Kush was not astonishing in itself. When Egypt lay divided, or beset by foes from elsewhere, the vile Kushites had always taken the opportunity to revolt. This time around, they seemed to be testing the spirit of Egypt first. The envoy had provoked Pharaoh's anger on purpose. He had expected to be condemned, and he had expected to escape Pharaoh's justice. That appeared clear.

The important thing was to learn what further plans he had made.

II

The advance which thou hast made towards the House is a prosperous advance; let not any baleful obstacle proceed from thy mouth against me when thou workest on my behalf.

— The Overthrow of Apep

Although he came rarely to the royal court, Kamose stood well in Pharaoh's favour. Thus he had been granted apartments of his own in the palace. He summoned his shaken acolyte there to question him.

"Tell me what happened, as the gods live, with no vapouring."

Two other persons were present; the Crown Prince, Rameses, and a well-shaped woman in the robe of a priestess, seated to one side on a couch, demure and silent.

The acolyte gulped. A rotund young man named Serkaf, he did not easily withstand shock or surprise. Being careful in duty, though, he applied himself to tell the story as his master ordered.

"Holy one, they took the Kushite out to destroy him, even as Pharaoh said. He was bound with strong cords and surrounded by spears. Then he spoke words in his devilish tongue, and the spears became lethal snakes! They turned on the men who held them! Being bitten, they fell down, writhing, and shortly they died. Then the serpents attacked the other soldiers, and in the confusion, the Kushite magician vanished. He was free of his bonds when men saw him last."

"Vanished?" Kamose said angrily. "He's seven feet tall and the hue of dates! However he escaped, he will not stay hidden long."

"Is that sure?" Rameses asked. "Clearly he's a magician of some power."

"Oh, Great One." Kamose softened his voice in respect. The prince might be a valiant soldier, but like most men of action he was too easily impressed by magic. "Clearly. Yet changing staves to serpents is not a monstrous feat. The priests of Thoth can do it. Serkaf here, my greenest acolyte, can do it. I'll have him demonstrate, if you wish."

"There is no need." Rameses drank wine cooled in the palace lake. "Well, was there more?"

Serkaf nodded jerkily. "A thing foul to repeat, mighty prince. Before he disappeared, the Kushite shouted threats against your sire, the Pharaoh. He declared the Royal Falcon would — would fly to his horizon — within the month."

Rameses hurled his wine-cup across the room with a blistering curse. "Words! Bluster! Vile and blasphemous, yet nothing but bluster! Who is this Kushite pig?"

Kamose nodded, bleakly speculative. "That is what I should most like to know, Great One. Who is he? Not a fool. He staged that outrageous brawl in the throne room so that none should forget him, knowing he would escape later — and he spoke words that none should forget, also. How if, unthinkably, he does plot the death of Pharaoh? And if it came to be? All would then know his end came from Kush."

"It must not happen!" Rameses had turned pale. "This miscreant — can he be human? Perhaps he is a demon, O Kamose."

The woman in the background lowered her eyes. Her lips moved in a very slight smile.

"Mortal or demon, he must be found quickly," Kamose said, "and thy father, Great One, must be protected day and night until that is achieved."

"What spies and bronze swords can do, will be done," Rameses vowed. "But you, wise Kamose, can you defend him with magic, if he should come under attack by magic?"

"That is a fearful trust to bear, Great One,"

Kamose said, "yet I will undertake it. If you and Pharaoh are prepared to calm the priests of Thoth for me. They will have fits with their legs in the air when they hear."

Rameses laughed shortly. "We will deal with the priests of Thoth, believe me."

When priest and acolyte had gone, Kamose sat scowling, barely noticing the cup of wine the woman placed before him. She seated herself and watched him from formidably deep black eyes. At last he stirred and tasted the wine.

"Guarding the Pharaoh against a wizard," she observed, "is a dangerous charge. One might fail."

"The priests of Thoth would like that." Kamose smiled darkly. "So might you. If I were destroyed, you would be free, lustful and voracious one."

"I'm sufficiently content in your service. I have lovers enough, and victims enough. That organisation of tomb-robbers —" She smiled. "Perhaps I can help in this matter too? You must discover where the Kushite hides, and I know the Delta well."

"You were its haunting terror until I curbed you, Mertseger. No, this I shall do without your help. It brought me much credit to rid the Delta of your depredations. I do not wish rumours to spread that the lamia has returned. Keep to your human shape and be discreet — or I shall be angry."

"This man changes rods into serpents," Mertseger said, and laughed a little. "I could show him a serpent." Opening her lovely mouth, she extruded a long forked tongue and hissed loudly.

"Do not so," Kamose ordered, adding ironically, "You are human, a priestess, and a woman of virtue. No, others may search for Tayo. I shall devote myself to protecting Pharaoh from whatever petty spells the Kushite may use against him. Two demon-spirits from the Duat whom I control can do that best; the Green Flame, and the Bone Breaker."

"Set them to stalking the palace halls and Pharaoh will surely die," Mertseger said maliciously, "not of spells, but of horror."

"Oh, they shall walk unseen," Kamose said, "and chase baleful influences from the Pharaoh's vicinity, since other beings of darkness fear them. Nearly all others," he amended, "as they in turn fear me."

Mertseger did not deny it. "What is the Living Horus to you, that he should continue living?" she asked idly. "You know he is not a god. You know the Nile would rise each year without him."

"The men who work the land do not," Kamose answered, "and there is too much disorder in Khem now. I dwell here too. My footsteps have been printed in enough foreign countries."

III

"You cannot escape me for I am your fate! There is only one means of escaping me and that is if you can dig a hole in the sand, which will remain full of water, and then my spell will be broken. If not death will come to you speedily, for you cannot escape."

— Story of the Doomed Prince

Kamose's eyes glittered with impatience and irritation. The man facing him also wore the vestments and regalia of an archpriest, though not the conventionalised black jackal's pelt which characterised the Temple of Anubis. On the contrary, he carried a gilded staff with a carved ibis-head. Despite the dignified finery, his face expressed little character, its most memorable feature being a soft, heavy mouth, on which rested a smug expression.

"You are a fool, Beba," Kamose said sourly. "You, and most of your priests of Thoth. But clearly you have gained the ear of Pharaoh in this matter, so if that is a triumph, enjoy it. I only beg that you will waste no more of my time."

Beba chuckled. "You may indeed have little left, O Kamose. If so, it is well. Did you suppose you could hide your evil magic from me, the chief servant of magic's ibis-headed lord? Long ago, unlawfully, you gained your own knowledge by stealing the scrolls written by Thoth himself! For that you were punished, and yet you learned not —"

Kamose took three forward steps, his face black with fury, and caught Beba's throat in the fingers of his right hand. Very softly he said, "Little man, do not speak of that again. You might find out what punishment is."

Beba pulled himself free, choking and alarmed. He retreated from his rival and answered between coughs, "Yes, you speak — like a man of violence, a worker of evil. You summoned demon-spirits into this palace! Why, unless to harm the Living Horus? But now he has commanded that you remove them. Your scheming has come to naught in the face of the servants of Truth, Kamose."

Kamose said harshly, his anger still blazing, "You serve Truth badly. Fools always do. The Green Flame and the Bone Breaker walked the palace for days, at my command, and invisibly, so as to cause no fear. If I meant harm to Pharaoh, it would have been done by this. My purpose with them was to banish and frighten other demon-spirits who might approach, sent by the Kushite. But none have come. It appears he was a petty conjurer from a savage land, a braggart, a liar, and no threat to Pharaoh. Therefore I have removed those demon-spirits as needless presences."

"You had to," Beba reminded him swiftly. "Pharaoh commanded it."

"At your persuasion. Consider that you have the better of me, then, be gleeful and revel in it. I have said already that you waste my time. If this is all —"

"It will never be all," Beba said vindictively. "You will be removed from your priestly office and brought low, Satni-Kamose."

"Not to your level. It is a measure of your soul that you use that vulgar nickname. Be gone."

Kamose brooded in the priest of Thoth's absence. The soft frog had overstepped indeed, when he dared mention the god's vengeance on Kamose for stealing his scrolls of magic from a hidden tomb. So long ago. All of a century ago. And still Kamose could scarcely think of it, how his wife and children had died, how —

Enough. He rejected the thoughts bitterly. The matter of his two demon-spirits called for attention. To invoke them, summon them from the Underworld, the Duat, and give them earthly substance, had been a dire, dreadful action. Even though the possibility of a threat to Pharaoh's life had justified it, that possibility seemed a mirage now. The Kushite "magician" had done nothing, which fairly well argued that he was not able to, beyond conjurer's tricks like turning rods to serpents.

The obvious course was to dismiss the demons wholly from the earth, not merely from Pharaoh's palace. Let them return to the caverns of night in the Duat. They were better there than in the realm of the living. Should they escape his control, they would either destroy him, or innocent fools for whose lives the law must hold Kamose to account.

Still, the situation was not yet wholly clear. It

might not be as simple as he had represented it to Beba — who in any case could only grasp simple issues, and not all of those. Kamose might still have tasks for the demon-spirits, before this affair ended. The risks involved in sending them away, and then bringing them back once more, if he should require to, made even his blood thicken, as with the deadly effect of hemlock.

Two things were sure. Because of Setekh-Nekht's dictum, he might not bring them to the palace. Nor might he allow them to roam at large, idle. However, there were temples of Anubis in the Delta, as in every place which boasted tombs and necropoli. A chapel existed even in this city of Pi-Rameses.

At midnight, within the chapel's walls, Kamose called the two by the light of bronze lamps shaped like dog's skulls, wherein burned oil mixed with powdered mummy from a traitor's grave. He drew blood from his arm with a copper knife. Raising it high, he then traced in the air a hieroglyph more antique than the pyramids. Its meaning was *relentless*.

The spirits responded.

The Green Flame appeared as a shape of emptiness, a shadow with thickness, somewhat human in outline and a bright, blazing emerald in colour. With it came a fierce dry heat more dessicating than the desert at noon.

Although the Bone Breaker did not scorch by its presence, it wore a form still more grotesque to behold. Also manlike, more or less, it had grey dead flesh as hard as leather and wore its bones

on the outside, like partial armour. Its head resembled a malformed, snouted skull with eyes and a tongue. If possible, its hands were less lovely still.

"Welcome," their master said ironically.

"What would you?" the Green Flame asked in a hissing, crackling voice. The other uttered the same question from a throat clogged, apparently, with putrescence.

Kamose had no wish to hold lengthy conversation with these beings. He said curtly, "Somewhere in the Delta a dangerous man is at large, an outlaw from Pharaoh's justice. He has murdered; what else I am not yet sure. Find and destroy him."

Both demons expressed pleasure. Kamose added repressively, "*This man only*," assured them of the pains they would suffer if they exceeded his command, and then described and named the Kushite envoy. The demons demanded to know how even they could find one man in the vastness of the delta.

"Have I not told you that he is no Egyptian? Have I not described him? Few men could be more conspicuous! Yet he has some cunning, and so — where does a man hide a leaf, if he is crafty?"

"Upon a tree," the Bone Breaker answered in its husky, phlegmy tones. "Among other leaves."

"Yes. Among Pharaoh's soldiers there is a corps of Kushite archers and another of spearmen. For the most part they are tall. Seek him first in their barracks, but remain unseen, and neither harm nor frighten any that is not the

man I designate."

"How shall we tell him from the rest?" the Green Flame asked in scorn.

"He's a magician, or what passes for a magician in Kush. You will smell sorcery on him. Besides, he is noble, not common — again, by Kushite reckoning. If he be not concealed among the soldiers, then seek him more broadly, but find him! I am not concerned to do your work for you!"

Raging with unvoiced hate, they departed. Fiercely and long though he had striven to leave normal human emotions behind — and the pain they caused — Kamose felt relieved by the demons' absence. The gods knew he had other things to do.

Counter the poison being poured in Pharaoh's ear by the priests of Thoth, for instance; they would be busy against him. How fortunate, he thought, that he enjoyed Pharaoh's favour to a degree, and that of Prince Rameses even more. But to become complacent about royal favour constituted a great step towards losing it. Even Egypt's greatest magician might not safely ignore politics.

IV

That which is an abomination unto me, that which is an abomination unto me, let me not eat. Let me not eat filth, and let me not drink foul water, and let me not be tripped up and fall in the Underworld.

— Papyrus of Nu

Setekh-Nekht, Pharaoh of Egypt, writhed on his couch and fought to breathe air grown hot and stifling. The pleasure lakes around the palace brought no cooling relief. Hideous dreams assailed him. Runnels of sweat poured from his skin; his fingers twisted the fabric beneath him.

Wildly, in his dreams, he looked for his royal protectors, the goddesses who warded the king. He found them, but not as they should have been. The Vulture hunched brooding on a plinth, her great wings folded, not outspread in guardianship.

Groaning, he turned in search of Wazt, his active defender, the Cobra who turned her burning eyes on his foes and shrivelled them with her glance. She coiled on the floor, head lowered, the hood flattened against her neck rather than distended in wrath. Malformed things crawled in the shadows.

"Help me! I am the Son of Ra! Let me not perish on account of my enemies!"

Bayet, the queen, mother of his heir, heard and awoke in distress. "My lord, I am here! What —"

His eyes opened, but he did not wake. Nor did he see her. For Setekh-Nekht, a naked figure huge in height strode from the shadows, strong past his power to resist, the shapes of evil pressing behind him. A dark hand closed on his shoulder and dragged him from his bed with such force that he screamed in pain. A long black corridor like the passage of a tomb opened before them. His assailant hauled him along like a child until they reached a chamber hewn from rough black granite.

"Do you know me, Lord of the Two Lands, you who made the brag that you are Lord of Kush as well? Do you know me? You condemned me to be thrashed with rods, and then to die impaled, but now it is I who sentence *you*!"

"No! Nekhebet, Wazt! Strike him down!"

Neither goddess answered, and the huge dark shape laughed in contempt. "Fool! Your protectors have gone! You yourself dismissed them at the urging of that other fool, the Archpriest of Thoth! The hour of your fate is here!"

There was a heavy rod in his hand. Setekh-Nekht remembered his divinity, his kingship, and his manhood. Rising to his feet against the awful strength of the hand that held him, he struck once, twice and again, strong blows that went home — *without effect*. Then the rod rushed down and snapped the bones of his arm. Further blows flattened him to the chamber's granite floor.

The terrified queen in Setekh-Nekht's bed heard the bones break, saw his forearm hang distorted from the couch's edge. She saw nothing else, no presence that might account for the injury, and he seemed to struggle against nothing, on a bed of tasselled linen. Yet huge wealed stripes appeared on his body. Bruises that bled, such as are caused by impact against rock, flowered on the Pharaoh's legs and back. One by one his ribs broke. The queen fought free from her trance of horror, and shouted for help with all her voice.

The Pharaoh seemed to hear. Briefly, his eyes cleared, and he whispered, "Bayet . . ." Then he croaked further words.

They were his last. Some unseen force hauled

him into a standing position and thrust him against the wall. Fearful impacts lashed across his taut belly, as from a smiting baton, breaking the organs within, liver, spleen and stomach.

The force holding Setekh-Nekht released him. Spewing bile and dark blood, he collapsed across the couch. Queen Bayet shrieked and shrieked. Even when her attendants rushed into the chamber, and guards clattered behind them, her screaming continued, rising higher.

By morning, all the city of Pi-Rameses knew that Pharaoh had died. As the Kushite threatened, Setekh-Nekht had flown to his horizon, sent there by loathsome murder. And considerably within the month.

V

As concerning the fight hard by the Persea tree in Annu, it concerneth the children of impotent revolt when justice is wrought on them for what they have done.

— Papyrus of Nebseni

Kamose made obeisance before the throne of Egypt, his dark eyes burning like anthracite. The Pharaoh's throne stood empty. Queen Bayet sat in the other, her face and bare breasts gashed in lamentation, looking at the Archpriest of Anubis with haunted eyes. Rameses stood beside her throne, resting a hand on her shoulder. He looked appalled and bewildered, but with his magician's eyes, Kamose saw the seeds of huge anger sprouting in his heart.

"My lord spoke before he died," Queen Bayet said like a stone image; except that stone does not bleed. "These were his words. *The priests of Thoth have failed me. Send for Kamose.*"

Despite his sardonic, self-contained philosophy, Kamose felt a rush of relief. Dying in such torment, Setekh-Nekht could hardly have known what he was saying. He could as easily have raved curses against Kamose for letting him die.

"I am here, Great One."

"What should we do?"

"The Kushite, Tayo, is a stronger magician than I believed. He has taken the earthly life of Pharaoh. The new Living Horus —" (Kamose bowed to young Rameses) "— must be guarded against his malice, before any other consideration. I shall surround him with spells and charges so potent that nothing can prevail against them."

"And the murderer?" Rameses asked.

"My demon-spirits are seeking him now. Soldiers, of course, with all the vizier's spies and agents, are combing the Delta. With reverence, Great One, this vile savage's apprehension can wait. Your divine life must be made safe at once."

"Yes." The queen's voice shook. "Listen, my son. Your father's *ka* was dragged from his body and thrashed to death in darkness. It must not happen to you!"

Kamose laboured nine days and nights, and nine more, and another nine, to ensure that safety. He kept strange terrible vigils, and invoked the Pharaoh's protecting goddesses anew, to watch over Rameses. He sacrificed a great bull hippopotamus to Set the Defender. At the end he vanished for three days, and returned gaunt, weary, sunken-eyed, the mark of great talons furrowed across his chest, but with a look of dark triumph stamped on his face.

"You are safe, Pharaoh," was all he would say.

Rameses, who *was* now officially Pharaoh, and the third to bear that name, looked into Kamose's eyes, and believed, and could scarcely resist a shudder.

"The magician of Kush has not yet been found," he said. When Kamose blinked, swaying on his feet, Rameses said quickly, "My friend! Forget I am a god, and rest before you fall!"

Thinking as best he could, with a brain that should have been shattered by his late experience, Kamose muttered:

"So? He laid his plans well. Perhaps he even had help from traitors. In his place — I should have quit the Delta — taken ship down the Red Sea."

"In due course we shall have him," Rameses said fiercely. "Let not your heart trouble, for I shall order the new Viceroy of Kush to bring him to justice."

"As Pharaoh speaks, let it be written," Kamose said hoarsely. "Well — if we cannot find the magician at once — we know where to find his master, and the one — who sent him on his mission."

"The King of Kush?"

"Yes."

Rameses felt the duties of a Pharaoh and a son pulling in different directions. "I cannot send a host to Kush, much less lead it, not even to avenge my sire! That would leave Egypt unguarded."

"In these days when it has no union." Kamose closed his eyes. "Grant me time to recover, Great One. Then leave Kush to me. When I have finished — they will take no more liberties here."

Kamose's recovery filled most of a year. The Nile rose and receded, the harvest was sown, ripened and reaped, before he was quite himself again. However, he did not wait that long to do as he had undertaken. He waited only days. He considered the King of Kush owed him a debt, and there were beings he could send with that message, his own sort of emissaries; beings who could not be made to wait indefinitely like soldiers in barracks, either. He commanded them and dispatched them.

They travelled by night. Dogs howled in the Delta as they passed. Soldiers on the mighty white walls of Hikuptah felt a cold wind blowing. At Abdu of the pilgrimages, and at Thebes where mighty Amun-Ra was worshipped in the greatest temple on Earth, evil dreams troubled the inhabitants. The demons came to Elephantine by the First Cataract, upper boundary of Egypt, but did not linger there. They travelled straight across the desert within that immense bend of the Nile where the gold of Kush was mined, by convicts and traitors. Their existence was torment, and death a happy release. The demons observed their pains, and in the night the miners heard them laughing. Then they went on. The journey was arduous — even for such as they — and they came to the palace of Kush filled with harsh rancour.

The monarch of Kush slept in his domed chamber, watched over by warriors who would walk into a furnace at his bidding, rich in beasts, gold and pride. No evil dreams troubled his sleep, as they had the Pharaoh of Egypt. First he awakened, and *then* his nightmare began.

Above him loomed a face of leering bone, and on his other side a blank head like a shape carved from the vacant air, burning emerald in hue. The king's warriors lay around him. They did not move. The nearest had a strangely shapeless head, as though his skull had been pulverised without one drop of brains or gore spilling forth.

This the king saw in a passing wild glance, but gave it no notice or thought. His mouth stretched wide to scream.

Fingertips of blunt grey bone closed on his throat, and squeezed with a kind of obscene delicacy, crushing the larynx just enough to prevent any sound above a whistling whisper. Air still reached his lungs. Breathing was not much impaired. The King of Kush in his demented terror failed to make this discovery for some time.

When he did, it brought him no joy.

His slaves found him at dawn. Every bone in his body had been broken, the large ones splintered lengthwise, the small ones crushed as in a press. Not one fragment protruded through his skin, which was neither torn nor broken anywhere. But his flesh had been dessicated dry, as though by days in the scorching desert air. His eyes, like grey pebbles sunk far back into his skull, yet seemed to stare appalled.

Words were seared in the plaster wall as though by fire. Written in the hieroglyphics of the Two Lands, they said: EGYPT'S ANSWER TO THE MURDER OF EGYPT'S PHARAOH.

Far away, the new Pharaoh leaned on a balcony of green malachite, looking over gardens and stone-quayed harbours. Kamose stood beside him. He now carried a sky-blue fan made from a single ostrich plume. This, a sign of great royal preferment, went with the title Fan-bearer at the King's Right Hand.

"My messengers have no doubt reached the King of Kush by now," he said. "No other will blaspheme against the life of a Pharaoh again. Or should they dare, you are protected, Lord of the Two Lands."

"That accursed envoy escaped," Rameses said. "He may have returned to Kush by now."

"Such is my hope."

"Your *hope*! Why?"

"The vile Kushites bury a king's greatest servants alive with him, to serve him in the hereafter." Kamose's smile was a chilling thing. "His magician and royal envoy should qualify as a great servant. It were fitting if Tayo should be given such a part in his king's obsequies." Ω

AUTHOR'S FOOTNOTE: Abdu of the Pilgrimages, where the body of Osiris was said to be buried, is modern Abydos; Hikuptah is Memphis; and Kush is the modern Sudan, more or less.

EMISSARIES OF DOOM

DEADLINE
by R.G. Evans

illustrated by Denis Tiani

It's going badly.

Outside the night birds begin to sing. Background noise at worst, their rising clamor creates only a minor distraction . . . but it will do.

My coffee has grown cold in the cup, and as I wince at its bitter chill I see my face reflected spectrally in the darkening window. Blank. Distant. Lost in my "poetry look," my father would say. "Goddamn book zombie."

My father.

For a man with such disdain for writing — *my* writing — he certainly had a way with words. Ironically, he dealt with his writing son with as much civility as Americans deal with their old and ill. Lock it up. Keep it hidden. Never talk about it with strangers.

Then along came Chastity.

Chastity LeMay, the potboiler to end all potboilers. Page after page of drivel, fluff and rubbish — Mickey Spillane meets *The Perils of Pauline* with a healthy dose of *007* thrown in for good measure. All the pulpy nonsense my father loved to read in all those terrible dog-eared paperbacks he'd leave in stacks on the back of the toilet for me to find, torturous traps set for his shameful poet son. But of course, I read them all, drinking in great sour drafts, cringing at their coarseness but reeling in their heady addictive spell.

Chastity LeMay. The only thing I ever wrote that my father admitted to liking. Every word of it written in longhand just for him.

But now the words seem to be dying, just as my father did. The note pad sits mockingly empty, and my fingers feel meaty and numb around the pencil.

It's going badly. The next chapter of *Chastity LeMay* — Chapter 427 — is due today, but the words just will not come.

Still, I'll have to hurry if I'm to finish it on time.

My father will be here soon.

Chastity was born out of ego and desperation, a child of scorn.

Her birth began with a phone call.

The electronic trill awakened me so abruptly that my hand, sodden and half-dead from sleep, knocked the receiver from the cradle. As I groped blindly for it, I glanced at the clock — almost three a.m., late even by my insomniac standards. Still groggy, I mumbled something incoherent into the phone.

"Todd?"

My brother's voice. Shocked into alertness, I bolted up in bed. Jerry and I only spoke in times of tragedy. The last time had been Mom's funeral nearly two years before. I wanted to tell him to leave me alone, that whatever it was, I didn't want to hear it. But my throat felt tight and dry, and I could only listen.

"Todd, it's dad. Cancer. The doctors say he's dying."

My family. We are all of us poets.

"He's in Briarwood, Todd."

"Briarwood?" I remembered my mother's last weeks spent in that soul-less place, the cloying scent of Pine-Sol covering the stench of death as unconvincingly as white-wash splashed on rotting wood. "How the hell could you put him in there after —"

"It's too much for Linda and me alone. We learned that with Mom. And you, well . . ."

"Yeah, and me." My father would sooner cut his own throat than admit he needed any help from me.

"You'd better go soon if you want to see him, Todd. He doesn't have long."

The phone clicked with a chilling finality, and I knew I would see Jerry soon.

At my father's funeral.

Briarwood Convalescent Home lay hidden well off the main road at the end of a secluded gravel track lined impressively on either side by towering elms. The car crunched along the gravel, sending up a white cloud of dust behind, obscuring the way in even further from any curious highway drivers. Driving reluctantly on, I thought of the old line about the three most important things in real estate being location, location, and location.

Briarwood's location was perfect. Just like its residents: out of sight, out of mind.

Out of *my* mind.

I thought about turning around, ignoring Jerry's phone call and saving myself and my father the trouble this visit would surely cause. Instead, I eased the car into a parking space, mechanically got out and went inside the home.

Sensory overload greeted me inside. The smell of disinfectant hung in the air like mustard gas, causing my nose to burn and making my eyes tear. Electronic bells chimed in cryptic sequences, calling attendants to rooms, sending nurses from station to station.

And, of course, the troops were all there. They sat hunched in wheelchairs at their posts along the corridor, slumping to one side or the other. Many slept, but some sat embroiled in conversations they had held decades ago, gesturing wildly as they spoke, breathing laboriously as they paused for their cruel children or unfaithful spouses or long dead parents to deliver their well-rehearsed lines. In a TV lounge to the left, a small crew huddled around a dusty Motorola gazing somnolently at Lassie coming home for the eight thousandth time. No familiar faces among them; they were this year's models.

My mother's class had all graduated long ago.

"May I help you?"

Startled, I pivoted and found myself eye-to-eye with a thin nurse, her face as ghostly pale as her uniform, her lipstick a stark red wound slashed across her face.

"Y-yes," I said. "Geisinger. Gerald Geisinger. I understand he was admitted yesterday. I'm his son."

Her nose wrinkled in disapproval as she scanned me from head to toe, her head twitching birdlike on the stalk of her neck. "Room 211."

Moving through the corridors and stairwells of Briarwood, I felt strangely dissociated but vaguely — sickeningly — at home, like Scrooge being led by a ghostly guide through his own past.

Or future.

But here I had no guide, so when I found myself nearing the wing where my mother had died, I stopped and considered taking a look into her room. I half-imagined I would see her there as she had been at the end: her cheeks sunken and gray; a gauzy, sticky film obscuring her left eye, her right swollen shut; her lips silently moving in one of the exclusive, one-sided conversations held by Briarwood's damned.

I took a deep breath and moved on to room 211.

My father's room was like all the others. Semi-private. White walls, white curtains, white heads lying in white beds. I walked past his roommate, a shapeless form crumpled under the sheets, stood between the curtained window and my father's bed, and looked down at him.

He looked very small lying there, but otherwise not much different than the last time I had seen him. Thick waves of white hair swept back from his high sun-spotted brow. A network of lines ("laugh lines" they would be called on anybody else, but on my father they were simply wrinkles) fanned out from the corners of his eyes, and two deep gorges were etched from the corners of his mouth down toward the hard angular ridges of his jaw. Suddenly, unexpectedly, I wanted to touch those lines, to feel the coarseness of that tanned leathery skin, to caress the face of the man that was my father. I reached out toward him —

He opened his eyes.

I jumped back as if some poisonous desert snake lay coiled on the pillow. The movement startled him, and his eyes moved frantically from side to side before squinting up at where I stood in the light of the window.

"Jerry?"

"No, Dad, it's me."

A shadow passed over his gray eyes and his head sunk back down into the pillow. "Oh."

One syllable told me volumes. Things hadn't changed. It was no better now than the last time we met. And why? What had I done to earn his resentment?

I wrote. I didn't farm. I wrote. I didn't twist lugs on an assembly line. I wrote. I didn't drive a forklift or carry freight over-the-road or make big ones out of little ones down at the quarry.

It was all ready to come out — I could feel myself preparing to lambaste this dying old man — when he spoke again.

"They took my glatheth. I can't thee a god-damned ting."

Then I saw that I was wrong. He didn't look the same at all. The Coke-bottle glasses he always wore lay on the night stand behind him just out of his reach. Without them, his eyes looked distant and weak and his whole face seemed withered, smaller. And the glasses weren't the only things "they" had taken: his upper plate had been removed, probably safely soaking in a cup in the night stand drawer. That explained his lisp. It also helped explain my sudden strange sensation that I was talking with a shrunken head left lying on the pillow.

"What time ith it?"

I looked at my watch. "Uh, it's —"

The words died. I saw my father withdraw a frail, palsied hand from beneath the sheets and squint at his bare wrist where there was no watch.

And then I knew.

It had become my mother's habit in her last days. Eight, nine times every hour, she would drag the tarnished old Westclock off the night stand, gaze forlornly into its scratched crystal, and put it back on the stand with a sigh that seemed to issue from the center of all her pain. Then, a few moments later, she would repeat the ritual, then sit fidgeting nervously until the next time she checked the clock. I never knew if she were counting the hours she had lain there, or imagining what minutes she had left.

And now her habit had become my father's.

"Damn it, I athked what time ith it?"

I told him and he sighed my mother's sigh.

"Can't thee the TV. There'th nobody here to talk to. And now they've thtole my glatheth. Can't even read."

I looked down into his pale eyes tangled in their net of wrinkles and realized with a pang of sadness that they had read their last trash novel.

Then, as if from another room, I head myself say, "Would you like me to read to you, Dad?"

He lowered his eyes. His shrunken little head sank forward slowly and his lips began to tremble and purse.

He would never be able to tell me yes.

"What shall I read to you?

But of course I knew the answer. Something containing cartoon-caricature men of action and the big, bosomy women they loved to date, berate, and use for bait. Throw in a little implausible intrigue and gratuitous violence for good measure, and there you'd have it: my father's perfect book.

"I'll be right back," I said.

The halls of Briarwood seemed less familiar as I left my father's room. The constant whiteness of the walls seemed to blur and turn fuzzy. The burning smell of disinfectant metamorphosed into the burning smell of black powder and the cool aroma of dry martinis. The faceless shadows that lined the halls in their wheelchairs assumed ominous expressions as they donned guises of drug lords, international terrorists, and double-agents. Even the severe desk nurse with the red

by R.G. Evans

wound lips seemed to soften into a feline Mata Hari, purring through poison-tinged lipstick.

Chastity LeMay was being born.

I took my note pad from my car and sat under the two big elms that towered in front of the home, oblivious to my surroundings. Words came furiously, my pencil moving across the pages so brutally that I wore the point blunt and had to pause to sharpen it three times. In less than an hour I stopped and held the pages in hands that trembled both from exertion and excitement. Then, my heart rising in my throat, I went back into my father's room.

He lay just as I had left him — shrunken, distant behind those sightless gray eyes — but impulse made me hide the notebook behind me until I was seated by the window and certain he couldn't see what I was holding.

"What time ith it?"

I forced the excitement out of my voice. "It's story time, Dad," I said.

Then I began to read.

It was a simple story, formulaic even. A beautiful girl locked in a room, escaping her captor by means of her feminine wiles. My voice rose and fell in the cadences of melodrama naturally built into such tales, and when I finished, I felt a little ashamed that I had actually been proud of such rot. I started to rip the pages out of the notebook when my father stirred in his bed.

"Oh, Toddy," he whispered. "How does it all *end*?

I looked up to see a man transformed. He had raised himself up on his elbows and leaned as far in my direction as he could without falling out of bed. His breath had quickened from excitement, and his lips had parted and quivered like a boy's on the verge of his first kiss. But his eyes ... they had begun to gleam like chips of gray ice and the distance in them was no longer inside the man, but far away — in a locked room where a fiery redhead sat awaiting her captor. I wondered how my father would have felt had he seen himself at that moment.

Because he was wearing my "poetry look."

"End?" I asked him. "What do you mean?"

"There's more to it," he said, more a plea than a statement of fact. "What happens next?"

I couldn't answer him. In my mind, the story was finished, a self-contained little adventure yarn of about two thousand words. A beginning, a middle, an end. *The* end. But how could I explain this to a man straining on his deathbed, desperate to find out "how does it all end?"

"Lie back and rest, Dad," I said, tucking him back into bed. "I'll read you the next chapter tomorrow."

And tomorrow. And tomorrow.

I added a second chapter to my little story and read it to my father the next day. Then I added a third and a fourth, all written in longhand — so disposable, unlike my poetry. Every day I would arrive at Briarwood at six and read my father the latest chapter of *Chastity LeMay*. Every day he would sit up beguiled until I was finished and then collapse back into bed, exhausted from the effort. It became our ritual, and I had written nothing else since the ritual began.

And not once did I tell him it was my story. He never asked and I never volunteered the information. My satisfaction came in the hypnotic power my story held over him, the way he sat entranced until I finished reading, even though the effort took its obvious toll on him. After each reading, he would shrink back into the pillow, ashen-colored and panting, noticeably weaker with each passing day.

But I didn't stop. It was *my* writing, and my father had finally begun to pay attention.

Summer gave way to an early fall, and harsh winds stripped the elms guarding Briarwood by Halloween. By mid-November, my daily visits became shrouded in darkness, and the spotless fluorescent-lit halls of Briarwood became an oasis of heatless light in the gloom of chill autumn evenings.

One night, braced against the cruel winds and armed with Chapter 283 of my magnum opus, I arrived at Briarwood earlier than usual. It was a long chapter — in which Chastity finally confronted one of her nemeses, Ben Al-Hasaad, in a battle to the death — and I wanted to be sure I would finish reading it to my father before visiting hours ended at eight o'clock. Most of the residents sat crowded into the tiny dining hall, slurping down the variety of puddings and strained fruits that served as dessert, but I knew that my father, unable to sit in either the dining hall chairs or a wheelchair, took his meals in his room, so I headed for the stairs.

Leaving the stairwell, I nearly collided with the stark, red-mouthed nurse I had become used to seeing behind the front desk. I apologized for my haste, but she continued to wear a look of stunned surprise.

"Really, I'm sorry," I said again. I held up the manuscript pages and smiled apologetically. "I guess I'm a little too eager for my dad to hear this."

The red smear disappeared as she pressed her lips into a tight little slit. Her eyes held a look I couldn't recognize. Anger? Pity? Sadness?

"We tried to call, Mr. Geisinger. Last night. Your father passed away shortly after you left yesterday. We tried to call, but we couldn't get through on your line."

Of course you couldn't get through, I started to say. I disconnect the phone at night so I can write undisturbed. Then I realized what she had said.

"My father? Dead? What have you done with him?"

"Your brother claimed the remains. He came right away. *He* tried to contact you too."

The red came back, an angry blotch of it curling beneath her nose. It seemed contagious: I could feel my cheeks filling with hot blood. She excused herself curtly and quickly walked away, leaving me alone in the false light of a place where I no longer belonged.

I don't remember turning around or walking down the steps or opening the door to leave Briarwood for the last time. My only memory is how cold the wind felt outside and how easily it caught the pages of Chapter 283 of *Chastity LeMay* as they fell from my hands, scattering like dead elm leaves in the night.

The numbness followed me home. I entered my apartment with all the energy of one of Briarwood's shambling residents. I noticed the dangling phone cord still disconnected from the night before. I imagined voices — the red nurse's, my brother's — straining mutely at the unplugged connector, unable to reach me. I saw by the clock that it was still several minutes till six. I saw the door of the cabinet where I keep a bottle of bourbon.

Even the bourbon couldn't cut through the numbness. Alone in the dark I drank, waiting for the burn, feeling nothing. Remotely I heard the clock begin to chime the hour as dull images floated up behind my eyes.

One: Chastity LeMay struggling valiantly against Ben-Al-Hasaad.

Two: my father's quivering lips and far-away dreamy eyes.

Three: the cold, shadowless hallways at Briarwood.

Four: the nurse's angry disappearing red lips.

Five: my brother signing release papers as attendants carried away my father's body.

Six: Chapter 283 fluttering away into the night —

Something moved in my apartment. I didn't hear is so much as *feel* it: a movement in the air — not wind, but something electric, firing past me, through me. Then a sound came from the bedroom. A rustle of fabric. The creak of a bedspring.

Someone was lying in my bed.

The numbness fled and a hot coil of panic tightened inside my chest.

"Who's there?" I called. My voice sounded thunderous in the darkness, and immediately I wished I could call the words back, just quickly — *quietly* — turn and run away.

Whoever it was didn't seem startled. I heard the bed groan as weight shifted on the mattress —

And then I heard the sound. It was deep and breathy at first, and I didn't recognize it as a voice right away. It grew louder, a sibilant whisper snaking through the dark.

Calling my name.

"toddy . . . taaaaaaaaaaaahhhhhdy . . . come . . . read . . . to . . . me. . . ."

The bourbon became a sudden hot geyser spewing up from my stomach, and I clamped my hand over my mouth to keep from retching. The bottle fell from my hand, but over the glugging of its spilled contents, I could still hear the voice.

"please, toddy . . . what . . . happens . . . next?"

My feet began to move. I didn't want them to, I screamed silently for them to stop, but they paid no attention. Step by step, they carried me toward one of two unwanted destinations.

The insane asylum.

Or a room where my dead father lay in my bed calling my name.

". . . taaaaaaaaahhhhdyyyy . . ."

I managed to stop outside the bedroom door. Sweat had erupted on my forehead and blood pounded in my ears. If I stepped inside and found nothing, did that mean I had lost my mind? And if I stepped inside and found my father lying in the bed, could that mean anything less?

I fumbled around the corner for the light switch, then thought better of the idea. Whatever lay waiting inside, I knew I didn't want to see it in the light.

I stepped inside.

Light streamed in from the streetlight outside my window, and the shadows cast by the wind-blown cedars outside make skittering spider-shapes on the wall, on the bed —

And on my father's face.

He looked as he had the last time I'd seen him: sallow, sunken-cheeked, hollow-eyed. The sheets rose and fell unevenly, and the sound of his labored breathing filled the room. I had to grab the door frame as my knees turned watery, and I felt the hot whiskey rising again in my gorge.

"toddy . . . what . . . happens . . . next?"

I looked into his eyes then and saw it. Distant hunger. Wherever he was, whatever he may have seen, it wasn't what he wanted. His eyes were focused on the sordid streets of Algiers where a fiery redhead named Chastity was making a stand against the villainous Ben Al-Hasaad.

"J-just a minute," I muttered.

My feet led me again. I shuffled into the other bedroom, the one I use as a study. Unconsciously, my hand reached out for the stack of note pads on the desk and peeled away a pad of blank pages.

Back in the other room, my dead father's breathing continued irregularly, painfully. I entered holding the blank note pad elevated in front of my chest, as an acolyte holds the Bible for a priest.

"toddy . . . ?"

"Just a minute, Dad." I cringed at the hollow sound of my own voice. I remembered the pages of Chapter 283 carried away by the wind and wondered exactly what I might do next.

I looked at the empty pages. Whether by a trick of memory brought on by stress or by the same mystery that had brought my father back, I could see the number "283" at the top of the first page. Beneath it, the words I had written the night before, the same words I had watched blow away earlier, seemed to shimmer and glow with their own light.

Then I heard my voice begin to read, and I heard my father struggle up onto his elbows, his rasping breath quieting immediately.

He stayed that way until I had finished reading Chapter 283.

When Chastity had succeeded in vanquishing Al-Hasaad, I heard my father settle back onto the bed. His breathing again became a painful hiss, and in the dancing spider-light from the window, I looked down into the distant pain of hunger in his eyes.

"oh, toddy . . . how . . . does . . . it . . . all . . . end?"

He seemed to sink deeper into the pillow, and deeper still. The bedsprings creaked and I saw the sheets settle down flush against the mattress.

And then he was gone.

Yes, Toddy, how *does* it all end?

There have been so many six o'clock rendezvous between Chapter 283 and tonight's scheduled installment, Chapter 427. Chastity and I have come a long way together. Her battles have taken her from Africa to the Mediterranean and all across Eastern Europe, and she has dealt with spies, thieves, lovers, murderers, and a rogue's gallery of other ne'er-do-wells, all in 144 chapters.

And I have written *and* read my father all 144 of those chapters. I don't seem to do much else, but I am so very tired.

And tonight it's going badly.

Lately, the words just don't seem to want to come. I don't *want* them to come. I don't want *him* to come.

But he will be here soon. Very soon I will feel a bristling in the air about me and a tingling electric warmth coursing through the very depths of my heart. From the next room, I'll hear a very fragile weight settling in the center of my bed, and a tremulous, airy voice will begin to call my name.

For the time being though, I look into the darkened window, my face reflecting sallow yellow light from the blank note pad, and I wonder just what will happen when the words stop coming.

Because it just may be tonight.

And then we'll both learn how it all ends. Ω

DRAGON'S EGG

Miraculously found
In the dark womb
Of a mountain cave,
Encrusted with limestone
From ceiling drippings,

A perfect, melon-sized
Egg of long ago,
Heavy to the holding,
Still warm to the touch
From inner whisper of fire

And if you softly press
An ear to its shell
You can faintly hear
A waiting heartbeat.

— K.S. Hardy

BLACK GHOST

Black ghost floating, circling high
Shrieks announce his passing by.
Shadow follows on the ground
Keeping pace, a silent sound.

Hunger drives his hollow heart
Visions sharp as needles dart.
Instincts heightened, claw and leap,
Desperate dreams disturb his sleep.

Black ghost rides unearthly breezes
Moisture falls below and freezes.
Violent purple clouds of fear
Reverberate and thunder near.

Ancient souls that roam the land
Sense the danger now at hand.
Spells and chants resound this day,
Auspicious omens point the way.

Black ghost spies the scurrying prey.
Dark eyes track its panicked way.
Talons tensing poised to strike,
Tear soft flesh with every spike.

Black ghost feasts on sacrifice,
Appeasing spirits with each slice.
Unfurled wings outstretched in flight,
A black star rising in the night.

— **Jill Bauman**

by Jill Bauman

TO CLOSE A DOOR
by George Barr

illustrated by George Barr

I pray for long life . . . I who have already lived a score of years more than anyone else I have ever known. It is not that I, in the long twilight of my life, have suddenly found the dawn of each new day imbued with a fresh sweetness to make me wish for its continuance. In all truth, I would long since have gladly breathed my last. Existence holds for me not the slightest promise of happiness. It is not joy for which I hope, but the dark pleasure of satisfaction. I would live to see proof that the measures I took against an unknown foe had the effect I planned. Then I will most willingly go to whatever punishment or reward my life has earned.

When first I saw Dorinhild's mirror turn dark, the candles were aglow and a cheerful blaze danced in the grate. Moonlight poured in a silver flood through wide-flung shutters and the room was a haven of brightness and warmth. Yet the glass which ought, by all the laws of the natural world, to have shown with that selfsame light and warmth, was a smoke-filled reflection of something and somewhere untouched by the cheer of that room.

None saw it but I: Dorinhild's aged nurse. The rest ate and drank, danced and laughed, rejoiced in Red Gerain's safe return from battle, joining my mistress — his wife — in welcoming the hero home from the war.

Many were the rich gifts he'd brought to his faithful and beautiful spouse: cloth woven with gold threads, strings of amber and pearl, spices from faraway lands, ointments rare and fragrant, and the crystal looking glass in its bronze knotwork frame.

These were among the spoils of that war, the bounty and the booty wrested by Gerain from the stronghold of that sinister lord who — so years of rumors told — had held the lands northward by his practices in the foul arts. Red Gerain had long laughed at such tales, and offered now his own victory as proof of their foolishness.

All the afternoon had his dear wife posed and strutted before the sorcerer's glass, displaying the new gowns and jewels to all our delight. Truly Dorinhild was beautiful. Always had she been beautiful — even when just a new born babe: the babe I cared for from the moment of her birth. There was a sweetness and joy that made her preening a means of sharing rather than a flaunting of newfound wealth. No one resented her good fortune. Rather, those of us who loved her

were glad to see her happy, considering her rich presents small compensation for the loneliness she'd suffered while Gerain had been at war.

In puzzlement I approached the mirror where it hung upon the wall. I could see my withered face in it, but darkly, as in a window which looked out upon the night. And — as though it were that window — I felt the creeping sense that something looked back at me from the other side . . . something which might burst through into the warmth and light . . . something dark, envious, and evil.

Fearfully I raised a hand to touch the glass and saw the darkness fade swiftly away. The mirror was cold to my touch . . . cold, with the feeling of ice upon a pond . . . the kind of ice which conceals beneath its sparkling surface the depths of ooze, and decay, and wriggling, cold-blooded, alien life.

When the guests had departed, long past the mid of the night, and Gerain and his lady prepared for the bed they had not shared for far too long a time, the thought came to me to cover the glass with a cloak. I did not, lest it be seen as a sign of mourning — an ill omen on our master's return.

The last to leave the room after all the muss of the celebration had been straightened, I was glad the master's great deerhound slept before the fire. I know not why I was so certain that evil had entered the house, for the mirror seemed naught but a glass, and the dog obviously sensed nothing amiss.

Alas for that faithful dog.

The morning found the walls encrimsoned by the poor beast's blood. Hard it was to believe that so much gore could have been contained within one mortal body — even a body as large as that dog's had been. That body itself was nowhere to

by George Barr

33

be found, though the casements and doors had been bolted against the night and those bolts were yet fast and true. Whatever had slain the creature had devoured it entire.

Our lord, Red Gerain, had loved that dog.

He was not a man to believe that which he could not see, and I well knew that he'd not listen kindly to my thoughts of what had slain his hound nor whence it had come. I kept my peace as he questioned each servant and bondsman who'd been within the house. Sure he was that someone had admitted a foe, then locked up tight again after that villain had done his bloody deed.

None could tell him ought to satisfy him, and dire punishments might have befallen many had not a serving wench brought to our master's attention the puzzling fact that — despite the rivers of blood which covered the room — there was not a single drop outside the house . . . neither on lintels nor doorsteps, nor anywhere in the dust. It gave him pause that a deed done so messily within the house could have been continued with such cleanliness outside.

The fact that caused all in the house to shudder was that, in all that spilt blood, there was not the print of a single foot. It did not seem that even a mouse could have picked its way across that floor without leaving a track.

More strange still — and it was something I alone noted and told to no one at that time — though the frame of Dorinhild's mirror was, like the wall upon which it hung, covered with clotting gore, there was not a droplet, a stain, nor a smudge upon the glass itself. It was as though the mirror had been set within its frame of bronze *after* the horror was over. How else could there be blood splashed over, around, and about it so thickly without a single drop touching the glass?

Most of the day was required to clean that room. Blood could be scrubbed from the stones and the tiles, but there was little hope that it could be washed entirely from draperies and cushions.

All that day I kept my eye upon the mirror but saw naught to give evidence of the truth of what I knew to be true.

A guard was ordered to stand attention through the night, and men patrolled about the house to make certain no intruder came again. To my great relief, the guard still lived come daylight, and he had seen or heard nothing untoward throughout the hours of the dark.

Three days passed with no clue to what had slain the dog, and no further strange happenings.

Our master and his lady, having naught else to blame, accepted that a madman had somehow gained entry to the house during the day before the doors were closed, had committed his foul deed, hidden somewhere inside, then escaped during the furor over what he had done.

I held my peace and watched the mirror.

On the fourth day Dorinhild's sisters came to visit: the ladies Faye, Artrude, and Rigga. Rigga, the youngest, brought with her a cradle and her nursing babe but four months old. It slept quietly, undisturbed by the talk and laughter.

Never for a moment was that babe left alone and unguarded. I myself never stepped foot from that room during the visit, and was seldom more than two or three paces from the cradle.

But in the midst of the ladies' conversation, I saw a movement from the corner of my eye. It was but a glimpse of something large that flashed past me, and I turned about to see the mirror once more dark and clouded.

Again I had that inexplicable feeling that something stared back at me. Then, before I could utter a sound, the darkness had faded and again the mirror was but a mirror.

It was several moments, as I looked about the room, before I noticed that the cradle was empty.

Rigga's sleeping babe was gone.

The land was searched for miles in all directions, as the supposition was that the abductor had come in through an open window and snatched the infant while the ladies chattered unaware. The unlikelihood of that was overlooked simply because there was no other explanation imaginable, and I — who was known to be nothing but a superstitious old woman — could not make anyone believe what I had seen.

On the coverlet where the babe had lain was a single spot of blood. From that, I knew that Rigga's infant would never be seen again. Had there not been so many others in the room when it was taken, I'd no doubt there'd have been the same splashing of gore as when the dog had died. But this time the creature — whatever it was — instead of devouring its prey on the spot, had dragged it back into its own stygian world to feed at its leisure.

I ignored, as well as I was able, all of the mourning, the recriminations, the threats, the preparations for vengeance should the abductor be taken . . . all of what I knew to be vain show.

The enemy was within the house and I had no proof to offer.

I had it in my mind to feign an accident while sweeping the room, to knock the mirror from the wall with my broom handle in hope it would shatter upon the tiles. I did not . . . because of thoughts I had whilst sweeping slowly toward it.

The mirror was of a size that — were it a hole in the wall — a man might have squeezed through it . . . but with difficulty . . . certainly not without attracting the attention of anyone nearby. Yet the movement I had glimpsed had seemed of something huge. It had been something large enough to have dismembered the great deerhound. It had, however, disappeared into that mirror in the blink of an eye. How, I wondered, was that possible?

Then I remembered a time when I was but a child and my brother, with his dip net, had drawn a small octopus up from the sea. I had never seen one and was fascinated by this soft, squirmy, living thing. It was almost large enough to fill a soup bowl yet it had managed without difficulty to escape, from the bag into which my brother put it, by squeezing its boneless body through a hole no larger than the nail on my thumb.

I knew not what form the creature from the mirror took, but I knew that the size of the doorway through which it came did not necessarily limit the size of the creature itself. Some forms of life could flow like water through almost any opening.

Therefore, I reasoned, breaking the cursed mirror might prove no hindrance to the demon which dwelt behind it. A chunk of amber is no less amber for being shattered by a mallet. The size of the piece has no bearing on its substance; the smallest particle of it is still amber. Thus, this doorway might still be a doorway in each of its broken parts, and the being which used it might merely flow through a smaller door than it had used previously. It would be too easy to lose or mislay one of the countless shards of a broken mirror, and I feared that each small piece might be as dangerous as the whole of it.

I thought that if, perhaps, the mirror might be cut precisely in half, and the two identically shaped pieces bound face-to-face, the doorway might then be effectively closed by becoming only a reentry to the place from which the creature had come.

But I knew of no way to cut a piece of glass that surely . . . that exactly. And I doubted there was

anyone I could convince of the necessity who would do it for me.

That night, as I was again the last to leave the room, I risked the master's displeasure and did hang a cloak over the glass. I wished there'd been a door I could bolt, but the big room opened upon a hall which led to the chambers of Gerain and Dorinhild, as well as to the stairway which wound up to the servants' quarters above.

In the morning I found the cloak upon the floor across the room from the mirror, but nothing else disturbed. Naught was said to me about it, but I supposed the master had flung the cloak away from where I'd hung it, and that he did not scold me because of my age and that I had expressed my fears to him. Though he thought me foolish for them, he at least doubted not my sincerity.

It was nearing midday when the kitchen maid said that she'd been unable to rouse the butler and feared that he was in a drunken stupor. His door was bolted and — after an hour of futile pounding — it took two strong men to break it down.

The sight which met our eyes was such as would give sleepless nights to even the strong of heart. The man's bed was a pool of congealing blood. Gore splashed the floor, the walls, and even the ceiling.

There was no sign of a struggle. Nothing was amiss within the room save for the blood which must have sprayed from that bed like spume from a breaking wave. That, and the fact that there was no other trace of the butler.

My fears — *my certainty* — were again ignored, this time because the man's window had not been locked. Though there was no sign of blood outside the casement nor on the ground beneath, the unlocked window was proof enough for Red Gerain that the assassin had entered and left through that portal.

It is a mystery to me why men will think that they *themselves* will retain their knowledge and wisdom to the end of their lives, when they are so certain that all others about them, whose hair has whitened and faces wizened with age, have utterly lost their senses so that all they may say is dismissed as the babbling of the aged. I have learned much in the years I have lived, and it was painful to me that my master saw me only as a muttering crone devoid of intellect. Had he hearkened to my warnings, I am full certain much would have been different in the remainder of his life . . . his, and my own.

The thing that had killed the butler had, I was sure, gained entry through the finger's-breadth space beneath the man's door. Within the room it had devoured its prey, then escaped by the same means to disappear through the glass into its own mad universe.

That I found red smudges on the inner rim of the bronze frame served only to convince my master that I had not cleaned the mirror as well as I ought after his dog had been slain. His view of the world did not allow him to see anything which might disturb that view.

As I stood before the glass, later that day, staring in impotent frustration into my own ancient eyes, again the mirror grew dark. I saw my face dim as the eyes of that reflection grew bright. They glowed back at me balefully, without intelligence, without understanding, but filled with an avidity that was shocking. My knees turned to water as I realized those were not my own eyes into which I gazed.

What reflection I could yet see in the smoky glass dissolved and I looked into the face of nightmare incarnate. I have tried many times to tell what I saw; I will not do so again. Things can only be described in terms of what they most resemble; there is no other way to put into someone else's mind a picture of what he has not seen. But details are not the whole of a thing, and to say that something had a *bit* of this, a *suggestion* of that, a *feeling* of something else . . . cannot convey the reality, nor even suggest the horror. I will not again attempt it. Suffice it to say, I would most willingly face the dread lord of Hell, himself, if I could be certain he did in no way resemble what I saw looking back at me from that bronze frame.

In fear of my very life, I fell to one side. And for the rest of my days I'll curse myself that I moved at all. I *should* have died. My death then and there would at least have convinced Red Gerain that I had spoken truth, and he might yet have acted in time to avert further disaster.

Alas, I lived.

Something vast, and alien, and awful poured through that opened portal, leaping past me to the next available prey. There was a flash of lightning movement, a swirl of golden hair, and . . . a sigh. No more than that; just a sigh. And my beloved Dorinhild, who could not have been more dear to me had I borne her myself, was

being pulled through that frame by . . . what? Hands? Paws? Tentacles? Of what? Sinew? Water? Smoke?

I pray that she died beneath that first slashing leap. I pray that she was not alive to feel herself torn asunder by being dragged sidewise through an opening so much too small to admit her. I pray she did not see the fountain of her blood which drenched us all.

Her lord and husband leapt toward her too late even to grasp the hem of her sleeve. His right arm plunged through that unholy doorway . . . and it closed upon him.

That arm was severed as by a headsman's ax, and only quick action by one of his men, binding the arm with a leather belt, saved his life at all.

For those who have wondered, that is how he lost his arm after the war he'd fought had left no scar upon him. I myself have wondered if the very fact that — throughout that war — he was *not* harmed, is not reason to suspect that his victory wasn't so hard-won as he believed. I cannot but wonder if he was not left deliberately alive in order that he might carry home his foe's means of ultimate revenge: that wretched, accursed glass.

I reached up one hand to touch a lock of Dorinhild's golden hair which hung from the surface of that mirror as though each strand had been dipped in hot beeswax. When my fingers brushed it, it fell away to scatter in the pool of her blood upon the floor.

Convinced at last, my master pointed at the glass which had been his proud gift to his wife, and with a croaking voice ordered it destroyed.

His man grasped an iron candlestick and swung it back above his head.

"No, My Lord," I begged, placing myself before it. "Let me! Let me dispose of it . . . and perhaps the demon, too. Please, My Lord!"

He looked hard into my eyes and saw, perhaps at last, that there was sane thought behind my words. "Do with it what you will," he said, "but take it from my house."

I snatched it off the wall and wrapped it in my blood-soaked apron. With no word of explanation, I ran with it from the house and up the path which led to the cliffs. It had come to me, when I saw the creature flow like water from that frame, what might be done to prevent its ever coming again into our world.

That nothing else had come out of that doorway after the demon, told me that it lived in a world with air like our own. Had it swum in a sea like the octopus my brother had captured so long ago, that sea would have poured forth from that open portal.

Thus, the sea became the answer.

I stood upon the cliffs overlooking the dark, wind-tossed waters. Those cliffs arose straight up out of the ocean with no shoreline, no beach, no slope at all. For my purpose it could not possibly have been too deep.

I tore the apron from the frame and with all my strength cast the mirror out as though it were a plate, to sail upon the wind . . . away from the cliffs and the chance that it might break before it reached the sea. I saw it strike the water on edge and it disappeared beneath the surface to sink — I hoped — a thousand fathoms into the black ocean.

When next the creature opened its portal into our world, the water would pour through, pushed by the weight of all the sea above it, in a torrent it could not stop nor swim through to wreak its vengeance upon us.

Perhaps — as I hoped — it would drown in that first fierce rush. In any event, I prayed it would be unable to close the door that it had opened.

I wondered . . . I wonder now . . . how long it will be before the waves break lower on the cliffs . . . before the sand of our shore stretches long miles out to sea as that sea drains away into the evil world from which that creature sprang. I pray I live long enough to see it happen . . . and to know that my Dorinhild is revenged. Ω

Popular Taste

What if haunters lurked in the dark
with night-gaunts on rubbery wings?
What if lines from a musty old book
conjured up hideous things?
What if a vampire on one drop of blood
could linger for thousands of years?
And what if Darkness had shape and a face
summoned by humankind's fears?

I think if we lived in a ghoul-haunted world,
where Cthulhu eldritchly shambled,
where razor-clawed fiends lurked under beds,
and Dracula thirstily rambled,
we'd find all such stuff to be just so mundane,
the uncanny so dreadfully boring,
that readers who crave excitement and thrills,
from writers would soon be imploring:

"Give us a tingling laundromat tale!
The deeds of a bold CPA!
Or spicy and sensuous sales clerk stories!
A pizza chef must save the day!
But *please* no more of this crypt-creeping crowd!
We tell you with every breath,
the vampire, the ghoul, the zombified corpse —
they've *been done,* all of them, quite *to death!*"

— **Darrell Schweitzer**

THE OLD MAN'S FINAL VISIT
by James Robert Smith

The Old Man sighed and watched his breath go puffing out, a long trail in the cold, black air. His antlered steeds heeded his strangely muffled commands as he took them speeding silently over weird lands. Below, hills covered in bare trees marked their passage on this night. Moonlight beamed and guided them along the way, the hills coming up beneath them as he took his sled down and down.

There were almost no roads in the gnarled and trackless country. There was no happy community feeding woodsmoke to the chilly sky to guide them in for another of their many visits. Here, there were only the cold hills and the trees grasping empty air like wizened old folk grasping for a last shred of life.

A lone house appeared from out of those arthritic trees and hooves skittered in nothingness as if to halt their descent to this awful place; but obediently they eased down to light upon the frozen, slate roof. The deer stood uncharacteristically still on their perch. Nostrils flared and huffed steam, and within their eyes there was a spark of fear.

The Old Man stood down from his great, solid sled, and he went along the tether, patting each one upon its furred muzzle and whispering words of encouragement. "Shhhhh," he said. "Sshhh." They calmed, but stared at those dark woods with fearful eyes.

He looked down, seeing through that unyielding roof, through those dark slates and into the house. Rooms stood cold and empty, floors untrod. But there was someone who waited. A pair of pale figures lay in the great bed of the master's room: male and female. The nursery bed was vacant, but something stirred the air: waiting.

Moonlight shined down and illuminated the pale trim of his coat. The cold light shone, glinting from his polished boots. And even his coat was a faint crimson in that frigid illumination. He went to the chimney and into it, descending its black throat. No warm fire welcomed him. Only the silence of a freezing, unlit place.

Magically, he unbent himself from the hearth, standing in an empty room that did not house a gay tree, that did not bear jolly stockings hanging in wait from the mantle, that did not hold cheer for those awaiting the wonder of this date.

His weight came down upon the ancient floor, and the wooden creaking fairly screamed his arrival in this silent night. Overhead, even the steeds skittered at the sound. He peered round, left and right. He blinked.

And there he was. The child was just there, in the doorway of the hall that led down from the attic. Little child torn away and left pale and cold in this dead place. He sighed and blinked again, and behind the child the two who had made it. The parents looked on with flinty gazes that reflected the moonlight and showed the dark, soul-free depths of their own damnation. A damnation with which their insatiable curse had marked their own little one.

"Come to me," the Old Man said, kneeling for this child who had been robbed of his childhood. He went down, prayerfully, his knees resting with a muffled thud, to rest. The un-child stared with the same diamond gaze of its parental companions.

There was a rasp of gloves on coat, and the Old Man revealed his warm, plump throat. "For you, little one," he whispered. Those small eyes glazed over with a crimson brighter than the coat that was drawn aside for it, and it glided silently across the floor where icy hands gripped ample flesh and white teeth flashed like little knives and a great, warm stream flowed: a gift.

The thing that was not a child felt the warmth flow in. It felt the glow of a home that had a fire burning cheerfully in the hearth. It felt the compassion that waxed between husband and wife and parent and child; and it knew the love that had once been its own before curse had chilled them all. Visions were imparted from countless homes, each happy place the Old Man had graced on his endless, night-long journey. There were trees and lights and healthy sustenance, and a sweetness that was not tinged with that coppery stain. There were colors: bright greens and yellows and blue and happy orange;

there was painted paper and glowing lights and ribbons and bows. And toys.

Cold, tiny fingers gripped the Old Man. The small body with the great hunger drew on and on, sucking down those wonderful visions. "These should have been yours," the Man thought, feeling the teeth holding tight to his great neck, letting his limitless strength hold him to this path.

Then, the sky began to pale, barely, in the east. Those cold fingers loosened their inhuman grip, and the small thing stepped away, a glimmer of something lost receding far and away and deep in its glassy eyes. Slowly, it backed away from the great, round figure, and it turned to the two who waited. It went to them and they knelt and licked at its face with white, dead tongues, something like pleasure shivering through them.

They were gone. Vanished back to their places there in that secluded, rotting place.

At the hearth, the Old Man drew his coat tight about his neck, and up that cold, black throat he went.

On his sled, drawn up and northward by his great steeds, he glanced back only once, and wished he could give something more...   Ω

THE CRUCIFIXION OF SATAN

On the road to Calvary,
a crown of thorns wedged
upon his thorny brow,
barbed tail wilted,
he disfavored us all
with a long-suffering stare.

He was a mere child
when it came to pain.
As we drove the nails
through his callused palms
he let loose with a growl
of obscenities that soon
turned to piteous screams.
His musculature writhed
with exaggerated tension.

As the blood drained
from his many wounds,
his scaled crimson hide
began to fade to salmon,
to the splotchy coral pink
of delicately boiled shrimp.

In death he was colorless.
Dull white as an old sheet.
Foul white as the maggots
that swarmed to feast
upon his decaying flesh.

We expected the heavens
to part with blinding light
and a clear proclamation
of our apocalyptic glory.
The sun remained veiled.
The skies stayed gray
with the silent threat
of rain that never rained.

We expected the balm
of goodness to anoint
all of our lasting days.
But little has changed
that we can acclaim.
Taste is less defined.
The pleasure in our
pleasures has failed.

Now we wait, the blood
sluggish in our veins,
the nights ever chill,
for evil to revive and
reanimate our tale.
With baited hearts
and souls gone pale
we anticipate the call
of his coming Resurrection,
the horripilating wail
of his maculate Ascension.

— Bruce Boston

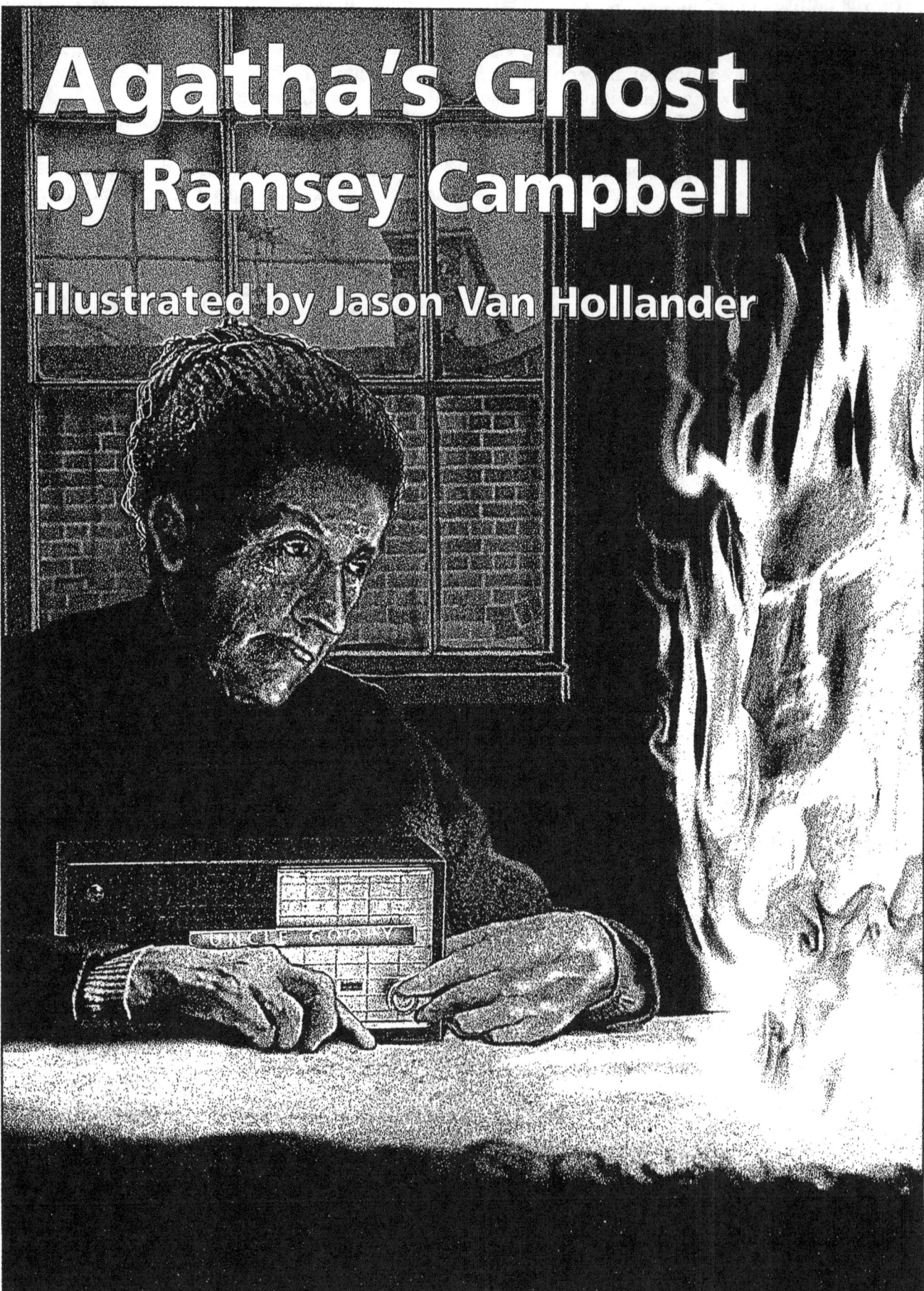

Agatha's Ghost
by Ramsey Campbell

illustrated by Jason Van Hollander

He'd done his best to hide her radio, but he'd forgotten to switch it off. That was the voice like someone speaking with a hand over their mouth she heard as she awoke. She was seated at the dining-table, on which he'd turned all four plates over and crossed the knives and forks on top of them to show that crosses were no use against him. She didn't know if it was daytime or the middle of the night, what with the glare of the overhead bulb and the grime on the windows, until she recognised the voice somewhere upstairs. It was Barbara Day, presenter of the lunchtime phone-in show.

Agatha eased her aching joints off the chair and lifted her handbag from between her ankles so that she could stalk into the hall. Was he lurking under the stairs? That had been his favourite hiding-place when he was little, and now, with most of the doors shut, it was darker than ever. She stamped hard on every tread as she made her slow way up to find the radio.

It was in the bathroom, next to a bath full almost to the brim. When she poked the water, a chill cramped her arm. Now she remembered: she'd been about to have her bath when the phone had rung, and she'd laboured downstairs just in time to miss the call, after which she'd had to sit down for a rest and dozed off. He'd got her into that state with his pranks — what might he try next? Then she heard Barbara Day repeat the phone number, and at once Agatha knew why he was so anxious to distract her. He was trying not to let her realise where she could find help.

She clutched her bag and the radio to her with both hands all the way downstairs. She sat on the next to bottom stair and trapped the bag between her thighs and the radio between her ankles before she leaned forward, dragging agony up her spine, to topple the phone off its rickety bow-legged table onto her lap. She pronounced each digit as she lugged the holes around the dial, but she was beginning to wonder if he'd distracted her so much she had dialled the wrong number when the bell in her ear became a woman's voice. "Daytime with Day," it announced.

"Barbara Day?"

"No, madam — just her researcher. Barbara is —"

"I'm quite aware you aren't she. I can hear her at this moment on the radio. May I speak to her, please?"

"Have you a story for us?"

"Not a story, no. The truth."

"I get you, and it's about . . ."

"I prefer to explain that to Miss Day herself."

"It's Ms, or you can call her Barbara if you like, but I need to have an idea what you want to talk about so I know if I can put you through."

Agatha had dealt with many secretaries when she was selling advertising for the newspaper, but never one like this. "I'm being haunted. Haunted by a wicked spirit. Is that sufficient? Is that worthy of your superior's time?"

"We'll always go for the unusual. Anything that makes people special. Can I take your name and number?"

"Agatha Derwent," Agatha began, then shook her fist. The paper disc had been removed from the centre of the dial. "My number," she cried, not having given it to anyone since she could remember, "my number," and grinned so violently the teeth almost came loose from her gums. "It's may I please go to the party."

"I'm sorry, I'm lost. Did you just say —"

"My number is may I please —" Since even talking at half speed seemed unlikely to communicate the message, Agatha made the effort to translate it. "It's three one six —"

"Double two three five. Got you. If you put your phone down now, Agatha, and switch your radio off we'll call you back."

Agatha planted the receiver on its stand and held them together. She wasn't about to switch off the radio when it might refer to her. She was listening to Barbara Day's conversation with a retired policeman who built dinosaur skeletons out of used toothbrushes, and staring at the darkest corner of the hall in case the twitch of spindly legs she'd glimpsed there meant that her persecutor was about to show himself, when the phone rang, almost flinging itself out of her startled grasp. "Agatha Derwent," she called at the top of her voice as she grappled with the receiver and found her cheek with it. "Agatha —"

"Agatha. We're putting you on air now, so can you switch us off and not say anything till Barbara speaks to you."

The minion's voice gave way to the policeman's, requesting listeners to send him all their old toothbrushes, and Agatha's sense of his being in two places simultaneously was so disconcerting that she nearly kicked the radio over in her haste to toe its switch. Then Barbara Day said in her ear "Next we have Agatha, and I believe you want to tell us about a ghost, don't you, Agatha?"

"I want everyone who's listening to know about him."

by **Ramsey Campbell**

"I'm holding my breath. I'm sure we all are. Where did you have this experience, Agatha?"

"Here in my house. He's always here. I'm sure he'll be somewhere close to me at this very moment," Agatha said, raising her voice and watching the corner next to the hinges of the front door grow secretively darker, "to make certain he hears everything I say about him."

"You sound a brave lady, Agatha. You aren't afraid of him, are you? Can you tell us what he looks like?"

"I could, but there'd be no point. He never lets me see him."

"He doesn't. Then excuse me for asking, only I know the listeners would expect me to, but how do you know it's a he?"

"Because I know who it is. It's my nephew Kenneth that died last year."

"Did you see a lot of him? That's to say, were you fond of each other?"

"I'd have liked him a great deal more if he'd acted even half his age."

"Will he now, do you think? I've often thought if there's life after death it ought to be our last stage of growing up."

"There's life after death all right, don't you wonder about that, but it's done him no good. It's more like a second childhood. He always liked to joke and play the fool with me, but then he started stealing from me, and now I can't see him he does it all the time."

"That must be awful for you. What sort of —"

"Clothes and jewellery and photographs and old letters that wouldn't mean a sausage to anyone but me. He had my keys more than once till I made certain my bag never left me, and now he's started putting things in it that aren't mine to show me it isn't safe."

"How old is he, Agatha? I mean, how old was —"

"Far too old to behave as he's behaving," Agatha said loud enough to be heard throughout the house. "Forty-seven next month."

"And forgive me for asking, but as one lady to another, how old would that make —"

"I'm retired from a very responsible job, maybe even more responsible than yours if you'll forgive my saying so. What are you trying to imply, that I'm growing forgetful? I'd know if I owned a brass candlestick, wouldn't I? Do you think anybody would be in the habit of keeping one of those in their bag? Or a mousetrap, or a tin of dog food when I've never owned an animal in my life because my father told me how you caught

diseases from them, or a plastic harmonica, or a tin of lighter fuel when all I ever use are matches?"

"I was only wondering if you might have picked up any of these items somewhere and —"

"That would be a clever trick for me to play, cleverer than any of his, since I haven't stirred out of this house for weeks. I bought enough tins to last me the rest of the year, and I've been waiting to catch him at his wickedness, but he thinks it's a fine game keeping me on edge every moment of the day and night. Do you know he whispers in my ear when I'm trying to get to sleep? I thought I could deal with him all by myself, but I won't have him wearing me down. One thing I'll tell you he's wishing I wouldn't: he doesn't want me to get help. He hid the phone directory, and he even tried to take away my radio so I wouldn't have your number. He doesn't want anyone to know about him."

"Well, all of us certainly do now, so I hope you feel less alone, Agatha. What kind of help —"

"Whatever has to be done to send him away."

"Do you think you ought to have a priest in?"

"I went to the one up the road, and shall I tell you what he said?"

"Do share it with us, please."

"He told me they don't —" Agatha made her voice high-pitched and supercilious. "— believe in such things as ghosts any more."

"Good heavens, Agatha, I'd have thought that was what they were supposed to be all about, wouldn't you? I'm sure some of our listeners must believe, and I hope they'll phone in with ideas. That was Agatha from the city centre, and let me just remind you if you need reminding of our number . . ."

At the start of this sentence Barbara Day's voice had recoiled from Agatha, who felt abandoned until the researcher came between them. "Thanks for calling. You can turn your radio on now," she said.

Agatha found the switch on the radio with one of the toes poking out of her winter tights before she fumbled the receiver into place. She returned the phone to its table as she levered herself to her feet with the arm that wasn't hugging her bag, in which she rummaged for her keys to unlock the front room. None of them fitted the lock, he'd stolen her keys and substituted someone else's — and then she saw that she was trying to use them upside down. He'd nearly succeeded in confusing her, but she threw the door triumphantly wide and grabbed the radio to carry it to her armchair.

When she lowered herself into the depression shaped like herself the chair emitted a piteous creak. It was the only one he hadn't damaged so that her friends would have nowhere to sit. He'd made the television cease to work, and she suspected he'd rendered the windows the same colour as the dead screen, to put into her head the notion that the world outside had been switched off. She knew that wasn't the case, because people who were on her side had started talking about her on the radio. Ben, who sounded like a black man, wanted Agatha to keep stirring a tablespoonful of salt in a glass of water while she walked through the entire house — that ought to get rid of any ghosts, he said. Then there was a lady of about her age who sounded the type she would have liked to have had for a friend and who advised her to keep candles burning for a night and a day in every room and corridor. That sounded just the ticket to Agatha, not least because she'd bought dozens of candles the last time she'd felt safe to leave the house. She'd stored them in — She'd bought them in case he started making lights go out again and pulling at the kitchen chair she had to stand on to replace the bulbs. She'd put them — The candlestick he'd planted in her bag would come in useful after all. The candles, they were in, they were in the kitchen cupboard where she'd hidden them, unless he'd moved them, unless he'd heard the lady tell her how to use them and was moving them at that very moment. Agatha grasped the arm of her chair, avoiding holes her nails had gouged in the upholstery, and was about to heave herself to her feet when Barbara Day said in a tone she hadn't previously employed "I hope Agatha is still listening. Go ahead. You're —"

"Kenneth Derwent. The nephew of Agatha Derwent who you had on."

The kick Agatha gave the radio sent it sprawling on its back as she did in the chair. Was there nowhere he couldn't go, no trick he was incapable of playing? He'd clearly fooled Barbara Day, who responded "We can take it you aren't dead."

"Not according to my wife. Just my aunt, and that's the kind of thing she's been making out lately. I must say I think —"

"Just to interrupt for a moment, does that mean everything your aunt said was happening to her —"

"She's doing it to herself."

Only Agatha's determination to be aware of whatever lies he told kept her from stamping on

the radio. "I did wonder," Barbara Day said, "only she seemed so clear about it, so sure of herself."

"She always has been. That's part of her problem, that she can't bear not to be. And I'm sorry, but you didn't help by talking to her as though it was all real, never mind letting your callers encourage her."

"We don't censor people unless they say something that's against the law. I expect you'll be going to see your aunt, will you, to try and put things right?"

"She hasn't let me in since she started accusing me of stealing all the stuff she hides herself. She won't let anybody in, and now you've had someone telling her to put lighted candles all round the place, for God's sake."

"I can see that mightn't be such a good idea, so Agatha, if you're listening —"

Agatha wasn't about to, not for another second. She threw herself out of the chair, kicking the radio across the room. It smashed against the wall, under the mirror he'd draped at some point with an antimacassar, and fell silent. She stalked at it and trampled on the fragments before snatching the cloth off the mirror in case he was spying on her from beneath it. She was glaring at the wild spectacle he'd driven her to make of herself when the phone rang.

She marched into the hall and seized the receiver, not letting go of her bag. "Who is it now? What do you want?"

"Agatha Derwent? This is the producer of Daytime with Day. I don't know if you heard some of our listeners who phoned in with suggestions for you."

"I heard them all right, and they aren't all I heard."

"Yes, well, I just wanted to say we don't think it would be such a good idea to put candles in your house. It could be very dangerous, and I'd hate to think we were in any way responsible, so if I could ask you —"

"I'm perfectly responsible for myself, thank you, whatever impression somebody has been trying to give. I hope you'll agree as one professional lady to another that's how I sound," Agatha said in a voice that tasted like syrup thick with sugar, and cut her off. She pinched the receiver between finger and thumb and replaced it delicately as a way of controlling her rage at the way she'd been made to appear. No sooner had she let go of it than the phone rang again.

She knew before she lifted the receiver who it had to be. The only trick he hadn't played so far was this. She ground the receiver against her cheekbone and held her breath to discover how long he could stand to pretend not to be there. In almost no time he said, "Aunt Agatha?"

"Are you afraid it mightn't be? Afraid I might have got someone in to listen to you?"

"I wish you would have people in. I wish you wouldn't stay all by yourself. Look, I'm going to come round as soon as the bank shuts, so will you let me in?"

"There's nobody but me to hear your lies now, so stop pretending. Haven't you done enough for one day, making everybody think —" Suddenly, as if she had already lit the candles, the house seemed to brighten with the realisation she'd had. "You are clever, aren't you. You've excelled yourself. All the things you've been doing are meant to make me look mad if I tell anyone about them."

"Listen to what you've just said, Aunt Agatha. Can't you see —"

"Don't waste your energy. You've confused me for the last time, Kenneth," she said, and immediately knew what he was attempting to distract her from. "You got out by going on the radio, and now you can't come back in unless I let you, is that it? You won't get in through my phone, I promise you," she cried, pounding the receiver against the wall. She heard him start to panic, and then his voice was in black fragments that she pulverised under her heel.

She knew he hadn't finished trying to return. She drew all the downstairs curtains in case he might peer in, she hauled herself upstairs along the banister to fetch a blanket that she managed to stuff into the tops of the sashes of the kitchen windows. Once the glass was covered she crouched to the cupboard under the sink.

He hadn't got back in yet — the candles were still there. She had to put her bag down and grip it between her wobbly legs each time she lit a candle with a match from the box that wasn't going to rattle her no matter how much it did so to itself. She stuck a candle on a saucer on the kitchen table, and found another saucer on which to bear a lit candle into the dining-room. The candle for the front room had to make do with a cup, because he'd hidden the rest of her dozens of saucers. Her resourcefulness must be angering him, she thought, for as she carried another cup with a flickering candle in it along the hall he began to ring the bell and pound the front door with the rusty knocker.

"Aunt Agatha," he called, "Aunt Agatha," in a voice that didn't stay coaxing for long. He tried sounding apologetic, plaintive, commanding, worse of all concerned, but she gritted her teeth until he started prowling around the outside of the house and thumping on the windows. "Go away," she cried at the blotch that dragged itself over the curtains, searching for a crack between them. "You won't get in."

He did his best to distress her by shaking the handle of the back door while he made his knuckles sound so hard against the wood that she was afraid he might punch his way through. The illusion must have been his latest trick, because all at once she heard his footsteps growing childishly small on the front path, and the clang of the garden gate.

She held onto the banisters for a few moments, enjoying the peace, though not once she became aware of his having made her smash the phone. If she hadn't, might he have been trapped in it for ever? Suppose he'd angered her so as to trick her into releasing him? She hugged the bag while she stooped painfully to retrieve the cup with the candle in it from the floor.

She was less than halfway up the stairs when the flame began to flutter. She took another laborious step and knew he was in the house. All his play-acting outside had been nothing but an attempt to befuddle her. "Stop your puffing," she cried as the flame dipped and jittered, "don't you puff me." It shook, it bent double and set the wax flaring, and now she was in no doubt that he wasn't just in the house; he'd crept up behind her — he was waiting for her to be unable to bear not to look. She swung around without warning and thrust the candle into his face. "See how you like —"

But he'd snatched his face away as though it had never been there. Nothing was in front of her except the air into which the cup and its candle thrust, too far. The shock loosened her grip on her bag. She tried to catch it and keep hold of the cup as the latter pulled her off her feet. The bag fell, then the candle, and she could only follow them.

She didn't know if the candle went out as she did. She didn't know anything for she didn't know how long. When she grew aware of darkness, she found she was afraid to discover how much pain she might be in. Then she understood that she was fully conscious, and there was no pain, nor anything to feel it. He'd got the best of her in every way he could. He'd stolen her bag, and her house, and her body as well.

She was in the midst of the remains of the house, a few charred fragments of wall protruding from the sodden earth. All around her were houses, but she couldn't go to her neighbours; she wouldn't have them see her like this, if they could see her at all. None of them had believed her when she'd tried to tell them about Kenneth. For a moment she thought he'd left her with nowhere to go, and then she realised who would believe in her: those who already had.

She heard their voices as they'd sounded on the radio. They weren't just memories, they were more like beacons of sound, and her sense of them reached across the night, urging her to venture out and find them. She felt as she had when she was very young and on the edge of sleep — that she could go anywhere and do anything. She was free of Kenneth at last, that was why; and yet now that he was gone she was tempted to play a few of his tricks, in memory of him and to prove she still existed. Maybe this was her second childhood, she thought as she scurried like the shadow of a spider across the city to seek out her new friends.   Ω

THE BOOK THAT MUST NOT BE READ

The page that must never be turned
In The Book That Must Not Be Read
Is writ in the blood of the author
In sentences best left unsaid.

'Twas penned without any quill
In the place that cannot be found
By the man who never was born.
Conundrums and cautions abound.

The parchment that must not be touched
Is filled with words not to speak.
The index is creeping and crawling
With references no one dare seek.

Those covers best left unopened
Are sealed by a lock without key.
The binding that no hand must fondle
conceals things not meant to be.

The names that must never be spoken,
The knowledge best left unknown,
The spells that must not be broken
By creatures of flesh and of bone,

Let them sleep in leather-bound covers,
Let them lie with the cold and the dead,
With the words that must never be uttered
In The Book That Must Not Be Read.

— **Joseph F. Pumilia**

OUR LADY OF THE UNICORN

Litanie en l'honneur d'Elle
"A mon seul désir." (To my one desire)
Motto from late mediæval tapestry.

I

She holds forevermore in fee
All tides, all treasures, of the sea,
But never would she flout or scorn
The empire of the rose and thorn,
Or yet the kingdoms of the dew,
Nor those of cypress and the yew.

She of the pure and only horn,
Our Lady of the Unicorn.

II

Where coldest ocean currents run
In seas below the midnight sun,
Cloud-borne, she hovers in the air
To watch the sport and frolic there
Of one-horned narwhals through the waves
Like jousting knights with ivory staves.

She of the pure and only horn,
Our Lady of the Unicorn.

III

Where gardens gleam with rose and leaf,
With promise of delight and grief,
She stands amid the shadowed brake
By fountains gushing near a lake,
To wait of that One sure to come,
Driven there by his heart's own drum.

She of the pure and only horn,
Our Lady of the Unicorn.

IV

Where morning dew and evening dew
With gems and filigree bestrew
Their traceries, their treasure-troves,
Upon the fields, upon the groves,
She skims above the level grass
Like phantom gliding over glass.

OUR LADY OF THE UNICORN

She of the pure and only horn,
Our Lady of the Unicorn.

V

Where graveyard cypress, graveyard yew,
And grimmest ilex-oak endue
The silent space between the tombs
With but the purest gloom of glooms,
She watches through the midnight hours
To heed the bloom of ebon flowers

She of the pure and only horn,
Our Lady of the Unicorn.

VI

Attended in her tented bourn
By maiden, lion, unicorn,
She looms inside the tapestry
Amid its figured imagery —
Where, summing all of love and fear,
The motto reads: *A mon seul désir.*

She of the pure and only horn
Our Lady of the Unicorn

VII

So thus and yea — yes, in this way —
To trumpets or to lutes at play,
Whether by night or yet by day,
She holds forever more in fee
All tides, all treasures, of the sea,
But never would she flout or scorn
The empire of the rose and thorn,
Or yet the kingdoms of the dew,
Nor those of cypress and the yew.

She of the pure and only horn
Our Lady of the Unicorn

Elle de l'unique et pure corone,
Voilá Notre-Dame á la Licorne.
— **Donald Sidney-Fryer**

CHRISTMAS STALKING
by James Van Pelt

illustrated by George Barr

I take the unusual assignments, so I wasn't all that surprised when a Tampa mob boss who was up to his elbows into skimming the profits of several prominent toy companies contacted me to make the Santa hit. The fat guy'd been cruising on luck for years anyway. He'd cold cocked the union movement among the elves, and he'd cut the dock workers and truckers out of his operation from the beginning, so he probably knew it was coming.

That Santa, though. He's a tough old son of a bitch. I suppose I should have known that. He's been a long time on the job

Seemed like a pretty easy score to me. I mean I've had to do some doozies. Picking off the Easter Bunny at 500 yards, for example. That took artistry. And the Tooth Fairy had eyes in the back of her head, but the fat guy, Hell, he's as big as a house, and I knew where he'd be and when he'd be there.

So I picked out my gear. Now a lot of guys go for single-shot rifles. Those finely bored Mausers are pretty popular. They break down easy, are dead accurate at any distance, and depending on your load, they can go for high penetration or knock down. I like the .45 caliber El-hal-Alamine however, a Turkish magazine loader that can zip twelve 540-grain titanium jacketed hollow points in four seconds on autoload. Of course, no one would clear the magazine all at once: it kicks hard and to the left, but I can put all twelve shots into a four inch circle at a thousand yards in fifteen seconds if the wind is calm.

To Hell with style points, I say. You've got a job to do, and you want to make sure it gets done. Nobody pays for a wounded mark, and there aren't any bonuses for saving on ammo in this profession. I don't care what the movies might make you think.

So I set up in a back-yard tree-house in Arden Hills, a pricey, Chicago subdivision filled with fake-colonial two-stories. From my vantage I had a clear bead on three chimneys, although I knew that I'd only get the one chance. My scope was a 60-power Verstaadt-Bern with a good anti-fog polish on the lenses. Cold weather

set-up, I couldn't risk condensation at a key point. Street lights would give me plenty of light, I figured. What I didn't figure on was the snow.

About 11:30, the front pushed through. I had a sleeping bag wrapped around my shoulders, and a thermos of Brazilian Black laced with a touch of rum beside me. Big, sloppy wet flakes fell at first. Christmas lights on the houses up and down the streets wrapped themselves in a layer of fuzzy color and visibility dropped right off. I didn't really mind at first until the snow swallowed my view of a suburban sweet tart whose unshaded bedroom window a block away I'd been scoping pretty regular. Guess it hadn't occurred to her when she went to shower that a guy with time on his hands would camp out in the neighbor's tree house. Then pretty soon all I've got for sure is the back of the closest house and its chimney. I'm getting nervous because I don't have time to set up somewhere new, and it'd be twelve months before the old boy would come out again. No hope for an off-season score. He's got that North Pole hidey-hole locked down tight as Fort Knox.

But the temperature kept dropping, and the flakes turned into those dry, little pellet things that sound like sand bouncing off your hat. I could see better, but it was darn cold, and the wind kicked up. I checked my load again. It's a habit. Don't want to be lined up for the chance and click on an empty chamber.

Somewhere I hear some caroling. Group of church kids, I suppose, since first it's "Hark the Herald Angels," and then "Silent Night," and then "Little Town of Bethlehem." I've got the piece resting on my knees, pointing in the right general direction, but my hands are jammed up under my arm pits. Can't wear gloves. Not even those thin-leathered Italian ones. Just never have been able to do that. You see a lot of wrong stuff in movies about aiming a rifle, and they all make it look easier than it is. It's in the squeeze, you know, and if I'm wearing gloves, my squeeze is off. Even at a hundred yards, I could miss. So now I've got all kinds of things to worry about.

It's getting way cold, and I'm thinking about temperature changes in my scope and barrel. Hell, the firing mechanism is filled with high-tech, mono-filament carbon alloys, and I don't know if they're tested at ten-below.

Then, there's the wind. It's steady, and not all that bad (if it weren't the dead of a Chicago winter!), but it's a cross breeze. On top of that, the visibility might go again.

These mob guys, they don't like disappointments. Hell, I can just see me now saying, "It was cold and windy." And he'd say, "Do you know how much you cost me this year?"

I hear those Tampa guys don't kill you before they dump you in the bay. They slice you up a bit, drop you a couple of miles off shore, then make bets on how far you can swim before the sharks get you.

So I'm sitting there with all of these bad thoughts running through my head, and it feels like my butt is turning into an ice sculpture, when the fat guy makes his appearance on the roof across the yard. It's spooky. Not a sound. No sleigh bells. Nothing. One minute it's a bare roof with snow curling around the chimney, and the next there's a regular stock-yard snorting steam into the frosty air, a honking big sleigh, and the fat guy slinging a bag over his shoulder.

I scope him. Cross hairs over his heart. He's got tiny glasses perched on his nose, and he's checking this list he's holding. The snow is bad — it's screwing up the light — and he's mostly a silhouette. I'm afraid I won't get the shot before he scoots down the chimney, but he checks the list twice, and I adjust for windage and squeeze real gentle.

He moved. The shot went anyway. I couldn't hold it back. The reindeer start, but they don't run. Their heads are up, ears up. Disciplined though: they don't go anywhere, and the fat guy is behind the chimney, peeking over the top in my direction.

I drop the cross hairs on him and take four more chances real quick. Three in the wind and one powders a hunk of mortar off the corner. He's gone. I'm hoping that maybe I got him and he's tumbled off the backside of the house, but I know I didn't. You can hear a bullet hit. None of these did.

So where is he? I scan the roof. Nothing. Just shadowy reindeer and the sleigh. Windows in the house are dark, but lights are popping on all over the neighborhood. Don't hear any caroling now. Then a curtain moves. Streetlight catches it. It's

him. How'd he get in? I swing the rifle down. Too late. He's long gone.

So I'm thinking, where's he going to go next, and all I figure is that he's got to come out the chimney.

I settle in, brace the rifle, and hold it steady on the target. Even in the blowing snow, it's clear. It's spooky how bad the light is, though. If it weren't snowing, the street lights would be enough, but everything is dark and indistinct now. The sleigh's a hump in the snowy eddies. The reindeer are black on black. My eyes water a little, so I blink them dry. Don't feel cold now. My cheeks are burning, while my hand is calm and cool. Finger resting on the trigger. Gun stock firmly placed. Head a bit to the side. Everything focused in on that bit of roof and the top of the chimney.

He's got to come. He has no choice.

Then, there's movement. A rounded silhouette pushes out the chimney. It's like candy. I empty the magazine, seven flat reports, starting from the top and working my way half way down the brick and mortar. I've got the penetration. Titanium jackets don't even flatten on the way through.

I watch for a second. He's slumped over the top.

Things are getting serious in the neighborhood though. Lights on all over the place. Some distant shouting. Doors opening. A couple of sirens in the distance. Wind picks up again and the snow is fierce.

My gun breaks down in three sections and goes into the case.

A job goes in parts: the setup, the chance, and the getaway. I'm getting ready to go down the tree when I glance up at the house. Something's moving at one of the windows. It opens. I grab just the scope out of my case and check it out.

I should have known. After all, he's been in the business a long time. It's the fat guy. He looks my way and waves. How'd he know I'd have the gun put away by now? Then he climbs up the side of the house. Pretty creepy to see a guy that big move like that. Then he pulls his bag out of the chimney. He piles it onto the sleigh, and he's gone.

You'll pardon me if I thought his "Ho, ho, ho," was a little mocking.

Five hours later, I unlock my condo, thinking about how much money I have deposited in accounts out of the states, and wondering if there's any chance of booking a flight during the heavy, holiday travel season. I turn on the lights, and there, nailed to my mantle, is a Christmas stocking. I live by myself, and I don't do Christmas decorations. I approach cautiously. In it is a brand new, Baush & Laumb night-vision riflescope. I turn its polished mechanisms over in my hand. If I'd predicted the snow, it's the tool I would have needed to make tonight's hit. I'd have known that wasn't the fat guy coming out of the chimney. Despite myself, I laugh. You've got to appreciate a guy with a sense of humor.

And the next day, while I'm talking to travel agents from my cell phone, and keeping on the move, I learn my Tampa employer got a Christmas stocking too. Santa paid him a visit. He knows who's been naughty and who's been nice, you know. Only his present wasn't so funny. Stocking blew up in his face.

Took it right off I hear. Ω

GNOME HOLIDAYS

The Gnome Queen has been trying to decide on her crown.

At the Gnome Ball they will be riding the lava floes
And receiving an embassage of other elementals.
She wants something formal but friendly
And unlikely to fall off
Going over cliffs.

Coals of fire are always attractive —
Earthflame for earthfolk —
On brows tough as asbestos —
Or diamonds, of course,
But gnomes always have diamonds.

Now, pearls are a rarity underearth,
Splendid as the foam,
But they might seem to imply more
About the current talks between the earth and merfolk
Then the Queen wishes to imply.

Then she catches sight of herself
In an obsidian cabinet, and laughs.
She is old, ages old, old enough for signs of wisdom,
Old enough for silver hair,
And, in a gnome, that's silver.
Her hair glitters in the light of phosphorescence.
She braids herself a coronet
Shining over her robe of cloth of gold.

— Ruth Berman

DEATH COMES IN THE WINDOW
by Chris Presta-Valachovic

Death is a wonderful bed-partner, all bony and white, and she doesn't snore. Her bones do poke from time to time, and her fingertips can be scratchy, but I'm used to that now — uppity women like me can get used to anything, once we realize the benefits. I just wish she'd quit whispering all those names at me and let me get some sleep.

It happened one night a while ago. I was lying in my queen-size waterbed, alone as usual and curled up in the scratchy cotton sheets, and staring up at my ceiling, which I'd painted black and covered with those cheap glow-in-the-dark plastic stars. It was a hot night, and I was sweating to soak the sheets. The window was wide open, but it didn't do any good — no fan in that window, not in my basement apartment. Living in this neighborhood means that one has to forego such comforts, if you want to wake up in the morning and find your fan still there and your screen unslashed.

'Course, it's stupid leave a window open to begin with, but I'm not one to be consistent, and I was too hot. Besides, after living in this neighborhood this long, there's nothing that could come in that window that I can't handle, and my neighbors sidestep me wide every morning because of it.

So I lay there, window wide open for the non-existent breeze and I could hear the regular police sirens, gunshots and yelling outside, down the street and next block over from the sound of it. But then I heard a different noise, scratching against the mesh of my window screen, and I turned my head towards my window, thinking someone's being really stupid to bust in here when I'm right there watching.

But then I stared at the window, for once surprised. The gleaming bony figure of Death crouched outside my window, its skeletal hands scratching at my window screen, to slash it open and get in. It peered in with shadows filling the eye-holes in its skull, as if it couldn't see in clearly — no surprise there. Despite the glow-in-the-dark cheapies on the ceiling, despite the full moon outside, my bedroom's in the shadow of the biggest stack of condemned bricks in the city, just across the alley.

I decided to let Bony know I was here, anyway. Perhaps then it'd run away and let me get back to trying to sleep. "What do you want, Bony?"

It actually jumped, all of its bones flying apart, then rattling back together. I could've sworn that skull-face looked sheepish, but I guess it had to save what was left of its face, for it gathered itself up and boomed out, in a hollow, echoing voice, "I've come for David!"

"Pipe down," I said. "No need to shout. I'm right here."

Naturally, it ignored me. "David!"

David's the drug-dealer next door, and I was thinking that if Bony offed David, then I'd be up all night from the noise of gunfire, sirens and agitated neighbors right outside my window. "There's no David here."

It peered in at me again. I could've sworn the shadowy eye-pits squinted. "Uh . . . Timothy?"

Oh, lord. Was it after me, then? But then again, Timothy was the block's meanest pimp, so maybe Death was just confused. But if Timothy bought it, I'd be walking to work through gang-fighting every morning, as all the young hoods scrambled to take over Timothy's sorry stable. "Nope. No one like that here, either."

"Joshua?"

No doubt about it. That bony face was peering at me and its eye sockets were squinted in puzzlement. So Bony wanted me, eh? Tough — I didn't want to go. But Josh was the local sneak thief. If he went instead of me, I'd have to bribe someone new to leave my apartment alone. I was getting tired of this. At this rate, I'd never get any sleep.

So I stalked over to the window and popped the screen out of the frame. Bony jumped, rattling in shock, but before it could do anything else, I'd snatched out to grab its neck vertebrae and squeezed those dry old bones, hard, and they froze my hands and turned my arms to icy lumps. I couldn't hold on too long; I had to end this quick.

Those shadowy eye-pits got just a touch bigger as Bony saw my body, my skin gleaming in the faint light of the moon shining over top of the condemned bricks. Its mouth gaped open in a bony, triumphant grin. "Marsha!"

Why the names? I thought fast and hard. Maybe if Death didn't know your name, it couldn't take you. It was worth a shot. "Nope," I said cheerfully. "Not even close."

Ever see bones deflate? "Jan? Marilyn? Sojourner?" When I went on grinning back, it looked desperate. "Don't suppose you'd give me a hint?"

"Nope," I said, sure of myself now. "You gotta get it right. That's the rules."

"You could come with me anyway," it said seductively. "I'll take you for a wild ride on a midnight stallion across the stars and we can skim the mountains and dance in the sky with the stars lighting our feet. . . ."

I knew a come-on line when I heard one. "Sorry," I said. "I like it here."

"Here?" Despite my grip on its neck, Bony gestured, taking in the slums, gunfire, endless sirens and sweating heat.

"It's not much," I agreed, "but it beats the alternative."

"I'm the alternative!" Bony sounded offended.

Now that I looked, those bones did look handsome, gleaming white and hard in the moonlight, and Bony was only doing its job. No need to offend it, after all. "It's just an old saying. You are kinda pretty."

"You must come with me," Bony said.

Whatever was left of a brain in that dead skull was surely one-track and stubborn. "Sorry. But you know the rules. You don't know, I don't go."

"But I must take someone tonight!" There was a touch of whine in that hollow voice.

"So why mess around here?" This time it was my gesture that took in the slums and sirens. "Lots of other folks around that are long past their time. Why not take the Pope? Or Dick Clark? Or Dennis Hopper?" At least then we might have a shot at getting a decent movie villain in Hollywood, but I didn't say that out loud.

"I'm just a minor-league Death," Bony said. "I'm not allowed to handle the big cases yet."

"There's more than one Death?"

"Of course." The way Bony said that, I felt ashamed for not thinking of it sooner. Of course, not thinking right now was the definite wrong way to go.

"City hospital's two streets over," I said. "Lots of folks there would love to go with you and bless you for your mercy."

"I'm not allowed mercy yet, either," Death said, in a small, whispery voice. "I've got eons before I work up to that level."

Feeling sorry for Death has got to be the weirdest shivery feeling in the world. But I did anyhow; it would give my neighbors a new reason to sidestep me. "Brother, you are between a rock and a hard place," I said sympathetically.

Those shadowy eye-pits narrowed just a touch. "Brother?"

Perhaps the moon gleamed brighter, perhaps the street light around the corner had decided to work for a change, but the light was now enough for me to get a real good look at the Death I gripped by the neckbones. Now I saw the curving cup of the pelvic bones and the wide-set hip bones and the long silvery hair clinging to its skull. "Sister," I said then, and made it sound apologetic.

"Then you'll let me take you?" She sounded as if she mistook my sympathy and apology for giving in.

"Not a chance," I said. "You ain't said my name yet."

Those bones deflated again. "Then let me go. I will report my failure to the One In Charge. She won't be happy with me this night." She sighed in a whispery shiver. "Again."

But I was looking around at my sweaty apartment, at my fan hidden in the corner instead of up in the useful window, and, more importantly, at my huge empty bed. Then I was looking at Death and her nicely curved bones and silky silver hair, and I started laughing as the idea came together in my head. I leaned over and whispered it to Sister Death, right into the holes in her skull where her ears should've been, and soon, she was laughing, too, her whispery chuckle shivering over my hearty giggling. Then I let my grip on her neckbones go, and she took my fleshy hand in her bony one.

Now I don't sleep alone, and there's a nice cool breeze blowing in my window from my fan each night. Almost every night, some fool tries to steal our breeze, but my sister Death takes care of that.

So each night, her quota is met, and the One In Charge has spoken of a promotion soon. My sister is now a happy Death, and we've gone for a couple of those wild rides on a midnight stallion, and I've shown her the pleasures of dancing to thumping disco in an crowded club. It's been a wonderful affair.

But each night, as the moon shines down on our bed and I'm settling down to sleep, she whispers a long string of names into my ear. Every night, I spend at least a couple hours saying "no, nope, not even close."

I don't think I'll be ready to say "yes" for a good long while. Ω

GRAND GUIGNOL
by Andy Duncan

illustrated by Allen Koszowski

1. Max

Charles is my friend, my brother, my right arm, my most valued assistant, my comrade in glory and trial since before the Armistice, and to say anything against him is almost more than I can bear — but today he brought me a sack of eyeballs of which, before God, not one was usable. Stress? Love? Syphilis? Who can say? I am saddened beyond speculation.

The instant I hefted the sack, I knew. A director senses these things. Yet to appease Charles, I dutifully held each eyeball, rolled it in my fingers, inspected it, flung it to the floor. Not one bounced — not one! Smack, smack, smack, like so many eggs. They surrounded my desk, gazing up at my shame.

The climax of *A Crime in the Madhouse* is so sublime, and to cut corners would be ruinous! The crones cackle . . . the victim shrieks and writhes, her arms pinned . . . the knitting needles flash . . . first one eyeball, then the other, is ripped free . . . they fall to the stage and bounce, roll, toward the edge, toward the front row. Ah! what a spectacle with which to launch our 1925 season! But if the eyeballs just plop, plop, like clots of pate from a drunkard's cracker — Is this what our patrons demand, deserve? Is this theatre? All this I pointed out to Charles, to no avail.

"Max, be reasonable. You send me for eyeballs, I bring you eyeballs. I bring you three score eyeballs at a good price, from the taxidermist in the rue Duperer. If we keep them on ice, we have enough to last for weeks, we have one less thing to worry about. Do you know, Max, how badly we need one less thing to worry about?"

"I have only *one* thing to worry about, Charles, and that is my *art*. I pay you a salary greater than the premier pays Marshal Petain to worry about everything *except* my art, and how do you repay me?"

"Max —"

"You kick me, you spit upon me!"

"Max —"

"You smear me with offal!"

"Max, you are a melodrama with no audience and a cast of one!"

Finally, of course, we embraced, we wept, we kissed like brothers, the stagehands outside the door applauded, and Charles did as he should have done before: He set out for the slaughterers in the Bois de Bologne. I have high hopes. For *The Garden of Torture* and *The Castle of Slow Death*, they provided commendable eyeballs, outstanding in every respect. Also, once, a truly remarkable liver.

But I still feel all is not well with Charles. Perhaps I will consult Dr. Binet when he calls this afternoon with the latest progress report on the sanity of our resident genius. How I wish he could persuade Andre to return to the theatre, to come in out of the damp! I am weary of transacting business with my star playwright in a cemetery. Pages blow away before we have revised them, surly mourners rout us from tomb to tomb, and Andre is so easily distracted by the play of light on marble, by the wink of a cherub. In my hour of need, all my comrades go mad! Did Aeschylus suffer so?

2. Andre

I am at home in this city of the dead. I stand on the hilltop and see all around me the spires, the turrets, the battlements of these silent narrow houses, grouped by gravel paths into thickets of gray. I press my palms against their cool gates and peer through the frosted glass at the flowers huddled into slender vases, at the precarious shrines stacked within. No balconied block on the Isle de St. Louis is more noble than these apartments of bronze and stone.

One tomb reminds me of Max's theatre. It is surrounded by a stone deck like a stage, and its angels are large and ridiculous. I sit here and eat my lunch, a cheese quiche and a lemon pastry bought from a cart propelled by a woman in crepe. I alternate bites of citrus and onion and wonder how rehearsals are going, and then I berate myself for wondering. Max will squat upon the stage and deposit his usual pile of miracles, and the patrons will stumble away fulfilled. Dr. Binet is right to tell me to stay away from that fetid little theatre in the rue Chaptal. He is acting as my amanuensis, delivering to Max the pages of my next play as they are completed. It is an adaptation of de Maupassant's "The Maker of Monsters," which will tax the company's skill with stage deformities. But they may make of it what they will; I no longer care. The true production is the one I envision alone, here in the center of Pere Lachaise. I have no actors to stable, no turnstiles to crank, no boulevardiers to appease. When I am done writing, the play is over.

3. Charles

While she is onstage, being strangled to death, I am in her dressing room, laying down a bouquet.

Or attempting to. Where to leave it? Like all the dressing rooms, this is little more than a closet, a vertical stall. The vanity is a jumble of overturned bottles, opened jars, and wadded handkerchiefs, every surface tacky with lipstick, rouge, and greasepaint. The two chairs are swaddled with layers of evil-smelling costumes, sleeves and bloomers all entwined. The lamp is wearing, at a flirtatious angle, a wig clotted with gore.

Finally I open the shallow drawer of the vanity, insert the clump of stems, and close the drawer so that the blooms jut out horizontally, sagging like broken fingers. It will have to do. I dare not be seen. Max would flay me alive, as in the climax of *The Horrible Experiment*. "Fraternizing with the enemy!" he would trumpet. Max suspects all actors of ongoing subversion, of plotting to overthrow their divinely appointed producer-director and launch another Commune. He suspects even the company's brightest light, its Bernhardt — Sonia Morel, glorious Sonia, beautiful Sonia, whose closet this is, who has been killed on our stage more than 10,000 times. I keep the books, and I know.

4. Binet

I did not know at first that Andre de Lorde was a playwright. At the time, I knew little of theatre, though I found it prudent several times a season to go on display in my box at the Opera. Andre was a patient of my embarrassingly earnest colleague Dr. Metenier, who would have had a prominent career had he not squandered so much of his time on patients. Metenier called the case the most absolute death fixation in his

experience and, in despair, sent Andre to me. In our first consultation, I saw that Andre would never be cured. He enjoyed the process of analysis too much. He perched on the edge of his chair like an excited child, eyes wide behind his spectacles, and gazed raptly at me as if I were the only visible object in the room. Later I saw this expression on the faces of actors standing in the dark awaiting their cue. He showed a rude lack of interest in the framed certificates and testimonials all around, however prominent and well-lighted. I waited, with steepled fingers, until the silence became unprofitable. Then I sighed and took up my pen.

"Let us suppose, Monsieur de Lorde, that you have a free afternoon in Paris. It is a lovely spring day. What would you do to pass the time? Where would you go?"

"Oh, any of several places, Doctor. Let's see. Well, recently I have been spending much of my spare time in the Place de la Nation."

"Could you be more specific? Do you shop, stroll, do you feed the birds?"

"I walk about, and I think about the guillotines."

"Pardon?"

"The guillotines. That plaza was the site of most of the executions during the Terror."

"Yes, but the Terror was a long time ago."

"I know, Doctor, but — well, while I'm walking, I try to imagine what it must have been like. Oh, I have seen executions in our modern day. I have accompanied my friend Max, who once worked for the police commissioner. But today only vile criminals are executed, and the atmosphere is so . . . sterile. Like the removal of a gangrenous limb in an operating room. Do you follow?"

"I'm not sure, Monsieur de Lorde."

"You may call me Andre."

I simulated gratitude. "Andre. Thank you. Please continue. The atmosphere, you say, is sterile?"

"Not so much sterile, I suppose, as . . . drab. The bureaucrats in their dusty grey suits, the mumbling priest, the journalists smoking and doodling rude pictures in their notebooks. Everyone, even the condemned man, looks bored, going through the motions, ready for everything to be over. There's not even as much blood as one would expect. The very arteries seem . . . inhibited."

"And this differs from the Terror?"

"Oh, yes! As the name implies. The prisoners went screaming to the stocks, and a thousand throats cheered each spurt of crimson. The Old Regime was a Hydra, and its coils spasmed for months after the first head had been severed. Each execution was a separate pageant, unlike any before or since."

"What an imagination! You envision all this, walking there with your hat and cane, with the newsboys yelling and the traffic roaring past?"

Andre smiled and shrugged. "Yes, it is silly, but I confess it. Call me a sentimentalist."

"Do you call yourself a sentimentalist?"

"No. Do you know what I read just this week, doctor? I read that puppeteers waited beside the guillotines to drag the corpses across the plaza to small stages made of pushed-together cheese crates. There they performed impromptu satiric plays, working the bodies like life-sized puppets." He sprang to his feet and stuck out both elbows, letting his forearms dangle, and did a loping dance about my office. His head flopped about as if his neck had, indeed, been severed. " 'Here is the merry Marquis, dancing at the ball!' Oh, how the crowd laughed."

I clapped slowly, forcefully, holding my arms aloft as if I were at the Opera. "You are most vivid and convincing, Andre. You should go on the stage."

His face fell, and he sat down heavily. "Acting? Pfagh! I am no *actor.*" His tone reeked of contempt.

"Forgive me. I meant no offense. What is your profession, Andre?"

"I am a *playwright.*" He leaned forward, fixing me with a Jacobean stare. "And I am looking, Dr. Binet, for a collaborator."

Thus it began. I provided Andre with case studies of the wretches I have treated in the lunatic asylums of France, and he turned their madness into melodrama. And so the brilliant Dr. Michael Binet, director of the Psychological-Physiological Laboratory of the Sorbonne, became a technical adviser to a back-alley theatre in Montmartre, the Grand Guignol.

Andre de Lorde, a fevered scribbler, saw his name in lights, while I saw my name on the back of the program, listed in small type with the milliners who designed the hats and the slaughterers who filled the buckets with grue.

I allowed my resentment to grow, swell, fester.

And now, thanks to Andre's unfortunate turn for the worse, I may at last claim a share of the credit I have so long deserved.

5. Sonia

I could be at the Theatre Antoine, the Odeon, the Gymnase, the Vaudeville, the Ambigu, even the Comedie Francaise. Why not? I could be playing Portia, Roxanne, Antigone. But no, I am throttled nightly by a bellowing, beery lout on a stage smaller than Max's bed.

"You witch! You strumpet! You will never leave me again!"

"Paul! What are you doing with that wire? Keep away from me! Keep away!"

"You left our baby to die, you slut!"

"Paul, no! No! — Aieeeeeeyeeeeeee!"

"Die! Die!"

"Augggggghhhhgugghhhhhh!"

"That blood is coming out very nicely, very nicely indeed." Max's voice in the dark is as bodiless and satisfied as God's. Near the back row, his cigarette glows.

"Eugenie used a bit more glycerin in the mix tonight, Max. Wait till you see how well it clots."

"Thank you, Camille, I look forward to it. Sonia, my dear, could you thrash your downstage leg a bit more? The front row will demand refunds en masse if they don't feel endangered. That's better. Your grimace, Octave, is much improved. You have studied the gargoyles as I suggested, yes? Yes. Can we hear that scrap of dialogue again? Let's return to — where should we resume, Camille?"

"Um, 'You left our baby to die, you slut.'?"

"Yes! From there, please, Octave."

"You left our baby to die, you — Augggg-ghhhhgugghhhhhh!"

"Octave. That's Sonia's line."

Octave crumpled, hands jammed into his groin.

"And you'll get another one just like it," I shouted, "if you ever again try to grope me onstage, you bastard!" I slung the prop wire into the wings, beribboning the curtains with blood. Octave whimpered.

"Sonia, my dear, our company is small and our resources limited. I must urge you not to kill any of your fellow performers until the season is over."

"Max, my dear, you are a miserable piece of shit!" I strode into the wings, shouldering aside poor little Eugenie, who cowered behind her cauldron of blood. I entered my dressing room, slammed the door, and righted the vanity mirror. I made fists and bounced on the balls of my feet. I bared my teeth like an ape, screwed shut my eyes, strained all my muscles, and hummed my rage.

Why do I stay? Max believes for love of art; the company believes for love of Max. Love! I love neither as much as I would love a role that did not require me to be strangled or boiled or gutted like a fish twice each evening plus matinees.

Most of all I would love a dressing room in which I could actually pace, large enough for me to admit more than one admirer at a time. One night King Carol of Rumania and his mistress, Mademoiselle Lupesco, came backstage to offer their compliments on my performance in *The Merchant of Corpses*.

Deposed monarchs require even larger retinues than active ones — their fiefdoms are rented suites and the lackeys who fill them — and so three rows of the theatre emptied to follow His Majesty and the mademoiselle into the dim and grimy corridors. I was forced to receive them in the passageway! Mademoiselle Lupesco could not precede the king into any room, and the king could not enter a woman's dressing chamber without a chaperone — as if I had space and air enough for a tryst! If His Majesty could maneuver that expertly, he would not be in exile. Even intimacy is too ambitious in this snuffbox.

I have given up on Max. At the theatre, his response is always the same. "What more will you demand of me?" he moans. He flings his hands outward, palms up, as if to receive the nails. "Are you not already renowned? Do you know what the newspapers call you? The High Priestess of the Temple of Horror!" As if this is a compliment. Away from the theatre, at his flat or at mine, Max has a different stock response, one more enjoyably physical, but it leaves my situation equally unresolved.

Here are more flowers. From Charles, no doubt. Poor Charles. He thinks his infatuation is so well hidden. He is as flamboyant, in his quiet way, as Max: He wants the drama of being a secret admirer. I am tempted to encourage him a little, but at this point in my life I need something more tangible than mute longing. Perhaps, indeed, something more than Max. I have told no one my vow: If I don't get a good notice from a serious reviewer this season, I will quit the company — and Max as well, ululate though he will.

In the meantime, I am at least learning new aspects of my craft. Eugenie is teaching me some of her more elaborate makeup tricks. The child really is talented. If I ever get to play Cordelia, I can also act as technical adviser to whoever

gouges out Gloucester's eyeballs. "More bounce! More bounce!"

I will not become hysterical.

6. Eugenie

Some nights Charles and I are the only ones left in the building, and he is kind enough to walk me home. I always finish my work first; Max leaves him quite a list. I push open the thick oak doors to the theatre proper — I have to lean with my whole body to budge them — and I sit in the middle, toward the back, where Max sits during rehearsals. I sit in the dark and wait for the outlines of the stage, the seats, the beams in the ceiling to appear, to resolve themselves into outlines of black and grey.

It is a curious thing. When I am not in my apartment, I have difficulty remembering what it looks like, even where it is. I keep the address pinned to the inside of my sleeve, on a folded scrap of butcher's paper, just in case. But I can always summon every pulley, every lamp, every alcove in this theatre. I don't need light to study their details. I asked Max once whether I simply could move my few belongings into the theatre, into the garret above the balcony, but he made popping noises and fluttered his hands and said it would not be proper. Surely he knows that I virtually live here already. I certainly live nowhere else. If I were able to sit here in the dark long enough, if there were enough hours in the night, I'm sure I eventually would be able to see not only the broad strokes of my surroundings, but the most minute flourishes carved into the farthest corner of the ceiling. It is all a matter of concentration, and at the same time of relaxing so that the images come to you, rather than straining yourself to meet them halfway. One night, as the theatre formed around me, one swatch of darkness became the shape of a man, and I recognized the spectacles of Monsieur de Lorde. He was sitting in the next row, facing the stage.

"They say no place on Earth is quite as dark as a darkened theatre," he said. "This frightens many people, Eugenie. Not you?"

"No, monsieur." I could not recall his addressing me before.

"That's good. Because at this time of night, in a darkened theatre, one can hear the most remarkable things, if one is open to hearing them. Did you know, Eugenie, that this building was once a convent?"

"Yes, monsieur. Charles — I mean, Monsieur Goudron — told me it had been gutted during the Terror. This hall used to be the chapel, and that's why angels are carved into the ceiling."

"Monsieur Goudron — I mean, Charles — is quite correct. I would share with you another part of that history, Eugenie, but I fear it would mean your following me upstairs, into the balcony. Upon my honor," he added, raising his hand, "I mean you no harm, and I will maintain my distance."

I was sure he could feel the warmth of my embarrassment even if he could not see its color. "Oh, I do not doubt you, Monsieur! I will follow you." We climbed the narrow stairs, which spiral up a chimneylike brick shaft. The darkness of the balcony was, if anything, more absolute than that below. Monsieur de Lorde sat, and so did I, at a proper distance of several feet. For many minutes we said nothing, only sat and looked at the oblong space above the stage. I believe that before I actually heard the murmuring, I felt it in my neck and arms, which prickled as if charged with electricity. The burbling was as faint as a trickle of water within the walls during a rainstorm, but there was no rain this night. The sounds had the tone and timbre of human speech, but the words, if words they were, were inaudible. I thought of Charles's mumblings as he tallied figures in Max's ledger.

"What is that sound, Monsieur?"

"This was their convent, and they are still here, still praying for us all." Monsieur de Lorde's voice was hushed. "Even during the uproar of performances, while this balcony is jammed with patrons, I can sit in this spot and hear the sisters. The terror continues, and so do the prayers."

Far from being frightened, I felt oddly consoled, as one feels when hearing a distant train. I was smiling when the lights came on. Charles was standing at the switch-box just inside the doorway below.

"There you are, Eugenie! Hello, Andre. My, you are a fine pair. Claiming your seats early for this weekend's show?" He laughed and swept a shock of hair out of his face. "Keep sitting up there in the dark like that," he said, "and you'll both be seeing things."

The murmuring had become so muted that my breathing drowned it out, but it continued, soft and frolicsome inside my ears.

by Andy Duncan

7. Max

I marvel that I can go on. Dr. Binet tells me that poor Andre no longer is well enough to see any of his friends, that he wanders the cemetery like a spectre, hardly eating, and — worst of all! — unable to write. Binet has been kind enough to pass me drafts of a play he himself is writing, *The Maker of Monsters*. Everyone is a playwright. Soon the concierges and streetcar drivers will be handing me scripts as well. Why does no one aspire to be a director? Because they watch me, study the terrible example that is my life, and they learn. Oh, the struggle!

Octave has left the company. He said terrible things — bloodcurdling things! — about Sonia. I could not bear it. Only three days before we open, we have no one to play Paul le Hirec, the insane sculptor who strangles his cruel and faithless wife in *The Dead Child*. Would that I were a dramaturge of ancient Greece, able to recast a play with a shuffling of masks! Would that I were in any other theatre, in any other age, than in this Sisyphean ordeal that occupies me now. Will the very slopes of Montmartre yawn wide to swallow us on opening night? I would not be surprised. The gods are against my endeavor. In the perfection of my art, I have angered the gods.

On the other hand, Charles could play the role. Excellent. It is decided. I will hand him the script today, and Sonia will rehearse with him tonight — all night, if necessary! Perhaps at her flat, where they will have some privacy. Charles will make the usual excuses, but I will not be swayed.

8. Charles

I woke sweating, naked and disoriented in a close and sultry bedchamber, sheets tangled about my legs. I sat up, startled, felt my stomach lurch, and lay down again, breathing deeply with my eyes closed. The sheets I lay upon were soothing, damp and cool, and I focused on the thin intersection of flesh and fabric, enjoying the contours of my body. I returned to the borderland between waking and sleeping, and wraiths of the evening before coiled around me. My body remembered before my mind how my night had been spent: a soreness in my upper arms and shoulder blades, an unusual coarseness in the play of my tongue along my palate, a detached numbness in my twitching penis. Eventually the room reshaped itself around the absent figure of Sonia, and then I remembered all, and smiled. I sat up, slowly this time, waited

a few seconds for my dizziness to pass, and padded unclothed to the doorway, where I looked across the sunny common room of a top-floor flat. At the far wall stood Sonia, with her back to me, bent over a countertop, intent on some project that she blocked with her body. She wore an abundant purple gown as generous as the matted sheets I had left behind; its drape revealed one bare shoulder. Her russet hair, streaked with grey, roamed long and loose; if I walked up behind and clasped her, her hair would enfold me down to my thighs. I moved softly across the room, my memory of the bedroom hours narrowing and intensifying this daytime moment, and just as I reached for her, she turned and smiled and held up her right forearm, to show that where her hand had been was a jagged, bleeding stump, flesh tattered, bone splintered and shining in the morning light. I screamed and lunged backward, falling, bruising my lower back as I hit the windowsill. I twisted and leaned out over the boulevard, my arms numb as I shuddered and heaved. Then her arms were around me, and her hands — both hands! — were caressing my forehead, my cheeks, my chin, and Sonia was saying: "It's makeup, that's all it is, one of Eugenie's tricks, she's been teaching me, I'm sorry, I'm so sorry, what was I thinking, I'm fine, Sonia's fine . . ." I slowly hauled myself into the room, leaving damp handprints in the grime of the windowsill, and sank to the floor, sobbing into her shoulder, my erection wedged between us like a lever.

9. Andre

Eugenie came to see me today. She found me leaning against Oscar Wilde's tomb, making notes toward an article on "Fear in Literature." The sunlight becomes her. I could not recall ever seeing her before outside the walls of the Grand Guignol. I was amazed but delighted to see her small, pale head cresting the hill, a breeze lifting what hair she has left. Why do young women crop their tresses so? I pocketed my notes on Poe and Baudelaire, stood, removed my hat and bowed from the waist not once, but twice. "Good afternoon, Mademoiselle," I said. "I trust you are well?"

The enthusiasm of my greeting flustered her and disconcerted me. Before I could make amends, she thrust at me a package wrapped in brown paper.

"I hope you will not think me forward, Monsieur de Lorde, but please accept this gift from your friends in the rue Chaptal."

I could think of nothing to say, so I bowed again, took the package and gestured her onto a bench. I gently shook the package as I sat beside her.

"I am surprised that Max has time for such gestures, in the final week of dress rehearsals." I slit the adhesive with a fingernail and began unfolding the paper.

"Monsieur, I must confess, Max knows nothing of this. I was building some props, and this one — well, this one turned out so fine that I felt I should present it to someone." I smoothed out the paper, revealing an ornate dagger of Chinese design.

"It is lovely," I said. "Fake, I hope?"

"Oh, yes, Monsieur, and with the usual spring blade." She slid the dagger gently from my lap, raised it above her head and, with surprising force, drove it to the hilt into her forearm. Then she lifted it slowly, allowing the dull and retractable blade to slip back out of the hilt that had concealed it. The illusion was flawless, as always.

"Wonderful," I said as she gravely handed back the weapon.

"The dagger is not loaded, Monsieur; I did not want to risk fouling your clothes. But here in the hilt is the reservoir that holds the blood — as much as a pint."

"Such craftsmanship. Dr. Binet will be impressed, as well. I will show it to him when he next visits."

"Oh, Monsieur, I beg you, don't tell Dr. Binet I was here! He will be at our opening Friday night, and he will be so angry."

"Hm? Angry? Whatever are you talking about, child?"

"Dr. Binet said that none of us were to contact you under any circumstances. He said your — your treatment required complete isolation. 'A break with his theatrical past,' he called it."

"How extraordinary!" I stood and walked a few deliberate paces on the gravel, like a lone duellist. "What, then, has Binet been doing with the manuscript of our latest collaboration? The adaptation of the de Maupassant story, about the awful woman who turns her babies into monsters? Is it locked away in a lab at the Sorbonne? Has he not been passing the pages to Max as they are completed?"

Eugenie frowned. "Collaboration, Monsieur? Dr. Binet has brought Max such a manuscript, yes, but he says it is his own work. He says your

illness prevents you from writing. Oh, I have said too much!" she said, standing. "I have upset you, Monsieur. You are all a-quiver, like the doctor at the climax of *The Kiss of Blood*. Please forgive me. I have spoken out of turn."

"Not at all, Eugenie, not at all!" I mopped my face with my handkerchief and took deep breaths, calming myself so as not to frighten the girl. "I thank you so much for the gift, Eugenie, and for visiting me today. I wonder, could I ask you to bring me one thing more?"

"Of course, Monsieur."

I held the dagger before me. "Might I have some blood with which to load this?"

10. Sonia

Opening night. My God, what next? Max and I were preparing ourselves in our usual superstitious way, perhaps indiscreetly, behind some balsa-wood trees backstage. I looked up, and there was Charles, pale and staring. I was going to have a conversation with him anyway — after what happened at my flat the other night — Oh! the folly! What was I thinking? — but I didn't want him to find out like this. And now, five minutes before the curtain, Charles is pacing and mumbling and rolling his eyes, ignoring all my entreaties and explanations. A frightening display. The stagehands think he is merely preparing for his role, but I wonder whether he will make it through the performance. I wonder whether I will.

11. Georges Choisy, On Theatre

A DARING NEW REALISM AT THE GRAND GUIGNOL

(*The World*, final edition, 9/21/25)

In recent months, much of the dramatic press in this most dramatic of cities has been devoted to new trends toward realism on our stages. We have seen a decided shift in dialogue this season, for example, from witty bourgeois repartee to rough, often crude, street argot, sometimes with electrifying results. No recent evening of realistic theatre, however, has so impressed this reviewer as tonight's season premiere at a most unlikely location: that venerable Temple of Horror, the Theatre of the Grand Guignol.

All the more remarkably, this overwhelming impression was made in the final minutes of the night's entertainment. Producer-director Max Mitchinn, with the daring of a master showman, began the evening in routine and traditional fashion: a series of short playlets of horror and broad comedy, including *A Crime in the Madhouse*, a new ghastliness from the clotted pen of Andre de Lorde. This included a particularly repellent eye-gouging in which the liberated orbs actually bounced into the front row, causing much commotion. So far, nothing to disconcert or surprise the dedicated "Guignolers," who roared and retched with their customary verve.

The climax of the evening, however, was something else entirely. Messieurs Mitchinn and de Lorde have newly shod a war-horse of their repertoire, *The Dead Child*, the story of a grief-maddened sculptor and his faithless wife. The new production eliminates all the violence but intensifies by many orders of magnitude the emotional power.

After a cataclysmic speech denouncing the perfidy of Woman, the sculptor collapses, howling in wordless grief and rage. Dazed, the wife slowly reaches out to him, holds him, and then her own tears come.

The sight of the devastated couple, the raving sculptor and his penitent wife, sobbing together in the center of the stage, holding each other with taut desperation as if encircling arms could possibly join the shards of their sundered lives, is a sight this reviewer will never forget. Nor, I suspect, will the majority of tonight's audience. The silence was as profound as that of a tomb. Never had the patrons seen such naked emotion laid bare in the theatre. The tatty backdrops, the prompter's box, the elbows rubbing my own to right and left, all dropped away like canvas scenery, and for a few anguished seconds I forgot my situation, and believed I was beholding a heartbreak as real and as wrenching as any I have experienced myself. At the curtain the applause was thunderous. The actors themselves seemed dazed as they emerged for a bow with the rest of the company.

As the sculptor, Charles Goudron made a stunning Paris debut. As the wife, Guignol veteran Sonia Morel, who so often sparkles in otherwise dull vehicles, proved herself worthy of comparison even to the great Bernhardt. One glows at the thought of the life force that Mademoiselle Morel would bring to the role of Antigone!

But the evening's revels were not ended. The lights came up, the patrons stood and rummaged for their belongings, and then the final, ultimate act of realistic drama took place, in the very aisles of the theatre itself, without the reassuring distance of

"A CRIME IN THE MADHOUSE," THE GRAND GUIGNOL, 1925

GRAND GUIGNOL

a stage! Two shouting men began grappling with one another in the middle of the seats.

When one of the men drew a dagger, I was at first frightened and tempted to summon the police. Then I was thrilled beyond words to recognize the assailant as none other than Monsieur de Lorde himself, and to realize that this must be a wonderfully satiric climax staged in the midst of the patrons.

This brief playlet ended comically. In true Guignol fashion, de Lorde shouted, "Die, Binet! Die!" and shoved his dagger into the chest of his gibbering partner, spraying a geyser of stage blood. After staring at the protruding hilt that quivered in the bubbling wound, the victim — wonderful reversal of expectations! — seemed to recover instantaneously. He fairly galloped up the aisle, yelling as he went, "Madman! Insane! Help! Help!" I am told the performance continued through the foyer, out the front door, and onto the pavement outside, until the gifted actor — whose name, I regret, was unavailable at press time — had vanished into the promenading crowds of the rue Chaptal . . .

12. Max

Our new season is a triumph. Sonia is radiant, and she and I test repeatedly the capacities of her dressing room. Charles is a matinee idol, standing in the stage door and signing autographs for crowds of adoring young women; a new gaiety fills the blind alley where patrons once stumbled only to vomit. Happily, this tradition continues as well — eleven last night, by Camille's count, a record. When the weather is bad, Andre and Eugenie spend an afternoon in the cemetery, stalking hand in hand among the tombs, visiting all their favorite dead. He and I, meanwhile, are at each other's throats on the staging of *The Maker of Monsters*, though Eugenie assures us that the plural of the title is not a problem, for she can produce hunchbacked urchins at will. It is like old times.

Late at night, Andre and Eugenie and Sonia and I sit in the balcony, rest from our labours, and bask in the murmur of the nuns. We toast the stage with cocktails of bicarbonate, and we see in the darkness a capering future, awash with drama and blood.   Ω

THE CRY OF THOSE WAITING UNDER THE BRIDGE

If not for the water
drip, drop, dripping
down the tendrils sagging
below the rotting bridge—
if not for the water
tip, tap, tapping
on the smooth stone protruding
from the cold and brackish stream—
if I had not been sitting on that stone
for countless days unending
listening to that
drip, drop, dripping—
if my blood were not the black water,
if my heart were not the smooth stone,
if my eyes were not holes a-gaping—

if only this world were fading
and this stinking stream rolling back upon itself
like a hand into a fist—
yes, if I could fall back into stone
and leave off this long waiting
drip, drop, dripping,
then I would let the stranger slowly walking,
trip, trap, tripping
across my bridge,
pass unharmed and unremembered,
but for this endless madness
drip, drop, dripping,
I will make this stranger a hero
in a tale I did not write.

— **David Sandner**

by Andy Duncan

AN IRON BRIDE
by Tanith Lee

Illustrated by Tom Simonton

Mirabeau said: "War is the national industry of Prussia." In the eighteenth and nineteenth centuries, Prussia asked her rich citizens to give up their gold and jewels to support a war, and rendered in their place, replicas of the ornaments in iron. These replicas were apparently so exquisite that other countries tried to copy the method — inadequately. None was as good, it seems, as war-mongering Prussia.

This stern city in the snow, who would think that it could ever be summer here? But once it was.

The lime trees had opened their parasols of aching green, birds flew about the red roofs, and in the gardens there were colored lamps at dusk, and soft music, and laughter. Along the boulevards carriages rattled. The sky was flowered with stars.

It was at the end of this lovely summer that they were to be married, Marten and Klovia. They had to wait a year, as was customary. But they had not minded so very much. Though young, both were possessed of a curious maturity. Meeting each other, they knew, each of them, that they would be together for the rest of their days, and, perhaps, beyond life. It was a love match, strange for their social position and era. They had been very lucky. Good luck always says, *Now I am with you, to the ending of the world.* And is believed.

Both were remarkable, he handsome and fair, she beautiful and very dark of hair and eyes. In this way, then, descending to some ballroom, he golden in his black clothes, and she crowned by night in her white dress and skin. They were the talk of the city, these two. No one wished them any ill. Sometimes perfection awakens in human beings an innate nobility and spiritual height. Marten and Klovia were like a talisman, like clear weather or a winter festival. Like a promise to everyone, of what might be.

And then there blew through the lavish corridor of summer the coarse trumpet note of war. Some had looked for it, and others, caught up in their own lives, not. The lovers raised their heads and saw, on the horizon, the march of men, banners, and cannon, and the black smoke that follows like a raven.

He held her in his arms. He said, "I'll soon come home. It will have to be an autumn wedding after all." She said, "Kiss me."

In the dark he went away, late in the night, but when the sun rose the next day, it did not rise for her. The light was gone.

Klovia's aunt came to the house of her mother. In the salon they drank tea, and beyond the doors, the charming garden stretched. Klovia did not eat the little cakes, and no one pressed her.

"It's been asked," said the aunt, who had once been beautiful, and now was only cruel.

"But surely —" said the mother.

"No. How can it be wrong to make a sacrifice for one's country?"

Klovia looked at her aunt stilly. In the green shade of the tree through which the sun, meaningless, was shining, the aunt glowed with purpose.

Klovia said, "I'll do it."

"Of course," said the aunt. "There you are. The young are sometimes able to teach us."

Klovia's mother put her hand dubiously to the golden pendant that hung about her own neck.

"Why do they need such things?"

"To pay for this war," said the aunt. "Do you think we should bow to our enemies?"

"But — a necklace —"

"It will be melted down. And look, do you see what's given in return? The badge of patriotism."

The aunt displayed the cruel black claws of her brooch. It was of iron. In return for an ornament of gold and pearls, they had given her an exact iron replica. It was very delicate, like a briar of thorns.

Klovia undid her golden bracelet and took the two filigree golden drops from her ears.

"What else do you have?" asked the aunt.

Klovia's mother said, "Wait —"

"Many things," said Klovia.

by Tanith Lee

"Fetch them," said the aunt imperiously.

As they walked along the boulevard in their slim, pale dresses, the aunt told Klovia of the virtue of what she did. It was the pride of women now to wear iron jewelry, showing they had given their riches for their country.

At a tall white building, they went in, and were treated most respectfully. Klovia placed her casket in the hands of a man who gasped in turn at this and her beauty. She was awarded a receipt written very carefully and stamped with the seal of the city.

Her aunt left her after this, and at home her mother wept over the loss of the jewels as if she had lost her son or husband.

Klovia looked at the bare column of her slender neck, her empty wrists, the white lobes of her ears. She did not know why she had done what she did. That she would be praised for it, faintly, distantly, annoyed her. This was irrelevant.

After a week, the iron jewelry came. It was brought ceremoniously, and the banner of her land nodded in the street as the things were presented. Every item had been faithfully copied.

Klovia set them out, the rings and earrings, bracelets and necklaces and combs. Like the sun, they had grown dark and hard.

A ball was held. Klovia entered. She wore midnight blue that was nearly black. At her throat and in her ears, delicate black metal, like traceries of ink. And the other women — all the same.

The men were like ghosts, only those the war had spared. Elderly men, invalids, the very young, the blind and halt and lame.

Klovia danced, and did not see who she danced with. All around the bright dresses and black iron jewelry.

On the terrace of the ballroom she looked up, and there was the black iron sky set with diamonds.

An old man said to her, "I fear you find me thirty years too late."

Klovia smiled at him. She realized that one day she too must be old and all things left behind, like shells on a beach. But she thought she would be old with Marten.

She left early. She said to her mother, "Don't ask me to go to such places anymore."

"But, my dear, you'll be talked about. It's our duty to maintain the spirit of the country."

Klovia went to her room and took out of a drawer a pair of gloves that belonged to Marten. She held them, but they were only gloves.

There had been one letter. It was full of repressed misery. She knew he would not write to her often, because there was only horror to tell her of. Even when he wrote of his love for her, it had become part of the horror, as if, by loving her, he had made himself the reasonable prey of war.

It seemed to her she did not exactly miss him or grieve. It was only as if half of herself had been cut away.

She took off the iron jewelry and went to bed and slept, for she was healthy and youthful still. Outside, a nightingale sang in a garden tree.

She dreamed she stood in the garden with Marten, as she had often done, and the nightingale sang on. When she touched her lover's hand, it was cold.

"What does the nightingale say?" she asked.

"That I love you."

But she knew it was no longer so. He had surely ceased to love her, for love had become a piece with the desperate darkness of war.

And when the sun rose in the dream, it was black, with rays like thorns.

After three months, Klovia knew she would never see Marten again. When acquaintances spoke of him, boldly, gladly, to cheer or please her, she smiled politely as she had to the old man at the ball. Marten in turn had became unreal. Perhaps he had never existed, and she and her mother, and all these other people, had simply imagined him. Before her stretched her life, which now had no meaning or interest. She had been trained from childhood, as rich women of her country had always been, to show nothing publicly of her deeper emotions, possibly not really to think of them.

Her gracious fortitude and bravery became a byword of the city. They understood, if she must not, what she had been deprived of.

The summer passed into a russet golden autumn.

There was a tall white church, and here Klovia and her mother and hundreds of others regularly went, to praise God for His grossly imperfect world and His faulty, erratic genius, and to thank Him for any occasional fortune or happiness they might have scavenged.

From this temple Klovia was coming out, when the news was brought to her, in front of five hundred people, on the steps, that Marten had been killed.

Klovia stood quite still in her dark red gown, holding the letter in her gloved hands that had a bracelet of black iron. The captain saluted her and spoke in ringing tones of Marten's courage, and how he had sacrificed his life for the honour of his land.

The crowd stood hushed. The crisp blue air was electric. Klovia nodded, and bowed her head.

"He is a hero," cried the captain. "His name will be remembered for ever."

A strange thing happened to Klovia. For a moment, only that, she could not remember Marten's name at all.

Klovia sat waiting through the autumn. She did not know for what she waited. Perhaps for them to bring her, again, the bad news.

Her mother wept copiously and even the maids in the fine house shed tears over the loss of Marten.

Klovia did not cry. It was as if she did not have the proper mechanism. She wondered if she had ever cried — in childhood certainly. She recalled as a child how her doll was broken — she had cried then. And when a favorite cat died, then too. But now her eyes were as empty as her life.

No one expected her to do anything in the way of social things. It was accepted that she would be reclusive. Only to the church was she still supposed to go, as she was supposed to pray to God, who had presumably permitted the death of Marten in horrible circumstances of blood and maiming, for the care of Marten's soul. She did go to church, but did not pray at all. She closed her eyes and thought of trivial things, that a new button must be sewn on her cuff, that she was thirsty.

However, every day, although no other social obligations were entailed, Klovia must rise and dress, breakfast and lunch and dine, attend her weeping mother, and listen to her mother's curious entreaties that she too, Klovia, should burst into loud sobbing.

"What is wrong with you?" cried Klovia's mother. "Are you unfeeling?"

But Klovia's aunt said, "Don't be foolish. Klovia's grief is assuaged by her pride in him. He died for his country."

Sometimes the war was mentioned. It was going very well.

One morning an important official arrived at the house. He showed Klovia and her mother a complex document with the seal of the city.

Klovia waited politely, looking at his face, and sometimes modestly lowering her eyes. But she did not hear much of what he said. She was thinking that the leaves would be gone from all the garden trees, turning them from gold to black.

"And today, this very evening, it will be brought here."

"It is a great honour," said Klovia's mother. "We are touched. My daughter is very sensible of this kindness."

Klovia raised her eyes, "It is more than I deserve," she said.

The official was gratified. He assured her that her stamina in loss had been an inspiration to the city. He went out.

Klovia's mother was flushed and excited. She exclaimed that she must send a message at once to the aunt.

Klovia said, "It . . . will come this evening."

"Yes. And a perfect likeness. No one else has been recognized in this way."

Klovia was puzzled. She lowered her eyes now to the complicated paper, and slowly read it. So she learned at last that she was to be given a life-size statue of her lover, Marten, modelled precisely to resemble him, and the face also, for a mould had been taken of this after death. Her city regretted that no valuable material was available because of the war. The statue was made of black iron.

As evening fell, the statue arrived with great circumstance, and was carried into the house and so out into the garden to a suitable site. After a lot had been said, and Klovia had made her thanks, she was left alone to stand beside the iron Marten, staring up into the face that had been constructed from a death-mask, and then its eyelids opened.

Indeed, it did look just like him, handsome and graceful, the high intelligent forehead and strong jaw, the classical mouth and nose, wide eyes, and fall of hair. There was a secretive, smiling look to the face, however, that he had never worn in life. He knew things now that living persons did not.

Night sank down to the grass, and Klovia was summoned into the lamplit house to dress and dine with her mother and aunt, and two or three officials.

After this, in her black necklace and bracelets, Klovia slipped out again, and stood under the trees, looking into the black eyes of Marten. No one tried to dissuade her.

Nevertheless, far into the night, she was called

again, to go through the decorum of undressing and lying down in bed.

About two in the morning, she descended through the house and let herself out once more. Once more she stood beside the statue.

The night was cold and crystalline with frost, and no nightingale sang, but Klovia did not think of this. Although when she touched the statue, the cold of it burned her.

It was the same height Marten had been. In the darkness it truly might have been he, except it had no light or warmth. It did not speak or move. It did not think.

Klovia had remained puzzled. She gazed on and on into the black face and eyes, trying to undo the riddle.

In place of her golden lover they had given her an iron bridegroom. What did this mean?

At last she gave it up, stopped considering it at all. She stepped between the statue's arms and stood against it, her hands loose at her sides, looking up even now, as if to receive the pressure of his kiss.

At the hour of arising, no one could find Klovia. They searched through the house and finally went out into the garden. Initially they did not discover her. However, at length, her mother noticed that the iron statue under the trees, the statue of Marten, had altered.

Presently Klovia's mother fell on the lawn in a faint. No one went to her aid for some while. They were arrested in contemplation of the statue — which overnight had become that of two persons, a handsome young man, and a lovely young girl, gazing up into his face as if awaiting some caress. Both figures were of black iron, and the frost webbed them over with a delicate filigree which, catching the sunlight, appeared to be made of gold.   Ω

FIELDS

In the dark heart of the forest
She weeps . . .
Her willow bangs
traipse, brush on aged icons —
Celtic stones frozen
under a froth of moss . . .
the gentle cover

She laid
over the wounded warriors
who nourished the Lady
in Her august glory,
Her crimson prime.

— J.W. Donnelly

HOME IS WHERE THE HEART IS

Love,
you say
you love me
from a place deep
within. I love
from an attic
over winding stairs
where a bearded crone
sits for my finger-blood
at the last spindle in Christendom;
from a parlor

where wing chairs warn
with tapestry smiles
how peach juice stains
forever;
from a cellar
where lidless reptiles
hug a cask of Italian sherry
and a hope chest, spilling
yellowed linen,
Love.

— Anne Sheldon

SINCE 1923: THE UNIQUE MAGAZINE
Spring 2000

ISSN 0898-5073
Cover by Dominic Harman

Weird Tales® is published 4 times a year by DNA Publications, Inc., in association with Terminus Publishing Co., Inc. Postmaster and others: send all changes of address and other subscription matters to DNA Publications, Inc., PO Box 2988, Radford VA 24143–2988. Editorial matters should be addressed to Terminus Publishing Co., Inc., 123 Crooked Lane, King of Prussia PA 19406–2570. Single copies, $4.95 in U.S.A. & possessions; $6.00 by mail to Canada, $9.00 by first class mail elsewhere. Subscriptions: 4 issues (one year) $16.00 in U.S.A. & possessions; $22.00 in Canada, $35.00 elsewhere, in U.S. funds. Publisher is not responsible for loss of manuscripts in publisher's hands or in transit; please see page 5 for more details. Copyright © 2000 by Terminus Publishing Co., Inc.; all rights reserved; reproduction prohibited without prior permission.

Typeset, printed, & bound in the United States of America.
Weird Tales® is a registered trademark owned by Weird Tales, Limited.

THE EYRIE

The Eyrie continues to need your letters!
We still want to hear from you by any means you choose, either by traditional paper mail or by e-mail, though if you send us a clay tablet, make sure there is enough postage on it, as we do not want to pay postage due. If delivery is made by ox-cart, be sure to include adequate fodder for the ox.

But seriously now, our address for e-mail is **owlswick@netaxs.com**. Make sure that the subject line reads "weird letter." But do *not* submit stories or poems this way. If we let people do that, considering the volume of submissions, our server would crash.

But we do want your letters.

What do we mean by supernatural? Even as different cultures create different gods, do they also create different spooks, "psychic powers," and occult phenomena? How much of this sort of thing is universal?

The belief in ghosts, for instance, probably arises from dreams. To a primitive, who does not distinguish between the "reality" of waking life and dreams, when a member of the tribe dies but then appears in a dream, it is evident then that the dead person still exists in another state or place, and can still interact with the living. The primitive would not say, "I dreamed of him," but, "He appeared to me in a dream." The dead man is seen as the one who initiated the action.

From this arises all the stories of ghosts,

prophetic apparitions, and the re-animated dead.

But how universal are ghosts?

We recently read with considerable fascination an article in an anthropology text, in which an American anthropologist, living among African tribesmen of an oral culture, decided to test the universality of a very famous story. He told the tribesmen the story of Hamlet. They enjoyed the white man's story; but eventually, however politely, they had to correct certain "errors."

It seems that the tribesmen didn't believe in ghosts. They didn't believe in individual survival after death at all, but held that we are all absorbed into nature when we die.

So that couldn't be the ghost of Hamlet's father on the battlements.

No, it had to be an apparition, sent by a witch. Furthermore, since they held that the first duty of a dead man's brother is to marry the widow and be a father to his children, the tribesmen regarded Hamlet's behavior as completely unreasonable. Claudius had behaved in an exemplary fashion toward him, so where was his complaint? After all, if it *couldn't* have been a ghost, what evidence was there that the former king, Hamlet Sr., had been murdered? In any case, if Hamlet *did* have a complaint, he had no business seeking revenge outside of his age-group. If he needed to take revenge, the socially acceptable course would be to ask another uncle — or someone else of the uncle's generation — to do the job. If youth took revenge on or otherwise criticized their elders, what would the world come to?

And then there was the matter of Ophelia. Obviously somebody drowned her (Laertes? King Claudius? Hamlet himself?) in order to sell her body to a witch, to pay for the conjuring of that apparition . . .

At this point the anthropologist found himself getting rapidly lost, and he had to conclude that maybe even the story of Hamlet isn't universal after all.

We note with interest that there is no telepathy in the Bible. Sure there is magic, and even necromancy (the Witch of Endor episode, in which King Saul has the witch raise up the ghost of Samuel); but there's no telepathy in either the Old or New Testaments. Is it possible that the ancient Hebrews and the peoples they came in contact with didn't believe in telepathy, or, indeed, had never even heard of the concept? Indeed, we can't think of any example of telepathy in ancient writings, either Hebrew or Graeco-Roman. Ghosts, spells, portents, witches, even a werewolf in *The Satyricon* (1st century A.D.), but most of the standard "psychic" powers that many modern people take as an article of faith are completely unknown.

The closest thing to ancient telepathy is a bit more like clairvoyance. The story goes (related in *The Life of Apollonius of Tyana* by Philostratus, 3rd century A.D.) that when the cruel emperor Domitian was being assassinated by a man named Stephanus in Rome (A.D. 96), the sage Apollonius, who was in Asia Minor at the time, suddenly stood up, shook his fist, and shouted, "Go Stephanus!"

Of course there was an agenda behind this story. Pagans tried to set up the wonder-working Apollonius as a rival to Christ, and pointed out that where Christ meekly submitted to crucifixion under Pontius Pilate, Apollonius had not merely told off an evil emperor, but lived to cheer his assassination from a distance. Well, never mind. The story does at least suggest that the ancients did believe that extraordinary people could do such things.

But telepathy and most of the standard psychic repertoire seem to have emerged from the Celtic countries — Scottish stories of "second sight" and the like — then entered both literature and the Spiritualist movement in the 19th century, ultimately becoming quasi-scientific in the 20th.

Similarly, there were no vampires in the an-

STAFF:

Publisher: Warren Lapine
Editors: George H. Scithers
& Darrell Schweitzer
Managing Editor: Carol Adams
Art Editor: Diane Weinstein
Assistant Editors: Kyle Phillips, Pat Buard,
Robert Waters, & Casey McCarthy
Computer Consultant: David J. Williams III
Typesetter: Owlswick Press
Printer: Morgan Publishing Co., Inc.

MANUSCRIPT SUBMISSIONS:

Before sending us your material, please send us a business-sized envelope, with postage affixed, addressed to you, for our guidelines.

The address for this and all other editorial matters: **Weird Tales®, 123 Crooked Lane, King of Prussia PA 19406-2570.**

The address for all new subscriptions, subscribers' changes of address, advertising, and any other money matters is: **DNA Publications, Inc., PO Box 2988, Radford VA 24143-2988.**

Yes; we read unsolicited submissions — but *only* if they are in standard manuscript format. To survive, all editors insist on a few Rules: each submission must be in proper format and must include a return envelope, addressed to you, with enough postage affixed to bring the manuscript back to you. If you want us to discard the manuscript if we don't buy it, tell us so, but include a business-letter-sized envelope, addressed to you, with proper postage affixed, so we can send you our comments. No loose stamps, please!

We recommend either or both of two books on writing (after all, we wrote one of them!): *On Writing Science Fiction: the Editors Strike Back!* by Scithers, Schweitzer, & John M. Ford; $19.50 in hardcover; and Barry B. Longyear's *Science-Fiction Writer's Workshop,* $9.50 in trade paperback, available from Owlswick Press, 123 Crooked Lane, King of Prussia PA 19406-2570. These prices include shipping & handling. If you live in Pennsylvania, please include 6% sales tax.

We are not responsible for manuscripts in our hands or in transit. You *must* keep a copy of every manuscript you send out. You *must* put your name and address on the first page of every manuscript. And please: *no* binders, folders, or padded envelopes; and especially: *no* registered or certified mail for which we would have to stand in line at the post office!

cient world, at least not vampires in the modern sense. There were *lamiae*, seductive, half-serpent women who seduced and devoured mortals, and in Roman folklore there was the *strix*, a kind of night-hag who drank the blood of children. "It is in Phlegon that we first find the hideous tale of the corpse-bride," H.P. Lovecraft intoned in "Supernatural Horror in Literature." Phlegon was a freedman of Hadrian (A.D. 117–138), whose *On Wonderful Events* has never been translated, but for the brief fragment Lovecraft read in L. Collison-Morley's *Greek and Roman Ghost Stories* (1912), which does indeed tell the story of a young man betrothed to a beautiful woman whom relatives later recognize to be someone who has died. She'd certainly be a vampire in modern fiction, but she has no fangs in Phlegon, or even in latter adaptations of the tale (dramas by Goethe and Anatole France, both entitled *The Bride of Corinth*) because the befanged, coffin-dwelling, cape-wearing vampire hadn't been invented yet.

Indeed, the vampire — with fangs, cape, and angst — is largely the invention of Bram Stoker, with substantial additions to the "rules" made by Hollywood and subsequent fiction. (Did you know that Stoker's Dracula can come out in daylight? He does at least twice.) The vampire of Eastern European folklore became the subject of what we might today call "the tabloid press" in the 18th century. There was enough of a "vampire flap" (excuse the pun and remember that vampires at this point had no connection with bats) in the Austro-Hungarian Empire that investigators were sent to the eastern provinces to find out what was behind it all. They found frightened peasants digging up and mutilating corpses which were alleged to fatten on the blood of the living, but still behaved quite differently from a modern "standard" vampire.

An 18th-century Austro-Hungarian vampire was hardly a suave, aristocratic seducer in evening clothes, but an obnoxious peasant corpse which sometimes grew enormously bloated with stolen blood while lying, uncorrupted, in its grave. Did it rise out of the grave at all? That's not clear. In modern terms, we might say that it moved by astral projection. No creaking coffin lids, no displaced earth . . . and no fangs. These vampires sometimes attacked their victims with their *fists*.

For sufficient detail to drive off the squeamish, see Paul Barber's *Vampires, Burial, and Death* (Yale University Press, 1988) which not only gives the whole story of the Austro-Hungarian vampire flap, but explains all the things that can happen to a corpse to make it bloat up with blood (and even make noises) without seeming to rot.

One traditional explanation for the lack of vampires in the ancient world is that vampires were created by the Devil to parody the resurrection of Christ, and since the Devil was not privy to God's plans, he couldn't do this until after the fact. *Ergo,* no B.C. vampires.

But it may also be that the stories (and the fears and beliefs that spawned them) which were to produce vampires took a while to evolve. Indeed they are still evolving. Notice how on *Buffy the Vampire-Slayer* the vampires' faces morph into a bestial, vaguely serpentine form when the vampires are in attack mode. That may well become standard in the future, as the black cape once was.

Then there are the variously exotic and disgusting Asian vampires, such as the ones in Lafcadio Hearn's *Kwaidan* whose heads separate from their bodies and fly around at night. Such beings mix with the human population by day, but may be detected by a red band around the neck when the head is about to come off. Other Asian vampires drag their entrails below the flying head; the worst one we've heard of is native to Thailand, where the head and entrails of a wicked person allegedly slither along the ground devouring excrement.

None of these vampires have anything to do with Dracula, Hollywood standards, or Buffy.

Ghosts, too, have evolved. In the ancient world they were sometimes a black outline of a person, or a walking skeleton, or merely an apparition of the person as he or she appeared in life. If you wanted to dress up like a ghost in ancient Greece or Rome, you would wear all black clothing, paint any exposed skin black, and don a skull mask.

Ghosts didn't acquire flowing white sheets until mass-production had made cloth cheap enough that people could afford to wrap corpses in shrouds, particularly during 19th century epidemics. Now that shrouds are out of fashion, most ghosts are sheetless again.

What is the point of all this?

It is that supernatural beliefs are temporally and culturally relative. What does this mean to the writer or reader of weird fiction? It means that we can pick and choose among various beliefs for story material, but this has to be done with some care. Modern psychic or New Age

IMAGINE CON

Sci-Fi, Fantasy, Horror, Comic & Toy Fair Convention

April 20-23, 2000 at the Virginia Beach Pavilion

Author Guest of Honor
Kevin J. Anderson

Artist Guest of Honor
Larry Elmore

Fan Guest of Honor
Ed Kramer

Gaming Guest of Honor
Gary Gygax

SPFX Guest of Honor
Terrence Masson

Media Guest of Honor
Ray Park

Guests of Literature
Rebecca Moesta
Jody Lynne Nye
Stephen Mark Rainey
Bud Webster

Media Guests
Richard Hatch
Anne Lockhart
Erin Gray
Yvonne Craig
Kari Wuhrer
Brinke Stevens
James Hong
Maggie Egan
Tom Savini

Other Featured Guests
Bernie Wrightson
Dorian Cleavenger
NeNe Thomas
More guests!

Events

Masquerade-Independent Film Festival-Gaming Tournaments-World Premieres-Dance-
Charity Auction-Art Show-Panels & Seminars-Live Theater Performances-
2-24 Hour Video Rooms-Giveaways-Dance-Party Floor-Art Auction-
Hall Costume Contest-Plus Much More!

"A Celebration of the Imagination!"

www.imaginecon.com for full details

beliefs would be inappropriate in Keith Taylor's ancient Egyptian stories, for example.

And we once got into a terrible argument with a writing student who wrote a story about a 19th century Pennsylvania coal miner who started having all sorts of psychic, New Age, neo-pagan experiences. No, we said. He's probably Irish. He's probably a poorly educated (and possibly illiterate) Catholic, who has never even *heard* of reincarnation, past lives, or channeling. Certainly he would address any strange happenings in a strictly Judeo-Christian context.

The student got very upset. She found our implied skepticism entirely too threatening. We hadn't even mentioned, let alone ridiculed, her belief in her own psychic abilities. We were talking about *fiction*. But she had made the classic mistake of the true believer. She had, like those African tribesmen listening to the story of Hamlet, assumed that her beliefs were universal through all time and geography. As long as she was going to assume that, she had no business writing fantasy, since in the fantastic or weird story there is an understanding between the writer and the reader that the story is made up. There is what we might call the agreement of artifice.

Whether one believes in the supernatural or not in real life, one has to be just a bit skeptical when writing fiction. One has to stand aside from the story, and pick and choose the elements which serve the interests of the story. It cannot be a matter of doctrine.

Ultimately the 2nd century satirist Lucian of Samosata said it best, in the preface to his famous *A True History* (which is anything but):

"I'm writing about things I neither saw nor heard from another, things which don't exist and couldn't possibly exist. So readers beware: don't believe any of it."

Congratulations are in order to **Bruce Boston,** whose poetry you have read in these pages many times before. The Science Fiction Poetry Association has now made Bruce its first **Grand Master Poet.** This award is both for outstanding achievement as well as for winning the most Rhysling Awards (also given by the SFPA) from 1985 to the present. We joked with Bruce, recalling what Joyce Carol Oates said when she got a Life Achievement Award from the Horror Writers of America a few years ago, "Does this mean everything I do from now on is posthumous?"

Not exactly. Bruce is the author of 24 books of fiction and poetry so far, the most recent of which was *Cold Tomorrows,* published by Gothic Press in 1998. Next up is *The Complete Accursed Wives,* assembling a series, some of which have appeared in *Weird Tales®.* It will be published by Dark Regions and Talisman, about the time you read this, at 100 pages, with five stories and thirty-five poems, plus five illustrations by Allen Koszowski. Send $8.95 to Talisman, Box 565572, Miami FL 33256–5572.

Is John Betancourt taking over the universe? Our former colleague's Wildside Press is now the top print-on-demand publisher in SF, Fantasy, and Horror. He is bringing out huge quantities of reprints, and some originals (some of those by your editor, Darrell Schweitzer, about which, see the ad elsewhere in this issue). All are handsome, well-bound trade paperbacks on good paper. Print-on-demand technology, which makes it possible to print and bind even single copies of a book, is going to revolutionize publishing in the next few years. Realistically, what the publisher does is order fifty or a hundred copies at once, sell those, then order some more. He doesn't have to spend all his money up front on inventory, and can merely put some of the profits back into the printing of more copies . . . and it goes on forever. Wildside has put out close to fifty titles in the last couple of months. It's a delight to see new editions of works by **R.A. Lafferty, Keith Roberts, Phyllis Ann Karr, Lin Carter, Mike Resnick, H. Rider Haggard, Theophile Gautier** . . . and as that list implies, it's a mix of modern authors' works and public-domain classics. There is some non-fiction, including S.T. Joshi's critical study of Lovecraft, *A Subtler Magick,* as well as reprints of several Schweitzer-edited anthologies of essays, starting with *Discovering Classic Fantasy Fiction.* And, the day before we did this editorial, your editor composed for Wildside Press introductions to new editions of the definitive Flying Dutchman novel, *The Phantom Ship* by Captain Frederick Marryat, and *The Witch of Prague,* an occult thriller by F. Marion Crawford, the author of the classic "The Upper Berth."

But for the *Weird Tales®* reader, perhaps the most intriguing Wildside reprint is their edition of the legendary *The Moon Terror* by A.G. Birch (actually an anthology, containing the title novel, plus three stories by other writers, one of them editor Farnsworth Wright and another Vincent Starrett). This book was originally published by

Weird Tales® itself in the late 1920s. Most issues from the '20s into the late '50s contained an ad for *The Moon Terror*.

Now you can see what the fuss was about, for just $15.00. (No charge for postage if you mention *Weird Tales*®. Write to Wildside Press, 522 Park Ave., Berkeley Heights NJ 07922 or check their web-page: http://www.wildsidepress.com.

Another book we recommend is *Science Fiction of the 20th Century* by Frank M. Robinson, published by Collectors Press (P.O. Box 2390986, Portland OR 97281). It's a large, coffee-table book (256 pp., $59.95). It is largely a publishing history, filled with illuminating anecdotes about the people who made the future happen in American popular culture. Its strongest point is truly spectacular color reproductions of book and magazine covers and movie posters (on virtually every page), many of which are the best (i.e. the cleanest and clearest) ever done. It's a beautiful volume to page through. After you're done that, settle down and read it, as the text itself is quite sound.

We have a letter from **Christopher Dunn**:
Thank you for your evisceration of the new

Haunting. *I mean it. Ever since seeing the trailers on TV and the review by Ebert and* Watch This Space *(I can't remember who the guest critic was that week) — a surprisingly mild review, by the way, for the damned thing — I've really longed to see it get what it deserved: sliced up in a grossout, popping–viscera–eyeball–gouging (even if you have to reach all the way into the mouth, à la Edward Lee) review by somebody. The Robert Wise film has been my personal standard for real fear and horror of the unknown, and for any haunted-house movie, since I first saw it in the '70s — and that was on TV with commercials every ten minutes. It's a true classic. And with hardly a trace of special effects. I have avoided seeing the current version, and it doesn't seem I am ever going to regret it. You're right in every detail about the damned thing: pure parasitism, and blood-sucking at that.*

I did have one thought about the Blair *movie, while I saw it and afterwards too. . . . Of all the authors of ghost stories I happen to be familiar with, the one who instantly came to mind, considering the use of suggestion and the general course of the story was — M.R. James.*

Now wait before you jump out of your chair. I know he was a minimalist, and he didn't go in for

screaming confrontations. James was, on the surface of his stories, quieter. But innocents innocently stirring up dreadful things and barely (if at all — remember "Count Magnus"? "A Warning to the Curious"?) surviving with their skins — that was the common theme in James. And under that quiet surface there were real horrors. I especially remember, in "Count Magnus," the little tale told by Herr Nielsen. And, of course, your suggestion of how The Blair Witch Project might have been handled, condensed, is exactly parallel to the way James actually did it. And he was a master of suggestion of terrible things.

And now, please, a moment of quiet: for some advice from a master, about poetry, Mr. Geis, and you. From the champion, if not the patron saint (hence the reverent quiet) of "vers libre":

" . . . what i have
always claimed is that manners and methods
are no great matter compared
with thoughts in poetry you cant hide
gems of thought so they wont flash"

But that poet always made sense, especially when you consider the effort he put into his writing. Archy the Cockroach was a genuine artist.

Your comparison of The Blair Witch Project with M.R. James is interesting. Yes, both do work from suggestion, though surely Blair Witch is by far the more primitive rendition. James would doubtless have approved of the effort, but if he had been writing the script, there would have surely been a more complete conclusion. His stories *ended* rather than just stopped.

Archy was certainly right. We have been fans of Don Marquis's poetical cockroach ever since a late-night rap session at a Clarion workshop many years ago, when Theodore Sturgeon, who had had even less sleep than the rest of us, suddenly out of the blue insisted that we all must read The Life and Times of Archy and Mehitibel. Yes, indeed, manners and methods are less important than content, which is what Archy seems to be saying. Our beef with much modern poetry is that there doesn't seem to *be* any accessible content.

Certainly we wouldn't insist that rhymed poetry is inherently *superior* to any other kind, keeping in mind:

He who stops and takes the time
to place his thoughts in metered rhyme

can still, with scarce a mental swivel,
turn out verse of purest drivel.

Samuel Lightcap of Philadelphia writes:
Regarding the demise of poetry in popular culture, please consider that this could be merely the product of a simple change in tastes. Both popular and high arts rarely have much staying power over the course of a century. Forms which do, such as classical music, have strong tendencies against radical innovation built into their communities. Mention Philip Glass in the wrong circles and listen to the deathly silence in response. And also consider that while anyone can write a poem (or a musical piece) it takes considerable skill to write a GOOD one.

As to Mr. Joshi's thoughts on what makes a horror story, I believe that the supernatural element is mandatory. That does not mean, for example, that the reader has to believe in ghosts, but that the character has to. Psycho is thus a horror story because Norman is convinced that his dead mother lives; it doesn't matter for purposes of this definition that the ghost is only in his mind. The Alienist is not a horror story, lacking this element, despite some gruesome elements. Please feel free to shoot holes in this notion.

Well, offered in the spirit of gentlemanly discussion: **Bang! Bang! Bang!** We tend to be suspicious of definitions which insist that this or that element or technique is absolutely necessary. Art is what the artist can get away with, if by "get away with" one means that he still arouses an emotional and intellectual response in the reader.

A horror story, then, is whatever seems horrific. That is, it is defined by the emotional response it creates, not by the elements that went into that emotional response. Admittedly this puts us smack on that very troublesome borderline between horror fiction and crime fiction (a region Cemetery Dance magazine exploits so capably), but we have to admit that some of Poe's most horrifying tales are non-fantastic: "A Cask of Amontillado," "The Pit and the Pendulum," "The Premature Burial," etc. And think of that spectacularly gruesome classic from the pages of the old-time Weird Tales®, "The Copper Bowl" by George Fielding Eliot, which will make you shudder for a long time, and certainly isn't fantastic, unless you have really elaborate theories about where the rat went.

We don't want to rule out non-fantastic horror. But at the same time let us say that a supernatural element in horror fiction is certainly *useful*, and especially in *Weird Tales®*, where the emphasis is on supernatural and fantastic horror.

Are the art-forms that last more than a century inherently conservative? Really? The lyric poem is not entirely dead, and it has been around for a very long time. Even the metrical romance hung in there for several centuries. The stage-play has been doing pretty well since Shakespeare's time, and has undergone occasional revolutions of form and content. The novel was invented in ancient Greece, and certainly suffered a hiatus during the Middle Ages, but it has been chugging along quite steadily since the 18th century. If nobody has the attention span to read anymore, why are the books (and trilogies, and series) getting longer?

But the numbers tell us something. 8,000 copies sold in hardcover is pretty good for the average novel. (Or 50,000 in paperback.) The average poetry book does well to sell 500 copies. The United States has a population of 250 million. Could it be that we have a reading public more the size you'd expect in Lichtenstein?

Chris Bevard of Springfield- LA, who edits a small-press horror magazine called *Flicker*, writes:

I've been a reader of Weird Tales *for quite some time, and there were a few points that I find necessary to address in your editorial concerning the comeback of Horror.*

In no way, shape, or form do I think we should "go for the gross-out," since this is usually quite unimaginative and usually burns out quickly. However, I have to say, in response to the question of how to get horror fans into Weird Tales, *that based on what I am seeing in the tastes and preferences of many new horror fans,* Weird Tales *is hardly the forum they should turn to for cutting edge horror. Don't take this statement the wrong way; I think* Weird Tales *is a wonderful magazine. Its attractive layout, covers, and content make for a finely-tuned magazine of fantasy and science fiction. But would I recommend it to a horror fan whose tastes lie in the realm of such contemporaries as Poppy Z. Brite, Charlee Jacob, or Douglas Clegg? Never. It wouldn't even cross my mind, because I cannot help but consider* Weird Tales *a fantasy magazine. It hasn't proven itself to me as anything otherwise in the course of my subscription.*

I like hardcore horror, and by this I don't mean

eye-popping, skull-crushing gore or explicit sex & language. "Visceral," however, does not always refer to gore, and I believe that if the horror genre is going to successfully move forward, more attention needs to be paid to raw and intense fiction by the likes of the aforementioned authors and others too numerous to list here. This is not to say that every story be filled with nonstop images of explosive mayhem, simply that such small press publications as Flicker, Mindmares, Flesh and Blood, Mightnight Carnival, *and* Deadbolt *(to name a few) are focussed on delivering pure horror — no fantasy, and no science fiction.*

For horror to survive as a viable and respected genre, it will require the uncompromising touch of authors such as Brite or Jacob to propel us forward, and it will also require markets that are clear in their intent. In short, it must be willing to take risks. I must confess, upon receiving a new issue of Weird Tales *in the mail, I sometimes wonder if I will find any stories that I consider "horror" inside. Rarely do I find "true" horror stories. Case in point, "Christmas Stalking," featured in your current issue. A very imaginative story, and I enjoyed it a great deal, but is it horror? I don't think so, and I don't think that any of my peers would think so either.*

Weird Tales can do whatever it wants; as I said, it's one of the better magazines out there in terms of production. The small press can work wonders over a period of time toward establishing authors firmly in the world of writing, but larger magazines with more pull need to step up to the challenge of ushering horror into its next phase of life. . . Every little bit helps, and if Weird Tales *wants to be a force in welcoming horror back into the collective consciousness with open arms, it should leave the fantasy and science fiction to others. A "chill up the spine" is preferable to a gross-out. The challenge is finding appropriate chills, something that, despite the occasional presence of such giants as Ramsey Campbell,* Weird Tales *seems to have a great deal of trouble locking in on.*

Uh, Mr. Bevard, meet Mr. Lightcap. One of you wants *no* fantastic content in *Weird Tales®*, the other insists that the supernatural is *essential* to true horror. This reminds us of the fable of the blind men and the elephant, and we'd have to conclude that Mr. Lightcap has hold of the larger part, but still not everything. Where we absolutely cannot agree with you, Mr. Bevard, is where you seem to insist that fantasy and science fiction preclude the possibility of horror. That being so, we are puzzled at your admiration of Ramsey Campbell, however well-placed, because virtually *all* of his work has fantastic content.

If there really are readers out there who don't know that horror can — and usually does — have fantastic content, I suppose we can, in a way, envy them, because of all the discoveries they have before them: Poe, Lovecraft, Machen, Le Fanu, Blackwood, M.R. James, Ray Bradbury, Harlan Ellison, Richard Matheson, Fritz Leiber, Stephen King, Thomas Ligotti . . . the list goes on and on. These readers have yet to stumble upon the mainstream of 19th and 20th century horror fiction.

Weird Tales® is part of that mainstream. It seems to us that the non-fantastic horror story, while certainly valid, is as specialized as the haiku. An entire magazine of such stories would be like a mystery magazine devoted entirely to locked room mysteries.

Would it satisfy you if we admit that *Weird Tales®* is not entirely focussed on horror? No, we didn't think "Christmas Stalking" was horror either. We thought it was funny. We will publish humor, sentimental fantasy, adventure fantasy, sword and sorcery, mythic fantasy . . . and, yes, horror, most of it supernatural or fantastic. This is what *Weird Tales®* has been about since it was founded in 1923. But we rarely publish science fiction. By our definitions, we have published exactly two science-fiction stories in the past twelve years, the last one being Michael Flynn's "Dragons" in issue #294, back in 1989. And that resulted from a "bet" between George Scithers and Stanley Schmidt to see who could find a story which was suitable for both *Analog®* and *Weird Tales®*. Stanley won.

Ross Eddy Osborn of Oklahoma City writes, about R.G. Evans's "Deadline":

I liked this grim-reaper tale for a few solid reasons. The opening hook, "It's going badly," held my attention at first; one has to find out what is going badly in a story titled "Deadline." The eerie work was surely chiseled out by personal experience, i.e., something looking over the author's shoulder, torment via his father's knifing criticism, a second string loved-one triangle, et cetera. The descriptive walk through the author's inner horrors was chilling. And his suspect fear, or craving of writer's block — which he so gracefully ground into his ghostly encounter — drove home like acidic ice. A job well done, I'd venture.

The Most Popular Story in issue #318 is, by a two-to-one margin, "Deadline" by R.G. Evans. Runner-up is "Christmas Stalking" by James Van Pelt. Third place went to "To Close a Door" by George Barr.

Forthcoming in future issues are stories by **Tanith Lee, Phyllis and Alex Eisenstein, Don Webb, Brian Stableford**, and **Keith Taylor**. We also have more of the popular Sekenre series by a certain **Darrell Schweitzer**.

See you next time.   Ω

SHADOWINGS
By Douglas E. Winter

Stories of Our Own

I am a man, and men are animals who tell stories. This is a gift from God, who spoke our species into being but left the end of our story untold. That mystery is troubling to us. How could it be otherwise? Without the final part, we think, how are we to make sense of all that went before, which is to say, our lives. So we make stories of our own, in fevered and envious imitation of our maker, hoping that we'll tell, by chance, what God left untold, and in finishing our tale, come to understand why we were born.

— Clive Barker, *Sacrament* (1996)

The Essential Clive Barker. New York: HarperCollins, 2000, 568 pp., $27.50.

Years ago, in a moment of quiet introspection, Clive Barker told me of a fond wish: that his creations might somehow take on a life of their own and wander out into the world — leaving him in solitude, and anonymity. "I would like one day to wander," he said, "in my last hour, through the collective unconsciousness, the culture of which I was a part, and find little places where I was. And none of these things would have 'This was made by Clive Barker' at the bottom. . . . Because that, finally, isn't the point."

Soon afterward, he found himself celebrating Halloween on West Hollywood's Santa Monica Boulevard. Among the partying throng was someone costumed as his most famous creation: "Pinhead" from the *Hellraiser* films. Giddy with drink, Barker decided to introduce himself. "I created you," he told the reveler, who replied: "Fuck off."

It was his wish come true, and also a fine metaphor for the Frankensteinian relationship between creator and creation that has marked the *Hellraiser* films. A few years later, however, the spurious Pinhead's answer might not have been so rude or uninformed. Clive Barker, with his ever-spiraling success, has become that figment of the popular imagination known as a

celebrity, with its share of pleasures — and perils.

In his most recent film, *Lord of Illusions* (1995), noir heroine Dorothea Swann laments: "Sometimes people get lost — even good people. Too much money, too much fame." Her words echo the sentiments of His Satanic Majesty in Barker's early play *The History of the Devil* (1980): "Do you know how difficult it is not to believe what people say about you? Not to become your own publicity?"

In the two dazzling but difficult decades that brought him from starving playwright to bestseller and Hollywood player, there have been temptations and moments of overindulgence, but Clive Barker did not lose himself in his fame. Indeed, as recent novels like *Sacrament* (1996) and *Galilee* (1998) suggest, perhaps, in making a public journey from innocence to experience, he found himself. That journey is now celebrated in *The Essential Clive Barker*, a unique retrospective that Barker personally assembled for readers, old and new.

Obviously the events of the past twenty years have changed Barker as a person and personality. "Inevitably," notes Doug Bradley, his longtime friend and collaborator (and, indeed, the actor who portrayed Pinhead on film). "He was successful, where he had not been so successful before. He was earning large amounts of money, where he had not been doing that before. He had

a lot of people beating a path to his door. He had a lot of people wanting a piece of his action, who had not been there before. And he had power that he had not had before. And you can't throw all those things at someone at once and expect them to remain the same person. Fundamentally, he didn't change at all. And that's been true right the way through. Granted, he used to be broke and lived in a flat up the road from me, and now he's a millionaire and lives in Beverly Hills. That re-defines people in obvious ways; but fundamentally, when I pick up the phone and talk to him, it's no different at all."

When, early in the 1990s, Clive returned home to Liverpool and visited Quarry Bank Grammar School for a television documentary, he made plans to meet his former teacher and mentor, Norman Russell, outside the Headmaster's Study. Russell was talking with a group of masters; as he recalls: "This figure in jeans was there waiting for the Sirs to finish speaking, and it was Clive — a man of great distinction and wealth and so on — but still waiting for Sir to finish talking. It was incredible. A lesser person couldn't do that. He seems to have bypassed all the nonsense that can go with success. It doesn't seem to have touched him at all. He could have

been quite insufferable if he wanted to be . . . but he's very kind to me."

That kindness has extended on to an ever-growing legion of readers and fans. Moved by the reading public's embrace of the *Books of Blood*, Barker decided to respond individually to each fan letter — a task that soon proved impossible. But popularity also had its price. On October 8, 1988, while promoting *Cabal*, Barker appeared at the Forbidden Planet bookstore in Greenwich Village. Lines snaked out of the store and around the block as people waited for hours to spend a few moments with Barker and have him sign their books. During the session, he was approached by a man some described as a "punk," but whom Barker recalls as a "perfectly normal-looking guy, who sounded quite articulate and self-possessed." The man suddenly slashed a razor blade along the veins of his own arm, offering the wound to Barker; nonplussed, Barker signed the book, then put his hand in the blood and pressed his wet palm into the book. The man was shown out of the store.

Fame also brought remarkable opportunities to advocate his vision in interviews and television appearances — and to create. He was asked to write, and possibly direct, the motion picture *Alien 3*; but he declined without hesitation, for the simple reason that it was *Alien 3*: the third entry in a series based on someone else's aesthetic and universe. While he felt perfectly comfortable in rejecting this high-paying, high-visibility offer, he is equally comfortable in contemplating a six-month hiatus to fashion a theatrical work that would be "so avant-garde that no one would want to see it" — or to propose writing a "bodice-ripper" of a romance novel or unabashed pornography.

Barker works without great concern for critics or the machinations of the culture industry, recognizing that, once he has committed his vision to the page or celluloid or canvas, the assessments of others are beyond control; he declines to expend emotion on anything but his next creation. "It's much more important," he says, "that somebody sees that what I'm doing is not like anybody else's than that they like it. Being liked as an artist is lower on my list of priorities than I would sometimes like it to be." It is idealism, perhaps — this belief that talent, if exercised, will win out; but he lived on welfare and his wits for ten years; and he has never forgotten what it meant to have labored in the shadows for so long, and then, at last, succeed. "If you believe in yourself," he insists, "you must do it." His inspiration is convincing in its simplicity, and he is its living example: dreams can become realities if you commit yourself to the task, intent on your own vision, and not that of artists you admire or a genre or the marketplace.

In a worthy summation of a twenty-year career as a professional writer — for the stage, books, and the screen — *The Essential Clive Barker* presents excerpts from Barker's writing that are organized around thirteen themes. None of the selections is new; instead, Barker has surveyed and selected elements of his prose that offer particular insight into his creative vision and the ways in which his stories and plays and novels intersect.

"Private Legends," the sizable essay that introduces *The Essential Clive Barker,* is alone worth the price of admission: a fine mingling of autobiography, creative manifesto and insights on the art and craft of prose, it is indeed essential to an understanding of his varied and prolific creations. The text that follows is an elaborate and edifying mosaic that offers a unique reading experience for even the most devoted fan.

As the introduction notes: "I don't expect anybody to pick this book up, begin on page one, and dutifully read on to the end . . . I think one of the pleasures of a collection like this is that it encourages a nomadic spirit. You wander here and there, guided only by some vague instinct." Nomads will find a rich selection of prose in these pages, and even constant readers may be surprised by the diversity of themes that Barker has deemed "essential."

Although the opening sections are devoted to the *sine qua non* of the fantastique — "Doorways" and "Journeys" — and subsequent themes include "Bestiary" and "Terrors" and "Making and Unmaking," two themes deserve special note. In "Old Humanity," Barker collects three worthy interludes from his early fiction (the novels *The Damnation Game* and *Weaveworld,* and the novelette "The Forbidden") that explore his fascination with the haunting of the modern by the ancient, particularly in our telling of stories, and the invention and evolution of myths and legends. In "Memory," he explores the power that nostalgia plays in his fiction — and the epic struggle of remembering and forgetting that he has confronted in life and in literature. As he notes here, and so eloquently: "The man who is remembering must take the responsibility for what he remembers."

By Douglas E. Winter

Gathered in these pages are stories, vignettes, set-pieces, mood-pieces, dreams, visions, nightmares, indulgences, insights: like the magical carpet of *Weaveworld,* a tapestry that is rich with fantasy, horror, and humanity. *The Essential Clive Barker* is a writer's reflection on the state of his art, and a perfect guide for readers who find the creative twists and turns of Barker's career either daunting or difficult, at times, to understand. And it is a fine bedside companion, best read, as he intended, in spare moments, paged through almost at random like the Bible or a book of poetry.

The diversity of content showcased in *The Essential Clive Barker* also underscores the aesthetic of evolution and re-invention that is the singular hallmark of Barker's creative life: from plays and musicals and pantomimes to short stories to novels to films to comic books to children's books to artwork to photography — a flux whose only constant is change.

When Barker chose to look back on his *Books of Blood,* more than a decade after their original publication, his reaction is instructive:

I look at these pieces and I don't think the man who wrote them is alive in me anymore.

We are all our own graveyards I believe; we squat amongst the tombs of the people we were. If we're healthy, every day is a celebration, a Day of the Dead, in which we give thanks for the lives that we lived; and if we are neurotic we brood and mourn and wish that the past was still present.

Reading these stories over, I feel a little of both. Some of the simple energies that made these words flow through my pen — that made the phrases felicitous and the ideas sing — have gone. I lost their maker a long time ago.

Although these words may have shocked and disappointed some readers, they were no surprise to Barker's friends.

As Doug Bradley notes: "Clive has always held horror near to his heart, never strayed far from it; but I knew, at the same time that Stephen King was saying that Clive was the future of horror,' Clive was saying, in his head, 'The hell I am!' "

Writing in *The Essential Clive Barker*, Barker revisits the pleasures and perils of his identification with horror:

I have, to be honest, an ambiguous response to that reputation. It has been all too often an easy peg for lazy journalists to hang a headline on; and for a certain order of reviewers, more interested in turning a phrase than exercising their intellects, it has been a stick to beat me with. But then if it hadn't been that it would have been something else; we all make rods for our own backs. I still enjoy crafting horror movies. It's a genre, which, for all its inanities, can still stir people up, which is always pleasing. It's such a primal form — it deals in the meat and bone of our existence — yet the moral issues it raises can be surprisingly complex: that's an attractive package.

As to writing horror, I think I'm done, barring a few pieces I still have in the works, designed to finish mythologies that still need closure. Of course I'll still go after a frisson if I see that the narrative offers me one; I just can't imagine devoting an entire novel to the business of scaring the reader. Sometimes, in fact, there's more potency in a darkness that creeps out of nowhere, its presence unsuspected, than in a fiction that announces from the first word that it intends to scare.

Curious words, it might seem, for a writer who announced his glee with the stuff of shock some fifteen years ago, when the *Books of Blood* shook the sudden and staid genre of horror; but these are also courageous words from a writer whose creative ambitions were cloistered by his own success — and who turned his back on the expected, spending years writing himself into freedom.

"I feel wiser the more I write," Barker says. "And I felt, even when I was making something like [his grammar school magazine] *Humphri*, that I was exploring myself and that I was explaining myself to myself, the way that any imaginative writer does. You feel emptied out by what you've made, but you also feel as though the journey to get there has made you, if it's any good, richer and stronger and more knowing and more self-knowing. The telling of stories is a particularly easy metaphor because it's the ultimate procedure: it's causality, it's connectedness, it's making sense where there apparently is not sense. It's saying: 'This is connected with this is connected with this is connected with this . . .' and before you know it, you've got a story. And you are like God, because you can put 'The End' on. And God puts 'The End' on, but we don't, in our own lives; we just have to wait it out."

In waiting it out, Clive Barker chooses to tell the stories that are uniquely his to tell, without concession to the conventions of commercialism or genre, urging us ever forward on new journeys of enlightenment. As he wrote in his most recent novel, *Galilee*:

I have to tell what I know. That's why I'm here; I have to tell people all that I've seen and felt, so that my pain is never repeated. So that those who come after me are like my children, because I helped shape them, and make them strong.

[Excerpted in part from *Clive Barker: The Dark Fantastic* by Douglas E. Winter, coming from HarperCollins in December]   Ω

We offer copies of *Weird Tales*® in full-cloth, hard-cover editions, numbered & limited to 200 copies or less, stamped in gold on the spine, & signed by the featured author & featured artist, & by the editors of the magazine. The text is printed on high-quality book paper. We offer the remainder of this stock at **$15** a copy!

    WT#292, signed by Keith Taylor, the featured author, & by Carl Lundgren, the featured artist.

☐ *WT*#296, signed by David Schow & Vincent DiFate.

☐ *WT*#297, signed by Nancy Springer & Frank Kelly Freas.

☐ *WT*#298, signed by Chet Williamson. This, our first multiple-artist issue (the previous ones were each illustrated by a single artist), contains the first reprint of Stephen King's first published story, "The Glass Floor." The issue is NOT signed by King, however.

We also offer cloth-bound, hard-cover copies of *Weird Tales*®, identical in quality to those described above, except that they are not signed, numbered, nor limited. We offer this stock in the titles listed below for just **$10** a copy!

☐ *WT*#291, the second issue of *Weird Tales*® since its revival in our hands. Tanith Lee is the featured author; Stephen Fabian, the featured artist.

☐ *WT*#293, with Avram Davidson as featured author, plus stories by Ian Watson & Keith Roberts; all art by Hank Jankus.

☐ *WT*#294, with Karl Edward Wagner's last Kane story; the whole issue is illustrated by J.K. Potter.

☐ *WT*#295, with Brian Lumley as the featured author & Vincent DiFate as featured artist.

And we have copies of a few issues of *Weird Tales*® in magazine (softcover) format: **$5** each, post paid (outside the USA & possessions, **$6** each).

☐ *WT*#293, with Avram Davidson as featured author, plus Ian Watson & Keith Roberts; all art by Hank Jankus.

☐ *WT*#297, stories by Nancy Springer, Thomas Ligotti, & John Brunner; all art by Frank Kelly Freas.

☐ *WT*#302, William F. Nolan, Brian Lumley, Robert Bloch, & Jason Van Hollander; cover by Bob Eggleton.

☐ *WT*#303, Thomas Ligotti, Tanith Lee, & Darrell Schweitzer; cover by Jason Van Hollander & Allen Koszowski.

☐ *WT*#304, John Brunner, Ramsey Campbell, Tanith Lee, S.P. Somtow; cover by Jill Bauman.

☐ *WT*#306, Nini Kiriki Hoffman, Tanith Lee, Lord Dunsany; all art by Nicholas Jainschigg.

☐ *WT*#307, two novellas by Ian Watson, plus stories by John Brunner & Fritz Leiber; cover by Paul Lehr.

☐ *WT*#313, Tanith Lee, Melanie Tem, Ian Watson, & Darrell Schweitzer; cover by Jason Van Hollander.

☐ *WT*#314, S.P. Somtow, Tanith Lee, David Schow & Brian Stableford; cover by Stephen Fabian.

☐ *WT*#315, Ian MacLeod, Tanith Lee, Thomas Ligotti, & Ramsey Campbell; cover by Jack Gaughan.

☐ *WT*#316, Tanith Lee, Thomas Ligotti, Ian Watson, & Lord Dunsany; cover by Jill Bauman.

☐ *WT*#317, Hugh B. Cave, Brian Stableford, Andy Duncan; cover by Rick Berry.

☐ *WT*#318, Ramsey Campbell, Tanith Lee, Andy Duncan, Keith Taylor; cover by Bob Eggleton

---

Worlds of Fantasy & Horror, **$5** each, post paid (outside the USA & possessions, **$6** each):

☐ *WoF&H*#1, Ramsey Campbell, Joyce Carol Oates, William F. Nolan, Lord Dunsany, & Morgan Llywelyn.

☐ *WoF&H*#3, Tanith Lee, Chet Williamson, & Lord Dunsany; cover by Ian Miller.

☐ *WoF&H*#4, Tanith Lee, Thomas Ligotti, & Ian Watson; Peter Straub interviewed; cover by Douglas Beekman.

Live in Pennsylvania? Add 6% for sales tax. If ordering hard-covers, please add **$3** per order for shipping.

Send your address with check or money order to us at:

Name: _____

Address: _____

More address: _____

City/State/Zip: _____

Terminus Publishing Co., Inc.
123 Crooked Lane
King of Prussia PA 19406-2570

HEART'S BLOOD
by William F. Nolan

illustrated by Stephen E. Fabian

Remember the shooting at that high school in Roanoke, Virginia, six years ago? The one where the 16-year-old student-body president mowed down a dozen of his classmates with an assault rifle? His name was Lucas Fraley, and when his friends were interviewed on TV they talked about how he was always so friendly and coöperative and how popular he was with everyone. Lucas never touched drugs or alcohol, they said. Just an all-around great guy.

I remember the way his mother looked on the TV newscasts: no make-up, her hair severely pulled back in a bun, standing stiff-backed in front of the camera, chin up, defiant as a pit bull, as she declared that Lucas had never given her a single day's worry, that he was her "perfect child."

Then what had gone wrong?

During a televised prison interview, young Fraley provided the answer. He was a good-looking boy, tanned and fit, with the dark, probing eyes of a serious student, and he spoke in calm, measured tones.

"I've always been very religious," he stated. "My family has belonged to the Full Holiness Gospel Church my whole life, and for the last two years I've served as Junior Pastor in the Sunday School. Seems like I always knew that my life's calling was to the ministry."

During a ninth-grade course in World History, Fraley developed what he admitted was a "total obsession" with Arthurian lore. "It was natural," he said, "once I discovered that King Arthur was my ancestor." Fraley explained that the celebrated King Arthur, who'd lived in Britain fourteen hundred years ago, was actually descended from the marriage of Jesus and Mary Magdalene. A thousand years after Arthur's death, the fabled monarch's descendants included England's King Charles II, who in his leisure hours 'had impregnated an unmarried palace servant girl named Elsbeth, then banished her and her unborn child to the New World colony of Virginia. "Her son by King Charles, born right here in Virginia, was my direct ancestor," Fraley said.

He'd hesitated at this point, his dark eyes flashing with sudden anger. "One night my girlfriend and I were playing Truth or Dare. She asked me what my greatest secret was, the thing I didn't want *anyone* to know. I told her that I was the direct descendant of Jesus Christ, and that I carried his genes within mine. I thought she'd understand, but instead she laughed at me. Then she told our friends and *they* started laughing at me. That's why they had to die. People should never laugh at a son of Jesus."

The newspapers had a field day.

SELF-STYLED SON OF JESUS CONFESSES
Mentally Disturbed Youth Attempts to Justify Killing Rampage

Fraley's father refused to be interviewed and wouldn't comment; his photo in the paper, with his dark eyes exuding religious zealotry, was chilling. A self-righteous, cold-hearted bastard if I ever saw one. After the shooting, the Fraleys separated, and later — despite the rigid precepts of the Full Holiness Gospel Church — Mrs. Fraley filed for divorce. Lucas had been their only child.

My parents had done the same thing . . . split up when I was in high school. My father went away somewhere and I never heard from him again. And like Lucas, I didn't have any brothers or sisters. The court gave custody of me to my mother, of course, but I didn't like it. Mom would get drunk on the weekends. When she was smashed, she'd kind of paw at me and want me to hug her. Spooky. So I took off on my own when I was eighteen.

I don't have good memories of my parents. All my good memories center around my grandparents on Mom's side. Devin and Keara Carrick were their names, but I never called them anything but Gramps and Granny.

They lived in Caxton, Missouri, for all of their adult lives. Came over to the U.S. as Irish orphans after World War I, when they were both still kids. Gramps eventually became Caxton's postmaster; Granny won dozens of state and county fair ribbons for her cooking.

Gramps and Granny were the reason we ended up shooting *The Friday Massacre* in Caxton. I wrote the film script, basing my screenplay on the actual Lucas Fraley killings, and although I fictionalized the story, I kept it authentic.

I believe in authenticity. Whatever I write about I research thoroughly. For this project, I wanted to see what it was like to actually shoot a rapid-fire assault rifle. I *needed* this experience in order to do full justice to my script. I couldn't legally buy one in California so a writer friend of mine bought the weapon in Texas, no questions asked, and drove it and the ammo west so I wouldn't have to deal with all the legal red tape.

When I tried out the rifle at a shooting range in the mountains I used real bullets, even though the actor in our film would be firing blanks. As the weapon spewed out its deadly rounds I was able to project myself into the persona of Lucas Fraley on that fateful Friday morning when he'd fired on his helpless classmates. It was a sick, ugly feeling.

When I finally stowed the rifle away in the trunk of my Lexus, safely disarmed, I had no desire to fire it again. I now had what I'd been after.

Authenticity.

I was pleased with my final draft of the script. Because this was a fictional take on the actual story, I'd changed all of the real names and added a romantic sub-plot between two of the teachers. The woman teacher gets wounded in the shooting, but she survives. I thought about killing her off, but decided against it. American audiences like happy endings.

I have great memories of visiting Gramps and Granny in Caxton each summer when I was young. Those were magical times and I've always considered Caxton to be my real home. Living with Mom in Kansas was a bummer.

Truthfully, Caxton is nothing much to look at. It's a sleepy little town nestled on the southern border of Missouri. Big shade trees on every street: maples, elms, oaks. Nice park, too, with a great playground for the kids. Gramps used to take me there and I'd spend hours riding the teeter-totter with him. I wore him out on those afternoons.

Granny spoiled me, for sure. At the beginning of each summer she'd always have a tall metal drum of her incredible ice cream waiting for me when I arrived. Butter brickle, my favorite. God, I can still taste it! She made it in her old-fashioned, hand-cranked freezer with triple-thick cream, farm-fresh egg yolks, and sugar which had been slowly infused with genuine vanilla beans.

Gramps liked to fish, and he'd take me out to Lake Louise, a few miles from town, and I'd row the boat across the dark green water, still as glass, until he told me to stop. Gramps knew the best places to catch fish. Down deep, near the rocks where they liked to hide. I hated baiting the hook with those wiggly gray worms, but I did it for Gramps because I loved him. You do a lot of things you don't want to do for the people you love.

They're both gone now, of course. Jan, my wife, never got to know them. Or Caxton, either. In fact, before we shot *The Friday Massacre* there, she'd never seen the town, but I'd told her about it, and I had photos of the place in Granny's faded yellow scrapbook that Jan always enjoyed leafing through. There was even a picture of Caxton's Main Street with some old cars parked at the curb in front of the post office, including "Bessy," Gramps' sun-faded '36 Dodge sedan that he would never part with. Granny was always after him to buy a new automobile, but he never budged. "Who needs a new car?" he'd say. "This is the one I used to drive you to high school in when you and I were sparkin'. Runs just dandy. Old things are better."

I always remembered him saying that. I guess it went in deep, because I collect antiques. Toys, furniture, old books. Actually, Jan and I spent a lot of our spare time hunting for antiques together. Just like me, she appreciated the past.

But the future can be just as fascinating as the past. Jan and I met because of the future, at a science-fiction preview in Hollywood. She'd always been as much a nut for sci-fi as I am. Strangers, we spent several hours sharing the same section of sidewalk down the block from the Egyptian Theatre, waiting in line, patiently, for the film to open. I'd asked her to hold my place while I went in search of a rest room and, when I returned, we began talking. We never stopped.

There was a twelve-year age gap between us, but never a generation gap. Women mature at a younger age than men do. Before the trip to Caxton we'd been married for a full decade, and we were just about to have our first baby. It had been a rough ten years for both of us because I'd been trying to get out of writing sitcoms for what had seemed like a century. Despite the excellent pay, I hated scripting those insipid episodes about skunks on a bus, broken toilets, and lost puppy dogs, writing for sour-faced producers who hadn't smiled since Abe Lincoln's second inauguration.

I was finally liberated when Lyle Samuels hired me to write *The Friday Massacre*. My first big-screen break. Jan and I celebrated at Musso & Frank's, giggling at each other, toasting the occasion with tall summer glasses of iced tea. We were sure that my days as a sitcom wage slave were over. I was free at last.

At my suggestion, Jerry Meins, our company location scout, flew from California to Missouri. To Caxton.

When he got back he told Lyle Samuels (our producer and director) that the town was definitely out as a location. Why? It seems that Caxton's only high school was closed, which meant that no students were available for crowd scenes. (We'd planned on using local talent to fill out the cast.)

"Not possible," I told Jerry. "When Gramps was alive, they had full enrollment. More than a hundred students."

Meins scowled. "How long since you were back there?"

"Thirty years," I admitted. "My last summer visit was just after I'd turned ten. The next winter, my grandparents both died in a traffic accident during an ice storm, so I never went back."

"A lot can happen in thirty years."

I shook my head. "Not in Caxton. It's always the same there. Gramps used to say that time stood still in Caxton."

"I'm tellin' ya, the town's like a graveyard," Jerry declared. "Even the elementary school's been shut down. Never saw a single kid on the street. And not many adults, either. Place gave me the creeps. Most of the stores are boarded over. Movie house is closed. So's the drugstore. Whole town's like an empty stage set."

I seized on that last sentence. "Makes it perfect for us," I said, turning to Samuels. "No hassle with crowds the way you had in Chicago. We'll have the place all to ourselves."

"Well . . . I dunno," Lyle mused. "I'd have to bus in a bunch of extras for the school scenes. And we'd need to spruce the place up. Make it look active." He hesitated. "And how do we know we can get permission to use the school?"

"Leave it to me," I said. "I'll personally go to Caxton and contact whoever it takes to swing the permit."

And that's what I did. My very pregnant wife stayed in California with her sister while I flew to St. Louis, then drove a rental car south to Caxton.

When I arrived I discovered that Jerry had been right. About the place being like a graveyard. Maybe a dozen cars downtown. A few businesses still open, including Annie's Eats, the local cafe. (I remembered how good her apple pie had been, but the original Annie was long dead by now. She'd been at least eighty when I'd seen her last.)

I waved hello to an old guy on a bicycle who just glared at me. The park was deserted and no kids were on the weed-grown playground. The teeter-totter had fallen over and the swings hung silent, with cobwebs between the chains.

My grandparents' house on Forest Avenue was

boarded up, but the boards in three of the windows had been broken, along with the glass underneath. The empty spaces looked like missing teeth in a wooden skull. Wild grass claimed the yard. The house had been willed to Granny's maiden aunt, but just before she died she hadn't been able to pay the property taxes so the house was now owned by the town of Caxton.

But some things hadn't changed. The bronze statue of Robert E. Lee still dominated the courthouse square, reminding me that this part of Missouri had supported the Confederacy during the Civil War. And City Hall looked exactly the same with its graceful Ionic pillars fronting the entrance.

I was halfway across the square when a hand gripped my shoulder. I turned, startled, to face a tall, beefy man in a dark uniform whose flushed face and ample gut evidenced a lifetime of too much greasy food. A walking coronary. He wore a wide-brimmed Stetson, and his badge read SHERIFF.

"You got ID?" he asked.

I produced my wallet, removed my California driver's license, and handed it to him. He looked it over, then gave it back.

"New in town, are ya?" His tone was affable, but there was menace and suspicion in his eyes. He wore a holstered revolver, and rested a meaty, sun-freckled hand on the butt of his weapon.

"I arrived this morning."

"Got business in Caxton?"

"I hope to have."

"What's *that* mean?"

"It means I need to talk to your mayor."

" 'Bout what?"

I ignored his question. "Have I broken some law?"

"Nope." His eyes were fixed on me. Folds of heavy flesh turned them into dark slits.

"Then I'm free to go?"

He shrugged his thick shoulders. "We don't get many strangers to town . . . but I guess you're all right."

"That's nice to hear," I said, turning back toward City Hall. I felt his eyes on me all the way to the entrance.

I've never liked small town cops.

Inside the municipal building, in the middle of the hall on the second floor, I located a frosted glass door that read MAYOR STAFFORD in gilt leaf. When I stepped inside, a dull-faced male office worker glanced up at me.

"I need to see the mayor," I told him.

His jaw tightened. "Mayor's busy. What business you got with him?"

"I came here from Los Angeles. Name's Cahill. I'm with a motion picture production company. We want to make a film in Caxton and we need a permit to use the high school."

"School's closed," he said tartly.

"I know. We'll open it again."

He stared at me. "We don't much appreciate strangers poking around."

"We won't be poking, we'll be filming," I said. "Besides, I'm no stranger. My grandparents lived right here in Caxton for most of their lives. Gramps was Devin Carrick, the town postmaster. He and Granny lived in the big white Victorian house at 33rd and Forest."

That didn't faze him. "We don't want you film people, an' that's final."

His stony attitude was beginning to annoy me. "Are you speaking for the mayor?"

"I'm speaking for all the folks in Caxton." His tone was strident.

The inner door opened and a tall, white-haired man peered out, like a bear from his cave. "What's the problem, Carl?"

"No problem," he said. "Except that this fella is from California and he wants to make a movie here in town. I told him no."

The mayor aimed a politician's smile in my direction. "I'm Byron Stafford. Named after the poet. You ever read Lord Byron?"

"Yes, I've read him," I said, returning his smile. "Happy to meet you, Mayor Stafford. I'm David Cahill."

We shook hands. His palm was sweaty.

"Come into my office, Mr. Cahill. Let's have us a little talk."

Stafford's office was crowded and stuffy, with gray walls, a glass-topped desk, two dark wooden file cabinets, three black-leather wing chairs, and several ashtrays that should have been emptied weeks ago. A framed portrait of Harry Truman loomed over the desk. The mayor offered me a cigar, but I told him no thanks, I didn't smoke.

"That's to your credit," he said. "My late wife was a chain smoker. She got me started."

On cigars? I wondered. I sat down in a leather chair as he lit a thick brown stogie.

When I reminded him, Stafford remembered the school shooting in Virginia. "Dreadful business," he said darkly. "Dreadful. The boy was obviously deranged."

I told him about my screenplay, how I hoped it

would exert a helpful influence and maybe keep some other kid from doing what Lucas Fraley had done. "This film will carry a strong, positive message for young people everywhere." I figured this was just corny enough to impress him.

"What do you want from me, Mr. Cahill?" he asked, puffing thoughtfully on his cigar.

"A permit to shoot at Caxton High School. We'll be happy to pay any fee you require. Shouldn't need it for more than two . . . maybe three weeks at the outside."

"I'm afraid the answer is no," he said, rolling the cigar in his fingers. "We're a quiet little town. Folks wouldn't take kindly to you Hollywood people comin' in and stirring up a ruckus. I'm sorry to tell you that strangers are not welcome here."

"Yeah, your sheriff made that clear. He treated me like a leper."

Stafford shrugged. "Oh, doncha mind Pete. He just enjoys bein' ornery. Pete's all right, once you get to know him."

"Uh-huh," I said.

"He just don't take to strangers."

"As I told your man here in the office, I'm no stranger. Used to visit my grandparents here in Caxton every summer. I want my wife to see the town. She's heard me talk so much about it."

"Any children?"

"Not yet, but Jan's about to have a baby."

Stafford pursed his lips. "Ah . . . the miracle of birth. How far along is she?"

"Eight months. She's due next month. That's one of the reasons I want Jan here on location with me. So that I'll be with her when she has our child."

The mayor stubbed out his cigar, got up, walked to the window. He stood there, gazing out for a full minute, hands clasped behind his back. Then he turned to me.

"Maybe I'm being unreasonable," he said. "I suppose there's no real harm in letting you make your film here." He smiled. "I'm sure we can work something out."

So that's how we got our permit. My talking about Jan seemed to soften the mayor's attitude. Probably had children of his own. Obviously, I'd said just the right thing.

It was early June, already hot and humid, but ideal for the film. School had been just about to end for the summer when Lucas Fraley went on his killing rampage, so we would be able to match the weather perfectly, giving us the precise look we were after.

Jan was excited about seeing Caxton, although I warned her that the town had changed a lot. She didn't care; she wanted to have our baby in the place I'd loved as a boy. A bond with my past. She repeated what Granny had said to me at the birth of a neighbor's child: "A new baby is the heart's blood of any marriage."

All indications were that Jan was going to have a trouble-free birth, but when she informed her obstetrician, Dr. Malloy, of our plans for the cross-country drive to Caxton, he was not pleased. Eventually Malloy reluctantly agreed to the trip, as long as we met his conditions:

1. Jan must have a sonogram to insure that the baby was healthy. (She did, which is when we found out that we'd be having a son. We named him Devin Michael, after Gramps.)

2. The medical facilities in Caxton must be approved by Malloy. (He had the Missouri hospital fax him their operating license, and he also talked to the doctor who would deliver Devin. In return, Malloy faxed Jan's medical records to the Caxton doctor.)

3. We had to carry a cell phone with us on the trip and make certain that each night's stopover was close to a major hospital in case Jan went into early labor. (She didn't, and we arrived in Caxton without a hitch. The trip had been great.)

I was optimistic about the future: my first produced screenplay, and our first child.

I had no way of knowing, back then, about the dark time that was coming.

Things began beautifully.

I'd taken a lot of photos before I left town. When Lyle Samuels saw them, he agreed with me that it was worth the cost of busing in the extras in order to shoot in town. Caxton had everything my script called for: a small, backwater Midwestern town, dozing under a hot summer sun, suddenly becoming the stage for an eruption of blood and violence. The match between locale and drama was seamless.

The production crew opened Caxton High and dressed it for the camera, closely followed by the cast and film crew who moved in so they could begin the shoot in mid-week. Time is money, and Lyle was determined to bring in *Massacre* under budget.

I've been to my fair share of locations and there's one thing you can always count on: an excited local audience crowding in to catch the action. Only this time, in Caxton, it was different.

Nobody in town seemed to give a hoot about watching us. Oh, sure, a few of the townspeople wandered by, looking hostile. Sometimes a car or truck would drive slowly past. The odd thing was, we didn't see a single woman or child during the entire shoot.

Strange. Damned strange.

Mayor Stafford showed up during the second week, while we were still shooting at the high school, to find out how the film was going. Earlier, he'd arranged for the house on Forest to be partially renovated for Jan and me so we could stay there while we were in town. Which I thought was very generous of him.

When the mayor arrived Lyle was busy directing a scene, so we met at the steps of the school. I told him we were right on schedule.

"Well, now . . . that's good to hear. Means your people will be moving out by the end of next week for sure."

"Right," I said. "After we're finished here, we'll be doing some pickup shots downtown. Local color. You're welcome to stand in as an extra. I might even write a speech for you."

The mayor chortled, shaking his head. "No-siree, Mr. Cahill, I'm no movie actor an' that's a flat fact."

"What about some of the others here in town?" I asked. "They could fill in for the crowd scenes."

"Afraid not," he said firmly. "Folks in Caxton like to keep to themselves. Our local theater shut down a few years ago, so nobody goes to the pictures anymore. We're not interested. We're not like you Hollywood people."

"There's one thing I've been really curious about," I said.

"What would that be?"

"Where are all the women and children? Usually, on a location shoot like this —"

"They keep to home," cut in Stafford. "An' speakin' of women, I was hoping to meet your wife. I'd consider it an honor."

"Of course," I said. "Jan's been taking it easy since we arrived. She's resting in the office trailer."

"Wouldn't like to disturb her."

"No, she's been wanting to meet you. C'mon, it's this way."

I led him across a snake-tangle of black electric cables toward our location office.

As we walked he told me how impressed he was with the way we'd fixed up Caxton High.

"Looks real smart . . . all spic-an'-span," he declared. "Like it was when it was open."

"Why did it close?" I asked. "It's the only high school in town. It would seem —"

He cut me off again. "A losing proposition. Not enough new students. Lotta folks started movin' to the big cities and took their kids along. Quiet little town like ours wasn't exciting enough for 'em . . . or maybe it's those big-city dollars they wanted. So we lost our students. Had to shut down. No choice, really."

I tapped lightly on the trailer door. "Company, Jan. It's Mayor Stafford."

Jan appeared in the doorway, smiling out at us. I never tired of seeing her smile. Radiant. That's the word for it. Jan was naturally pretty, but when she smiled, she was radiant.

The mayor offered her his hand. "Mighty happy to meet you, ma'am."

She nodded. "David's told me about your coöperation," my wife said. "Without you, we wouldn't be here. Without the permit, I mean. And your opening David's grandparents' house to us . . . we really appreciate it!"

"Pleased to be of service, Mrs. Cahill."

We stepped inside and Jan awkwardly shifted her weight, then sat down gingerly on the couch, folding her hands across her distended stomach. "I must look a sight," she said to Stafford, who sat down in the armchair across from her. "I'm almost due."

"Now, don't you go talking that way," the mayor chided. "In the Lord's eyes, all pregnant women are beautiful. Human birth is a miracle and a blessing."

Jan took my hand. "That's exactly what this baby is going to be," she said. "A blessing."

"Amen," nodded Stafford.

"Can I offer you anything?" I asked him. "There's some cold beer in the fridge."

"Tempting," he said. "But I'm due back to the office. Got a town to run."

"Caxton is a wonderful place," said Jan. "I don't know why anyone would ever want to leave it."

The mayor agreed, thanked us for our hospitality, and exited the trailer.

"He seems like a really nice man," Jan said.

Our key sequence at Caxton High was underway.

Billy Pitts, who was playing "Alex Staley," the student killer, pulled an assault rifle from his hallway locker, then ran down the stairs, camera following, to the school cafeteria.

Our set designer had done his job and the scene

looked totally real. Teenaged extras jostled one another in the food line as they filled their trays with sandwiches, milk, and cookies, while others were at the cafeteria tables, talking and laughing and generally showing off for each other. A typical teenaged din.

Then Pitts burst in with his rifle and began firing, setting off instant panic. Bodies fell everywhere. The cafeteria turned into a slaughter house.

"Cut!" shouted Lyle Samuels. From the floor, several "dead" students sat up as the action ceased.

Lyle walked over to Pitts. "You're supposed to be nuts, Billy . . . over the edge, freaked out. Where's the madness, the rage? I want to see it in your face. You're *killing* people, for Christ's sake! You're not at some church picnic."

"Sorry," muttered Pitts, head down. "Guess I lost focus."

Lyle sighed heavily. "All right . . . we'll take it again from you coming through the door. Just keep telling yourself, 'I'm a nutcase . . . I'm a nutcase.' Got it?"

"I got it," Pitts responded.

The next take was perfect.

We used up three bottles of ketchup in this sequence. That's one thing about the film business which has remained constant in the wake of a multitude of technical advances: on most movie sets, blood is still ketchup.

What I couldn't know then was how much real blood would be spilled before this trip was over.

After three weeks of shooting we were done. Our school scenes had been filmed and our love story told. Cast and crew had performed at top level and Lyle had directed with force and precision. My script had attained vivid life. And despite the fact that we had been virtually ignored by the local citizens, we had all the location shots we needed. Lyle would do a few interiors and some pickup crowd stuff back in L.A. to fill in the gaps, but the basic work was finished.

The Friday Massacre was a wrap.

Jan and I said good-bye to everyone that weekend as they boarded the charter bus for the trip north to the airport in St. Louis. We'd be seeing them back in California within the next thirty days.

"You sure you want your kid born in a spooky town like this?" Lyle asked Jan.

"Absolutely," she said "Besides, I'm so far

by **William F. Nolan**

along now, I'd probably give birth on the plane if I tried to go back with you."

"Well, it's your baby," said Lyle. "Me, I'm damned glad to be getting out of here. Jerry Meins had it right: this place gives me the creeps."

"That's silly," Jan declared. "Caxton is a lovely little town. No wonder David's grandparents lived here for so many years."

"To each his own," shrugged Lyle. He kissed Jan on the cheek, then shook my hand. "See you both in L.A."

"Right," I said. "Have a good trip back."

And we were left alone in Caxton.

Anxiously, we awaited the birth of our son. Once Devin was born and Jan had recovered, our newly-formed family would drive back to California.

Everything was in order. I'd checked with the local hospital when we'd arrived in Caxton and they had assured me they were ready to take Jan in on a moment's notice. Once she went into labor they would send an ambulance for her.

I visited the maternity ward. It was clean and modern, but I was shocked to find that all of the bassinets were empty. No babies. When I questioned a male nurse (all the nurses were male!), he told me that births were rare in Caxton these days, then hurried away before I could question him further.

The house on Forest had unleashed a flood of memories for me and I kept expecting my grandparents to step through the door, their faces shining with happiness, their arms outstretched to hug me. But of course, that didn't happen. They were gone, and no ghosts had been left behind. Unless you counted their heavy Victorian furniture. At night, with the full midsummer moon casting an ivory glow on chairs and sofas and tables, the furniture *did* seem to take on a ghostly aura.

Jan adored the house. Her fascination for antiques found full expression here. "Isn't it simply wonderful?" she'd exclaim at a new discovery, and I'd agree.

But somehow I failed to share her joy. Without the warm presence of Gramps and Granny, the house on Forest seemed cold, almost . . . sinister. Crazy word for the beloved old Victorian mansion I'd so loved as a kid, but I couldn't shake a mounting sense of unease. And things about Caxton I'd never particularly noticed when I was a kid — the too-lush greenery, humidity so bad I

was never really dry, and the nearly deafening sound of millions of noisy insects — now seemed oppressive.

In truth, I was looking forward to the day we could leave.

A week later, near midnight, Jan went into labor. The contractions were steady and evenly spaced when I phoned the hospital. They would send an ambulance immediately, I was told.

It rolled up to the house in less than ten minutes, siren blaring and red lights flashing, with a crew of two rushing attendants.

"The ambulance is here," I told Jan. "Everything's going to be fine."

She gave me a pained smile. "Men should have babies. Then they'd know what women go through."

The attendants quickly placed Jan on a gurney, covered her with a blanket, and transferred her to the back of the ambulance. I started to climb in beside her when one of the attendants, a burly fellow with football shoulders, put a restraining hand against my chest.

"Sorry, but we're not allowed to transport unauthorized individuals."

"What do you mean, 'unauthorized'?! She's my *wife*. I belong with her."

"Not permitted," snapped the second attendant. He looked equally tough.

I grabbed his jacket collar and thrust my face close to his. "To hell with your authority, I'm going along!"

He wrenched free and punched me in the stomach. Hard. As I doubled over, gasping for breath, the ambulance sped away, its siren wailing.

"Can't let them do this," I muttered, heading for my car. I jumped behind the wheel of the Lexus, fired the engine, and gunned after them.

The house on Forest was less than two miles from the hospital, straight down Troost Avenue, and I expected to see the ambulance pull off Troost for the hospital's emergency entrance, but it didn't. It passed the hospital and kept right on going.

I was shocked and angry. What was happening here? Where were they taking Jan? She was in labor! The situation was insane and I could make no rational sense of it.

The ambulance raced ahead of me like a white phantom through the night, increasing speed as it cleared the outskirts of town.

Helpless and frustrated, I continued the pursuit, but when the vehicle abruptly swung sharp-left, onto a rutted dirt road leading into the hills, I cut my lights before I followed. Let them think they'd lost me.

In the midnight blackness, without being able to see the road surface, I drove blindly, following the dim glow of their taillights. At the top of the hill the ambulance slowed and stopped. I pulled the Lexus into an area of heavy brush and cut the engine.

The hill had been bulldozed to form a wide, flat plateau, surrounded by thick trees which looked ancient. A low-roofed brick building sat at one edge of the clearing, while in the center, there was a structure of some kind. I moved closer through the obscuring wall of wild undergrowth.

A group of white-robed figures, each bearing a flaming torch, emerged from the building, led by a tall man whose bright crimson robe was trimmed in ermine. They moved to the center, to what I could now see was a stone edifice. It reminded me of those archaic altars archaeologists excavate at prehistoric sites. My attention was also drawn to a thick book, bound in rich leather and ribbed in gold, which had been placed on the top stone by two of the group.

The figure in red turned to face the others and I drew in a sharp breath: Mayor Stafford! Face flushed and eyes flashing, he raised his hand. "Let the women come forth to share in this miracle," he intoned.

From the building at the edge of the clearing came the women of Caxton. They walked single file, like zombies, heads down, trancelike, as they moved to surround the altar.

Stafford kept talking in the measured tone of a tent-show preacher at a Sunday revival: "We are blessed on this auspicious occasion with one who is new among us and who will deliver a child unto us." He gestured. "Bring her forth."

Jan, groaning and writhing in pain and on the verge of delivering, was carried from the ambulance to the altar.

Christ! She was going to give birth here and now. And there was nothing I could do about it.

They spread a red cloth covering across the altar and placed her upon it. Two of the tranced women moved in to assist with the birth. Jan was struggling and crying out: "No! No . . . leave me alone!"

Stafford poured thick liquid from a gold urn into a tall, jeweled chalice. He elevated the vessel and spoke some words I couldn't hear, then brought it to Jan's lips. He forced her to swallow

the liquid, and Jan's struggles ceased. Obviously, it was some kind of sedative.

Then, as I watched helplessly, my child was born. Jan cried out once in pain, and I saw a glistening round head emerge from between her legs. Then the rest of the small body followed. The umbilical cord was severed and the tiny infant was lifted into the air for all to see. Our son!

The baby began to cry in the cool night air and a soft murmur swept through the robed figures. Jan's head fell back against the blanket as she lapsed into unconsciousness.

My throat was dry and my heart was pounding like a flesh drum inside my chest. The scene was surreal, nightmarish, beyond anything I could have believed possible.

And then the true horror began.

Our baby was placed on the highest point of the altar, directly in front of Stafford. He reached into the folds of his crimson robe and brought forth a short-bladed knife, set with flashing jewels along the ornate handle. The blade glittered wickedly in the torchlight as he raised it above his head.

"This woman has delivered unto us the fruit of her womb so that we may all partake of it. As warriors in ancient times devoured the heart of the slain beast to attain fresh life, so will we benefit in sharing together the heart's blood of this newborn child. I shall now read from the *Sacred Book of Brotherhood . . .*"

The robed figures clasped hands as Stafford opened the thick, leatherbound book.

"And ye shall drink of the newborn and devour its heart so that its radiant energy may flow into thee. This life force, pure and uncorrupted, shall renew and sustain thee. So it has ever been. So shall it ever be."

He bowed his head, as did all of his unholy cult. The group began rhythmically chanting.

I was already running desperately for the Lexus, knowing that I had only bare seconds.

At the car, I keyed open the trunk and snatched up the assault rifle, quickly loading it. Then I plunged back through the thick green overgrowth, bursting wildly from the high grass to confront the robed figures.

Now we'd see whose blood was spilled!

I squeezed the trigger as the robed figures broke away from the altar.

Die, you bastards. Die!

Like rows of scythed wheat they fell under the relentless rain of bullets from my weapon.

When I reached Jan and our baby, Mayor

Stafford — wounded in one shoulder and his face convulsed with rage — rushed at me, the jeweled knife raised.

"You sick son of a bitch!" I shouted as I cut him down with a short, savage burst from my rifle.

Somehow, in a numbed haze, I managed to get Jan and our baby into the Lexus, then drove away rapidly from the blood-soaked plateau, heading straight for Bridge Road and the Interstate. And I'd grabbed the *Sacred Book*. I'd need it to prove that all this was real.

Jan was weak, but she insisted on clutching our child close to her chest. Bonding with our newborn seemed to give her strength. But she didn't speak and her eyes were glazed with shock and exhaustion.

"Everything's all right now," I said. "We'll soon be clear of this hellhole. It's over."

But it wasn't.

We were about to crest the hill on Bridge Road when I saw them. Pete the sheriff and three of his uniformed deputies.

They'd angled their two patrol cars in the middle of the bridge, forming a barrier. Pete brandished a shotgun, and the deputies had unholstered their revolvers.

I rolled the Lexus to a stop a few hundred feet short of the bridge.

"I can smash through them," I told Jan. "Just make sure you and the baby are secure because it's going to be rough."

"They want my baby," she said numbly.

"Sure they do! The whole town's in on this. But don't worry, honey. They'll never —"

I suddenly felt cold steel pressing against the skin of my neck.

Stafford's knife! Jan must have taken it from his body at the altar. She was holding the razored blade at my throat, and the glaze in her eyes took on new meaning for me. She had the same trance-like expression I'd seen on the faces of the Caxton women.

"Whatever was in that chalice," I said slowly. "It *changed* you."

"I don't want to kill you, David. Give up the baby and let us have the *Sacred Book*."

She kept the blade at my throat as she eased open the passenger door and gestured to the sheriff and his men.

They advanced toward us, moving cautiously. For all they knew, I might be armed. But I wasn't. I'd discarded the empty assault rifle back on the hill.

I looked at the innocent pink face of our baby.

No, dammit. No! I twisted away from Jan and knocked the knife from her hand. It skittered to the floor of the car. I dived for it, came up with the knife in my grasp. Jan lunged for it, then gasped. The sudden thrust had driven the blade into her heart. She slumped back and fell from the car, onto the roadway, as blood coursed from the mortal wound.

I was devastated. My beautiful Jan, the dearest thing in my existence, lost to me forever! A huge part of my life had suddenly been chopped away, and I looked into a black void. How could I live without her?

The baby, a voice deep within me responded. *You must live for the baby.*

I slammed the passenger door and locked it. Little Devin was crying, but safe. As the engine of the Lexus roared to life, Pete smashed the butt of his shotgun against the driver's window. Another blow would shatter it.

I jammed my foot against the accelerator pedal and the Lexus surged forward, spinning Pete into the road. His deputies were firing at me as I gained speed, aiming for the center of the bridge.

"It's all here, I tell you! Right in these pages! Their history . . . rituals . . . everything!"

I was at the F.B.I. office in St. Louis, talking to a trio of hard-faced federal agents. On the way, I'd examined the *Sacred Book* and had been stunned by its contents.

"They call themselves the Brotherhood," I said. "And they've taken over Caxton."

"So everybody in town is really a *snake*, eh?" asked the first agent, a lean six-footer. He was perched on the edge of a straight-back chair, the sleeves of his sweat-soaked shirt rolled up. The other two stood behind him. I was at a table in the small, summer-hot room, the book opened in front of me.

"Not snakes, *reptilians*," I said. "Physically, they look like ordinary human beings."

"How'd they get to be . . . reptilians?" asked the second agent. He was shorter, and balding prematurely for his age.

"It took millions of years of genetic evolution," I explained. "These creatures go all the way back to the dinosaur. Dinosaurs didn't disappear from the Earth . . . they *evolved*."

"Uh-huh," nodded the third agent, a young guy who looked like he was fresh out of college. "How come they eat babies? Part of their diet?"

"Without a periodic intake of the blood of a

newborn child, the reptilians can't maintain human form in this dimension."

The first agent grunted. "So now you're saying these reptilians are from another *dimension?*"

"No. They originated right here on Earth, but they'll be forced *into* another dimension if they don't continue to drink the blood of newborns."

"Where do all these 'newborns' come from?" asked the college guy.

"Mostly from their own females. They use women as breeders, to produce babies. Probably from human semen. Artificial insemination."

The tall agent: "These women . . . they don't mind having their kids served up as snake meat?"

"The females are kept in a trance state. Mental slaves under mind control. They're probably forced to drink the same stuff my wife did."

"So what, exactly, was in that drink she had?" asked the second agent. "Snake blood?"

"I don't know," I said, "but I *do* know it altered Jan's mind. She wanted to give them our baby, wanted me to hand him over to the sheriff."

The young agent's brows went up. "You mean ole Pete Adams? You're saying Pete's actually a reptile? A *snake*-sheriff?" The other two were grinning.

"The whole town's involved, and he's one of them."

The first agent was now pacing the room. "You tell us that your wife tried to kill you with a 'ritual knife,' but ended up stabbing herself. Right?"

"Right," I nodded.

"Where's the knife now?"

"I left it in Jan's body on Bridge Road . . . it's buried in her chest."

"You've got some problems, Mr. Cahill. If we do find your wife's body, you'll likely be facing a murder count. And if the rest of what you've said is true — about your shooting all those folks on the hill — you'll be charged with mass murder."

"I had no choice. They were going to sacrifice my child! Read this book! It's all in here."

They ignored the book and stared at me.

"Check out the wreckage on Bridge Road," I demanded. My voice was shrill. "Check that hill outside of Caxton. The bodies are *there.*"

They checked Bridge Road. No Jan. No wreckage. The hill had been raked clean of blood and there were no bodies. The altar? Simply an old stone well.

There was nothing in Caxton to back up my incredible story.

Nothing.

What happened on that hot summer night in Missouri completely changed my life.

When I'd begun my screenplay, Lucas Fraley had seemed remote, the stuff of TV and news headlines, far removed from my world of reality. Yet now I, too, had used an assault rifle to deadly effect. We had, each of us, killed living creatures. Of course the circumstances were entirely different, but there was a dark parallel, proof that any of us can resort to overt violence when the brain commands it.

I gave up Hollywood, got out of the entertainment industry. No more scripts. No more location shoots. No more small towns. I moved to New York, the biggest city in North America, to raise my son. With Jan's and my savings I began investing in commercial real estate and the stock market. That's how I've been able to make a living for Devin and me.

I've never gotten over Jan's death. Her sweet smile still haunts my mind.

And what of the reptilians in Caxton?

I'd killed most of their breeders, so there weren't enough newborns to sustain them. Unable to maintain human form, the reptilians were forced from Earth into another dimension.

No more blood. No more human sacrifices.

By now, they're gone forever.

At least that's what I believe. Pray God it's true.   Ω

ELDRITCH

Deep in the ocean of my mind
Dead Lovecraft must lie dreaming —
Recently, Unspeakably
I fear he may be waking.
So slowly, so subtly has
He started to raise his head —
Insinuating himself with words
I never would have chosen
Like "Hideous" "Unknowable"
And even "Eldritch"
(Wasn't that the first name of some
Activist in the sixties?)
Going on and on and on when one
        or two sentences would suffice . . .
I want to learn forgotten languages
Never intended for th human tongue.
I want to go to my travel agent
And book a perilous journey
To an Unknown Place
("I don't want to go to Hawaii!
I want to go to someplace Antique
And Uncharted!")
I've developed a terror of university libraries
Especially those with Rare Book collections —
Piles of old dusty book do more than
Make me allergic. They drive me MAD.
I avoid at all costs visiting small, isolated

New England towns
Especially if the inhabitants
Look a little *unusual*.
I blanch at the sight of anything withered,
Or grey, or decaying.
Fearful of the sight of fungi,
I search my shower daily for signs of invasion
I cannot bear to eat mushrooms.
The thought of Athlete's Foot
Fills me with horror.
I will not eat at seafood restaurants
For fear they might serve me Calamari
(It took me days to recover
From my last visit to the Aquarium).
I want to know the genealogies of all my friends
To make sure there isn't
Any *inbreeding* lurking there.
Deep in the ocean of my mind
Dear Lovecraft must be waking —
I want to invent my own mythology!
I want to make poltically incorrect statements
About mentally ill individuals of Arabic descent!
I want to grab a pen and scribble
Pages and *pages* of lurid prose
STOP ME! IN GOD'S NAME STOP ME
BEFORE IT'S TOO LATE . . .

— **Melissa Pinol**

THE PLACE OF SKULLS
(a graveyard for endangered species)

In bright pink dusk
    pale sea gulls
    Hover
        over
the Place of Skulls:

Acrid musk,
and marble stones,
Twined in clover,

with ghost-white bones;
an elephant tusk,
a rhino horn;
the skeleton of
a unicorn,
and the scaly husk
    of a demon's hide,
    tossed above
as the demon died.
In dark red dusk:
    grey ghost gulls
    shimmer
        over
the Place of Skulls.

— **W. Paul Ganley**

THE KISSING OF FROGS

Rank with the stench of pond water!
Cold and slimy! Humpbacked and no-necked!
The thought of kissing a frog disgusted her.
Yet a prince was a different matter all together.
Tall and handsome. Square-jawed.
        Straight as a wall.
His dark eyes laughing seductively into hers.
Her cheek pressed against
        his gold-braided tunic.
His royal purple cape enclosing her
        like a shelter
as he held her safe
        within his long strong arms.
Oh how she yearned to kiss a prince!

The thought of kissing a frog disgusted her.
Yet she knew she would never kiss a prince
unless she set about the kissing of frogs.
So with sovereign ambition she steeled herself
to the daily horrors of amphibian osculation.
She kissed wood frogs and leopard frogs.
Pickerels and tree toads and bull frogs.
Ancient croakers and adolescent squeakers
that were nothing more
        than tadpoles at heart.

And after a time she began to grow
accustomed to the kissing of frogs.
Their wall-eyed, bug-eyed stare that seemed
to both fix upon her and gaze around her.
How they at first squirmed
        within her grasp
until their small solidly muscled bodies
settled into the warmth of her palms.

It was not nearly so bad as she thought
it might be and there was even much
that could be said for the kissing of frogs.
The tender thump-ba-da thump-ba-da
of their tiny three-chambered hearts.
The way their slender prehensile tongues
sometimes darted between her teeth and
curled against the roof of her mouth to tease
that ticklish spot just above her incisors and
send delightful shivers
        winging down her spine.
The taste of their cool skin like baby lettuce.

Then one day when she least expected it,
when she had already abandoned all hope,
she felt thick lips pressing upon her lips

and a thickening tongue against her own.
She started back and he stood before her.
Tall and handsome (though somewhat stooped
and not as comely as she had once imagined).
Square-jawed
        (with a hint of four-o'clock shadow).
His gold-braided tunic
        (only gold cloth of course).
His royal purple cape
        (a bit wrinkled it must be said).
His dark eyes leering at her
        as his head wobbled
back and forth upon its stalk of a neck.

As he reached to encircle her in the shelter
of his long strong (though ungainly) arms,
she could spy the dots of stubble on his chin
and feel his breath like a furnace wind.
She could see the long black hairs
sprouting like the roots of pond grass
(or a nest of writhing disembodied
spider legs) from his open collar.
She recalled the way his tongue,
fat and fleshy and artless, had filled
her mouth and left no room to breathe.
The thought of kissing him disgusted her
and she roughly pushed him away.

She knew at once that he was not for her.
Even if he were a real prince
        (which she doubted).
Even if he agreed to keep his collar buttoned
and that paddle of a tongue to himself.
Even if she could somehow learn to tolerate
his outrageously pale and hirsute flesh,
she knew he could never be the one for her.

And after all, there was a great deal
that could be said for the kissing of frogs!

— **Bruce Boston**
— **illustrated by George Barr**

by **Bruce Boston**

PASSING THE NARROWS
by Frank Tuttle

illustrated by Vincent Di Fate

The *Yocona* surged ahead, paddle-wheel churning, cylinders beating like some great, frightened heart.

"Dark as Hell and twiced as hot," muttered Swain from the shadows behind the clerk's map-table.

A ragged chorus of ayes answered. The Captain checked his pocket watch; ten o'clock sharp. Old Swain and his hourly announcements hadn't lost a minute in twenty years.

The Captain snapped his pocket watch shut and peered out into the darkness. There, to port, loomed a hulking mass of shadow twice the height of any around it — Cleary's Oak, last marker before the riverboat landing at Float. "We're an hour from Float, Mr. Barker. Notify the deck crew we'll be putting in for the night."

"Aye, Cap'n."

"She won't like that," said Swain, whispering. "Fit to be tied, she'll be. Full of fire and steam."

"Who, Swain?"

"You know who. The wand-waver. The Yankee."

"Go back to sleep."

"I heard her talkin' while the boys were hauling me up the deck," said Swain, gesturing with the stump of his missing right arm. "Said she was aimin' to make Vicksburg 'fore the moon came again. Said she had orders, and papers, and —"

"I give the orders here, Swain. Not any damn Yankee wand-wavers."

Swain cackled. The *Yocona* churned past Cleary's Oak, picking up speed as the Yazoo River turned narrow and straight. The Captain rang three bells, and the thump-thump-thump of the pistons slowed.

The *Yocona*'s running lamps began to touch the trees on each bank of the Yazoo River. Shadows whirled and twisted, caught mid-step in some secret dance before fleeing back into the impenetrable murk beyond the first rank of trees. Some few seemed to run just ahead of the light, capering and tumbling like shards of a nightmare given flesh and let loose to roam.

The shadows reminded the Captain of Gettysburg and Oxford and a hundred other haunted ruins left in the wake of the war. The Yazoo River was the only safe route through the countryside now, unless you were a sorcerer, a Yankee, or a fool.

"Eyes ahead, boys," said the Captain, softly. "They're only there if you look."

The pilothouse door flew open and slammed like a rifle-shot. The Captain whirled, cursing.

In the dim red glow of the pilothouse night-lamps, the Yankee in the doorway looked little more real than the shadows in the trees. A long blue Union sorcerer's robe and hood concealed all angry green eyes and long, pale hands.

"Why are we stopping at Float?" said the sorceress.

"Warned you," whispered Swain.

The sorceress stepped forward and glared down at Swain. "You are the Captain of this vessel?"

Swain guffawed. "No ma'am," he said. "I'm the clerk. If you want a freight book marked or a Federal river-map copied I'll be happy to oblige." Swain cocked his head. "Tell the truth, now — don't them robes get awful hot?"

The sorceress turned, traded frowns with the Captain.

"You gave the order to put ashore at Float?" she said.

"I did," said the Captain.

"You will rescind your order. We will proceed on to Vicksburg. Tonight. With all possible speed."

The Captain turned his back to the sorceress and listened to the paddle wheels for a time. Far off in the night, he heard the shriek of another riverboat's steam-whistle.

"Get off my bridge," said the Captain, staring out into the shadows. "Get off, and stay off."

"We go to Vicksburg."

"Tomorrow. First light. Not before."

The sorceress stepped forward. "I am an official representative of the United States government," she said. "I have Papers of Empowerment which authorize me to commandeer this vessel, if necessary. Is it?"

"Just like a Yankee," said Swain. "Comman-

by Frank Tuttle

33

deerin' stern-wheelers without no notion of how to steer one. How far you reckon you'd get before you found a sand-bar or a snag?"

"Vicksburg," snapped the sorceress.

"Hell," said Swain. "In pieces, you might." Swain scooted himself sideways on his bench, grinning as he saw the sorceress look down at the stumps of his legs and then look quickly away.

Another steam whistle rang out, and another. "Hear that?" asked Swain. "Two more boats puttin' in at Float. Probably twenty there, maybe more, every one of 'em losin' time and money by stoppin' for the night." Swain cackled. "Ain't many things tighter than a Mississippi river-boat master's fist, wand-waver, and there's some that would steer for Hell itself if they thought the devil had a penny in his britches. But not a one of 'em will pass the Yazoo Narrows without a moon, and that's a fact."

"One will tonight," said the sorceress. "Or he'll get off and watch me take his craft. I don't care which." Papers rustled. "This is a Presidential writ, Captain," she said. "This craft and my cargo are going on to Vicksburg. Tonight. Any further obstruction will be met with force. Is that clear?"

"Go to Hell," said the Captain, not turning. "Go to Hell and take Lincoln with you."

Paddle-wheels churned. Tiny flickers of light played over the backs of the sorceress's hands.

"We'll need half a hour at Float to unload the passengers and such of the crew that ain't eager to die, ma'am," said Swain. "Course, since Yer Mightyness is in a hurry, we could just throw the women an' babies off now."

The sorceress let out her breath in a long weary sigh. The glow at her fingers vanished. "You may have half an hour at Float," she said. "No more."

The Captain was silent. The sorceress turned and stepped through the open door and then turned again to fix the Captain's back with a glare. "I will forget your insubordination if there are no further difficulties between us, Captain," she said. "And I may have neglected to mention that you will be reimbursed for any losses you incur if passengers remain behind." The Captain didn't stir.

"The War is over," muttered the Sorceress. "Why can't you people accept the peace?"

"I reckon," said Swain, nodding toward the haunted night beyond the pilothouse, "because it ain't any too peaceful south of Memphis these days, yer Yankeeship."

The door slammed. The sorceress's heavy foot-falls faded, buried under the *Yocona's* steady throbbing.

"Well, Captain," said Swain quietly, "Guess I just saved your ass from the Yankees. Again."

The Captain shook his head and lit a cigar. Purple-grey smoke drifted wraithlike through the pilothouse. "You believe the stories about the Narrows, Swain?" asked the Captain. "Because if you do, you just sent us all to Hell."

Swain pulled himself back into the darkness behind the map table. "Bound for it anyway, ain't we?" he said. "This way, maybe we get to take a Yankee wand-waver with us."

The Captain took a long draw of the cigar and watched the shadows tumble all the way to Float.

The River turned. The *Yocona* followed, and the lights blazing at Float vanished, one by one. As the lamp lights failed, a chorus of steam-whistle blasts rang out, hanging in the thick, moist night air until they, too, were swallowed up by the river and the night.

"At least we got a proper send-off," muttered Swain. "We bein' doomed heroes and all."

"Quiet, Swain," said the Captain.

"They'll be talkin' about us for years to come, they will," said Swain. "We'll be the ones that dared the Narrows on a moonless night. Vanished without a trace — 'cept some nights, you can still hear the *Yocona's* pistons, throbbin' and thrashin' deep down in the river —"

"Swain!"

Boots scuffed planks just beyond the pilot-house door. After a moment, someone knocked.

A match scratched and flared as the Captain lit a fresh cigar.

"She'll just barge in anyway, Cap'n," said Swain. "Might as well invite her in, polite-like."

The door opened. "May I enter?"

"Step right up, ma'am," said Swain before the Captain's silence lingered too long. "You'll want a good place to watch from."

The sorceress entered and stood before the map-table. "And for what," she said, "am I to watch, sir?"

"You'll know it when you see it, wand-waver. And don't be sirrin' me — name's Swain. Mister Swain, if you're bein' formal, which you might well be since you're the one goin' to get me killed."

"You could have stayed with the others at Float," snapped the sorceress. "If you are con-

vinced this vessel is doomed, why did you remain aboard?"

"Shut up, Swain," said the Captain. "You talk too damn much."

"At last," said the sorceress. "Something the good Captain and I agree upon."

"Oh, do you now?" said Swain. "Well, to Hell with both of you. We're headed for the Yazoo Narrows in the middle of a moonless night and if I feel like talkin' I'll talk. What do you know about the Narrows anyway, wand-waver? Anything?"

"I've heard the Narrows mentioned," said the sorceress. "Just after the War, it was even surveyed as a possible site for arcane unlatching. But the survey team found only a mild residual charge, natural in origin."

Swain hooted. "Surveyed it, did they? Brought a boatload of wand-wavers over it in broad damn daylight, they did. Broad damn daylight. We told 'em. Oh, yes. We told 'em it only stirred on moonless nights, but they was Yankees an' officers and too damn smart to pay mind to the likes of us."

The sorceress shook her head. "Arcane concentrations do not vary by day or night —"

"This ain't no arcane concentration, Yer Yankeeship."

"Then what is it, Mister Swain?"

"It's a haunt, ma'am. A powerful one. You ever hear of the *Winney*?"

"The *Winney*? No."

"She was a hospital boat. One of ours. Had two hundred or more wounded on board, most of 'em civilians from towns your hero Sherman paid visit." Swain leaned into the night-lamp's glow. "Well, the *Winney* hit the Narrows just as one of them Yankee ironclads rounded the bend. The *Winney's* master came out on deck with a white flag. One of your boys picked him off with a miniball while the rest opened up with artillery. The *Winney* went down, crew and wounded and rats and all. No survivors."

"Utter nonsense," said the sorceress.

"Some say the dead of the *Winney* come up from the mud on moonless nights, lookin' to take their vengeance. And they ain't too picky about who they take vengeance on, anymore."

"Ridiculous, Mr. Swain," she said. "If that story is the basis of your fears, then I am truly relieved."

"That's just the popular version," said Swain. "I didn't say I believed it. I just thought you'd appreciate it, bein' of the Yankee persuasion and all." Swain winked at the sorceress's glare. "No, ma'am, I tend toward the story a Choctaw medicine man told me years before the War even broke. The red men called the Narrows Nusi ma Kosh. Means "That Which Sleeps." You wouldn't catch them within ten miles of the Narrows after sunset."

"Primitives —"

"Don't go calling 'em names, wand-waver," said Swain. "They was here before you. Long before. So maybe there's something down there, way under that black Mississippi mud. Something older than the Choctaw and older than the Union. Maybe it was sleepin'. And maybe the War and you wand-wavers done about woke it up." Swain chuckled. "But I reckon you'd call that superstitious primitive hillbilly nonsense, wouldn't you?"

"No, I would not," she said. "But there are many sites that exhibit natural concentrations of arcane energy. Stonehenge, for instance —"

Swain's open hand slapped the map-table. "This ain't natural, wand-waver," he said. "It ain't Stone-henge, it ain't natural, and it ain't goin' away just because your precious Union don't want it between you and Vicksburg."

"You have no evidence —"

"Madam," snapped the Captain. "Be silent."

The sorceress bristled.

The Captain motioned toward the river ahead. "Listen, madam," he said. "Listen, and tell us what you hear."

The sorceress was silent for a moment. "I hear the throbbing of the pistons, and the hiss of steam, and the churning of your paddle wheel."

Swain's eyes grew wide. "Damn," he muttered.

"I fail to see the significance of this," said the sorceress.

"The bugs," said Swain. "Think back to Float. Bugs were so loud you could hardly hear a shout. Always are, on summer nights. 'Cept tonight."

The sorceress listened, searching past the surge and thrash of the *Yocona* for any hint of sound from the forest.

"How far are we from the Narrows, Captain?"

"Two hours."

The sorceress sighed. "There are certain measures I can take, Captain. Precautions."

The Captain snorted. "Wand waving."

"If you must call it so," said the sorceress. "Your vessel will not be permanently affected."

The Captain shrugged. The sorceress turned and marched out of the pilothouse.

The Captain pulled out his pocket watch and opened the cover. "You're late, Swain," he said. "It's three minutes after midnight, and you've said nothing about the weather."

"Go to Hell, Cap'n." said Swain.

"Yes," said the Captain. Strange lights slanted across the Yocona's foredeck, raked the riverbank, spun back. "It appears I'll do just that." He yanked a bell-pull, and an instant later Barker's voice sounded from a voice-tube.

"Cap'n?"

"The wand-waver is laying spells," said the Captain. "Stay out of her way. Pass the word."

"Yessir."

"I want every lamp we've got lit, Mr. Barker. Inside and out. All of them. They are to remain lit until we reach Vicksburg."

"Yessir. Every lamp."

A glowing tangle of spell-stuff snaked across the Yocona's crowded foredeck, writhing and curling and flowing among the cotton bales and flour-kegs and tightly-lashed crates like a thick, inquisitive fog. The larger filaments anchored themselves to the Yocona's railings and bolts and hand-holds, covering her until the vessel was enveloped in a ragged, drooping luminescent web.

"Ain't seen that since them Union ironclads shelled us at Mobile Bay," said Swain. "Remember that, Cap'n?"

"I remember," said Swain.

"We damn near got one of 'em, didn't we?"

"Damn near."

The sorceress appeared on the foredeck, weaving her way through bales and crates. She stopped, threw back her hood, and lifted her hands.

The Yocona lurched, wallowed to port, and shook from her stern to her bow. A jar of pencils flew from the map table and scattered on the deck. The pilothouse night-lamps dimmed and flickered before guttering back to life.

The Captain clenched the wheel and cursed. Voices and bangs rang out of the boiler room voice tube. Swain cackled.

"She might not believe in the Narrows, but I reckon the Narrows believes in her."

The Captain spat out his cigar. "Barker!" he bellowed. "Full stop! And get those men back to their posts."

The Yocona shuddered again. Ten-inch oak beams creaked and moaned as though coming back to brief, agonized life. Deep within the Yocona's frame came a crack like a cannon shot as one of the eighty-foot chains that tied stern to bow stretched and broke.

A flash of silent lightning lit the foredeck and the river and the leaning, moss-shrouded willow-trees.

The lightning also touched the sky. In that instant, it seemed to the Captain that something huge beyond all reason was rising up to hang over them.

The sorceress shouted, her words strange and angry.

The river boiled suddenly, thrashing and filling the air with the stench of just-raised mud and old, wet rot.

Swain leaned close to the window beside him, straining to see into the night while alternately mumbling prayers and cursing his missing legs.

"God help us, Captain," he said, after a moment. "God help us. It's awake."

The Captain wrestled with the Yocona's wheel and followed Swain's wide-eyed gaze. There, just at the periphery of the Yocona's running lights, he saw movement, saw men. Men in uniform. Confederates.

They lurched and stumbled and fell, always moving toward the river. Some clutched rifles, some pulled crude litters. One bore a tattered flag.

The lightning flared again, and the flag unfurled long enough for the Captain to pick out crossed rifles against a blue starburst — the same flag the Captain's son died under at Billings.

The flag bearer reached the edge of the river. A face more bone than flesh lifted up and grinned at the Yocona's running lamps.

"It's me, Paw," came a voice from the ruined throat, somehow sounding over the screams and the steam-engines and the thrashing of the river. "It's me! I'm coming back to you, Paw! Comin' right over!" Then the flag bearer stumbled, the flag fell, and both were swallowed by the thick brown water.

The Yocona shuddered again, then jerked as though falling a hand's breadth. On the fore-deck, the sorceress stumbled, caught herself, and hurled a fistful of light up into the night.

She shouted a word. The explosion blinded the Captain, sent Swain sprawling to the deck, and

shattered every window, every door-pane, every dining-room mirror on the *Yocona*. When the Captain could see again, the river was calm, the forest was empty, and the sky was wide and full of stars.

"Damn damn," snarled Swain. "Get me a chair, Cap'n. Glass all over down here."

The Captain stared ahead, unheeding.

"Damnit, Lester, help me up!" said Swain. "Quit lookin'! It ain't there if you don't look!"

The Captain moved slowly to Swain, caught him by his arm, and lifted Swain back into his customary seat. "Much obliged," muttered Swain as he sat. "Now you might do some steerin' before we climb the bank."

Broken glass crunched as the Captain darted for the wheel.

"That's better," said Swain. "I was afraid ol' Swain might be the only one aboard with his head still latched on tight."

"You might be," said the Captain. Outside the pilothouse, men shouted and cursed. A dozen small fires sprang up across her decks, only to wink out at a wave from the weary sorceress.

The Captain steered the *Yocona* to the middle of the Yazoo River and bent to retrieve his damp cigar-stub. "I saw my son, out there," he said around the cigar.

"He ain't out there, Cap'n. You know that."

"He was with the others. Went in the water."

"No!" barked Swain, slapping the map table. "No, he didn't. Nobody did. He's dead, Cap'n, and that's a damn shame. But he's at rest, not wandering around some damnfool haunt two hundred miles from Billings." Swain spat and shook his head. "That thing out there looks inside you, Cap'n. It looks inside and it sees what you want or what scares you, or both. And then it shows you things, if you're fool enough to look."

The Captain fumbled for a match, scratched it, touched it to the cigar. "What did you see, Mr. Swain?"

Swain spat. "I saw a face, Cap'n, way up in the sky. That, and a pair o' legs and an arm that looked awful familiar."

The Captain turned. "Legs and an arm?"

"The legs was wearin' pants, Cap'n. Pants and fancy-like boots. Jest a standin' there on the deck. I never seen nothin' so foolish in all my life. Damn near said so."

Barker appeared at the pilothouse door, poked his head in through the broken door-pane. "Cap'n?" he said.

"Yes, Mr. Barker?"

"Fin and Poke are gone, sir. Went over the side. Wade says something came up out of the water and took Pete. It's just me an Wade and six or so of the others."

"Get the men off the deck, Mr. Barker," said the Captain. "And keep them off. Get some planks. Board up the windows in the boiler room, get in, and nail the door shut."

"Yessir." Barker paused. "Are we turnin' back for Float?"

Barker whirled, yelped, and stepped aside. The sorceress opened the door and entered the pilothouse. Her robes trailed smoke, and the scent of burnt hair wafted from her, and her face was covered with a dirty sheen of sweat.

"I reckon," said Swain mildly, "that some folks have words that need eatin'."

"Quiet, Swain," said the Captain. He turned away from the river and faced the sorceress. "I trust you were not injured, madam," he said.

"Not permanently," she replied. Her voice was hoarse, and she began to cough.

The Captain reached into his jacket and produced a battered silver whiskey flask. "For your throat, madam," he said.

The sorceress took the flask. "Thank you," she said, and took a long drink.

"The Narrows ain't done yet," said Swain. "So don't you two start no victory drinkin' just yet."

"Is he correct?" said the Captain.

"He is," rasped the sorceress. "We were attacked. It faced unexpected magic, and it retreated, but it will try again. You were right all along, Mister Swain," she said. "That Which Sleeps is waking, and it was our doing." She took another draw from the flask. "Another brilliant example of contained Union military sorcery."

Swain goggled. "I don't know which I like less," he said. "The Cap'n offering Yankees his good Kentucky whiskey or Yankees bad-mouthing their war heroes."

The Captain squinted into the night. "The river grows troubled," he said. "And we're nearly to the Narrows proper." He took the flask from the sorceress. "Madam," he said. "Your mission.

Are you willing to turn back, now that you've seen what we face?"

The sorceress shook her head. "I cannot turn back," she said. "Or wait. There can be no delay."

"What's in them crates of yours?" said Swain. "Lincoln's favorite undershorts?"

"You may all leave," she said. "Put in at the riverbank. I can provide you with protection that will see you safely through the forest, back to Float."

Another match flared as the Captain lit a fresh cigar. "Will lives be lost if you and your crates fail to reach Vicksburg tonight?" he asked.

The sorceress nodded. "Lives will be lost," she said. "Innocent lives."

The Captain sighed and waved out the match. He stared into the shadows, silent for a moment. Then he pulled out his pocket-watch.

"I had this inscribed with my son's name, madam," he said, holding the watch forth. "For his seventeenth birthday. I didn't know it, but while the jeweler was engraving the letters my son lay dying in the mud at Billings. Ironic, no?"

The sorceress shook her head. "I am truly sorry for your loss, sir. Truly, I am." She leaned against the map table and wiped her face with her sleeve. "I can't bring anyone back, Captain. No one can. But if my cargo fails to make Vicksburg tonight an outbreak of yellow fever is going to take hundreds, perhaps thousands, of more young lives. That I can stop. If we keep going."

The Captain snapped the pocket watch shut. "Then damn the Narrows," he said. "Damn the Narrows. Damn the haunt. Damn them both." He stuck his head through the glassless pilothouse window. "Mr. Barker!" he bellowed. "Mr. Barker!"

"Cap'n?" came a faint reply.

"Stoke her up, boys," he said. "Stoke her like the devil is at our heels, because he just might be."

"Yessir," said Barker. "Fine serving with you, sir."

"Always a smart-ass, that boy." The Captain stepped away from the window. "What can we do to assist you, madam?" he said.

"Remain calm," she said. "Keep control of your craft. Beyond that, I simply do not know."

The *Yocona* surged and lifted as a single tall hump of water rushed past. The sorceress sighed and straightened. "It begins," she said. "I must return to the cargo deck."

"Good luck, madam," said the Captain. "I trust you will share a proper drink with me, once we reach Vicksburg."

"Give 'em Hell, your Yankeeship," said Swain. "No offense," he added, at the Captain's glare.

The sorceress lifted an eyebrow. "Thank you, gentlemen," she said. The *Yocona* heaved as another trough of black water surged past. Frantic pounding sounded below as Barker and his engine crew redoubled their efforts to barricade the boiler room.

The sorceress opened her mouth, shut it, and marched out into the dark.

"Damn, Cap'n, what's got into you?" said Swain. "I was half-expectin' you to drop down on one knee and polish her boots."

"We lost the war, Swain."

Swain snorted. "Do tell? Hell, I thought we was engaged in a long-term strategic withdrawal."

"We lost," said the Captain. "Lost the war and lost your limbs and lost my son. Lost our lives." The Captain sighed. "I'm tired of losing, Matthew. Tired to death of it."

Swain spat. "So now you reckon on fightin' the Narrows with a broke-down paddle-wheeler, a cripple, an' a lady Yankee wand-waver with more guts than sense?"

The Captain chewed his cigar and said nothing.

"Oh Hell," muttered Swain. Moans began to sound from the trees on either bank, and the muddy Yazoo river-water began to roil and foam, disturbed by dark forms writhing just below the surface.

The *Yocona* heaved and yawed. Ragged man-shapes began to march clumsily out of the forest, pacing the *Yocona*, stumbling to keep up with her running lamps.

Swain peered out and broke into a short fit of laughter. "There they are, Cap'n," he said. "Off to port, right next to the headless gent. My legs. Got 'em a fine pair of boots." Swain leaned out the window and began to shout. "Ya did better without the rest o' me, boys!" he yelled. "I'da never bought ya high-steppers like that!"

The forest answered with a volley of screams. Screams, and the shriek and thump of artillery, and the sporadic pop-pop of rifles.

The sorceress moved to stand in front of the pilothouse. An aura flared around her, growing and spinning and wheeling about her like a flock of tame thunderstorms. Each of her hands was lost in a fierce, hissing glare that left streaks across Swain's vision.

The sorceress spoke a word.

The stars vanished. Swain cursed, and when he stopped searching the sky for the stars he saw that the riverbanks were gone, and the trees, and every trace of the land beyond. Instead, in every direction there was water — smooth, still, black water, not river but sea, yet not like any sea Swain had ever seen.

The sorceress stumbled, fell to her knees. The glow surrounding her faded; her hands, invisible before, showed clearly through the failing radiance.

The Captain gasped. Swain peered over his shoulder, out into the black sea.

There, on the horizon, something was emerging from the water, rising up to fill the grey and starless sky.

"God have mercy," whispered the Captain.

The sorceress shouted and lifted her right hand. The harsh light returned, and from it a narrow strand of silent lightning rose up to hang dancing in the empty sky.

The *Yocona* reeled as though struck. Swain caught the map table and hung on. The Captain was tossed away from the wheel, sent sprawling to the glass-covered deck.

Swain squeezed his eyes shut against the gargantuan thing still rising from the sea. "Is this what you call a last stand, Cap'n?" he shouted. "Layin' on the floor, bleedin'? Is this the way you want to die?"

The *Yocona* heaved again. Swain opened his eyes long enough to see that the sorceress had risen to her feet, and though only faint flashes of light shone about her, she was facing the shadow, hands uplifted, chanting broken words in a hoarse, spent voice.

The monstrous form grew, looming closer, moving like a bank of thunderheads. The oily waters broke into slow and shallow waves. The *Yocona's* pistons slowed; from below, Swain could hear hissings and grindings that spoke of ruptured cylinder casings, or worse.

The sorceress's chant broke into a fit of coughing. The strand of lightning dropped from her hand and was extinguished as it fell in wide coils against the vast obsidian sea. Barker's voice rang

out faintly from the boiler room; he recited half-remembered Psalms interspersed with exhortations clearly meant for the *Yocona's* failing steam pistons.

Outside, the sorceress forced herself to stand. Her robes smoked. No glow played about her hands now; and though she spoke, her words lacked the echo of power that always accompanied sorcery. At first, Swain thought she was praying. Then he heard a snatch of words and realized the Yankee wand-waver was trying to sing.

The sea boiled. The sky shrank, still filling with the thing from the sea.

"Mine eyes," Swain bellowed, "have seen the glory of the coming of the Lord."

The sorceress turned, her weary green eyes gone suddenly wide. She smiled with cracked and bloody lips. "That's a Yankee war song you're singing, Mr. Swain," she said. "Hardly words for a Confederate veteran to die with."

Swain laughed. "Good as any, ma'am," he said. "I reckon Ol' Scratch yonder might even choke on 'em."

The Captain moaned and stirred.

"Get up, Captain," said Swain. "Me and my Union friend are startin' us a choral group."

The Captain grabbed the edge of the map-table and lifted himself up. Blood trickled down the right side of his face and oozed in drips from his woolly beard.

He stared out, past the pilothouse and the sorceress, at the thing still rising from the water.

"It's over, Cap'n," said Swain. "All over, and high time."

The *Yocona* rolled and heaved. Swain laughed again, and began beating out a rhythm on the map table.

"He is trampling out the vintage where the grapes of wrath are stored,
"he hath loosed the fateful lightning of his terrible swift sword —"

The Captain pulled out his hip-flask, drained it, and threw the battered silver flask — a memento of the Fifth Infantry — out in a long arc above the black waters. His voice joined Swain's, and the faint, coarse rasp of the sorceress.

"Glory, glory, hallelujah,"
"glory, glory, hallelujah,
"His truth is marching on."

by Frank Tuttle

The sky was all but gone. The black water around the *Yocona* churned and swirled and rose, sending icy spray into the pilothouse and snuffing out the running lamps.

The Captain opened the voice tube to the boiler room. Voices, booming and muffled, rose up from it, some singing, some praying, Barker's rising above the rest in a sing-song litany of 'Come on girl come on come on.' "

"Goodbye, Cap'n," said Swain. "You were a good man and a good friend and if there's a whiskey house in Hell I'll buy the first round."

"The War is over, Swain," said the Captain. "Call me Lester."

Swain grinned. "Glory, glory, hallelujah," he shouted. "Now let's all go home."

The sorceress licked her lips, lifted her hands, and with one final broken cry she hurled a word out against the dark.

The word echoed, and the dark sea tilted, and with a lurch the *Yocona* plunged bow-first into a sudden and deep abyss.

Hands gripped Swain's shoulders. Something raked his face, raked it again. Swain woke and swatted and fought with both hands until he remembered he had only one.

"Hold him!" came a voice. Swain opened his eyes. The Captain stood over him, a bloody rag in his hand. "Calm down, Swain," he said. "You got a gash on your fool head I'm trying to doctor."

Swain relaxed. "Thought we was dead," he said. "Thought that thing in the water —"

"Shut up, damnit," snapped the Captain, looping the rag around Swain's temple and pulling it tight. "Can't get this thing tied with your jaws flapping like buzzard wings." Thick fingers nimbly made a knot. "There. You'll live. Can you sit up?"

"Don't need no nurse-maid," snapped Swain, offering his hand. "Just give me a hand-up."

Barker spoke from beyond the pilothouse door. "I can give you quarter ahead, Cap'n," he said. "For a while."

"Good work, Mr. Barker," said the Captain. "Give us all you can."

Barker yelled. The deck shuddered, and after a moment the *Yocona's* paddle-wheel screeched and began to turn.

"I better get back there," said Barker. "Got to ride herd on the old girl."

Swain peered around. He saw darkness, but there — there were stars, and the outlines of

trees against a half-clouded sky. The *Yocona's* running lamps were dark, but someone had lit a single lantern on the hurricane deck and hung it on a broken rail.

"You have a horrific singing voice, Mr. Swain," said the sorceress. Swain turned to find her slumped in the corner of the pilothouse, wrapped in a blanket and the Captain's long coat. "Still, I thank you."

"You're welcome, ma'am," said Swain. "Now would you kindly explain why we're here on the Yazoo instead of — wherever we was?"

The sorceress smiled. "I would, if I could," she said. "But my recollection is equally at fault. I remember speaking a final word, and then darkness. Until your Mr. Barker found me wedged between two cotton bales."

"Must a' been quite a word you said," said Swain. "Knocked Old Scratch right back to Hades."

The sorceress shook her head. "Hardly, Mr. Swain. Hardly. For some reason, the Narrows — whatever it is — lost its grip. My word had little, if anything, to do with that."

"Musta been my singin', then. Never could carry a tune."

"Agreed. That's what I'll put in my official report," said the sorceress. "Hostile spirit entity repelled by one Mr. Swain and his rendition of 'The Battle Hymn of the Republic.' "

Swain snorted. The Captain chuckled. The sorceress went on. "I jest, gentlemen, but that may not be far from the truth," she said. "The Narrows lost its grip on us when we joined together in song."

"The War fed the Narrows," said the Captain. "Woke it and fed it. Maybe it let go when we let our wars go. Who knows?" he grinned. "We won one, Swain," he said. "Somehow, we won this time."

Swain grinned. "'Bout time we was made war heroes," he said.

The Captain snorted. "It's about time we just let it pass," he said. "Time to let it end." He pulled out his pocket watch, held it clenched in his fist. "Goodbye, James," he said. "Goodbye."

He threw the watch through the open window, watched it glitter and tumble and then vanish in the dark.

"Mister Barker!" he bellowed.

"Yessir," came a reply.

"Do we have a whistle?"

"Nosir," shouted Barker. "But I can —"

"Fix it," shouted the Captain. "Make it loud.

Let's wake them up in Vicksburg, right before dawn. I want them to jump up cussing all the way to Farish Street."

"Jump up cussing, right away sir."

The Captain bent, rummaged in the ledger-desk, produced a whiskey bottle and three miraculously clean shot glasses. "Join me in a toast," he said, proffering a glass to the sorceress and another to Swain. "To victories won, to wars forgotten."

The captain poured. "To peace," said the sorceress. "To peace, and healing, and courage."

"To busted down steamboats, Yankee wand-wavers, and crippled old Rebs," said Swain. "Forever and ever amen." He drank.

The *Yocona's* whistle sounded, long and high and loud. The Captain smiled. "Again, Mister Barker," he yelled. "Make a racket all the way."

The *Yocona* churned ahead, whistle shrieking triumph all the way to the bluffs of Vicksburg. Ω

PHOBOS

Master of depravity, embodiment of sin,
I stalk the misty caverns where the winter storms begin.
I lurk, behind the nightmares, at the bottom of your brain.
But at night, *you'll* hear me scratching at your bedroom windowpane.

They think that I am dead and gone, a victim of our age,
But they'll never stop my laughter while the winter storms still rage!
I'm on the moons of Mars, and at the bottom of the seas.
But at night, *you'll* hear my laughter when the wind blows through the trees.

They let me reign in Paris! Ah, that was the best of times.
They made me a judge in Salem, and I made up all the crimes.
I marched before the soldiers on the highway from the Reich.
But at night, *you'll* see my shadow when you hear the lightning strike.

I've hunted side by side with Grendel, Fafnir, Jaws, King Kong.
I howl out in the moonlight when the full moon waxes strong.
I haunted Edgar Allan Poe with dreams of Death and Doom.
But at night, *you'll* hear boards creaking, as I creep up to your room.

Now, perhaps you don't believe in things that bump you in the night,
And perhaps ghoulies and ghosties leave you quite devoid of fright.
So, perhaps, when *you* crawl into bed, you'll never hear a sound.
But at night,
When lights are out;

DON'T

TURN

AROUND!

—Bruce Glassco

ELVIS DIED FOR YOUR SINS
by Sarah A. Hoyt

> "It's whom I'm dreamed that remains eternal
> *It's him whom I shall return.*"
> — Fernando Pessoa

Mid afternoon in Eternal Life, the only New Age store in Lythia Springs, Colorado, tended to be quiet.

We were through with the lunch-time rush of power-vegetarian executives and not yet up to the late-afternoon rush of college students in search of books on the Hermetic Order of the Golden Dawn or those convenient Ouija board kits.

I'd taken my sandals off, grabbed a ricecream popsicle from the freezer at the back of the store and sat down in the window seat behind the magical-crystal-jewelry counter, with my knees drawn up and the long skirt of my Indian print dress demurely drawn down to hide all but my toes.

My eyes half closed, I heard the rumbling talk coming from the book section.

"Archetypes can come alive. You really must read this book; it takes the thesis of the Golden Bough one step further. You know, the one about the divinization of dead chieftains. It maintains that not only did humanity worship these . . . beings, but that they were actually called into existence by this worship and assumed, not the flawed mortal envelopes in which they had truly existed, but perfect archetypes."

A male voice. Probably a college professor, I thought, from the boring, slow, *I'm going to impart this knowledge whether you want it or not* tone. My first husband had been a college professor. I made a face at the memory.

"Oh, you mean they would take the form expected of them, like John Keel claims happens with UFOs and men in black and fairies . . ." A young woman's voice. Buttering the guy up for the kill? Trust me, honey, not worth it.

"Yes, in a way. They're brought to life by the collective subconscious. Perhaps they existed in another form, some spiritual form." A bout of nervous laughter. "I'm not sure I like the idea of all those idolized rock stars and actors walking around long after death, not even in archetype form. And yet, the idea is so elegant, like some-

thing out of Jung, something resonating of the shared collective subconscious —"

He continued, on and on, in slow, rolling language, full of names and quotes. His female companion listened in silence and presumed raptness. I sighed and ate my ricecream and kept my mouth shut. The pickups that took place in this store were as unusual as everything else.

"Mariann?"

I opened my eyes.

My boss, Elroy Peters, owner of Eternal Life, stood by the batik curtain that hid the store area from our warehouse and staff kitchen, which had once been the servants' quarters of this converted Victorian. A tall man with snow-white hair, thin to the point of gauntness, Elroy stood as always with his hip tilted to one side and his lower lip poked out, in a way that reminded me of someone, but I could never make out whom. His pruned old face showed worry. "Hasn't Jonni shown up yet?"

I shook my head.

"Wasn't she supposed to have been here at ten?"

I nodded.

"It's not like her," Elroy said. "She might be many things, but she's also punctual to the minute." He normally spoke in an odd way that Jonni called *chewing on the words.* Agitation made it even worse, and brought out his too-perfect-to-be-true, good-ol'-boy southern accent.

And he had some reason to be agitated. Jonni, our resident college-student-ditsy-blonde, had never been this late. And Elroy, rightly or wrongly, thought that he was responsible for all of us.

"I've called her," I said. "But there was no answer."

Elroy frowned, threw back a white cowlick. "Mark supposed to come in?"

"At two," I said.

"Tell me when he gets in . . . maybe we can go out and see if there's anything wrong with Jonni." He disappeared into the back, so fast that he gave the impression of walking through the virulently colored batik curtain.

"Miss?" came a young man's voice.

I turned away from the curtain that hung motionless, as though no one had gone near it, and looked at the young man who stood at the other end of the counter. "Yes?"

"I'm . . . I'm not sure how to put this," he said. He had wild green eyes and wilder hair and beard in a shade of red not normally seen outside Crayola boxes. His voice came out in odd fits and starts. "But . . . my spirit just took over this body. I'm an advanced soul from the Gorianth sphere and I'm here to lead humanity, but I'm not sure —"

Ah, a walk-in. Our daily bread. I took a final bite of my ricecream. "You want walk-ins. Book section. Fourth set of shelves to the right, in the sun-room area. We have several books that will give you further insight into humanity on Earth and what you're expected to tell them."

"Thanks," he said, flashing odd, metal-capped teeth.

I watched his retreating back for so long that I missed Mark's approach until he came behind the counter and almost within touching distance. "Problem?" he asked.

"Nah," I said. "A walk-in. From the Gorianth sphere."

Mark raised his perfect black eyebrows over his bright blue eyes. "No kidding. Another one? It's the tenth since the psychic fair."

"Yeah." I looked at the stick for my ricecream. The licked-clean stick said LIFE IS SENSELESS WITHOUT BELIEF. *Well, then,* I thought to myself, *I shouldn't work at a New Age store. Nothing jades you quicker.* "Elroy wanted to know when you came in."

Mark frowned. He took off his bright blue tapestry jacket, shoved it out of sight under the counter. "Why?"

"Jonni hasn't come in. I think he had some idea of going out and checking on her."

"She had an argument with her boyfriend last night," Mark said, pulling out the schedule sheet to write in the time he'd arrived. "At the Catering Turnip."

Mark played his acoustic guitar and sang his own songs at the Catering Turnip, a vegetarian restaurant. He was such a nice guy I'd never had the courage to tell him that he was too late to be the next Bob Dylan. Even Bob Dylan didn't want to be Bob Dylan anymore.

"Big row," he said, looking up at the clock on the wall and writing down a time ten minutes earlier. "He left her to pick up the check, and she didn't have any cash and I had to lend her money. She left in tears. I expected to hear the entire soap opera today."

I found my sandals with my feet. It didn't sound good. As I made my way to the back I thought that the more I heard about this, the less I liked it. Jonni always took her boyfriends so seriously and she picked them with the same recklessness that led other people to play Russian roulette. "If the guy who wants to be possessed calls, tell him we don't have any particular relationship with supernatural entities and he'll have to find his own way to damnation," I told Mark just before I ducked through the batik curtain.

"What?" he asked, for once surprised.

"Some guy who wants instructions on how to become possessed," I said. "He's trying to get over a fundamentalist upbringing, he says. He called five times this morning. Probably will call again, trying to get a different answer."

Mark gave me a bewildered half smile, as if not sure whether to believe me.

I opened the batik curtain and went through, letting it swing closed behind me.

Elroy was half-hidden by a pile of cardboard boxes marked: BLUE GREEN ALGAE. HANDLE WITH CARE.

"Mark is here," I told him. "If you want to go out or whatever."

"Come with me," he said. "To take care of business."

I hesitated. Like everyone in this store, Elroy was all right but slightly different, like his whole concept of reality hung slightly askew. And I had never fully got over the impression that one day, one of the people who worked here was going to pull out a big ritual knife and sacrifice me to the god or goddess of his or her choice.

"In case I need help, young 'un. Come on."

"You could take Mark," I demurred.

But Elroy shook his head. "And leave you here alone? Not right for a young lady."

After two failed marriages and in my mid-thirties, I didn't really feel like a young lady, but I bit back my response. I didn't particularly want to hang around and talk to the possession aspirant, either.

I made a quick detour to inform Mark that I'd be going with Elroy and left through the front door.

Elroy waited in the parking lot, warming up

his car, a white Eldorado with huge tailfins and pink accents. Inside, teddy bears in pastel colors filled all except the driver's seat. I tried not to bat an eye since, as I said, people at the Eternal Life store were odd. I started to push the teddy bears off the seat onto the floor. Elroy gave me a freezing glare, took the teddy bears and put them in the back seat, next to ten hundred or so of their near relatives.

"You know where Jonni lives?" I asked, as he started up his car.

He nodded and mumbled, "Employment application."

As though he thought I'd suspect him of an illicit affair with Jonni, who must be all of seventeen. I told him about what Mark had said of Jonni, to forestall any more such nonsense.

We drove deeper into the old Victorian district of Lythia Springs, past the zone where houses were converted into shops, through the zone where the houses were houses, each one with a tended lawn to rival the most conventional of suburbs and on to the zone of houses chopped up into apartments, with beer cans on the window sills, and dried-up, dusty front yards.

Elroy pulled up in front of a narrow, violet townhouse.

As he got out of the car, the sun shone on his belt buckle, a huge gold-and-fake-jewels affair with the initials EP picked out in would-be rubies. I shook my head. I'd never noticed the thing. Then again, I didn't normally go around staring at my boss's belt buckle.

I walked up the maltreated concrete steps to the violet door. Elroy looked in the fly-specked window to the left. "Too dirty," he mumbled. "Can't see a darn thing."

I rang the bell, tried the massive brass doorknob.

"Is it open?" Elroy asked.

"No," I said, giving the doorknob a final shove.

"Here," he said. "Let me try."

"Be my guest." I stepped back and he took my place. The sun shone off something, probably his belt buckle, enveloping the knob in a blinding white light. He turned the knob. "It was unlocked after all."

The door opened with a mighty creak.

I frowned at the doorknob and followed Elroy into the dark living room. It was decorated in Early College Student, with sheets of batik in reddish brown tenting the ceiling, covering the walls, and draped over the two shapeless sofas.

On the right hand sofa, Jonni lay. "Jonni," I called, making my way around piles of books and mounds of dirty clothes. "Jonni."

She lay on her stomach, in her long T-shirt nightgown, and she didn't move. Her long blonde hair covered her face.

"Jonni," I called. But even before I knelt by her side and put my hand on her cold, cold neck to feel for an nonexistent pulse, I knew that she was dead. The cause wasn't that far to seek, either. Several empty, prescription-labeled bottles lay scattered on the floor near the sofa.

Shocked, gasping, not sure yet what I felt, I yelled out, "She's dead. Don't touch anything." Just as if this were some stupid murder mystery.

Elroy stood by the sofa, staring down at Jonni's body. "I knew something had gone wrong," he said.

"Just don't touch anything," I told him, feeling tears well up in my eyes, moist, warm tears roll down my face. Damn, what did Jonni want to go and do this for? She was so young, so pretty. And, unlike me, she hadn't thoroughly fucked up her life, yet. She should have at least tried her hand at fucking it up further, before giving it up. I stumbled to the kitchen, blinded by tears, looking for a phone. I had to call 911. I had to get the police out here.

"She's not dead," Elroy said. "She just needs waking up."

I didn't even attempt to argue. No one that cold could be alive.

In the kitchen, a narrow cubicle with a stove and a sink piled up with dirty dishes, I found a small, white wall-phone and managed to blink away enough of my tears to dial. I'd no more than dialed the nine when I stopped.

From the living room came the sound of Elvis singing, "Are you lonesome tonight?" A bright light shone through the kitchen doorway.

Damn, I'd told Elroy not to touch anything. Did he have to go and turn on Jonni's music, and every damned light? Damn the man.

I slammed the phone down and walked into the living room, to give him what for.

And stopped. He hadn't turned on any music. Nor the lights.

Elvis, or a reasonable facsimile thereof, stood in the middle of the living room, dressed in a white-sequined polyester jump suit, leaning over Jonni and singing, "All my dreams fulfill." Light shone around and from him.

And Jonni, Jonni who had been cold and dead, sat on the ratty batik sofa and stared up at Elvis, her eyes full of wonder, her cheeks red.

I couldn't speak. I could take walk-ins. I could take attempted possession. I could take a hundred different things, but Elvis materializing in Jonni's living room was just too much. To say nothing of this resurrection business.

I leaned against the wall and wondered what had been in that ricecream bar.

Elvis took off his scarf and handed it to Jonni.

Jonni — a dazed, enchanted-looking Jonni — clapped enthusiastically.

"Jonni?" I managed to say.

The light went out. I blinked. It wasn't Elvis. Only Elroy, who stood there, with his hip poked out, his lower lip sticking forward in a rakish pout. "See?" he said, turning around. "I told you she just needed waking."

I shook my head. Side-effects of working in a New Age store. You eventually went as nuts as the customers.

I approached Jonni gingerly. She had been dead. I was sure she had been dead. "Are you all right?" I asked her.

"Yeah," she said, in her thin, little-girl voice. "Yeah. I had a bad argument with Pete and I took some sleeping pills and slept late, that's all. You guys want me to come in to the store?"

"Yes," Elroy said, unequivocal. "Why don't you go get dressed?"

"I'll go with you," I volunteered, not willing to let her out of my sight, lest she should revert to a dead state. I followed her up a rickety stair and into a messy room, where I watched her change into a pair of jeans and T-shirt. And heard the full account of her row with Pete, told in a strangely detached voice.

"And Elroy woke you?" I asked, bringing her back to the present.

"Yes," she said, and wrinkled her perfect brow. "Only . . . I didn't even know he was an Elvis impersonator."

Elvis impersonator? So, she'd seen it too? Were hallucinations shared, now?

I led Jonni downstairs and out the door, to the car.

Elroy had cleared a space for her in the back by piling the teddy bears in unholy confusion on one side of the back seat. He sat her down with unusual solicitude, then opened the door for me.

Once I was in and we'd started the drive back to the store, he said, "I hope I never catch you taking sleeping pills again, young 'un. I don't want you taking any of that trash. That stuff can kill you."

I almost told Elroy that we'd all seen the this-is-your-brain-on-drugs commercial, but it struck me that Jonni, whose full name was Jonnitan and whose parents had met in a hippie commune, *might never* have heard any anti-drug speech from someone she respected. So I let Elroy ramble on in his odd, chewed-up speech.

He sounds just like Elvis, I thought. And his gestures, his hip-positioning, his lower-lip pouting, his disapproving sneer. All of them are just like Elvis. "So, you were an Elvis impersonator, when you were young?" I asked him, when I thought that Jonni had enough sermonizing. Besides, he'd started quoting the gospels mixed up with vintage New Age sayings and stuff about a higher plane.

My question brought him up short. He turned to stare at me. "A what?"

"An Elvis impersonator," I said, just as the weird thought ran through my mind that there had been no impersonation involved. Looking down, I saw that he wasn't wearing any belt buckle, certainly not a huge, gold-and-jewels one. Had I dreamed that, too?

I was so shocked that when I paid mind to Elroy again, he had launched off in another sermon of some sort, this one apparently directed at me, "— besides, young lady, unlike some people I don't go through life playing no phony role. It's just that sometimes you're required to be what people need, what people think you should be, and in a way to expiate and to cleanse the sins of who you were or they think you were. For instance, all those ricecreams you eat —"

"I pay for them," I protested.

"Damn right you do. You can die of overweight, you know. And besides, as my mama used to say —"

He had parked in front of the store by the time he finished his sermon. I almost ran out of the car, confused, baffled, feeling like I was having a weird dream and definitely very tired of Elroy's sermon.

Mark was at the counter, on the phone, with a pile of books in front of him and a pricing gun in his hand. He looked up and mouthed at me, "Jonni?"

"She's fine. She's coming in," I said. I wanted to tell him she'd been dead and Elroy had taken on Elvis' form and resurrected her, but then Mark would just tell me I'd been working for Eternal Life too long. And maybe I had.

"Well, ma'am, if you are possessed by a malevolent entity, I'd say you definitely should quit your job with the nuclear power plant," Mark said, into the phone.

I moved in beside him, took the price gun from his hand, determined to start work and forget what must have been a dream, had to have been a dream.

Looking down at the cover on the first book on the pile, I gasped.

Mark covered the mouthpiece on the phone.

"Elroy had them vanity published. Isn't it a hoot?"

I looked at the cover again, speechless.

It showed a figure in a white jump suit, surrounded by light. On the top it said Elroy Peters. And on the bottom, in black letters, was the title: *Elvis Died for Your Sins.* Ω

ABDUCTION

Dan's old felt fedora
still grows from the hatstand
where he left it three years ago. "I'm off"
he said, as he left
with his huge bundle of keys
and a sappy smile. "I'm off
to get a cake for Pete's birthday
and a couple of six-packs, I guess." I nodded,
once. I was pissed off, mildly so,
for no good reason I can remember. All they found
was a concentric series of circular
burn marks. And one sneaker,

        carefully untied.
        There was no foot in it.
        I made certain to ask.
        I suppose they might have lied.

I still get calls
from the Ufologists, the New Atlanteans,
the Rosicrucians and the occasional
        would-be
        Illuminati.

Hard Copy offered money, NASA offered nada,
but was unexpectedly sympathetic.

        ("Happens more often
        than you might think."
        said one grizzled G-man.)

What bothers me most
is what happened to all those keys
and who has them
and what they unlock.

— **Sam Henderson**

The Classic Horrors

. . . and, what is to me more curious, at the side of this den, against the wall, was crouching the anatomy or skeleton of a human being . . .

"The Ash Tree" by M.R. James

Allen Koszowski

WHAT YOU WISH FOR
by Stephen Dedman

Illustrated by Jill Bauman

Roy woke suddenly, and realised that he was still in Mapurtiti. Partly it was the heat — that, and the residual stink from the kangaroo his predecessor had left in the 'fridge over the Christmas holiday, when the house had been empty and the electricity turned off. The interior of the 'fridge had been green with decay when Roy had arrived in January, and despite his repeatedly scrubbing it and the kitchen, and buying the local store's entire stock of air-fresheners, he'd never entirely dispelled the reek. Replacing the 'fridge would have taken more money than he had and, he suspected, a ream or two of paperwork to the Education Department. Burying the carcass had been the most nauseating work he'd ever done; he'd dry-heaved for hours.

He lay on the bed, the sheet plastered to his body, the stench and the hot dry air moved only by a rattling table fan. The Department had promised him that the housing was air-conditioned as well as furnished — but the air-conditioner had been vandalised during the holiday. Boredom, after the school day was finished (and worse still, over the weekend), was as much a problem as the heat and the lingering stench; the town had no bookshop, and no library except the school library and a rack of rental videos in the general store. The television that had come with the house only received one channel — irregularly — and was too old to be compatible with his VCR. There was no phone jack in the house for his modem; the nearest was a solar-powered phone booth outside the school. Worst of all, Heather was a thousand klicks away, and there were almost no single women living near the town, except in the aboriginal community. There was one part-time prostitute living on the other side of Mapurtiti, but she was ten or fifteen years his senior and, worse still, had a daughter in his class. Privacy, he realised, was as scarce in small towns as books, especially for newcomers like himself.

Roy lay there for a moment and listened, wondering what had wakened him, then decided that it wasn't important and rolled over. He closed his eyes, then opened them again and fumbled for the switch on the reading lamp. Something — someone? — was standing in the doorway.

"Hello."

The voice was softly feminine, and sounded faintly familiar. "Heather?" he blurted out, before finding the light-switch. A few seconds later, he could see that it wasn't Heather, or anyone else he recognised.

"No," she said, taking a step closer. The lamp didn't quite dispel the shadows from her face, but she looked close to his own age, several years too young to be the mother of any of his students. Apart from that, Roy could only be sure that she was slim and fairly tall, with shoulder-length dark-brown hair, and as naked as he was. She looked down from his face to his crotch and back again, and her smile widened into something that might have been a grin. Roy looked down, and realised that it was too late to bother pulling the sheet up. "Who are you, and what are you doing in here?"

"Who were you expecting?"

"Nobody."

"That's me." She sat on the bed, near his feet. "What's the problem?"

*This **must** be a dream*, he thought, *an intense — what do they call them? **lucid** dream*. He looked at her more closely, trying to read her expression. She was conventionally pretty, but apart from her smile and her enormously dilated pupils, he saw no signs of any emotion. A quick, almost involuntary, glance at her nipples was slightly more informative. "Don't you like me?" she asked.

"I don't know you," he said, hoping he didn't sound as ridiculous as he felt.

"Does that matter?"

"It does to me."

She nodded, without her expression changing at all. "Do you prefer blondes?" she asked. "Pale skin? Blue eyes?"

He shrugged. He didn't have any strong preferences, as far as looks went; he'd decided while still a teenager that, like Phebe in *As You Like It*, he was 'not for all markets' and couldn't afford to restrict himself to women of any particular type. He also believed that personality was far more important than minor details of appearance — especially if, like Heather, they insisted on making love in the dark. He was about to speak when he noticed that the woman on the bed had suddenly become blonde. She giggled at his expression as her golden hair became curlier and longer and her features flowed into a fair likeness of Pamela Lee Anderson. "Is this better?" she cooed. Roy merely stared. "Or would you prefer Cindy Crawford? Elle McPherson? Sandra Bullock?"

"Who are you?"

"Who do you want me to be?"

He took a deep breath. "Okay. Do you have a name? — and *don't* ask me what I want it to be."

"Why not?"

"I don't like being lied to."

She raised an eyebrow in what seemed perfectly genuine astonishment. "Really? Most men love it."

"Really," he said, though with less force than he'd intended. The woman's breasts deflated noticeably, a few faint stretch marks appeared, her smile became a few lumens less radiant and her pupils contracted. "Is this better?"

He took a deep breath. "Look, who are you — or if that's too difficult, *what* are you — and why are you here?"

"You can call me Mara, if you like," she said, after a moment's hesitation. "If you want to believe I'm a dream, or a fantasy, that's fine. As for why I'm here . . ." she reached down for his cock and stroked it gently, making him gasp.

"What if I don't want you?"

"I can come back when you're asleep," she suggested. "Most men I've known sleep more soundly than you; maybe they work harder. I was here a week ago, but maybe you don't remember. But while you're awake, I can be whatever you want me to be. You must have *some* fantasies."

I can't believe I'm arguing with a dream, he thought, then shook his head. Mara wandered over to the bookshelf, looking at his small collection of videotapes; she held up his copy of *Bram Stoker's Dracula* and crooned, "Winona Ryder?" Her hair became dark in an instant.

"I'd prefer Sadie Frost," he replied, without thinking. She looked over her shoulder at him, then shrugged.

"Sorry; her I don't know. Is there anyone else?"

"Mia Kirshner?" A slight shake of the head.

"Mathilda May? Angelina Jolie? Beatrice Dalle? Amy Yip? Joey Lauren Adams? Uma Thurman?"

"What movie?" She turned around; her hair was auburn, her body stunning — a twentieth century Botticelli Venus, à la *The Adventures of Baron Munchausen.* "I can't do costumes, not while you're awake; if you want those, you'll have to provide them yourself. The same with whips, handcuffs, or any other toys . . ."

Roy tried to answer, but his mouth felt too dry. "Okay," she said, kneeling beside the bed. "What do you want to do?"

The old thermometer in the classroom read 110° Fahrenheit, 43 point something Celsius, but at least the clock said 3:23, only seven more minutes of the school week remaining. The children slumped over their desks merely stared at him listlessly, somehow reptilian, though he knew that — like reptiles — they could move quickly enough when motivated. He knew better than to try to teach them anything in this sort of weather, and was vaguely flattered that any of them had bothered to show.

When the bell rang, the children looked up hopefully, and he nodded. "Okay, see you all on Monday. Don't forget your maths homework." He could hear younger children already walking out of Ms Kickett's room next door, not running until they reached the sun-baked quadrangle. He sighed, packed his books into his desk, switched off the rickety ceiling fans, and walked out. Ms Kickett and Mrs Bach were already in the tiny staff-room, helping themselves to cold water from the 'fridge. "You look exhausted," said Debbie Kickett, her dark face gleaming with sweat. "Water?"

"Thanks. I'm not used to this heat."

Mrs Bach shrugged. "We have at least another month of that ahead; it doesn't start to cool down until March. What are you doing over the weekend? Going anywhere?"

Roy shook his head. The nearest town worthy of the name, Meekatharra, was two hours away on mostly unpaved roads — an unpleasant prospect in his un-airconditioned Datsun. "Just doing lesson plans, I guess, and maybe some reading. What about you?"

"Working on my book," said Mrs Bach.

"What sort of book?" he asked after a moment's silence, suspecting that it was expected of him.

"A historical novel. I'd like to write a history of the town, but most of it was never written down

— or if it was, the records were lost. You might not think it, but this must have been a terribly exciting place about a century ago, during the gold rush. Four or five thousand men camped on a dozen acres. All that's left now is the cemetery and the other holes in the ground; the area was all but mined out by 1915. Most of the men enlisted, and almost none of them came back." Roy nodded. There were still mines around Mapurtiti, but with the price of gold at a record low, few of them were being worked. Rich deposits of arsenic had kept the town alive for a few decades, but those mines had also closed. "The difficult part is finding names for the characters; so many of the men used the name 'Smith,' it becomes rather confusing. But there was plenty of material — a lot of fights and murders," Bach continued, almost wistfully, "sometimes two or three a month — mostly over gold, or cards, or — um — lover's tiffs. And those are just the ones we know about; no one thought too much of it if someone disappeared, and there are plenty of places around here where you could bury a body without it being found for a century or more. But these things happen when there aren't enough women around to provide a civilising influence."

"What about the Yamidji women?"

"They didn't go near the mines," replied Debbie Kickett. "There's a . . . a taboo that seems to pre-date the gold rush days. Sometimes the white men would catch them while they were out gathering food, and sometimes they'd come to the tribal camp with food or booze to trade, but that was dangerous — and illegal, after there were police in town."

Mrs Bach looked at her as though she was about to speak, then shrugged. "What sort of taboo?" asked Roy.

"I don't really know. Secret men's business, probably, but no one will tell me. I haven't been initiated into the tribe; I'm actually from Perth myself." She yawned, glanced at her watch, then gulped down another large glass of water. "No point staying around here any longer. Have a good weekend."

Roy slept fitfully for the next few days, and not merely because of the heat. Mara returned on Thursday morning; she still bore a resemblance to Uma Thurman, but it was coarser, the legs longer, the breasts larger, the nipples enormous and almost scarlet, a faint hint of pornographic parody to her hourglass figure. Roy stared at her as she sashayed across the room, wondering how

many other men she'd been close to, how many had imposed their fantasies onto her.

"Hi, lover," she crooned. "Miss me?"

"Yes," he replied. He had no reason to believe she could read his mind, but she could obviously read his body.

She grinned, and cupped her breasts. "So, what do you want tonight?"

"What do *you* want?"

The grin didn't change, but he had a strong impression of something darker crawling around behind it. "I don't fantasize," she said, softly. "My needs are simple." She knelt beside the bed, craned her neck, and licked the tip of his cock. "Would you rather I were somebody else? I never knew a man who didn't want a harem. You want a blonde? A brunette? A black girl, maybe?"

He looked at her. "Do you know Jessica Harper? *Phantom of the Paradise?*"

"No, but I know Jessica Rabbit." Her breasts ballooned to a preposterous size, while her hair and lips and nipples became bright carnadine. "So, what's up, Doc?" she giggled. "Don't worry, it still feels like flesh. Tastes good, too," she said, sliding up onto the bed until her enormous boobs were hanging just above his face. "So, anything special you'd like to do?"

A few minutes later, he rolled off her and lay on his back, staring at the constellation of cracks in the ceiling. "Hey," she said.

"What?"

"You probably don't know this, but it's not polite not to look at your partner after sex."

"If you can persuade her to leave the light on," he muttered.

"What?"

"Nothing." He turned towards her, saw her licking his semen from her cleavage with a tongue like a sentient pink necktie. The image would have been frightening if it hadn't been so funny. "Is that all you need?" he asked. "A little protein?"

She grinned again, and for an instant, her teeth looked alarming long and sharp and white. "Not all," she said. "Do you want me to come back, Roy?"

The weather became cooler over the next week, though Debbie noticed that he obviously wasn't sleeping any better as a result, and commented on it in the staff room during the lunch break. "Don't you think you might be pushing yourself too hard?" she asked.

"What?"

"Lesson plans, or whatever it is you're doing. I know there's not much else to do around here *but* work, and that it's your first year in the real world, but you've got to learn to play it by ear, or you'll do yourself some damage." She shook her head. "This isn't what you had in mind, is it?"

"What?"

"Teaching. It's not something you always wanted to do."

"Oh, I don't mind teaching," he said. "I'd expected to teach high school English and drama, but there weren't any vacancies this year, so I took what I could. I had to borrow a lot of money to get through university, and I couldn't afford to be unemployed for a year or ten. But, no, this wasn't in my plans. I'd expected to be able to take students to the theatre, train a debating team . . . I miss the cinemas, the bookshops, Japanese restaurants, Planet Video, the internet . . . I even miss the beach a lot more than I'd expected; I don't think I've ever been this far inland in my life."

"What sort of films do you like?"

"Cult movies, especially old horror films." He smiled, remembering how as a boy, his goth babysitter had brought horror videos and let him watch them if he 'behaved' — which usually meant letting her bring her boyfriend around and fuck on his parents' waterbed. He liked to blame her for infecting him with a passion for vampires, *The Rocky Horror Picture Show,* and other cinematic weirdness; he still owned several books that she'd lent him and not picked up, and that he'd never had the heart to get rid of.

"And your girlfriend?"

"What?" He snapped out of his reverie. "Yeah, I miss her too . . . though we sort of broke up when I came here and she stayed in Perth. I miss all my friends."

The next weekend he drove down to Meekatharra to pick up the adapter for the television to show videos. While he was there, he dropped into a book exchange and bought some magazines: *Fox, Score, D-Cup, Oriental Dolls, Celebrity Skins.* The middle-aged woman behind the counter commented that she hadn't seen him in there before, and he muttered something about passing through. He spent the night in the motel, enjoying the air conditioning, and drove back to Mapurtiti first thing in the morning.

Mara re-appeared a few minutes after midnight on Wednesday, this time in the likeness of Marilyn Monroe. "Didn't have time to change," she said. "There's an old guy who likes — but you probably don't want to hear about him. So, who do you want me to be tonight?"

He reached under the bed for the copy of *Oriental Dolls,* and turned to the pictorial of an especially pretty porn star, a callipygous Asian woman with a beautiful elfin face and long black hair.

Mara looked at the pictures, and smiled as she transformed into a clone-copy of the woman. "Nice," she said, "very nice," then turned around and looked up at Roy from between her legs. "Is this what you had in mind?" she asked, her hands on her lovely rump, opening herself to his view. "Don't worry, it's perfectly safe." She giggled. "It's even legal, and if it weren't, I wouldn't tell anybody. I won't even scream, unless you want me to. Or do you want to spank me first?" He said nothing. "You teachers don't get to do that any more, do you?"

"Why the Hell are you here?"

She looked innocent. "Don't you know the saying? Never look a gift whore in the mouth. Come *on.* Your head may be saying no, but your cock isn't listening to it. Come *ON!* Trust me, you'll think more clearly afterwards." Roy didn't move, and finally Mara turned around again and sat on the bed. "Okay, okay. If it's missionary position you want, again, fine, but do *something* or I'm going to fuck off and never come back, and you wouldn't want that, would you?"

"Why are you here?" he asked again, stubbornly.

"I told you; to get laid. It's why I exist, how I feed. If there's nothing for me here . . ."

"Feed?" A faint memory murmured in the back of his brain.

"Uh-huh. Oh, not on flesh; a few mouthfuls of protein won't get me very far. If you're worried, you can wear a condom, that's not a problem; Hell, we could do it over the phone, if you had a phone. I feed on lust and fantasy; I am what I eat." She licked her lower lip, slowly.

"Why are you telling me this?"

"You want to talk, that's okay, lots of men like talking. You said you didn't want to be lied to, so I'm telling you the truth. We aim to please."

"We?"

"Did I ever say I was unique? I have sisters in every city, everywhere where the feeding is good. It's not as good here as it once was, but I get by." She looked down at her slender body. "Are you sure this is what you want? I can't stay here all night."

The next week, he picked another porn star from another magazine, a more voluptuous darker-skinned woman, but the same act. It lasted longer, though that didn't make any apparent difference to Mara's enjoyment. The week after that, a blonde with huge, nearly spherical breasts. That lasted little more than a minute, and when he looked at her afterwards, lying on her back with the huge domes sitting on her chest like half-deflated basketballs, her ribs prominent, he noticed the scars under her breasts where her implants had been inserted. "What's wrong?" she asked, her tongue flicking out like a chameleon's.

He shrugged. "I guess some fantasies are better not realised."

"Nah. Some — a lot — don't work twice once you've tried them, but that's not the same thing. Don't forget, I *live* on fantasies."

"What do you do when they all stop working?"

"Almost never happens. Men will always create new fantasies — why do you think there are always new magazines, new videos? — and if that fails, every man I've ever known has fantasies he hasn't dared tell anybody else about, but he'll tell them to me — and not just tell them, usually. They may be old fantasies, adolescent lusts buried away for decades, but that doesn't worry me."

"You like your food rotten?"

"Matured," she said, and transformed back into the Asian woman from a fortnight before. "Like wine. Is this better? Or should I just go?"

"Will you come back?"

Her smile became wider, much too wide for that pretty face, until it reminded him of a horror movie he'd seen as a boy. "Yes," she said, "yes, of course."

Mara didn't return for nearly two weeks; she didn't offer an explanation, and Roy didn't ask. He chose three porn stars from a magazine — their obviously fake names and ridiculous 'quotes' made it easier to think of them as fantasies, not real women — and had Mara assemble that night's perfect woman Frankenstein-style from spare parts; this one's pretty face and creamy skin, another's spectacular but natural torso, a third's peach-shaped ass, Barbie-doll legs and shaven cunt. The sex was less time-consuming than the creation, and less satisfying, but good enough that he thought he might be on the right track. "I won't be here next week," he said, with genuine regret in his voice. "It's the Easter break; I'll be going back to Perth for a few days." She said nothing. "I'll be back the

Saturday after Easter." Mara looked at him coolly, then shrugged. The gesture might not have been intended as seductive, but the movement of her breasts dragged his gaze downwards. "I promise," he said.

Roy arrived back in the city early on Easter Saturday — Shut-In or Shitten Saturday, to the Victorians, and after a drive of more than a thousand klicks, much of it on unsealed roads, he was feeling both shut-in and shitty. Two long showers and an interrupted sleep at his parents' Mount Lawley home improved his mood only slightly, and he was still looking distinctly corpse-like when Heather arrived at seven.

Dinner, at one of their favourite Japanese restaurants, was awkward; Heather had found a job at a Catholic girl's college, and everything she said seemed to emphasize the distance between them. They both soon regretted having pre-booked seats for *Romeo and Juliet,* but tried to tough it out. After the show, they walked back down Pier Street to the car park, both wondering if it would be wiser not to spend the night together. "Are you seeing anybody else?" he asked.

"No. Oh, I go out to movies and shows with friends occasionally, but no one special. What about you?"

"In Mapurtiti? You must be joking. There's nobody there; the town's been dying for more than fifty years."

"Aptly named, then?"

"What?"

"Mapurtiti. It means 'Spirits of the Dead.' "

"Oh; I thought it might be something to do with Nefertiti — you know, 'The Beautiful One has Come.' Where did you hear that?"

"A lecture at the Art Gallery, last month. Of course, that might be in another dialect; I didn't get a chance to ask." She opened her door, sat down, and fastened her seat belt. Roy leaned over, kissed her, reached for her breast, then gently bit her neck. She neither repelled him nor reciprocated, and after a few seconds, he returned to his own side of the car.

"Are you tired?" she asked. "I mean, you've had a long drive down here . . ."

"Not too tired."

"Okay," she said, neutrally. An hour later, they were both staring at the ceiling of her bedroom. "I'm sorry," he said.

"Can I turn out the light now?"

"Sure." She turned away from him, and reached for the switch. "I'm sorry," he repeated, sourly, "I really thought it would help. Why do you insist on doing it in the dark, anyway? Do you have to pretend I'm somebody else?"

"Roy . . ." She considered rolling over and touching him to comfort him, but decided against it.

"Is that it?"

"No. It's me, not you; I don't much enjoy looking at myself, and I think . . . no, forget it."

"Forget what?"

She sighed. "I like the way sex feels, but not the way it looks; it looks . . . gross."

"Gross?"

"Well . . . sometimes, yes. Sometimes it looks violent. Sometimes it just looks funny. Okay, maybe I'm a hopeless romantic or something, but I wish it looked like it *felt.* Why do you like having the light on?"

"I like to see who I'm with."

"Why? Can't you remember?" He didn't reply. "That was meant to be a joke."

"Ha ha."

They lay there for another few minutes, not speaking. "Do you want me to drive you home?" she asked, eventually.

"Don't you want me here?"

"Not while you're like this, no."

"It'll be better in the morning. . . ."

"I don't think so, Roy. I'd rather you left."

"Fine. I'll call a cab."

"I can drive you . . ."

"No, I don't want to put you out. I'll call you, okay?" He was still feeling frustrated and flaccid, tense in all the wrong places. As the cab drove towards Northbridge, he considered going to a strip show, or maybe a brothel, but decided against it; live girls and mass-market fantasies weren't what he wanted, needed. Memories of Mara were more potent than sordid fleshy reality. He went straight home, paid the driver, and hurried into his bedroom where he masturbated until he felt like screaming.

He spent the next few days watching videos and shopping for another car, finally choosing an old but unbeaten Land Rover with air conditioning. He stuffed his suitcase with books and videos and skin magazines and left three days earlier than he'd originally planned. Mara came to him the morning after he arrived back in Mapurtiti; she still wore the top-heavy, long-limbed, angel-faced Frankenhooker body. "You knew I'd be here, didn't you?" he asked.

"It seemed likely. Not certain, but likely."

"I nearly went looking for your sisters. Where can I find them?"

She smiled beatifically. "You don't. We find you. Oh, you can try calling the phone sex lines, or the escort agencies, or some of the sex shops that offer private strips, and there's a *small* chance you'll get lucky, but we can't work crowds, we never have addresses, and you'll never see us during the day. So, what do you want tonight? Another mix and match?"

"No . . . ," he said, after a moment's thought. He reached for his wallet, and removed the photo of Heather. Mara looked at it dubiously. "I can't see her body," she said, her face broadening into Heather's, her hair turning from black to ash-blonde. "You'll have to describe it."

"Oh . . . about five five, rather plump . . . no, the breasts sag more than that, no lower, yeah that's okay . . . fatter thighs, wider across the hips . . . her nipples are paler than that, with almost no areolae, and the pubic hair's sort of mousy brown, the stuff on her head is dyed . . . yeah. Yeah."

"This is what you want?" asked Mara, her voice and expression neutral.

Roy nodded. Jesus, he thought, she's even uglier than I am; no wonder she hates having the light on. "That's great. Now get turn around and get down on your hands and knees. Make that elbows and knees. Yeah. Yeah. Now, her voice . . . nah, forget it, just don't say anything unless I tell you to. Yeah."

She returned a week later, still looking like Heather, and he asked her to change into somebody else, *anybody* else. She transformed instantly into the likeness of a pretty dark-haired girl of about ten. "No, Jesus, that's worse! Can you do, oh God I don't know, Drew Barrymore? Look, I'm sorry about last time," he said, as she changed yet again.

"Don't be."

"I mean it."

"So do I. That's why I'm here?"

"What?"

"Fantasies you don't like to admit to are the best sort, the tastiest. Lust is nice, but shame . . . shame is even better."

"I don't understand."

"For some men, it's a particular woman. Best friend's wife. Teacher. Mother, sister, daughter. Little girls, little boys. She-males. Hermaphrodites. Amputees. Corpses; you remember my Marilyn Monroe?" She smiled. "One of the most delicious I can remember was from a young man who used to go out at nights with his best friend bashing gays, then go home and fantasize about sucking his best friend's cock. Sometimes it's not a person that's important, but an act. Violence. Humiliation. Whatever. Often it's incredibly old, a first sexual urge, and incredibly deeply buried or suppressed. You're coming closer to yours; you should be ready in a few more weeks. Real flesh isn't good enough for you any more, is it?"

"And what happens then?"

"Do you still want me to tell you the truth?"

"Yes!"

She shrugged. "It depends. Sometimes it burns out all other desires, and sometimes *all* desire. Some commit suicide, though not many. Some recover. I don't know what *you'll* do."

"And what do you do?"

"Eventually, I stop coming back. After all, the best is gone; all that's left are the dregs."

"And you're not scared that telling me this is going to warn me?"

She threw back her head and laughed loudly. "Oh, sure. Like putting warnings on cigarette packs? Face it, you're hooked . . . but okay, I'll make you a promise; I won't come back until you know you want me, whatever it costs. Now, what do you want to do?"

Mara returned three weeks later, this time in the exaggerated likeness of a comic-book super-heroine, unrecognisable without her costume. "Teenagers," she explained. "So, what's it going to be?"

"You think I'm ready?"

She grinned. "You've been ready for weeks; I waited until you were about to boil over. This must be *good.*"

He shrugged. "I've been doing some reading. About succubi." She looked innocent. "Sexual vampires," he explained. "They're supposed to turn into incubi on the other side of the world, carrying the sperm they've stolen from men to impregnate witches."

Mara laughed. "Yes, I've heard that one. It comes from the idea that sperm is sacred; besides, it helped explain how so many nuns mysteriously became pregnant. I can be male if men want me to be, but I don't do it regularly. Is that what you want?"

"One of the books mentioned your name," he continued. "Mara. It's the Danish word for succubus, or vampire; she visits sleeping men, and if they fall in love with her, she strangles them. It's where the 'Nightmare' comes from."

"Really? I didn't know that. 'Mara' was just what one of the miners called me — I'm not sure where he was from — and I liked the sound of it. We have to take names the same way we take faces, so I took that one."

"What happened to this miner?"

"Oh, I strangled him while he was dreaming," she replied, her tone sugary with feigned innocence. "It's what he wanted. What do *you* want?"

"So you *are* a succubus?"

She yawned. "If you like. I'm what men want me to be. I didn't make up the stories; they did."

Roy reached for the remote control for the video. "Can you switch the TV on?"

"Sure. What are we watching?"

"*Dracula.*" He pressed the 'Play' button, and they watched as Keanu Reeves wandered through the ruined castle to the bedroom where he met Dracula's brides. Mara smiled as she saw the women emerge from the dark sheets. "Is that what you want?"

He nodded. "The blonde?" He slid off the bed, and she lay down, face up, and pulled the sheet over her. A moment later, she slid out slowly from between the sheets, to see Roy standing over her with a short fire-hardened wooden spear and a rubber mallet.

He plunged the spear down between her breasts with all his strength, then swung the mallet, forcing the spear down until the point emerged between her back ribs. She stared up at him, as he dropped the mallet and reached under the bed for the axe.

She screamed, but there was no one around to hear, and the axe fell a moment later, decapitating her. Roy dropped the axe as Mara's head rolled off the bed and fell at his feet, but he didn't move until he was sure he felt no desire to ever enact that fantasy again.

Burying the carcass was the most nauseating work he'd ever done — he dry-heaved for hours — but he was confident that it would never be found. He stayed in Mapurtiti until the end of the year, then accepted a job in a high school in North Perth.

He lives alone, but is careful never to be alone with anyone, especially after dark. And sometimes, late at night, he calls a phone sex line or an escort agency and listens for a few seconds, but he always hangs up without speaking. Ω

VILLANELLE

On lonely beach and windswept dune
where bleached bones lie among sea-wrack
strange beasts are howling at the moon.

Whistling a thin and eldritch tune
the last magician walks the track
over lonely beach and windswept dune.

Where the shingle curves like a silver spoon
she hears the baying of the pack —
the beasts that howl beneath the moon.

She prays that dawn is coming soon.
The stars are cold and the sky is black
over lonely beach and windswept dune.

And then beside the dark lagoon
she feels their breath upon her back —
the beasts that howl beneath the moon.

She writes in the sand a single rune.
The earth shifts, the heavens crack.
Over lonely beach and windswept dune
she howls like a beast beneath the moon.

— Eileen Kernaghan

CONCERNING THE FATE OF PHILIP, EMISSARY OF POPE ALEXANDER III TO PRESTER JOHN

This much might well be true,
that the pope wrote a letter,
dated September 22, 1177,
and entrusted his physician, Philip,
to deliver it, commanding him
to seek out the fabled domain
of John, Priest, Lord of the Four Indias,
most puissant Christian monarch of Asia,
and secure an alliance against the Saracens.

Philip never returned.
It is easy enough to imagine
that loyal and learned man
butchered by bandits,
or rotting in a dungeon far away,
or dying obscurely in some God-forsaken village
while strangers shook their heads sadly,
unable to comprehend a single word of his delirium,
and then placed the letter, unopened,
at the feet of a barbarous stone idol
until wind and rain and mice did the rest.
Or maybe the wastelands just swallowed him up.

No, I say.
We must demand more than that.
Let us insist, at least,
that brave Philip reached the wild marches of Asia,
encountering whole wandering herds
of seven-horned bulls,
and lions of red, green, black, and blue,
and griffins, which carry off oxen,
and Yllerion, which have wings like razors,
and, of course, unicorns.

Let us say, too,
that he crossed the Sea of Sand,
as Alexander did, carried aloft
by one of those griffins,
and came at last
to the river of precious stones,
and the land of shadow,
and the country of headless men,
whose eyes grow beneath their shoulders,
and other such marvels as are described
by numerous excellent authors.

I am certain that he beheld the Phoenix,
dying, burning, resurrected,
and I think that he secured a drop
of that holy oil
which bleeds from a dry tree,
a mere day's journey from the Earthly Paradise.

And I have dreamed that Philip was received kindly
at the court of Prester John,
and allowed to rest,
while the pope's letter was read.

What then? He did not return.
Prester John's answer remains a mystery.
There *are* mysteries, after all.
I merely insist on certain standards
so the trackless waste
won't swallow us all.

— **Darrell Schweitzer**

— **illustrated by George Barr**

TALES FROM WESTON WILLOW
by Ian Watson

illustrated by George Barr

The line-up of ales in the Wheatsheaf Inn wasn't too impressive, so I settled for a bottle of Satzenbrau. Nor was the decor much to speak of. Outside, the pub was old stone, but inside it was tatty modern. Over the bar hung a joke TEXAS FLYSWATTER fully three feet long. Beside the darts board dangled a nude pin-up calendar from the local garage. A joke clock ticked off the time backwards, its numerals arranged in reverse order. Polished brass shell cases lined one window ledge, darts' and skittles' trophies another.

More congenially, the Wheatsheaf resembled a large living room for an extended, garrulous family of villagers.

I soon found myself in conversation with a stout, grey-haired woman in her late fifties. She wore dark glasses. A harnessed Labrador lay snoozing by her seat.

All *I* had said to her was, "May I share this table?"

"You'll be Mr Campbell from Manor Cottage?" was the reply. She chuckled as if she could see my surprise. "Anyone can hear the Scots in your voice. So who else could it be?"

"Word travels fast. We've hardly been here a week, Mrs, er . . . ?"

"It's Prestidge. Mrs Prestidge. I hear you're an author as well as being a history teacher."

"Well, I've done a couple of detective stories set in the eighteenth century. The last one was about a jewel theft: *The Rape of the Rock.*"

"What name do you write under?"

I sighed silently. "My own."

"You'll find our village *interesting*, Mr Campbell."

Ominous words. I noticed how some of the locals were watching us with interest. One hairy fellow grinned at me. Nodding in Mrs Prestidge's direction, he tapped his head; signifying that she was wise, or that she was a bit batty?

"Let me tell you about Charlie and his wife Ann, who moved here from the city."

I didn't wish to be rude. Quite soon I was riveted . . .

FOXED

"Charlie was a jogger. Now, you don't see too many pavements here in the countryside, and the roads can be a bit narrow and twisty, but Charlie kept up his jogging. Every evening throughout the summer, and on Saturday and Sunday mornings too, he could be seen in his russet track suit completing his six miles. He would head out of the village by the road to Briarley, then cut across a field footpath and down the rutted green lane to the edge of Red Ditch Farm. From the farm he trotted along a ride through Neapton Wood owned by the Forestry Commission, all flanked by firs, to Thumpton Pool where a girl once drowned herself, but that's another matter. From Thumpton Pool a bridleway took him back into the village for a welcome shower. His trainers were usually filthy by then. He needed to buy several pairs.

"In the autumn, the darkening of the evenings forced him to limit his running activities to weekends. We don't have many street lights, you'll have noticed. To compensate, Charlie would get in a game of squash most afternoons before driving home. An accountant for the Heritage Hotels group, that's what he was. Of a Saturday and Sunday he sometimes went round his familiar course twice. Winter brought a bonus. The ground hardened. Running was much easier now along the formerly muddy stretches.

"With winter, too, came the Hunt. They meet at different likely villages around the country, not more than twice at any one place during the season, though that's not to say you don't see huntsmen and women passing through on horseback more often, or pulling their horseboxes behind their Range Rovers if they're from further off. When they meet here, it's in the car park outside. The girls from the Grange serve the trays of sherry. Oh, the crisply jacketed fellows and ladies on their expensive hunters with tightly plaited crests and tails! Young girls on ponies too.

"Neither Charlie nor Ann cared for hunting, nor thought it picturesque. It was with a sense of righteous annoyance at the tetchy pomp of many of the riders that Charlie watched the Hunt set

by Ian Watson

off from the village that Saturday morning, then himself set out at ninety degrees to the route of the hunt for his customary run.

"Charlie had passed by Briarley and was jogging along the green lane when he heard faint halloos coming closer. He saw hunters leaping a distant hedge, the dogs racing ahead of them across the bare brown soil of Red Ditch Farm. In the next field which was a pasture, sheep were panicking, and maybe one or two of the silly muttons would stifle to death in a ditch; but the Hunt would pay up. Did you know it costs the price of a smart car to kill a single fox by hunting, and often as not it gets away? Though sometimes it's broken-breathed, a shadow of itself. You always pay for what you do, Mr Campbell.

"As the dogs neared the barns there came a check and a casting about. Presently, as Charlie jogged on, the quarry itself popped through a gap in the hedge along the green lane. Charlie paused. The animal halted in the middle of the lane. It flicked a glance at Charlie as though he was an irrelevance to it that day — but he wasn't — then stared sharply back the way it had come, panting. Its tongue hung right out. As though the animal had all the time in the world, it squatted and loosed some droppings. Maybe it did so out of fear, or to lighten the load. Or maybe for another reason! Huntsmen admire the patience and pluck and quick wits of the fox. I heard one tell a farmer he could no more shoot a fox than he could strike a woman. Another saw a vixen bring her cubs on to his lawn, and the huntsman put out food for them. In fact he gave the fox family the choice of a dead kitten, a dead pigeon, and a stale loaf. Would you believe, they all went for the loaf? Oh yes, hunting folk feel affection for their clever quarry.

"This particular quarry darted away through the opposite hedge. Not wishing to be trampled by hunters crashing across the lane, Charlie picked up speed to a full sprint. As he was rounding a bend he glanced back and spotted foxhounds wriggling through the first hedge. These checked again. For some unaccountable reason the lead dog gave tongue and began to lope his way. The other dogs followed, yapping.

"Charlie realized that he must have trodden in those fresh fox droppings and was now laying down a strong fresh scent. This amused him. He was in no danger, being recognizable to any foxhound for what he was. He could give their poor prey a head start — if the idiots followed him far enough!

"Running as fast as he could into Neapton Wood, he diverted from his usual route down another ride. Behind, the dogs cried. He could hear the muffled pounding of horses along the green lane. Beyond the Forestry plantings was the parkland of Marston Hall, a great undulating sward where mature oaks, sycamores, and chestnuts grew. Charlie didn't know, but Marston Hall is the home of the Master of Foxhounds, the Honourable Jeremy Brett. Scaling a five-bar gate, Charlie ran for the nearest trees. He fancied that their leafless lower branches might knock a few unwary riders off. Pausing briefly, he saw the dogs fanning out behind. The Master's horse took the gate in its stride, followed by others. Of course, the Master saw Charlie — the man pointed with his whip. The foxhounds checked again. They snuffled and clawed at a hole in the ground between tree roots. Could it be another den, with a new scent? While the dogs stopped, and one younger hound tried to squirm into the earth, Charlie took the chance to put more distance between himself and the Hunt, though by now his heart was pounding. But for the fact that he was gasping through an open mouth, he would probably have gritted his teeth with determination.

"As he breasted a rise, a horn blew, and riders pointed to where he was. They gestured at him, seeing him for what he was, yet now urging the hounds on. The riders drummed on their saddles and shouted. Hounds raised their muzzles to proclaim a deep, throaty music.

"As the pack flooded down the rise behind him in full cry, Charlie spotted a tree which he could scramble into.

"He pulled himself up, from branch to branch.

"Moments later, the pack reached the tree and bayed around the base, rearing, scratching.

"Recovering his breath, Charlie laughed at them.

"The core of the Hunt — those horses which had stayed the obstacle course — soon arrived at the tree. The flushed faces of the riders remained curiously blank, as though Charlie wasn't there at all. Some riders patted and slapped their steaming mounts, but no one said anything. No one quite looked him in the eye.

"Then the red-coated Master stood up in his stirrups and, reaching, he grasped Charlie's ankle."

"Ann saw the Hunt return through the village. A young girl rode proudly beside the Master. Ann was disgusted to see blood smeared on the girl's cheeks. She had been blooded, a custom which Ann thought had died out. Instead of riding past, the Master dismounted at their gate. Doffing his riding cap, he strode up the front path.

" 'Mrs Fox,' he said when she opened the door, 'I'm afraid there's been a terrible accident.' "

"Is Ann still living here, Mrs Prestidge?"

"What do you think? She moved away. There's others who haven't ever moved away."

"Wait a bit. Didn't Mrs Fox call the police?"

"No need. We have our own constable right here in the village, Mr Tate."

"Yes, but — "

"Poor Charlie died of a heart attack, didn't he? All that running wasn't good for him. That's why he tumbled out of the tree."

"But you said . . . And the blood on that girl's cheek!"

Mrs Prestidge chuckled. "If only the dogs could have known his name, what would they have thought?"

Her glass was empty. Likewise, mine.

"Can I buy you a drink, Mrs Prestidge?"

"Rum and black, please."

I elbowed through to the bar for her rum and blackcurrant and another bottle of the German lager for myself. The skinny, hyperthyroid land-lady — I gathered her name was June — winked a bulgy eye at me.

"Having a good time, love?" As if I was in the process of picking up Mrs Prestidge, who was almost old enough to be my mother!

I contented myself with saying, "Fascinating."

I set the rum and black in front of my informant, who heard the clink of glass, and sniffed, and thought, then cautiously reached and captured the drink.

"Cheers, Mr Campbell." She sipped. "And some," she repeated, "did not leave here at all."

"Such as Charlie Fox?"

"Oh no, I was thinking of Paul and Ruth Andrews down at Centre Point, and of course their daughter Julia too . . ."

CENTRE POINT

" 'I always thought that Centre Point was a building in London!' Ruth joked to the secretary of the Women's Institute, who had called round. Ruth and Paul were still in the midst of moving in to the huge old ex-vicarage; the last few tea-chests weren't yet cleared.

"The stone building dated back to Tudor times. With the departure of the most recent vicar, the Church Commissioners had put the unwieldy edifice on the market. When a new vicar arrived to take up his duties, he would live in a neat little bungalow. Until then, Archdeacon Hubble — who had retired to the village from Cambridge-shire, to an imposing rose-clad house in two acres — was taking services in St Mary's. Paul had grand ideas of converting the house to include a couple of independent luxury flats as well as their own domain.

"Mrs Armstrong had said to Ruth, 'Welcome to Centre Point.'

" 'We're almost on the edge of the village,' Ruth pointed out.

"The visitor smiled, 'We have our centre point, too, and it's here.'

" 'Oh, do you mean in the sense that the church is a centre of village life? So therefore the vicarage — '

" 'Not really,' Mrs Armstrong said vaguely. She peered through open doors. The former vicarage had huge rooms with high ceilings and two enormous oak staircases front and back. To Ruth's eye one particular dark patch of ceiling above the rear stairwell looked almost perversely inaccessible.

" 'What'll you be doing with this vast house then, Mrs Andrews, since you only have one child?'

" 'From the first moment that the Andrews arrived in the village they had become accustomed to friendly, though searching questions.

" 'We'll probably split it into three, Mrs Armstrong. One part for us. We'll either sell or rent the others.'

"Mrs Armstrong frowned. 'You'd need to make a lot of alterations. This house is over three hundred years old.'

"Ruth took her remarks in good part. The other day she had dug up some raggy spiraea which was blocking the front path of the overgrown garden. Another neighbor had rushed across with a plate of scones an hour later and had spoken about the vicarage garden as though there was a preservation order on every single plant.

"Ruth grinned. 'All those weird old statues in the garden need a bit of rethinking. They're sim-

ply lost in the bushes — though, from the look of them, I don't know that they're worth finding.'

" 'Those statues are loved in the village, Mrs Andrews. They belong here.'

"Oh yes, thought Ruth. The preservation order mentality again."

"Paul was in insurance. After he had come home and they'd had dinner and Julia was tucked up safely in bed, the couple did some more unpacking. At nine o'clock Paul left to wander along to the Wheatsheaf here, where he was already integrating beautifully, so he claimed.

"You'll have noticed what a lot of people drive to the pub, even if they're only coming quarter of a mile. But Paul, as I say, knew about risks — "

"Such as being nabbed by Constable Tate?" I interrupted.

"He wouldn't dream of it. Has to live here with his missus and nippers, doesn't he? Patrol car from town, maybe — lurking up a lane. Why, last month a fellow was driving back home at twelve down Marston Lane when a patrol car blazed up behind him, floodlights full on. He stopped, hitched himself up three inches taller, marched round and stared at the back of his van, just in case a light was out, which it wasn't, then he stepped up to the police and demanded, 'Do you think I stole this van? Do you think I have something stolen hidden in the back?' Actually he was carrying a computerized thingy for controlling crop spraying. The police took a look and said, 'What's that?' He said to them, 'You wouldn't bloody know if I told you.' But that's by the by.

"Paul returned home at eleven, seeming tipsy.

" 'You know, Ruthy,' he said, 'I don't think we ought to shift any of those statues.'

" 'They're so *ugly*,' she protested. 'Shapeless. They look like those people at Pompeii who were covered in slag. Mrs Armstrong was round today telling me what I shouldn't do. Have the chaps been getting at you in the pub? It's our garden, Paul. It's our house.'

" 'They were telling me how this house got its nickname. It's because it *is* the centre of everything. The centre's in this very house.'

" ' What nonsense. The centre of England is in Meriden, isn't it?'

" 'No, not the centre of *England*. The centre of the universe, Ruthy. That's why the last vicar left. He couldn't compete. Having custody of that in his own house was too big for him.'

" 'They're kidding you, Paul. They must be laughing their heads off. What do they know about the universe? Ever heard of Galileo? The earth moves — millions of miles around the sun. If the universe had a centre, and goodness knows where it might be, it can't possibly stay in one spot on earth.'

" 'Maybe it can.' He grinned feebly. 'What do you know about the universe?'

" 'I know that a village is the centre of its own universe! This is ridiculous. You've made a fool of yourself. Did they slip something in your beer? Oh, it isn't ghosts or witchcraft in villages nowadays. No yokels here! They've wised up. They're going to try and control us by telling us we're sitting on the centre of the whole damn universe! I wonder who dreamed up this crazy joke. It *is* a joke, you know. Wise up, Paul. Climb into bed, wake up tomorrow, watch the sun rise.'

" 'I shouldn't have told you.'

" 'They told you not to tell me? That's even richer. What happened tonight? Was it the village boys' initiation ritual? Did you all pull up your trouser legs? They were pulling *your* leg, Paul.'

" 'No one who didn't know would believe it . . .' He seemed to be holding back some further foolishness. 'We aren't sitting on the centre, Ruthy. It's up near the ceiling, over the back staircase; that bit which you can't get to.'

" 'I'll tell you one thing. You're going to get to it tomorrow evening. You're going to bring the extending ladder inside, and you're going to stick yourself up there to get rid of the cobwebs — and out of your brains too.'

" 'No! I can't.'

" 'If you don't, husband mine, I'm leaving this house the morning after and taking Julia with me. I am not living here, to be manipulated by all and sundry.' "

Mrs Prestidge paused. "I was here in the 'sheaf that night. Well, they weren't kidding him, not a bit. Not Fred and John." She turned her head towards the bar as though she could see. "Ah, but that was before . . . another event. Yes, Paul was faced by a big risk now. Whether to act unwisely — or to risk losing his wife. I think she might have meant that threat. Don't you? Marriages are so much looser nowadays."

One thing I thought was that Mrs P was a dab hand at imitating voices. But how did she know so intimately what had happened inside the vicarage after Paul returned? Unless Paul himself — or even Ruth — had later been her informant . . .

* * *

"Paul passed a fairground on the way home from work, so as a peace offering he brought back a gas balloon with a funny face on it. Julia squealed with delight.

"Then he wrestled the ladder in through the back door and extended it fully up the stairwell. His hands were shaking. It was a very heavy ladder.

"The phone rang, for Paul. The doorbell, for Ruth. Mrs Armstrong hovered outside with news about the Women's Institute drama group. Has Mrs Armstrong been to see your wife yet, Mr Campbell? Your Jill, isn't it? We do like people to join in."

I shrugged, then remembering Mrs P's condition I said, "I'm not sure. Jill hasn't said." I was starting to imagine more than your usual WI of jam and Jerusalem — rather, a secret society for village women! Did these villagers try to control newcomers by separating husband from wife? If so, in our case they wouldn't succeed.

"Mrs Armstrong'll be round," Mrs Prestidge assured me. "I'll remind her." She resumed her story. "While Paul and Ruth were both through at the front of the house, a cry of 'Look at me!' came from the rear. Excusing herself hastily, Ruth ran back.

"The balloon had escaped up to the ceiling. Little Julia was high up the ladder, reaching for the dangling string. She was really at risk.

" 'Don't move, Julia!' cried Ruth. 'Paul, leave the phone! Come here!'

"Mrs Armstrong trotted through inquisitively behind Paul.

" 'Oh Lord,' she exclaimed. 'Oh dear.'

"Julia caught, and lost, the string. The balloon bobbed away. Ignoring her mother, the girl climbed even higher.

"A flash of light blinded the onlookers — as if Julia had touched some exposed wiring!

"Their little girl no longer stood on the ladder. Up top only a mass of white slag perched, in her vague shape and size."

"The village takes care of its own. Constable Tate and Archdeacon Hubble both came. They both *knew*.

" 'Whoever reaches the centre of the universe cannot move away in any direction,' the Archdeacon said wistfully. 'This is the centre of absolute motion. So they're trapped there. We can shift them, but they themselves can never move again. They're eternal.'

" 'Nobody can prove as that's your little girl,'

the Constable told the Andrews bluntly. 'Outsiders would assume as you'd . . . got rid of her. We can sort this out with your coöperation. The last vicar didn't leave. He got reckless. Others too, over the centuries since the first happening while this place was being built. Vicar's in your garden along with the rest of them.' "

"What the hell *is* up there?" Paul demanded.

" 'It's the centre of things,' Hubble repeated gently. 'Has to be somewhere, doesn't it? You're in charge of it now.' "

"With Tate's help, Paul moved the small new statue out into the shrubbery. It looked very ancient and worn out.

"Ruth would sit by the window, weeping. Outside, rain would fall on the blurred Pompeii cast of Julia. All the statues would seem to weep."

"If you like to, Mr Campbell, you can visit those statues. If you call on Mr and Mrs Andrews they'll show you round their garden. They won't leave each other now, nor leave Julia."

"Mm," I said.

"All newcomers to the village have the right to see, just the once, to satisfy theirselves."

"Has a new vicar arrived yet?"

"Ah, that can take a number of years. Our Archdeacon doesn't mind helping out. Besides, we hold joint benefice services with the parishes of Briarley and Marston."

Services, yes. Rituals. But what did these villagers truly believe?

"This Hubble must be a peculiar chap, considering what you say he knows." Not that I credited this latest offering from Mrs P, but she could tell a good yarn, and I had driven past the old vicarage; my eye had been caught by the shapeless objects vaguely visible here and there in the shrubbery.

"The Archdeacon's one of us," she said and tilted her empty glass. Mrs P could certainly sink a few drinks.

"Another one?" I asked. And another story?

She nodded. When I got to the bar, June was holding up eight fingers twice to tell a bald, weatherbeaten, middle-aged bloke how much two

pints of Mild cost. He paid over a palmful of silver and was toasted by a moon-faced contemporary with an unruly gray thatch. This drinking companion said nothing as such, merely gesturing with his glass.

The bald bloke bellowed back, "Cheers!" then he too fell silent. It was pretty noisy in the pub, what with everyone else chattering, piped pop songs playing, and a darts match in progress.

THREE MONKEYS

"Well, Mr Campbell, we decided that our little village of Weston Willow was going to walk off with the trophy in the County Inter-Village Quiz this year. Last year and the previous year we'd been knocked out in the first round.

"The questions are always fairly vicious. Can you say offhand who designed Nelson's column? It was William Railton, in 1843. Do you know the collective noun for moles? It's a 'labour' of moles. Seems plausible enough once you know the answer.

"This year, thanks to our three monkeys, we were through to the final round . . ."

"Richard was the instigator of Project Monkey. He's the secretary of our village hall. You'll meet him — Richard's always on the look-out for new committee members. He has to organize our end of the quiz, get a team together, liaise with rival villages, contact the quizmasters. The Rural Community Council arranges the roster of teams and sets the questions; and Sterling Property Services sponsor it. The county newspaper hosts the grand final at the college in town.

"Richard had come across a pile of paperback quiz books in the secondhand bookshop and discovered to his delight that all the questions we had suffered from in previous years had been cannibalized from these. Naturally he bought the lot, imagining that our team could get some practice in.

"The flaw in this plan soon became obvious. Each book included approximately two thousand questions and answers, a total of ten thousand in all.

"One thing you soon learn in a village, Mr Campbell, is that there's always someone who can turn their hand to anything you want. This doesn't only apply to ordinary things, but to exotic items. I really do believe, if you wanted a small space rocket built in your back garden, someone would turn out to be, or have been, a guided missile engineer.

"At a meeting in the village hall we marshalled our collective talent.

"Richard works for a computer firm which is trying to sell home computers to farmers. He would provide a new prototype micro-memory. With all of us mucking in, we could load the tiny box for instant access to all ten thousand answers.

"Martin's company specializes in micro-electronics, including bugging devices. We weren't supposed to know about this aspect, but of course we all did. Martin could rig up a hearing aid to receive whispered radio messages from Richard. Unfortunately Martin could only gimmick one hearing aid. Stock security was tight at his company — and perhaps three deaf team members might have seemed excessive, don't you think?

"We also had our three monkeys: Lucy, Fred, and John. For the purposes of the quiz they were going to become Blind Lucy, Dumb Fred, and Deaf John.

"Deaf John would wear the hearing aid, to receive the computer answers from Richard in the audience. Richard would be hidden amongst our supporters.

"According to the rules any unanswered question goes to the next team member before being passed over to the opposition. Here, we slyly hedged our bets. Dumb Fred would be printing his answers on one of those 'magic writing' slates which erases itself when you pull it out. If Blind Lucy didn't know the answer and Dumb Fred did, he would scrawl it on his slate under the table for Blind Lucy to squint at out of the side of her dark glasses. Those would hide the movements of her eyes.

"Naturally we didn't ever score *full* marks, but we won all the preliminary rounds. At last the night of the grand final came, in a lecture theatre at the college. Prizes were set out on a table midway between the tables of the two contending teams: a silver cup and souvenir pen sets. Of course there was particular interest in the fact that we had fielded three disabled candidates, who had done startlingly well so far.

"Blind Lucy was guided to her seat by Dumb Fred, who gestured Deaf John to his.

"The question master summarized the rules; and battle commenced. We were up against Milton Langford. Their team were hot shots: a headmistress, a bank manager, and an estate agent. They had won the quiz in the two previous years, and now they stared across at our disadvantaged trio with a mixture of sympathy and amusement.

"The questions rolled on.

" 'Who was the highest scorer for England against Australia in the first innings at Lords in 1909?'

"Deaf John fielded that one easily, 'J. H. King.'

" 'What is Kepler's Third Law?'

"Dumb Fred didn't know, so Deaf John trotted out: 'The squares of the periodic times of planetary orbits vary as the cubes of the semi-major axes.' Right!

" 'In which county does the river Itchen reach the sea?'

"This was tricky. Blind Lucy had no idea of the answer, but most happily Dumb Fred genuinely did. Squinting, Blind Lucy read from his writing tablet, 'Hampshire.'

"Milton Langford didn't do badly at all, but they could hardly match our performance. We won by 115 points to 98, and all the while Blind Lucy managed to remain convincingly blank, and Dumb Fred suitably tongue-tied, and Deaf John gratifyingly hard of hearing. During the presentations John even added to the illusion by tapping his hearing aid, with a puzzled look on his face."

"Afterwards Dumb Fred led Blind Lucy out to our rented minibus which was in the college car park, waving Deaf John along with sweeps of his other arm. The doors were slammed, and off we drove. As soon as we were safely isolated out on the dark highway, Richard — who was driving — began to laugh triumphantly. Or to cackle triumphantly; it was that kind of laugh.

"But as he laughed, Blind Lucy cried out in a strangled voice, 'Don't you understand? I can't *see!* I can't see a thing. I'm blind!' She tore off her black glasses. 'There's nothing! Nothing.'

"Deaf John shouted. 'Eh? Eh?'

"Dumb Fred mouthed at his fellow passengers, noiselessly."

The moon-faced chap and his drinking companion had edged up close to our table. The former was listening keenly. His bald friend stared blankly at Mrs Prestidge.

"You're Blind Lucy, aren't you?" I cried at her.

"That I am, Mr Campbell." She laid her spectacles carefully on the table and gazed at me with sightless, whitened eyes. "And here is Deaf John and that's Dumb Fred. Weston Willow's a special village, you see, being so close to the centre of you-know-what. Mostly our village *appears* like anywhere else. Just you look out of the corner of your eye, though! Hereabouts things are given, and things are taken away, if you follow me. We shouldn't have drawn attention to ourselves outside the village. The village didn't like that. That's what went wrong. That's why something was taken away from us."

"Look here," I protested, while John and Fred crowded closer, "you used *technology* to cheat in the quiz. You didn't use magic or something!"

"Weston Willow doesn't wish any attention drawn to itself; that's the simplest I can say. I could tell all kinds of tales, Mr Campbell. These three tonight are just the icing on the cake. Odd things happen here, and that's a fact. You'd hear the stories soon enough. You tell stories, don't you, being a writer?"

"Detective," I mumbled. "Eighteenth century."

"We had an eighteenth century here too, same as everywhere else. Soon enough you'd be sending your eighteenth century investigator here to try to plumb a mystery." Her hand snaked out unerringly and caught my wrist. "You mustn't tell on us, must you?

I felt paralysed by her clutch. My eyes glazed with tears. For a few moments I couldn't see a thing; everything went blank.

"I can see through your eyes, Mr Campbell," I heard Mrs Prestidge whisper.

My vision snapped back into focus. A man's hand gripped my shoulder.

"I can hear through your ears," murmured John. Music had died in the room. Conversation, too. The locals were all looking at me.

No sooner did John release me than my shoulder was seized.

"I can talk through your mouth," I said. This was my own voice — but those weren't my words!

The pressure subsided. Lucy Prestidge reclaimed her dark glasses and hid those eyes like glass baubles filled with ashes.

The piped music and the chatter both resumed, the locals once again engrossed in each other's lives. Lucy Prestidge smiled at me. Her eyes were invisible, but her mouth stretched, her cheeks swelled and creased into a smile.

"Shall I tell you another tale, Mr Campbell?

Not to be told elsewhere ever, in any form, do you promise?"

I nodded.

Promises. Ten-year-old promises. It's already half a decade since Jill and I moved away from Weston Willow. We came all the way to Edinburgh, where I'd been born. Surely far enough away in time and space!

Nowadays I'm head of history in a large comprehensive. I did manage to write one further novel about my eighteenth-century detective, Montague Hamilton, but it was the novel for which I already had ideas when we moved to Weston Willow. After that the drought in my imagination commenced — while simultaneously a forbidden reservoir was filling up.

No more novels. I was sure, and Jill too was sure, that I should have been able to break through to become a full-time writer, quitting teaching forever. Indeed the mystery novel which might have propelled me over this threshold was waiting inside me, blocked only by my promise to Lucy Prestidge. It in turn blocked the possibility of any other different novel. The frozen embryo within me prevented any other fertilization. The visit of Montague Hamilton to the Manor House of Weston Willow for a hunting party, the mysterious disappearances, the events at the vicarage, a distillation and transmutation of everything I picked up from Blind Lucy and the other locals during five years' residence; if only I dared to tackle this material. I knew I would be free. If only I could break the seal upon my lips — or upon my typing fingers.

Surely the seal existed only in my imagination. So far as publicity went, didn't I now live in Edinburgh, in another country, Scotland? And wouldn't I faithfully change the name of Weston Willow to Milton Mandeville, or Chipping Charlford, or whatever?

A week ago the school holidays started, and I began to type *The Undeserted Village*. Just as I had echoed Alexander Pope in the case of the jewel theft, now I echoed Oliver Goldsmith. And the story flowed, how it flowed.

Three nights ago I woke in the early hours to find that my left forearm and hand were paralysed. That arm lay on top of the bedspread like a lump of rubber. I needed no Montague Hamilton to deduce that I had not squeezed the blood flow by sleeping upon the arm. Nor was the night air cold; I had not chilled my exposed flesh. It was as if part of my body had died.

Bemused, I used my right hand to lift the dead limb and shook it about. A dentist might have needled it full of novocaine. No demon dentist prowled the darkened bedroom, where only Jill and I lay. I listened to Jill's breathing; she sounded deeply asleep.

Sensation returned suddenly. Feeling flooded back fully and immediately without any prickling interval of pins and needles. One moment dead meat, the next living flesh. Something had slipped a sleeve over my arm which blocked off all feeling, which nullified the nerves. Suddenly the sleeve was snatched away. Puzzled, I drifted back to sleep.

Two nights ago, after writing some more, I woke to find the whole of my right arm dead. After five minutes the limb came alive again.

Last night, after another five pages of *The Undeserted Village*, both my legs died. For ten minutes I lay in terror, paralysed from the waist down.

I consulted a medical book today. I did find a rare disorder known as periodic paralysis. Yet it didn't seem as though I ought to suffer from this. I also came across a reference to hysterical paralysis. Can it be that I'm doing this to myself?

I fear that isn't the case.

Nor do I know whether the nightly symptoms would cease if I abandoned my book, if I deserted *The Undeserted Village*. How can I abandon it? What do I tell Jill? What do I tell myself? That I'm a failure? That I've found a perfect excuse to be a failure?

What I did today at my desk was to set those first chapters aside for the moment and to type up this brief account instead. Just in case.

I never told Jill all that I learned in Weston Willow — for instance the way in which Dumb Fred spoke through my own lips, that night in the Wheatsheaf. Jill's reaction would have been similar to Ruth Andrews' — before her daughter was turned into a shapeless statue. I'm sure that Fred did borrow my vocal chords, my tongue; that it wasn't just a trick. I'm sure that it happened. I wonder whether Jill knows any secrets that she never confided to me, through fear of . . . who can say what? Most of the time, of course, our life in the village was ordinary and normal.

This has taken till eleven-thirty. I shall leave the pages in full view. And now that I have done, I shall climb upstairs to join Jill in bed. She will be asleep. Soon I will also be asleep — until I waken up. Ω

SINCE 1923: THE UNIQUE MAGAZINE

Summer 2000

ISSN 0898-5073

Cover by Jill Bauman

Weird Tales® is published 4 times a year by DNA Publications, Inc., in association with Terminus Publishing Co., Inc. Postmaster and others: send all changes of address and other subscription matters to DNA Publications, Inc., PO Box 2988, Radford VA 24143–2988. Editorial matters should be addressed to Terminus Publishing Co., Inc., 123 Crooked Lane, King of Prussia PA 19406–2570. Single copies, $4.95 in U.S.A. & possessions; $6.00 by mail to Canada, $9.00 by first class mail elsewhere. Subscriptions: 4 issues (one year) $16.00 in U.S.A. & possessions; $22.00 in Canada, $35.00 elsewhere, in U.S. funds. Publisher is not responsible for loss of manuscripts in publisher's hands or in transit; please see page 5 for more details. Copyright © 2000 by Terminus Publishing Co., Inc.; all rights reserved; reproduction prohibited without prior permission.
Typeset, printed, & bound in the United States of America.
Weird Tales® is a registered trademark owned by Weird Tales, Limited.

THE EYRIE

We want your letters! You may e-mail *Weird Tales®* at owlswick@netaxs.com, or send ordinary mail to us at 123 Crooked Lane, King of Prussia PA 19406-2570. Make sure to put "weird letter" in the subject line. However, *do not* send unsolicited story submissions by e-mail.

Also, visit us on our new Web site:
dnapublications.com

The World Horror Convention, 2000

There are times for referring to oneself in the plural — a prerogative traditionally reserved for kings and queens, emperors, and editors — but there is also a time for dropping the "we," as when it doesn't make sense, as in, specifically, a report on the World Horror Convention (held May 11–14th in Denver) because one of us went and one of us didn't. That is to say Darrell went. *I* who am writing this went. There, just to prove that I can do it. *We* did not go, and are reminded of the old joke in which two people are talking. "Are you schizophrenic?" says the first. "We don't think so," says the second.

Yours the Above-Named spent four days in Denver, and, as is rather typical of such ex-

periences, did not see much of the city except out of a hotel window. The old part of the city was not in evidence. It looked like a brand-new, very nicely designed generic American shopping mall.

But the reason for not wandering out all that much is not merely that the tourist attractions don't seem all that strong — an art museum, the Molly Brown House, she of Unsinkable fame — but because the convention itself held so much interest. For one thing, there was the schedule. I was on the program for an hour, then off for an hour, then on again, or so it seemed, time also being demanded by important program items — an hour and a half of Harlan Ellison, a presentation by Dan Simmons, with a reading from the script of the movie of *Children of the Night* — plus attempts to get into the dealer's room (some of that actual Work, soliciting advertising for *Weird Tales®*) so that time flew by. There wasn't always even time for meals. Of course, though, sufficient edibles were available at the Hospitality Suite that it is only a joke that the calories taken in at a convention don't count. I managed one interview, with Neil Gaiman. I sold some books and

copies of this magazine. I signed books. I had other people sign my copies of their books. I managed to acquire more, so that in the end I was profoundly grateful for the wheeled luggage which had been a gift from my mother-in-law.

Conventions are like that. When enough high-talent people of similar interests get together, things come to a boil, and don't stop boiling until it is all over, with formal program items in the day and parties at night. It is a time for schmoozing, networking, seeing old friends, making new ones. Yours Truly made a controversial remark on one of the panels, that there is a limit to the benefits of networking. You can go to conventions to meet editors, find out who is publishing what, swap notes with other writers, but it's my (actually *our*) experience that hardly anyone has ever sold a story to *Weird Tales®* by coming up to one of the editors and saying, "Hey, I have this story I want to talk to you about." That will get a noncommittal reply of "Well, go ahead and send it to me." One of the rules is that you *never*, unless by prior arrangement, hand an editor a manuscript at a convention, hoping to get special attention that way. What's he going to do? Carry it around to parties? Lose it? No, send it to the office.

One of the pleasures of such a convention is meeting one's authors, which in (both of) our experience tends to happen after the fact. In Providence last Autumn at the World Fantasy Convention, I met Sarah Hoyt, whose work we'd already bought. In Denver, I sat at the autographing next to Ken Rand, author of "Refuge" in this issue. He is now a friendly face, where he had been an unfamiliar name on a manuscript. I also met Carrie Vaughn, whose great "Dr. Kitty Solves Your Love Problems" will be appearing here soon, and at least found someone who knew Frank Tuttle, author of last issue's "Passing the Narrows" and was able to pass on the word that his story had proven popular.

Editors don't particularly buy stories from people they know. They get to know people they buy stories from. It's not the same thing.

A few random notes about the convention:

Harlan Ellison was given a special World Horror Grandmaster Award from the convention, which is not the same as the Stoker Award Life Achievement (also given out at the convention), which went to Charles L. Grant and the (sadly) late Edward Gorey. Harlan was in fine form. His public lectures are not to be missed. He is one of those people, like Lenny Bruce or Mark Twain, who has turned his own life into the source of his art. In public he does a kind of stand-up comedy, as Twain did, full of great stories and biting satire. He has terrific control of the audience.

On panels Harlan may have seemed like the resident Luddite, as much of the talk seemed to be about the Internet and the glories of on-line publishing, which leave him unimpressed. He wanted to talk more about art and about writers making a living (this latter something conspicuously *not* happening from on-line publications) rather than technowhiz wonders.

He has a point. Our own (both of our) view is that the Internet is a wonderful billboard, but do not confuse the billboard with the product. The product is the physical object, the magazine you're holding in your hands, which is easier and more convenient to read, and for which you're more likely to be willing to pay money. There are two problems with on-line publications, the first being that just *anyone* can post something on a web-

STAFF:
Publisher: Warren Lapine
Editors: George H. Scithers & Darrell Schweitzer
Managing Editor: Carol Adams; Art Editor: Diane Weinstein; Assistant Editors: Kyle Phillips, Pat Buard, Robert Waters, Casey McCarthy, & Donica Collier; Computer Consultant: David J. Williams III
Typesetter: Owlswick Press; Printer: Morgan Publishing Co., Inc.

MANUSCRIPT SUBMISSIONS:
Before sending us your material, please send us a business-sized envelope, with postage affixed, addressed to you, for our guidelines. The address for this and all other editorial matters:
Weird Tales®, 123 Crooked Lane, King of Prussia PA 19406-2570.
The address for subscriptions, subscribers' changes of address, advertising, and any other money matters is:
DNA Publications, Inc., PO Box 2988, Radford VA 24143–2988.
Visit us on the Web at: dnapublications.com
Yes; we read unsolicited submissions — but *only* if they are in standard manuscript format. To survive, all editors insist on a few Rules: each submission must be in proper format and must include a return envelope, addressed to you, with enough postage affixed to bring the manuscript back to you. If you want us to discard the manuscript if we don't buy it, tell us so, but include a business-letter-sized envelope, addressed to you, with proper postage affixed, so we can send you our comments. No loose stamps, please!

We recommend either or both of two books on writing (after all, we wrote one of them!): *On Writing Science Fiction: the Editors Strike Back!* by Scithers, Schweitzer, & John M. Ford; $19.50 in hardcover; and Barry B. Longyear's *Science-Fiction Writer's Workshop*, $9.50 in trade paperback, available from Owlswick Press, 123 Crooked Lane, King of Prussia PA 19406-2570. These prices include shipping & handling. If you live in Pennsylvania, please include 6% sales tax.

We are not responsible for manuscripts in our hands or in transit. You *must* keep a copy of every manuscript you send out. You *must* put your name and address on the first page of every manuscript. And please: *no* binders, folders, or padded envelopes; and especially: *no* registered or certified mail for which we would have to stand in line at the post office!

site and call it "published." Now if Ellen Datlow (another of the convention's guests of honor), the former editor of *Omni*, posts something on the **scifi.com** website she edits, we'll take it seriously, but we still wish the results would be published on paper. The second problem is that on-line fiction, once it's no longer posted, is the equivalent of ice-sculpture. You can perhaps preserve it in the freezer (i.e. archive) for a while, but otherwise it's gone as if it had never existed.

The question came up and I answered it honestly: Would *Weird Tales*® buy a story which had been previously "published" on-line? Yes, as long as it has been off-line for at least a month. Then we're willing to consider it an unpublished story. The irony is that one of the Stoker Award winners, "Five Days in April" by Brian Hopkins (Best Long Fiction) from something called *Chiaroscuro* is by our (George's and my) definition an unpublished story, which could be submitted and sold to *Weird Tales*®.

Nevertheless, this was clearly the year of the Internet. The Best Non-fiction Stoker went to an on-line news magazine, Paula Guran's *Dark Echo*. There was also much talk of print-on-demand technology, which is the salvation of reprint publishers and the small press. Rather than investing thousands of dollars, for a few hundred one can print, say, a hundred copies of a book, then sell those, then print more as needed. Virtual inventory, without risk. Great! The production values can be very good indeed. Print on demand is the secret of success

for Wildside Press, whose catalogue is bound into this issue.

Other Stoker Awards went to more traditional material: *Mr. X* by Peter Straub (novel); *Wither* by J.G. Passarella (first novel); "Aftershock" by F. Paul Wilson (short story, from *Realms of Fantasy* for December 1999); Douglas Clegg's *Nightmare Chronicles* (story collection); Neil Gaiman's *Sandman; The Dream Hunters* (comic book); *The Sixth Sense* (screenplay); J.K. Rowlings's *Harry Potter and the Prisoner of Azkaban* (for young readers); Harlan Ellison's tape collection of his readings; *I Have No Mouth and I Must Scream* (other media); and Christopher and Barbara Roden (special publisher award, for Ash-Tree Press). It was particularly gratifying to see *The Sixth Sense* defeat *The Blair Witch Project*, since the virtues of the latter, whatever they may be, can hardly be said to be in the writing. It hardly even has a script, but *The Sixth Sense* is beautifully and perfectly written.

The other overwhelming thought that arose from the World Horror Convention is that horror is no longer a mainstream, New York publishing phenomenon. It is definitely on the mend from a low point of a few years ago, but it is still a small genre — much smaller than mystery or science fiction, for example. Walking into the dealer's room in Denver, one immediately sees that just about all the publishers in the field were there (indeed as many tables were taken by publishers as by book dealers) and none of them were from New York, except for Leisure books (which did not have a table, though the

Leisure editor was at the convention).

There has been some talk in the Horror Writers of America that the Stoker Banquet should not again be held at the World Horror Convention, but either in New York or Los Angeles, "where the action is."

This is surely a mistake, because award banquets, unsupported by a convention, are expensive and there is the risk of an embarrassingly small turnout (Horror is, after all, a field with very few full-time writers), and also because *That's not where the action is.* Leisure Books is the only mass-market paperback house with a horror line. Tor and New American Library do the occasional horror book, as do other mainstream houses (Peter Straub, for example, is published by Random House), but there are more horror publishers in Minneapolis (Fedogan & Bremer and Dreamhaven) than there are in New York. The magazines in the field, *Weird Tales*®, *Cemetery Dance*, Paula Guran's new *Horror Garage* (which made its debut at the convention) are all published far from New York. Horror has already done what the more literary end of science fiction and fantasy may soon do. It has cut itself entirely adrift from the New York publishing scene. For better or for worse it bravely seeks its own destiny.

To demonstrate this, let me list some of the really neat volumes picked up which made my mother-in-law's wheeled suitcase so essential. You won't find these in your local bookstore, but you can doubtless order them all on-line. (The Internet again, in its proper rôle, as a promotional tool.) All these books are de-

luxe hardcovers, much better made than anything from New York publishers outside of perhaps Library of America or Heritage Press. Most are limited editions.

The Death Artist by Dennis Etchison. 190 pp. $30.00. A collection of this distinguished author's stories, the first in some years. From Dreamhaven Books, 12 west Lake St., Minneapolis MN 55408.

Dark Detectives edited by Stephen Jones. 395 pp. $29.00. A fine collection of psychic detective stories, new and old, with authors ranging from William Hope Hodgson to Neil Gaiman. Fedogan & Bremer, 3721 Minnehaha Ave. South, Minneapolis MN 55406.

The Boar by Joe R. Lansdale. 169 pp.$40.00. A short novel, set in Texas during the Great Depression, originally written as a young adult book. Suspense, coming of age, a killer beast, etc. Subterranean Press, P.O. Box 190106, Burton MI 48519.

The Monster Maker by W.C. Morrow. Edited by S.T. Joshi and Stefan Dziemianowicz. 304 pp. $40.00. The weird stories from Morrow's legendary *The Ape, the Idiot, and Other People* (1897) plus many more, previously uncollected. Morrow was a brilliant predecessor of (and briefly mentor to) Ambrose Bierce. "The Monster Maker" and "Over the Absinthe Bottle" are classics (and were reprinted in *Weird Tales®* in 1928 and 1933, respectively) but the rest are only now rediscovered. From Midnight House, 4128 Woodland Park Ave. N., Seattle WA 98103.

Reunion at Dawn by H.R. Wakefield. Edited by Peter Ruber. 176 pp. $40.00. Wakefield was one of the great British ghost-story writers of the early 20th century, a peer of E.F. Benson or Algernon Blackwood. Here's an entire volume of unknown, previously unpublished material from the Arkham House files, which August Derleth once intended to publish. Not all the stories are good, but they round out the body of an important writer's work. The publisher is also doing a uniform reprinting of Wakefield's earlier books. Ash-Tree Press, P.O. Box 1360, Ashcroft, British Columbia V0K 1A0, Canada.

Santa Steps Out by Robert Devereaux. 252 pp. $39.95. You may remember Devereaux's off-the-wall "Ridi Bobo" in *Weird Tales®* #306. Well now he's got a novel truly too hot for traditional publishing to handle, as is attested in the twin introductions by insiders David G. Hartwell and Patrick LoBrutto (two of the most experienced New York editors). Very adult, dark, perverse. The secret (frequently sexual) adventures of Santa Claus, a premise that sounds silly but somehow isn't. "One of the most interesting and unusual literary artifacts of the late 20th century in America," says Hartwell. Dark Highway Press, 2519 S. Shields #117, Fort Collins CO 80526.

Tagging the Moon: Fairy Tales fro L.A. by S.P. Somtow. 280 pp. $25 (trade edition). $55.00 (limited edition). These are *not* fairy tales in the usual sense, but beautiful, eerie, terrifying, sometimes hilarious stories set in Hollywood and Los Angeles. One of them, "The Hero's Celluloid Journey" appeared in *Weird Tales* #315.

Now, resuming the mask of our royal, imperial, or editorial we, let us look at some recent letters:

Ann Chaput writes: *About 319, my favorite part of this issue was The Eyrie. I took both Anthropology and history this semester and enjoyed the stuff about Shakespeare in the Bush and about the history of horror. "Passing the Narrows" was my favorite story — I enjoyed the mix of history, horror, and fantasy. I loved "Tales from Weston Willow" because it's nice to relax with a story of fantasy after the tense moments reading horror. I loved the cover art — creepy AND colorful!*

Well, that balance of shifting from horror to fantasy and back is certainly what we are trying to achieve. Incidentally, the article about telling *Hamlet* to the African tribe was called "Shakespeare in the Bush," so presumably you've read it, since we did not give the title. The author is Laura Bohannan (not having the piece on hand when we wrote, we incorrectly referred to the anthropologist as "he") and the source was *Applying Cultural Anthropology* ed. Podolesfsky and Brown, Mayfield Publishing, 1997.

Tim Sinniger of Bend, Oregon writes: *It was great to see William F. Nolan grace your pages again with his fiction. He is my favorite writer and his new story "Heart's Blood" is right up there with my favorites, like his story "Broxa," which you published in 1991. I love the way Nolan's characters get into your mind. His lead character turns empathy for a student guilty of a high school massacre and takes you with him spiraling into his lead* character's own nightmare! Fabulous writing! I for one would like to see more of William F. Nolan in your magazine, only let's not wait so long next time.

Timothy Walters also liked the Nolan story, even if it was *not the most original entry. Several aspects of its plot reminded me of other fiction and film projects. Fortunately the author's seasoned storytelling ability transforms a potentially pedestrian tale into an impressive thriller. As events unfolded I began to suspect that Caxton was home to a sinister band of Satanists, but Nolan's surprising denouement isntead reveals a town overrun with reptilian creatures who hunger for the hearts and blood of infants.*

The author, **William F. Nolan** remarks that the setting of "Heart's Blood" is:*. . . a combination of Sikeston (where I acted in Roger Corman's The Intruder and Kansas City (my birthplace). Although K.C. was certainly no small town when I lived there, my perception was that of growing up in a small town within a large city. Our "town" consisted of a seven-square-block area. Here we had our church, our grade and high schools, shops, cafes, and movie theatres. I would visit downtown K.C. the way one visits a distant city.*

All this had a profound effect on me.

I moved to California in 1947, but many of my horror tales have been centered in the Missouri of my childhood. The area continues to haunt me . . .

I traveled to Sikeston, at the southern tip of Missouri, in the summer of 1961 for my supporting rôle in the Corman film. With Charles Beaumont (who wrote the screenplay), we spent 18 days filming at the local high school, etc. and got a hostile reception from the locals. Thus I write from experience as well as imagination.*

Leigh Kimmel of Indianapolis writes: *The editorial about the changing nature of the supernatural over the centuries and across cultures was of particular interest to me as a hsitorian. One of the greatest difficulties that a historian must overcome is that of getting into the mindset of another time. Much bad history (especially in the popular press) has been turned out by writers who have looked at past events through the eyes of the present, never appreciating just how differently our ancestors thought about themselves and their world. The offenses often get even worse in historical and historically-based fiction, viz. the laughalble romance that had its 17th century heroine spouting modern psychobabble about "actualizing her selfhood." Sometimes it's a problem of the writer for whom these things are a matter of belief and doctrine (as with the African tribesfolk and the New Ager) but all too often it is more a problem of simple laziness — the writer has never gone to the trouble to try to look beyond his present-day assumptions and really get into the heads of the people of the time in order to create a believable character who belongs there, rather than just a present-day mind in period clothing.*

Exactly. One reason we so admire Gene Wolfe's *Soldier of the Mist* and *Soldier of Arete* is that they present another time (Greece, 5th century B.C.) so convincingly from its own per-

spective. This is surely the essence of both good historical writing and good fantasy, and one reason we (as writers and as editors both) are so drawn to books written in other cultures, removed by distances of time and place. To an ancient Greek, for instance, the assumptions of what "everybody knows" about how the world works are quite different. The writer has to learn to seize on those differences, and, if he's writing an imaginary-scene fantasy, invent them.

Not everybody is happy with everything we do in *Weird Tales*®. **Dorothy P. Cobb** found the Nolan story last issue *severely flawed* because, she felt, the human evil in the story (which *causes you to wonder about the human condition and the evil things that everyday people are capable of doing*) did not mesh quite with the baby-eating lizards (*Inhuman, you can simply dismiss.*) She continues, *Perhaps Nolan would have done better if he had focused more on human religious fanaticism. I realize he was trying to do something by comparing the narrator and*

Fraley, but killing evil cultists who are trying to kill your son (and who turn out to be inhuman anyay) and mowing down your classmates whom you've probably known for years, out of a belief that you are descended from Jesus Christ, aren't really all that comparable.

George M. Gismondi takes us to task for jumping all over Chris Bevard: *It seems to me that what Mr. Bevard is commenting on is not the presence or absence of a fantastic element in horror fiction, but the absence of true horror in horror fiction. Intentionally or not, most writers have abandoned the Art of the Horror Tale so much appreciated by fans of the genre, in which the sole purpose of the work is, simply, to scare the hell out of the reader. Characterization, setting, plot all contribute to the effectiveness of the story, but the intrinsic value of the pure horror narrative is determined by how difficult it is to click off that light switch after you've finished reading. In these jaded times, evoking genuine fear through the printed page is more difficult than ever, but it is disheartening that just about everyone seems to have stopped trying. Scare me — I dare you!*

Yes, we must admit, on reflection , that we *were* a little unfair to Mr. Bevard, setting him up against the following letter like that, and the challenge is a valid one. We do prefer to scare people with fantastic elements, most of the time. *Cemetery Dance* scares you with non-fantastic elements much of the time. There is room for both.

Samuel Lightcap passes on the startling news that there are two Lovecraft poems, "The Well" and "Alienation" (both part of "Fungi from Yuggoth") in Library of America's *American Poetry: The Twentieth Century*. Lovecraft even rates half a page of bio-notes. Which presumably means that the Old Gent is officially Literature after all. That he achieved this with poetry is actually rather astonishing.

Elaine Weaver remarks on the definition of horror that *it is the emotional plot elements that shape a story. Like you, I hope that our fellow fans will explore the full depth of the genre. It's ironic, though — I had always thought an open mind is what draws readers to* Weird Tales *in the first place.*

She then asks if we are using the Internet to promote the magazine.

Yes, definitely. There are occasional stories and columns posted on the DNA website, the address of which is at the front of this column. But remember: the website is our billboard. This magazine is the product!

Author **Richard A. Lupoff** had this to say about Frank Tuttle's "Passing the Narrows": *. . . certainly an unusual story, and a most impressive one . . . Tuttle showed remarkable restraint in the fantastic elements of a truly outstanding piece.*

A fine story, a fine writer — I've not encountered Tuttle's byline before, but I will look for it in the future!

The Most Popular Story in issue #319 was a neck-and-neck race. We received a gratifying number of letters and votes. For a while there William F. Nolan's fans made the voting *unanimous* in the first-place voting for "Heart's Blood." But with a sudden burst in the final lap . . . the winner is "Passing the Narrows" by Frank Tuttle by eight points. Nolan is second. Third place went to "Tales from Weston Willow" by Ian Watson. This is the second time in three issues that first place went to a new writer.

Coming up soon. We have in inventory fine stories by **Tanith Lee, Ian Watson, Richard Lupoff, Sarah Hoyt, Phyllis and Alex Eisenstein** and many more. There are new entries in popular series, your editor's own "Sekenre" series as well as *Keith Taylor's* "Kamose" tales of ancient Egyptian intrigue and sorcery.   Ω

THE DEN

by S.T. Joshi

After a considerable hiatus, Arkham House has, in the last three years, resumed the publication of books. The departure of Jim Turner (who died suddenly and unexpectedly in 1999 just as he was developing his own imprint, the Golden Gryphon Press) appears for a time to have produced a state of confusion at Arkham House; but now, with Peter Ruber — a friend of Derleth's during the latter's last decade of life — as editorial adviser, the publishing company that August Derleth founded — and which he did not expect to survive him — is renewing its claim as the preeminent small press in our field.

During the past three years Arkham House has issued (or reissued) seven books. Three of these can be dealt with briefly. The reprint of Lovecraft's *Selected Letters III* (1997), which had inexplicably been out of print for a decade and a half, was very welcome. *New Horizons: Yesterday's Portraits of Tomorrow* (1999) is an insubstantial but entertaining science fiction anthology that August Derleth had conceived, apparently in the early 1960s, but never issued; it has now been capably assembled, with introduction and biographical notes, by Joseph Wrzos. My own *Sixty Years of Arkham House* (1999) is an exhaustive updating of Derleth's *Thirty Years of Arkham House* (1970), with a complete author and title index to every Arkham House, Mycroft & Moran, and Stanton & Lee publication. A fourth volume — *Lovecraft Remembered* (1998), Peter Cannon's superlative compilation of memoirs of Lovecraft — I have discussed previously in this column. The three other books require more extended commentary.

Robert Bloch's *Flowers from the Moon and Other Lunacies* (1998) is a volume of uncollected stories (mostly dating from the 1930s and 1940s) edited by Robert M. Price. This is, decidedly, a very mixed bag — there are good reasons why Bloch himself did not reprint some of these tales

in his own collections when he was alive. But Price has found some gems that deserve our attention: the title story, a bizarre horror/SF amalgam, with even a little hard-boiled mystery mixed in; "Be Yourself," a typically Blochian mixture of humor and horror; the early tale "The Dark Isle" (1939), almost an echo of a Robert E. Howard sword-and-sorcery tale, albeit with Romans rather than barbarians. Price's brisk and scintillating introduction, full of a wordplay that Bloch himself would have enjoyed, is itself almost worth the price of admission.

Perhaps the most interesting volume published recently by Arkham House is *Dragonfly*, a first novel by Frederic S. Durbin. At a minimum, it is a testimonial that slushpile submissions do, on rare occasions, make it into print. We are here introduced to a ten-year-old girl, nicknamed Dragonfly, who, in falling down the laundry shute of her home, stumbles into a huge and complex fantasy world called Harvest Moon beyond or underneath the basement. The premise sounds rather like C. S. Lewis's *The Lion, the Witch and the Wardrobe*, but Durbin's Harvest Moon is a much darker place, presided by the evil Samuel Hain who, with numerous scoundrelly cohorts, literally feeds off other people's pain and is seeking to force himself into our world. Dragonfly gathers her own set of offbeat sidekicks to foil their efforts. As a horror-fantasy amalgam, *Dragonfly* is a marked success. Durbin is gifted with a prodigious fantastic imagination — indeed, perhaps a bit too gifted: after a time the endless succession of bizarre events begins to weary the reader through sheer surfeit. Durbin will need to be a bit more disciplined in the use of fantastic imagery; sometimes less really is more. But the verve, panache, and assurance with which *Dragonfly* is written make us marvel that it could be a first novel; Durbin is a "find" in whom Arkham House can rightly be proud.

I have one further reservation on *Dragon-fly*, however, and that concerns the increasing frequency of its mentions of God, prayer, and the like toward the end. At one point a character blithely affirms, in regard to some relatively minor event: "That was the hand of God." This is, I think, an aesthetic and philosophical mistake. It is too easy for the fantasy writer — who is, after all, himself a kind of god of his imagined universe — to attribute some event or incident to God; it makes the reader suspect that the author didn't have the cleverness to account for the incident in any other way. Later we are soberly asked to accept the myth of the Tower of Babel as a literal explanation for the proliferation of human languages throughout the world. Durbin is at perfect liberty to believe whatever religion he wishes, but he would be well advised to keep it out of his writing. The last thing one would wish to see is a writer of Durbin's undoubted talents restricting his imagination to the narrow confines of some religious dogma.

Arkham House's Masters of Horror (2000) is the most challenging and provocative volume published by Arkham House in many years. Edited by Peter Ruber, it gathers stories or other works by twenty-two of the leading Arkham House authors over the first thirty years of its existence, along with lengthy biographical/critical notes on the authors. Ruber's prose is, I fear, somewhat slipshod, and much of this book appears to have been written and compiled in considerable haste. More than any other volume published recently by Arkham House, it could have benefited from a good copy editor. But it suffers greater problems than this.

Ruber's manifest intention is to defend August Derleth on many fronts. There is something charming in this endeavor — it is always good to see friends stand up for each other, especially when one of them isn't around to defend himself; but Ruber's defense — as embodied in a lengthy introduction, "The 'Un-Demonizing' of August Derleth" — seems curiously off the mark. No one in his right mind would deny that Derleth spent a considerable portion of his own money in keeping Arkham House afloat for its first three decades. As to the actual success — either aesthetic or commercial — of the books that Derleth chose to publish, the record is much more mixed: a good many literarily outstanding books appeared, but Arkham House also published a number of books (usually by pulp writers with whom Derleth was acquainted) that do not speak well of Derleth's critical judgment; other books (some of them quite respectable on an aesthetic level) remained in print for many years, although that merely indicates the radical divergence of genuine literary merit and popular appeal.

But Ruber fails to come to grips with the true sources for many critics' complaints about Derleth, most of them focusing around his handling of the Lovecraft material. These complaints center around four points: (1) his careless editing of Lovecraft's texts, resulting in thousands of textual or typographical errors in the editions of the 1960s; (2) his ruthless (and possibly illegal) control of the Lovecraft literary rights; (3) his dissemination (by way of books, articles, and introductions) of highly misleading views of Lovecraft the man and writer, specifically relating to the "Cthulhu Mythos," which was largely Derleth's own invention; (4) his grinding out of those truly awful "Cthulhu Mythos" pastiches (including the deceitful "posthumous collaborations" with Lovecraft), which may well have "kept Lovecraft's name alive" during the 1940s and 1950s but also ended up casting disrepute upon Lovecraft's own work. Ruber never discusses any of these points — although some of them are alluded to in a long letter by Stefan Dziemianowicz quoted by Ruber — and therefore his attempt to "undemonize" Derleth is incomplete. Some defense could possibly be made on these issues, but the fact that Ruber does not even address them reveals a strange oversight as to the true sources of Derleth's current unpopularity in certain circles.

Ruber states repeatedly that Derleth was forced to publish Lovecraft's works himself when mainstream publishers like Scribner's refused to do so. Since Ruber has paid no attention to my discussion of this point in *H. P. Lovecraft: A Life* (1996), and since it gets to the very heart of Derleth's founding of Arkham House, it may be worth summarizing my arguments. Let us consider the precise wording of Derleth's own comment on the submission of the immense *Outsider and Others* to Scribner's: "Since Charles Scribner's Sons were then my publishers, I sent the manuscript to them. They were sympathetic to the project and recognized the literary value of Lovecraft's fiction; but in the end they were forced to reject the manuscript because the cost of producing so bulky a book, combined with the public's then sturdy resistance to buying short story collections and the comparative obscurity of H. P. Lovecraft as a writer, made the project financially prohibitive" (*Thirty Years of Arkham House*). Is it not clear from this that, had Derleth submitted a smaller book of Lovecraft's best stories, Scribner's would have been much more receptive? Only six years after publication of *The Outsider and Others*, Derleth did exactly that in assembling Lovecraft's *Best Supernatural Stories* for the World Publishing Company — an edition that sold *more than 67,000 copies in hardcover in a year and a half,* an incredible figure for the time. It is safe to say that a volume of this kind published by Scribner's — a far more prestigious firm than World — would have made a huge difference in Lovecraft's recognition, and perhaps in the course of weird fiction as a whole. But Derleth was so fixated on publishing *The Outsider and Others* as he had originally compiled it that he found himself unable to compromise on this vital point.

An overriding problem with Ruber's whole account is its parochialism — not merely focusing entirely on Derleth, but failing to contextualize the history of weird fiction within the general literary trends of the period. Ruber speaks blithely of the "legitimization of genre fiction" engendered by the pulp magazines in the 1920s, when in fact the very opposite occurred: the existence of the pulps led to the ghettoizing of the genres of mystery, fantasy, horror, and science fiction, as these genres disappeared almost entirely from mainstream magazines. It is telling that no writer except Lovecraft and Ray Bradbury has emerged from the weird fiction pulps to gain a genuine foothold in American literature; Clark Ashton Smith and Robert E. Howard are considerably to the rear, and Seabury Quinn, E. Hoffmann Price, and other hacks are not even on the map, nor do they deserve to be. (Derleth has a small niche for his mainstream work, but not for his weird work.) It is a plain but depressing fact that the overwhelming majority of the material published in the pulps — weird, detective, science fiction, mystery, or what have you — was subliterate rubbish that deserves the oblivion that has overtaken it. Arkham House contributed, in its small way, to this ghettoization: after his first several publications garnered hostile or condescending reviews in the mainstream press, Derleth refused to send out review copies of Arkham House books to standard news-

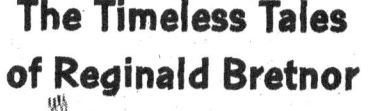

by S.T. Joshi

papers and magazines (except to sympathetic reviewers such as Vincent Starrett), making these books virtually invisible in the general literary community.

Ruber's biographical notes on the authors he covers tend to be harsh, dogmatic, and intolerant — compounded, in some cases, by an inadequacy of research that results in numerous errors large and small. Ruber chides the Derleth-haters for failing to conduct "serious research" on their subject; but Ruber's own work is subject to much the same criticism, especially in regard to Lovecraft, Smith, and other figures, and his comments are on occasion scarcely above the level of the fan criticism he excoriates. Their only worthy feature is the abundance of quotations from Derleth's unpublished letters, which are unfailingly crisp, lively, and pungent ("The trouble with _____ _____ is that he's a dumb bastard"). Arkham House or some other enterprising publisher should certainly consider a volume of Derleth's selected letters.

The worst of the biographical notes is the one on Lovecraft, which is crude to the point of caricature. Ruber (as did L. Sprague de Camp) continually calls Lovecraft a "schizoid personality"; but given that Ruber is not a psychiatrist and that, even if he was, he never had the chance to analyze Lovecraft, the remark is only indicative of Ruber's profound failure to understand Lovecraft's mentality. Also like de Camp, Ruber seems to regard Lovecraft's unprofessional stance as an inherent failing. To be sure, it was a very different stance from that of the resolutely professional August Derleth, but (aside from Lovecraft's immense superiority as a weird writer, and as a thinker, to Derleth) it is very largely Lovecraft's aesthetic integrity — his refusal to sell himself out to commercial or pulp markets — that has ensured the literary recognition of his work. No one is writing dissertations on E. Hoffmann Price or Seabury Quinn.

Ruber speaks derisively of the large quantity of criticism, both biographical and critical, devoted to Lovecraft in the past two or three decades; certainly, he seems to have read little of it himself, if the errors peppering his account are any indication. One example among many: "'The Dunwich Horror' was reportedly so gruesome for its time that readers [of *Weird Tales*] and censorship groups filed complaints with the magazine." In fact, this incident pertains to the publication of C. M. Eddy's "The Loved Dead," which was revised by Lovecraft, in the May-June-July 1924 issue. Ruber also claims that when, in New York, Lovecraft lacked money he "simply sold some of his furniture and books." This never happened. Ruber then makes the outrageous claim that Lovecraft, in his final years, was "perfectly at ease letting his aunt, Mrs. Gamwell, pay for the roof over his head out of the small income she had." This is a pure fantasy. Lovecraft had his own portion of the inheritance from his grandfather, as well as a small mortgage in the western part of the state, not to mention his work as a revisionist and ghostwriter; these, rather than his sparse sales of professional fiction, were the sources of Lovecraft's income — he never borrowed any money from his aunt, who herself was unemployed and living off her meager inheritance.

Ruber admits that he has not even read Lovecraft's complete fiction, so it is hardly surprising to find him making the astounding claim that "since so much of [Lovecraft's] work was derivative of the past and firmly rooted in the tradition of Edgar Allan Poe, it cannot be said that his stories were experimental — or that he brought any true innovation to the genre." Can Ruber really be unaware of Lovecraft's pioneering amalgamation of horror and science fiction in his later work — an innovation that influenced generations of writers in both genres, from John W. Campbell to Arthur C. Clarke to Stephen King to Ramsey Campbell? It would appear that Ruber is intent on demoting Lovecraft as an indirect means of vaunting Derleth; but to do so by uttering falsehoods about Lovecraft does not seem a very effective means to accomplish this end.

Ruber seems to have a particular problem with authors who didn't exhibit the maniacal dynamism of Derleth. Hence, Lovecraft "was virtually without ambition and pathetically idled away most of his waking hours writing letters"; Clark Ashton Smith was "a lazy and unambitious person"; Donald Wandrei led an "unfulfilled" life — presumably because he didn't write more stories. Who is Ruber to cast these imperial judgments on the personal lives of authors he does not understand or sympathize with? If Lovecraft "idled away" his time writing letters, that was his prerogative: maybe he *liked* writing letters. All that the lazybones Smith accomplished was to produce about 1500 poems (including some of the finest poetry written in his century), 130 or so short stories or novelettes, hundreds of paintings and sculptures, and sundry other things. Ruber can't help tallying up the appalling amounts of subliterate trash produced by his favored pulpsmiths. ("Arthur J. Burks was the consummate professional pulp story writer; he could write any type of story to order at a moment's notice.") Quantity production is not, in itself, admirable. Smith's *The Hashish-Eater* or Lovecraft's "The Shadow out of Time" is, aesthetically, in itself worth more than the complete charlatanries of Seabury Quinn. You would never know it from Ruber, but there are higher literary values than merely the ability to write an "entertaining" story.

Ruber's biographical notes on other writers are less egregiously error-riddled than the one on Lovecraft, but errors nonetheless crop up. He is, of course, considerably better when dealing with the pulp hacks dear to his heart. And the typos! Ordinarily a reviewer does not comment on a flaw that has blemished virtually every book for the past five hundred years, but the number and severity of the errors in this volume call for comment. This is probably the worst proofread book in Arkham House history, with the exception of Lovecraft's *The Horror in the Museum and Other Revisions* (1970), which was essentially a set of uncorrected proofs. At one point we are introduced to Donald Wanfrei. There is a comical alteration in the spelling of E. Hoffmann Price's middle name — sometimes with two *n*'s, sometimes with one. Price's life dates are given (in prominent display type) as 1998–1988: he must have been the prototype of Algernon Blackwood's "The Man Who Lived Backwards."

As for the actual contents of the anthology, Ruber is hampered by his need to find contributions by his "masters" not previously included in Arkham House books. As a result, many trivial and ephemeral items are included. Clark Ashton Smith's two-page Arabian Nights tale, "Prince Alcouz and the Magician," is so slight that it is immediately forgotten after it is read. Among the British authors published by Arkham House, Ruber made the error of choosing the mediocre H. Russell Wakefield (largely because Ruber himself discovered a mass of unpublished Wakefield stories at Arkham House) rather than such superior writers as Algernon Blackwood or Lord Dunsany. There are unpublished stories by David H. Keller and by Derleth and Mark Schorer, but they don't amount to much. The stories by E. Hoffmann Price, Arthur J. Burks, Seabury Quinn, Carl Jacobi, and many others are pure hokum. Ramsey Campbell's "Property of the Ring" is far from being his best story; but, alone in the volume (with, of course, the exception of Bradbury's classic "The Small Assassin"), it actually deals with the genuine emotions of real human beings, rather than the conventionalized emotions of stick figures. If one did not have independent knowledge of the genuinely meritorious work of most of these writers, one would never know from the contents of this book that they were "masters" of anything but hackwork and mediocrity.

If Peter Ruber plans to continue being Arkham House's editorial adviser, he had better give up his devotion to pulp rubbish — or, at any rate, cease to recommend its republication — and focus on truly sound weird literature, whether of the past or of the present. Only in that way will Arkham House recapture its position as the flagship small press in our field.

(Publishers and authors should feel free to send books for review to my home address, 10 West 15th Street #312, New York, NY 10011.)

Ω

THE INCUBUS OF THE ROSE
by Brian Stableford

illustrated by George Barr

Conrad Othman had lived on the island for four years before the bitter winter came that served as a backcloth to the events which I am about to relate. He was a composer of music for strings and woodwind. Few of his compositions required more than four instrumentalists and many were duets which sought to use the contrasting temperaments of two instruments that were not conventionally required to play in harness to generate productive tension. His work was too ethereal, some might say too *eerie*, to be popular with the island's aristocratic patrons, but its quality was appreciated by the cognoscenti.

Conrad played wind instruments himself, although he was a little way short of first rate. He had difficulty finding string-players, because he rarely wrote for the violin or cello. Harps posed a particular problem because there were so few performers available, but Conrad was too attentive to the dictates of his muse to let the pattern of his compositions be guided by the ready availability of players. Dorothea Rosa was universally recognised as the best harpist on the island, but she preferred to operate as a soloist. Her reluctance to lend her services to Conrad owed something to envy of the fact that he was a better composer for her own instrument of choice than she could ever be, although the fact that she was an exclusive lesbian also had something to do with it. I suppose she must have refused him at least a dozen times before she finally agreed, reluctantly, to accompany him.

Conrad had, in the end, to win Dorothea's agreement by the only means possible: by producing a piece so cunningly adapted to her tastes and talents that she would be avid to play it. He used other instruments of seduction as well, of course — he flattered her outrageously, sent her expansive bouquets of her favourite moss roses and procured rare books from the mainland that she needed for her library — but all that would have been in vain had he not eventually been able to lay before her a score that accomplished everything she had been striving for, unsuccessfully, in her own compositions.

I was at the first performance of the Rose Duet, as were such diehard Othman aficionados as the physician Fion Commonal and the funeral director Emmaus Partibus. I was glad to be there, because there was a rare relief in being able to escape my studio. My current commission was to paint the twin sons of the Duke of Dellacrusca, whose unsupervised journey to the island had provided their first experience of freedom from direct supervision. They were the most restless and mischievous sitters I had ever encountered. Hecate Rain was also at Othman's that night, although her presence owed more to her friendship with Dorothea than her appreciation of music. As a word-obsessed poet, Hecate preferred her music accompanied by lyrics.

It is easy enough for humans to conceive of themselves as divided beings, in whom the dictates of reason and emotion are constantly in conflict. Our scrupulous "higher selves" often seem to be under threat from the urges of our "baser instincts". All of Conrad's compositions tended to reproduce some such division in their opposition of strings to woodwinds, and they were clearest of all in his duets. He always cast his woodwinds in the nobler role, as representatives of more conscientious yearnings, while the fulsome harps or guitars against which their questing pipings were set always played an earthier and more voluptuous part. The piece Conrad had written in order to seduce Dorothea Rosa to play for and with him exaggerated this distinction to a new limit.

The harp part in Conrad Othman's Rose Duet had been conceived with Dorothea firmly and centrally in mind. Although Conrad cannot have made the slightest attempt to decode or psychoanalyse the sequence of sounds, he had the kind of genius that allowed him to transmute her emotional landscape into music more effectively than she had ever been able to do herself. What Dorothea played that night — with consummate skill and total absorption — was a truer representation of the complexity of her own eroticism than she had ever found before. Like any great composition, it was both powerful and plaintive,

by Brian Stableford

because it rejoiced in the discovery of the self even while it yearned for evolution, and also because it recognised that while imperfect humanity is only capable of limited achievement, the human imagination is more than capable of desiring the impossible.

Conrad's instincts had informed him that he might spoil the seductive effect of his duet if he put too much of himself into his own part — but it was his composition. He wanted the totality of the piece to be his own reflection as well as Dorothea's, and he wanted his own reflection to be paramount. I have already described Conrad's music as "ethereal" and "eerie" but neither word is adequate to convey the import of the flute's contribution to the Rose Duet. The harp part was voluptuous in a frankly exceptional fashion, but the flute part was so far beyond the commonplace complements of voluptuousness as to have forsaken all recognition of the flesh. It was an escapade of pure spirit, of that hopeful part of human consciousness that cannot believe that it will die, conceiving of itself entirely in terms of immortality, irrepressibility and incorruptibility.

There was no implication in the flute part of the Rose Duet to offend the lesbian sensibilities of Dorothea Rosa, but the measure of Conrad Othman's accomplishment was that it actually exerted an attractive force upon them. The flute part was not in the least *disconnected* from the harpist's part; it seemed, in fact, to be a kind of completion that the harp part required, even if that part lacked the intelligence to express a yearning for it. As the players gave themselves to the music, in the wholehearted way that is only possible in real performance, they could not help but be transformed by it, if only for a little while. In time, the effect would have worn off, as all effects do — we are only human, after all — but in the immediate aftermath of their playing it formed a kind of bond between Conrad and Dorothea that neither them had conceived of before.

Eight days had passed before Conrad sought me out in my favourite covert in the Sprite, where I was sipping absinthe.

"That stuff will be the death of you, Master Rathenius," he observed.

"I have built up an impressive tolerance," I assured him. "My body has made its peace with wormwood, and would now be quite desolate without it. Are we no longer on first name terms, Conrad? I did not know that I had offended you."

The depth of the sigh he let loose as he sat beside me informed me that it was embarrassment that had prompted his thoughtless formality.

"I beg your pardon, Axel," he said. "My mind is so agitated that even my habits are confused. I have fallen victim to an absurd infatuation."

"Why absurd?" I asked, although I already knew.

"Absurd," he said, "because I allowed it to grow out of all proportion. I have been wooing the lady with presents and compliments for months, having fooled myself into thinking that I only wanted her to play for me. Doubly absurd because I knew all along that she prefers the company of her own sex, and would never allow a man to make love to her."

It would have been a waste of time to offer conventional commiserations or to ask him why he had brought his problem to me.

"The question you have to ask," I told him, "is whether that preference is the greater of two attractions or the lesser of two repulsions."

"What difference does it make?" he retorted. Even great artists can be unsubtle in matters unconnected to their art.

"If it were the greater of two attractions," I said, "the task before you would be to discover an even greater attraction, and to equip yourself with it — but you have already done that, I think, and it has only served to complicate the issue. Am I right in supposing that the problem is not that Dorothea does not reciprocate your love, but that she feels unable to consummate it in spite of her reciprocation?"

He stared at me as if I were a magician, although I had not said anything that was less than obvious.

"She swears that since we performed the Rose Duet she loves me with an intensity she never thought to feel for anyone," he confirmed. "She insists, however, that what she loves is my genius, my soul and my intelligence. It is, she claims, a purified emotion far finer than any mere matter of the flesh. She says that what she feels for me could only be sullied and spoiled by bodily intercourse. All nonsense, of course — but she believes it. How can I persuade her that she is sublimating an affection which is solidly rooted in the material, and which demands material satisfaction?"

"With great difficulty," I told him, "given that you have already done your utmost to persuade her of the opposite."

"She has heard no such argument from me, I can assure you!"

"Of course not," I said. "Had she heard it as an argument it would probably have sounded fatuous. The problem is that she heard it in a far more immediate — and hence far more persuasive — form. She heard it in the dialogue between your flute and her harp: a dialogue unconfined by mere matters of language and anatomy. You took care to incorporate a certain unusual voluptuousness into her part, but your own part set echoes of the flesh firmly aside. That aspect of you with which she fell in love is not something which demands material satisfaction but something which comes perilously close to denying any such possibility."

He hesitated, with furrowed brow, before answering. "That was not my intention," he said, finally.

"Not consciously," I admitted. "But you did it very well. There is no higher achievement in art than to communicate a keen sense of the impossible, and the tragedy of its unattainability. I was near to tears myself."

"But that is not what I felt," he insisted. "It was, I admit, the music that transformed my inchoate desire into aching lust, but it is certainly not lust for anything extraordinary, let alone anything impossible of attainment."

"That is because you identified yourself too fully with the flute part, thus creating a sense in which you could only listen to the harp. As a member of the audience, I could only play the eavesdropper, hearing both. Dorothea, on the other hand, identified herself completely with the harp, and she could only listen to the flute. While you fell in love with her voluptuousness, she fell in love with your lack of it." I could have pointed out that the simplest way out of his predicament was to wait until both effects were dulled by time, but that would not have been the best advice to offer *for art's sake;* it would merely have been the advice most likely to minimise the cumulative sum of Conrad's misery.

Conrad thought about my analysis for a few moments, and then said: "I still don't understand the distinction between the lady's preferences being the greater of two attractions or the lesser of two repulsions."

"Because the former would give you no chance of success, given that you have already found the greater attraction and laid it before her. Mercifully, Dorothea's lesbianism is a matter of peculiar fastidiousness rather than animal magne-

tism. She is not powerfully attracted to women in a sexual sense — she merely finds their material attentions more easily bearable than those of men. Were there another subspecies even more bearable, she would readily accept the advances of its members — not very avidly, I dare say, but as gladly as she can."

"But there is no such subspecies," Conrad said. He was not an unimaginative man, but he could not exercise his imagination in other than musical terms. "And if there were, I would not be a member of it."

"What there is, and what you are, need not trouble us overmuch," I said. "Even Dorothea's firm and long-held beliefs need not enter the equation. The question is: what illusion can she be made to accept, however tentatively, for a little while?"

"What *illusion?*" he echoed, and then repeated the question with the emphasis differently laid. "Well, then, *what* illusion?"

"Whatever illusion already haunts her dreams," I said. "Whatever illusion her unconscious mind attaches to the lusts which disturb her in spite of her fastidiousness."

"And how are we supposed to find that out?" he wanted to know.

"We have already found it in your music," I said, "which has answered her unadmitted desires more successfully than her own. You have said yourself that she loves your genius, your soul, your intelligence. We have only to confront her with what she believes to be your disembodied spirit, and she will surrender to you utterly."

"You mean," he said, slowly, "that I have to convince her that I am a ghost. How on earth am I to do that?"

"Not so much a ghost," I said, "as an incubus. As for the means, you must appear to have died. Such things can be arranged, if you know the right people. Fion Commonal and Emmaus Partibus, for instance."

Conrad had never been one of the many residents of the island who entertained doubts about my greatness as a painter, but it was a delight nevertheless to see him look at me with a new expression on his face: the humble expression of a clever man who realises that   is confronted by amazing ingenuity.

Given that there are so few prescriptions which actually work in more than a morale-boosting way, all physicians must be artists first and artisans second. Having been so long on the island, Fion Commonal was as far removed from the rudely mechanical as any doctor in the Empire. He was also the attending physician at the World's Stage Theatre, where his duties had forced him to become a master of dramatic artifice. When I explained to him that we must contrive a swift but artful apparent death for Conrad Othman he was only too willing to agree.

"We might have him run through in a duel," he suggested. "I have been experimenting with several new kinds of blood, and no one fakes a belly-wound better than I. On the other hand, I have an excellent concoction that will bring on a very real but perfectly safe fever. Used in connection with a salve for turning healthy skin pallid it provides a perfect facsimile of the point of death. Which would you prefer?"

"Both," I said, without hesitation. "But the wound should not be in the belly. It should be to the left of the heart, as if the thrust had been turned aside by the ribs, and it should be gangrenous as well as bloody. That will allow it to serve as the ostensible cause of the fever."

"We would need another duellist," Commonal mused. "It will not be easy to find a volunteer. To be the killer of Conrad Othman, if only for a little while, would attract a great deal of opprobrium on the island."

"A hired killer might be better," I agreed. "A mysterious masked man. No one would hire an assassin to kill a master musician, of course, so Conrad must be hurt while coming to the aid of a more plausible victim. It would add to the poignancy of the occasion if the man he saves were to be some high-born but utterly unworthy rapscallion. You can safely leave the casting of the parts of assassin and intended victim to me."

Commonal nodded understandingly. "The Dellacrusca brats!" he said, his tone expressing his satisfaction with the choice.

"The Dellacrusca twins," I confirmed, "will be only too delighted to be assisted in the discovery of a new kind of mischief."

Genius does not pause when inspiration commands. Within twenty-four hours the entire island was abuzz with the news that a hired assassin had been dispatched from the capital to murder the elder of Dellacrusca's twin sons, in order to carry forward some half-forgotten blood-feud, and had caught up with the boy on the balcony of the Sprite. The younger son would have been the heir apparent if the thrust had struck home, but the great composer Conrad Othman had made a bold attempt to disarm the masked man. Thwarted in his purpose, the killer had disappeared after the mysterious fashion of his kind, but the dagger must have been poisoned, for the glancing blow that Conrad had suffered had not been as lucky as it first appeared. He had been carried to his bed, and the question of whether he would survive the night was not yet settled.

Although it was only November, that winter was too cold to allow rumours to flow with their usual alacrity. Commonal and I had to wait a full thirty minutes longer than I had anticipated before Dorothea Rosa came hammering at the door of Conrad's house, demanding to be allowed to see him. At first, Commonal refused, telling her that Conrad was too sick to recognise his visitors, let alone converse with them, and that the infection in his wound created a danger of contagion. Dorothea had to plead with him very ardently — which she did most affectingly, considering that her flooding tears rendered her all-but-helpless, and by the time she was finally let in she was in no condition to detect any imposture.

Conrad's part was by no means difficult — dying is easy, as any tragedian will tell you — but he played it superbly. He babbled a little, refused to recognise Dorothea for a full five minutes, while she sobbed hysterically, and then put on a show of clearing his senses. For just a moment his wildly wandering eyes fixed upon her face, and he whispered her name once before collapsing upon his pillows in a moderately convincing faint.

It was then that I took Dorothea by the shoulders and steered her gently from the room.

"He knew me!" she exclaimed. "Even in the extremity of his distress, he knew me!"

"Pray that you have given him the strength to live," I said, as I hustled her through the door and closed it behind us. "He loves you with all the passion he can muster. That might just be enough to pull him through."

"And I refused him!" she mourned. "Oh, if I had but known! What is my niceness compared to the suffering of a man like that! If he lives, I swear that he shall have me. If he lives, I shall deny him nothing."

THE INCUBUS OF THE ROSE

"Shhh!" I said, urgently, pretending that it was for her sake. The last thing I wanted was to put the idea into Conrad Othman's mind that he need not see my little drama through to its intended conclusion. "Go home, Dorothea, and try to sleep. I shall sit up with him all night, and I will keep Commonal to his task. I will bring you news in the morning myself. You have my promise."

"Thank you, Master Rathenius," she said. "If you can only tell me that he is saved, I shall be in your debt forever."

Artistry is much rarer among funeral directors than among physicians, but as the island's principal practitioner Emmaus Partibus had perforce to specialise in arranging the funerals of artists, and he was well used to rising to such occasions. The service, procession, interment and wake that we planned together was mostly of my own devising, but he added a few professional touches which rounded off my script to perfection.

Instead of lilies, we decided that the flowers accompanying the coffin must be roses: the moss roses that were Dorothea's favourite. I, of course, would provide the principal oration, offering a fulsome tribute to Conrad's achievements and an intimate account of his last days. There would be two others, both poetic — classic pieces only, both to be delivered by male mourners. This decision annoyed Hecate Rain, who would have loved an opportunity to read one of her own elegies, but I did not want Dorothea's attention to be in any way distracted and Hecate can be heart-rendingly attractive when she is in an elegiac mood.

The most important aspect of any musician's funeral is the music. Instead of the conventional hymns and dirges, convention demanded that the music played during the service must be Conrad's finest pieces, but here I intruded one of my most delicate strokes of genius. I decreed that each piece should be performed *without the part that Conrad would ordinarily have played,* so that their incompleteness would demonstrate his absence more obviously and more sensitively than any mere appearance could ever have contrived. The climax of this eccentric concert was, of course, to be provided by Dorothea Rosa performing the Rose Duet, for once and once only, as a solo.

The whole affair went off very well, but from my own viewpoint everything that followed Dorothea's performance at the church was anti-

climactic. The procession was tedious, the interment as empty of effect as the coffin, and I was so quiet at the wake that I almost spoiled my reputation by engendering the suspicion that I must, after all, have a soft heart. Perhaps I could have roused more enthusiasm for my own part had Dorothea not played hers to such perfection, but she was magnificent — so unexpectedly clever, in fact, that I felt quite unable to take the whole credit for her work, even though I had contrived the situation. While I listened to her, I was convinced that she would never play better.

Under normal circumstances, there is a profound dissatisfaction in listening to a piece played without one of the instruments for which it was designed. The fact that I had heard the Rose Duet played as it was meant to be played only a few days earlier should have made Dorothea's rendering of the harp part seem even more jejune, but these were not normal circumstances. Had I believed — as Dorothea and almost all her fellow mourners did — that Conrad was really dead I honestly believe that I would have been able to hear that half-duet as a work of genius in its own right, all the more wonderful for the fact that its context could never be reproduced. Even as things were, I could see that it was uniquely brilliant.

I often close my eyes when listening to music, thus alleviating the risk of being distracted by any haphazard glimpse of something beautiful. As a painter, I am unusually vulnerable to visual distraction. While Dorothea played her solo version of the Rose Duet, however, I kept my eyes firmly fixed on her face. I watched the grief and sadness that had marked her features ever since I took her news of Conrad's death deepen by degrees as she transported herself into a private realm where she could not help but feel the force of Conrad's absence more keenly than anyone in her audience. Then I watched her expression change, becoming calmer and strangely joyous, and I knew that in her mind she could hear the missing part, perhaps more clearly than she could have heard it if it had really vibrated the air around her. I watched her forge a new link with Conrad in spite of his absence: a new union. It was a marriage truly made in Heaven, even though there is no Heaven, save for the idea that haunts the human imagination.

I have wrought this miracle, I said to myself — but I could not quite believe it. I knew that I had merely been the facilitator, and that Dorothea alone had wrought the miracle, because Dorothea alone had the will and the art to do it. I had to remind myself, instead, that my plan was unfolding as neatly as I could possibly have expected.

Perhaps I should have worried that it was proceeding a little too well, and remembered how fate delights in cheating us when we are at our most confident, but I was too self-satisfied for that. I thought, once the empty coffin had been laid in the waiting grave, that the difficult part of the scheme was concluded and that its momentum was now unstoppable.

I was absolutely right, of course — more absolutely, as it turned out, than I had anticipated or thought possible.

As soon as Dorothea was ready to leave Conrad's wake I volunteered to see her home. It was not late, but the winter dark always falls too eagerly for comfort; she was grateful for the offer.

"I believe I have misjudged you, Master Rathenius," she said, as we walked. "I never believed that you could be so deeply affected by the death of a mere acquaintance."

"There was nothing mere about Conrad Othman," I assured her.

"True," she agreed. "He was the finest man I knew — the only one, I think, whose finer qualities transcended his fleshly manhood. I wish that I had known him more intimately than time and pride permitted."

"Life is too short," I observed. "No matter what we achieve, we all die with an infinity of experience untasted. You and I must be thankful that we are artists. The majority, I think, die too contentedly, with that infinity of lost experience not merely untasted but unsuspected."

"Should we be thankful for that?" she asked. "Is not ignorance bliss? Would we not be happier if we did not know the true measure of our loss?"

"Of course we would," I said. "But what have you and I to do with that vulgar kind of happiness? Should the blind be glad that they have been spared the sight of the world's misfortunes? We should be grateful for every glimpse imagination gives us of possibilities unrealised and potentials unfulfilled, for they are a more precious

form of wealth than any mere coin or completed achievement. We are artists, Dorothea. We are the true humans, the hope and soul of the race. The extremity of your grief may be tearing you apart, but so it should — and you should be delighted to be torn, for that is the measure of your sensitivity and the measure of Conrad Othman's worth as musician *and* man."

"As musician and man!" she echoed, plaintively. "I only loved the musician, no matter how he strove to make me love the man. What a miser I am! What a pusillanimous, uncharitable soul is mine! I have been a fool, Axel: a self-protective fool."

"I do not believe it," I lied. "I heard you play today, and I watched you too. I heard and I saw what you really are, and I know your true capacity. You are no miser, Dorothea, and no coward either. Conrad Othman may have died before making that discovery, but if his dying helped you to make it, he did not die in vain. Here is your house — I should bid you farewell."

I did not, of course. I let her invite me in — and when she gave way to her distress and sank down upon a couch, I volunteered to show myself out, Having reconnoitred very carefully when I visited her to bring her news of Conrad's death, I knew exactly which window to unlock and exactly where to hide once I had loudly closed the door without actually passing through it. We are fortunate on the island not to have been reached by the new fashions in decoration that have all-but-banished screens and tapestries from the capital in favour of padded wallpaper; I had no difficulty in making my way back to the room where she had cast herself down — the same room in which her servants had re-established her harp, having carried it back from the church — and secreting myself behind a screen.

I knew that I would have to be patient, but I also knew that my wait would not be in vain. For an hour she could not move, and when she could her first thought was to revive herself with brandy. Had I thought it necessary, I might have contrived to have the brandy drugged, but I had faith in her artistic temperament. I knew that there was no danger of her lacking imagination — alas, I had not seen the contrary danger that she might possess too much.

I knew that Dorothea would fret for a while and weep for a while, that she would flutter aimlessly around the room twice or thrice, and throw herself down on her couch at least twice or thrice more. I knew that she would consume at least three glasses of brandy, that she would strike her breast and worry the hem of her black gown, that she would sob and mutter and bite her lip — but I knew that all such gestures would be a mere *tuning up*. I knew that she would torture herself only by way of preparation, and that there was only one way in which her frustration and self-abuse could eventually find proper expression.

In the end, two hours after midnight, she went to the harp. At the darkest hour of her distress, she went to play her part of the Rose Duet.

As soon as she sat down, she was listening. As soon as her fingers touched the strings, she was reaching out with every fibre of her being into the great unknown, hoping to hear the complementary voice of the flute.

And she heard it. From the very beginning, she was playing a duet — although I, the audience, could only hear the harp.

I had given Conrad very strict instructions as to the precise moment when he should begin to play outside Dorothea's window, adding a real instrument to the one that was already sounding in her imagination. I thought that I had judged the moment to perfection, and I was annoyed at first when the flute joined in some seven minutes early — but as the piece proceeded, I came to understand that I had been wrong. I am a painter by vocation, and although I consider myself a connoisseur of half a dozen other arts I have not the special expertise of a great player or a great composer. I realised, once the duet was half way through, that the flautist had added the audible to the imaginary at a moment even more appropriate than the one I had identified, and I was generous enough to extend my honest congratulation to the unseen player.

I had expected to see Dorothea start slightly when the notes she heard in her mind were supplemented by something more robust, but she gave no sign of any awareness of change. She continued playing quite seamlessly, She played no better than she had in the church, but she played more intently, as musicians tend to do when they believe that they are playing for themselves alone. Now that I could hear both instruments instead of only one, I was able to savour the Rose Duet as it was meant to be savoured, and I had no doubt that this was a stronger and more sincere performance than the one I had heard at the debut — but I could not help comparing it slightly unfavourably with

the incomplete performance I had heard in the Church. The new performance was deeply moving and perfectly executed, but there is sometimes a superabundance in emotional harmony and perfection: a saturation which is not entirely to be preferred to the best kind of tragic breakage. I had to tell myself that what I was hearing was best regarded as the second movement of a collective whose first had been played in the church.

When it was finished, it was all that I could do to quiet the reflex which bade my hands applaud — but it had to be suppressed, for the third movement was yet to be played, and the true climax of my collaborative composition still remained to be achieved.

I was sufficiently captivated by the magic of the moment not to be anxious when I did not hear the slightest creak from the window I had carefully unlocked. I was not surprised when it seemed as if the incubus that had been Conrad Othman really had materialised out of the shadows behind the couch on which Dorothea had lain down before she began to play.

She ran towards him as soon as she saw him, and gladly admired the way he glided around the couch, so that he could meet her in front of it and topple her into its tender embrace.

Although my vantage was good, too many candles had guttered and died while Dorothea played to allow me to see very clearly what was happening on the couch. I did not mind; too much light would have lent their performance a suggestion of cheap pornography, while the shadows helped to ennoble their intercourse far above that level. I could hear perfectly well, and I was left in not the slightest doubt that the intercourse in question was munificently material and exceedingly earthy.

Whatever Dorothea's previous proclivities might have been, and however they had been inspired, I knew that there was nothing for her in this experience but ecstasy. She believed — had I not given her every reason to believe? — that her playing had summoned a response even from beyond the grave, and that Conrad Othman had been allowed to return to earth for a single hour in order to complete that which had been left incomplete before. And if she believed it, was it not true *for her?* Was she not artist enough to be an authentic creator? Had she not genius enough to make the impossible real, if only for a moment? And was I not privileged to have had a part in the making of such an art-work? Was I not entitled to congratulate myself as the true author of the drama that I had already titled, if only privately. "The Incubus of the Rose"?

Yes, yes, yes, yes and yes. All of that, *and more.*

What *material* difference does it make, after all, that the incubus she summoned was not Conrad Othman at all? What *material* difference does it make that Conrad Othman — the *living* Conrad Othman — had been unable to take up his position outside Dorothea Rosa's window, because he had been rudely seized and detained by the secret spies the Duke of Dellacrusca had set to watch over his twin sons during their first experience of apparent freedom, who were very anxious to know exactly how and why the younger had been persuaded to put on a mask and make a very convincing pretence of trying to assassinate the elder?

I must emphasize at this juncture that it was no part of my plan that anyone should suffer any serious injury. I did not expect Dorothea Rosa to be grateful to me when she discovered that Conrad had been introduced to her bed by a cunning ruse, and I did not suppose that she would easily forgive Conrad, but I had faith in her as an artist. I sincerely believed that when her immediate anger had abated, she would realise that I had, after all, gifted her with a unique experience of considerable value. Even if she refused to entertain the idea that her new sexual experience had advanced her sentimental education considerably, I felt sure that her memory of those two remarkable performances of the incomplete Rose Duet would be infinitely precious.

I had, of course, envisaged that Conrad would remain with her after completing his deceptive seduction, and would soon reveal to her that he was, in fact, still alive. I was surprised when he disappeared, leaving Dorothea alone on the couch — and surprised, too, that I had somehow failed to notice his withdrawal — but it did not seem to be so terrible a violation of my script. I assumed that he had been temporarily overcome by the enormity of his own experience and that he would return as soon as he had composed himself.

I, of course, stole quietly away, using the window that I had unlocked for Conrad. I went stealthily, because I had carefully omitted to mention to Conrad that I intended to watch his performance, and I did not want him to catch me descending from the sill. I was glad that he was not there, because I knew no better.

It was not until he roused me from my own bed, two hours after dawn, to show me his bruises and complain bitterly at the manner in which Dellacrusca's bully-boys had interrogated him, that I belatedly realised that my scheme had gone awry.

I was so starved of sleep that I nearly blurted out a demand to know who had played the flute outside Dorothea's window and then made love to her, if he had not, but I remembered just in time that he was not supposed to know that I had remained in the house after seeing Dorothea home. It is hardly surprising, though, that while I kept silent that very question possessed my brain like an irresistible fever.

I am, of course, a thoroughgoing materialist. I know full well that there is no world beyond the grave — neither Heaven, nor Hell, nor purgatory — and I have never believed for an instant that ghosts routinely walk the earth, or that incubi and succubi are anything but the product of dream-driven appetite. On the other hand, I *do* believe in the force of the human imagination and the capacity of art to communicate that force.

It did not astonish me to learn that Dorothea Rosa had the ability to conjure up a phantom of Conrad Othman, even though Conrad Othman was not actually dead, and then to play the Rose Duet with the phantom's accompaniment, and even to enjoy physical intercourse with the phantom. I will admit that it did surprise me, a little, to discover that she also had the ability to make me see and hear the phantom too, but when I had time to reflect I could see that it made sense. I heard her playing, and was as conscious as she was of the absence implied by her playing alone. I am a painter, well used to the employment of my mind's eye in seeing the possible within and beyond the actual. If the incubus of the rose was a *folie*, it had every right and reason to be a *folie à deux*. If it could be material to Dorothea's ear and eye and touch, there was no reason why it should not be equally material to mine.

Although I am a great artist, I am — alas! — only human. It took time for me to work all this out, and while I was making the calculation I did

not have time or space in my thoughts for anything else. I simply had no opportunity to address the next question, which was: what would Dorothea do next, in the circumstances as I now understood them?

Perhaps I would have guessed, and perhaps not. It makes no difference now, and would have made none then.

In the event, Fion Commonal came hammering at my door two hours after Conrad Othman — while Conrad was still with me — to bring us the news that minutes after waking on her couch and beholding the cold grey light of the winter dawn, Dorothea Rosa had swallowed a draught of poison strong enough to kill a horse.

It was not such a terrible tragedy as everyone seemed to think. Dorothea was in her thirties. Not only had her looks begun to fade but — more importantly — her talent had already peaked. Had it not been for my little drama she might never have played as well as she had on the day and night of Conrad's false funeral, and she would certainly never have played so well again. She killed herself because she felt that there was nothing left for her on earth, and because she wanted to enjoin herself for all eternity with the phantom she had conjured from the vasty deep. In that, I presume, she succeeded, insofar as any success was possible. I do not say that she was not to be pitied or mourned, and I would certainly have been glad to see her appear alive and well the day after her funeral to declare that it had all been a joke designed in reprisal — but I still insist that if there are ways to die that are better than others, then Dorothea Rosa's was far from the worst.

Nobody agreed with me then, of course, and the lapse of time has not yet persuaded anyone to change sides. Emmaus Partibus was not grateful for the opportunity to stage two of the finest funerals that the island has ever seen within a single week, and Conrad Othman was not grateful for the opportunity to excel himself at Dorothea's funeral service almost to the extent that she had excelled herself at his. Hecate Rain was not grateful for the opportunity to make up for being omitted from the list of orators at Conrad's funeral by presenting the primary oration at Dorothea's. The twin sons of the Duke of Dellacrusca were not grateful to discover that their ostensible lack of supervision had been deceptive, and that their clandestine watchers would be reporting every detail of their bad behaviour to the Duke. All in all, I walked abroad in a distinctly frosty atmosphere for months, and not only because the winter turned out to be exceptionally harsh.

But what else could I have done, given that my only loyalty was and always will be to the cause of art?

All artists thrive on love, but there are different ways in which they draw its nourishment. Some feed on piquant challenge, some on the joyous zest of first consummation, some on the heady riot of intense engagement, some on the fierce pain of parting and some on the mellow melancholy of remembered loss. Rare indeed is the opportunity for *any* artist to make a singular banquet of all those nutriments, but Dorothea Rosa achieved it — and if Conrad Othman did not, the incubus of the rose more than made up for his omission.   Ω

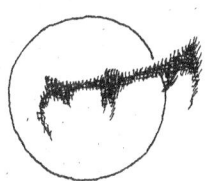

STEEL ANIMAL MOON

steel animal moon . . .
claw crescent / space-tempered fang
sunk into night's throat

— **Ann K. Schwader**

ONE BAD 'HOOD
by Michael R. Gist

"Won't bend that way."

Ralph pushed harder.

"I'm tellin' ya, it won't work."

"Maybe if you'd help," Ralph said, "we could both . . . together . . ."

Harry dropped his end and sighed. "Look here. See that scaly part? That's not gonna fold, no matter how hard you push. Now lower, along the tail . . . that'd work."

Ralph set down his side and wiped his sweaty brow with a clean white handkerchief. Disposal wasn't a very pretty job in the Mob, or very prestigious. But a guy had to start somewhere.

Straightening his suit and tie, Ralph studied the fire blazing in the basement furnace. "That doesn't look hot enough to me."

"You're gonna start that again?"

"That hide . . ."

"Don't get skittish on me."

Ralph eyed his older partner. Harry's street-hardened face was impassive. To him, it was just another job.

"What about the ropes?" Ralph asked.

Harry leaned over and tugged.

In response, bulky muscles flexed against their restraints. But the heavy cable held fast.

Ralph reached down and pulled up, before taking hold. "It still don't seem right."

Harry grabbed his shoulders. "This is our street isn't it?"

"Yes."

"And nobody works our street but us, right?"

"But . . ."

"No buts. Am I right or am I *right?*"

Ralph looked down, sheepishly. "You're right."

"Okay. So you get his tail this time." Harry grabbed the horns, one in each hand.

Ralph went around and folded the tail. "But this was *Satan* . . ."

Harry fixed Ralph in his gaze. "So he shoulda known this was a bad neighborhood, shouldn't he? You bet he should!"

Ralph picked up the hooves. "Okay, then. On a count of three."

"One.

"Two . . ."   Ω

BAD BOY
by James Robert Kimsey

At midnight, the boy walked to the last booth at the Swap Meet, just as the old, old man was closing up, and snarled, "Your money or your life," as he whipped out his switch-blade knife and jabbed it menacingly at the old man.

"Thanks!" the old, old man replied with a chuckle. "I've waited forty years for some young boy like you to make me this deal. . . . You may have my life, and . . ."

The old, old man — a wizard, of course — moved a finger, lightning flashed, and the old, old man became a boy . . .

. . . and the boy with the switch-blade became an old, old man.

"Thanks again," said the wizard from another time and place. He chuckled as he drew his young, muscular body up tall. "I do love the Swap Meets you have here in America."   Ω

The Classic Horrors

It was a twilit grotto of enormous height, stretching away farther than any eye could see; a subterraneous world of limitless mystery and horrible suggestion.
"The Rats in the Walls" by H.P. Lovecraft

ALLEN K. '00

WEIRD TALES TALKS WITH NEIL GAIMAN
by Darrell Schweitzer

Interviewer's note: This was recorded at the World Horror Convention in Denver, May 11–14 2000. Neil won a Stoker Award for the *Sandman* comics, but the real tribute to him and to his talent came the previous evening, when he conducted a *three hour* reading of the entirety of his new children's book, *Coraline,* about 28,000 words. It's a beautiful, eerie story, somewhat reminiscent of the best work of John Bellairs, author of *The Face in the Frost.* But what was most astonishing was that Neil, who is undeniably a good reader, held the audience completely spellbound for that long, when they normally would have been at the Friday night parties. It was an amazing experience, comparable to the best Harlan Ellison readings, or the time Fritz Leiber read "The Haunter of the Dark" in Providence at the first World Fantasy Convention in 1975, only blocks away from where the events in the story "actually happened." Neil's three-hour reading is probably *not* going to start a tradition, because very few other people could actually do it. This interview was recorded in the Green Room on Saturday afternoon, a much calmer and more ordinary time for such things.

Weird Tales: Our readers may know you less well than comic-book readers —

Gaiman: — the guy who wrote the introduction to the Lovecraft Dream Cycle book.

WT: Something like that. Or they've seen a pirated American tape of *Neverwhere* by now. So, could you give a brief outline of the high points of your career up to the moment?

Gaiman: My career to date, by Neil Gaiman, age thirty-nine and a half. I started out in England as a journalist. While working as a journalist, I collaborated with Kim Newman on a book called *Ghastly Beyond Belief,* a book of science-fiction and fantasy quotations, the worst of. I then did a biography of Douglas Adams, while still supporting myself as a journalist, called *Don't Panic.* Then I threw my lot in for fiction, and did mainly graphic novels and comics for the next ten years. I started with a book called *Violent Cases,* then did a monthly comic called *Sandman,* which won the World Fantasy Award and sundry other awards. But the best book I did during that time was one with Dave McKean

called *Mr. Punch,* which is a fantasy about Punch and Judy and memory and childhood. I also wrote a bunch of short stories. I won the International Horror Critics Guild Award for *Angels and Visitations.* I have been nominated for various World Fantasy Awards and Stokers and suchlike along the way. I did a TV series called *Neverwhere,* then turned that into a novel in England and rewrote it as a novel for America. I then did a fairy story called *Stardust,* and am now hard at work on a novel called *American Gods,* which is late; and I just handed in a very, very creepy, scary children's story called *Coraline.* That's pretty much my career to date. I've done a few other things along the way.

WT: You may be the best-known comic-book writer in the world. There aren't a lot of them who actually become *famous* in any case. So you must be doing something special.

Gaiman: I think Alan Moore may be the best known of us. I was very very lucky because the period in which I was writing mainstream comics happened to coincide with the period in which Alan Moore wasn't, which meant that I got to win every best writer award in everything, which was great fun. But, yes, I suppose I am. The odd thing right now about being me is that there are people who have discovered me from different places and different directions. There are *Sandman* people who have no idea that I have done anything else. There are people who found me through *Neverwhere.* As far as they are concerned, that is my first novel. There are people who discover me from one place and not another. To some of them I am the guy who wrote the introductions to the Dunsany books, or who wrote *Stardust,* so to them I'm a Dunsanian scholar and fantasist.

WT: There are people who probably know you as a Lovecraftian humorist, for "Shoggoth's Old Peculiar."

Gaiman: That was so bizarre. It was nominated for a World Fantasy Award last year, which was very nice, albeit very, very puzzling. Luckily it was up against "The Specialist's Hat" by the lovely Kelly Link, which was a story I much preferred. I was very, very happy when it won. It was one of those nice occasions, because I couldn't think of what I'd do if I did get the award except get up and say, "I think this is really Kelly Link's," and hand it over to her.

WT: But yours is a story of great charm. Lovecraft somehow readily lends himself to humor.

Gaiman: Lovecraft was the inspiration for the very first piece of fiction I remember writing and being pleased with. I'm not saying that it was any good, but the first thing that I wrote that I was pleased with was an attempt to write Cthulhu's autobiography, as dictated to Mr. Whateley. I gave it to a fanzine called *Dagon* and they published it in the mid-'80s. Horror and humor are so close anyway, but Lovecraft lends himself because he takes it so seriously and his readers take it so seriously. You only have to twist half a turn to the left and the material becomes screamingly funny. Witness that wonderful —

WT: *Scream for Jeeves* by Peter Cannon?

Gaiman: No, I wasn't even thinking of *Scream for Jeeves,* which is also wonderful, and is coincidentally based, oddly enough, on a gag that I must have come up with about the same time as Peter Cannon did. I'd written a letter to *Dagon* afterwards and said, "I'm glad people liked this Cthulhu biography so much. When I get around to it I will reveal the letters that have come into my possession, the Wodehouse-Lovecraft letters." I started talking about the musical they collaborated on, because Wodehouse actually was in New York and, I believe, a *Weird Tales* reader during the '20s. He was out there working on musicals. Wouldn't it have been fun if he'd written to Lovecraft and said, "Would you like to collaborate?" And I talked about "Cthulhu Springtime," which was the musical they collaborated on. Let me see if I can remember some of the lyrics. I quoted a few:

Although I'm just a bird in a gilded cage,
kept captive like some parakeet or love,
when a maiden meets a giant lipophage,
her heart gets chewed and broken like that old
    adage.
I'm just a fool who thought that Cthulhu could fall in
    love.

I explained how there was only one performance of the musical, the dreadful thing that happened to the theatre, and how nothing has ever been built there since. I had an enormous amount of fun with it. I was going to say that coming into this convention [the World Horror Convention in Denver], there was that wonderful

table in the dealer's room full of Cthulhupoid stuff, jokey stuff, including a Cthulhu to go on the back of your car instead of a Darwin or a fish, that sort of stuff. It's very Cthulhupoid.

WT: Were you warped by Lovecraft early in life like everybody else?

Gaiman: Oh yes. I was eleven or twelve. I was very lucky. Grafton books, or Granada Books had just brought the whole Lovecraft corpus back into print, about 1972 or 1973 in England. The first story of his I ever read was "The Outsider." That is such a great story. You know, the thing coming up into the light and then discovering it's the ghoul after scaring everybody. But yes, I discovered HPL and thought he was great. And then I picked up Clark Ashton Smith and thought, I don't like you. You don't do it for me. Whatever it is I'm reading Lovecraft for and getting off on, I'm not getting from Clark Ashton Smith. It was really disappointing because the Smith books had these gorgeous covers. There was Averoigne and Zothique and all that. I'd buy all the Smith books and I loved the ideas behind them. A couple years later I discovered Jack Vance and *The Dying Earth,* and thought, yes, this is better. But probably I am a philistine. Probably if I went back and read Clark Ashton Smith now I'd go, "Oh what a fine and beautiful writer." I was missing it all. But possibly not.

WT: Other than to supply quotes for *Ghastly Beyond Belief,* did these inform your sensibility and influence what you wrote?

Gaiman: Definitely. Everything you read as a kid is important. Everything you read as a kid is shaping you, particularly if you're going to be a writer. When I look back now, there are some things that are just key books. Judy Merril's *SF 12.* It had "The Star Pit" by Delany. It had Lafferty's "Narrow Valley." It had Aldiss's "Confluence." It had some William Burroughs in it. I read that when I was 11 or 12. I didn't understand half of it. It didn't matter. It was shaping things inside my head. Running into Roger Zelazny mattered. Moorcock when I was nine was deeply, horribly important. Zelazny and Lafferty and Harlan Ellison and all those guys by the time I was ten or eleven, again, awfully, awfully important. I would be a very different writer without them. What is odd is that I expected that I'd be a science-fiction writer. When I was a kid, if you'd asked me what I was going to do, that's what I would have said. I expected to be Larry Niven. I figured I'd write cool, hard-science things, despite the fact that I never actually wrote SF for pleasure. When I turned around somewhere in my early thirties and found that I seemed to be a fantasy and horror writer, I was almost surprised.

WT: I think that the reason for that, for most Baby-Boomers, is that when we were kids science fiction was much more predominant. There was very little fantasy and horror available. Therefore when you encountered fantastic fiction, it was under the umbrella of science fiction. I also thought I was going to be a science-fiction writer, and look what happened.

Gaiman: I think that's exactly right. The stuff that actually was the drug we were responding to — not even that, the true awe. When you hit the true awe, it all came under the SF rubric. Books were packaged with spaceships on the cover. You go back and reread Zelazny now, and it's very obvious that he's not writing SF. He's writing fantasy. What is "A Rose for Ecclesiastes" anyway? It's a fine and beautiful fantasy.

WT: In those days, indeed, fantasy was something you had to sneak in, either as a children's book or as science fiction.

Gaiman: Yes.

WT: Now we may have the opposite problem. Not only is fantasy predominant, it's expected to be published in ten fat volumes. I wonder if somebody really could get a fine and beautiful *short* fantasy novel published now.

Gaiman: I don't know how fine and beautiful it is, but that was my intention with *Stardust.* The joy for me with *Stardust* was that it is a hair under 60,000 words. People say to me, "When you get to the end and you do that stuff where they're coming home, all of the sudden you take half a page and you list some of the cool things that happen to them. Why didn't you take five chapters to tell that?" And I reply that it would have turned it into a different book. I wanted to write a Dunsany book. I wanted to write something that came in at 60,000 words, that was a small, elegant book in which everything happened.

WT: I think the reason you got away with it is that you're famous and you have clout. You have to have clout nowadays to get a short book into print. Anybody can have a long book, but if it's short, the publishers and bookstore buyers are going to have to be really convinced that it's going to sell, even if it doesn't weigh in by the pound.

Gaiman: Oh, I think so. And even then the publisher did some very peculiar things. And bless them. They want to maximize their sales and so forth. But they put this enormous typeface in, so they could get it to 350 pages instead of the 200 pages that it probably would have been much happier at.

WT: How did you make the transition from writing comic scripts to writing novels? They are very different media, after all.

Gaiman: One of the things I did was that, all the time while I was writing comics, I still kept a foot in the prose camp. I didn't get to write a lot of prose, but I wrote "Chivalry." I wrote "Troll Bridge" and "Murder Mysteries." Some solid short stories that got anthologized and picked up for Year's Best anthologies, that kind of thing. So I was always writing the shorts. By the time I had finished *Sandman, Neverwhere* was happening. I had been working on that for five years, and I was then able to send the scripts off to Avon and say, "I'm going to be writing this novel. It's going to be based on these scripts." So I think that from that point of view, nobody was in any doubt. But a lot of people have real problems moving from medium to medium. I don't know why that is, but I've watched it happen. There were some people, like Harlan Ellison, who are storytellers. If you say, "Tell it as a 30-minute episode for TV," and they can, and you say "Tell it as a big-budget movie" and they can. If you say "Tell it as a piece of stripped-down prose" and they can. You say "Tell it as a comic," and they can do it. There are many, many more people who are fine novelists, but when you say, "Good, now write me a 15-page comic," and it's appalling. Or they cannot write screenplays. They cannot make the transition, or they cannot bring the magic from one medium to another.

WT: One of the differences might be — correct me if I'm wrong because you have written comics and I have not — that in a comic or a screenplay, you are expecting someone else to supply the visuals and much of the atmosphere, and therefore you concentrate on dialogue. By contrast, the worst screenplay writer ever would have been H.P. Lovecraft, because he was all visuals and atmosphere. He did, in his prose, all the things that art or photography would do, and less of what the script would do.

Gaiman: I disagree with you, and I think that one of the problems we get with people moving from one medium to another, especially into comics, is that's what they assume. They think that the artist is going to put in all the detaily stuff and all they have to do is worry about writing cool dialogue. What you have in comics that you don't have in prose is control over how the information is received. You have control over the rhythm of the information, just putting it down, beat by beat, in panels. When I'm writing a script, I'm writing a letter to an artist, telling him what I want, what I'm trying to do, what I want in each panel, what effect we're trying to do. The thing that I miss in prose more than anything else, that is like a piece of the toolkit that you have in comics that you don't have in prose, is the silent panel. Just the beat after somebody says something, or you just pull back and somebody is standing there on their own without saying anything. You don't have to describe them anymore. You don't have to add anything else in. You just have a beat. I keep trying to do that in prose. How can I get that exact effect? I still haven't figured it out.

WT: You could skip a space. Or you could vary the rhythm of the prose drastically, as in a long, screaming tirade followed by a one-sentence paragraph that says, "Nothing happened."

Gaiman: It's one of those things that you can do in comics and you can approximate and move around it in prose. And there are things you can do in prose that you can't do in comics. You can really go into someone's head and start mucking around behind the eyes.

WT: I am reminded of a comment Lord Dunsany made. He saw a script which had a gorgeous description of a sun setting over a landscape, and this had to be crossed out, so that it just said, "Sun sets, left." This is what I mean by the visuals being supplied by somebody else, in that case the stage designer and the director.

Gaiman: Yes, that's very true. The advantage in doing a comic is that I can describe that sunset to an artist and see how close I can get it. If I just say, "Sunset," I might get anything. But one of the media that I love most is radio plays. There you can do both. You can do all the things you can do in prose and all the things you can do in comics, strangely. You have control over timing and beat, and you have the immediacy of films, but the audience is still building the pictures in their heads.

WT: You've got the visuals.

Gaiman: Exactly. I did an adaptation of my story "Murder Mysteries," which is about a murder committed in Heaven before the Fall, and about the angel investigating this murder. I adapted that for the Sci Fi Channel, SciFi.Com. We put together a wonderful cast starring Brian Dennehy as the angel private eye. It is lovely listening to it because you can do things on the radio. At one point they're walking around this city of angels and they come into this hall in which the universe is being constructed. At one point the hero falls through the universe as it's being built. How many millions of dollars would it take to achieve that on the screen?

WT: Someone made the comment that there are some things you just can't do in any medium other than radio. It might have been Robert Bloch who said it. The example given was a scene in a radio play in which they filled up Lake Erie with whipped cream and a fleet of helicopters lowers a giant maraschino cherry on top. If you did that in a movie, it would just look silly, but the mind's eye can produce it effectively.

Gaiman: Exactly. You're doing it in people's heads. The one that really didn't work, I remember was from *The Hitch-Hiker's Guide to the Galaxy.* When they did the line in the radio play, "Ford, you're turning into an infinite number of penguins," it was marvelous. But when they did the TV show and tried to show Ford turning into an infinite number of penguins, it was one of the most embarrassing moments in the whole show.

WT: Horror also works this way, and often does better on the radio.

Gaiman: Horror always exists as this wonderful balancing act between showing the monster and not showing the monster. What Clive Barker did that was so brilliant when the *Books of Blood* came out — it really felt like a breath of fresh air — was not only did he show the monster, but the monster that came on was cooler than the one that you'd imagined. That, I think, was lovely. Then everybody started showing the monster. Unfortunately their imaginations and their descriptive powers were not up to Clive's. I think that mostly monsters are best kept in the shadows.

WT: There is the basic aesthetic problem that once you've shown everything, you've shown everything and there is nothing more. I am sure we have all seen any number of movies that play all their cards early. Then unless they have a strong plot, they're dead.

Gaiman: Completely. The weird thing right now about *American Gods,* my new novel, is that it is probably a fantasy novel. I don't think it is horror, though it has enough horror in it to upset some people. I got some lovely letters from ladies who were romance fans. They were big fans of *Stardust.* They have their newsletters and they have their web sites, and they praised them to the heavens. And I cannot see them liking *American Gods* at all. So word fifteen is "fuck." You're not through the first sentence before you get the word "fuck" because I just want to tell everybody that this is not a sweet book, and it's not a friendly book, and it's not a nice Victorian love story. If you have any trouble, *put it down now.* You have your out in the first sentence.

WT: So you'll get a different audience with every book. Do the *Neverwhere* readers like *Stardust*?

Gaiman: I don't think so. Some of them did and some of them didn't. The wonderful thing about my time in comics was that I did train a core readership in understanding that what I was going to do next was not what I did last. If you don't like it, that's probably okay, because there's a good chance you will like what I do after that. And I'm not going to do the same thing over and over and over again. So I trained people. Except, of course, that all the *Sandman* people went out and picked up *Neverwhere* and said, "Uh, it's not *Sandman*. We don't like this." The *Neverwhere* people said, "We love this. We've never read anything like it." Then they picked up *Stardust* and said, "Oh, this isn't *Neverwhere*. We don't know if we like this or not." Meanwhile, most of the people who picked up *Smoke and Mirrors*, my short-story collection, liked it, because even if there are short stories or whatever in there that you don't like, there's enough stuff in there that you probably would. It keeps them happy.

WT: Sooner or later you get the publisher offering you five million dollars for another *Neverwhere* sequel, and another, and another. You can get trapped that way, as Frank Herbert did with *Dune*. We all should hope to have this problem that people keep offering us millions ... but what do you do in the face of this Faustian temptation?

Gaiman: I don't know. The big problem with me in *Neverwhere* is that I'd love to do another *Neverwhere* novel. I have at least two or three stories in the series going on in my head. But there are other things that I'd like to write first, which is why they aren't getting written. What I might do — I'm thinking that when the current novel is finished, I could do a book of three novellas. One would be a *Stardust* novella, one would be a *Neverwhere* novella, and one would be an *American Gods* novella. This is not an attempt to cash in on my audience, but because I have these bloody stories floating around in my head.

The *Stardust* one is really peculiar because they get to go to Hell in a hot air balloon. There's a *Neverwhere* story called "How the Marquis Got His Coat Back." They're all nineteen to twenty thousand word stories, which is a really irritating length to write anything at all, because nobody really wants that. So I will probably end up doing three in a book. But, yes, the financial thing is horrible. You can really get trapped into what Joe Straczynski calls "The velvet trap," the Rod Serling thing. They give you an awful lot of money, and then your standard of living goes up to that awful amount of money, and then they've got you. Somebody who is earning twenty-five thousand a year, go and offer them a million and they can turn you down with a clear conscience. I turned down a ten million dollar deal a few years ago with a clear and easy conscience, because I didn't want to do it. I didn't like the amount of things I'd have to give away to do it. Once you get trapped at a certain level, I can see how the whole *Dune* thing would come in. Roger writing more and more Amber books. You look at them, especially the last batch of Amber books, and they really weren't very good. They didn't read like he was writing them because he wanted to write them. Then all of a sudden he did *A Night in Lonesome October* which he really did want to write.

WT: Then someone could come to you and ask you to do an on-going weekly series of *Neverwhere*. Has that happened?

Gaiman: There's a movie that's happening right now, that is being directed by a guy called Richard Loncraine. I wrote about eight drafts of the script until I got very tired of writing drafts of the script, and I stepped aside, and I believe they've got Andrew Birkin writing the script. Then I will either come back or not come back at the end to give it a dialogue polish.

WT: To get back to an interesting comment you made before we started this interview ... you said that one of the things you really wanted to read was all the works of Robert Aickman, cover to cover. This will probably surprise some of your fans. It's a different sensibility. What do you see in Robert Aickman that makes him essential?

Gaiman: I think that Aickman is one of those authors that you respond to on a very primal level. If you're a writer, it's a bit like being a stage magician. A stage magician produces coin, takes coin, demonstrates coin vanished. [Gaiman is doing this as he speaks, quite capably.] If you're a professional stage magician, you're not going,

"Oh boy! He vanished the coin!" You're thinking that was a smooth or a not smooth French Drop. Or, "Look, he did that sleight. I haven't seen that one done in a while." Or, "Look, there's a reverse French Drop." That tends to be what you do as a fiction writer, reading fiction. You'll go, "Oh, look. He's setting that up." You're in the position of a stage magician in the audience. You may admire the way something is done, but you never worry if that woman is going to get cut in half. Reading Robert Aickman is like watching a magician work, and very often I'm not even sure what the trick was. All I know is that he did it beautifully. Yes, the key vanished, but I don't know if he was holding a key in that hand to begin with. I find myself admiring everything he does from an auctorial standpoint. And I love it as a reader. He will bring on atmosphere. He will construct these perfect, dark, doomed little stories, what he called "strange stories." I find the same with Lafferty. We were talking about Lafferty earlier as somebody who I'd love to read. I am hoping someone will do the complete short stories of R.A. Lafferty. What is interesting is that when you read the early Lafferty, the closer he comes to what one might consider a normal story, the less successful he is. I think that with Aickman, that the closer he comes to something that somebody else could have written, the less successful he is.

WT: What I find curious about both of these writers is that they are authors one admires very much but you don't really understand. Does anybody really understand either Lafferty or Aickman?

Gaiman: God? Certainly, if there is one. But no, I think that the joy of Lafferty and the joy of Aickman is the joy of people who exist completely independent of everything else. I love Stephen King. I think that Steve is an astonishing storyteller. And I also think that he's a really good writer. I think that he's written books that were sloppy and I think that he's written books that were really good. But I think that he's a really good wordsmith. I think that he's a better wordsmith than he gives himself credit for. But Steve is comprehensible. That is one reason why he is a very popular writer, because you understand what he is talking about. You can connect to it. You can draw the dots. You can see where it works. I can understand why Peter Straub responded to Robert Aickman, because Straub loves jazz. Steve loves rock. Stephen King is rock & roll. Aickman is jazz. And Lafferty is something played in an Irish bar on an instrument

that you're not quite sure what it is and you're humming the tune but you don't remember the words as you walk out.

WT: Another thing about these writers is that you can tell they're not faking you out. There are many writers who will just plop down a mass of almost random words and say, "Well this is really very profound, and if you don't understand it you must be an ignoramus." You somehow know with Lafferty or Aickman that this is not the case.

Gaiman: Avram Davidson is another one of those. You're not being faked out. And Gene Wolfe. If you're going to put together four people who belong on the same page, I would have said Lafferty, Aickman, Gene Wolfe, and Davidson. If you don't get it, it's your fault somehow. Go back and read it again. You'll get there. I remember Aickman's "Mark Ingestre: The Customer's Tale." I wound up researching. Who was Lord Lovatt? What is his tie-in to Mrs. Lovett? What is the significance to all this stuff? How does it tie in to Sweeney Todd? I finally got to the point where I went, "You know, I do understand this." I don't think I've ever put as much effort into any other story by Aickman, but one assumes that it's there for the repaying, in the same way that a good Gene Wolfe story tends to return what gets put into it.

WT: These are all brave or oblivious writers. They are taking risks. If you do what they do, you run the risk that lots of lazy readers will take their money elsewhere, and lazy publishers will anticipate this and not publish you.

Gaiman: I don't think I am one of them. I may occasionally visit from time to time, but at the end of the day I am probably in the Stephen King camp. I'm a storyteller. The coolest thing for me is the telling of a story. The moments that matter are the moments when I get to surprise myself, the giving to people points of view they haven't had before. A very strange thing caught me with *American Gods*, because I needed a prose style which was really meat-&-potatoes, very straightforward, very, very basic. And I got very tired of it very fast. So I started writing short stories to go into the body of the text, set in the past. For each of them I can write beautiful, elegant prose, and not to worry about the stripped-down, Elmore Leonard stuff that the novel is in.

WT: I think that you have to keep your readers in mind, but ultimately you have to take these risks for the sake of the book. But many people won't notice anyway. It's always been my theory that the reason that many really bad books get published is that a lot of readers are completely style-deaf. They just skim it. So somebody whose prose is like fingernails on the blackboard can get published and become a bestseller.

Gaiman: I think that's true. I'm not really one of those people. I tend to write for very small audiences. My audience can be me. If I am writing a short story, the audience can be the editor who solicited the story.

WT: The downside is that if most people are style deaf, they'll never know if you're writing beautifully.

Gaiman: That's very, very true. But I also figure that there are enough people out there who can tell the difference. James Branch Cabell once said that a man crafts a beautiful sentence for the same joy you get from playing a good game of solitaire. You don't craft a beautiful sentence for the multitude. You craft a beautiful sentence for your own satisfaction.

WT: You've somehow managed to become very popular. You've had your cake and eaten it too.

Gaiman: I guess I have. I don't quite know how, and I don't necessarily want to investigate too hard. I think I'm very lucky. There are two kinds of saying "I think I'm very lucky." One is a self-deprecating way, and what you're actually saying is that I think I'm very clever and I think I'm very good, so I'm going to say I'm very lucky and you can all go, "No, no, no! He's not lucky. He's brilliant." I think I'm very lucky, just because the stories I like to tell happen to be the same stories that people like to read. I don't think I could change the kinds of stories I like to tell. So if public readership tastes did not happen to coincide with what I like to write, I would still be writing the same stuff, and I would simply not be selling anything. [Laughs.] I am fortunate that at this juncture, I'm telling stories people like to read. Whether or not this will continue, I don't know. There is a wasteland in literature which is filled with authors, good authors and bad authors, who told the right story at the right time, and briefly were famous, briefly were popular.

WT: One example I can think of is Joseph Hergesheimer, who most people know from dedications and introductions in James Branch Cab-

ell books. He woke up one morning in 1929 and he had no audience.

Gaiman: Completely. But Cabell himself was a minor writer, with some critical acclaim, who wrote *Jurgen,* had one line in some New York newspaper saying, "This guy Cabell is getting away with murder; all the chorus girls are reading this filthy book he's written." The New York Society for the Suppression of Vice under Mr. Sumner busted *Jurgen,* took the plates, sued the publisher. Cabell and the publisher won the case, and Cabell was now a best-selling author. There was a line in *The New Yorker,* if memory serves, saying that "while the literary laurels of the future are all in doubt, there is one name from our time that will ring out forever into the future and that is the name of James Branch Cabell. And by 1950, everything except *Jurgen* was out of print and he was writing for tiny university presses.

WT: Even now there are only occasional reprintings.

Gaiman: They reprint the fantasies, but there are Cabell books which are finer than some of his fantasies that have not been back in print since 1929.

WT: Another one the critics of that era were certain would be one of the great novels, if not the greatest novel of the 20th century, was Walter de la Mare's *Memoirs of a Midget.* It didn't happen.

Gaiman: It didn't happen, but that was the one they all pointed to. Like *Messer Marco Polo* by Donn Byrne. Yes, but tastes change. You write for your time. I write for me, at the end of the day. I am my audience. I write to amuse myself, in the very, very fundamental sense that it passes the time, it staves off boredom, and I don't know that there's anything else out in the world that I am actually any good at. And I have too much of a work ethic to sit and watch television all day, or else there isn't enough good TV, and I get bored. So I've got myself a little cabin now, twenty minutes from home, overlooking a lake. I get in my car and I drive my twenty minutes, and I settle down, and I write. There is no phone in there and there is no TV in there, and all the books are books that relate to whatever I am working on. And I write, or I make cups of tea.

WT: Thanks, Neil. Ω

WILDSIDE PRESS

MYSTERIES • SUSPENSE • SCIENCE FICTION
CLASSICS • MUSIC • COOKING • REFERENCE

SPRING 2000 CATALOG

A WORD FROM THE PUBLISHER

Welcome to the Wildside! This is the largest catalog we've ever sent out, and it's going to thousands of new readers. Let me take a minute to introduce our company and tell you what we're about. (Wildside isn't your usual run-of-the-mill publisher . . . not by a long shot.)

My wife and I started Wildside in 1989 as a hobby to publish affordable signed, limited edition books. In part it was a rebellion against overpriced thousand-copy "special" signed editions costing $75.00 or more. (Our average price for a signed limited hardcover edition was only $35.00... and sometimes less.) My wife and I garnering two special World Fantasy Award nominations for our efforts, and two of our books won World Fantasy Awards for Best Collection of the Year...a pair of short story collections by Bradley Denton, which are featured later in this catalog.

In mid 1999, I decided to devote myself full-time to publishing. Since August of that year, Wildside Press has brought out more than 200 new titles...and we should top 500 by the end of 2000. From novels to short story collections to non-fiction and reference works, from science fiction to mystery to romance—quality and affordability remain our watchwords.

Here in this catalog you will find important new works by hot young writers like Bruce Holland Rogers and Amy Sterling Casil alongside books by current masters like Anne McCaffrey, Alan Dean Foster, and Mike Resnick (to name just a few). World Fantasy Award-winner Darrell Schweitzer, who edits *Weird Tales* magazine, is reprinting his novels, short story collections, and scholarly non-fiction anthologies through Wildside. And we are rescuing long out-of-print works by important genre writers like Avram Davidson, R.A. Lafferty, and Keith Roberts before they are forgotten.

And we have begun a fantasy classics reprint program, Wildside Fantasy Classics, to bring back "lost" masterpieces of the fantasy field. Featured are titles by H. Rider Haggard, Lafcadio Hearn, William Morris, and many more.

Please take a moment to look through our catalog; from mysteries to science fiction to romance—from reference books to author studies to popular non-fiction . . . we're sure you'll find something you'll enjoy!

—John Betancourt. *Publisher*

Our authors include . . .

John Gregory Betancourt
Lloyd Biggle, Jr.
Robert Bloch
Nelson S. Bond
Chris Bunch
Lin Carter
Amy Sterling Casil
F. Marion Crawford
Avram Davidson
Grania Davis
L. Sprague de Camp
David Dvorkin
Leonore Dvorkin
Tom Easton
Rosemary Edghill
John M. Ford
Alan Dean Foster
Esther Friesner
H. Rider Haggard
Joe L. Hensley
Roby James
S.T. Joshi
Phyllis Ann Karr
Marvin Kaye
R. A. Lafferty
Tanith Lee
Morgan Llywelyn
Katherine MacLean
Barry Malzberg
David Mason
Anne McCaffrey
Brian McNaughton
Ward Moore
William Morris
Ray Faraday Nelson
Mike Resnick
Keith Roberts
Alan Rodgers
Bruce Holland Rogers
Darrell Schweitzer
George Scithers
S. P. Somtow
Lois Tilton
Lawrence Watt-Evans
Robert Weinberg
Leslie What
F. Paul Wilson

& many more!

MYSTERIES AND SUSPENSE

David Dvorkin

- *New York Times* best-selling author
- Writes *Star Trek* novels as well as mysteries

Time for Sherlock Holmes, by David Dvorkin

In the 1920s, Sherlock Holmes discovered how to render Dr. Watson and himself immortal. Unfortunately, in the previous century, his nemesis Professor Moriarty had stolen a time machine from its inventor and jumped forward. As decades pass, Holmes and Watson travel into space to save humanity from their old enemy. Great for mystery readers and science fiction fans alike!

"[A] really wild one. . . . Doyle to Wells to Dvorkin — nice triple play!" —*New York Times Book Review*

"Somewhere, Arthur Conan Doyle may be loving all of this. For us, it's a lot of fun." —*Arizona Republic*

ISBN: 1-58715-0735 (Trade paper, $15.95)

❊

The Cavaradossi Killings, by David Dvorkin

On the run from the Chicago mob he was part of for 20 years, Tom Hamilton returns to his Colorado hometown. But when a singer is murdered during a local opera performance, Tom is drawn into the case almost against his will and better judgment, stirring up old passions and hatreds—and endangering his life!

ISBN: 1-58715-126X (Trade Paper, $15.95)

About Ray Faraday Nelson

- Writes science fiction as well as mysteries.

Dog-Headed Death, Ray Faraday Nelson

When a wealthy shipping magnate is murdered in his Egyptian mansion, several members of his family, including a son and daughter, have the means, motive, and the opportunity. But this isn't a contemporary tale—rather, it is set in the first century A.D., in Alexandrian Egypt, at a time when the upstart Christian believers were battling the established religion of Mother Isis/Father Osiris-Serapis for converts. Enter Centurion Gaius Hesperian, a reflective and compassionate member of Emperor Nero's palace guard who, with his lieutenants and soldiers, is sent to Alexandria and charged with solving the crime . . .

Carefully researched for period detail, it includes members of the extended Memnon family, the Apostle Mark, Parthian spies, and many more colorful and authentic characters.

ISBN: 1-58715-0816 (Trade Paperback, $15.00)

JOE L. HENSLEY

- Former judge turned mystery writer
- Most popular series features Donald Robak

Robak's Cross, by Joe L. Hensley

The seventh mystery in the Robak series.

ISBN: 1-58715-0336 (Trade Paperback, $15.00)

❊

Robak's Fire, by Joe L. Hensley

Murder, arson, a crooked town...and Don Robak. Now the sides are even!

ISBN: 1-58715-0344 (Trade Paperback, $15.00)

❊

Robak's Firm, by Joe L. Hensley

Not to be confused with *Robak's Fire*, this book is a collection of Hensley's finest mystery stories.

ISBN: 1-58715-0352 (Trade Paper $15.00)

❊

A Killing in Gold, by Joe L. Hensley

As Donald Roback turns from lawyer to amateur detective his safe, comfortable life-style is threatened by murder, theft, and danger!

ISBN: 1-58715-0360 (Trade Paperback, $15.00)

❊

The Poison Summer, by Joe L. Hensley

A young lawyer searches for justice in two deaths.

ISBN: 1-58715-0379 (Trade Paperback, $15.00)

❊

Song of Corpus Juris, by Joe L. Hensley

Violence and intrigue surround a small town lawyer as he defends a beautiful young woman accused of murder.

ISBN: 1-58715-0387 (Trade Paper, $15.00)

❊

Final Doors, by Joe L. Hensley

Fifteen short stories, collected for the first time.

ISBN: 1-58715-0395 (Trade Paper, $15.00)

❊

Rivertown Risk, by Joe L. Hensley

Corruption, politics, and murder make uneasy bedfellows!

ISBN: 1-58715-0409 (Trade Paper, $15.00)

❊

Outcasts, by Joe L. Hensley

Another fine detective novel from Joe L. Hensley.

ISBN: 1-58715-0417 (Trade Paper, $15.00)

MARVIN KAYE

- *Best-selling suspense writer*
- *Author of many books on toys, games, and magic*

A Lively Game of Murder, by Marvin Kaye

In this first Hilary Quayle mystery novel, industrial espionage and dirty business dealings lead to murder at New York City's annual American Toy Fair trade show. Beautiful, headstrong Hilary and her Archie Goodwin-like secretary Gene, solve the mystery of three Scrabble tiles clutched in a dead man's fist.

This book offers a fascinating inside look at the American toy, hobby, game industry, for which the author used to be a leading journalist.

ISBN: 1-880448-718 (Trade Paperback, $15.00)

Bullets for Macbeth, by Marvin Kaye

In this unique tour de force, glamorous PR agent Hillary Quayle returns to solve the 350-year-old hotly-disputed scholarly puzzle of the Third Murderer's identity in Shakespeare's Scottish play while her lover Gene catches the killer in a spectacular production at Madison Square Garden. Acclaimed as the most convincing solution to the centuries-old Shakespearean problem by theatre and literary scholars, including Isaac Asimov, Jose Ferrer, Dr. O. B. Hardison, Jr. (late director of The Folger Shakespeare Library in Washington), *Bullets for Macbeth* has been singled out as an important Shakespearean murder mystery in two articles in *The Armchair Detective* magazine. It was adapted by the Stratford Ontario Shakespeare Festival in its staging of Macbeth.

ISBN: 1-880448-734 (Trade Paperback, $15.00)

The Soap Opera Slaughters, by Marvin Kaye

While Hilary Quayle and Gene are having a lovers' quarrel, Gene falls in love with Hilary's lookalike cousin. Meanwhile, a killer stalks *Riverday*, a popular TV soap opera, pushing its writer off the roof, poisoning a star on camera, and bashing the producer with his own Emmy award! This book features a rare inside look of how a TV soap operas works, with details drawn from the author's visits to the sets of *Another World*, *Days of Our Lives*, and *Ryan's Hope*.

ISBN: 1-880448-726 (Trade Paperback, $15.00)

My Son the Druggist, by Marvin Kaye

Marty Gold, a good-natured New York City pharmacist, has his hands full coping with his father's anger over Marty's religious doubts, his mother's meddling in Marty's love life (or lack of it), and the police's suspicion that Marty deliberately poisoned one of his own customers.

ISBN: 1-880448-70X (Trade Paperback, $15.00)

My Brother the Druggist, by Marvin Kaye

While visiting his sister in Washington, Marty Gold's young traveling companion is kidnapped and it's up the amiable New York pharmacist to rescue the boy from a cold-blooded criminal.

ISBN: 1-880448-696 (Trade Paperback, $15.00)

POPULAR FICTION

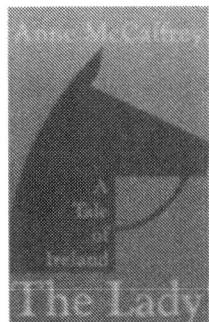

The Lady, Anne McCaffrey

Set in Ireland, *The Lady* is the saga of a family of weathy horsebreaders, their lives, loves, and triumphs. A terrific change of pace from the *New York Times* best-selling author of *The White Dragon*.

ISBN: 1-58715-0174 (Trade Paperback, $19.95)

Ring of Fear, by Anne McCaffrey

A contemporary romance from the best-selling author of the *Pern* series.

ISBN: 1-58715-0166 (Trade Paperback, $15.00)

Apart From You, by Leonore Dvorkin

Indiana University, 1968. Temporarily separated from her liberal-minded fiancé, Elizabeth Nye begins an affair, only to find herself caught in a complex web of love, lies, and belated remorse. This brilliant first novel explores several varieties of deception, alienation, and miscommunication. Sibling rivalry and infidelity take emotional center stage.

ISBN: 1-58715-0743 (Trade Paperback, $15.95)

YOUNG ADULT

Forgetting Places, by S.P. Somtow

A sensative and touching story of a boy dealing with the death of his older brother. But when messages from the dead boy start arriving, it's the start of an adventure of self-discovery and healing. A brilliant break-through novel by the author of *The Aquilliad* and *Vampire Junction*.

ISBN: 1-58715-145-6 (Trade paperback, $13.95)

The Bear Who Found Christmas, by Alan Rodgers

Joey Robins loved his toy bear. Joey loved the bear so hard and long and pure, so deeply and so truly and so powerfully, that the bear began to grow a heart. Nobody ever would have known about Bear at all, in fact, if Joey hadn't lost him in the hotel beside the haunted shopping mall on Christmas Eve . . . And so begins a great quest, as the toy bear tries to find his way home. A timeless classic for all seasons.

Alan Rodgers won the Bram Stoker Award. He is the best-selling author of *Fire* and *Night*.

ISBN: 1-58715-107-3 (Trade Paper $12.95)

SCIENCE FICTION & FANTASY

BRADLEY DENTON COLLECTIONS!

The Calvin Coolidge Home for Dead Comedians, by Bradley Denton

A Conflagration Artist, by Bradley Denton

These two collections, originally published in hardcover as a set, won the World Fantasy Award for Best Collection of the Year. Each volume is a selection of the best of Denton's short fiction—some fantasy, some science fiction, all excellent—plus two original stories written just for these books.

Calvin: ISBN: 1-880448-890 (Trade Paperback, $17.00)
Artist: ISBN: 1-880448-904 (Trade Paperback, $17.00)

BOOKS BY MIKE RESNICK
• **Hugo and Nebula Award-winner**
• **Best-selling author**

A Safari of the Mind, by Mike Resnick

16 stories by Mike Resnic, including several of his most popular award-winners, spanning the genres of science fiction and fantasy. Included are the classic "Seven Views of Olduvai Gorge," "The 43 Antarian Dynasties," and even such fun pieces as "A Limerick History of Science Fiction." Introduction by Kristine Kathryn Rusch.

ISBN: 1-58715-0069 (Trade Paper, $15.00)
ISBN: 1-58715-0077 (Hardcover $30.00)

❊

Alternate Skiffy, edited by Mike Resnick & Patrick Nielsen Hayden

The latest of Resnick's alternate histories is devoted to the science fiction field—such what-if premises as "What is H.P. Lovecraft became editor of *Weird Tales?*" and "What if Fritz Leiber became a successful actor instead of writer?" Lots of fun! Contributors include Frederick Pohl, Barry Malzberg, Mike Resnick, Greg Cox, David Langford, and more.

ISBN: 1-880448-548 (trade paperback, $12.50)

ABOUT DARRELL SCHWEITZER
• **Editor of *Weird Tales***
• **World Fantasy Award-winner**
• **Author of *The Mask of the Sorcerer***

Necromancies & Netherworlds: Uncanny Stories, by Darrell Schweitzer & Jason Van Hollander

Bold fantasies of a land where men have overthrown the gods. "If you're at all uncertain about what is meant by "phantasmagoric," this book will set you right." —*Interzone*

ISBN: 1-880448-65-3 (Hardcover $30.00)
ISBN: 1-880448-66-1 (Trade Paperback, $15.00)

❊

The Shattered Goddess, by Darrell Schweitzer

An epic quest, as a young hero tries to escape his destiny at the end of time. "Few writers can genuinely touch the quality of nightmare . . . the fear that, formless and almost banal, stems from the sleeping mind. John Bellairs did it with *The Face in the Frost* . . . James Blaylock can do it. And now there is also *The Shattered Goddess.*—Mary Gentle

ISBN: 1-880448-80-7 (Trade Paperback, $15.00)

❊

We Are All Legends, by Darrell Schweitzer

"... although it's written as a series of discontinuous episodes, there's a sense of progression and a conclusion. Moorcock's *Elric* stories make up a novel in much the same way, and these stories also appeared separately in a variety of magazines and anthologies before being collected . . . Nor does the similarity end there, for the protagonist, Sir Julianthe Later and Lesser Apostate (as he styles himself) has a similar sense of damnation, deriving from the murder of one who loved him." —*Interzone*

". . . what a brilliantly berserk, schizoid universe Schweitzer has manufactured for his characters! *We Are All Legends* contains none of the cosy cuteness of standard fantasy worlds. It's a place of metal teardrops, phantom gargoyle armies, desolation and terror, and the details ring true . . ." — S.P. Somtow

ISBN: 1-880448-83-1 (Trade Paperback, $15.00)

❊

Groping Toward the Light, by Darrell Schweitzer

Fantastic and macabre poetry by Darrell Schweitzer. Illustated by Jason Van Hollander Available May 30, 2000.

ISBN: 1-58715-108-1 (Trade Paper, $15.00)
ISBN: 1-58715-109-X (Hardcover, $30.00)

※

Nightscapes: Tales of the Ominous and Magical, by Darrell Schweitzer

A new collection of short stories, illustrated by Jason Van Hollander.

ISBN: 1-58715-060-3 (Hardcover $35.00)
ISBN: 1-58715-061-1 (Trade Paperback, $17.00)

※

The White Isle, by Darrell Schweitzer

Schweitzer's first novel, an alternate world fantasy as a young man masters the art of magic, then comes face to face with the dread god of death when his wife dies and he cannot bear to live without her.

ISBN: 1-58715-134-0 (Trade Paperback, $15.00)

ABOUT LLOYD BIGGLE, JR.
- *Classic science fiction author*
- *Writing career spans 4 decades*

All the Colors of Darkness, by Lloyd Biggle, Jr.
ISBN: 1-880448-742 (Trade Paperback, $15.00)

※

Watchers of the Dark, by Lloyd Biggle, Jr.
ISBN: 1-880448-75-0 (Trade Paperback, $15.00)

※

This Darkening Universe, by Lloyd Biggle, Jr.
ISBN: 1-880448-76-9 (Trade Paperback, $15.00)

※

The World Menders, by Lloyd Biggle, Jr.
ISBN: 1-880448-77-7 (Trade Paperback, $15.00)

※

Monument, by Lloyd Biggle, Jr.
ISBN: 1-58715-051-4 (Trade Paperback, $15.00)

※

The Still, Small Voice of Trumpets, by Lloyd Biggle, Jr.
ISBN: 1-58715-052-2 (Trade Paperback, $15.00)

※

The Fury out of Time, by Lloyd Biggle, Jr.
ISBN: 1-58715-053-0 (Trade Paperback, $15.00)

※

The Light that Never Was, by Lloyd Biggle, Jr.
ISBN: 1-58715-054-9 (Trade Paperback, $15.00)

※

Silence is Deadly, by Lloyd Biggle, Jr.
ISBN: 1-58715-055-7 (Trade Paperback, $15.00)

※

The Rule of the Door, by Lloyd Biggle, Jr.
ISBN: 1-58715-0328 (Trade Paperback, $15.00

ABOUT R.A. LAFFERTY
- **Nebula Award-winning author**
- **"Lafferty is a totally unique writer. That Wildside seems determined to reprint virtually all of his major work is cause for celebration." —Aboriginal SF**

Past Master, by R.A. Lafferty

A Hugo Award finalist, in which Sir Thomas More is resurrected on another planet to sort out the human condition. ("A minor miracle," Judith Merril wrote, "that a serious philosophical and speculative work could be written so colorfully and so lyrically.")

ISBN: 1-880448-99-8 (Trade Paper, $15.00)

※

Lafferty in Orbit, by R.A. Lafferty

This collection assembles all of Lafferty's stories from the anthology series *Orbit* in a single volume. Introduction by Damon Knight.

ISBN: 1-880448-68-8 (Trade Paper, $15.00)

※

Iron Tears, by R.A. Lafferty

Fifteen stories by R.A. Lafferty.

ISBN: 1-58715-127-8 (Trade Paper, $15.95)

※

Nine Hundred Grandmothers, by R.A. Lafferty

Perhaps the best introduction to Lafferty, this book contains many of his finest stories.

ISBN: 1-880448-97-1 (Trade Paper, $15.00)

※

Sindbad: The Thirteenth Voyage, by R.A. Lafferty

Short novel depicting the heretofore unknown thirteenth voyage of Sindbad, as only Lafferty could tell it!

ISBN: 1-880448-64-5 (Trade Paper, $15.00)
ISBN: 1-880448-91-2 (Hardcover $35.00)

※

Does Anyone Else Have Something Further to Add?, by R.A. Lafferty

Subtitled "Secret Places and Mean Men," this volume assembles more of Lafferty's unique stories.

ISBN: 1-880448-92-0 (Trade Paperback, $15.00)

※

The Devil is Dead, by R.A. Lafferty

"...an amazing fantasy like no other you've read. If Lafferty were Spanish this would be Magic Realism and the toast of the literati, who are missing this one, and all the rest." —*Aboriginal SF*

ISBN: 1-880448-95-5 (Trade Paper, $15.00)

※

Fourth Mansions, by R.A. Lafferty
ISBN: 1-880448-96-3 (Trade Paper, $15.00)

ABOUT PHYLLIS ANN KARR
• Popular short fiction writer

Idylls of the Queen, by Phyllis Ann Karr
Queen Guinevere is accused of murder!
ISBN: 1-58715-0123 (Trade Paperback, $15.00)

✳

Frostflower and Thorn, by Phyllis Ann Karr
First in a fantasy series following the adventures of the sorceress Frostflower and the warrior-woman Thorn...
ISBN: 1-58715-0131 (Trade Paperback, $15.00)

✳

Frostflower and Windbourne, by Phyllis Ann Karr
Second in the fantasy series...
ISBN: 1-58715-014X (Trade Paperback, $15.00)

✳

At Amberleaf Fair, by Phyllis Ann Karr
Death and deception at the annual fair land a toymaker in trouble for a murder he didn't commit...
ISBN: 1-58715-0158 (Trade Paperback, $15.00

ABOUT JOHN GREGORY BETANCOURT
• Best-selling Star Trek author
• More than one million books in print

The Blind Archer, John Gregory Betancourt
Betancourt's first novel. Ker Orrum longed for a life of magic. When an Oracle tells of a journey and a gem, his fate is sealed. Vowing to challenge the mighty god known as the Blind Archer, he sets out to win his fortune . . . and finds a destiny few would envy. Pawn to wizards and gods, blinded and helpless, he accidentally opens a gateway and sets an ancient evil loose on the world . . . an evil which only he can defeat!

"Ker is reminiscent of Ged of Earthsea and Paul of Dune. Rollicking adventure!"
—Jessica Amanda Salmonson, author of the *Tomoe Gozen Saga*
ISBN: 1-58715-0190 (Trade Paperback, $15.00)

✳

Johnny Zed, by John Gregory Betancourt
In an America only a few years away, Congress has seized power and eliminated the Presidency, ruling by decree. Small terrorist cells work ceaselessly toward the restoration of democracy, headed by the mysterious figure known only as "Johnny Zed".

Embraced by cyberpunk fans, adapted for gaming by role-playing gamers, *Johnny Zed* is an fast-paced political novel.
ISBN: 1-58715-0441 (Trade Paperback, $14.00)

✳

Rememory, by John Gregory Betancourt
Set in the same universe as *Johnny Zed*, and with some overlapping minor characters, *Rememory* follows a band of catmen (humans surgically altered to resemble giant cats) as they prowl the animalform underworld. When they steal a cargo from dogmen smugglers, though, they get more than they bargained for: a secret government shipment of decapitated heads, which hold a secret that just might topple the government!

"A fast-paced future mystery, more than worth the time to read." —*Locus*
ISBN: 1-58715-0204 (Trade Paperback, $14.00)

ABOUT BRIAN McNAUGHTON
• World Fantasy Award-winning author
• International Horror Guild Award-winning author

The Throne Of Bones, by Brian McNaughton
This book won the World Fantasy Award and International Horror Guild Award for Best Collection of the Year.

About *The Throne Of Bones*, Alan Rodgers writes in his introduction: "Imagine what Tolkien's *Lord of the Rings* would have been if Tolkien had tried to tell that story sympathetically from the point of view of the human denizens of Mordor. That's the book you hold in your hands. It's special stuff."

"McNaughton's world is a mixture of mythology and pre-history, a land of unpronounceable but strangely sensible names, a dark place filled with old caves in which to shelter from storms, ruined and empty cities and endless inhospitable deserts, through which all manner of hideous creatures roam—some vaguely human and others not vaguely anything—and all of them on the lookout for warm flesh... Either to eat or for some other reason too horrific even to consider." —Peter Crowther, *Interzone*
AVAILABLE MAY 30, 2000.

ABOUT ALAN DEAN FOSTER
• Internationally best-selling author
• Creator of the *Commonweath* series

Into the Out Of, by Alan Dean Foster
An African Massai *laibon* goes to America to find two special people and bring them back to Africa to stop an evil force from coming through to our world. One of Foster's very best novels, highly recomended.
ISBN: 1-58715-0476 (Hardcover $35.00)
ISBN: 1-58715-0484 (Trade Paperback, $17.00)

To the Vanishing Point, by Alan Dean Foster
The road to hell may be an Arizona highway!
ISBN: 1-58715-045X (Trade Paperback, $17.00)
ISBN: 1-58715-0468 (Hardcover $35.00)

The Man Who Used the Universe, by Alan Dean Foster

From crimelord to ruler of an interstellar empire, the tale of one man who can bring peace to the universe . . . But at his own price! One of Foster's very best works.

ISBN: 1-58715-0492 (Trade Paper, $17.00)
ISBN: 1-58715-0506 (Hardcover $35.00)

ABOUT CHRIS BUNCH
- **Best-selling fantasy author**

The Empire Stone, by Chris Bunch

First in a new fantasy trilogy, debuting in a limited edition (only 2500 copies) hardcover from Wildside Press.

ISBN: 1-58715-0565 (Hardcover $39.95)

ABOUT DAVID MASON
- **Classic fantasy author**
- **In the tradition of Robert E. Howard**

Kavin's World, by David Mason

In the grand sword & sorcery tradition of Conan, David Mason starts the saga of a new fantasy hero: Prince Kavin. Forced from his home by an unholy army, Kavin sets sail in a white ship to raise an army and regain his homeland. One of the finest books of its type.

ISBN: 1-58715-0654 (Trade Paperback, $15.00)
※

The Return of Kavin, by David Mason

Hundreds of years after the events in *Kavin's World*, a sorceror tries to bring Kavin back . . . but is this the same great warrior, or another entirely?

ISBN: 1-58715-0662 (Trade Paperback, $15.00)
※

The Shores of Tomorrow, by David Mason

Mason's only overtly science fiction novel, as a band of settlers are kidnapped from a parallel Earth, only to discover theirs is but one of of an infinite number of parallel worlds in the Multiverse. Winning their freedom, they set out to find they way home—and destroy the evil empire which captured them! One of Mason's best.

ISBN: 1-58715-0646 (Trade Paperback, $15.00)
★

The Deep Gods, by David Mason

He was just a norman man, until he got pulled into a fantastic universe . . .

ISBN: 1-58715-062X (Trade Paperback, $15.00)
※

The Sorceror's Skull, by David Mason
ISBN: 1-58715-0638 (Trade Paperback, $15.00)
※

ABOUT DAVID BISCHOFF
- **Popular science fiction author**

Philip K. Dick High, by David Bischoff

Quinn Roberts is a model teenager. This handsome high-school football quarterback has got everything going for him . . . Until he discovers his whole universe is a sham!

ISBN: 1-58715-0751 (Trade paperback, $13.95)

ABOUT LIN CARTER
- **Author of nearly 100 fantasy and science fiction books**
  - **Creator of *Thongor of Lemuria* and the *World's End* series**

The Man Who Loved Mars, by Lin Carter

An homage to the work of Leigh Bracket, depicting a impossible Mars of high adventure and romance.

ISBN: 1-58715-0301 (Trade Paperback, $14.00)
※

The Nemesis of Evil, by Lin Carter

The first "Zarkon, Lord of the Unknown" novel–a tribute to Doc Savage, full of fantastic pulp action/adventure!

ISBN: 1-58715-0573 (Trade Paperback, $14.00)
※

Invisible Death, by Lin Carter

The second "Zarkon, Lord of the Unknown" novel.

ISBN: 1-58715-0581 (Trade Paperback, $14.00)
※

The Volcano Ogre, by Lin Carter

The third "Zarkon, Lord of the Unknown" novel.

ISBN: 1-58715-059X (Trade Paperback, $14.00)
※

The City Outside the World, by Lin Carter
ISBN: 1-58715-0670 (Trade Paperback, $14.00)
※

Beyond the Gates of Dream, by Lin Carter
ISBN: 1-58715-0786 (Trade Paperback, $14.00)
※

Destination Saturn, by Lin Carter
ISBN: 1-58715-0794 (Trade Paperback, $14.00)
※

Tower of the Medusa, by Lin Carter
ISBN: 1-58715-0808 (Trade Paper, $14.00)
※

The Wizard of Zao (Kylix II), by Lin Carter
ISBN: 1-58715-0859 (Trade Paper, $14.00)
※

The Quest of Kadji, by Lin Carter
ISBN: 1-58715-0867 (Trade Paper, $14.00)
※

Tower at the Edge of Time, by Lin Carter
ISBN: 1-58715-093-X (Trade Paper, $14.00)

✳

Time War, by Lin Carter
ISBN: 1-58715-0948 (Trade Paperback, $14.00)

✳

The Black Star, by Lin Carter
ISBN: 1-58715-0956 (Trade Paperback, $14.00)

ABOUT ESTHER FRIESNER
- *Popular editor of the "Chicks in Chainmail" anthology series.*
- *Author of more than 20 fantasy novels*

Up the Wall and Other Stories, by Esther Friesner

The queen of comic fantasy shows her serious side, with the collection of Arthurian stories.
ISBN: 1-58715-0964 (Trade paperback, $15.00)
ISBN: 1-58715-097-2 (Hardcover, $35.00)

ABOUT ALAN RODGERS

New Life for the Dead, by Alan Rodgers

Rodgers' first short story collection assembles many of his best works, including the Bram Stoker Award-winner, "The Boy Who Came Back from the Dead."
ISBN: 1-58715-105-7 (Trade Paperback, $15.00)

✳

Ghosts Who Cannot Sleep, by Alan Rodgers

Rodgers' second collection of short fiction features some of the best stories from recent years, including "Mama Ghost." *"'Mama Ghost' really must be one of the best, and certainly one of the most disturbing, horror stories written during the last decade and a half."* —Peter Straub, Author of *Ghost Story*
ISBN: 1-58715-106-5 (Trade Paperback, $15.00)

ABOUT AMY STERLING CASIL
- *Winner of the Writers of the Future Competition*

Without Absolution, by Amy Sterling Casil

Without Absolution is Casil's first story collection. She is the only four-time finalist and winner of the Writers of the Future Contest, and frequent contributor to *The Magazine of Fantasy and Science Fiction*. Explore imagination's shores, from Mona Lisa's smile to the magic of a newborn's eyes.

Dave Wolverton calls Amy's work "powerful, compelling, and often gut-wrenching."
ISBN: 1-58715-117-0 (Trade Paperback, $15.00)

ABOUT BRUCE HOLLAND ROGERS
- *Two-time Nebula Award-winning author*

Wind Over Heaven, by Bruce Holland Rogers

The first collection from this two-time Nebula Award-winner ranges from the kitchen of a fine restaurant where the saucier cooks up alternative medicine to the battlefields of World War II, from secret societies of New Orleans during Mardis Gras to the predations of witches on Wall Street. Includes a story that won the Pushcart Prize and the Bram Stoker Award, plus two stories nominated for the Nebula Award. A tour de force from one of the hottest new writers in the field.
ISBN: 1-58715-118-9 (Trade paperback, $16.00)

ABOUT LOIS TILTON
- *Popular Star Trek author*
- *Best-selling horror novelist*

Written in Venom, by Lois Tilton

From Norse myth, this is the god Loki's story of revenge on Odin and the others who imprisoned him . . .
ISBN: 1-58715-1197 (Trade paperback, $16.00)

ABOUT TOM EASTON
- *Dr. Thomas A. Easton is Professor of Life Sciences at Thomas College in Waterville, Maine.*
- *By the author of Taking Sides: Clashing Views on Controversial Issues in Science, Technology and Society.*

Gedanken Fictions: That's Stories on Themes in Science, Technology, and Society, edited by Thomas A. Easton

A collection of classic science fiction stories dealing with classic themes sin science fiction.
ISBN: 1-58715-0697 (Trade Paperback, $17.50)

✳

The Electric Gene Machine, by Tom Easton
ISBN: 1-58715-070-0 (Trade paperback, $15.95)

The world is terrified of genetically modified foods, but Baby, you ain't seen nothin' yet! Genetic engineering is a technological infant, barely taking its first tiny steps toward a century of pumpkin houses, flying moving vans, sports cars that run away and go to sea, and garbage disposals that want careers as singers. And that's just the beginning of the future sketched in these stories and the five novels of Tom Easton's "Organic Future."

✳

Sparrowhawk, by Tom Easton

First volume of the "Organic Future" series.

The genetic engineers aren't about to stop with genetically modified food. It won't be long before they're playing with

houses and vehicles too, and someone is trying to kill gengineer Emily Gilman! The Chickadee at the bird feeder is the size of a Piper Cub, a Sparrow airliner is gobbling Buggies on the highway, a Mack truck is lunging across the sidewalk, and detective Bernie Fischer is flying his modified Sparrowhawk to the rescue.
ISBN: 1-58715-1200 (Trade Paperback, $15.95)

❋

Greenhouse, by Tom EAston

Second volume of the "Organic Future" series.

Can Tom Cross and his friends—including Freddy the ex-garbage disposal and professional singer—save his mother from the half-human flowers who are plotting to rule the world with the aid of genetically modified honeysuckle?
ISBN: 1-58715-1200 (Trade Paperback, $15.95)

❋

Woodsman, by Tom Easton

Third volume of the "Organic Future" series.

Freddy the Pig is now human, but the Luddite "Engineers" are determined to destroy him and all his genetically modified friends. If they can survive the concentration camps, there's a starship waiting. A prophetic foreshadowing of the current anti-genetic-engineering fervor.
ISBN: 1-58715-1227 (Trade Paperback, $15.95)

❋

Tower of the Gods, by Tom Easton

Fourth volume of the "Organic Future" series.

The gengineers have created a new intelligent species on the world of First-Stop, Tau Ceti IV. But before they can leave the Racs to their own destiny, Pearl Angelica, their plant-human hybrid emissary, must survive one last contact with Earth and its Luddite "Engineers."
ISBN: 1-58715-1235 (Trade Paperback, $15.95)

❋

Seeds of Destiny, by Tom Easton

Fifth volume of the "Organic Future" series.

Centuries after the gengineers left First-Stop to their creations, the Racs, Earth's anti-gengineering fanatics are on their way to hunt down the gengineers and destroy all their works. Fortunately the Racs are on the verge of space travel. They have a fighting chance, if they can just stop fighting over whether tailed or tailless Racs were the first creations of their gods and learn to use the heritage the gengineers left behind.
ISBN: 1-58715-1243 (Trade Paperback, $15.95)

❋

ABOUT KEITH ROBERTS
- **One of the most critically praised British science fiction writers**
- **Author of several classic novels, including *Pavane* and *The Chalk Giants***

Lemady, by Keith Roberts

A semificationalized autobiography, covering publishing in England in the 1960s.
ISBN: 1-58715-031-X (Trade Paper, $15.00)
ISBN: 1-880448-63-7 (Hardcover $30.00)

❋

Winterwood, by Keith Roberts

A collection of ghostly tales.
ISBN: 1-58715-082-4 (Trade Paper, $15.00)

❋

Kaeti & Company, by Keith Roberts

The first collection of Kaeti stories, one of Roberts' most popular and endearing characters.
ISBN: 1-58715-083-2 (Trade Paperback, $16.50)

❋

Kaeti on Tour, by Keith Roberts

The second Kaeti collection picks up where the first left off.
ISBN: 1-58715-084-0 (Trade Paperback, $17.50)

❋

The Grain Kings, by Keith Roberts

Collection of related science fiction stories.
ISBN: 1-880448-84-X (Trade Paperback)

❋

The Furies, by Keith Roberts

Classic SF novel of killer wasps gone wild...
ISBN: 1-880448-85-8 (Trade Paperback, $15.00)

❋

The Inner Wheel, by Keith Roberts
ISBN: 1-880448-86-6 (Trade Paperback, $15.00)

❋

The Chalk Giants, by Keith Roberts
ISBN: 1-58715-098-0 (Hardcover $35.00)
ISBN: 1-58715-099-9 (Trade Paperback, $15.00)

❋

The Furies, by Keith Roberts
ISBN: 1-58715-100-6 (Hardcover $35.00)
ISBN: 1-880448-62-9 (Trade Paperback, $15.00)

❋

Kiteworld, by Keith Roberts
ISBN: 1-880448-87-4 (Trade Paperback, $15.00)

❋

Grainne, by Keith Roberts
ISBN: 1-58715-131-6 (Trade Paperback, $15.95)

❋

The Lordly Ones, by Keith Roberts
ISBN: 1-58715-132-4 (Trade Paperback, $15.00)

PRAISE FOR THE ORGANIC FUTURE BY THOMAS A. EASTON

"Brilliant, compelling ... a fascinating bioengineered future!"
—Mike Resnick

"An interesting mix of hard science and wild speculation ... Fascinating action-adventure... A lot of fun."
—Otherrealms

"Well thought out ... Quite interesting."
—Locus

"A strictly human future in designer genes .. A lot of fun."

ABOUT AVRAM DAVIDSON

- *One of the most celebrated science fiction authors of all time*
- *Winner of the Hugo Award, the Edgar Award, and the World Fantasy Award*
- *"Davidson had one of the most original imaginations in the history of American SF and fantasy ... and he deserves to be enjoyed by generations of ordinary readers rather than left to the dubious mercy of SF academics." —Booklist*
- *"[Avram Davidson is] a true teller of tales." —Ray Bradbury*

Clash of Star-Kings, by Avram Davidson

On a remote mountain in Mexico, two alien forces, dormant for centuries, face off in a deadly confrontation that will decide Earth's fate!

On one side, the Great Old Ones, who had benevolently ruled the land in the days of the Toltecs, before the coming of the cruel Aztecs. On the other side, the Huitzili, who had come from the distant Evil Stars to teach the Aztecs conquest and war. In return, they demanded endless human sacrifice, human blood, and human hearts. And now, if they gain control of the awesome secret power within the mountain, they will plunge the entire Earth into endless barbarism!

ISBN: 1-58715-076-X (Trade Paperback, $15.00)

⁂

Joyleg, by Avram Davidson and Ward Moore

There are governments that want to know his secret. There is evidence that he is more than 200 years old. And indeed he does have a secret—one that will cause the history of the world to be rewritten!

Joyleg is a joyous prophetic novel, one of the first great science fiction collaborations and a recognized classic of the field.

ISBN: 1-58715-077-8 (Trade Paper, $15.00)

⁂

Ursus of Ultima Thule, by Avram Davidson

Swarthy, hairy, ostracized by others of his tribe, Arnten set off to lead a life of proud and lonely independence in his primitive world of Thule—Ultima Thule—where men huddled in animal skins against the arctic cold and used crude clubs and spears to kill the giant prehistoric animals that roamed the land.

But Arnten—"The Bear"—was quicker of body and sharper of mind than his fellow men, and he had a special destiny: a path beset with mortal dangers and evil witchery he

must overcome to save himself, his world, and his woman, from the evil one called "The Wolf."

Rich with weird beauty, mystery, and magic—this is a classic novel from one of the 20th centuries most acclaimed storytellers of fantasy and science fiction!

ISBN: 1-58715-136-7 (Trade Paperback, $15.00)

⁂

The Kar-Chee Reign and Rogue Dragon, by Avram Davidson

Earth was old, her riches gone. Her children had left her, all but a few who lived peacefully off the land.

And then came the Kar-Chee, to crack Earth open and suck out what remained of her richness, threatening the twilight of the old planet with an evil beyond anything that had gone before.

With them they brought their servants, beasts so cruel and horrible that men could recall their like only from ancestral nightmares, naming them "Dragons ..."

ISBN: 1-58715-137-5 (Trade Paperback, $17.50)

⁂

Rork!, by Avram Davidson

Ran Lomar wanted to be left alone. That's why he volunteered for duty on Pia 2, the most remote planet in the galaxy.

His assignment was simple. Redwing, a plant used as a medical fixative, grew only on Pia 2, and less and less was being harvested. Lomar's job was to find out why—and fix the problem at once.

It seemed like a simple job. But Lomar hadn't counted on the strange inhabitants of Pia 2—the Tacks, the Tame ones and the Wild ones, and the mysterious "rorks" that everyone feared!

ISBN: 1-58715-138-3(Trade Paperback, $15.00)

⁂

The Island Under the Earth, by Avram Davidson

"A world of living legend, peopled by centaurs, golems, harpies, and primitive but shrewd humans...all this in a mysterious realm of Starflux and Earthflux, closer to the primordial chaos than the world we know, and told in a style at once familiar and fantastic, homely and horrific. I was completely caught up in the saga." *—Fritz Leiber*

"It's always exciting to discover a new dimension in the work of a writer you think you know pretty well. The Island Under the Earth reveals that Avram Davidson is at one of those points of discovery and renewal. He's opened out into pure, funny, stimulating fantasy with something more than grace and easiness." *—Peter S. Beagle*

ISBN: 1-58715-139-1 (Trade Paperback, $15.00)

⁂

Masters of the Maze, by Avram Davidson

Nate Gordon entered the inner room, closed the door, pulled up the wall, stepped through, pulled it down after him.

He took five or six uncertain steps . . .

Afterwards, though how long afterwards he knew not, he came out in ancient Mesopotamia, where the priestess was waiting . . .

Then, ice and snow gusted on a plain where the great red mammoths fled away . . .

And he stood facing men with green beards at a strange crossroads on another world . . .

And the Maze had not yet done with him!
ISBN: 1-58715-140-5 (Trade Paperback, $15.00)

❋

The Enemy of my Enemy, by Avram Davidson

Jerrod Northi—pirate, rogue, and a citizen of Pemath—was desperate enough to go through the transformation.

It cost 100,000 units for the Craftsmen to endow him with the Seven Signs: green eyes, long fingers, long ears with tips, a smooth and hairless body, full mouth, slender feet, and a melodious voice. It was a rather steep price, even for Northi, but he would pay it somehow.

For Jerrod Northi had powerful enemies. Since being attacked by deadly leeris, he knew the cost of missing this opportunity to find refuge in the land of Tarnis might be even higher . . . perhaps even his life!
ISBN: 1-58715-141-3 (Trade Paperback, $15.00)

❋

Marco Polo and the Sleeping Beauty, by Avram Davidson & Grania Davis

Ten years in the service of Kublai Khan . . . Marco, Niccolo, and Maffeo Polo have seen magic and miracles—and accumulated riches beyond their wildest dreams. Yet all they now want is to return to their beloved Venice.

Unfortunately, as the only Westerners in the glittering Mongol court, they are favorites with the Khan of Khans. And before he will allow them to leave, they must undertake one strange, final quest...

Kublai is beginning to suffer the ravages of old age. Tales have reached him of a mysterious princess who sleeps forever, yet remains forever young . . . Surely she holds the secret of immortality.

Bring me the princess, he tells the Polos, *and you are free!*

"Marvelous! A kaleidoscopic Cathayan Nights' Entertainment, full of enchantments and wonders." *–Poul and Karen Anderson*
ISBN: 1-58715-142-1 (Trade Paperback, $15.95)

❋

Peregrine: Primus, by Avram Davidson
ISBN: 1-58715-143-X (Trade Paperback, $15.00)

Peregrine: Primus is a picaresque fantasy best described as the Davidsonian approach to the curiously modern amorality of the Dark Ages. It is the first of two novels describing the adventures of Peregrine, bastard son of the pagan king of Sapodilla, which, as all men know, was adjacent to both Navarre and to Pannonia, and was the last remaining bastion of pagan orthodoxy in what that generation considered the encroaching sea of Christian heathenism.

Peregrine: Primus is not only Avram Davidson at his best—but also a delightful approach to the other side of history!

❋

Peregrine: Secundus, by Avram Davidson

Once more Peregine discovers new friends and new adventures, in the classic sequel to *Peregrine: Primus.*
ISBN: 1-58715-144-8 (Trade Paperback, $15.00)

ABOUT GRANIA DAVIS
- **Frequest collaborator with Avram Davidson**
- **Acclaimed fantasist**

The Rainbow Annals, by Grania Davis

"Davis has written a novel that is an unalloyed delight—effortlessly readable, funny, touching, and enchanting in the way that only folklore and tall tales can be."
–Publishers Weekly

He came from a jeweled mountain in the center of the universe . . .

The Monkey Prince was a god of awesome power and curiosity who somersaulted through the dimensions of time to reach the harsh, snow-peaked Earthland of Dza. There he searched for the secret of Chos, key to perfect knowledge and compassion. And there he met the demoness Drolma, who took his heart in an instant and claimed it for all eternity.

Their passionate union spawned generations of mortals destined to follow in their exalted quest: to search for Chos, and to forever wage battle with the Black Shen, master of monsters, black magic, and nightmares—the evil destroyer of all love and wonder!
ISBN: 1-58715-149-9 (Trade Paperback, $15.00)

Moonbird, by Grania Davis

On an island near Bali lived a young man named Madai, a fisherman's son. One day he found a magical moonstone Garuda, who gave him healing powers, and took him flying to mythic realms. There he met the demoness Rangda, who tried to destroy the one he loved best. Now he had to choose between the joys of the flesh, or the shadow world of the spirits to save his beloved.

ISBN: 1-58715-150-2 (Trade Paperback, $15.00)

ABOUT S.P. SOMTOW
* *John W. Campbell Award-winner*

Forgetting Places, by S.P. Somtow
A sensative and touching story of a boy dealing with the death of his older brother. But when messages from the dead boy start arriving, it's the start of an adventure of self-discovery and healing. A brilliant break-through novel by the author of *The Aquilliad* and *Vampire Junction*.

ISBN: 1-58715-145-6 (Trade paperback, $13.95)

ABOUT RAY FARADAY NELSON
* *Mystery and science fiction writer*

The Ecolog, by Ray Faraday Nelson
ISBN: 1-58715-146-4 (Trade Paperback, $15.00)
✳
TimeQuest, by Ray Faraday Nelson
ISBN: 1-58715-147-2 (Trade Paperback, $15.95)
✳
Then Beggars Could Ride, by Ray Faraday Nelson
ISBN: 1-58715-148-0 (Trade Paperback, $15.00)

WILDSIDE FANTASY CLASSICS

Some Chinese Ghosts, by Lafcadio Hearn
A classic collection of ghost stories from Lafcadio Hearn.
ISBN: 1-58715-000-X (Trade Paperback, $15.00)
ISBN: 1-58715-0018 (Hardcover - $35.00)
✳
One of Cleopatra's Nights, by Theophine Gautier
A major fantasy collection from French author Theophile Gautier, containing his classics stories "The Mummy's Foot," "One of Cleopatra's Nights," and many more. Translated into English by Lafcadio Hearn.
ISBN: 1-880448-59-9 (Trade Paperback, $19.50)
✳
Well at World's End volume I, by William Morris
William Morris's classic fantasy, hailed as his masterpiece. One of the best fantasy novels ever written. Introduction by Lin Carter and John Betancourt
ISBN: 1-58715-088-3 (Trade Paperback, $17.50)
✳
Well at World's End volume II, by William Morris
The second (and concluding) volume of Morris's epic.
ISBN: 1-58715-089-1 (Trade paperback, $17.50)
✳
The Phantom Ship, by Capt. Frederick Marryat
The first—and perhaps definitive—novel about the Flying Dutchman of legend is a classic fantasy novel, long unavailable. Introduction by Darrell Schweitzer.
ISBN: 1-58715-090-5 (Trade Paperback, $17.50
✳
F. Marion Crawford - The Witch of Prague
Classic fantasy novel from the author of *Wandering Ghosts*.
ISBN: 1-58715-091-3 (Trade Paperback, $17.50)
✳
The Best of Weird Tales: 1923, edited by Marvin Kaye and John Gregory Betancourt
The best stories from the 1923 issues of *Weird Tales*, assembled for the first time (and many reprinted for the first time anywhere!) Includes work by H. P. Lovecraft, Farnsworth Wright, and many more.
ISBN: 1-880448-53-X ($12.00, trade paperback)

✳
Al Azif, by Abdul Alhazred
The legendary cursed book, now available in a facsimile edition. Introduction by L. Sprague de Camp.
ISBN: 1-58715-043-3 (Trade Paperback, $24.95)

H. Rider Haggard Classics...

Heu-Heu, or the Monster, by H. Rider Haggard
ISBN: 1-58715-151-0 (Trade Paperback, $19.50)
✳
Colonel Quaritch, V.C., by H. Rider Haggard
ISBN: 1-58715-110-3 (Trade Paperback, $19.50)
✳
Child of Storm, by H. Rider Haggard
ISBN: 1-58715-111-1 (Trade Paperback, $19.50)
✳
Jess, by H. Rider Haggard
ISBN: 1-58715-112-X (Trade Paperback, $19.50)
✳
Eric Brighteyes, by H. Rider Haggard
ISBN: 1-58715-026-3 (Trade Paperback, $19.50)
✳
Marie, by H. Rider Haggard
ISBN: 1-58715-028-X (Trade Paperback, $19.50)
✳
Queen of the Dawn, by H. Rider Haggard
ISBN: 1-58715-125-1 (Trade Paperback, $19.50)
✳
The Ancient Allan, by H. Rider Haggard
ISBN: 1-58715-103-0 (Trade Paperback, $19.50)
✳
Swallow, by H. Rider Haggard
ISBN: 1-58715-104-9 (Trade Paperback, $19.50)
✳
More H. Rider Haggard books are forthcoming. Sign up for our e-mail mailing list (on our web site, www.wildsidepress.com) to keep up with news of future releases.

BOOKS ON H.P. LOVECRAFT

A Subtler Magick: The Writings and Philosophy of H.P. Lovecraft, by S.T. Joshi

A comprehensive overview of H. P. Lovecraft's life and thought, followed by detailed discussions of all his major stories, from "The Tomb" (1917) to "The Haunter of the Dark" (1935), as well as chapters on Lovecraft's poetry, essays, and letters. Written by the leading scholar on Lovecraft and the editor of his collected fiction, essays, and poetry.

ISBN: 1-880448-610 (Trade Paperback, $19.95)

※

H.P. Lovecraft: Decline of the West, by S. T. Joshi

An exhaustive discussion of H. P. Lovecraft's philosophical thought—including his metaphysics, ethics, aesthetics, and politics—and its relevance to the understanding of his horror tales. Included are discussions of Lovecraft's atheism, his political evolution from monarchy to socialism, and his theory of weird fiction.

ISBN: 1-58715-0689 (Trade Paperback, $19.95)

About S.T. Joshi

- **Winner of Bram Stoker Award and the British Fantasy Award**
- **Leading authority on H.P. Lovecraft**
- **Author of numerous other studies on horror and fantasy writers**

BOOKS ON WRITING

On Writing Science Fiction: The Editors Strike Back! by George Scithers, Darrell Schweitzer, and John M. Ford

One of the best books ever written on writing commercial science fiction, with detailed commentary on the art of writing—and every topic is amply illustrated with an example short story which the editors originally purchased for publication in *Isaac Asimov's Science Fiction Magazine*. (Each is a first sale by its author). For someone interested in the craft of writing, this book is an excellent place to start.

ISBN: 1-880448-78-5 (Trade Paperback, $17.50)
ISBN: 1-880448-79-3 (Hardcover, $27.50)

About the Editors

- **George H. Scithers has won four Hugo Awards and one World Fantasy Award for his editing work, which spans 5 decades:** Isaac Asimov's Science Fiction Magazine, Amazing Stories, *and* Weird Tales.
- **Darrell Schweitzer is an accaimed author and critic as well as the current editor of** Weird Tales. **He won a World Fantasy Award for** Weird Tales.
- **John M. Ford worked on** Isaac Asimov's Science Fiction Magazine *before departing for a new career as a best-selling novelist. He won a World Fantasy Award for* The Sleeping Dragon.

PULP MAGAZINES

The Weird Tales Story, by Robert Weinberg

The history of *Weird Tales* magazine from 1923 to 1955, by one of the world's greatest authorities on pulp magazines. Includes chapters on the history of the magazine, the writers, the editors, and more—amply illustrated with photos, covers, and artwork from the magazine.

ISBN: 1-58715-1014 (Oversized Trade Paperback, $24.95)

※

The Moon Terror, by A. G. Birch

Originally published in 1927 in *Weird Tales* magazine, *The Moon Terror* is a fascinating period piece sure to interest all collectors of pulp fiction!

ISBN: 1-58715-113-8 (Trade paperback, $15.00)

※

The Best of Weird Tales: 1923, edited by Marvin Kaye and John Gregory Betancourt

The best stories from the 1923 issues of *Weird Tales*, assembled for the first time (and many reprinted for the first time anywhere!) Includes work by H. P. Lovecraft, Farnsworth Wright, and many more.

ISBN: 1-880448-53-X ($12.00, trade paperback)

※

Best of Weird Tales: The Termus Years, edited by John Gregory Betancourt

Selection of some of the finest stories from the most recent incarnation of *Weird Tales*. Authors include Robert Bloch, Ramsey Campbell, Brian Lumley, Tanith Lee, and many more—a virtual Who's Who of modern fantasy and horror! More than 500 pages of classic fiction.

No ISBN. ($8.00, trade paperback)

MUSIC AND COOKING

Mystic Rhythms: The Philosophical Vision of Rush, by Robert M. Price and Carol Price.

A detailed look at and analysis of the lyrics and philosophy of the rock band Rush.
ISBN: 1-58715-1022 (Trade Paperback, $15.00)

❋

Cooking Out of this World, edited by Anne McCaffrey

A cookbook written by science fiction writers (with many unusual yet delicious recipes!)—contributions from such luminaries as McCaffrey, Le Guin, Anderson, Ellison, Niven, Davidson, and many, many more. Beyond the recipes, you will find stories *about* the recipes and how they were invented, mixed with liberal doses of literary anecdotes, memoirs, and a lot of unique writing.
ISBN: 1-880448-432 (Trade paperback, $10.00)

❋

To Serve Man, by Karl Wurf

It's a real "cookbook for people," filled with cannibal recipes such as Texas Cowboy with Chili!

This book was published with the permission of Damon Knight, author of the classic story "To Serve Man" that was later adapted by *The Twilight Zone* TV show.
ISBN: 1-880448-823 (Trade Paperback, $14.00)

BOOKS ON LITERATURE

Pathways to Elfland, by Darrell Schweitzer

One of the first book-length studies of Irish fantasist Lord Dunsany, including looks at his most famous works, detailed listings of uncollected material, and scholarly analysis of themes and recurring imagery. First time in trade paperback.
ISBN: 1-58715-1332 (Trade Paperback, $17.50)

❋

Windows of the Imagination, by Darrell Schweitzer

The first collection of essays from the editor of *Weird Tales* magazine, covering everything from cults to fantastic literature in Schweitzer's always entertaining style.
ISBN: 1-88044-860-2 (Trade Paperback, $16.00)

❋

Discovering Classic Horror Fiction I, edited by Darrell Schweitzer

Essays on early horror writers: Arthur Machen, William Hope Hodgson, Walter de la Mare, Robert W. Chambers, H. Russell Wakefield, J. Sheridan LeFanu, August Derleth, more.
ISBN: 1-58715-0026 (Trade Paperback, $15.00)
ISBN: 1-58715-0034 (Hardcover , $30.00)

❋

Discovering Classic Fantasy Fiction, edited by Darrell Schweitzer

Essays on early fantasy writers: Dunsany, Cabell, A. Merritt, Collier, Blackwood, and L. Frank Baum.
ISBN: 1-58715-0042 (Trade Paperback, $15.00)
ISBN: 1-58715-0050 (Hardcover, $30.00)

❋

Discovering Modern Horror Fiction I, edited by Darrell Schweitzer

Essays on 20th century horror writers: Stephen King, Shirley Jackson, Ramsey Campbell, Russell Kirk, Karl Edward Wagner, Manly Wade Wellman, Roald Dahl, more.
ISBN: 1-58715-0107 (Trade Paperback, $15.00)
ISBN: 1-58715-0115 (Hardcover $30.00)

❋

Discovering Modern Horror Fiction II, edited by Darrell Schweitzer

More essays on 20th century horror writers: Peter Straub, Ray Bradbury, Fritz Leiber, Robert Bloch, Robert Aickman, Joseph Payne Brennan, Chelsea Quinn Yarbro, and many more.
ISBN: 1-58715-0085 (Trade Paperback, $15.00)
ISBN: 1-58715-0093 (Hardcover, $30.00)

❋

Speaking of Horror: Conversations with Masters of Horror, by Darrell Schweitzer

Interviews with famous horror writers, including Ramsey Campbell, Tanith Lee, Thomas Ligotti, Brian Lumley, William F. Nolan, Manly Wade Wellman, and F. Paul Wilson.
ISBN: 1-880448-815 (Trade Paperback, $15.00)

About Darrell Schweitzer

- *World Fantasy Award-winner*
- *Editor of Weird Tales magazine*
- *Popular fantasy author*

SCIENCE FICTION CLASSICS

Lancelot Biggs: Spaceman, by Nelson S. Bond

He was the nicest, most helpful spaceman on the Venus cargo run . . . and just happened to be the biggest menace in all of space! A cult classic science fiction novel, originally published in science fiction pulp magazines int he 1950s.
ISBN: 1-58715-152-9 (Trade Paperback, $15.00)
AVAILABLE AFTER MAY 30, 2000.

ABOUT KATHERINE MacLEAN
• **Nebula Award-winning author**

The Diploids, by Katherine MacLean
MacLean's first collection of short work, featuring the title story and 6 others. MacLean was a regular contributor to John W. Campbell's classic magazine *Analog*.
ISBN: 1-58715-128-6 (Trade Paperback, $15.00)

✳

Missing Man, by Katherine MacLean
The first novel from Nebula Award-winner Katherine MacLean, frequent *Analog* contributor, is an exciting future thriller.
ISBN: 1-58715-129-4 (Trade Paperback, $15.00)

✳ ✳ ✳ ✳
INFORMATION FOR
LIBRARIES AND BOOKSTORES

Bookstores: Wildside Press books are available through Ingram Distributors (usually as a special order). Wholesale orders should be placed through Ingram whenever possible. For more information, please contact: sales@wildsidepress.com

Libraries: You may order directly through Wildside Press, or through another company that deals with Ingram or with us directly, such as Brodart. For more information, please contact: librarysales@wildsidepress.com

QUANTITY	TITLE	PRICE
	SUBTOTAL:	
	In New Jersey? Please add 6% state sales tax. TAX:	
	$3.50 for the first 2 books, $1.00 per additional book. SHIPPING:	
	TOTAL:	

Enclosed is payment of $_____ paid via:

[ ] Check   [ ] Money Order   [ ] Credit Card

Credit Card No:_____

Exp: __ / __ Name on Card:_____

Order from:

WILDSIDE PRESS
P.O. Box 45
GILLETTE, NJ 07933-0045

Mail books to this address:

Name: _____

Address:_____

Address:_____

Address:_____

You can also order our books online! Visit our web site at www.wildsidepress.com

WILDSIDE PRESS
PO Box 45
Gillette, NJ 07933-0045
www.wildsidepress.com

FIRST CLASS MAIL

TO:

GAINFUL EMPLOYMENT
by Warren Lapine

Brin cursed as he raced through the forest after his horse. The damn beast seemed to delight in running off whenever it could. A few moments ago, Brin had spotted some strange tracks. He'd dismounted to check them out and off Fluffy had run. The only thing that made him feel more stupid than owning a horse named Fluffy was running through the forest shouting its name. He'd tried to rename the horse, but the stubborn animal refused to answer to anything else.

It wouldn't have been so bad, but Fluffy had picked the worst possible time to run away. This forest was dangerous and Brin had broken his sword, just below the hilt, chopping wood for a breakfast fire yesterday. He should have been using a hand ax, but he'd sold his so that he and Fluffy could eat. As an adventurer, Brin was a total failure. If he didn't find gainful employment soon, he might have to eat Fluffy. Things couldn't get much worse.

Wrong!

It began to rain. Brin's rusty chain mail started to feel like it weighed three hundred pounds. "Fluffy, when I get my hands on you . . ."

Brin's words died off as he ran smack into the biggest red dragon he had ever seen. Well, to be honest, it was the only dragon, of any color, that he had ever seen. The dragon turned its head to look at Brin as Brin scrambled to his feet, covered in mud.

"My, aren't we in a hurry," the dragon said menacingly. Without thinking, Brin drew his sword. The dragon laughed. "My friend, your sword has no blade."

Brin looked at the pommel in his hands and swallowed. The only option left, it seemed, was to run away.

"I wouldn't try and run if I were you," the dragon said. "You wouldn't get any farther than your horse did."

"You ate Fluffy?"

"Fluffy?"

"My horse."

"You named your horse Fluffy?"

"No, he already had the name when I bought him," Brin said defensively.

"I hope you didn't pay very much for him; he was a miserable little morsel. I'm still quite hungry."

"I don't suppose there's any chance that you'd consider letting me go?"

"Truthfully, you've come to me at precisely the right time."

"Oh?"

"Yes, I was just considering how best to go about hiring a knight, though you don't look like much of a knight."

"Don't let my appearance fool you," Brin lied. "I'm a damn fine knight."

"And Fluffy was a damn fine horse."

"Well, are you going to eat me or give me a job?" Brin demanded, letting his temper get the better of him.

"A bit testy, aren't we?"

"Well?"

"Have you heard of Jeras the Invincible?"

"Of course, who hasn't? He's the greatest swordsman that's ever lived."

The dragon snorted. "His reputation's a bit overblown. If you had the magic armor that he has, people might say that you were the greatest swordsman that ever lived."

"Hey wait a minute. If you're worried about Jeras you must be Dresbin, Bane of Knights," Brin said in disbelief.

If a dragon could be said to smile, Dresbin smiled. "Yes, I am Dresbin, called Knights' Bane. And you, my friend, are going to help me out of the predicament that I find myself in."

"You mean with Jeras?"

"Yes."

"I can't believe it! You're afraid of Jeras."

"I most certainly am not. Jeras is a popinjay. He doesn't go anywhere without his 'Gathering of Honor.' Haven't you ever wondered why he travels with all those other knights?"

"No."

"Well, he does it so that no one will call him out."

"Then what's your problem?"

"His armor and his new sword."

"New sword?"

"Yes, the wizard that enchanted the blade informs me that it will cut through my scales like butter."

"Why on earth did he tell you that?"

"For the same reason you humans do anything: greed. I paid him."

"You paid him for information?"

"Certainly."

"So, where do I come in?"

"I want you to pretend to kill me."

"Come again?"

"I want you to go through the motions of killing me."

"I must be missing something."

"Once Jeras says that he is going to do a thing he doesn't stop until he has done it. He's told everyone that he will not rest until I'm dead. With that blasted armor of his, I can't touch him. God knows I've tried. The two of us have done battle five times. It always ends the same. Neither of us can harm the other. But now that he has this new sword, Jeras has the upper hand."

"So?"

"Little man, you are dense. If I fight him again, he will kill me. If I run from him, he'll track me down and he will kill me. Now, if he thinks I'm dead, he'll find someone else to bother and I can move on to greener pastures."

"So what's your proposal?"

"In two weeks, Jeras should be arriving in Cramford. When he does, I want him to see you charge at me with a lance and strike me down."

"Won't he check to make sure you're dead?"

"Cramford sits on the bank of the Amasis river. You'll knock me into the river and I'll just drift away."

"Do you really think that will work?"

"Jeras is not a bright man. I'm sure it will work."

"What do I get out of this?"

"You get to live."

"In case you've forgotten, you ate my horse and I don't have a sword. I have to look like a knight of substance if I am to pull this off."

"Yes, I suppose you do. Come here, little man. You may pry three gems out of my scales as payment."

Brin moved up to Dresbin slowly and held his breath as he plucked three fist sized gems from Dresbin's scales. He didn't breathe again until after he had stepped back. Being this close to a dragon, even one that didn't plan to eat him, was taking its toll on Brin.

"Now, little man, meet me in Cramford in two weeks time. Should you fail me, you will wish you had never been born." With that, Dresbin took wing and disappeared.

Brin sat heavily on a log. He was working for a dragon; this was going to take some getting used to. Well, at any rate, it was gainful employment.

Two days later, Brin found himself in Cramford. The first thing he did was find a money changer. He had to turn these gems into currency.

The money changer looked up as Brin walked in. He didn't even try to hide his distaste. "I believe you are in the wrong establishment," he said icily.

Brin pulled out one of his gems. "No, I have the right place. I need this changed into currency."

The little, bald money changer took the gem from Brin impatiently and examined it, then turned purple and dropped his glasses. "Excuse me," he said, bending to pick them up. A few moments later he came back up with them. "I can give you one hundred gold pieces for this."

"One hundred gold pieces?" Brin said in mock outrage. "It must be worth a hundred times that!" He didn't believe that for a second, but haggling was haggling.

The money changer nodded. "Just checking, how about five thousand pieces of gold?"

"Five thousand?" Brin choked in disbelief.

"No, no of course not, then, seven thousand five hundred."

Brin's eyes bulged.

"You drive a hard bargain, young man. Ten thousand pieces of gold, that's my final offer."

"D-done," Brin finally managed to stammer.

Later he purchased the finest charger that he had ever seen. The horse's name was Thunder. Now that was a proper name. After buying new clothes, he purchased the best sword and lance that money could buy. Then it was time for armor. He entered the first armorer's shop he happened upon. A dwarf was busily making a suit of chain mail.

"Can I help you?" the dwarf asked politely.

"Yes, how much for a suit of chain no, make that plate mail."

"One thousand pieces of gold."

"Will platinum do?"

"Certainly," the dwarf said smiling.

"Good, I could never carry that much gold, too heavy you know." Brin counted out the money.

"Let me take some measurements from you and you'll have your mail in two months."

"I can't wait two months, I need the armor next week."

"Can't be done."

Brin counted out another thousand gold pieces worth of platinum coins and handed them to the dwarf. "I need the armor next week."

"Next week, you say. Then next week it is."

The week passed by slowly, but Brin didn't mind. He was having a good time getting used to being a wealthy, successful knight. Finally, however, his armor was ready. He'd never worn plate before. The stuff was heavy! But it was what all the respectable knights were wearing these days.

Then it was time to get to work. Brin practiced with his new weapons and horse every day near the river. He wanted to look convincing for his big performance.

By the third day he was starting to think he might be able to handle this knight business after all.

By the time Brin actually saw Dresbin flying towards Cramford, he was feeling downright cocky.

The cockiness lasted for all of three seconds. Houses began to erupt into flames as Dresbin passed. He sure was making this look convincing. People were running about screaming and crying in terror. Dresbin landed near the river bank and shouted, "Come, gentle knight, protect the good people of Cramford."

Brin could see a group of knights riding towards him at a full gallop. Jeras and his Gathering of Honor would be moments too late.

Brin took a deep breath and lowered his lance. "For King and Country," he shouted in his loudest voice and charged. Thunder didn't like the idea of charging at a dragon. It was all Brin could do to keep the horse on track. Thinking about it, Brin didn't much like the idea of charging Dresbin either. What if the dragon changed his mind? What if he decided to torch them? After all, if he waited until the last second to burn Brin to a crisp, it might still look as though Brin had managed to lance him just before being consumed by the dragon's breath. And as everyone knew, a dead man could tell no tales.

Brin and Thunder came closer and closer to Dresbin. Dresbin let out a roar and a jet of flame just missed Brin. The heat was tremendous. Then with a crash, Brin and Thunder collided with Dresbin. The impact threw Brin from the saddle and slammed him to the ground, knocking him cold.

Brin awoke to see Jeras kneeling over him. "He yet lives," Jeras shouted to his companions.

Brin moaned and looked about. "Where is the dragon? Did I kill it?"

"Yes, bold knight, you did indeed kill the dragon," Jeras answered. "I'm afraid you struck him such a mighty blow that his carcass slipped into the river and was washed away by the current. The fish shall feast tonight."

"Then I have no trophy? No proof that I killed a dragon?"

"Young knight, you didn't kill just any dragon, you killed Dresbin the mightiest dragon that ever lived. It is true, you have no trophy as proof of your noble deed; but, fear not, you have the word of Jeras that you killed Dresbin. No other proof is necessary."

"Yes, your word is all I need," Brin said, hamming it up.

"What is your name, most noble knight?"

"Brin."

"Then arise, Sir Brin, Slayer of Dragons."

Brin did so, appreciating the promotion. He tried to look as noble as possible.

"Brin, as I am sure you know, I travel with only the bravest and noblest of knights. I would be honored to have you among my honor guard."

"You mean a job?"

"I suppose you could call it that. I prefer to think of it as a Gathering of Honor." Ω

REFUGE
by Ken Rand

illustrated by Vincent Di Fate

Adjoa Oyono accepted the basket of enchanted threads from Daura Rumfa because she feared refusing the gift would displease the old fetish priestess. Who knew what wrath might spew from those wrinkled old lips if she became angered.

Besides, Daura had said, flashing a toothless smile, the blanket she wove would earn Adjoa the respect of Kairaba village women, and of women from villages all along the N'Goko River. Adjoa coveted such respect in the secrecy of her heart. But she was only the second daughter of the second wife of Osei Oyono, a poor fisherman with little stature in Kairaba affairs, and she was still unmarried even after some cousins had borne their second sons. Daura Rumfa knew many secrets, including the contents of Adjoa's heart. Daura Rumfa was never wrong.

Still, Adjoa felt apprehensive. Daura had never paid her much attention before. Why now? Adjoa hid her disquiet behind a smile, and as circumspect as she could manage, tried to learn — why now? Why me?

Daura did not answer Adjoa's probing questions. Or if she did, Adjoa did not understand the answer. The old crone often spoke her juju in riddles.

"But I don't understand," Adjoa said.

"I know, child-woman."

"But what does it do? The enchantment, what does it —"

"It is for a door, of course," Daura responded, brow furrowed in exasperation, knobby knuckles anchored on hips. "A door, you know, child-woman? You go through a door to get from *here* to *there*. You understand?"

Adjoa nodded, puzzled. Another soldier truck passed on the road beyond Kairaba's eastern edge, going north. The truck raised fine, red dust in a rooster tail that hung in the morning heat like fog. The soldiers sang a vulgar song.

Daura stood in the shaded doorway of Adjoa's mother's hut, her bent and bony frame propped against a walking stick as gnarled as she, and between phlegmy coughs, described how Adjoa must weave the threads into the blanket. "You must space the threads out as evenly as you can among the wool threads you already have. Weave them *this* way," her hands fluttered like wizened butterflies, "and *this* way, so they form a loose net, you understand? Make it so a grown person cannot touch the blanket without also touching at least one place where the threads cross one another. See the pattern?"

Adjoa said she understood, but Daura repeated her instructions again, as if Adjoa had not. Unconsciously, Adjoa touched the side of her too-large nose, as if to hide it.

She kept her gracious smile in place as she stood in the wake of the old crone's fishy breath and repeated the instructions back, word for word, until Daura nodded, satisfied. Then Daura gave her the basket of enchanted threads and hobbled away.

Adjoa sat in the shade of her mother's hut before her loom and watched the old woman go. Other villagers bade the woman greetings as she passed and she replied in her grizzled way, cheery to this one and curt to that, not at all to another.

When Daura disappeared back into her own hut beneath the old mangroves near the riverbank, the women of Kairaba converged on Adjoa. "What did old Daura give you?" they asked. "What did she want?"

Adjoa lifted the basket and showed them. "She gave me these threads and bade me weave them into my new blanket." Adjoa had just started a new blanket to replace the old tattered and patched one now hanging across her mother's hut's door. "She told me how to do it."

Eyebrows rose among the women as they chattered. "Why did she do this?" one said. "Why didn't she give this to someone else?" another said. None said "Why you, granddaughter of a slave?" But Adjoa could see the question in their eyes, the tilt of their head and the tone of their voice. She touched her nose and looked away.

Adjoa knew her neighbors didn't respect her. Her ancestry, her ugliness, and her unmarried status offended them. They didn't respect her as a weaver and her father was poor. Now the old juju woman paid attention to her. Perhaps they

were jealous. In her secret heart, Adjoa smiled. She shifted her iro higher over her breasts and straightened her back.

"She said the threads were enchanted."

Eyebrows rose until the whites of the women's eyes showed. Jaws dropped and the women chattered with animation. They probed Adjoa with more questions, speculated when she shrugged, unable to answer them.

"Go ask Daura yourself," Adjoa said. "She wouldn't answer me." She knew none would dare. None did.

In time, the women disbursed to their own activities, leaving Adjoa alone. The sun rose higher and she shifted the tarp under which she sat for shade. Another soldier truck rumbled past, heading to the war up north. The soft road dust lifted by the truck's passing drifted west, across the village and toward the river.

She examined the tarp weave as she shifted it. A poor weave. She sighed and admitted to herself that she was indeed a poor weaver.

And of questionable heritage.

So why me? And what enchantment am I being asked to weave into my mother's doorway?

Adjoa sat and examined the threads in the basket. They were thick and dark, tacky, like tar-coated vine. The threads smelled oily. They smelled like something dead.

No, not vine, Adjoa decided. The gut of some small animal, stretched to a fine thinness, dried but still supple, and coated with tar or something like tar. Adjoa could not say from which animal the gut-threads had been taken. She pictured in her mind the animals she'd seen villagers, including her father and uncles, lay before Daura's door, wart hog, monkey, and cane rat among them. She knew the old woman often wore antelope hides like a cloth iro, and used baboon knuckle bones to cast fortunes. She wore a necklace of owl's feet. But she couldn't guess the source of the threads she'd been told to weave into her new blanket.

What would her mother say? Would she be angry? Even if so, Adjoa could not have refused the priestess without insulting her.

She wove, setting the juju threads in place this way and that way, just as the old crone had instructed.

She had made progress on the blanket, a quarter of the way done, when the sun began dropping behind the sapele and obeche trees across the N'Goko River. The air glowed red in the dust hanging foglike over Kairaba from the constant passage of soldier trucks taking more government troops north. She abandoned the loom and joined her sister and mother in preparing the evening meal. Her mother, Jankeh, and her father's first wife, Sireng, had spent the day at market, but they had heard about the priestess's morning visit to Adjoa. The women's interest showed like cankers, more pronounced because they said nothing about it, as the women worked at the oven baking catfish and rice cakes.

Adjoa's father, Osei, joined the family just before sunset, a net half full of perch and catfish over one shoulder. He sat and ate, talking with two brothers and several older sons and their cousins. They talked about the war up north, things their neighbors on the river had heard on the radio at the village a few kilometers south where the electricity ended. Chief Yakubu stopped by and chatted.

As the women cleaned up, Osei spoke at last to Adjoa. "What's this I hear about Daura giving you something today?"

The children were shooed off under the care of Binta, Adjoa's sister. Both Osei's wives stayed to listen.

Adjoa told her story and showed her father and her family the blanket she'd started on. The women wrinkled their noses at the faint dead-something odor in the enchanted weave.

Osei gave a look to the chief, and to his kin, silently asking them to leave so he could confer with his spouses and child in private. They left.

Sireng nodded, brow furrowed and lips turned down. "Daura could not help when my first boy-child died."

"But our fishing has been good," Osei reminded her. "Our catch has always been as good as other's." They all spoke in whispers in the doorway of the hut. It rained.

"I have not been blessed with sons," Jankeh complained.

"Jankeh, my second wife," Osei said, "Our youngest daughter will marry well, I think."

A silence followed. No one needed to speak for Adjoa to hear the unspoken: "But our eldest daughter will never marry." Adjoa touched her nose.

A jet airplane roared by, unseen above the rain clouds. Heading north.

"My husband and honored first wife," Jankeh said, "all Daura does is not good." She did not use the word "black magic," but those listening knew what she meant.

"And Daura didn't say why this enchantment?" Osei asked.

"No, father," Adjoa said. "It's for the door, she said. That's all she would say."

"This may not be a good thing," Sireng said, ample bosom rising in a sigh.

Adjoa's mother and father nodded in agreement. They looked around to see if anyone observed their conference. Except for the patter of rain, the ever-present calls of jungle life, the bells on a few goats tethered near, and the occasional chicken clucking, the village of Kairaba stood silent.

"You must not hang this blanket over the door," Osei said to his second wife.

Jankeh nodded, silent, obedient.

"But father —" Adjoa began.

Osei turned eyes burning with disapproval on his daughter. The ugly one.

Adjoa gulped in a dry throat, took a breath, and pressed on. "Daura gave the threads to me. She gave them. To me. Wouldn't she be angered if I didn't do as she bade?"

Silence followed.

"It would not be good to anger her," Osei said.

"What must we do?" Jankeh asked, a nervous quake in her voice.

"We must find out why she wants Adjoa to cover our doorway with this enchantment."

"How do we do that?" Jankeh persisted.

Again, silence reigned.

Osei spoke. "Adjoa, you know you are not the best weaver in Kairaba."

Adjoa nodded.

"No one would be surprised if you took long to weave this blanket. Take a long time. Make mistakes, even more than you usually do. Start over. Often."

"What will this accomplish?" Jankeh asked.

"Daura will not know if Adjoa is deliberately going slow or if the slowness comes from poor craftsmanship. She may suspect we've conspired to delay her juju. She may then speak to Adjoa, maybe say why she wants this thing done."

Sireng nodded. "I can call Adjoa away from her weaving often to help in my kitchen."

"And my net is old," Osei added. "Perhaps it will need mending soon."

Osei and Sireng looked at Jankeh, who shrugged. "I too will discover ways to delay Adjoa's weaving. Maybe this will work. Maybe Adjoa will then say why she wants this enchantment done on our doorway. But what if —"

Again, an eloquent silence descended.

"It is decided," Osei said. "We will do this."

The family went to their beds. From the north came the low rumble of artillery. Or perhaps it was just thunder. The night was warm, but Adjoa felt a chill. The rain ceased.

In the morning, Daura hobbled by to check on Adjoa's weaving progress. She peered through watery eyes at the blanket, the weave uneven, sloppy. She did something fluttery with her owls' feet necklace, uttered a phlegmy cough and whispered to Adjoa: "Respect of all, child-woman. Remember. Respect of all."

Adjoa found herself minutes later industriously working at the blanket, her family's scheme forgotten.

It wasn't until Sireng returned from the river, a bundle of wash atop her head and little Abubakar asleep against one hip, that Adjoa realized she'd forgotten to slow her weaving to provoke some revelation from the juju woman.

"Help me with the wash," Sireng demanded. Her tone brought Adjoa out of her concentration on weaving, made her suddenly aware of the concentration. How long ago had she spoken to the crone? The sun had climbed above the tall palms and she now sat outside their shade. That long.

Embarrassed and annoyed with herself, Adjoa joined Sireng sorting the wash and putting it away. As she did so, she thought, and realization came: Daura had enchanted her, forcing her to concentrate on weaving.

Or something like that.

Yes, she decided, that must be it. Her own desire to earn the respect of all Kairaba women had nothing to do with her industriousness. Nothing at all.

Still, she found herself rushing to help sort and put away the wash. While this annoyed Sireng, she could think of nothing more to keep Adjoa busy and further delay the weaving, so she dismissed Adjoa after a while: "Remember. Work as slowly and as poorly as you can. Accept any excuse to do something else. I'll try to find ways to call you away."

Adjoa nodded, expression grim. Then she hurried to the loom; her hands and feet became blurs.

More trucks passed north on the road outside Kairaba. Among the troop trucks, Adjoa saw a few ambulances. The air became heavy with dust. Rain fell and cleared the air.

Soon, Jankeh came by Adjoa's loom and bade her help with the marketing. This took all afternoon and Adjoa didn't return to the loom until almost dark. She had just sat down for a few passes of her shuttle before dark when Sireng called her to help with the evening meal.

So, the process continued for a few days. Adjoa would rise with the sun, begin a few lines on the loom, get called away for some task by her mother or Sireng and return to the loom only to be called away a few minutes later for some other domestic chore that required her assistance.

The days passed hot and wet.

Daura visited often, and her promises to Adjoa of earning the respect of Kairaba women became more urgent as the blanket remained unfinished.

More troops went north and a few ambulances returned south.

"You will earn the respect of —" The old woman stopped and stood back from Adjoa, peering down her long nose. "It isn't working. You don't care if others respect you or not, do you? That is why you work so slowly. Isn't it? You are not interested in being respected."

Adjoa stopped weaving. She refused to meet Daura's eyes. She couldn't speak.

"So," Daura said. "This is good. Better than I expected. You'll do well. Perhaps. The truth, then; would it encourage you to work harder, faster, if I told you the truth about these threads, what they're for?"

Adjoa nodded, still afraid to speak.

"Hmph. Just so, then. I will tell you a story —"

The old woman coughed and the cough racked her body. Adjoa stood patiently, hands folded, until the fit passed and Daura spat a wet, gray, thumb-sized lump on the ground.

"A story," Daura rasped. "There once was a cane rat who lived on the banks of the Sanga. This cane rat was ugly. He had a hunched back and a nose like yours. He was skinny, not like his plump cousins.

"Now it happened that a cobra came to live along the banks the Sanga, where it had heard that there were many fat cane rats to eat. When the fat cane rats heard that the snake was coming to eat them, they became frightened. 'What should we do?' they cried.

"The ugly cane rat was not frightened. He spoke up and invited everyone to hide in his burrow.

" 'Why should we hide in your burrow?' his cousins asked.

" 'Because I will stand outside and tell the snake that you are all hiding in my burrow. He will laugh at me and say, "Nobody would hide in your burrow. You are too ugly." Then he will go away because I am also too skinny to eat.'

"So his cousins hid in the ugly cane rat's burrow, the snake came, the ugly cane rat told him his cousins were hiding in his burrow, the snake laughed and went away."

It took a moment before Adjoa realized Daura had finished. "I don't understand."

Daura gripped her elbow. It hurt. She drew nose to nose with Adjoa, sunken eyes burning, breath like dead fish. "The soldiers. They're coming. You must work quickly. You must hang the blanket —"

The old woman doubled over, spasmed by another coughing fit. She shook her head as Adjoa moved to help, struggled to speak again but gave it up. She hobbled away, coughing and ashen-faced, back to her own hut.

From the north, Adjoa heard rumbles. She saw clouds, but she knew the rumbles were not thunder.

That evening, Adjoa told her family the story Daura had told her. They discussed it for a while but came to no conclusion. Osei went off to talk with Yakubu.

The next day, Adjoa rose before the sun and went to her loom, weaving as fast as she could in the predawn dark. Her mother found an errand before the morning meal and kept her busy all morning. Adjoa worked on the loom between chores and errands. By nightfall, the blanket was almost finished.

Daura hadn't visited all day.

Daura often stayed inside her hut for days at a time, her presence evident only in a thin curl of pungent smoke escaping through the peak of her roof, and her chanting in Hausa and French drifting across the village like bird twittering. But today the village gossips found the priestess's hut quiet.

Even the chief looked concerned. Yakubu had gone to her hut, stood at her door, and called. "Daura? I would talk with you about something important. Will you come out and sit in the shade with me, or will you let me come in?"

She seldom let anyone enter her hut. She enjoyed sitting in the shade of an iroko tree and chatting with the chief and others. But she did not answer.

Nobody dared even whisper that the old woman had died. For a reason she could not name, Adjoa feared she had.

That fear grew deeper and harder in Adjoa's stomach, until she had to go see. Had to.

She'd been told to stop weaving to tend to her infant cousin Abubakar while her mother traded with a peddler who rode his bicycle up and down the road along the river, selling needles, buttons, mirrors, knives and other things. She knew Jankeh could have taken the baby with her, that leaving Abubakar with her was just another way to delay the weaving. She had nodded obediently, left the loom and took the child.

As soon as her mother disappeared among the huts east of the village toward the road, Adjoa hiked Abubakar on her hip, shifted her iro above her knees with the other hand, and ran to Daura's hut.

Without thinking or pausing to gather courage, Adjoa pushed back the blanket over the doorway and entered the hut.

She let the blanket fall back into place and stood a step inside the door, listening, letting her eyes adjust to the windowless dark. She remembered to breathe. "Daura?" she whispered, heart in her throat. The air hung stagnant, stifling, and Adjoa broke out in sweat. The room stank of urine, dead things, and rotted fruit. In the dark, she heard a rasping, like a dog snoring.

Abubakar whimpered softly.

Outside the door, the usually bustling village had gone quiet. Adjoa knew her neighbors watched, waiting for her to report on whatever she'd found inside Daura's hut.

As Adjoa's eyes adjusted to the lightless interior, she looked around. She saw metal and clay cooking pots at the center of the room by the oven. A low wooden table sat to one side, littered with pots, baskets, glass jars, and tin cans. Leaves, roots and bark of various kinds stuck out of the containers like a tiny jungle and littered the floor nearby.

She smelled dried kaga nut paste, heard beads clatter as a lizard darted somewhere in the gloom, saw a string of snake heads dangling against a back wall. Owls' feet. A long tail; lion maybe. A cluster of horns. A large dried skin tacked against a side wall. A basket of cassava flour.

The snoring sound came again. It came from a hide pile at the far side of the hut. The hides moved.

"Daura?"

A phlegmy grunt answered.

Adjoa settled Abubakar into a fold of her iro to free her hands. She stepped forward until she stood over the hide mound where, she now could see, Daura lay.

Daura lay naked, flaccid breasts barely moving

with each labored breath struggling from her bony chest. Her eyes were glazed over as if coated with river slime and her hand and mouth jerked and spasmed as if of their own will.

It occurred to Adjoa that Daura lay in a juju trance and she ought to run away. Run, before whatever thing Daura was conjuring got her, or before Daura awoke and became angered that Adjoa had invaded her hut. After all, she'd only come to find out if Daura was alive. Nothing more. She could leave, tell the chief, her mother and neighbors —

Suddenly, a bony hand flew out to grab Adjoa's wrist.

Adjoa stifled a scream. She tried to jerk away from the cold, skeletal thing holding her, but could not.

"Is it finished?" the old crone rasped.

"What?"

"The blanket — the door. Is it finished?"

"No, Daura. But only a few —"

"Finish it. *Finish it.*" Daura's fingers bit into Adjoa's wrist, hurting her.

"I will, Daura. I promise."

"Quickly. *Quickly*, do you hear?"

"Yes, Daura, I —"

"They're coming." Daura's lips twitched, spittle flying.

"Who? Who's coming?" Adjoa wanted to leave, to run. But the bony hand imprisoning hers held fast, a steel band. Abubakar began fidgeting, whimpering.

"The soldiers. From the north."

"That's good, isn't it? Then the war is over? We won?"

"No. The others. The soldiers flee."

"Oh." Adjoa fought for breath, for words. "But surely, they'll just go by, to the city. Surely, they'll —"

"Burn, rape, murder, torture. And then the rebels come. More death, more pain."

"Maybe if we're quiet —"

"I've seen them. *Seen* them, you hear? No soul behind their empty eyes, no heart behind their howling, like hyenas. Blood coating their hands and arms. They are coming. Soon." Daura's voice had risen, become more powerful with each word.

"What must I do?"

"Finish it."

"The blanket?"

"The door. Finish it. *Quickly*. Hang it across the door of your hut. Then bid all to enter. *All.*"

"But my hut is small. How —"

Daura's hand dropped away, a shuddering

dead leaf. "Enchanted. Room for all." The old woman seemed to wither, weakening even as Adjoa watched.

Adjoa felt dizzy. The air hung still, hot. She had questions to ask before Daura died. She felt ghoulish in asking, but Adjoa felt the old woman's terror — and that prompted an urgency that overrode her own discomfort, her need to see to Abubakar, who'd relieved himself down Adjoa's back.

"I will finish it. But why? Why me? Why not Yakubu? People will believe their chief. They will not follow me."

"Remember the ugly cane rat? Do as he did. Tell Yakubu. He knows the story. He will believe."

"I will tell him." Adjoa turned to go. At the door, she hesitated. "But why me? Is it because I'm —"

"Because you are ugly, like the cane rat, like me? I am ugly because I am old, dying. But I have always been ugly. That is why I am a priestess. When I was your age, I met a juju man who taught me. You can be juju. If you want. But that is not why I chose you."

"Then why —"

"Because you care. You have a good heart."

Daura said nothing more and Adjoa stood silent for a moment ignoring the whining baby on her back. Daura had gone still and Adjoa felt sure she'd died. She shivered. Outside, she heard her neighbors rustle and mutter, waiting.

Adjoa pushed back the blanket over the hut door, where Osei, Sireng and her mother stood, eyes filled with concern. Behind them, it seemed the entire village stood, waiting.

Adjoa handed Abubakar to her younger sister, Binta, who took the baby to the river to clean him. Adjoa's mother started to speak, shook away the words, and reached for her daughter, hugging her.

Yakubu spoke. "We could hear you. We could hear her too, but we couldn't make out the words. What did she say?"

In the shade of an iroko tree, Adjoa told her family, neighbors and Yakubu what Daura had said. She left out no detail. The villagers talked at length about it.

They argued. Some men, including Osei and several of Adjoa's uncles, vowed to fight if soldiers or rebels came into the village as Daura predicted they would. Others said they would flee into the jungle or take their boats down river. No one said they would hide in Adjoa's mother's hut.

"But if you believe what Daura says about the war coming here," Adjoa said, "why don't you believe when she says you can hide safely in my mother's hut behind the enchanted blanket Daura bade me weave?"

"Adjoa," Osei said, warning in his voice. Osei glared at her with disapproval before Adjoa realized she'd spoken without being asked. She touched her nose and bowed her head, pulling her ori tight around her knees. She felt thankful the sun had fallen beyond the N'Goko and no one could see her face.

"I believe," Jankeh said.

"And I," Binta said.

A few others joined in, but not many. Only women. "Adjoa," Osei said, "you may go."

Adjoa rose, nodded to her father and mother without meeting their eyes and walked back to her loom, silence behind her; she felt the villager's eyes boring into her back.

She'd wanted to talk about Daura. She wanted to go back into her hut and see if she'd died. But she could no more ask about it, ask what to do, than she could disobey her father.

Adjoa's fingers and feet soon became lost in the soothing rhythm of weaving. Only a few rows remained before the blanket was done. She worked fast in the dark.

It started to rain. Above the rain's hiss, Adjoa heard a truck approaching from the north. She heard the truck's brakes squeak to a stop on the road beyond the fringe of palm trees and bamboo at the eastern edge of the village. Men shouted.

Gunfire.

Screams.

Adjoa's heart rose to her throat as she stood. Several village men ran past toward the road, including Yakubu and Osei. Some carried machetes. Adjoa stood frozen, listening to men shouting and cursing, women screaming in the near distance. And the stuttering pop-pop-pop of gunfire.

Before she heard the truck roar away, Adjoa fought back an urge to run away and hide in the jungle, or run to the road, to see what had happened. Instead, she sat back down at the loom. She forced her shaking hands to do their job, weaving, weaving, mechanically, feet dancing. She had to finish the blanket. Quickly.

She did not look up as villagers passed, returning from the road and the senseless slaughter there. She heard women wailing, men cursing and old Kobina screaming in pain. She listened but did not look up.

Yao and uncle Kwesi dead, and old Kobina wounded, a bullet in his leg. The soldiers were drunk, she heard someone say. Deserters, another said. More are coming. The rebels aren't far behind.

Daura had been right.

The rain stopped.

Adjoa's fingers blurred across the loom, her fingers and arms ached, thighs and calves burned, sweat poured into her eyes and she blinked furiously but did not stop weaving.

She felt a cloth dab at her forehead, saw her mother out of the corner of her eye.

Adjoa nodded thanks but her fingers continued weaving.

"Can we not cover the doorway now?" Jankeh asked.

"No," Adjoa said. "Daura said it must be finished."

"How soon?"

"Soon."

From the corner of her eye, Adjoa saw villagers gathered around, felt more standing behind her. She heard babies wailing, Kobina's painful cries, a few women weeping.

"I have brought Daura," Adjoa heard Yakubu say. She did not look up. She heard a low rumbling from the north. More trucks coming.

Quickly. Quickly.

"Finish, child-woman," Daura hissed, voice like dry rushes in a hot wind. "Quickly."

Adjoa nodded, hands and feet flying. She felt relief, knowing the fetish priestess still lived, but she did not look up or hesitate. The truck noise grew louder, closer.

"You all must go into the hut," Daura said. "When the blanket is hung, all must go inside. *All.* Do not look out. Stay inside until you have all slept seven times."

Adjoa heard muttering, heard Yakubu shushing the mutterers.

"Seven times. No less. I have seen, do you hear? I have seen. Not just the soldiers and the rebels burning, killing. Not just here and at the other villages along the river. I have seen a fire in the sky. A poison toadstool grows in a land far, far away. It is made of light and death. It grows so high it touches the stars and shoots off deadly spores. The spores drift from a far away land across the ocean beyond the capital. The spores descend on the village, bring death to men, women, animals — all living things. Many toadstools, bringing death to the whole jungle. I've seen it."

"America," someone said. "Atomic bombs," another said.

Yakubu shushed them.

Truck lights could be seen a half kilometer to the north.

Adjoa finished the blanket and stiff arms dropped to her side. Sireng pulled it from the loom and handed it to Adjoa's mother. Jankeh pulled the old blanket away from the doorway, tied the new blanket in place and people began streaming into the hut. They didn't push or jostle. They moved quietly through the hut doorway, fearful eyes darting toward the north and east before they disappeared inside.

Adjoa sat frozen with fatigue before her loom, watching the people enter her mother's hut. *How can they fit in there?*

A few trucks roared past on the road. Adjoa heard some stop.

She struggled to stand on numb legs. Yakubu gripped her elbow, steadying her. Adjoa noticed Yakubu carried Daura's frail body in his other arm like a baby.

Adjoa nodded thanks as she found her feet, walked shakily to the doorway. As she lifted the blanket to enter, she heard soldiers shouting from the other end of the village by the road. Gunfire.

"I will stay," Daura said to Yakubu, who stood right behind Adjoa, ready to enter the hut.

"No, Daura, you —"

"To tell the soldiers you are all inside. If I do not, how can they not believe me and go away?"

"But Daura —"

"*Put me down.*"

Yakubu put the old priestess down in front of Adjoa's mother's hut's doorway and stepped inside the hut behind Adjoa.

Adjoa and Yakubu squatted behind the blanket, listening.

They heard the soldiers whooping, cursing, firing their rifles. They heard a soldier ask Daura where everybody had gone. They heard Daura tell them the villagers had all hidden in the hut where she sat. They heard men laughing.

They heard a gunshot.

In time, the shouting and shooting died down and the soldiers could be heard driving away. Through chinks in the hut walls, Adjoa could see huts burning.

"Will my hut catch fire?" Jankeh asked, voice trembling.

"I don't think so," Adjoa said.

"What will happen?" Osei asked.

Adjoa looked up from where she squatted inside the doorway. Her father had asked for her opinion. She stood, facing him in the shadows cast by the light from the fires outside the hut. Behind and around her father and her family, she saw moving shadows; the villagers standing, sitting and squatting in family groups. A baby squalled somewhere and old Kobina whimpered in dull pain. The walls near the door were dim, and she couldn't see the familiar contour of the ceiling above her, but Adjoa felt as though the comforting closeness of the hut where she'd spent her whole life had somehow expanded. She felt dizzy, as if standing on the edge of an endless savanna. When she spoke, it sounded as though she stood outside under the stars, rather than inside a small hut.

"We will stay here. We will not look out. When we have all slept seven times, we will go out. Just as Daura said."

Nobody spoke.

In time, families wandered farther into the hut's shadowy depths to claim their own space. Adjoa wandered around and discovered each family had settled twenty to thirty meters from the next family. Some women had brought food with them and Jankeh had a full larder. They had little, but everyone shared. No one felt like eating much anyway.

Before everyone slept that first night, Yakubu asserted his leadership and men dug a latrine for all to use against the hut wall several hundred meters away from the door. The next day, the space by the door became the village meeting place, where Yakubu sat and spoke with the men.

Sometimes, Adjoa would sit with the men and sometimes they would ask her opinion on this or that. They didn't talk about the visions Daura said she'd seen and they didn't talk about the war or the shooting and killing they'd witnessed or heard. They talked about childhood memories, told stories and played games. Or they sat in silence, content to be together, safe. When they spoke, the villagers spoke softly.

Even children stifled their playful shouts. The younger ones sat quietly in the arms of mothers, sisters, or aunts. None cried.

The hut interior never brightened, as if the sun never rose outside.

Old Kobina slowly recovered from his wound and began hobbling about on a walking stick his wife fashioned for him.

On the morning of the eighth day, after the villagers had slept inside their refuge seven times, Yakubu pushed back the blanket covering the hut door and squinted into the bright light of day outside. Adjoa stood looking past his shoulder, her father and family clustered close and the other villagers gathered around, close.

The air smelled humid and musty. Monkeys chittered. A dog barked somewhere and chickens pecked and clucked at the ground before the door.

Yakubu stepped out, Adjoa on his heels. The others followed.

The jungle had overgrown the village and all the huts except Jankeh's had vanished as if they had never been. On the ground two meters in front of the door, stark white rib bones protruded from a shallow mound of pale dust. Among the bones, an owls' feet necklace lay. Daura Rumfa's.

"But we have only been inside for seven days," Osei said.

"No," Adjoa said. She tugged her ori aside, bent over to pick up the necklace. "We have been away from the world for . . . generations." As Adjoa fingered the necklace, she knew. "The war ended long ago. The danger is past. We are safe now."

"Who won?" Yakubu asked.

"Daura won."

"I don't understand," Yakubu said.

"I know," Adjoa said. She slipped the necklace over her head and let it fall in place around her neck. Ω

AN UNLIKELY MATCH

A lithsome, alluring young fetch,
  replied to a rummy old letch,
      "Beware, Sir; I'm Jewish,
      "and if you feel woo-ish
"I'll haunt you and likely will kvetch."

— **Darrell Schweitzer & Marilyn Mattie Brahen**

CALLUM'S FEAST
by Noreen Doyle

illustrated by Allen Koszowski

"I won't have Redmane Mabryd coming onto Da's land! I won't!"

Callum heard his own voice crack in the fierceness of the whisper. Shivering beneath a foxskin cape which had belonged to his father, he crouched beside his cousin in the faded, prickly heather of the moor. Wind whipped off the sea with the cold promise of winter, though it was only Year End and winter lay two full months away. What Callum would give if it were only winter already. Were it any time of year but the End.

He said, "Redmane brought nothing but misery upon poor Da. Now he comes walking onto Surry lands like some uncle of mine home for dinner, when Da's just a month 'neath the cairn. Do you hear me, Barric?"

"I hear you," his cousin said and dug a calloused thumb into the fur of his boots. "But I'll listen to you only when you start talking sense."

Barric waved to men dismounting ponies on the next hilltop. Each of the chieftains gathered here tonight, even Barric, was a big man, and each had broad shoulders from swinging axes into trees and laying stone boundary walls and punting into the Wetmeadow to cut peat.

"It is sense I'm talking," Callum muttered. He shrugged his narrow shoulders and the fox-skin cape slid from his back. He marvelled at the big men greeting each other with hard claps to the arm, always first and always hardest from Redmane Mabryd. Try as he might, like a rabbit caught by a snake, Callum could not wrench his eyes from Redmane.

A head taller than any other man, with a chest as great around as a holy oak tree and corded arms and thighs to match, among these big men Redmane Mabryd loomed a giant. Only the wind had ever braided his hair. He had been born with it, they said, a great shock of flame on a big-boned babe his mother died pushing from her womb. Some went so far as to say that he had been born with the wild beard that draped down so low that when he stood bare-chested none could see his navel.

Each step he took shook the earth beneath Callum's feet. Each swing of one corded arm or the other landed like a blow upon Callum's back.

"*He* can go home," Callum said. He turned his back on the men, sat down and dug his heels into the dirt.

"You don't have any choice, Callum," replied Barric, sounding less curt than before but perhaps a little more pitying. Callum did not want pity. "Redmane is a chieftain just like the rest of the guests. The laws of Year-End hospitality say you can't keep him out,"

"The *guests* must have a choice, then! Let them all go to someone else's land for the feast."

Barric clucked his tongue with thinning patience. "Your father was Champion of the Year-End Feast last year. That means that he would have been host this year. If he'd lived."

"But he didn't. And I don't want to be host. Let one of my uncles be host."

Callum thrust a thumb toward the cream-colored glow of neep-lanterns on another hill. In the light of candles housed in turnip shells carved fancy with faces, gathered the women, the children, and those men not privileged to join the feast. They were having dinner of their own, of turnip hollowings and boiled fish.

"Your da's brothers are not here because they cannot be. They are not chieftains," Barric replied.

"You're a chieftain, Barric. You take the Right Knife!"

Callum took a knife from his belt. It was terribly old, made not of iron like an everyday knife but of stone, and it was duller than featherdown. For all that it was the pride prize of the chieftains, won fairly last Year End by Callum's father, who had openly boasted that he looked forward to passing it along to the next Champion, whosoever that may be — Redmane not excepted. There was honor in that, his father would have said in his great gravelly voice. If he had lived.

Barric did not take the Right Knife. "You're the host, Callum Surry, like it or not. Nobody will challenge you, anyway. The laws of Year-End hospitality forbid fighting. But I'll see that Redmane makes no trouble for your grandmother."

Barric tousled Callum's hair and ran off to join the other chieftains.

Callum envied his cousin, a man with a man's braids and a good start on a man's beard. At scarcely fourteen (or perhaps a little less; his sisters used to tease that he would never be old enough to be a man, though they had said nothing of that since Da's death), Callum still had his hair cut short by his grandmother or one of his sisters every other fortnight. Callum would try to be out with the sheep or occupied in the far garden but they always found him. Only a little fuzz fringed his upper lip, like the down on his forearms. But now, beard or no, like it or no, he had to play the part of a man.

There on the hill Redmane Mabryd stood with arms akimbo, waiting for Barric to catch up, but his gaze wandered farther and came to rest where Callum hid like a rabbit. He was, Callum knew, looking for the son of Adalthic Surry.

Like a rabbit Callum could slip away through the stones that dotted the scrubby moorlands where foxes hunted and shaggy cattle roamed wild. This time no one would find him: not his grandmother, not his cousin, not Redmane Mabryd.

He said to the wind and the spirits who rode it tonight, "O Da, why did you have to die?"

He heard no answer. The stare of Redmane Mabryd had, perhaps, frightened the spirits away.

His father would never have fled. No, Adalthic Surry lived a hero's life unto death, but that did not make Callum feel any better.

One month ago Adalthic had gone up into the hills to drive the cattle home from the summer pastures. That was the cycle of life on the Surry lands: the cattle grazed up-country in summer, and wintered in byres near the village. Every family had a cow or three, from the poorest broom-maker to chieftains like Adalthic. While women and children brought in the harvest, men took care of the cattle.

It should have been easy work. Dogs did most of it, and the cattle knew the way home by themselves. But it had not been easy this year. Robbers had ambushed Callum's father not far from this very spot. They stole his rings and clipped off his long grey braids, but Adalthic got the cattle home before he died.

Callum watched Barric escort the other chieftains toward a flat hilltop on which a small, licking bonfire had been kindled. Redmane

Mabryd walked long-strided until he overtook Barric and it appeared that he, not Barric, was leading. They were silhouettes along the crest of the hill, a giant followed by big men.

For years Redmane Mabryd had argued with Callum's father over who should graze a certain pasture where a brook ran cold and clear beneath an ancient stone bridge. Redmane Mabryd always lost, but these arguments still made Adalthic an unhappy man. Callum hated Redmane for that.

And he feared him for that too. The argument was one more thing Callum inherited from his father.

He drew himself tall, shook his trimmed mop of black hair. His hand patted the dull Right Knife, then fell upon the hilt of his iron blade. Yes, it should have been Redmane Mabryd, not Callum's father, murdered by robbers on this lonely stretch of road.

Callum snagged his father's fox-skin cape from the ground and threw it over his shoulders. It was too big but did not drag in the grass until he went downhill, and then the twiggy heather and earth-knobs caught at it and held fast. Not even big enough to wear your da's fox-skin cape, Callum mourned. And they expect you to bear up under his duties.

He joined the men at three long, wooden tables, each hewn from a single log and set to span across north-mossed stones dragged into the fields by giants jealous of men's round stone houses. While others sat on benches, Callum sat on the hard, unyielding seat of his father's oaken chair. Once it had had a pillow dyed with woad, but that had gone under the cairn beneath his da's head.

Eleven chieftains stared at him. Callum might as well have not been there by the way Redmane Mabryd stared through him.

And still he wished he were not. The swelling apple of his throat bobbed up and down when he tried to swallow his spit. He could hide beneath the table, if they turned their eyes for just a minute!

But his father would not like that; surely his spirit was amongst the wind-borne tonight, this thin Year End. It would disgrace the family, and the family was here too, not only the men and the wind-borne spirits. Staving darkness with neep-lanterns, gathered on a hilltop between here and home were the women and children who had prepared for this night, and who could now only watch its bonfire and shadows with the common men. They would be cold tonight. Callum remembered how cold it was, bonfireless in the autumn heather.

He could not disgrace his father, not before these chieftains, and not before the women and children and common men. As the eldest son of Adalthic Surry, Callum was chieftain here, not a little boy shivering in exile. And he was dreadfully frightened.

Callum mumbled words his father should be saying with a loud, kinglike voice. "Whosoever has fought and defeated the strongest foe during this year past will become Champion of the Year End." He took the stone knife from his belt. There were more words to say. Remaltha and Barric had practiced him for three days but he could remember none of the invocations, made to gods not yet real to Callum because he had no long hair nor any beard. He could remember only the very last line — his favorite for it being the last. Callum said, "Only the Champion can use the Right Knife to carve the beast and claim it for himself."

To prove its magic, Callum held up a hunk of butter molded into a ball. With his iron knife he easily sliced it into two pieces. He sliced his thumb, too. Blood fell in one great droplet onto the table. The chieftains laughed. Redmane Mabryd had the sky's laugh, full of thunder and spit. Every tooth in his great, broad head showed. They looked sharp. Maybe he sharpened them on the stones that dotted his own poor pastures.

Three times Callum dropped the butter. It was salty and stung the cut on his thumb. Finally he put it in a bowl and touched it with the stone blade.

With the Right Knife he could not incise the slightest mark in its slippery surface which yielded so easily to his fingers. The butter might as well have been stone itself.

The men banged the tables with their fists and cheered the magic. Soon one of them would own three prizes: the magic knife, the entire beast of the feast, and the name "Champion."

Barric leaned close to speak behind his palm. "Be careful of what they say about dragons. To prove that he's telling the truth, a man must have proof or three witnesses of his deed. Anything less and he's talking about a dream."

"But how do I know which has been a stronger enemy? I've never fought but my own sisters before. I don't know if it's harder to fight pirates or dragons. If I choose the wrong man, the Right Knife won't cut for him and I'll look very stupid.

by Noreen Doyle

So will Da, for having had such a clod-pated son. I want to be out with the cattle!"

"Do what you can. If something goes wrong, your grandmother Remaltha will become judge. It's the law."

Callum made his best effort to beetle his brows, yet he had not so much muscle nor depth of skin to draw into furrows as Adalthic, nor even Barric, and Callum knew that he could draw not so much as a wrinkle across his smooth forehead. "No chieftain wants a wisewoman telling him his business!"

Redmane Mabryd surged into Callum's view and roared, "What are we challenging each other for? An empty table? Where's the beast?"

Callum's face drained as white as the moon. He cried, "Bring out the beast of the feast!" and his voice cracked.

Four near-grown boys carried a groaning plank of wood to a wide boulder about which clustered the tables. They were all chieftains' heirs who would sit around the bonfires of future Year Ends. Having delivered their burden they ran back to the women and children and common men.

Never before had Callum seen a beast of the feast whole and uncarved. To carry the beast was an honor Callum had never performed. He had become a chieftain before he was old enough to serve as chieftain's heir.

The beast filled the air with the smell of pork and spices. It was enormous, glistened with fat and was black with herbs his sisters had carefully tended all summer, picked when ripest to the taste and dried from the rafters.

Could they see it, he wondered, from their hillside?

He remembered his father coming home from the Pelanid lands, having won the beast last Year End. Adalthic's belly was distended, his beard slick with grease, and he feasted on the remains — alone — for six days thereafter. At no other time had Adalthic Surry denied his son something from his plate. "When you're Champion, Callum, you can taste it," he had said, gnawing out the marrow of a foreleg. "Not before."

The men did not take their eyes from the beast of the feast. Perhaps it was small compared to others, perhaps it dwarfed them, but Callum could not say. Redmane Mabryd drew a hand across its blistering hot skin. His palm — rough from labor, thickened like the sole of a foot — came away slick and he pretended to lick it clean. The others jeered.

"Back off, Mabryd. I hope that Surry kitchen hollowed out enough turnips and boiled enough fish for the rest of you," Chieftain Kethelric Muroy said, flashing a lock of hair cut from a Crissenman pirate. "Tonight that roast goes whole into my own gut!"

"No, mine, you young seal-pup, for slaying that sea-drake," said Artan Pelanid. He was an old chieftain, the father, it was said, of twelve daughters and but two sons, one of whom had gone over to the Crissenmen. Artan maintained his pride and lands intact nonetheless; he was so firm a man.

Barric leapt over the table to stand firmly between Redmane and the beast. "This beast," he said, "is only a suckling pig compared to the Haunting Boar of Elwirthy Dun."

"Bah!" said Redmane, resuming his seat. His beard rustled over his voice, thick and trembling like a thicket in an autumn wind. Callum wondered at how brave Adalthic had been to maintain his own against this giant. "Men have told that tale for a hundred years and they've all been liars. The beast won't be yours, Barric, any more than was the Haunting Boar."

Barric smiled anyway, and spoke in a sing-song way: "It plagued our lands for a hundred years, slew our youth and birthed our fears. It could no longer be so.

"Alone I went to Elwirthy Dun when our planters had just begun to set the seed which come Year End we'd reap. And the Haunting Boar came a-charging from the crumbles of the keep. With this devil's knife-teeth at my thigh along the ruins of one wall ran I, playing as the mouse might with the cat. Up the high, down the low, I jumped and he ran, scraping stones. His great long tooth it sliced the wall and behind my every step another rock did fall."

"Bah!" said Redmane Mabryd. "We all know the earth-shaking brought down the last of the walls of Elwirthy Dun."

Barric sang on: "At the cliff I stood before him, over the surging of the tide. I called him, 'Charge!' and charge did he, so then I stepped aside. Down into the sea — down and down and down — went he!"

Laughing at Barric's cleverness of foot and of tongue, men nevertheless chanted, "Proof! Proof!" They beat their jasper seal-rings atop the tables.

Barric pulled from his bag a broken tusk, scraped to a point like a knife sharpened on stone. He held it beside the tusk on the beast of the feast. It measured four times the length and twice the girth.

Redmane Mabryd glowered, but he did not argue. Nor did anyone else.

Each of the twelve chieftains tried to better Barric's story. Everyone knew that Kethelric Muroy had driven off the Crissenmen, for everyone had watched the battle from the beach; he scarcely needed the captain's lock of hair. Lem Lorrin had four claws from the bear that had tried to eat his baby girl. But Artan had not one scale, not so much as a slimy barb, from the sea-drake that nearly wrecked his ship.

Divyn Rusk spoke of the fires in his holy oak lands (this brought a moment's reflection and a murmur of "Yes, a worthy tale for this night"), and so on it went.

"Speak up, Redmane," Barric said. "You've been quiet tonight."

Redmane Mabryd rose slowly like a giant roused from slumber by the pale light of a winter morning. He studied his hands, turned them over as if they were wonderful things. "The Haunting Boar was a ferocious beast, no doubt. And who doubts the courage and strength needed to drive off Crissenmen or a bear or fire the immortal foe! But who was stronger than all of these, until a short while ago? It was Adalthic Surry."

"Get on with it," Kethelric Muroy grumbled. "You can't win over the judge by flattering his dead father!"

"Each of us knows how strong Adalthic was," said Redmane, "how cunning and how brave."

"Redmane!" the chieftains yelled. "Get on with it! Don't keep the beast waiting!"

Redmane Mabryd smiled and lifted his blistered hands and they did seem like wonderful things, great meaty things, useful things compared to Callum's, whose were more like a babe's than those of one who had done anything in life. "For many years this foe stole from me my milk and yes my meat. This foe pinched the grass from my cattle's stomachs, snatched cold clear water from their tongues. A long journey it forced on us, should we wish to cross the river. Every season I met him and let this foe defeat me, until he thought me no trouble and he did not pay me mind. It was then that I slew this foe."

He turned his pale blue eyes upon Callum. They were at once wet and hard, like sea-slicked stones, glittering and frightful, eager to dispatch a passerby into the black brine. "Tell me how great was the foe whom I defeated. I slew Adalthic Surry."

Callum leapt up to stand on his father's chair. "Proof!" he cried, slapping the table with his palm, for he had no seal-ring with which to beat the wood. "Proof!"

Redmane Mabryd threw at the table a scrap of cloth. It landed so that Callum's final blow upon the table struck it instead: he felt something long and firm, paired with things small, hard and a little sharp.

Its leather drawstrings fell apart when Callum tugged. There, laid out in linen, were his father's rings and locks of his braided grey hair.

"So," said Redmane Mabryd with lips framed with flaming hair, "who will claim the beast of the feast tonight, Chief Callum Surry?"

Callum trembled. They had laid his father beneath a cairn, yet here lay more of him. Here lay his hair — so soft, Callum remembered snuggling it when he was a littler boy, remembered his father letting his sisters practice braiding upon it, so patient was he. Here lay his rings — old silver, his grandfather's silver, beaten out of Crissenman coins. Here lay his tale. The end of it. The cause of his family's grief.

Redmane Mabryd was just a short leap away. His chest would be soft as hot butter for the iron knife. Callum's hand closed about the hilt. The glow of the neep-lanterns danced on the hill beyond, the cold stone of the Right Knife stung his hands, and the smell of the beast of the feast filled his nostrils with all the rest of the signs of the Year End and all its hospitality and laws. Callum stood still but for the tears pouring from his eyes.

"What's wrong, Chief Callum?" said Redmane Mabryd. "Can't you tell who was the greater? An old boar or your own brave father?"

Even before Callum could speak, the men began arguing and pushing. Some were yelling for swords and daggers which they had left behind with their ponies. Fighting was forbidden at the Year-End Feast; nothing was worse than starting a new year with bloodshed. It ruined crops and brought bad rains for the winter.

"Redmane cheats! He's a murderer!" one man said.

"But he's right! Adalthic was the strongest of all!" cried another. "Murder isn't a charge to settle at the Year End."

"Here, now!" came a woman's voice, and the men's collapsed to silence.

Callum's grandmother stood beside the beast of the feast. Remaltha leaned against a gnarled staff cut from an oak tree and carved into thick seaman's knots. The wind stirred her heavy grey cloak and her hair, which was long and braided like a man's, for she had upon her chin the scant growth of a man's beard, the mark of an eldress wisewoman. There were pale lights too in the darkness, the women and children and common men with their neep-lanterns, come in a little closer to see. "Why should you grown men act like little boys fighting over table scraps?"

Barric came forward, taut-drawn like a ready bow. "Redmane started it!"

She tipped the staff left and right. "I want to hear what happened tonight. Callum, tell me."

Callum came around the table to fall before his grandmother. "I've wanted to run away and hide since the feast started! Even before I knew what he'd done, I wanted Redmane to die for all the trouble he made for Da. Then he was rude to Barric, and I hated him! And when Redmane said he had killed Da, I wanted to cut out his heart! But I didn't. I can't, for all my heart screams that Redmane deserves to die! I hide behind the laws of Year-End hospitality, that's all."

There. He had displayed his cowardice. Now Remaltha would scold him and disown him and send him off the Surry lands with a curse upon his small shoulders as only an eldress wisewoman could. Had only he given the Right Knife to Redmane, none of this would have come to pass. His grandmother had suffered enough, losing her son. Now, to endure this foolishness on account of her grandson!

Remaltha wandered around the tables, brimming with purpose. She halted before Redmane Mabryd and thrust her knotty staff into the dirt. "Callum, give me the Right Knife."

"Yes, make Remaltha judge," the chieftains murmured. Even Redmane Mabryd was happy with this.

"Tell me your tales," Remaltha said, taking the Right Knife in her thin-fingered fist. The men repeated them, one by one, without so much fanciness as before. Rhymes became plain speech, riddles and tricks of tongue had no part to play. Even in their bare bones the tales told of courage. I should have listened to them more closely, Callum thought. I should have learned something about their courage, for I certainly have none of my own.

Redmane grinned with ready satisfaction, and Callum slumped into his father's chair, lower still until he was out of it. He would burst into flames if he sat there, if he dared to take the place of brave-unto-death Adalthic Surry. Of course

Remaltha would think that her son Adalthic was stronger than a boar or bear or Crissenmen. Why did she even ask to hear what the others might say?

His first chance to be a man, and he had failed it miserably.

Remaltha held out the Right Knife to Callum. "Carve the beast of the feast, Champion."

"What's this?" Redmane bellowed. "He can't win the contest! He's the judge!"

"By your own calling, I am the judge," Remaltha said.

Flushed red as an autumn apple, Redmane Mabryd snatched off the Right Knife from Remaltha's whithered hand. Two broad steps brought him up beside the beast of the feast and he raked the stone blade across the crackled skin.

It did not furrow the grease.

Redmane Mabryd roared like the pounding surf and stormed up to Remaltha, raging about wisewoman trickery which had unmanned the Right Knife, threatening to behead her with bare hands if need be. The neep-lanterns of women and children and common men shrank into the darkness again.

The other chieftains fell upon him and he fought like a bear.

"Naich! Naich! Stop your fighting!" Remaltha cried, striking stone with her knotted staff. "Do you want crops to suffer the blight next harvest? Would you have the pastures wash out in early rains?"

Redmane Mabryd did not care. He ripped through them, surging like a salmon fighting the river. His corded arms swept everywhere at once, like flames in the holy oak wood, and the chieftains fell from him only to surge again like salmon themselves. Callum had imagined that only gods might fight in so quicksilver a fashion, and he realized that Barric and the rest were eager only to spill no blood.

Someone with half his wits had fetched Redmane's pony — could it have been his sisters? Callum heard a high voice soothe the animal — and this sparked the others from their thrust-and-retreat. With great difficulty (did salmon ever leap as pairs, much less by dozens?) they threw him over its back, four men holding the pony still while six held Redmane Mabryd, and the last men locked his hands and feet in a grommet beneath the creature's belly. They fell off at that moment, and Kethelric Muroy gave the flurried pony a slap to the rump, and off it rode across the pastures, while Redmane Mabryd howled. The wind whipped up to join him, and the spirits took up his cry, or perhaps it was only the wind whistling through dry grass, stones dragged by giants and planks dragged by men.

"By the time he works himself free," Kethelric said, "that poor creature will have taken him halfway back to his own lands, and that's some fair hours' ride. It'll be daylight then, and he'll be fair game."

"We'll all be fair game," Barric said, pinching his nose to stem a trickle of blood. They watched until the pony pounded over the last hill. The night air, however, billowed Redmane Mabryd's cries long after. "He broke the law of Year-End hospitality, aye, but all the same Redmane earned the haunch. Adalthic was stronger than anything the rest of us fought."

Remaltha, who spared not one glance to the fleeing pony and its rider, inspected the beast of the feast. "The rest of you Redmane fairly beat, of that I have no doubt. But of all the tales of strength and courage I have heard here tonight, Callum's was by far the best."

"Callum's? But he did not *do* anything!" said Barric.

"Yes, and that can be the hardest thing of all. Callum defeated his own passion, and a stronger enemy no man has ever met. Has Redmane ever done that?" She fixed them with a stare, all at once. "Have any of you?"

Barric bowed his head. The other chieftains shrugged.

His grandmother said. "Callum, take the Right Knife."

Callum looked at the knife in his hands. Just an hour ago he had not been able to cut butter with it and here his grandmother expected him to carve the beast! In a moment she would look just as foolish as Callum.

With trembling hands, Callum held the Right Knife. He pressed it against the meat, and the juices flowed.

"Go on," his grandmother whispered.

The chieftains stood in silence, watching with weighted stares.

Callum pressed a little harder. More juice, tempting and hot, seeped from the skin. But the Right Knife did not cut.

Then, with a sudden **snap!** and splatter of hot fat the brown skin split. The Right Knife sliced through the meat.

Barric clapped Callum hard on the shoulder. "Get the Champion his plate! Eat up, Callum! Tonight the feast is yours!"

Callum carved white slices from the beast and handed the first to Remaltha. He trotted toward the glow of the neep-lanterns. From their cold darkness he brought the women and the children and common men to the bonfire, and no chieftain could gainsay him, for the beast belonged to none but Callum.

"I think," said Champion Callum Surry, passing around his wooden plate, "that tonight we share."   Ω

THE HORLA
(as it might happen to a Heinlein hero)

I was smoking like a chimney
  As I waited for the beast.
And my wife said, "All this smoking
  Isn't helping in the least."

"Dear," I said, "we face a monster
  Who can stalk us all unseen.
But I've got an Army pistol
  And a seven-round magazine.

"Now you say that I've been smoking
  Till the air is turning blue —
Well, that's just what I intended.
  Now let's see what smoke can do."

Then the shutter creaked and shattered,
  And the window cracked and broke,
And I saw the Horla coming —
  He was outlined by the smoke!

So I shot him in the brisket,
  And put two rounds in each head,
Then a couple in the belly
  Just to make sure he was dead.

Now he's buried in the garden,
  And it's like I tell my wife:
"When you smoke, it stinks the house up,
  But it just might save your life!"

— **Kenneth W. Meyer**

IN THE STREET OF THE WITCHES
by Darrell Schweitzer

illustrated by Stephen E. Fabian

Tsarag Vin was fourteen years old when he first came to the Street of the Witches. But he never returned from it. Someone did, who looked like him, who remembered what he remembered and shared his longings; but this was someone else, for truly it is said that whosoever dwells among the Witches, even for a single night, is irrevocably changed.

I know this to be true, for I have dwelt there a long time.

I am your host, the storyteller, one of the characters in the story, whose identity will be clear enough in time.

Be patient then. The Street of the Witches weaves through the back alleys and shadows of every city in the world, every city which ever was and ever will be.

It is a path through the labyrinth. It is the labyrinth.

by Darrell Schweitzer

I

Tsarag's transformation began subtly, as his teacher, the learned Meras, was telling a story about the Street of Witches, as warning and edification and entertainment; something about a mighty hero of old who ventured there to gain the remedy to a great peril, knowing full well that he must sacrifice himself in the winning of it. But the honor of the Nine Gods or the safety of his city . . . or something high-sounding and terribly important . . . would not be denied.

The boy's attention wandered. He gazed out the window, to where workmen were loading huge bales onto sledges for winter transport. Even when the White River was frozen, the merchants of House Vin were always busy.

"Am I boring you, Lord?" said the teacher.

But Tsarag wasn't even paying attention to the men loading the sledges. He gazed beyond the wooden wall of the Vin compound, to the outer city beyond. He didn't answer.

Tsarag's ten-year-old brother Amasdag made a face. "He's thinking about his *girl*friend . . . He wants to get *married*. . . ."

The teacher said sternly, "That is quite ridiculous. The heir to House Vin will marry the bride selected for him by his father, for the good of all." Then he smiled toward Tsarag and added, "Besides, that won't be for a few years yet."

"I'm sorry," said the elder brother. "I don't feel well. Go on with the story."

He left Meras to edify Amasdag. Amasdag stuck out his tongue after his departing brother. Outside in the corridor, Tsarag Vin wept and slammed his fist into the wall and demanded of the Winter Gods how they could be so cruel.

He wasn't the same after that. He wasn't ever the same.

For in fact Tsarag Vin was secretly in love with the beautiful Azrekia of House Zevas, the great rival of House Vin. Only one trading family could occupy the inner citadel of White Nevasderat. That one family was Vin. Vin barges plied the river in summer, all the way down to the Crescent Sea. Vin horsemen patrolled the banks. House Zevas was an upstart, a mediocrity, its master consumed with envy.

Yet the heir to Vin had clandestinely met and fallen in love with the daughter of his father's enemy. It was an impossible, ridiculous situation —

And it is not entirely the story I wish to tell.

* * *

In the night, Tsarag Vin awoke from terrible dreams. He sat up, drenched in sweat, shivering in the silence, the dream fading even as he sat there, until he could recall only screams and a burning mask which hovered in the air and inexorably settled over his own face, smothering him.

Amasdag stirred under the furs beside him, but did not wake. Meras slept on in his chair by the fireplace.

A spark popped among the embers.

Tsarag slipped out of bed, listening to the faint creaking of the rafters overhead, certain he could hear the snow itself as it fell.

A sudden gust of wind buffeted the shutters. The embers stirred and glowed.

Tsarag shivered, pulling a heavy woolen tunic over himself, then padded barefoot across the wooden floor.

His faithful dog lay by the fire, whimpering and snorting in its sleep. He knelt down to comfort the animal, which raised its head lazily and stared at him.

"Quiet. I have to go."

The dog made to get to its feet, but Tsarag pushed it down gently.

"No. Stay here. They need you to protect them."

And as he spoke, he made a sign, to invoke the protection of Vohg-Zemad, foremost among the Winter Gods, who had always shown favor to House Vin. The boy needed protection and he was afraid, but he knew also that he must go alone, like the hero in Meras's jumbled story, without even the company of a dog, though he did not know why he had to go, or exactly where . . . it was something about the dream, and the burning mask —

For a Destiny or a geas or a weird, or whatever you want to call it was upon him; and perhaps he had never awakened at all, but passed from layer to layer of his dream, into true and prophetic vision, even as the soul journeys from Leshé, *which is dream, into* Tashé *which is death, and beyond, like a sailor on an endless, unknowable sea —*

He was compelled. He went. The burning mask spoke his name, summoning him.

Like the hero in the story, he set forth, and did not question.

He dressed himself stealthily and made his way out into a corridor, past his parents' bedroom, past sleeping servants, and across the great hall, where retainers and guests lay snoring on the tables and benches. On the walls all around hung the shields and trophies of House Vin, even the stuffed head of a fabulous beast some ancestor had slain. In the darkness the jumble of them suggested a tangle for thorn-bushes at a forest's edge.

It was quite an undertaking for the eldest son of the Lord of Vin to sneak out by himself on a winter's night. Servants could be beaten for allowing such a thing to happen. But there had been a great feast that night and they were all drunk. And the boy was small, and silent afoot. He knew the way through hidden doors, a secret stair, a tunnel.

He went out into the night, very much afraid, yet unafraid, as one is in a dream. The air, laden with snow, stung his face. The cold seemed to reach through his thick boots to grab his ankles with frigid, iron-hard fingers.

He was no giant like his father — or the hero in Meras's story today — but he was a native of this land and accustomed to dark and cold. Many a foreigner could get lost in the wooden maze that was Nevasderat, a city of concentric rings of stockades and log houses, rippling out from the citadel and House Vin. There was even a word for such unfortunates, who perished just trying to cross the street or find the privy — *tagheri,* which meant "dancing statue," since the frozen corpse always seemed to be in some absurd position when found, as if interrupted in a revel.

But Tsarag Vin was Nevasderati himself, and would therefore never be *tagheri.*

He went on. A sudden howling wind sent an avalanche of snow sliding down from a rooftop onto him. He fell to his knees, then caught hold of a barrel and pulled himself up.

In the dream, which he remembered, in the seeming dream which never ended, the burning mask was before him, like a lantern gleaming through the snow and darkness. Again it spoke his name, and again he felt that compulsion which only makes sense in dreams, which holds the dreamer in place when he would flee, or drives him on without any recourse or mercy or explanation.

The boy replied, "Azit Azim," invoking the Horned One, who watches over travelers.

The mask vanished. Tsarag clung to the edge of the barrel for a second, then shook the snow off himself.

It was then that he heard the screaming, like no sound he had ever heard from a human throat before, something more intense, more horrible, as if all the despair and all the world's pain were summed up in that single cry —

And the voice was a young one.

It was nearby.

It was at his feet.

He crouched down and cleared away the snow from a little window, then watched, appalled and sickened but unable to turn away from the scene in the cellar down below: a boy about his own age bound naked onto a wooden table, while hideous women in scarlet cloaks gathered around him, burning him with white-hot irons, slashing him with knives, while the boy screamed all the more and so struggled against his bonds that his wrists and his feet were bloody. The witches — for Tsarag did not doubt that was who they were — tore away the boy's flesh. They opened him like a bag. They tossed aside what must have been internal organs like so much garbage.

(*Has to be dead now,* Tsarag told himself. *This is impossible. It should have stopped. It can't go on.*)

Yet the screaming went on, that hopeless, sub-animal scream, as two of the witches, wearing thick gloves to protect their hands, carried a steaming vessel to the table and poured molten metal into the boy's open belly.

(*Dying. Dead. Impossible!*)

The screaming stopped. The witches cut the boy's bonds. He sat up on the table, his face now filled with more than human fury.

Then it was Tsarag Vin who cried out, as the boy on the table glared directly at him. Their eyes met. It seemed that the other wore his own face, as if he were looking into a mirror.

"Behold, you will become as I," the naked boy seemed to be saying, but only it was a dream-voice, more remembered than actually heard.

Tsarag screamed and fell back from the window and could only lie there, waiting for death; but the light in the snow winked out as one of the witches curtly pulled down a blind, and there was only silence and darkness and cold.

Tsarag put his hands to his face, to make sure it was still there.

He rose. He went on. He knew that he had come to the Street of the Witches, because it was his time to arrive there, like the hero in his teacher's tale. The Street only revealed itself out of whim, out of mystery —

Once, as the snow whirled in front of his face, he saw a silver carriage drift by, borne aloft by naked, winged men, whose flesh was all the color of ice. Their wings made a hushed, steady sound, like snow and wind buffeting fastened shutters.

A curtain rippled. A lady leaned out from the carriage. She wore a scarlet robe and a silver crown.

She held up the burning mask, which now gleamed like white-hot metal. She heaved it into the air, and then she was gone, and the mask was gone, and the snow was blinding.

When Tsarag could see again, he had come out of an alley into a street lined with brightly-lit shops. Lanterns swayed in the wind, snow swirling around them.

The street was empty, yet he heard, carried on the wind, fragments of incomprehensible conversation, laughter, music, a single voice shouting, a murmur of many voices. He turned and turned again as people in fantastic costumes flickered in the periphery of his vision: a king in tattered yellow and red, wearing a crown the color of bone; and another king, all in black, his face black as the night, his eyes like fire, black dogs licking his hands. Here was a yellow-faced woman all in black silk, her bare arms covered with glowing tattoos; and, again, a barbarian all in furs, with an axe over his shoulder; and a man who seemed half machine, whirring, lurching, making clicking sounds as he walked, his robe like a patch cut out of a clear night sky, filled with stars.

And there was one who had no face at all, whose upraised hood was hollow as a cave, but for a single candle within. This one held the burning mask in pale hands, and called out the name of Tsarag Vin.

The boy stepped sideways, into a shop filled from floor to ceiling with wooden puppets, all of them intricately carven and painted, swaying on their strings in the draft as if alive.

They too called out the name of Tsarag Vin.

But Tsarag Vin was close to tears now. He wanted this dream to end. He wanted to go home. He pleaded. But the puppets laughed at him, and something huge and wooden rose from behind a counter within the shop and a painted face spoke,

saying, "Tsarag Vin, this is your home now. You have no other."

He screamed and ran out into the night, and all but collided with the burning mask yet again.

Now someone was wearing it, someone who was very small and thin, an old woman perhaps, or a child, clad only in a very loose, thin white robe that streamed in the wind and didn't seem at all adequate for a Nevasderati winter.

This person took hold of Tsarag's hand, and the touch was solid and warm. It was a young hand, firm. Tsarag allowed himself to be led through deep drifts, along the Street of Witches. Now women in red cloaks emerged from every doorway, regarding him. Then, by some transition he could not follow, he wasn't outdoors anymore, but in a dark corridor. The burning mask had faded to a sullen red glow. It did not light the way. But as he and his companion passed, pale hands, floating in the darkness, uncurled themselves, revealing white flames flickering from the upraised palms.

By this faint light he gained a better impression of his companion: slender, somewhat shorter than he, with very long, black hair that trailed behind on the air, even as the white robe trailed. Impossibly, the stranger was barefoot, and did not seem to feel the cold.

Perhaps it was a corpse that had borne him away, he thought, but corpses are not warm to the touch, nor do they smell faintly of sweat.

Then there was another transition he could not follow, as if a curtain had parted before him, and the light was somehow different. Snow still swirled around him, but through it he saw some other place which was not Nevasderat, but a city of squat, black stone buildings interspersed with the occasional tower, and, impossibly, palm trees.

The other bade him sit, and they squatted down in a courtyard amid carven stone crocodiles. Still the snow fell, and Tsarag Vin felt the frigid night air; certainly the snow on his boots and fur trousers did not begin to melt; but the masked other did not shiver. That gown was thin as spider-silk; through it a bare thigh flashed, then narrow shoulders. The front was open and he could make out faintly luminous scars crisscrossing the bare chest, but there was something indefinable here, something about the light and the way the other moved, and the shadows, so that he could not tell if this was a boy or a girl, even when the other removed the mask.

The light of the mask went out utterly. It was a delicate thing, like a dead, autumn leaf.

The stranger crushed it into nothingness, then opened dark hands, and white flames danced from scarred palms; and Tsarag Vin could make out a round, soft, olive-colored face, and dark, dark eyes he could look into forever.

The other wore a lot of jewelry. Silver bands rattled on both wrists and ankles.

"Do not be afraid," said the other. The voice, like everything else, was soft, ambiguous, and strangely accented.

Tsarag Vin thought of the hero in his teacher's story. It was just a story, but it reminded him to be brave.

"I am Tsarag Vin. My father is the greatest prince of Nevasderat. He will reward you richly if you take me home." Already Tsarag Vin was convinced that tonight's adventure, if it were other than just a dream, was a disaster, to be escaped if he could. The best he could hope for was making it back home before his absence was discovered.

But the other laughed and said, "Have you considered that a name can be a weapon? Now you have revealed your secret to me."

"You give me your name now. We'll bargain."

The other shrugged and held up burning hands, "But you have already paid me, without asking for anything in return. What kind of bargain is that? But I did not bring you here to haggle over names. I have many. I contain multitudes. One of my names is Julna of Kadisphon."

Tsarag swallowed hard and tried to contain his surprise, lest it grow into fear. *Kadisphon* was proverbial. *As far as Kadisphon* was to say *to the end of the Earth.* Julna, he supposed, was a girl's name in some barbarous tongue.

Tsarag spoke. "I want to ask —"

"Why?" said Julna of Kadisphon.

"I want to —"

"In the Street of the Witches?"

"Why am I here?" said Tsarag.

"Because you came."

"But —"

"Because we brought you here. Is that more satisfactory?"

"Who —?"

"Because it served our purpose."

Now Julna of Kadisphon held fire in one hand and a bowl in the other. She — and yet Tsarag wasn't entirely sure this was a *she,* as if Julna of Kadisphon were a shadow-thing, too indeterminate for the eye to define — offered the bowl and said, "Drink."

Tsarag Vin knew his stories.

"If I drink, I'll remain here forever. Everybody knows that."

"You are already here forever. If you don't drink, you will never even seem to leave. Go on. It is merely water."

Reluctantly, Tsarag drank. The water was warm. It was just water.

"Now take the bowl with you and go."

"What?"

"Just go. There are no bargains —"

"I want to know —"

"No explanations."

II

There are no explanations. There can be no explanations. Even the witches do not understand, though they have delved deeper into the shadows than anyone, though they have learned and heard the speech of the Shadow Titans, of whom even the gods are afraid. Their art is like a storm, like a tide; it flows through them toward its own ends.

No answers. Only mystery.

Tsarag Vin awoke, but not in his bed. He sat up in a snowdrift by a barrel and a log wall. He still held the bowl in his hand. He stuffed it into his pocket and got to his feet. He knew after taking but a few steps that he must be in some shabby, outer district of Nevasderat.

He began to run, from fear of more immediately comprehensible things. He had been out all night. His teacher, Meras, would be blamed, possibly even put to death, for the wrath of the Lord of Vin could be terrible and there was no law restraining him, only custom, and the custom was that the occupant of the citadel was not restrained.

Surely everyone would be frantic. There must be house-guards out looking for him, turning the whole city upside down.

He knew where he was now. He ran from the Black Circle, where foreigners and no-accounts dwelt; then crossing the Brown Circle, where stood the shops of free craftsmen who were not

associated with any house; and the Red, the place of the lesser trading houses, including House Zevas; and on through Silver Nevasderat, where rose the towers of the nobles, where visiting kings might rest; and finally he plunged through the gate into the White Citadel, home of House Vin.

There a guard caught him by the hood of his coat, laughing, and swung him around.

"And where do you think *you* are going, my bold young sir?"

For a moment, Tsarag couldn't reply. It was an impossible thing, as if a wooden statue had not merely spoken, but squandered its miraculous ability on something completely stupid.

He squirmed, then said, "Let me go. I have to get inside."

"Not here you don't. Only family and servants." The guard scrutinized him up and down. "And you don't seem to be either."

He scrutinized the guard, and it was then that he became more and more alarmed. Something wasn't right. These guards wore *tazams*, loose, sleeveless garments over their furs, on which were displayed the emblem and colors of the reigning house. Of course they did, but the Vin emblem was a fiery eagle, and the Vin colors were yellow and white. These men wore blue and green, with the emblem of a coiled snake.

He had seen those colors and that snake before, but never here.

He could have apologized for coming to the wrong house, but he knew it *wasn't* the wrong house. There was only one White Citadel. He looked past the gathering company of curious guards — all of whom wore blue and green, with snakes — and *of course* he recognized the courtyard where he and his brother had raced their dogs, and the shed where the sledges were stored, and his mother's window, surrounded by white-painted, wooden lilies.

There was no mistake.

These men wore the colors of House Zevas. He had seen them many times, when he had come, disguised, to visit his beloved Azrekia.

That was impossible. If somehow the Zevas warriors had stormed House Vin during the night and won an equally impossible victory, the yard would be heaped with corpses and still swarming with armed men and captives. There'd be broken doors, burnt roofs, much destruction, because the men of House Vin would not give up easily.

No.

He struggled. The guards laughed. He threatened. He told them he was the son of the lord of this place, if they had somehow forgotten, and still they laughed.

Then a sledge pulled up and a man got out. The guards stood at attention. Someone said, "My Lord!" and rattled off an explanation.

It was Lord Duraine Zevas, Azrekia's father. He wore a peaked cap and a coat embroidered with serpent signs. He looked into Tsarag's face and spoke in a kindly voice, as if, somehow, he had no idea who this boy was and had never heard of House Vin. All he said was, "You mustn't make this disturbance, child. You don't belong here. You know that."

Tsarag at fourteen didn't like being called a child. But that was nothing. It was nothing too, that Lord Zevas somehow didn't recognize him. In fact that was fortunate, if somehow House Zevas *had* supplanted House Vin during the night.

But then there was a girl beside him. It was Azrekia, Tsarag's own beloved. *She* didn't know him either. Of course she couldn't have said anything, but he saw it in her eyes. She was first bemused, then puzzled, then a little afraid. He made the secret sign they had between them and she did not recognize it.

All *she* said, to her father, was, "If this boy is hungry, maybe we should let him go around to the kitchen —"

There was a dog beside her. It was — or had been — *his* dog. It whined, and almost seemed to sense something strange or strangely familiar, but Azrekia put her hand on its head and the beast was still.

Tsarag broke free of the guards and ran away from the White Gate, back into the outer city, tears streaming down his face. He ran until his breath came in painful gasps, until the cold air tore at his lungs and he could run now more. Then he stopped, and leaned against a wall in the snow, and tried to puzzle out what had happened. He prayed to the Winter Gods, asking their forgiveness, if this were all some punishment they'd set upon him for whatever sin. No, he didn't think it was that. No, he didn't think this was a dream either. Somehow, somewhere, between last night and now, he had indeed awakened, but not into quite the same city, quite the same world. He stopped people on the street and demanded to know of House Vin, and no one knew what he was talking about. When he claimed to be the son of the greatest prince in all

White Nevasderat, they made signs against him, to ward off bad luck, because they took him to be mad.

He spent much of the day in a furious rage, trying to find the Street of the Witches, determined to kill Julna of Kadisphon.

Of course he did not find it.

Once, in his desperation, he went into a shop and asked a metal smith if he knew the way to the Street of the Witches, and the man was silent for several minutes, then came toward Tsarag with a silver knife, making signs in the air with the tip of it as he did.

"Just let me cut your throat," he said, "and you shall go to the Witches soon enough."

Tsarag escaped, but his quest went nowhere. He swore terrible revenge, as the son of a great lord (or a hero in a story) might be expected to do, but nothing came of that either, and nightfall found him exhausted, unable to convince anyone that he was a person of any account. There was no place for him to sleep other than a derelict barn, now inhabited by beggars. There he was accepted with some suspicion, and even ladled a little soup out of the common pot, which he drank from the bowl the witch Julna had given him.

As he sat there, someone reached over and fondled his fine coat, but he was too weary, too despairing to care.

In the morning he woke up outside in the snow, with blood on his face and a lump on his head. His coat was gone, and his heavy woolen tunic, and his boots, and even his socks.

He wandered, barefoot, shivering in his undershirt, begging from house to house, from shop to shop for someone who would help him restore House Vin to its rightful place. He promised many rewards. People laughed and threw snow at him. Someone came up from behind and wrapped bright ribbons around his neck, the mark of a lunatic. A kindly woman gave him rags to tie around his bleeding feet.

When he tried to sell the bowl he had received from the witches, a shopkeeper merely shrugged and said, "It's cheap southern ware. From the Delta." He waved at his own shelves, which were full of such bowls. "And, look, yours is chipped."

He sat on a barrel at a street corner with the bowl in his lap, to beg, and while the sun was high, he could stand it, and he gathered a few coins, but as the sun set, the cold was too much, and he knew he would become *tagheri*, one of those grotesque, dancing, frozen corpses before another dawn arrived.

It was dark by the time he reached the White Citadel again. This time he avoided the main gate, but went to a humbler entrance. His feet were bleeding again and his hands were numb.

He pounded on the kitchen door for what seemed forever. When it finally opened, the blast of warm air nearly knocked him over. He held up his bowl to beg, but the doorway was swaying crazily and he couldn't make sense of the babbling voices around him, and he fell forward.

III

No explanations. Mystery. Next, Tsarag Vin grew into manhood, in a mere blinking of the eye of eternity.

But it is never as simple as that.

Planning his revenge, although unsure exactly what or against whom, Tsarag Vin bided his time. The servants at the kitchen door lifted him up, laid him in a warm bed, and later gave him hot broth. He soon recovered and was made one of them. It didn't make any difference that he told them who he really was, for none had heard of House Vin, much less considered it a threat to House Zevas.

No, the Lord of Zevas was by all accounts a kindly man, charitable to the unfortunate, a man who, despite his high position, had no enemies. He was a master at pleasing everyone. He was even, incredibly enough in the rough-and-tumble world of Nevasderati commerce, honest.

So Tsarag Vin became the least of the many servants in House Zevas. He scrubbed pots. He carried out the stinks. He spread new rushes over the floor of the great hall. His tasks brought him, like a ghost, to places he had known all his life, and no one recognized him. He could not enter the master bedroom — where his parents had slept — because he was not allowed.

He wondered if his parents were alive, somewhere else, or if they had merely ceased to exist.

He even regretted the loss of his younger brother, Amasdag.

Once he saw a familiar toy on a shelf, a wooden horse, with wheels. One of the wheels was half

gone. He remembered how it had gotten that way, when he was eight and Amasdag four, and Amasdag had flung the horse, which was *his*, Tsarag's, down a flight of stairs. How he'd pummelled his brother then, until Meras pulled them apart.

Now he looked at the toy, and dared not touch it, and wept for Amasdag.

He grew. A year passed, two, three. He was rarely close to the Zevas princes, for he was the least among the servants, usually left in the kitchen or the stables during great events. He saw the master, most of the time, only from a distance.

He watched Azrekia from afar. He might as well have been on the Moon.

But once he met her in a corridor, and he could hardly bear to look on her, but he managed to say, "Do you not know me?" Again he made the secret sign they had between them.

She looked at him oddly. "Should I?"

He made the sign again.

She smiled, and said, "Yes, you were the boy at the gate —"

But before she could say anything more he seized her in his arms and kissed her as hard and as passionately as he could, remembering all their secret meetings, their fears, their shared dangers, how they had planned, desperately, impossibly, to marry in secret, then run away together —

She pushed him away and slapped him across the face.

"How *dare* you? You forget yourself! How *dare* you?"

He couldn't explain. He couldn't find the words. He felt like a helpless, stuttering fool.

"Very well then," she said, suddenly more amused than angry, "I shall assume that you were briefly driven mad by my beauty. It has been known to do that. I, being a great lady, forgive you. But you must not come near me again. You must not forget who I am and who you are. Is that understood?"

All he could do was look down at his feet and mutter, "Yes, Lady."

And, laughing, she swept along the corridor and was gone.

She was gone from his life. He was without hope.

But he did not forget who she was and who he was, and that transformed him. He brooded by himself. He cursed the air. He cried out in his sleep, amid terrible dreams. At an age when most

of the servants married others of their class, he took no interest, refused all offers, and gradually came to neglect his appearance and his manner, until he was seldom let out of the cellars or the kitchen, and he did not come close to Lady Azrekia. Lord Zevas heard of the change that had come over him, but did not choose to turn him out. He ordered Tsarag closely watched, and those who watched him could only report that their quarry was elusive. Sometimes, at night especially, he seemed to vanish into thin air.

Though he was no longer a prince here, he still knew the secret ways, the trapdoors, the secret stair, the tunnel that led under the wall into a warehouse in Red Nevasderat.

Tsarag, in his rage, stole away from the house every night. He didn't seem to need to sleep. Fury and pain filled him. He was always dreaming now, almost useless for work. Somehow he was fed. Most of the time, no one knew where he was.

He was tempted three times:

Julna of Kadisphon came to him, walking in a dream, darkness trailing behind like a cloak.

"Curse the Winter Gods," said Julna of Kadisphon, "for they have sent you only ill-fortune."

"I will curse them," said Tsarag Vin.

"Spare not your enemies, nor ever forgive them, for they will neither spare nor forgive you."

"I shall be revenged on them," said Tsarag Vin.

"Take evil as your good," said Julna of Kadisphon, "for this is pleasing to the Titans of Shadow, who alone can aid you. Despair then, of all else."

"I curse. I shall be revenged. I despair."

He was seeking the Street of the Witches. He knew from the tales that those who seek such a place, those who deserve to find it, who *do* find it, are the most depraved of human beings. Those who are abducted there, or who find it by seeming accident, may be almost otherwise — but never entirely innocent, or else they wouldn't have been of any interest to the witches, who find that dark door within the soul and pry it open, so that the Titans — those opposite and equal shadows of the gods, of whom even the gods are afraid — may be made manifest and chaos speak to the world like a ravening wind.

So it was in the stories. Now it was more than florid rhetoric.

He sought the witches through his own evil.

He seldom returned to House Zevas at all anymore, and when he did it was only to haunt the place, to cause fear. He dwelt in the city, disguised among the beggars, then in dark houses, among secret guilds. He became a robber, then a murderer, then the terror of much of Nevasderat. He became a black magician, someone who tore up newly-dug graves and arranged the corpses in ridiculous positions, as *tagheri,* and bound the souls of those departed into the corpses, so that he could force secrets out of them, not secrets which would advance his cause, but merely those which would cause pain.

He felt that he was on fire. He loathed himself. He could not look at himself in a mirror, and smashed all mirrors he encountered.

But he went on, for he was the son of a great lord, someone from whom a tremendous, dramatic revenge is to be expected.

Ghosts followed him, howling in the streets.

Heroes came from afar to slay him, so great and terrible was his reputation, but none could find the tomb in which he dwelt by day, and he killed the heroes, one by one, and devoured their hearts.

Still he sought the Street of the Witches in every part of the city. He searched every night. Sometimes he glimpsed it from afar, and ran toward it, but it was never there when he should have reached it.

He killed those he encountered by chance in the night, offering up their souls to the witches and to the Shadow Titans, that he might become evil enough.

He did not hate Julna of Kadisphon anymore. No, he wanted to become like her, to be devious and terrible, to jerk people around, like puppets on strings, to ruin their lives for the pure sport of doing so.

For thus the world is filled with darkness and ruin. Thus are the Shadow Titans nourished.

IV

He never found the Street of the Witches. Instead, he built it afresh within his soul.

And Julna of Kadisphon came to him in the darkness, as he slept in a coffin, among the absurd, dancing, frozen dead in a secret tomb. She crawled to his side. He felt her filmy, spider-silk garment brush over him, her jewelry scrape against him as she caressed him gently. He felt her warmth as she whispered in his ear that he had done well, that she was very pleased. Her long hair fell against his face.

He knew that he loved her now. He hated Azrekia. He desired only Julna, the witch of Kadisphon, who had directed his whole life, who had shown him how to be happy.

She told him as much.

She told him what he had to do, to consummate all her desires, and his.

She pressed a bronze dagger into his hand.

When he reached for her with his other hand, she was gone.

He awoke then, covered with sweat, from a long and terrible dream. For a moment he was afraid, unable to understand how he had come to dwell in a pit among defiled corpses, and he remembered all his crimes, but he remembered, too, what he had been before he had committed them, and he wept, trying to figure out if he was a madman dreaming he was sane, or a sane man dreaming he was mad.

It was all a story, he told himself, and he was the hero.

It was all a story, and it wasn't true. No, not really.

He dreamed that he was a boy who wandered out into the city streets one wintry night and nearly froze to death, and everything that happened afterward was no more than delirium as he lay there, dying, or else as he lay in his bed slowly nursed back to health by those who loved him. But he awoke once more in a pit full of corpses and no one loved him except the witch of Kadisphon, and Kadisphon was at the end of the Earth; and the Shadow Titans loved him because he had despaired and cursed the gods, and he was dreaming, a madman who dreamed he was sane, a sane man who dreamed he was mad, good and evil all swirling together like paint stirred in a pot.

He couldn't see the pattern anymore.

Therefore he washed himself and put on clean clothing (beneath which he concealed the knife) and walked through Nevasderat, drawing little notice. He wasn't a ragged boy anymore, but a tall, broad-shouldered man with a jet-black beard. Only his eyes were strange. Anyone who looked into his face turned quickly away.

All the while he heard Julna of Kadisphon

whispering inside his mind. She was telling him a story.

And in this story, he came to White Nevasderat, to the citadel of House Zevas. He waited until nightfall, knowing the hour at which the lord and lady and their guests took supper, and when they retired, and when the servants, too, would likely be in bed.

Late, then, he tapped gently but insistently on the kitchen door. At last an old woman came.

"I have a message for the lord of this house."

The woman looked at him, befuddled, half asleep, and finally said, "Well take it around to the front gate. Can't it wait?"

He grabbed her hair and slit her throat.

"No, it cannot."

The knife hummed and trembled in his hand, for it was a witch-knife, forged in some unfathomable darkness between the stars, where only the Titans of Shadow look on.

He entered into the house, silently, knowing the secret ways.

There was only one light burning. He drew near and saw the old teacher, Meras,, up late in his study, paging through a book.

Meras looked up when Tsarag stood in the doorway.

"Yes?"

"Teacher, do you know me?"

"No. Should I?"

"Probably not. But you can help me. I am writing a story."

"Splendid! Will you recite it before the house?"

"I will perform it."

"A masque, then?"

"Something like that. But I am not sure how it should end." And Tsarag briefly related all his adventures and deeds.

Meras shuddered and was silent for a time, then said. "The ending must be a tragedy, for this Tsarag has sought the Street of the Witches, and whether he found it or not, he is surely damned. Your matter is perhaps too dark for a popular tale — for the happy ending is always more pleasing — but perhaps if you end with a strong moral, you can perhaps bring it off."

"Thank you," said Tsarag Vin softly. Then he cut off the old man's head with the bronze knife and placed the head on the teacher's desk next to the book. He dipped a pen in the murdered man's blood and spent an hour writing out an account of the tragedy of his life on the volume's endpapers.

But even then the thought came to him, like a whispered temptation: what if the tragedy did not end? What if it merely stopped? He had done so much evil thus far, and it could not be undone, but what if, at this point, he merely walked away? What if he simply did no more?

That was the boy, Tsarag Vin, talking, he who was almost innocent.

But the man, Tsarag Vin, he who was damned, knew better. He gazed into the dead eyes of his old teacher and Meras seemed to agree. There had to be an ending.

Therefore he rose and took the witch-knife in his hand, and made his way stealthily to the bedchambers of the master of the house and of the master's lady. With that knife he cut out the hearts of Lord and Lady Zevas as they slept, and did it so cunningly, by hideous arts he had learned, that they did not exactly die, but passed from nightmare into something which was neither life nor death, even as the soul passes from *Leshé*, dream, into *Tashé*, death, and beyond, into the unknowable —

With his hideous art he caused their hearts to burn as he held them in that cheap, chipped Deltan bowl he had once brought back from the Street of the Witches. And Lord and Lady Zevas screamed in their dreams, beyond death, while flames crackled out of the gaping holes in their chests and their bodies lit up like huge paper lanterns. They rose from their beds and drifted about the house like spirits of the dancing, ridiculous dead, causing terror wherever they came.

The outcry awakened Azrekia. Her maid, who slept beside her, screamed as she looked up at the bearded stranger looming over them. A single stroke of the knife silenced the maid, and another beheaded her; and Tsarag Vin stood over Azrekia, holding up the bloody head as if it were an offering, and he said softly, "I loved you once, dearest Azrekia."

But Azrekia only struggled and tried to get away. He wrestled with her on the bed and he cut out her heart with the witch-knife, somewhat more sloppily, so that she actually died before he had finished. But he imprisoned her spirit there in the burning corpse and heard her moans and her pleadings come out through her dead, open mouth.

Then Tsarag withdrew from the room slowly, like one walking in a dream, and he made his way to the great hall, which was deserted but for the burning corpse of Lady Zevas, who had blundered among some benches and gotten tangled there. She bumped against a pillar again and again, like a confused moth.

Tsarag ignored her. He sat down in the chair at the head of the great table, the place reserved for the lord of the house, and he spoke in a loud voice, to no one in particular, "Behold, I welcome you to House Vin, for I am the lord of this place and I have restored my family's name and honor."

V

Enough of this. It is too horrible. I have to bring it to an end.

I have to clean up the mess.

Tsarag Vin heard a soft footstep and looked to one side. He saw that Julna of Kadisphon had come to him, as he had always seen her, in her almost translucent gown of spider-silk, her long hair flowing behind her in some imperceptible, magical wind, the jewelry on her wrists and ankles clinking softly as she moved.

Her eyes were so dark. He gazed into them and it seemed that he looked beyond the Earth itself, beyond *Leshé*, which is dream, and *Tashé*, which is death, beyond the belly of the great god Surat-Kemad who devours all things at the end of time; that god whose teeth are the stars, whose mouth is the night sky. He beheld, then, the night sky and the stars rippled, like a curtain stirred by a wind, and the black sky parted like a curtain, and out of the deeper darkness which the eye cannot fathom, he saw, rising up like leviathans drawn to the light of the Moon from out of a midnight sea, the very Shadow Titans themselves, their faces so vast and terrible that even the gods cannot look upon them; and he knew their names and their aspects and their titles: the Titans of Desolation and Wrath and Earthquakes; and Sedengul, bringer of storms to the soul; and Arvadas, Lord of Lust; and Vedatis, the wildest of all, sender of dark dreams.

He prayed to Vedatis, most especially.

Drawn to these, his soul and his mind utterly subsumed into darkness, Tsarag Vin took Julna of Kadisphon in his arms and kissed her passionately, begging to be one with her forever.

"I have done as you told me," he said. "I have despaired of any love but yours."

But something happened. Suddenly the Titans vanished and Julna of Kadisphon was gone, as abruptly as if a door had been slammed in his face.

He could see nothing at all in those dark eyes: just eyes now. Someone else was there.

The one he held in his arms moved differently.

The slender hands pushed him away and, unresisting, he let go, but the spider-silk gown tore and came away in his hands. He stood holding it, gaping stupidly at the impossible, at the ridiculous.

Only a *tagheri* corpse could have laughed, though.

For one thing, the person naked before him was a boy.

For another, that boy, his dark flesh crisscrossed with faintly luminous scars, held a glowing mask in his hands. He put it on his face and the mask came alive in fire, and the features were those of Tsarag Vin as he had once been, only screaming now, in infinite despair.

And the boy reached out his hand and uncurled his fingers, and a white flame danced on his palm. A wind blew, inside that great hall, the air swirling around and around, as motes of light gathered, as those motes resolved themselves into the silently screaming ghosts of all those people Tsarag Vin had murdered and would not allow to rest.

Then the boy said, "Know that I am not Julna of Kadisphon, although such a one is within me. I have many names, for I contain multitudes. But foremost I am Sekenre the sorcerer, and I have come to make an ending."

And this is the ending I made. It was only the best I can do. I weep at its inadequacies.

And is it not often claimed that a sorcerer cannot weep?

Is it not said that no sorcerer can ever atone?

I took Tsarag Vin by the hand and led him outside, into the Street of the Witches, which was all about, for he had created it in his mind. The snow was deep and drifting. I know the wind bit at his flesh, but I was naked and felt only the cool night air of the otherwise hot and dusty City of the Delta far to the south. It was one of the many miracles of the Street of the Witches that Tsarag Vin and I met, though he was on the other side the Crescent Sea in some icy land I had never seen.

by Darrell Schweitzer

Such are the least of the miracles, in the Street of the Witches.

He and I walked past the shop where the wooden puppets laughed and called out his name.

Women in red gowns emerged from every doorway, gazing hungrily, their eyes filled with terrible darkness. Even I could not look on them.

"Why are you here?" Tsarag Vin demanded of me. "You are not one of their number."

I explained to him that a witch serves the darkness of her own will. She has made a pact. Her soul is all the more corrupted because she is not compelled. She is wholly consumed. But sorcery is a contagion, like a cancer. The sorcerer contains multitudes. Whosoever kills a sorcerer becomes that sorcerer, joining together within himself the soul and mind of that sorcerer and all the others that sorcerer has murdered. The physical body does not age. It is preserved, by sorcery, like a dead thing in a bottle, although it is alive and may be slain. The one who killed and swallowed the sorcerer is still, in some small sense, himself. Thus, three hundred years ago, a fifteen-year-old boy called Sekenre was made to kill his father, a sorcerer, and the boy became his father, who was called Vashtem, and he became Balredon, and Tannivar, and Talno and so many others, whom his father had already murdered, and more, whom he had to murder in the course of his subsequent adventures. Among the great riot of voices within him was Julna of Kadisphon, who was also a member of the Witches in good standing and therefore an abomination. But Sekenre, struggling to remain Sekenre, is, although unclean, at least capable of greater moral complexity.

"All this was her doing, not mine," I said. "I can only begin to comprehend what her purpose was, and I fear I cannot undo what she has done."

"How did she do it?"

"Somehow, when I was asleep, she seized the body and did these things. I saw them only as one in a dream. Now I have awakened, and shut her away again inside myself. In time, I will pry her secrets out of her."

And he said to me, "Sekenre, how may I be redeemed?"

I led him by the hand.

The witches gathered around us. I too put on a red gown and moved among them, and they took me for Julna of Kadisphon and were not alarmed, though they hated and feared Sekenre.

In a cellar room, we bound Tsarag Vin naked to a wooden table. We stripped away his years, and he was a child again. We burned his flesh with iron and cut him with our witch-knives. We opened him like a sack and poured molten silver into his gut and sewed him up.

His screaming stopped then. He looked up, at the window. I saw someone peering in and pulled down the shade.

"It is over," I whispered into his ear.

I took off the burning mask, and let its ashes float away on the air.

Now the tale is of Sekenre and is set in the hot and dusty Delta, beyond the Crescent Sea, where few Nevasderati ever venture.

There Sekenre walked into the great, silent temple of Bel-Hemad, the god of spring and renewal, and of forgiveness. He moved like a ghost, his bare feet silent on the marble floor. He wore, in the fashion of the Delta in that time, a brilliantly dyed, loose-sleeved shirt that reached to mid-thigh, and baggy, white trousers torn off at the knees, his long hair tied behind in a braid; and he wore no jewelry. He might have been taken for a common street youth of that place. It suited him to appear as such.

But the god knew otherwise. The god could see that the sorcerer was unclean.

No god will listen to a sorcerer's prayers.

For the sorcerer cannot pray any more than he can weep.

That's what they say, anyway.

Therefore, to atone, Sekenre could only place the heart of Tsarag Vin (which he had stolen from the Witches) in the chipped, earthen bowl and place it at the feet of Bel-Hemad.

He left, as an offering, the toy horse with the broken wheel.

He could only hope that the god would understand, and that on some night, either in a year or a hundred years, there would be a ghost waiting in the temple of Bel-Hemad, and it would be the ghost of that young boy who went into the Street of the Witches in what might have been a dream, and never returned.

The monster, who came back, had ceased to exist.

But the god could grant this much, even to a sorcerer, that Sekenre might lead the ghost of the boy Tsarag to the shore of the Black River, into the Land of the Dead, where he might join with his parents, with his brother Amasdag, with his teacher Meras and with Azrekia who truly loved him, and dwell in the great House of Vin (which is a dream) forever. Ω